YOUNG HORNBLOWER
Three Complete Novels

C. S. FORESTER

Young Hornblower

THREE COMPLETE NOVELS

Mr. Midshipman Hornblower

Lieutenant Hornblower

Hornblower and the *Atropos*

BOSTON

LITTLE, BROWN AND COMPANY

LIBRARY OF CONGRESS CATALOG CARD NUMBER 60–12205
PRINTED IN THE UNITED STATES OF AMERICA

Mr. Midshipman Hornblower

Contents

ONE *Hornblower* and the Even Chance 9

TWO *Hornblower* and the Cargo of Rice 33

THREE *Hornblower* and the Penalty of Failure 54

FOUR *Hornblower* and the Man Who Felt Queer 69

FIVE *Hornblower* and the Man Who Saw God 83

SIX *Hornblower* the Frogs, and the Lobsters 98

SEVEN *Hornblower* and the Spanish Galleys 125

EIGHT *Hornblower* and the Examination for Lieutenant 143

NINE *Hornblower* and Noah's Ark 157

TEN *Hornblower* the Duchess, and the Devil 173

One

HORNBLOWER
and the Even Chance

A JANUARY GALE was roaring up the Channel, blustering loudly, and bearing on its bosom rain squalls whose big drops rattled loudly on the tarpaulin clothing of those among the officers and men whose duties kept them on deck. So hard and so long had the gale blown that even in the sheltered waters of Spithead the battleship moved uneasily at her anchors, pitching a little in the choppy seas, and snubbing herself against the tautened cables with unexpected jerks. A shore boat was on its way out to her, propelled by oars in the hands of two sturdy women; it danced madly on the steep little waves, now and then putting its nose into one and sending a sheet of spray flying aft. The oarswoman in the bow knew her business, and with rapid glances over her shoulder not only kept the boat on its course but turned the bows into the worst of the waves to keep from capsizing. It slowly drew up along the starboard side of the *Justinian,* and as it approached the main chains the midshipman of the watch hailed it.

"Aye aye," came back the answering hail from the lusty lungs of the woman at the stroke oar; by the curious and ages-old convention of the navy the reply meant that the boat had an officer on board—presumably the huddled figure in the sternsheets looking more like a heap of trash with a boat cloak thrown over it.

That was as much as Mr. Masters, the lieutenant of the watch, could see; he was sheltering as best he could in the lee of the mizzenmast bitts, and in obedience to the order of the midshipman of the watch the boat drew up towards the main chains and passed out of his sight. There was a long delay; apparently the officer had some difficulty in getting up the ship's side. At last the boat reappeared in Masters' field of vision; the women had shoved off and were setting a scrap of lugsail, under which the boat, now without its passenger, went swooping back towards Portsmouth, leaping on the waves like a steeplechaser. As it departed Mr. Masters became aware of the near approach of someone along the quarterdeck; it was the new arrival under the escort of the midshipman of the watch, who, after pointing Masters out, retired to the main chains again. Mr. Masters had served in the navy until his hair was white; he was lucky to have received his commission as lieutenant, and he had long known that he would never receive one as captain, but the knowledge had not greatly embittered him, and he diverted his mind by the study of his fellow men.

So he looked with attention at the approaching figure. It was that of a skinny young man only just leaving boyhood behind, something above middle height, with feet whose adolescent proportions to his size were accentuated by the thinness of his legs and his big half-boots. His gawkiness called attention to his hands and elbows. The newcomer was dressed in a badly fitting uniform which was soaked right through by the spray; a skinny neck stuck out of the high stock, and above the neck was a white bony face. A white face was a rarity on the deck of a ship of war whose crew soon tanned to a deep mahogany, but this face was not merely white; in the hollow cheeks there was a faint shade of green—clearly the newcomer had experienced seasickness in his passage out in the shore boat. Set in the white face were a pair of dark eyes which by contrast looked like holes cut in a sheet of paper; Masters noted with a slight stirring of interest that the eyes, despite their owner's seasickness, were looking about keenly, taking in what were obviously new sights; there was a curiosity and interest there which could not be repressed and which continued to function notwithstanding either seasickness or shyness, and Mr. Masters surmised in his far-fetched fashion that this boy had a vein of caution or foresight in his temperament and was already studying his new surroundings with a view to being prepared for his next experiences. So might Daniel have looked about him at the lions when he first entered their den.

The dark eyes met Masters', and the gawky figure came to a halt, raising a hand self-consciously to the brim of his dripping hat. His mouth opened and tried to say something, but closed again without achieving its object as shyness overcame its owner, but then the newcomer nerved himself afresh and forced himself to say the formal words he had been coached to utter.

"Come aboard, sir."

"Your name?" asked Masters, after waiting for it for a moment.

"H–Horatio Hornblower, sir. Midshipman," stuttered the boy.

"Very good, Mr. Hornblower," said Masters, with the equally formal response. "Did you bring your dunnage aboard with you?"

Hornblower had never heard that word before, but he still had enough of his wits about him to deduce what it meant.

"My sea-chest, sir. It's—it's for'rard, at the entry port."

Hornblower said these things with the barest hesitation; he knew that at sea they said them, that they pronounced the word "forward" like that, and that he had come on board through the "entry port," but it called for a slight effort to utter them himself.

"I'll see that it's sent below," said Masters. "And that's where you'd better go, too. The captain's ashore and the first lieutenant's orders were that he's not to be called on any account before eight bells, so I advise you, Mr. Hornblower, to get out of those wet clothes while you can."

"Yes, sir," said Hornblower; his senses told him, the moment he said it, that he had used an improper expression—the look on Masters' face told him, and he corrected himself (hardly believing that men really said these things off the boards of the stage) before Masters had time to correct him.

"Aye aye, sir," said Hornblower, and as a second afterthought he put his hand to the brim of his hat again.

Masters returned the compliment and turned to one of the shivering messengers cowering in the inadequate shelter of the bulwark. "Boy! Take Mr. Hornblower down to the midshipmen's berth."

"Aye aye, sir."

Hornblower accompanied the boy forward to the main hatchway. Seasickness alone would have made him unsteady on his feet, but twice on the short journey he stumbled like a man tripping over a rope as a sharp gust brought the *Justinian* up against her cables with a jerk. At the hatchway the boy slid down the ladder like an eel over a rock; Hornblower had to brace himself and descend far more gingerly and uncertainly, into the dim light of the lower gundeck and then into the twilight of the 'tween-decks. The smells that entered his nostrils were as strange and as assorted as the noises that assailed his ears. At the foot of each ladder the boy waited for him with a patience whose tolerance was just obvious. After the last descent a few steps—Hornblower had already lost his sense of direction and did not know whether it was aft or forward—took them to a gloomy recess whose shadows were accentuated rather than lightened by a tallow dip spiked onto a bit of copper plate on a table round which were seated half a dozen shirt-sleeved men. The boy vanished and left Hornblower standing there, and it was a second or two before the whiskered man at the head of the table looked up at him.

"Speak, thou apparition," said he.

Hornblower felt a wave of nausea overcoming him—the after-effects of his trip in the shore boat were being accentuated by the incredible stuffiness and smelliness of the 'tween-decks. It was very hard to speak, and the fact that he did not know how to phrase what he wanted to say made it harder still.

"My name is Hornblower," he quavered at length.

"What an infernal piece of bad luck for you," said a second man at the table, with a complete absence of sympathy.

At that moment in the roaring world outside the ship the wind veered sharply, heeling the *Justinian* a trifle and swinging her round to snub her at her cables again. To Hornblower it seemed more as if the world had come loose from its fastenings. He reeled where he stood, and although he was shuddering with cold he felt sweat on his face.

"I suppose you have come," said the whiskered man at the head of the table, "to thrust yourself among your betters. Another soft-headed ignoramus come to be a nuisance to those who have to try to teach you your duties. Look at him"—the speaker with a gesture demanded the attention of everyone at the table—"look at him, I say! The King's latest bad bargain. How old are you?"

"S–seventeen, sir," stuttered Hornblower.

"Seventeen!" The disgust in the speaker's voice was only too evident. "You must start at twelve if you ever wish to be a seaman. Seventeen! Do you know the difference between a head and a halliard?"

That drew a laugh from the group, and the quality of the laugh was just noticeable to Hornblower's whirling brain, so that he guessed that whether he said "yes" or "no" he would be equally exposed to ridicule. He groped for a neutral reply.

"That's the first thing I'll look up in Clarke's *Seamanship,*" he said.

The ship lurched again at that moment, and he clung onto the table. "Gentlemen," he began, pathetically, wondering how to say what he had in mind.

"My God!" exclaimed somebody at the table. "He's seasick!"

"Seasick in Spithead!" said somebody else, in a tone in which amazement had as much place as disgust.

But Hornblower ceased to care; he was not really conscious of what was going on round him for some time after that. The nervous excitement of the last few days was as much to blame, perhaps, as the journey in the shore boat and the erratic behaviour of the *Justinian* at her anchors, but it meant for him that he was labelled at once as the midshipman who was seasick in Spithead, and it was only natural that the label added to the natural misery of the loneliness and homesickness which oppressed him during those days when that part of the Channel Fleet which had not succeeded in completing its crews lay at anchor in the lee of the Isle of Wight. An hour in the hammock into which the messman hoisted him enabled him to recover sufficiently to be able to report himself to the first lieutenant; after a few days on board he was able to find his way round the ship without (as happened at first) losing his sense of direction below decks so that he did not know whether he was facing forward or aft. During that period his brother officers ceased to have faces which were mere blurs and came to take on personalities; he came painfully to learn the stations allotted him when the ship was at quarters, when he was on watch, and when hands were summoned for setting or taking in sail. He even came to have an acute enough understanding of his new life to realise that it could have been worse—that destiny might have put him on board a ship ordered immediately to sea instead of one lying at anchor. But it was a poor enough compensation; he was a lonely and unhappy boy. Shyness alone would long have delayed his making friends, but as it happened the midshipmen's berth in the *Justinian* was occupied by men all a good deal older than he; elderly master's mates recruited from the merchant service, and midshipmen in their twenties who through lack of patronage or inability to pass the necessary examination had never succeeded in gaining for themselves commissions as lieutenants. They were inclined, after the first moments of amused interest, to ignore him, and he was glad of it, delighted to shrink into his shell and attract no notice to himself.

For the *Justinian* was not a happy ship during those gloomy January days. Captain Keene—it was when he came aboard that Hornblower first saw the pomp and ceremony that surrounds the captain of a ship of the line—was a sick man, of a melancholy disposition. He had not the fame which enabled some captains to fill their ships with enthusiastic volunteers, and he was devoid of the personality which might have made enthusiasts out of the sullen pressed men whom the press gangs were bringing in from day to day to complete the ship's complement. His officers saw little of him, and did not love what they saw. Hornblower, summoned to his cabin for his first interview, was not impressed—a middle-aged man at a table covered with papers, with the hollow and yellow cheeks of prolonged illness.

"Mr. Hornblower," he said, formally, "I am glad to have this opportunity of welcoming you on board my ship."

"Yes, sir," said Hornblower—that seemed more appropriate to the occasion than "aye aye, sir," and a junior midshipman seemed to be expected to say one or the other on all occasions.

"You are—let me see—seventeen?" Captain Keene picked up the paper which apparently covered Hornblower's brief official career.

"Yes, sir."

"July 4th, 1776," mused Keene, reading Hornblower's date of birth to himself. "Five years to the day before I was posted as captain. I had been six years as lieutenant before you were born."

"Yes, sir," agreed Hornblower—it did not seem the occasion for any further comment.

"A doctor's son—you should have chosen a lord for your father if you wanted to make a career for yourself."

"Yes, sir."

"How far did your education go?"

"I was a Grecian at school, sir."

"So you can construe Xenophon as well as Cicero?"

"Yes, sir. But not very well, sir."

"Better if you knew something about sines and cosines. Better if you could foresee a squall in time to get t'gallants in. We have no use for ablative absolutes in the navy."

"Yes, sir," said Hornblower.

He had only just learned what a topgallant was, but he could have told his captain that his mathematical studies were far advanced. He refrained nevertheless; his instincts combined with his recent experiences urged him not to volunteer unsolicited information.

"Well, obey orders, learn your duties, and no harm can come to you. That will do."

"Thank you, sir," said Hornblower, retiring.

But the captain's last words to him seemed to be contradicted immediately. Harm began to come to Hornblower from that day forth, despite his obedience to orders and diligent study of his duties, and it stemmed from the arrival in the midshipmen's berth of John Simpson as senior warrant officer. Hornblower was sitting at mess with his colleagues when he first saw him—a brawny good-looking man in his thirties, who came in and stood looking at them just as Hornblower had stood a few days before.

"Hullo!" said somebody, not very cordially.

"Cleveland, my bold friend," said the newcomer, "come out from that seat. I am going to resume my place at the head of the table."

"But—"

"Come out, I said," snapped Simpson.

Cleveland moved along with some show of reluctance, and Simpson took his place, and glowered round the table in reply to the curious glances with which everyone regarded him.

"Yes, my sweet brother officers," he said, "I am back in the bosom of the family. And I am not surprised that nobody is pleased. You will all be less pleased by the time I am done with you, I may add."

"But your commission—?" asked somebody, greatly daring.

"My commission?" Simpson leaned forward and tapped the table, staring down the inquisitive people on either side of it. "I'll answer that question this once, and the man who asks it again will wish he had never been born. A board of turnip-headed captains has refused me my commission. It decided that my mathematical knowledge was insufficient to make me a reliable navigator. And so Acting-Lieutenant Simpson is once again Mr. Midshipman Simpson, at your service. At your service. And may the Lord have mercy on your souls."

It did not seem, as the days went by, that the Lord had any mercy at all, for since Simpson's return life in the midshipmen's berth ceased to be one of passive unhappiness and became one of active misery. Simpson had apparently always been an ingenious tyrant, but now, embittered and humiliated by his failure to pass his examination for his commission, he was a worse tyrant, and his ingenuity had multiplied itself. He may have been weak in mathematics, but he was diabolically clever at making other people's lives a burden to them. As senior officer in the mess he had wide official powers; as a man with a blistering tongue and a morbid sense of mischief he would have been powerful anyway, even if the *Justinian* had possessed an alert and masterful first lieutenant to keep him in check, and Mr. Clay was neither.

Twice midshipmen rebelled against Simpson's arbitrary authority, and each time Simpson thrashed the rebel, pounding him into insensibility with his huge fists, for Simpson would have made a successful prizefighter. Each time Simpson was left unmarked; each time his opponent's blackened eyes and swollen lips called down the penalty of mast heading and extra duty from the indignant first lieutenant. The mess seethed with impotent rage. Even the toadies and lickspittles among the midshipmen—and naturally there were several—hated the tyrant.

Significantly, it was not his ordinary exactions which roused the greatest resentment—his levying toll upon their sea-chests for clean shirts for himself, his appropriation of the best cuts of the meat served, nor even his taking their coveted issues of spirits. These things could be excused as understandable, the sort of thing they would do themselves if they had the power. But he displayed a whimsical arbitrariness which reminded Hornblower, with his classical education, of the freaks of the Roman emperors. He forced Cleveland to shave the whiskers which were his inordinate pride; he imposed upon Hether the duty of waking up Mackenzie every half hour, day and night, so that neither of them was able to sleep—and there were toadies ready to tell him if Hether ever failed in his task. Early enough he had discovered Hornblower's most vulnerable points, as he had with everyone else. He knew of Hornblower's shyness; at first it was amusing to compel Hornblower to recite verses from Gray's "Elegy in a Country Churchyard" to the assembled mess. The toadies could compel Hornblower to do it; Simpson would lay his dirk-scabbard on the table in front of him with a significant glance, and the toadies would close round Hornblower, who knew that any hesitation on his part would mean that he would be stretched across the table and the dirk-scabbard applied. The flat of the scabbard was painful, the edge of it was agonising, but the pain was nothing to the utter humiliation of it all. And the torment grew worse when Simpson instituted what he aptly called "The Proceedings of the Inquisition," when Hornblower was submitted to a slow and methodical questioning regarding his home life and his boyhood. Every question had to be answered, on pain of the dirk-scabbard; Hornblower could fence and prevaricate, but he had to answer and sooner or later the relentless questioning would draw from him some simple admission which would rouse a peal of laughter from his audience. Heaven knows that in Hornblower's lonely childhood there was nothing to be ashamed of, but boys are odd creatures, especially reticent ones like Hornblower, and are ashamed of things no one else would think twice about. The ordeal would leave him weak and sick; someone less solemn might have clowned his way out of his difficulties and even into popular favour, but Hornblower at seventeen was too ponderous a person to clown. He had to endure the persecution, experiencing all the black misery which only a seventeen-year-old can experience; he never wept in public, but at night more than once he shed the bitter tears of seventeen. He often thought about death; he often even thought about desertion, but he realised that desertion would lead to something worse than death, and then his mind would revert to death, savouring the thought of suicide. He came to long for death, friendless as he was, and brutally ill-treated, and lonely as only a boy among men—and a very reserved boy—can be. More and more he thought about ending it all the easiest way, hugging the secret thought of it to his friendless bosom.

If the ship had only been at sea everyone would have been kept busy enough to be out of mischief; even at anchor an energetic captain and first lieutenant would have kept all hands hard enough at work to obviate abuses, but it was Hornblower's hard luck that the *Justinian* lay at anchor all through that fatal January of 1794 under a sick captain and an inefficient first lieutenant. Even the activities which were at times enforced often worked to Hornblower's disadvantage. There was an occasion when Mr. Bowles the master was holding a class in navigation for his mates and for the midshipmen, and the captain by bad luck happened by and glanced through the results of the problem the class had individually been set to solve. His illness made Keene a man of bitter tongue, and he cherished no liking for Simpson. He took a single glance at Simpson's paper, and chuckled sarcastically.

"Now let us all rejoice," he said. "The sources of the Nile have been discovered at last."

"Pardon, sir?" said Simpson.

"Your ship," said Keene, "as far as I can make out from your illiterate scrawl, Mr. Simpson, is in Central Africa. Let us now see what other *terrae incognitae* have been opened up by the remaining intrepid explorers of this class."

It must have been Fate—it was dramatic enough to be art and not an occurrence in real life; Hornblower knew what was going to happen even as Keene picked up the other papers, including his. The result he had obtained was the only one which was correct; everybody else had added the correction for refraction instead of subtracting it, or had worked out the multiplication wrongly, or had (like Simpson) botched the whole problem.

"Congratulations, Mr. Hornblower," said Keene. "You must be proud to be alone successful among this crowd of intellectual giants. You are half Mr. Simpson's age, I fancy. If you double your attainments while you double your years, you will leave the rest of us far behind. Mr. Bowles, you will be so good as to see that Mr. Simpson pays even further attention to his mathematical studies."

With that he went off along the 'tween-decks with the halting step resulting from his mortal disease, and Hornblower sat with his eyes cast down, unable to meet the glances he knew were being darted at him, and knowing full well what they portended. He longed for death at that moment; he even prayed for it that night.

Within two days Hornblower found himself on shore, and under Simpson's command. The two midshipmen were in charge of a party of seamen, landed to act along with parties from the other ships of the squadron as a press gang. The West India convoy was due to arrive soon; most of the hands would be pressed as soon as the convoy reached the Channel, and the remainder, left to work the ships to an anchorage, would sneak ashore, using every device to conceal themselves and find a safe hiding place. It was the business of the landing parties to cut off this retreat, to lay a cordon along the water-front which would sweep them all up. But the convoy was not yet signalled, and all arrangements were completed.

"All is well with the world," said Simpson.

It was an unusual speech for him, but he was in unusual circumstances. He was sitting in the back room of the Lamb Inn, comfortable in one armchair with his legs on another, in front of a roaring fire and with a pot of beer with gin in it at his elbow.

"Here's to the West India convoy," said Simpson, taking a pull at his beer. "Long may it be delayed."

Simpson was actually genial, activity and beer and a warm fire thawing him into a good humour; it was not time yet for the liquor to make him quarrelsome. Hornblower sat on the other side of the fire and sipped beer without gin in it and studied him, marvelling that for the first time since he had boarded the *Justinian* his unhappiness should have ceased to be active but should have subsided into a dull misery like the dying away of the pain of a throbbing tooth.

"Give us a toast, boy," said Simpson.

"Confusion to Robespierre," said Hornblower, lamely.

The door opened and two more officers came in, one a midshipman while the other wore the single epaulette of a lieutenant—it was Chalk of the *Goliath*, the officer in general charge of the press gangs sent ashore. Even Simpson made room for his superior rank before the fire.

"The convoy is still not signalled," announced Chalk. And then he eyed Hornblower keenly. "I don't think I have the pleasure of your acquaintance."

"Mr. Hornblower—Lieutenant Chalk," introduced Simpson. "Mr. Hornblower is distinguished as the midshipman who was seasick in Spithead."

Hornblower tried not to writhe as Simpson tied that label on him. He imagined that Chalk was merely being polite when he changed the subject.

"Hey, potman! Will you gentlemen join me in a glass? We have a long wait before us, I fear. Your men are all properly posted, Mr. Simpson?"

"Yes, sir."

Chalk was an active man. He paced about the room, stared out of the window at the rain, presented his midshipman—Caldwell—to the other two when the drinks arrived, and obviously fretted at his enforced inactivity.

"A game of cards to pass the time?" he suggested. "Excellent! Hey, potman! Cards and a table and another light."

The table was set before the fire, the chairs arranged, the cards brought in.

"What game shall it be?" asked Chalk, looking round.

He was a lieutenant among three midshipmen, and any suggestion of his was likely to carry a good deal of weight; the other three naturally waited to hear what he had to say.

"Vingt-et-un? That is a game for the half-witted. Loo? That is a game for the wealthier half-witted. But whist, now? That would give us all scope for the exercise of our poor talents. Caldwell, there, is acquainted with the rudiments of the game, I know. Mr. Simpson?"

A man like Simpson, with a blind mathematical spot, was not likely to be a good whist player, but he was not likely to know he was a bad one.

"As you wish, sir," said Simpson. He enjoyed gambling, and one game was as good as another for that purpose to his mind.

"Mr. Hornblower?"

"With pleasure, sir."

That was more nearly true than most conventional replies. Hornblower had learned his whist in a good school; ever since the death of his mother he had made a fourth with his father and the parson and the parson's wife. The game was already something of a passion with him. He revelled in the nice calculation of chances, in the varying demands it made upon his boldness or caution. There was even enough warmth in his acceptance to attract a second glance from Chalk, who—a good card player himself—at once detected a fellow spirit.

"Excellent!" he said again. "Then we may as well cut at once for places and partners. What shall be the stakes, gentlemen? A shilling a trick and a guinea on the rub, or is that too great? No? Then we are agreed."

For some time the game proceeded quietly. Hornblower cut first Simpson and then Caldwell as his partner. Only a couple of hands were necessary to show up Simpson as a hopeless whist player, the kind who would always lead an ace when he had one, or a singleton when he had four trumps, but he and Hornblower won the first rubber thanks to overwhelming card strength. But Simpson lost the next in partnership with Chalk, cut Chalk again as partner, and lost again. He gloated over good hands and sighed over poor ones; clearly he was one of those unenlightened people who looked upon whist as a social function, or as a mere crude means, like throwing dice, of arbitrarily transferring money. He never thought of the game either as a social rite or as an intellectual exercise. Moreover, as his losses grew, and as the potman came and went with liquor, he grew restless, and his face was flushed with more than the heat of the fire. He was both a bad loser and a bad drinker, and even Chalk's punctilious good manners were sufficiently strained so that he displayed a hint of relief when the next cut gave him Hornblower as a partner. They won the rubber easily, and another guinea and several shillings were transferred to Hornblower's lean purse; he was now the only winner, and Simpson was the heaviest loser. Hornblower was lost in the pleasure of playing the game again; the only attention he paid to Simpson's writhings and muttered objurgations was to regard them as a distracting nuisance; he even forgot to think of them as danger signals. Momentarily he was oblivious to the fact that he might pay for his present success by future torment.

Once more they cut, and he found himself Chalk's partner again. Two good hands gave them the first game. Then twice, to Simpson's unconcealed triumph, Simpson and Caldwell made a small score, approaching game, and in the next hand an overbold finesse by Hornblower left him and Chalk with the odd trick when their score should have been two tricks greater—Simpson laid his knave on Hornblower's ten with a grin of delight which turned to dismay when he found that he and Caldwell had still only made six tricks; he counted them a second time with annoyance. Hornblower dealt and turned the trump, and Simpson led—an ace as usual, assuring Hornblower of his re-entry. Hornblower had a string of trumps and a good suit of clubs which a single lead might establish. Simpson glanced muttering at his hand; it was extraordinary that he still had not realised the simple truth that the lead of an ace involved leading a second time with the problem no clearer. He made up his mind at last and led again; Hornblower's king took the trick and he instantly led his knave of trumps. To his delight it took the trick; he led again and Chalk's queen gave them another trick. Chalk laid down the ace of trumps and Simpson with a curse played the king. Chalk led clubs of which Hornblower had five to the king queen—it was significant that Chalk should lead them, as it could not be a singleton lead when Hornblower held the remaining trumps. Hornblower's queen took the trick; Caldwell must hold the ace, unless Chalk did. Hornblower led a small one; everyone followed suit, Chalk playing the knave, and Caldwell the ace. Eight clubs had been played, and Hornblower had three more headed by the king and ten—three certain tricks, with the last trumps as re-entries. Caldwell played the queen of diamonds, Hornblower played his singleton, and Chalk produced the ace.

"The rest are mine," said Hornblower, laying down his cards.

"What do you mean?" said Simpson, with the king of diamonds in his hand.

"Five tricks," said Chalk, briskly. "Game and rubber."

"But don't I take another?" persisted Simpson.

"I trump a lead of diamonds or hearts and make three more clubs," explained Hornblower. To him the situation was as simple as two and two, a most ordinary finish to a hand; it was hard for him to realise that foggy-minded players like Simpson could find difficulty in keeping tally of fifty two cards. Simpson flung down his hand.

"You know too much about the game," he said. "You know the backs of the cards as well as the fronts."

Hornblower gulped. He recognised that this could be a decisive moment if he chose. A second before he had merely been playing cards, and enjoying himself. Now he was faced with an issue of life or death. A torrent of thoughts streamed through his mind. Despite the comfort of his present surroundings he remembered acutely the hideous misery of the life in the *Justinian* to which he must return. This was an opportunity to end that misery one way or the other. He remembered how he had contemplated killing himself, and into the back of his mind stole the germ of the plan upon which he was going to act. His decision crystallised.

"That is an insulting remark, Mr. Simpson," he said. He looked round and met the eyes of Chalk and Caldwell, who were suddenly grave; Simpson was still merely stupid. "For that I shall have to ask satisfaction!"

"Satisfaction?" said Chalk, hastily. "Come, come. Mr. Simpson had a momentary loss of temper. I am sure he will explain."

"I have been accused of cheating at cards," said Hornblower. "That is a hard thing to explain away."

He was trying to behave like a grown man; more than that, he was trying to act like a man consumed with indignation, while actually there was no indignation within him over the point in dispute, for he understood too well the muddled state of mind which had led Simpson to say what he did. But the opportunity had presented itself, he had determined to avail himself of it, and now what he had to do was to play the part convincingly of the man who has received a mortal insult.

"The wine was in and the wit was out," said Chalk, still determined on keeping the peace. "Mr. Simpson was speaking in jest, I am sure. Let's call for another bottle and drink it in friendship."

"With pleasure," said Hornblower, fumbling for the words which would set the dispute beyond reconciliation, "if Mr. Simpson will beg my pardon at once before you two gentlemen, and admit that he spoke without justification and in a manner no gentleman would employ."

He turned and met Simpson's eyes with defiance as he spoke, metaphorically waving a red rag before the bull, who charged with gratifying fury.

"Apologise to *you*, you little whippersnapper!" exploded Simpson, alcohol and outraged dignity speaking simultaneously. "Never this side of Hell."

"You hear that, gentlemen?" said Hornblower. "I have been insulted and Mr. Simpson refuses to apologise while insulting me further. There is only one way now in which satisfaction can be given."

For the next two days, until the West India convoy came in, Hornblower and Simpson, under Chalk's orders, lived the curious life of two duellists forced into each other's society before the affair of honour. Hornblower was careful—as he would have been in any case—to obey every order given him, and Simpson gave them with a certain amount of self-consciousness and awkwardness. It was during those two days that Hornblower elaborated on his original idea. Pacing through the dockyards with his patrol of seamen at his heels he had plenty of time to think the matter over. Viewed coldly—and a boy of seventeen in a mood of black despair can be objective enough on occasions—it was as simple as the calculations of the chances in a problem at whist. Nothing could be worse than his life in the *Justinian*, not even (as he had thought already) death itself. Here was an easy death open to him, with the additional attraction that there was a chance of Simpson dying instead. It was at that moment that Hornblower advanced his idea one step further—a new development and startling even to him, bringing him to a halt so that the patrol behind him bumped into him before they could stop.

"Beg your pardon, sir," said the petty officer.

"No matter," said Hornblower, deep in his thoughts.

He first brought forward his suggestion in conversation with Preston and Danvers, the two master's mates whom he asked to be his seconds as soon as he returned to the *Justinian*.

"We'll act for you, of course," said Preston, looking dubiously at the weedy youth when he made his request. "How do you want to fight him? As the aggrieved party you have the choice of weapons."

"I've been thinking about it ever since he insulted me," said Hornblower temporising. It was not easy to come out with his idea in bald words, after all.

"Have you any skill with the small-sword?" asked Danvers.

"No," said Hornblower. Truth to tell, he had never even handled one.

"Then it had better be pistols," said Preston.

"Simpson is probably a good shot," said Danvers. "I wouldn't care to stand up before him myself."

"Easy now," said Preston, hastily. "Don't dishearten the man."

"I'm not disheartened," said Hornblower. "I was thinking the same thing myself."

"You're cool enough about it, then," marvelled Danvers.

Hornblower shrugged.

"Maybe I am. I hardly care. But I've thought that we might make the chances more even."

"How?"

"We could make them exactly even," said Hornblower, taking the plunge. "Have two pistols, one loaded and the other empty. Simpson and I would take our choice, without knowing which was which. Then we stand within a yard of each other, and at the word, we fire."

"My God!" said Danvers.

"I don't think that would be legal," said Preston. "It would mean one of you would be killed for certain."

"Killing is the object of duelling," said Hornblower. "If the conditions aren't unfair I don't think any objection can be raised."

"But would you carry it out to the end?" marvelled Danvers.

"Mr. Danvers—" began Hornblower, but Preston interfered.

"We don't want another duel on our hands," he said. "Danvers only meant he wouldn't care to do it himself. We'll discuss it with Cleveland and Hether, and see what they say."

Within an hour the proposed conditions of the duel were known to everyone in the ship. Perhaps it was to Simpson's disadvantage that he had no real friend in the ship, for Cleveland and Hether, his seconds, were not disposed to take too firm a stand regarding the conditions of the duel, and agreed to the terms with only a show of reluctance. The tyrant of the midshipmen's berth was paying the penalty for his tyranny. There was some cynical amusement shown by some of the officers; some of both officers and men eyed Hornblower and Simpson with the curiosity that the prospect of death excites in some minds, as if the two destined opponents were men condemned to the gallows. At noon Lieutenant Masters sent for Hornblower.

"The captain has ordered me to make inquiry into this duel, Mr. Hornblower," he said. "I am instructed to use my best endeavours to compose the quarrel."

"Yes, sir."

"Why insist on this satisfaction, Mr. Hornblower? I understand there were a few hasty words over wine and cards."

"Mr. Simpson accused me of cheating, sir, before witnesses, who were not officers of this ship."

That was the point. The witnesses were not members of the ship's company. If Hornblower had chosen to disregard Simpson's words as the ramblings of a drunken ill-tempered man, they might have passed unnoticed. But as he had taken the stand he did, there could be no hushing it up now, and Hornblower knew it.

"Even so, there can be satisfaction without a duel, Mr. Hornblower."

"If Mr. Simpson will make me a full apology before the same gentlemen, I would be satisfied, sir."

Simpson was no coward. He would die rather than submit to such a formal humiliation.

"I see. Now I understand you are insisting on rather unusual conditions for the duel?"

"There are precedents for it, sir. As the insulted party I can choose any conditions which are not unfair."

"You sound like a sea lawyer to me, Mr. Hornblower."

The hint was sufficient to tell Hornblower that he had verged upon being too glib, and he resolved in future to bridle his tongue. He stood silent and waited for Masters to resume the conversation.

"You are determined, then, Mr. Hornblower, to continue with this murderous business?"

"Yes, sir."

"The captain has given me further orders to attend the duel in person, because of the strange conditions on which you insist. I must inform you that I shall request the seconds to arrange for that."

"Yes, sir."

"Very good, then, Mr. Hornblower."

Masters looked at Hornblower as he dismissed him even more keenly than he had done when Hornblower first came on board. He was looking for signs of weakness or wavering—indeed, he was looking for any signs of human feeling at all—but he could detect none. Hornblower had reached a decision, he had weighed all the pros and cons, and his logical mind told him that having decided in cold blood upon a course of action it would be folly to allow himself to be influenced subsequently by untrustworthy emotions. The conditions of the duel on which he was insisting were mathematically advantageous. If he had once considered with favour escaping from Simpson's persecution by a voluntary death it was surely a gain to take an even chance of escaping from it without dying. Similarly if Simpson were (as he almost certainly was) a better swordsman and a better pistol shot than he the even chance was again mathematically advantageous. There was nothing to regret about his recent actions.

All very well; mathematically the conclusions were irrefutable, but Hornblower was surprised to find that mathematics were not everything. Repeatedly during that dreary afternoon and evening Hornblower found himself suddenly gulping with anxiety as the realisation came to him afresh that tomorrow morning he would be risking his life on the spin of a coin. One chance out of two and he would be dead, his consciousness at an end, his flesh cold, and the world, almost unbelievably, would be going on without him. The thought sent a shiver through him despite himself. And he had plenty of time for these reflections, for the convention that forbade him from encountering his destined opponent before the moment of the duel kept him necessarily in isolation, as far as isolation could be found on the crowded decks of the *Justinian.* He slung his hammock that night in a depressed mood, feeling unnaturally tired, and he undressed in the clammy, stuffy dampness of the 'tween-decks feeling more than usually cold. He hugged the blankets round himself, yearning to relax in their warmth, but relaxation would not come. Time after time as he began to drift off to sleep he woke again tense and anxious, full of thoughts of the morrow. He turned over wearily a dozen times, hearing the ship's bell ring out each half hour, feeling a growing contempt at his cowardice. He told himself in the end that it was as well that his fate tomorrow depended upon pure chance, for if he had to rely upon steadiness of hand and eye he would be dead for certain after a night like this.

That conclusion presumably helped him to go to sleep for the last hour or two of the night, for he awoke with a start to find Danvers shaking him.

"Five bells," said Danvers. "Dawn in an hour. Rise and shine!"

Hornblower slid out of his hammock and stood in his shirt; the 'tween-decks was nearly dark and Danvers was almost invisible.

"Number One's letting us have the second cutter," said Danvers. "Masters and Simpson and that lot are going first in the launch. Here's Preston."

Another shadowy figure loomed up in the darkness.

"Hellish cold," said Preston. "The devil of a morning to turn out. Nelson, where's that tea?"

The mess attendant came with it as Hornblower was hauling on his trousers. It maddened Hornblower that he shivered enough in the cold for the cup to clatter in the saucer as he took it. But the tea was welcome, and Hornblower drank it eagerly.

"Give me another cup," he said, and was proud of himself that he could think about tea at that moment.

It was still dark as they went down into the cutter.

"Shove off," said the coxswain, and the boat pushed off from the ship's side. There was a keen cold wind blowing which filled the dipping lug as the cutter headed for the twin lights that marked the jetty.

"I ordered a hackney coach at the George to be waiting for us," said Danvers. "Let's hope it is."

It was there, with the driver sufficiently sober to control his horse moderately well despite his overnight potations. Danvers produced a pocket flask as they settled themselves in with their feet in the straw.

"Take a sip, Hornblower?" he asked, proffering it. "There's no special need for a steady hand this morning."

"No thank you," said Hornblower. His empty stomach revolted at the idea of pouring spirits into it.

"The others will be there before us," commented Preston. "I saw the quarter boat heading back just before we reached the jetty."

The etiquette of the duel demanded that the two opponents should reach the ground separately; but only one boat would be necessary for the return.

"The sawbones is with them," said Danvers. "Though God knows what use he thinks he'll be today."

He sniggered, and with overlate politeness tried to cut his snigger off short.

"How are you feeling, Hornblower?" asked Preston.

"Well enough," said Hornblower, forbearing to add that he only felt well enough while this kind of conversation was not being carried on.

The hackney coach levelled itself off as it came over the crest of the hill, and stopped beside the Common. Another coach stood there waiting, its single candle-lamp burning yellow in the growing dawn.

"There they are," said Preston; the faint light revealed a shadowy group standing on frosty turf among the gorse bushes.

Hornblower, as they approached, caught a glimpse of Simpson's face as he stood a little detached from the others. It was pale, and Hornblower noticed that at that moment he swallowed nervously, just as he himself was doing. Masters came towards them, shooting his usual keen inquisitive look at Hornblower as they came together.

"This is the moment," he said, "for this quarrel to be composed. This country is at war. I hope, Mr. Hornblower, that you can be persuaded to save a life for the King's service by not pressing this matter."

Hornblower looked across at Simpson, while Danvers answered for him.

"Has Mr. Simpson offered the proper redress?" asked Danvers.

"Mr. Simpson is willing to acknowledge that he wishes the incident had never taken place."

"That is an unsatisfactory form," said Danvers. "It does not include an apology, and you must agree that an apology is necessary, sir."

"What does your principal say?" persisted Masters.

"It is not for my principal to speak in these circumstances," said Danvers, with a glance at Hornblower, who nodded. All this was as inevitable as the ride in the hangman's cart, and as hideous. There could be no going back now; Hornblower had never thought for one moment that Simpson would apologise, and without an apology the affair must be carried to a bloody conclusion. An even chance that he did not have five minutes longer to live.

"You are determined, then, gentlemen," said Masters. "I shall have to state that fact in my report."

"We are determined," said Preston.

"Then there is nothing for it but to allow this deplorable affair to proceed. I left the pistols in the charge of Doctor Hepplewhite."

He turned and led them towards the other group—Simpson with Hether and Cleveland, and Doctor Hepplewhite standing with a pistol held by the muzzle in each hand. He was a bulky man with the red face of a persistent drinker; he was actually grinning a spirituous grin at that moment, rocking a little on his feet.

"Are the young fools set in their folly?" he asked, but everyone very properly ignored him, having no business to ask such a question at such a moment.

"Now," said Masters. "Here are the pistols, both primed, as you see, but one loaded and the other unloaded, in accordance with the conditions. I have here a guinea which I propose to spin to decide the allocation of the weapons. Now, gentlemen, shall the spin give your principals one pistol each irrevocably—for instance, if the coin shows heads shall Mr. Simpson have this one—or shall the winner of the spin have choice of weapons? It is my design to eliminate all possibility of collusion as far as possible."

Hether and Cleveland and Danvers and Preston exchanged dubious glances.

"Let the winner of the spin choose," said Preston at length.

"Very well, gentlemen. Please call, Mr. Hornblower."

"Tails!" said Hornblower as the gold piece spun in the air.

Masters caught it and clapped a hand over it.

"Tails it is," said Masters, lifting his hand and revealing the coin to the grouped seconds. "Please make your choice."

Hepplewhite held out the two pistols to him, death in one hand and life in the other. It was a grim moment. There was only pure chance to direct him; it called for a little effort to force his hand out.

"I'll have this one," he said; as he touched it the weapon seemed icy cold.

"Then now I have done what was required of me," said Masters. "The rest is for you gentlemen to carry out."

"Take this one, Simpson," said Hepplewhite. "And be careful how you handle yours, Mr. Hornblower. You're a public danger."

The man was still grinning, gloating over the fact that someone else was in mortal danger while he himself was in none. Simpson took the pistol Hepplewhite offered him and settled it into his hand; once more his eyes met Hornblower's, but there was neither recognition nor expression in them.

"There are no distances to step out," Danvers was saying. "One spot's as good as another. It's level enough here."

"Very good," said Hether. "Will you stand here, Mr. Simpson?"

Preston beckoned to Hornblower, who walked over. It was not easy to appear brisk and unconcerned. Preston took him by the arm and stood him up in front of Simpson, almost breast to breast—close enough to smell the alcohol on his breath.

"For the last time, gentlemen," said Masters, loudly. "Cannot you be reconciled?"

There was no answer from anybody, only deep silence, during which it seemed to Hornblower that the frantic beating of his heart must be clearly audible. The silence was broken by an exclamation from Hether.

"We haven't settled who's to give the word!" he said. "Who's going to?"

"Let's ask Mr. Masters to give it," said Danvers.

Hornblower did not look round. He was looking steadfastly at the grey sky past Simpson's right ear—somehow he could not look him in the face, and he had no idea where Simpson was looking. The end of the world as he knew it was close to him—soon there might be a bullet through his heart.

"I will do it if you are agreed, gentlemen," he heard Masters say.

The grey sky was featureless; for this last look on the world he might as well have been blindfolded. Masters raised his voice again.

"I will say 'one, two, three, fire,'" he announced, "with those intervals. At the last word, gentlemen, you can fire as you will. Are you ready?"

"Yes," came Simpson's voice, almost in Hornblower's ear, it seemed.

"Yes," said Hornblower. He could hear the strain in his own voice.

"One," said Masters, and Hornblower felt at that moment the muzzle of Simpson's pistol against his left ribs, and he raised his own.

It was in that second that he decided he could not kill Simpson even if it were in his power, and he went on lifting his pistol, forcing himself to look to see that it was pressed against the point of Simpson's shoulder. A slight wound would suffice.

"Two," said Masters. "Three. Fire!"

Hornblower pulled his trigger. There was a click and a spurt of smoke from the lock of his pistol. The priming had gone off but no more—his was the unloaded weapon, and he knew what it was to die. A tenth of a second later there was a click and spurt of smoke from Simpson's pistol against his heart. Stiff and still they both stood, slow to realise what had happened.

"A misfire, by God!" said Danvers.

The seconds crowded round them.

"Give me those pistols!" said Masters, taking them from the weak hands that held them. "The loaded one might be hanging fire, and we don't want it to go off now."

"Which was the loaded one?" asked Hether, consumed with curiosity.

"That is something it is better not to know," answered Masters, changing the two pistols rapidly from hand to hand so as to confuse everyone.

"What about a second shot?" asked Danvers, and Masters looked up straight and inflexibly at him.

"There will be no second shot," he said. "Honour is completely satisfied. These two gentlemen have come through this ordeal extremely well. No one can now think little of Mr. Simpson if he expresses his regret for the occurrence, and no one can think little of Mr. Hornblower if he accepts that statement in reparation."

Hepplewhite burst into a roar of laughter.

"Your faces!" he boomed, slapping his thigh. "You ought to see how you all look! Solemn as cows!"

"Mr. Hepplewhite," said Masters. "Your behaviour is indecorous. Gentlemen, our coaches are waiting on the road, the cutter is at the jetty. And I think all of us would be the better for some breakfast; including Mr. Hepplewhite."

That should have been the end of the incident. The excited talk which had gone round the anchored squadron about the unusual duel died away in time, although everyone knew Hornblower's name now, and not as the midshipman who was seasick in Spithead but as the man who was willing to take an even chance in cold blood. But in the *Justinian* herself there was other talk; whispers which were circulated forward and aft.

"Mr. Hornblower has requested permission to speak to you, sir," said Mr. Clay, the first lieutenant, one morning while making his report to the captain.

"Oh, send him in when you go out," said Keene, and sighed.

Ten minutes later a knock on his cabin door ushered in a very angry young man.

"Sir!" began Hornblower.

"I can guess what you're going to say," said Keene.

"Those pistols in the duel I fought with Simpson were not loaded!"

"Hepplewhite blabbed, I suppose," said Keene.

"And it was by your orders, I understand, sir."

"You are quite correct. I gave those orders to Mr. Masters."

"It was an unwarrantable liberty, sir!"

That was what Hornblower meant to say, but he stumbled without dignity over the polysyllables.

"Possibly it was," said Keene, patiently, rearranging, as always, the papers on his desk.

The calmness of the admission disconcerted Hornblower, who could only splutter for the next few moments.

"I saved a life for the King's service," went on Keene, when the spluttering died away. "A young life. No one has suffered any harm. On the other hand, both you and Simpson have had your courage amply proved. You both know you can stand fire now, and so does everyone else."

"You have touched my personal honour, sir," said Hornblower, bringing out one of his rehearsed speeches. "For that there can only be one remedy."

"Restrain yourself, please, Mr. Hornblower." Keene shifted himself in his chair with a wince of pain as he prepared to make a speech. "I must remind you of one salutary regulation of the navy, to the effect that no junior officer can challenge his superior to a duel. The reasons for it are obvious—otherwise promotion would be too easy. The mere issuing of a challenge by a junior to a senior is a court-martial offence, Mr. Hornblower."

"Oh!" said Hornblower, feebly.

"Now here is some gratuitous advice," went on Keene. "You have fought one duel and emerged with honour. That is good. Never fight another—that is better. Some people, oddly enough, acquire a taste for duelling, as a tiger acquires a taste for blood. They are never good officers, and never popular ones either."

It was then that Hornblower realised that a great part of the keen excitement with which he had entered the captain's cabin was due to anticipation of the giving of the challenge. There could be a morbid desire for danger—and a morbid desire to occupy momentarily the centre of the stage. Keene was waiting for him to speak, and it was hard to say anything.

"I understand, sir," he said at last.

Keene shifted in his chair again.

"There is another matter I wanted to take up with you, Mr. Hornblower. Captain Pellew of the *Indefatigable* has room for another midshipman. Captain Pellew is partial to a game of whist, and has no good fourth on board. He and I have agreed to consider favourably your application for a transfer should you care to make one. I don't have to point out that any ambitious young officer would jump at the chance of serving in a frigate."

"A frigate!" said Hornblower.

Everybody knew of Pellew's reputation and success. Distinction, promotion, prize money—an officer under Pellew's command could hope for all these. Competition for nomination to the *Indefatigable* must be intense, and this was the chance of a lifetime. Hornblower was on the point of making a glad acceptance, when further considerations restrained him.

"That is very good of you, sir," he said. "I do not know how to thank you. But you accepted me as a midshipman here, and of course, I must stay with you."

The drawn, apprehensive face relaxed into a smile.

"Not many men would have said that," said Keene. "But I am going to insist on your accepting the offer. I shall not live very much longer to appreciate your loyalty. And this ship is not the place for you—this ship with her useless captain (don't interrupt me) and her worn-out first lieutenant and her old midshipmen. You should be where there may be speedy opportunities of advancement. I have the good of the service in mind, Mr. Hornblower, when I suggest you accept Captain Pellew's invitation—and it might be less disturbing for me if you did."

"Aye aye, sir," said Hornblower.

Two

HORNBLOWER
and the Cargo of Rice

THE WOLF was in among the sheep. The tossing grey water of the Bay of Biscay was dotted with white sails as far as the eye could see, and although a strong breeze was blowing, every vessel was under perilously heavy canvas. Every ship but one was trying to escape; the exception was His Majesty's frigate *Indefatigable,* Captain Sir Edward Pellew. Farther out in the Atlantic, hundreds of miles away, a great battle was being fought, where the ships of the line were thrashing out the question as to whether England or France should wield the weapon of sea power; here in the Bay the convoy which the French ships were intended to escort was exposed to the attack of a ship of prey at liberty to capture any ship she could overhaul. She had come surging up from leeward, cutting off all chance of escape in that direction, and the clumsy merchant ships were forced to beat to windward; they were all filled with the food which revolutionary France (her economy disordered by the convulsion through which she was passing) was awaiting so anxiously, and their crews were all anxious to escape confinement in an English prison. Ship after ship was overhauled; a shot or two, and the newfangled tricolour came fluttering down from the gaff, and a prize crew was hurriedly sent on board to conduct the captive to an English port while the frigate dashed after fresh prey.

On the quarterdeck of the *Indefatigable* Pellew fumed over each necessary delay. The convoy, each ship as close to the wind as she would lie, and under all the sail she could carry, was slowly scattering, spreading farther and farther with the passing minutes, and some of these would find safety in mere dispersion if any time was wasted. Pellew did not wait to pick up his boat; at each surrender he merely ordered away an officer and an armed guard, and the moment the prize crew was on its way he filled his main topsail again and hurried off after the next victim. The brig they were pursuing at the moment was slow to surrender. The long nine-pounders in the *Indefatigable's* bows bellowed out more than once; on that heaving sea it was not so easy to aim accurately and the brig continued on her course hoping for some miracle to save her.

"Very well," snapped Pellew. "He has asked for it. Let him have it."

The gunlayers at the bow chasers changed their point of aim, firing at the ship instead of across her bows.

"Not into the hull, damn it," shouted Pellew—one shot had struck the brig perilously close to her waterline. "Cripple her."

The next shot by luck or by judgment was given better elevation. The slings of the fore topsail yard were shot away, the reefed sail came down, the yard hanging lopsidedly, and the brig came up into the wind for the *Indefatigable* to heave-to close beside her, her broadside ready to fire into her. Under that threat her flag came down.

"What brig's that?" shouted Pellew through his megaphone.

"*Marie Galante* of Bordeaux," translated the officer beside Pellew as the French captain made reply. "Twenty four days out from New Orleans with rice."

"Rice!" said Pellew. "That'll sell for a pretty penny when we get her home. Two hundred tons, I should say. Twelve of a crew at most. She'll need a prize crew of four, a midshipman's command."

He looked round him as though for inspiration before giving his next order.

"Mr. Hornblower!"

"Sir!"

"Take four men of the cutter's crew and board that brig. Mr. Soames will give you our position. Take her into any English port you can make, and report there for orders."

"Aye aye, sir."

Hornblower was at his station at the starboard quarterdeck carronades—which was perhaps how he had caught Pellew's eye—his dirk at his side and a pistol in his belt. It was a moment for fast thinking, for anyone could see Pellew's impatience. With the *Indefatigable* cleared for action, his sea-chest would be part of the surgeon's operating table down below, so that there was no chance of getting anything out of it. He would have to leave just as he was. The cutter was even now clawing up to a position on the *Indefatigable's* quarter, so he ran to the ship's side and hailed her, trying to make his voice sound as big and as manly as he could, and at the word of the lieutenant in command she turned her bows in towards the frigate.

"Here's our latitude and longitude, Mr. Hornblower," said Soames the master, handing a scrap of paper to him.

"Thank you," said Hornblower, shoving it into his pocket.

He scrambled awkwardly into the mizzen chains and looked down into the cutter. Ship and boat were pitching together, almost bows on to the sea, and the distance between them looked appallingly great; the bearded seaman standing in the bows could only just reach up to the chains with his long boat hook. Hornblower hesitated for a long second; he knew he was ungainly and awkward—book learning was of no use when it came to jumping into a boat—but he had to make the leap, for Pellew was fuming behind him and the eyes of the boat's crew and of the whole ship's company were on him. Better to jump and hurt himself, better to jump and make an exhibition of himself, than to delay the ship. Waiting was certain failure, while he still had a choice if he jumped. Perhaps at a word from Pellew the *Indefatigable's* helmsman allowed the ship's head to fall off from the sea a little. A somewhat diagonal wave lifted the *Indefatigable's* stern and then passed on, so that the cutter's bows rose as the ship's stern sank a trifle. Hornblower braced himself and leaped. His feet reached the gunwale and he tottered there for one indescribable second. A seaman grabbed the breast of his jacket and he fell forward rather than backward. Not even the stout arm of the seaman, fully extended, could hold him up, and he pitched head foremost, legs in the air, upon the hands on the second thwart. He cannoned onto their bodies, knocking the breath out of his own against their muscular shoulders, and finally struggled into an upright position.

"I'm sorry," he gasped to the men who had broken his fall.

"Never you mind, sir," said the nearest one, a real tarry sailor, tattooed and pigtailed. "You're only a featherweight."

The lieutenant in command was looking at him from the sternsheets.

"Would you go to the brig, please, sir?" he asked, and the lieutenant bawled an order and the cutter swung round as Hornblower made his way aft.

It was a pleasant surprise not to be received with the broad grins of tolerantly concealed amusement. Boarding a small boat from a big frigate in even a moderate sea was no easy matter; probably every man on board had arrived head first at some time or other, and it was not in the tradition of the service, as understood in the *Indefatigable,* to laugh at a man who did his best without shirking.

"Are you taking charge of the brig?" asked the lieutenant.

"Yes, sir. The captain told me to take four of your men."

"They had better be topmen, then," said the lieutenant, casting his eyes aloft at the rigging of the brig. The fore topsail yard was hanging precariously, and the jib halliard had slacked off so that the sail was flapping thunderously in the wind. "Do you know these men, or shall I pick 'em for you?"

"I'd be obliged if you would, sir."

The lieutenant shouted four names, and four men replied.

"Keep 'em away from drink and they'll be all right," said the lieutenant. "Watch the French crew. They'll recapture the ship and have you in a French gaol before you can say 'Jack Robinson' if you don't."

"Aye aye, sir," said Hornblower.

The cutter surged alongside the brig, white water creaming between the two vessels. The tattooed sailor hastily concluded a bargain with another man on his thwart and pocketed a lump of tobacco—the men were leaving their possessions behind just like Hornblower—and sprang for the main chains. Another man followed him, and they stood and waited while Hornblower with difficulty made his way forward along the plunging boat. He stood, balancing precariously, on the forward thwart. The main chains of the brig were far lower than the mizzen chains of the *Indefatigable,* but this time he had to jump upwards. One of the seamen steadied him with an arm on his shoulder.

"Wait for it, sir," he said. "Get ready. Now jump, sir."

Hornblower hurled himself, all arms and legs, like a leaping frog, at the main chains. His hands reached the shrouds, but his knee slipped off, and the brig, rolling, lowered him thigh deep into the sea as the shrouds slipped through his hands. But the waiting seamen grabbed his wrists and hauled him on board, and two more seamen followed him. He led the way onto the deck.

The first sight to meet his eyes was a man seated on the hatch cover, his head thrown back, holding to his mouth a bottle, the bottom pointing straight up to the sky. He was one of a large group all sitting round the hatch cover; there were more bottles in evidence; one was passed by one man to another as he looked, and as he approached a roll of the ship brought an empty bottle rolling past his toes to clatter into the scuppers. Another of the group, with white hair blowing in the wind, rose to welcome him, and stood for a moment with waving arms and rolling eyes, bracing himself as though to say something of immense importance and seeking earnestly for the right words to use.

"Goddam English," was what he finally said, and, having said it, he sat down with a bump on the hatch cover and from a seated position proceeded to lie down and compose himself to sleep with his head on his arms.

"They've made the best of their time, sir, by the Holy," said the seaman at Hornblower's elbow.

"Wish we were as happy," said another.

A case still a quarter full of bottles, each elaborately sealed, stood on the deck beside the hatch cover, and the seaman picked out a bottle to look at it curiously. Hornblower did not need to remember the lieutenant's warning; on his shore excursions with press gangs he had already had experience of the British seaman's tendency to drink. His boarding party would be as drunk as the Frenchmen in half an hour if he allowed it. A frightful mental picture of himself drifting in the Bay of Biscay with a disabled ship and a drunken crew, rose in his mind and filled him with anxiety.

"Put that down," he ordered.

The urgency of the situation made his seventeen-year-old voice crack like a fourteen-year-old's, and the seaman hesitated, holding the bottle in his hand.

"Put it down, d'ye hear?" said Hornblower, desperate with worry. This was his first independent command; conditions were absolutely novel, and excitement brought out all the passion of his mercurial temperament, while at the same time the more calculating part of his mind told him that if he were not obeyed now he never would be. His pistol was in his belt, and he put his hand on the butt, and it is conceivable that he would have drawn it and used it (if the priming had not got wet, he said to himself bitterly when he thought about the incident later on) but the seaman with one more glance at him put the bottle back into the case. The incident was closed, and it was time for the next step.

"Take these men for'rard," he said, giving the obvious order. "Throw 'em into the forecastle."

"Aye aye, sir."

Most of the Frenchmen could still walk, but three were dragged by their collars while the British herded the others before them.

"Come alongee," said one of the seamen. "Thisa waya."

He evidently believed a Frenchman would understand him better if he spoke like that. The Frenchman who had greeted their arrival, now awakened and suddenly realising he was being dragged forward, broke away and turned back to Hornblower.

"I officer," he said, pointing to himself. "I not go wit' zem."

"Take him away!" said Hornblower. In his tense condition he could not stop to debate trifles.

He dragged the case of bottles down to the ship's side and pitched them overboard two at a time—obviously it was wine of some special vintage which the Frenchmen had decided to drink before the English could get their hands on it, but that weighed not at all with Hornblower, for a British seaman could get drunk on vintage claret as easily as upon service rum. The task was finished before the last of the Frenchmen disappeared into the forecastle, and Hornblower had time to look about him. The strong breeze blew confusingly round his ears, and the ceaseless thunder of the flapping jib made it hard to think as he looked at the ruin aloft. Every sail was flat aback, the brig was moving jerkily, gathering sternway for a space before her untended rudder threw her round to spill the wind and bring her up again like a jibbing horse. His mathematical mind had already had plenty of experience with a well-handled ship, with the delicate adjustment between after sails and headsails. Here the balance had been disturbed, and Hornblower was at work on the problem of forces acting on plane surfaces when his men came trooping back to him. One thing at least was certain, and that was that the precariously hanging fore topsail yard would tear itself free to do all sorts of unforeseeable damage if it were tossed about much more. The ship must be properly hove-to, and Hornblower could guess how to set about it, and he formulated the order in his mind just in time to avoid any appearance of hesitation.

"Brace the after yards to larboard," he said. "Man the braces, men."

They obeyed him, while he himself went gingerly to the wheel; he had served a few tricks as helmsman, learning his professional duties under Pellew's orders, but he did not feel happy about it. The spokes felt foreign to his fingers as he took hold; he spun the wheel experimentally but timidly. But it was easy. With the after yards braced round the brig rode more comfortably at once, and the spokes told their own story to his sensitive fingers as the ship became a thing of logical construction again. Hornblower's mind completed the solution of the problem of the effect of the rudder at the same time as his senses solved it empirically. The wheel could be safely lashed, he knew, in these conditions, and he slipped the becket over the spoke and stepped away from the wheel, with the *Marie Galante* riding comfortably and taking the seas on her starboard bow.

The seaman took his competence gratifyingly for granted, but Hornblower, looking at the tangle on the foremast, had not the remotest idea of how to deal with the next problem. He was not even sure about what was wrong. But the hands under his orders were seamen of vast experience, who must have dealt with similar emergencies a score of times. The first—indeed the only—thing to do was to delegate his responsibility.

"Who's the oldest seaman among you?" he demanded—his determination not to quaver made him curt.

"Matthews, sir," said someone at length, indicating with his thumb the pigtailed and tattooed seaman upon whom he had fallen in the cutter.

"Very well, then. I'll rate you petty officer, Matthews. Get to work at once and clear that raffle away for'rard. I'll be busy here aft."

It was a nervous moment for Hornblower, but Matthews put his knuckles to his forehead.

"Aye aye, sir," he said, quite as a matter of course.

"Get that jib in first, before it flogs itself to pieces," said Hornblower, greatly emboldened.

"Aye aye, sir."

"Carry on, then."

The seamen turned to go forward, and Hornblower walked aft. He took the telescope from its becket on the poop, and swept the horizon. There were a few sails in sight; the nearest ones he could recognise as prizes, which, with all sail set that they could carry, were heading for England as fast as they could go. Far away to windward he could see the *Indefatigable's* topsails as she clawed after the rest of the convoy—she had already overhauled and captured all the slower and less weatherly vessels so that each succeeding chase would be longer. Soon he would be alone on this wide sea, three hundred miles from England. Three hundred miles—two days with a fair wind; but how long if the wind turned foul?

He replaced the telescope; the men were already hard at work forward, so he went below and looked round the neat cabins of the officers, two single ones for the captain and the mate, presumably, and a double one for the bosun and the cook or the carpenter. He found the lazarette, identifying it by the miscellaneous stores within it; the door was swinging to and fro with a bunch of keys dangling. The French captain, faced with the loss of all he possessed, had not even troubled to lock the door again after taking out the case of wine. Hornblower locked the door and put the keys in his pocket, and felt suddenly lonely—his first experience of the loneliness of the man in command at sea. He went on deck again, and at sight of him Matthews hurried aft and knuckled his forehead.

"Beg pardon, sir, but we'll have to use the jeers to sling that yard again."

"Very good."

"We'll need more hands than we have, sir. Can I put some o' they Frenchies to work?"

"If you think you can. If any of them are sober enough."

"I think I can, sir. Drunk or sober."

"Very good."

It was at that moment that Hornblower remembered with bitter self-reproach that the priming of his pistol was probably wet, and he had not scorn enough for himself at having put his trust in a pistol without repriming after evolutions in a small boat. While Matthews went forward he dashed below again. There was a case of pistols which he remembered having seen in the captain's cabin, with a powder flask and bullet bag hanging beside it. He loaded both weapons and reprimed his own, and came on deck again with three pistols in his belt just as his men appeared from the forecastle herding half a dozen Frenchmen. He posed himself in the poop, straddling with his hands behind his back, trying to adopt an air of magnificent indifference and understanding. With the jeers taking the weight of yard and sail, an hour's hard work resulted in the yard being slung again and the sail reset.

When the work was advancing towards completion Hornblower came to himself again to remember that in a few minutes he would have to set a course, and he dashed below again to set out the chart and the dividers and parallel rulers. From his pocket he extracted the crumpled scrap of paper with his position on it—he had thrust it in there so carelessly a little while back, at a time when the immediate problem before him was to transfer himself from the *Indefatigable* to the cutter. It made him unhappy to think how cavalierly he had treated that scrap of paper then; he began to feel that life in the navy, although it seemed to move from one crisis to another, was really one continuous crisis, that even while dealing with one emergency it was necessary to be making plans to deal with the next. He bent over the chart, plotted his position, and laid off his course. It was a queer uncomfortable feeling to think that what had up to this moment been an academic exercise conducted under the reassuring supervision of Mr. Soames was now something on which hinged his life and his reputation. He checked his working, decided on his course, and wrote it down on a scrap of paper for fear he should forget it.

So when the fore topsail yard was reslung, and the prisoners herded back into the forecastle, and Matthews looked to him for further orders, he was ready.

"We'll square away," he said. "Matthews, send a man to the wheel."

He himself gave a hand at the braces; the wind had moderated and he felt his men could handle the brig under her present sail.

"What course, sir?" asked the man at the wheel, and Hornblower dived into his pocket for his scrap of paper.

"Nor'east by north," he said, reading it out.

"Nor'east by north, sir," said the helmsman, and the *Marie Galante*, running free, set her course for England.

Night was closing in by now, and all round the circle of the horizon there was not a sail in sight. There must be plenty of ships just over the horizon, he knew, but that did not do much to ease his feeling of loneliness as darkness came on. There was so much to do, so much to bear in mind, and all the responsibility lay on his unaccustomed shoulders. The prisoners had to be battened down in the forecastle, a watch had to be set—there was even the trivial matter of hunting up flint and steel to light the binnacle lamp. A hand forward as a lookout, who could also keep an eye on the prisoners below; a hand aft at the wheel. Two hands snatching some sleep—knowing that to get in any sail would be an all-hands job—a hasty meal of water from the scuttlebutt and of biscuit from the cabin stores in the lazarette—a constant eye to be kept on the weather. Hornblower paced the deck in the darkness.

"Why don't you get some sleep, sir?" asked the man at the wheel.

"I will, later on, Hunter," said Hornblower, trying not to allow his tone to reveal the fact that such a thing had never occurred to him.

He knew it was sensible advice, and he actually tried to follow it, retiring below to fling himself down on the captain's cot, but of course he could not sleep. When he heard the lookout bawling down the companionway to rouse the other two hands to relieve the watch (they were asleep in the next cabin to him) he could not prevent himself from getting up again and coming on deck to see that all was well. With Matthews in charge he felt he should not be anxious, and he drove himself below again, but he had hardly fallen onto the cot again when a new thought brought him to his feet again, his skin cold with anxiety, and a prodigious self-contempt vying with the anxiety for first place in his emotions. He rushed on deck and walked forward to where Matthews was squatting by the knightheads.

"Nothing has been done to see if the brig is taking in any water," he said—he had hurriedly worked out the wording of that sentence during his walk forward, so as to cast no aspersion on Matthews and yet at the same time, for the sake of discipline, attributing no blame to himself.

"That's so, sir," said Matthews.

"One of those shots fired by the *Indefatigable* hulled her," went on Hornblower. "What damage did it do?"

"I don't rightly know, sir," said Matthews. "I was in the cutter at the time."

"We must look as soon as it's light," said Hornblower. "And we'd better sound the well now."

Those were brave words; during his rapid course in seamanship aboard the *Indefatigable* Hornblower had had a little instruction everywhere, working under the orders of every head of department in rotation. Once he had been with the carpenter when he sounded the well —whether he could find the well in this ship and sound it he did not know.

"Aye aye, sir," said Matthews, without hesitation, and strolled aft to the pump. "You'll need a light, sir. I'll get one."

When he came back with the lantern he shone it on the coiled sounding line hanging beside the pump, so that Hornblower recognised it at once. He lifted it down, inserted the three-foot weighted rod into the aperture of the well, and then remembered in time to take it out again and make sure it was dry. Then he let it drop, paying out the line until he felt the rod strike the ship's bottom with a satisfactory thud. He hauled out the line again, and Matthews held the lantern as Hornblower with some trepidation brought out the timber to examine it.

"Not a drop, sir!" said Matthews. "Dry as yesterday's pannikin."

Hornblower was agreeably surprised. Any ship he had ever heard of leaked to a certain extent; even in the well-found *Indefatigable* pumping had been necessary every day. He did not know whether this dryness was a remarkable phenomenon or a very remarkable one. He wanted to be both noncommittal and imperturbable.

"H'm," was the comment he eventually produced. "Very good, Matthews. Coil that line again."

The knowledge that the *Marie Galante* was taking no water at all might have encouraged him to sleep, if the wind had not chosen to veer steadily and strengthen itself somewhat, soon after he retired again. It was Matthews who came down and pounded on his door with the unwelcome news.

"We can't keep the course you set much longer, sir," concluded Matthews. "And the wind's coming gusty-like."

"Very good, I'll be up. Call all hands," said Hornblower, with a testiness that might have been the result of a sudden awakening if it had not really disguised his inner quaverings.

With such a small crew he dared not run the slightest risk of being taken by surprise by the weather. Nothing could be done in a hurry, as he soon found. He had to take the wheel while his four hands laboured at reefing topsails and snugging the brig down, and the task took half the night, and by the time it was finished it was quite plain that with the wind veering northerly the *Marie Galante* could not steer northeast by north any longer. Hornblower gave up the wheel and went below to the chart, but what he saw there only confirmed the pessimistic decision he had already reached by mental calculation. As close to the wind as they could lie on this tack they could not weather Ushant. Shorthanded as he was he did not dare continue in the hope that the wind might back; all his reading and all his instruction had warned him of the terrors of a lee shore. There was nothing for it but to go about; he returned to the deck with a heavy heart.

"All hands wear ship," he said, trying to bellow the order in the manner of Mr. Bolton, the third lieutenant of the *Indefatigable*.

They brought the brig safely round, and she took up her new course, close hauled on the starboard tack. Now she was heading away from the dangerous shores of France, without a doubt, but she was heading nearly as directly away from the friendly shores of England—gone was all hope of an easy two days' run to England; gone was any hope of sleep that night for Hornblower.

During the year before he joined the navy Hornblower had attended classes given by a penniless French *émigré* in French, music, and dancing. Early enough the wretched *émigré* had found that Hornblower had no ear for music whatever, which made it almost impossible to teach him to dance, and so he had endeavoured to earn his fee by concentrating on French. A good deal of what he had taught Hornblower had found a permanent resting place in Hornblower's tenacious memory. He had never thought it would be of much use to him, but he discovered the contrary when the French captain at dawn insisted on an interview with him. The Frenchman had a little English, but it was a pleasant surprise to Hornblower to find that they actually could get along better in French, as soon as he could fight down his shyness sufficiently to produce the halting words.

The captain drank thirstily from the scuttlebutt; his cheeks were of course unshaven and he wore a bleary look after twelve hours in a crowded forecastle where he had been battened down three parts drunk.

"My men are hungry," said the captain; he did not look hungry himself.

"Mine also," said Hornblower. "I also."

It was natural when one spoke French to gesticulate, to indicate his men with a wave of the hand and himself with a tap on the chest.

"I have a cook," said the captain.

It took some time to arrange the terms of a truce. The Frenchmen were to be allowed on deck, the cook was to provide food for everyone on board, and while these amenities were permitted, until noon, the French would make no attempt to take the ship.

"Good," said the captain at length, and when Hornblower had given the necessary orders permitting the release of the crew he shouted for the cook and entered into an urgent discussion regarding dinner. Soon smoke was issuing satisfactorily from the galley chimney.

Then the captain looked up at the grey sky, at the close reefed topsails, and glanced into the binnacle at the compass.

"A foul wind for England," he remarked.

"Yes," said Hornblower, shortly. He did not want this Frenchman to guess at his trepidation and bitterness.

The captain seemed to be feeling the motion of the brig under his feet with attention.

"She rides a little heavily, does she not?" he said.

"Perhaps," said Hornblower. He was not familiar with the *Marie Galante* nor with ships at all, and he had no opinion on the subject, but he was not going to reveal his ignorance.

"Does she leak?" asked the captain.

"There is no water in her," said Hornblower.

"Ah!" said the captain. "But you would find none in the well. We are carrying a cargo of rice, you must remember."

"Yes," said Hornblower.

He found it very hard at that moment to remain outwardly unperturbed, as his mind grasped the implications of what was being said to him. Rice would absorb every drop of water taken in by the ship, so that no leak would be apparent on sounding the well—and yet every drop of water taken in would deprive her of that much buoyancy, all the same.

"One shot from your cursed frigate struck us in the hull," said the captain. "Of course you have investigated the damage?"

"Of course," said Hornblower, lying bravely.

But as soon as he could he had a private conversation with Matthews on the point, and Matthews instantly looked grave.

"Where did the shot hit her, sir?" he asked.

"Somewhere on the port side, for'rard, I should judge."

He and Matthews craned their necks over the ship's side.

"Can't see nothin', sir," said Matthews. "Lower me over the side in a bowline and I'll see what I can find, sir."

Hornblower was about to agree and then changed his mind.

"I'll go over the side myself," he said.

He could not analyse the motives which impelled him to say that. Partly he wanted to see things with his own eyes; partly he was influenced by the doctrine that he should never give an order he was not prepared to carry out himself—but mostly it must have been the desire to impose a penance on himself for his negligence.

Matthews and Carson put a bowline round him and lowered him over. He found himself dangling against the ship's side, with the sea bubbling just below him; as the ship pitched the sea came up to meet him, and he was wet to the waist in the first five seconds; and as the ship rolled he was alternately swung away from the side and bumped against it. The men with the line walked steadily aft, giving him the chance to examine the whole side of the brig above water, and there was not a shot hole to be seen. He said as much to Matthews when they hauled him on deck.

"Then it's below the waterline, sir," said Matthews, saying just what was in Hornblower's mind. "You're sure the shot hit her, sir?"

"Yes, I'm sure," snapped Hornblower.

Lack of sleep and worry and a sense of guilt were all shortening his temper, and he had to speak sharply or break down in tears. But he had already decided on the next move—he had made up his mind about that while they were hauling him up.

"We'll heave her to on the other tack and try again," he said.

On the other tack the ship would incline over to the other side, and the shot hole, if there was one, would not be so deeply submerged. Hornblower stood with the water dripping from his clothes as they wore the brig round; the wind was keen and cold, but he was shivering with expectancy rather than cold. The heeling of the brig laid him much more definitely against the side, and they lowered him until his legs were scraping over the marine growths which she carried there between wind and water. Then they walked aft with him, dragging him along the side of the ship, and just abaft the foremast he found what he was seeking.

"Avast, there!" he yelled up to the deck, mastering the sick despair that he felt. The motion of the bowline along the ship ceased. "Lower away! Another two feet!"

Now he was waist-deep in the water, and when the brig swayed the water closed briefly over his head, like a momentary death. Here it was, two feet below the waterline even with the brig hove-to on this tack—a splintered, jagged hole, square rather than round, and a foot across. As the sea boiled round him Hornblower even fancied he could hear it bubbling into the ship, but that might be pure fancy.

He hailed the deck for them to haul him up again, and they stood eagerly listening for what he had to say.

"Two feet below the waterline, sir?" said Matthews. "She was close hauled and heeling right over, of course, when we hit her. But her bows must have lifted just as we fired. And of course she's lower in the water now."

That was the point. Whatever they did now, however much they heeled her, that hole would be under water. And on the other tack it would be far under water, with much additional pressure; yet on the present tack they were headed for France. And the more water they took in, the lower the brig would settle, and the greater would be the pressure forcing water in through the hole. Something must be done to plug the leak, and Hornblower's reading of the manuals of seamanship told him what it was.

"We must fother a sail and get it over that hole," he announced. "Call those Frenchmen over."

To fother a sail was to make something like a vast hairy doormat out of it, by threading innumerable lengths of half-unravelled line through it. When this was done the sail was lowered below the ship's bottom and placed against the hole. The inward pressure would then force the hairy mass so tightly against the hole that the entrance of water would be made at least much more difficult.

The Frenchmen were not quick to help in the task; it was no longer their ship, and they were heading for an English prison, so that even with their lives at stake they were somewhat apathetic. It took time to get out a new topgallant sail—Hornblower felt that the stouter the canvas the better—and to set a party to work cutting lengths of line, threading them through, and unravelling them. The French captain looked at them squatting on the deck all at work.

"Five years I spent in a prison hulk in Portsmouth during the last war," he said. "Five years."

"Yes," said Hornblower.

He might have felt sympathy, but he was not only preoccupied with his own problems but he was numb with cold. He not only had every intention if possible of escorting the French captain to England and to prison again but he also at that very moment intended to go below and appropriate some of his spare clothing.

Down below it seemed to Hornblower as if the noises all about him—the creaks and groans of a wooden ship at sea—were more pronounced than usual. The brig was riding easily enough, hove-to, and yet the bulkheads down below were cracking and creaking as if the brig were racking herself to pieces in a storm. He dismissed the notion as a product of his overstimulated imagination, but by the time he had towelled himself into something like warmth and put on the captain's best suit it recurred to him; the brig was groaning as if in stress.

He came on deck again to see how the working party was progressing. He had hardly been on deck two minutes when one of the Frenchmen, reaching back for another length of line, stopped in his movement to stare at the deck. He picked at a deck seam, looked up and caught Hornblower's eye, and called to him. Hornblower made no pretence of understanding the words; the gestures explained themselves. The deck seam was opening a little; the pitch was bulging out of it. Hornblower looked at the phenomenon without understanding it—only a foot or two of the seam was open, and the rest of the deck seemed solid enough. No! Now that his attention was called to it, and he looked further, there were one or two other places in the deck where the pitch had risen in ridges from out of the seams. It was something beyond his limited experience, even beyond his extensive reading. But the French captain was at his side staring at the deck too.

"My God!" he said. "The rice! The rice!"

The French word *"riz"* that he used was unknown to Hornblower, but he stamped his foot on the deck and pointed down through it.

"The cargo!" he said in explanation. "It—it grows bigger."

Matthews was with them now, and without knowing a word of French he understood.

"Didn't I hear this brig was full of rice, sir?" he asked.

"Yes."

"That's it, then. The water's got into it and it's swelling."

So it would. Dry rice soaked in water would double or treble its volume. The cargo was swelling and bursting the seams of the ship open. Hornblower remembered the unnatural creaks and groans below. It was a black moment; he looked round at the unfriendly sea for inspiration and support, and found neither. Several seconds passed before he was ready to speak, and ready to maintain the dignity of a naval officer in face of difficulties.

"The sooner we get that sail over that hole the better, then," he said. It was too much to be expected that his voice should sound quite natural. "Hurry those Frenchmen up."

He turned to pace the deck, so as to allow his feelings to subside and to set his thoughts running in an orderly fashion again, but the French captain was at his elbow, voluble as a Job's comforter.

"I said I thought the ship was riding heavily," he said. "She is lower in the water."

"Go to the devil," said Hornblower, in English—he could not think up the French for that phrase.

Even as he stood he felt a sudden sharp shock beneath his feet, as if someone had hit the deck underneath them with a mallet. The ship was springing apart bit by bit.

"Hurry with that sail!" he yelled, turning back to the working party, and then was angry with himself because the tone of his voice must have betrayed undignified agitation.

At last an area five feet square of the sail was fothered, lines were rove through the grommets, and the working party hurried forward to work the sail under the brig and drag it aft to the hole. Hornblower was taking off his clothes, not out of regard for the captain's property but so as to keep them dry for himself.

"I'll go over and see that it's in place," he said. "Matthews, get a bowline ready for me."

Naked and wet, it seemed to him as if the wind blew clear through him; rubbing against the ship's side as she rolled he lost a good deal of skin, and the waves passing down the ship smacked at him with a boisterous lack of consideration. But he saw the fothered sail placed against the hole, and with intense satisfaction he saw the hairy mass suck into position, dimpling over the hole to form a deep hollow so that he could be sure that the hole was plugged solid. They hauled him up again when he hailed, and awaited his orders; he stood naked, stupid with cold and fatigue and lack of sleep, struggling to form his next decision.

"Lay her on the starboard tack," he said at length.

If the brig were going to sink, it hardly mattered if it were one hundred or two hundred miles from the French coast; if she were to stay afloat he wanted to be well clear of that lee shore and the chance of recapture. The shot hole with its fothered sail would be deeper under water to increase the risk, but it seemed to be the best chance. The French captain saw them making preparations to wear the brig round, and turned upon Hornblower with voluble protests. With this wind they could make Bordeaux easily on the other tack. Hornblower was risking all their lives, he said. Into Hornblower's numb mind crept, uninvited, the translation of something he had previously wanted to say. He could use it now.

"*Allez au diable,*" he snapped, as he put the Frenchman's stout woollen shirt on over his head.

When his head emerged the Frenchman was still protesting volubly, so violently indeed that a new doubt came into Hornblower's mind. A word to Matthews sent him round the French prisoners to search for weapons. There was nothing to be found except the sailors' knives, but as a matter of precaution Hornblower had them all impounded, and when he had dressed he went to special trouble with his three pistols, drawing the charges from them and reloading and repriming afresh. Three pistols in his belt looked piratical, as though he were still young enough to be playing imaginative games, but Hornblower felt in his bones that there might be a time when the Frenchmen might try to rise against their captors, and three pistols would not be too many against twelve desperate men who had makeshift weapons ready to hand, belaying pins and the like.

Matthews was awaiting him with a long face.

"Sir," he said. "Begging your pardon, but I don't like the looks of it. Straight, I don't. I don't like the feel of her. She's settlin' down and she's openin' up, I'm certain sure. Beg your pardon, sir, for saying so."

Down below Hornblower had heard the fabric of the ship continuing to crack and complain; up here the deck seams were gaping more widely. There was a very likely explanation; the swelling of the rice must have forced open the ship's seams below water, so that plugging the shot hole would have only eliminated what would be by now only a minor leak. Water must still be pouring in, the cargo still swelling, opening up the ship like an overblown flower. Ships were built to withstand blows from without, but there was nothing about their construction to resist an outward pressure. Wider and wider would gape the seams, and faster and faster the sea would gain access to the cargo.

"Look'ee there, sir!" said Matthews suddenly.

In the broad light of day a small grey shape was hurrying along the weather scuppers; another one followed it and another after that. Rats! Something convulsive must be going on down below to bring them on deck in daytime, from out of their comfortable nests among the unlimited food of the cargo. The pressure must be enormous. Hornblower felt another small shock beneath his feet at that moment, as something further parted beneath them. But there was one more card to play, one last line of defence that he could think of.

"I'll jettison the cargo," said Hornblower. He had never uttered that word in his life, but he had read it. "Get the prisoners and we'll start."

The battened-down hatch cover was domed upwards curiously and significantly; as the wedges were knocked out one plank tore loose at one end with a crash, pointing diagonally upwards, and as the working party lifted off the cover a brown form followed it upwards—a bag of rice, forced out by the underlying pressure until it jammed in the hatchway.

"Tail onto those tackles and sway it up," said Hornblower.

Bag by bag the rice was hauled up from the hold; sometimes the bags split, allowing a torrent of rice to pour onto the deck, but that did not matter. Another section of the working party swept rice and bags to the lee side and into the ever-hungry sea. After the first three bags the difficulties increased, for the cargo was so tightly jammed below that it called for enormous force to tear each bag out of its position. Two men had to go down the hatchway to pry the bags loose and adjust the slings. There was a momentary hesitation on the part of the two Frenchmen to whom Hornblower pointed—the bags might not all be jammed and the hold of a tossing ship was a dangerous place wherein a roll might bury them alive—but Hornblower had no thought at that moment for other people's human fears. He scowled at the brief check and they hastened to lower themselves down the hatchway. The labour was enormous as it went on hour after hour; the men at the tackles were dripping with sweat and drooping with fatigue, but they had to relieve periodically the men below, for the bags had jammed themselves in tiers, pressed hard against the ship's bottom below and the deck beams above, and when the bags immediately below the hatchway had been swayed up the surrounding ones had to be pried loose, out of each tier. Then when a small clearance had been made in the neighborhood of the hatchway, and they were getting deeper down into the hold, they made the inevitable discovery. The lower tiers of bags had been wetted, their contents had swelled, and the bags had burst. The lower half of the hold was packed solid with damp rice which could only be got out with shovels and a hoist. The still intact bags of the upper tiers, farther away from the hatchway, were still jammed tight, calling for much labour to free them and to manhandle them under the hatchway to be hoisted out.

Hornblower, facing the problem, was distracted by a touch on his elbow when Matthews came up to speak to him.

"It ain't no go, sir," said Matthews. "She's lower in the water an' settlin' fast."

Hornblower walked to the ship's side with him and looked over. There could be no doubt about it. He had been over the side himself and could remember the height of the waterline, and he had for a more exact guide the level of the fothered sail under the ship's bottom. The brig was a full six inches lower in the water—and this after fifty tons of rice at least had been hoisted out and flung over the side. The brig must be leaking like a basket, with water pouring in through the gaping seams to be sucked up immediately by the thirsty rice.

Hornblower's left hand was hurting him, and he looked down to discover that he was gripping the rail with it so tightly as to cause him pain, without knowing he was doing so. He released his grip and looked about him, at the afternoon sun, at the tossing sea. He did not want to give in and admit defeat. The French captain came up to him.

"This is folly," he said. "Madness, sir. My men are overcome by fatigue."

Over by the hatchway, Hornblower saw, Hunter was driving the French seamen to their work with a rope's end which he was using furiously. There was not much more work to be got out of the Frenchmen; and at that moment the *Marie Galante* rose heavily to a wave and wallowed down the farther side. Even his inexperience could detect the sluggishness and ominous deadness of her movements. The brig had not much longer to float, and there was a good deal to do.

"I shall make preparations for abandoning the ship, Matthews," he said.

He poked his chin upwards as he spoke; he would not allow either a Frenchman or a seaman to guess at his despair.

"Aye aye, sir," said Matthews.

The *Marie Galante* carried a boat on chocks abaft the mainmast; at Matthews' summons the men abandoned their work on the cargo and hurried to the business of putting food and water in her.

"Beggin' your pardon, sir," said Hunter aside to Hornblower, "but you ought to see you have warm clothes, sir. I been in an open boat ten days once, sir."

"Thank you, Hunter," said Hornblower.

There was much to think of. Navigating instruments, charts, compass—would he be able to get a good observation with his sextant in a tossing little boat? Common prudence dictated that they should have all the food and water with them that the boat could carry; but—Hornblower eyed the wretched craft dubiously—seventeen men would fill it to overflowing anyway. He would have to leave much to the judgment of the French captain and of Matthews.

The tackles were manned and the boat was swayed up from the chocks and lowered into the water in the tiny lee afforded on the lee quarter. The *Marie Galante* put her nose into a wave, refusing to rise to it; green water came over the starboard bow and poured aft along the deck before a sullen wallow on the part of the brig sent it into the scuppers. There was not much time to spare—a rending crash from below told that the cargo was still swelling and forcing the bulkheads. There was a panic among the Frenchmen, who began to tumble down into the boat with loud cries. The French captain took one look at Hornblower and then followed them; two of the British seamen were already over the side fending off the boat.

"Go along," said Hornblower to Matthews and Carson, who still lingered. He was the captain; it was his place to leave the ship last.

So waterlogged was the brig now that it was not at all difficult to step down into the boat from the deck; the British seamen were in the sternsheets and made room for him.

"Take the tiller, Matthews," said Hornblower; he did not feel he was competent to handle that overloaded boat. "Shove off, there!"

The boat and the brig parted company; the *Marie Galante,* with her helm lashed, poked her nose into the wind and hung there. She had acquired a sudden list, with the starboard side scuppers nearly under water. Another wave broke over her deck, pouring up to the open hatchway. Now she righted herself, her deck nearly level with the sea, and then she sank, on an even keel, the water closing over her, her masts slowly disappearing. For an instant her sails even gleamed under the green water.

"She's gone," said Matthews.

Hornblower watched the disappearance of his first command. The *Marie Galante* had been entrusted to him to bring into port, and he had failed, failed on his first independent mission. He looked very hard at the setting sun, hoping no one would notice the tears that were filling his eyes.

Three

HORNBLOWER
and the Penalty of Failure

DAYLIGHT crept over the tossing waters of the Bay of Biscay to reveal a small boat riding on its wide expanses. It was a very crowded boat; in the bows huddled the French crew of the sunken brig *Marie Galante,* amidships sat the captain and his mate, and in the sternsheets sat Midshipman Horatio Hornblower and the four English seamen who had once constituted the prize crew of the brig. Hornblower was seasick, for his delicate stomach, having painfully accustomed itself to the motion of the *Indefatigable,* rebelled at the antics of the small boat as she pitched jerkily to her sea-anchor. He was cold and weary as well as seasick after his second night without sleep—he had been vomiting spasmodically all through the hours of darkness, and in the depression which seasickness brings he had thought gloomily about the loss of the *Marie Galante.* If he had only remembered earlier to plug that shot hole! Excuses came to his mind only to be discarded. There had been so much to do, and so few men to do it with—the French crew to guard, the damage aloft to repair, the course to set. The absorbent qualities of the cargo of rice which the *Marie Galante* carried had deceived him when he had remembered to sound the well. All this might be true, but the fact remained that he had lost his ship, his first command. In his own eyes there was no excuse for his failure.

The French crew had wakened with the dawn and were chattering like a nest of magpies; Matthews and Carson beside him were moving stiffly to ease their aching joints.

"Breakfast, sir?" said Matthews.

It was like the games Hornblower had played as a lonely little boy, when he had sat in the empty pig-trough and pretended he was cast away in an open boat. Then he had parcelled out the bit of bread or whatever it was which he had obtained from the kitchen into a dozen rations, counting them carefully, each one to last a day. But a small boy's eager appetite had made those days very short, not more than five minutes long; after standing up in the pig-trough and shading his eyes and looking round the horizon for the succour that he could not discover, he would sit down again, tell himself that the life of a castaway was hard, and then decide that another night had passed and that it was time to eat another ration from his dwindling supply. So here under Hornblower's eye the French captain and mate served out a biscuit of hard bread to each person in the boat, and filled the pannikin for each man in turn from the water breakers under the thwarts. But Hornblower, when he sat in the pig-trough, despite his vivid imagination, never thought of this hideous seasickness, of the cold and the cramps, nor of how his skinny posterior would ache with its constant pressure against the hard timbers of the sternsheets; nor, in the sublime self-confidence of childhood, had he ever thought how heavy could be the burden of responsibility on the shoulders of a senior naval officer aged seventeen.

He dragged himself back from the memories of that recent childhood to face the present situation. The grey sky, as far as his inexperienced eye could tell, bore no presage of deterioration in the weather. He wetted his finger and held it up, looking in the boat's compass to gauge the direction of the wind.

"Backing westerly a little, sir," said Matthews, who had been copying his movements.

"That's so," agreed Hornblower, hurriedly going through in his mind his recent lessons in boxing the compass. His course to weather Ushant was nor'east by north, he knew, and the boat close hauled would not lie closer than eight points off the wind—he had lain-to to the sea-anchor all night because the wind had been coming from too far north to enable him to steer for England. But now the wind had backed. Eight points from nor'east by north was nor'west by west, and the wind was even more westerly than that. Close hauled he could weather Ushant and even have a margin for contingencies, to keep him clear of the lee shore which the seamanship books and his own commonsense told him was so dangerous.

"We'll make sail, Matthews," he said; his hand was still grasping the biscuit which his rebellious stomach refused to accept.

"Aye aye, sir."

A shout to the Frenchmen crowded in the bows drew their attention; in the circumstances it hardly needed Hornblower's halting French to direct them to carry out the obvious task of getting in the sea-anchor.

But it was not too easy, with the boat so crowded and hardly a foot of freeboard. The mast was already stepped, and the lug sail bent ready to hoist. Two Frenchmen, balancing precariously, tailed onto the halliard and the sail rose up the mast.

"Hunter, take the sheet," said Hornblower. "Matthews, take the tiller. Keep her close hauled on the port tack."

"Close hauled on the port tack, sir."

The French captain had watched the proceedings with intense interest from his seat amidships. He had not understood the last, decisive order, but he grasped its meaning quickly enough when the boat came round and steadied on the port tack, heading for England. He stood up, spluttering angry protests.

"The wind is fair for Bordeaux," he said, gesticulating with clenched fists. "We could be there by tomorrow. Why do we go north?"

"We go to England," said Hornblower.

"But—but—it will take us a week! A week even if the wind stays fair. This boat—it is too crowded. We cannot endure a storm. It is madness."

Hornblower had guessed at the moment the captain stood up what he was going to say, and he hardly bothered to translate the expostulations to himself. He was too tired and too seasick to enter into an argument in a foreign language. He ignored the captain. Not for anything on earth would he turn the boat's head towards France. His naval career had only just begun, and even if it were to be blighted on account of the loss of the *Marie Galante* he had no intention of rotting for years in a French prison.

"Sir!" said the French captain.

The mate who shared the captain's thwart was protesting too, and now they turned to their crew behind them and told them what was going on. An angry movement stirred the crowd.

"Sir!" said the captain again. "I insist that you head towards Bordeaux."

He showed signs of advancing upon them; one of the crew behind him began to pull the boat hook clear, and it would be a dangerous weapon. Hornblower pulled one of the pistols from his belt and pointed it at the captain, who, with the muzzle four feet from his breast, fell back before the gesture. Without taking his eyes off him Hornblower took a second pistol with his left hand.

"Take this, Matthews," he said.

"Aye aye, sir," said Matthews, obeying, and then, after a respectful pause, "Beggin' your pardon, sir, but hadn't you better cock your pistol, sir?"

"Yes," said Hornblower, exasperated at his own forgetfulness.

He drew the hammer back with a click, and the menacing sound made more acute still the French captain's sense of his own danger, with a cocked and loaded pistol pointed at his stomach in a heaving boat. He waved his hands desperately.

"Please," he said, "point it some other way, sir."

He drew farther back, huddling against the men behind him.

"Hey, avast there, you," shouted Matthews loudly; a French sailor was trying to let go the halliard unobserved.

"Shoot any man who looks dangerous, Matthews," said Hornblower.

He was so intent on enforcing his will upon these men, so desperately anxious to retain his liberty, that his face was contracted into a beast-like scowl. No one looking at him could doubt his determination for a moment. He would allow no human life to come between him and his decisions. There was still a third pistol in his belt, and the Frenchmen could guess that if they tried a rush a quarter of them at least would meet their deaths before they overpowered the Englishmen, and the French captain knew he would be the first to die. His expressive hands, waving out from his sides—he could not take his eyes from the pistol—told his men to make no further resistance. Their murmurings died away, and the captain began to plead.

"Five years I was in an English prison during the last war," he said. "Let us reach an agreement. Let us go to France. When we reach the shore—anywhere you choose, sir—we will land and you can continue on your journey. Or we can all land, and I will use all my influence to have you and your men sent back to England under cartel, without exchange or ransom. I swear I will."

"No," said Hornblower.

England was far easier to reach from here than from the French Biscay coast; as for the other suggestion, Hornblower knew enough about the new government washed up by the revolution in France to be sure that they would never part with prisoners on the representation of a merchant captain. And trained seamen were scarce in France; it was his duty to keep these dozen from returning.

"No," he said again, in reply to the captain's fresh protests.

"Shall I clout 'im on the jaw, sir?" asked Hunter, at Hornblower's side.

"No," said Hornblower again, but the Frenchman saw the gesture and guessed at the meaning of the words, and subsided into sullen silence.

But he was roused again at the sight of Hornblower's pistol on his knee, still pointed at him. A sleepy finger might press that trigger.

"Sir," he said, "put that pistol away, I beg of you. It is dangerous."

Hornblower's eye was cold and unsympathetic.

"Put it away, please. I will do nothing to interfere with your command of this boat. I promise you that."

"Do you swear it?"

"I swear it."

"And these others?"

The captain looked round at his crew with voluble explanations, and grudgingly they agreed.

"They swear it too."

"Very well, then."

Hornblower started to replace the pistol in his belt, and remembered to put it on half-cock in time to save himself from shooting himself in the stomach. Everyone in the boat relaxed into apathy. The boat was rising and swooping rhythmically now, a far more comfortable motion than when it had jerked to a sea-anchor, and Hornblower's stomach lost some of its resentment. He had been two nights without sleep. His head lowered on his chest, and then he leaned sideways against Hunter, and slept peacefully, while the boat, with the wind nearly abeam, headed steadily for England. He was awakened late in the day when Matthews, cramped and weary, was compelled to surrender the tiller to Carson, and after that they kept watch and watch, a hand at the sheet and a hand at the tiller and the others trying to rest. Hornblower took his turn at the sheet, but he would not trust himself with the tiller, especially when night fell; he knew he had not the knack of keeping the boat on her course by the feel of the wind on his cheek and the tiller in his hand.

It was not until long after breakfast the next day—almost noon, in fact—that they sighted the sail. It was a Frenchman who saw it first, and his excited cry roused them all. There were three square topsails coming up over the horizon on their weather bow, nearing them so rapidly on a converging course that each time the boat rose on a wave a considerably greater area of canvas was visible.

"What do you think she is, Matthews?" asked Hornblower, while the boat buzzed with the Frenchmen's excitement.

"I can't tell, sir, but I don't like the looks of her," said Matthews doubtfully. "She ought to have her t'gallants set in this breeze—and her courses too, an' she hasn't. An' I don't like the cut of her jib, sir. She—she might be a Frenchie to me, sir."

Any ship travelling for peaceful purposes would naturally have all possible sail set. This ship had not. Hence she was engaged in some belligerent design, but there were more chances that she was British than that she was French, even here in the Bay. Hornblower took a long look at her: a smallish vessel, although ship-rigged. Flush-decked, with a look of speed about her—her hull was visible at intervals now, with a line of gunports.

"She looks French all over to me, sir," said Hunter. "Privateer, seemly."

"Stand by to jibe," said Hornblower.

They brought the boat round before the wind, heading directly away from the ship. But in war as in the jungle, to fly is to invite pursuit and attack. The ship set courses and topgallants and came tearing down upon them, passed them at half a cable's length and then hove-to having cut off their escape. The ship's rail was lined with a curious crowd—a large crew for a vessel that size. A hail came across the water to the boat, and the words were French. The English seamen subsided into curses, while the French captain cheerfully stood up and replied, and the French crew brought the boat alongside the ship.

A handsome young man in a plum-coloured coat with a lace stock greeted Hornblower when he stepped on the deck.

"Welcome, sir, to the *Pique*," he said in French. "I am Captain Neuville, of this privateer. And you are—?"

"Midshipman Hornblower, of His Britannic Majesty's Ship *Indefatigable*," growled Hornblower.

"You seem to be in an evil humour," said Neuville. "Please do not be so distressed at the fortunes of war. You will be accommodated in this ship, until we return to port, with every comfort possible at sea. I beg of you to consider yourself quite at home. For instance, those pistols in your belt must discommode you more than a little. Permit me to relieve you of their weight."

He took the pistols neatly from Hornblower's belt as he spoke, looked Hornblower keenly over, and then went on.

"That dirk that you wear at your side, sir. Would you oblige me by the loan of it? I assure you that I will return it to you when we part company. But while you are on board here I fear that your impetuous youth might lead you into some rash act while you are wearing a weapon which a credulous mind might believe to be lethal. A thousand thanks. And now might I show you the berth that is being prepared for you?"

With a courteous bow he led the way below. Two decks down, presumably at the level of a foot or two below the waterline, was a wide bare 'tween-decks, dimly lighted and scantily ventilated by the hatchways.

"Our slave deck," explained Neuville, carelessly.

"Slave deck?" asked Hornblower.

"Yes. It is here that the slaves were confined during the middle passage."

Much was clear to Hornblower at once. A slave ship could be readily converted into a privateer. She would already be armed with plenty of guns to defend herself against treacherous attacks while making her purchases in the African rivers; she was faster than the average merchant ship both because of the lack of need of hold space and because with a highly perishable cargo such as slaves speed was a desirable quality, and she was constructed to carry large numbers of men and the great quantities of food and water necessary to keep them supplied while at sea in search of prizes.

"Our market in San Domingo has been closed to us by recent events, of which you must have heard, sir," went on Neuville, "and so that the *Pique* could continue to return dividends to me I have converted her into a privateer. Moreover, seeing that the activities of the Committee of Public Safety at present make Paris a more unhealthy spot even than the West Coast of Africa, I decided to take command of my vessel myself. To say nothing of the fact that a certain resolution and hardihood are necessary to make a privateer a profitable investment."

Neuville's face hardened for a moment into an expression of the grimmest determination, and then softened at once into its previous meaningless politeness.

"This door in this bulkhead," he continued, "leads to the quarters I have set aside for captured officers. Here, as you see, is your cot. Please make yourself at home here. Should this ship go into action—as I trust she will frequently do—the hatches above will be battened down. But except on those occasions you will of course be at liberty to move about the ship at your will. Yet I suppose I had better add that any harebrained attempt on the part of prisoners to interfere with the working or well-being of this ship would be deeply resented by the crew. They serve on shares, you understand, and are risking their lives and their liberty. I would not be surprised if any rash person who endangered their dividends and freedom were dropped over the side into the sea."

Hornblower forced himself to reply; he would not reveal that he was almost struck dumb by the calculating callousness of this last speech.

"I understand," he said.

"Excellent! Now is there anything further you may need, sir?"

Hornblower looked round the bare quarters in which he was to suffer lonely confinement, lit by a dim glimmer of light from a swaying slush lamp.

"Could I have something to read?" he asked.

Neuville thought for a moment.

"I fear there are only professional books," he said. "But I can let you have Grandjean's *Principles of Navigation*, and Lebrun's *Handbook on Seamanship* and some similar volumes, if you think you can understand the French in which they are written."

"I'll try," said Hornblower.

Probably it was as well that Hornblower was provided with the materials for such strenuous mental exercise. The effort of reading French and of studying his profession at one and the same time kept his mind busy during the dreary days while the *Pique* cruised in search of prizes. Most of the time the Frenchmen ignored him—he had to force himself upon Neuville once to protest against the employment of his four British seamen on the menial work of pumping out the ship, but he had to retire worsted from the argument, if argument it could be called, when Neuville icily refused to discuss the question. Hornblower went back to his quarters with burning cheeks and red ears, and, as ever, when he was mentally disturbed, the thought of his guilt returned to him with new force.

If only he had plugged that shot hole sooner! A clearer-headed officer, he told himself, would have done so. He had lost his ship, the *Indefatigable's* precious prize, and there was no health in him. Sometimes he made himself review the situation calmly. Professionally, he might not—probably would not—suffer for his negligence. A midshipman with only four for a prize crew, put on board a two hundred ton brig that had been subjected to considerable firing from a frigate's guns, would not be seriously blamed when she sank under him. But Hornblower knew at the same time that he was at least partly at fault. If it was ignorance—there was no excuse for ignorance. If he had allowed his multiple cares to distract him from the business of plugging the shot hole immediately, that was incompetence, and there was no excuse for incompetence. When he thought along those lines he was overwhelmed by waves of despair and of self-contempt, and there was no one to comfort him. The day of his birthday, when he looked at himself at the vast age of eighteen, was the worst of all. Eighteen and a discredited prisoner in the hands of a French privateersman! His self-respect was at its lowest ebb.

The *Pique* was seeking her prey in the most frequented waters in the world, the approaches to the Channel, and there could be no more vivid demonstration of the vastness of the ocean than the fact that she cruised day after day without glimpsing a sail. She maintained a triangular course, reaching to the northwest, tacking to the south, running under easy sail northeasterly again, with lookouts at every masthead, with nothing to see but the tossing waste of water—until the morning when a high-pitched yell from the fore topgallant masthead attracted the attention of everybody on deck, including Hornblower, standing lonely in the waist. Neuville, by the wheel, bellowed a question to the lookout, and Hornblower, thanks to his recent studies, could translate the answer. There was a sail visible to windward, and next moment the lookout reported that it had altered course and was running down towards them.

That meant a great deal. In wartime any merchant ship would be suspicious of strangers and would give them as wide a berth as possible; and especially when she was to windward and therefore far safer. Only someone prepared to fight or possessed of a perfectly morbid curiosity would abandon a windward position. A wild and unreasonable hope filled Hornblower's breast; a ship of war at sea—thanks to England's maritime mastery—would be far more probably English than French. And this was the cruising ground of the *Indefatigable,* his own ship, stationed there specially to fulfill the double function of looking out for French commerce-destroyers and intercepting French blockade-runners. A hundred miles from here she had put him and his prize crew on board the *Marie Galante*. It was a thousand to one, he exaggerated despairingly to himself, against any ship sighted being the *Indefatigable.* But—hope reasserted itself—the fact that she was coming down to investigate reduced the odds to ten to one at most. Less than ten to one.

He looked over at Neuville, trying to think his thoughts. The *Pique* was fast and handy, and there was a clear avenue of escape to leeward. The fact that the stranger had altered course towards them was a suspicious circumstance, but it was known that Indiamen, the richest prizes of all, had sometimes traded on the similarity of their appearance to that of ships of the line, and, by showing a bold front, had scared dangerous enemies away. That would be a temptation to a man eager to make a prize. At Neuville's orders all sail was set, ready for instant flight or pursuit, and, close-hauled, the *Pique* stood towards the stranger. It was not long before Hornblower, on the deck, caught a glimpse of a gleam of white, like a tiny grain of rice, far away on the horizon as the *Pique* lifted on a swell. Here came Matthews, red-faced and excited, running aft to Hornblower's side.

"That's the old *Indefatigable*, sir," he said. "I swear it!"

He sprang onto the rail, holding on by the shrouds, and stared under his hand.

"Yes! There she is, sir! She's loosing her royals now, sir. We'll be back on board of her in time for grog!"

A French petty officer reached up and dragged Matthews by the seat of his trousers from his perch, and with a blow and a kick drove him forward again, while a moment later Neuville was shouting the orders that wore the ship round to head away directly from the *Indefatigable*. Neuville beckoned Hornblower over to his side.

"Your late ship, I understand, Mr. Hornblower?"

"Yes."

"What is her best point of sailing?"

Hornblower's eyes met Neuville's.

"Do not look so noble," said Neuville, smiling with thin lips. "I could undoubtedly induce you to give me the information. I know of ways. But it is unnecessary, fortunately for you. There is no ship on earth—especially none of His Britannic Majesty's clumsy frigates—that can outsail the *Pique* running before the wind. You will soon see that."

He strolled to the taffrail and looked aft long and earnestly through his glass, but no more earnestly than did Hornblower with his naked eye.

"You see?" said Neuville, proffering the glass.

Hornblower took it, but more to catch a closer glimpse of his ship than to confirm his observations. He was homesick, desperately homesick, at that moment, for the *Indefatigable*. But there could be no denying that she was being left fast behind. Her topgallants were out of sight again now, and only her royals were visible.

"Two hours and we shall have run her mastheads under," said Neuville, taking back the telescope and shutting it with a snap.

He left Hornblower standing sorrowful at the taffrail while he turned to berate the helmsman for not steering a steadier course; Hornblower heard the explosive words without listening to them, the wind blowing into his face and ruffling his hair over his ears, and the wake of the ship's passage boiling below him. So might Adam have looked back at Eden; Hornblower remembered the stuffy dark midshipman's berth, the smells and the creakings, the bitter cold nights, turning out in response to the call for all hands, the weevilly bread and the wooden beef, and he yearned for them all, with the sick feeling of hopeless longing. Liberty was vanishing over the horizon. Yet it was not these personal feelings that drove him below in search of action. They may have quickened his wits, but it was a sense of duty which inspired him.

The slave deck was deserted as usual, with all hands at quarters. Beyond the bulkhead stood his cot with the books upon it and the slush lamp swaying above it. There was nothing there to give him any inspiration. There was another locked door in the after bulkhead. That opened into some kind of boatswain's store; twice he had seen it unlocked and paint and similar supplies brought out from it. Paint! That gave him an idea; he looked from the door up to the slush lamp and back again, and as he stepped forward he took his claspknife out of his pocket. But before very long he recoiled again, sneering at himself. The door was not panelled, but was made of two solid slabs of wood, with the crossbeams on the inside. There was the keyhole of the lock, but it presented no point of attack. It would take him hours and hours to cut through that door with his knife, at a time when minutes were precious.

His heart was beating feverishly—but no more feverishly than his mind was working—as he looked round again. He reached up to the lamp and shook it; nearly full. There was a moment when he stood hesitating, nerving himself, and then he threw himself into action. With a ruthless hand he tore the pages out of Grandjean's *Principes de la Navigation,* crumpling them up in small quantities into little loose balls, which he laid at the foot of the door. He threw off his uniform coat and dragged his blue woollen jersey over his head; his long powerful fingers tore it across and plucked eagerly at it to unravel it. After starting some loose threads he would not waste more time on it, and dropped the garment onto the paper and looked round again. The mattress of the cot! It was stuffed with straw, by God! A slash of his knife tore open the ticking, and he scooped the stuff out by the armful; constant pressure had almost solidified it, but he shook it and handled it so that it bulked out far larger in a mass on the deck nearly up to his waist. That would give him the intense blaze he wanted. He stood still, compelling himself to think clearly and logically—it was impetuosity and lack of thought which had occasioned the loss of the *Marie Galante,* and now he had wasted time on his jersey. He worked out the successive steps to take. He made a long spill out of a page of the *Manuel de Matelotage,* and lighted it at the lamp. Then he poured out the grease—the lamp was hot and the grease liquid—over his balls of paper, over the deck, over the base of the door. A touch from his taper lighted one ball, the flame travelled quickly. He was committed now. He piled the straw upon the flames, and in a sudden access of insane strength he tore the cot from its fastenings, smashing it as he did so, and piled the fragments on the straw. Already the flames were racing through the straw. He dropped the lamp upon the pile, grabbed his coat, and walked out. He thought of closing the door, but decided against it—the more air the better. He wriggled into his coat and ran up the ladder.

On deck he forced himself to lounge nonchalantly against the rail, putting his shaking hands into his pockets. His excitement made him weak, nor was it lessened as he waited. Every minute before the fire could be discovered was important. A French officer said something to him with a triumphant laugh and pointed aft over the taffrail, presumably speaking about leaving the *Indefatigable* behind. Hornblower smiled bleakly at him; that was the first gesture that occurred to him, and then he thought that a smile was out of place, and he tried to assume a sullen scowl. The wind was blowing briskly, so that the *Pique* could only just carry all plain sail; Hornblower felt it on his cheeks, which were burning. Everyone on deck seemed unnaturally busy and preoccupied; Neuville was watching the helmsman with occasional glances aloft to see that every sail was doing its work; the men were at the guns, two hands and a petty officer heaving the log. God, how much longer would he have?

Look there! The coaming of the after hatchway appeared distorted, wavering in the shimmering air. Hot air must be coming up through it. And was that, or was it not, the ghost of a wreath of smoke? It was! In that moment the alarm was given. A loud cry, a rush of feet, an instant bustle, the loud beating of a drum, highpitched shouts—"*Au feu! Au feu!*"

The four elements of Aristotle, thought Hornblower, insanely, earth, air, water, and fire, were the constant enemies of the seaman, but the lee shore, the gale, and the wave, were none of them as feared in wooden ships as fire. Timbers many years old, and coated thick with paint, burnt fiercely and readily. Sails and tarry rigging would burn like fireworks. And within the ship were tons and tons of gunpowder waiting its chance to blast the seaman into fragments. Hornblower watched the fire parties flinging themselves into their work, the pumps being dragged over the decks, the hoses rigged. Someone came racing aft with a message for Neuville, presumably to report the site of the fire. Neuville heard him, and darted a glance at Hornblower against the rail before he hurled orders back at the messenger. The smoke coming up through the after hatchway was dense now; at Neuville's orders the after guard flung themselves down the opening through the smoke. And there was more smoke, and more smoke; smoke caught up by the following wind and blown forward in wisps—smoke must be pouring out of the sides of the ship at the waterline.

Neuville took a stride towards Hornblower, his face working with rage, but a cry from the helmsman checked him. The helmsman, unable to take his hands from the wheel, pointed with his foot to the cabin skylight. There was a flickering of flame below it. A side pane fell in as they watched, and a rush of flame came through the opening. That store of paint, Hornblower calculated—he was calmer now, with a calm that would astonish him later, when he came to look back on it—must be immediately under the cabin, and blazing fiercely. Neuville looked round him, at the sea and the sky, and put his hands to his head in a furious gesture. For the first time in his life Hornblower saw a man literally tearing his hair. But his nerve held. A shout brought up another portable pump; four men set to work on the handles, and the clank-clank, clank-clank made an accompaniment that blended with the roar of the fire. A thin jet of water was squirted down the gaping skylight. More men formed a bucket chain, drawing water from the sea and passing it from hand to hand to pour in the skylight, but those buckets of water were less effective even than the stream from the pumps. From below came the dull thud of an explosion, and Hornblower caught his breath as he expected the ship to be blown to pieces. But no further explosion followed; either a gun had been set off by the flames or a cask had burst violently in the heat. And then the bucket line suddenly disintegrated; beneath the feet of one of the men a seam had gaped in a broad red smile from which came a rush of flame. Some officer had seized Neuville by the arm, and was arguing with him vehemently, and Hornblower could see Neuville yield in despair. Hands went scurrying aloft to get in the fore topsail and fore course, and other hands went to the main braces. Over went the wheel, and the *Pique* came up into the wind.

The change was dramatic, although at first more apparent than real;

with the wind blowing in the opposite direction the roar of the fire did not come so clearly to the ears of those forward of it. But it was an immense gain, all the same; the flames, which had started in the steerage in the farthest after part of the ship, no longer were blown forward, but were turned back upon timber already half consumed. Yet the after part of the deck was fully alight; the helmsman was driven from the wheel, and in a flash the flames took hold of the driver and consumed it utterly—one moment the sail was there, and the next there were only charred fragments hanging from the gaff. But, head to wind, the other sails did not catch and a mizzen trysail hurriedly set kept the ship bows on.

It was then that Hornblower, looking forward, saw the *Indefatigable* again. She was tearing down towards them with all sail set; as the *Pique* lifted he could see the white bow wave foaming under her bowsprit. There was no question about surrender, for under the menace of that row of guns no ship of the *Pique's* force, even if uninjured, could resist. A cable's length to windward the *Indefatigable* rounded-to, and she was hoisting out her boats before even she was fully round. Pellew had seen the smoke, and had deduced the reason for the *Pique's* heaving-to, and had made his preparations as he came up. Longboat and launch had each a pump in their bows where sometimes they carried a carronade; they dropped down to the stern of the *Pique* to cast their jets of water up into the flaming stern without more ado. Two gigs full of men ran straight aft to join in the battle with the flames, but Bolton, the third lieutenant, lingered for a moment as he caught Hornblower's eye.

"Good God, it's you!" he exclaimed. "What are you doing here?"

Yet he did not stay for an answer. He picked out Neuville as the captain of the *Pique,* strode aft to receive his surrender, cast his eyes aloft to see that all was well there, and then took up the task of combatting the fire. The flames were overcome in time, more because they had consumed everything within reach of them than for any other reason; the *Pique* was burnt from the taffrail forward for some feet of her length right to the water's edge, so that she presented a strange spectacle when viewed from the deck of the *Indefatigable.* Nevertheless, she was in no immediate danger; given even moderate good fortune and a little hard work she could be sailed to England to be repaired and sent to sea again.

But it was not her salvage that was important, but rather the fact that she was no longer in French hands, would no longer be available to prey on English commerce. That was the point that Sir Edward Pellew made in conversation with Hornblower, when the latter came on board to report himself. Hornblower had begun, at Pellew's order, by recounting what had happened to him from the time he had been sent as prize master on board the *Marie Galante.* As Hornblower had expected—perhaps as he had even feared—Pellew had passed lightly over the loss of the brig. She had been damaged by gunfire before surrendering, and no one now could establish whether the damage was small or great. Pellew did not give the matter a second thought. Hornblower had tried to save her and had been unsuccessful with his tiny crew—and at that moment the *Indefatigable* could not spare him a larger crew. He did not hold Hornblower culpable. Once again, it was more important that France should be deprived of the *Marie Galante's* cargo than that England should benefit by it. The situation was exactly parallel to that of the salvaging of the *Pique.*

"It was lucky she caught fire like that," commented Pellew, looking across to where the *Pique* lay, still hove-to with the boats clustering about her but with only the thinnest trail of smoke drifting from her stern. "She was running clean away from us, and would have been out of sight in an hour. Have you any idea how it happened, Mr. Hornblower?"

Hornblower was naturally expecting that question and was ready for it. Now was the time to answer truthfully and modestly, to receive the praise he deserved, a mention in the *Gazette,* perhaps even appointment as acting-lieutenant. But Pellew did not know the full details of the loss of the brig, and might make a false estimate of them even if he did.

"No, sir," said Hornblower. "I think it must have been spontaneous combustion in the paint locker. I can't account for it otherwise."

He alone knew of his remissness in plugging that shot hole, he alone could decide on his punishment, and this was what he had chosen. This alone could re-establish him in his own eyes, and when the words were spoken he felt enormous relief, and not one single twinge of regret.

"It was fortunate, all the same," mused Pellew.

Four

HORNBLOWER
and the Man Who Felt Queer

This time the wolf was prowling round outside the sheep fold. H.M. Frigate *Indefatigable* had chased the French corvette *Papillon* into the mouth of the Gironde, and was seeking a way of attacking her where she lay anchor in the stream under the protection of the batteries at the mouth. Captain Pellew took his ship into shoal water as far as he dared, until in fact the batteries fired warning shots to make him keep his distance, and he stared long and keenly through his glass at the corvette. Then he shut his telescope and turned on his heel to give the order that worked the *Indefatigable* away from the dangerous lee shore —out of sight of land, in fact. His departure might lull the French into a sense of security which, he hoped, would prove unjustified. For he had no intention of leaving them undisturbed. If the corvette could be captured or sunk not only would she be unavailable for raids on British commerce but also the French would be forced to increase their coastal defences at this point and lessen the effort that could be put out elsewhere. War is a matter of savage blow and counter blow, and even a forty gun frigate could strike shrewd blows if shrewdly handled.

Midshipman Hornblower was walking the lee side of the quarterdeck, as became his lowly station as the junior officer of the watch, in the afternoon, when Midshipman Kennedy approached him. Kennedy took off his hat with a flourish and bowed low as his dancing master had once taught him, left foot advanced, hat down by the right knee. Hornblower entered into the spirit of the game, laid his hat against his stomach, and bent himself in the middle three times in quick succession. Thanks to his physical awkwardness he could parody ceremonial solemnity almost without trying.

"Most grave and reverend signor," said Kennedy. "I bear the compliments of Captain Sir Ed'ard Pellew, who humbly solicits Your Gravity's attendance at dinner at eight bells in the afternoon watch."

"My respects to Sir Edward," replied Hornblower, bowing to his knees at the mention of the name, "and I shall condescend to make a brief appearance."

"I am sure the captain will be both relieved and delighted," said Kennedy. "I will convey him my felicitations along with your most flattering acceptance."

Both hats flourished with even greater elaboration than before, but at that moment both young men noticed Mr. Bolton, the officer of the watch, looking at them from the windward side, and they hurriedly put their hats on and assumed attitudes more consonant with the dignity of officers holding their warrants from King George.

"What's in the captain's mind?" asked Hornblower.

Kennedy laid one finger alongside his nose.

"If I knew that I should rate a couple of epaulettes," he said. "Something's brewing, and I suppose one of these days we shall know what it is. Until then all that we little victims can do is to play unconscious of our doom. Meanwhile, be careful not to let the ship fall overboard."

There was no sign of anything brewing while dinner was being eaten in the great cabin of the *Indefatigable*. Pellew was a courtly host at the head of the table. Conversation flowed freely and along indifferent channels among the senior officers present—the two lieutenants, Eccles and Chadd, and the sailing master, Soames. Hornblower and the other junior officer—Mallory, a midshipman of over two years' seniority—kept silent, as midshipmen should, thereby being able to devote their undivided attention to the food, so vastly superior to what was served in the midshipmen's berth.

"A glass of wine with you, Mr. Hornblower," said Pellew, raising his glass.

Hornblower tried to bow gracefully in his seat while raising his glass. He sipped cautiously, for he had early found that he had a weak head and he disliked feeling drunk.

The table was cleared and there was a brief moment of expectancy as the company awaited Pellew's next move.

"Now, Mr. Soames," said Pellew, "let us have that chart."

It was a map of the mouth of the Gironde with the soundings; somebody had pencilled in the positions of the shore batteries.

"The *Papillon,*" said Sir Edward (he did not condescend to pronounce it French-fashion), "lies just here. Mr. Soames took the bearings."

He indicated a pencilled cross on the chart, far up the channel.

"You gentlemen," went on Pellew, "are going in with the boats to fetch her out."

So that was it. A cutting-out expedition.

"Mr. Eccles will be in general command. I will ask him to tell you his plan."

The grey-haired first lieutenant with the surprisingly young blue eyes looked round at the others.

"I shall have the launch," he said, "and Mr. Soames the cutter. Mr. Chadd and Mr. Mallory will command the first and second gigs. And Mr. Hornblower will command the jolly boat. Each of the boats except Mr. Hornblower's will have a junior officer second in command."

That would not be necessary for the jolly boat with its crew of seven. The launch and cutter would carry from thirty to forty men each, and the gigs twenty each; it was a large force that was being despatched, nearly half the ship's company.

"She's a ship of war," explained Eccles, reading their thoughts. "No merchantman. Ten guns a side, and full of men."

Nearer two hundred men than a hundred, certainly—plentiful opposition for a hundred and twenty British seamen.

"But we will be attacking her by night and taking her by surprise," said Eccles, reading their thoughts again.

"Surprise," put in Pellew, "is more than half the battle, as you know, gentlemen—please pardon the interruption, Mr. Eccles."

"At the moment," went on Eccles, "we are out of sight of land. We are about to stand in again. We have never hung about this part of the coast, and the Frogs'll think we've gone for good. We'll make the land after nightfall, stand in as far as possible, and then the boats will go in. High water tomorrow morning is at 4:50; dawn is at 5:30. The attack will be delivered at 4:30 so that the watch below will have had time to get to sleep. The launch will attack on the starboard quarter, and the cutter on the larboard quarter. Mr. Mallory's gig will attack on the larboard bow, and Mr. Chadd's on the starboard bow. Mr. Chadd will be responsible for cutting the corvette's cable as soon as he has mastered the forecastle, and the other boats' crews have at least reached the quarterdeck."

Eccles looked round at the other three commanders of the large boats, and they nodded understanding. Then he went on.

"Mr. Hornblower with the jolly boat will wait until the attack has gained a foothold on the deck. He will then board at the main chains, either to starboard or larboard as he sees fit, and he will at once ascend the main rigging, paying no attention to whatever fighting is going on on deck. He will see to it that the main topsail is loosed and he will sheet it home on receipt of further orders. I myself, or Mr. Soames in the event of my being killed or wounded, will send two hands to the wheel and will attend to steering the corvette as soon as she is under weigh. The tide will take us out, and the *Indefatigable* will be awaiting us just out of gunshot from the shore batteries."

"Any comments, gentlemen?" asked Pellew.

That was the moment when Hornblower should have spoken up—the only moment when he could. Eccles' orders had set in motion sick feelings of apprehension in his stomach. Hornblower was no maintopman, and Hornblower knew it. He hated heights, and he hated going aloft. He knew he had none of the monkeylike agility and self-confidence of the good seaman. He was unsure of himself aloft in the dark even in the *Indefatigable,* and he was utterly appalled at the thought of going aloft in an entirely strange ship and finding his way among strange rigging. He felt himself quite unfitted for the duty assigned to him, and he should have raised a protest at once on account of his unfitness. But he let the opportunity pass, for he was overcome by the matter-of-fact way in which the other officers accepted the plan. He looked round at the unmoved faces; nobody was paying any attention to him, and he jibbed at making himself conspicuous. He swallowed; he even got as far as opening his mouth, but still no one looked at him and his protest died stillborn.

"Very well, then, gentlemen," said Pellew. "I think you had better go into the details, Mr. Eccles."

Then it was too late. Eccles, with the chart before him, was pointing out the course to be taken through the shoals and mudbanks of the Gironde, and expatiating on the position of the shore batteries and on the influence of the lighthouse of Cordouan upon the distance to which the *Indefatigable* could approach in daylight. Hornblower listened, trying to concentrate despite his apprehensions. Eccles finished his remarks and Pellew closed the meeting.

"Since you all know your duties, gentlemen, I think you should start your preparations. The sun is about to set and you will find you have plenty to do."

The boats' crews had to be told off; it was necessary to see that the men were armed, and that the boats were provisioned in case of emergency. Every man had to be instructed in the duties expected of him. And Hornblower had to rehearse himself in ascending the main shrouds and laying out along the main topsail yard. He did it twice, forcing himself to make the difficult climb up the futtock shrouds, which, projecting outwards from the mainmast, made it necessary to climb several feet while hanging back downwards, locking fingers and toes into the ratlines. He could just manage it, moving slowly and carefully although clumsily. He stood on the foot rope and worked his way out to the yard-arm—the foot rope was attached along the yard so as to hang nearly four feet below it. The principle was to set his feet on the rope with his arms over the yard, then, holding the yard in his armpits, to shuffle sideways along the foot rope to cast off the gaskets and loose the sail. Twice Hornblower made the whole journey, battling with the disquiet of his stomach at the thought of the hundred-foot drop below him. Finally, gulping with nervousness, he transferred his grip to the brace and forced himself to slide down it to the deck—that would be his best route when the time came to sheet the topsail home. It was a long perilous descent; Hornblower told himself—as indeed he had said to himself when he had first seen men go aloft—that similar feats in a circus at home would be received with "ohs" and "ahs" of appreciation. He was by no means satisfied with himself even when he reached the deck, and at the back of his mind was a vivid mental picture of his missing his hold, when the time came for him to repeat the performance in the *Papillon*, and falling headlong to the deck—a second or two of frightful fear while rushing through the air, and then a shattering crash. And the success of the attack hinged on him, as much as on anyone—if the topsail were not promptly set to give the corvette steerage way she would run aground on one of the innumerable shoals in the river mouth to be ignominiously recaptured, and half the crew of the *Indefatigable* would be dead or prisoners.

In the waist the jolly boat's crew was formed up for his inspection. He saw to it that the oars were properly muffled, that each man had pistol and cutlass, and made sure that every pistol was at half-cock so that there was no fear of a premature shot giving warning of the attack. He allocated duties to each man in the loosing of the topsail, laying stress on the possibility that casualties might necessitate unrehearsed changes in the scheme.

"I will mount the rigging first," said Hornblower.

That had to be the case. He had to lead—it was expected of him. More than that; if he had given any other order it would have excited comment—and contempt.

"Jackson," went on Hornblower, addressing the coxswain, "you will quit the boat last and take command if I fall."

"Aye aye, sir."

It was usual to use the poetic expression "fall" for "die," and it was only after Hornblower had uttered the word that he thought about its horrible real meaning in the present circumstances.

"Is that all understood?" asked Hornblower harshly; it was his mental stress that was making his voice grate so.

Everyone nodded except one man.

"Begging your pardon, sir," said Hales, the young man who pulled stroke oar. "I'm feeling a bit queer-like."

Hales was a lightly built young fellow of swarthy countenance. He put his hand to his forehead with a vague gesture as he spoke.

"You're not the only one to feel queer," snapped Hornblower.

The other men chuckled. The thought of running the gauntlet of the shore batteries, of boarding an armed corvette in the teeth of opposition, might well raise apprehension in the breast of a coward. Most of the men detailed for the expedition must have felt qualms to some extent.

"I don't mean that, sir," said Hales indignantly. "'Course I don't."

But Hornblower and the others paid him no attention.

"You just keep your mouth shut," growled Jackson. There could be nothing but contempt for a man who announced himself sick after being told off on a dangerous duty. Hornblower felt sympathy as well as contempt. He himself had been too much of a coward even to give voice to his apprehensions—too much afraid of what people would say about him.

"Dismiss," said Hornblower. "I'll pass the word for all of you when you are wanted."

There were some hours yet to wait while the *Indefatigable* crept inshore, with the lead going steadily and Pellew himself attending to the course of the frigate. Hornblower, despite his nervousness and his miserable apprehension, yet found time to appreciate the superb seamanship displayed as Pellew brought the big frigate in through these tricky waters on that dark night. His interest was so caught by the procedure that the little tremblings which had been assailing him ceased to manifest themselves; Hornblower was of the type that would continue to observe and to learn on his deathbed. By the time the *Indefatigable* had reached the point off the mouth of the river where it was desirable to launch the boats, Hornblower had learned a good deal about the practical application of the principles of coastwise navigation, and a good deal about the organisation of a cutting-out expedition—and by self-analysis he had learned even more about the psychology of a raiding party before a raid.

He had mastered himself to all outside appearance by the time he went down into the jolly boat as she heaved on the inky-black water, and he gave the command to shove off in a quiet steady voice. Hornblower took the tiller—the feel of that solid bar of wood was reassuring, and it was old habit now to sit in the sternsheets with hand and elbow upon it, and the men began to pull slowly after the dark shapes of the four big boats; there was plenty of time and the flowing tide would take them up the estuary. That was just as well, for on one side of them lay the batteries of St. Dye, and inside the estuary on the other side was the fortress of Blaye; forty big guns trained to sweep the channel, and none of the five boats—certainly not the jolly boat—could withstand a single shot from one of them.

He kept his eyes attentively on the cutter ahead of him. Soames had the dreadful responsibility of taking the boats up the channel, while all he had to do was to follow in her wake—all, except to loose that main topsail. Hornblower found himself shivering again.

Hales, the man who had said he felt queer, was pulling stroke oar; Hornblower could just see his dark form moving rhythmically backward and forward at each slow stroke. After a single glance Hornblower paid him no more attention, and was staring after the cutter when a sudden commotion brought his mind back into the boat. Someone had missed his stroke; someone had thrown all six oars into confusion as a result. There was even a slight clatter.

"Mind what you're doing, blast you, Hales," whispered Jackson, the coxswain, with desperate urgency.

For answer there was a sudden cry from Hales, loud but fortunately not too loud, and Hales pitched forward against Hornblower's and Jackson's legs, kicking and writhing.

"The bastard's having a fit," growled Jackson.

The kicking and writhing went on. Across the water through the darkness came a sharp scornful whisper.

"Mr. Hornblower," said the voice—it was Eccles putting a world of exasperation into his *sotto voce* question, "cannot you keep your men quiet?"

Eccles had brought the launch round almost alongside the jolly boat to say this to him, and the desperate need for silence was dramatically demonstrated by the absence of any of the usual blasphemy; Hornblower could picture the cutting reprimand that would be administered to him tomorrow publicly on the quarterdeck. He opened his mouth to make an explanation, but he fortunately realised that raiders in open boats did not make explanations when under the guns of the fortress of Blaye.

"Aye aye, sir," was all he whispered back, and the launch continued on its mission of shepherding the flotilla in the tracks of the cutter.

"Take his oar, Jackson," he whispered furiously to the coxswain, and he stooped and with his own hands dragged the writhing figure towards him and out of Jackson's way.

"You might try pouring water on 'im, sir," suggested Jackson hoarsely, as he moved to the after thwart. "There's the baler 'andy."

Seawater was the seaman's cure for every ill, his panacea; seeing how often sailors had not merely wet jackets but wet bedding as well they should never have a day's illness. But Hornblower let the sick man lie. His struggles were coming to an end, and Hornblower wished to make no noise with the baler. The lives of more than a hundred men depended on silence. Now that they were well into the actual estuary they were within easy reach of cannon shot from the shore—and a single cannon shot would rouse the crew of the *Papillon,* ready to man the bulwarks to beat off the attack, ready to drop cannon balls into the boats alongside, ready to shatter approaching boats with a tempest of grape.

Silently the boats glided up the estuary; Soames in the cutter was setting a slow pace, with only an occasional stroke at the oars to maintain steerage way. Presumably he knew very well what he was doing; the channel he had selected was an obscure one between mudbanks, impracticable for anything except small boats, and he had a twenty foot pole with him with which to take the soundings—quicker and much more silent than using the lead. Minutes were passing fast, and yet the night was still utterly dark, with no hint of approaching dawn. Strain his eyes as he would, Hornblower could not be sure that he could see the flat shores on either side of him. It would call for sharp eyes on the land to detect the little boats being carried up by the tide.

Hales at his feet stirred and then stirred again. His hand, feeling round in the darkness, found Hornblower's ankle and apparently examined it with curiosity. He muttered something, the words dragging out into a moan.

"Shut up!" whispered Hornblower, trying, like the saint of old, to make a tongue of his whole body, that he might express the urgency of the occasion without making a sound audible at any distance. Hales set his elbow on Hornblower's knee and levered himself up into a sitting position, and then levered himself further until he was standing, swaying with bent knees and supporting himself against Hornblower.

"Sit down, damn you!" whispered Hornblower, shaking with fury and anxiety.

"Where's Mary?" asked Hales in a conversational tone.

"Shut up!"

"Mary!" said Hales, lurching against him. "Mary!"

Each successive word was louder. Hornblower felt instinctively that Hales would soon be speaking in a loud voice, that he might even soon be shouting. Old recollections of conversations with his doctor father stirred at the back of his mind; he remembered that persons emerging from epileptic fits were not responsible for their actions, and might be, and often were, dangerous.

"Mary!" said Hales again.

Victory and the lives of a hundred men depended on silencing Hales, and silencing him instantly. Hornblower thought of the pistol in his belt, and of using the butt, but there was another weapon more conveniently to his hand. He unshipped the tiller, a three foot bar of solid oak, and he swung it with all the venom and fury of despair. The tiller crashed down on Hales' head, and Hales, an unuttered word cut short in his throat, fell silent in the bottom of the boat. There was no sound from the boat's crew, save for something like a sigh from Jackson, whether approving or disapproving Hornblower neither knew nor cared. He had done his duty, and he was certain of it. He had struck down a helpless idiot; most probably he had killed him, but the surprise upon which the success of the expedition depended had not been imperilled. He reshipped the tiller and resumed the silent task of keeping in the wake of the gigs.

Far away ahead—in the darkness it was impossible to estimate the distance—there was a nucleus of greater darkness, close on the surface of the black water. It might be the corvette. A dozen more silent strokes, and Hornblower was sure of it. Soames had done a magnificent job of pilotage, leading the boats straight to that objective. The cutter and launch were diverging now from the two gigs. The four boats were separating in readiness to launch their simultaneous converging attack.

"Easy!" whispered Hornblower, and the jolly boat's crew ceased to pull.

Hornblower had his orders. He had to wait until the attack had gained a foothold on the deck. His hand clenched convulsively on the tiller; the excitement of dealing with Hales had driven the thought of having to ascend strange rigging in the darkness clear out of his head, and now it recurred with redoubled urgency. Hornblower was afraid.

Although he could see the corvette, the boats had vanished from his sight, had passed out of his field of vision. The corvette rode to her anchor, her spars just visible against the night sky—that was where he had to climb! She seemed to tower up hugely. Close by the corvette he saw a splash in the dark water—the boats were closing in fast and someone's stroke had been a little careless. At the same moment came a shout from the corvette's deck, and when the shout was repeated it was echoed a hundred fold from the boats rushing alongside. The yelling was lusty and prolonged, of set purpose. A sleeping enemy would be bewildered by the din, and the progress of the shouting would tell each boat's crew of the extent of the success of the others. The British seamen were yelling like madmen. A flash and a bang from the corvette's deck told of the firing of the first shot; soon pistols were popping and muskets banging from several points of the deck.

"Give way!" said Hornblower. He uttered the order as if it had been torn from him by the rack.

The jolly boat moved forward, while Hornblower fought down his feelings and tried to make out what was going on on board. He could see no reason for choosing either side of the corvette in preference to the other, and the larboard side was the nearer, and so he steered the boat to the larboard main chains. So interested was he in what he was doing that he only remembered in the nick of time to give the order "in oars." He put the tiller over and the boat swirled round and the bowman hooked on. From the deck just above came a noise exactly like a tinker hammering on a cooking pot—Hornblower noted the curious noise as he stood up in the sternsheets. He felt the cutlass at his side and the pistol in his belt, and then he sprang for the chains. With a mad leap he reached them and hauled himself up. The shrouds came into his hands, his feet found the ratlines beneath them, and he began to climb. As his head cleared the bulwark and he could see the deck the flash of a pistol shot illuminated the scene momentarily, fixing the struggle on the deck in a static moment, like a picture. Before and below him a British seaman was fighting a furious cutlass-duel with a French officer, and he realised with vague astonishment that the kettle-mending noise he had heard was the sound of cutlass against cutlass—that clash of steel against steel that poets wrote about. So much for romance.

The realisation carried him far up the shrouds. At his elbow he felt the futtock shrouds and he transferred himself to them, hanging back downward with his toes hooked into the ratlines and his hands clinging like death. That only lasted for two or three desperate seconds, and then he hauled himself onto the topmast shrouds and began the final ascent, his lungs bursting with the effort. Here was the topsail yard, and Hornblower flung himself across it and felt with his feet for the footrope. Merciful God! There was no footrope—his feet searching in the darkness met only unresisting air. A hundred feet above the deck he hung, squirming and kicking like a baby held up at arm's length in its father's hands. There was no footrope; it may have been with this very situation in mind that the Frenchmen had removed it. There was no footrope, so that he could not make his way out to the yard-arm. Yet the gaskets must be cast off and the sail loosed—everything depended on that. Hornblower had seen daredevil seamen run out along the yards, standing upright, as though walking a tightrope. That was the only way to reach the yard-arm now.

For a moment he could not breathe as his weak flesh revolted against the thought of walking along the yard above the black abyss. This was fear, the fear that stripped a man of his manhood, turning his bowels to water and his limbs to paper. Yet his furiously active mind continued to work. He had been resolute enough in dealing with Hales. Where he personally was not involved he had been brave enough; he had not hesitated to strike down the wretched epileptic with all the strength of his arm. That was the poor sort of courage he was capable of displaying. In the simple vulgar matter of physical bravery he was utterly wanting. This was cowardice, the sort of thing that men spoke about behind their hands to other men. He could not bear the thought of that in himself—it was worse (awful though the alternative might be) than the thought of falling through the night to the deck. With a gasp he brought his knee up onto the yard, heaving himself up until he stood upright. He felt the rounded, canvas-covered timber under his feet, and his instincts told him not to dally there for a moment.

"Come on, men!" he yelled, and he dashed out along the yard.

It was twenty feet to the yard-arm, and he covered the distance in a few frantic strides. Utterly reckless by now, he put his hands down on the yard, clasped it, and laid his body across it again, his hands seeking the gaskets. A thump on the yard told him that Oldroyd, who had been detailed to come after him, had followed him out along the yard—he had six feet less to go. There could be no doubt that the other members of the jolly boat's crew were on the yard, and that Clough had led the way to the starboard yard-arm. It was obvious from the rapidity with which the sail came loose. Here was the brace beside him. Without any thought of danger now, for he was delirious with excitement and triumph, he grasped it with both hands and jerked himself off the yard. His waving legs found the rope and twined about it, and he let himself slide down it.

Fool that he was! Would he never learn sense and prudence? Would he never remember that vigilance and precaution must never be relaxed? He had allowed himself to slide so fast that the rope seared his hands, and when he tried to tighten his grip so as to slow down his progress it caused him such agony that he had to relax it again and slide on down with the rope stripping the skin from his hands as though peeling off a glove. His feet reached the deck and he momentarily forgot the pain as he looked round him.

There was the faintest grey light beginning to show now, and there were no sounds of battle. It had been a well worked surprise—a hundred men flung suddenly on the deck of the corvette had swept away the anchor watch and mastered the vessel in a single rush before the watch below could come up to offer any resistance. Chadd's stentorian voice came pealing from the forecastle.

"Cable's cut, sir!"

Then Eccles bellowed from aft.

"Mr. Hornblower!"

"Sir!" yelled Hornblower.

"Man the halliards!"

A rush of men came to help—not only his own boat's crew but every man of initiative and spirit. Halliards, sheets and braces; the sail was trimmed round and was drawing full in the light southerly air, and the *Papillon* swung round to go down with the first of the ebb. Dawn was coming up fast, with a trifle of mist on the surface of the water.

Over the starboard quarter came a sullen bellowing roar and then the misty air was torn by a series of infernal screams, supernaturally loud. The first cannon balls Hornblower had ever heard were passing him by.

"Mr. Chadd! Set the headsails! Loose the fore tops'l. Get aloft, some of you, and set the mizzen tops'l."

From the port bow came another salvo—Blaye was firing at them from one side, St. Dye from the other, now they could guess what had happened on board the *Papillon.* But the corvette was moving fast with wind and tide, and it would be no easy matter to cripple her in the half-light. It had been a very near-run thing; a few seconds' delay could have been fatal. Only one shot from the next salvo passed within hearing, and its passage was marked by a loud snap overhead.

"Mr. Mallory, get that fore-stay spliced!"

"Aye aye, sir!"

It was light enough to look round the deck now; he could see Eccles at the break of the poop, directing the handling of the corvette, and Soames beside the wheel conning her down the channel. Two groups of red-coated marines, with bayonets fixed, stood guard over the hatchways. There were four or five men lying on the deck in curiously abandoned attitudes. Dead men; Hornblower could look at them with the callousness of youth. But there was a wounded man, too, crouched groaning over his shattered thigh—Hornblower could not look at him as disinterestedly, and he was glad, maybe only for his own sake, when at that moment a seaman asked for and received permission from Mallory to leave his duties and attend to him.

"Stand by to go about!" shouted Eccles from the poop; the corvette had reached the tip of the middle ground shoal and was about to make the turn that would carry her into the open sea.

The men came running to the braces, and Hornblower tailed on along with them. But the first contact with the harsh rope gave him such pain that he almost cried out. His hands were like raw meat, and fresh-killed at that, for blood was running from them. Now that his attention was called to them they smarted unbearably.

The headsail sheets came over, and the corvette went handily about.

"There's the old *Indy!*" shouted somebody.

The *Indefatigable* was plainly visible now, lying-to just out of shot from the shore batteries, ready to rendezvous with her prize. Somebody cheered, and the cheering was taken up by everyone, even while the last shots from St. Dye, fired at extreme range, pitched sullenly into the water alongside. Hornblower had gingerly extracted his handkerchief from his pocket and was trying to wrap it round his hand.

"Can I help you with that, sir?" asked Jackson.

Jackson shook his head as he looked at the raw surface.

"You was careless, sir. You ought to 'a gone down 'and over 'and," he said, when Hornblower explained to him how the injury had been caused. "Very careless, you was, beggin' your pardon for saying so, sir.

But you young gennelmen often is. You don't 'ave no thought for your necks, nor your 'ides, sir."

Hornblower looked up at the main topsail yard high above his head, and remembered how he had walked along that slender stick of timber out to the yard-arm in the dark. At the recollection of it, even here with the solid deck under his feet, he shuddered a little.

"Sorry, sir. Didn't mean to 'urt you," said Jackson, tying the knot. "There, that's done, as good as I can do it, sir."

"Thank you, Jackson," said Hornblower.

"We got to report the jolly boat as lost, sir," went on Jackson.

"Lost?"

"She ain't towing alongside, sir. You see, we didn't leave no boat-keeper in 'er. Wells, 'e was to be boatkeeper, you remember, sir. But I sent 'im up the rigging a'ead o' me, seeing that 'Ales couldn't go. We wasn't too many for the job. So the jolly boat must 'a come adrift, sir, when the ship went about."

"What about Hales, then?" asked Hornblower.

" 'E was still in the boat, sir."

Hornblower looked back up the estuary of the Gironde. Somewhere up there the jolly boat was drifting about, and lying in it was Hales, probably dead, possibly alive. In either case the French would find him, surely enough, but a cold wave of regret extinguished the warm feeling of triumph in Hornblower's bosom when he thought about Hales back there. If it had not been for Hales he would never have nerved himself (so at least he thought) to run out to the main topsail yard-arm; he would at this moment be ruined and branded as a coward instead of basking in the satisfaction of having capably done his duty.

Jackson saw the bleak look in his face.

"Don't you take on so, sir," he said. "They won't 'old the loss of the jolly boat agin you, not the captain and Mr. Eccles, they won't."

"I wasn't thinking about the jolly boat," said Hornblower. "I was thinking about Hales."

"Oh, 'im?" said Jackson. "Don't you fret about 'im, sir. 'E wouldn't never 'ave made no seaman, not no 'ow."

Five
HORNBLOWER *and the Man Who Saw God*

WINTER HAD COME to the Bay of Biscay. With the passing of the Equinox the gales began to increase in violence, adding infinitely to the labours and dangers of the British navy watching over the coast of France; easterly gales, bitter cold, which the storm-tossed ships had to endure as best they could, when the spray froze on the rigging and the labouring hulls leaked like baskets; westerly gales, when the ships had to claw their way to safety from a lee shore and make a risky compromise between gaining sufficient sea-room and maintaining a position from which they could pounce on any French vessel venturing out of harbour. We speak about the storm-tossed ships. But those ships were full of storm-tossed men, who week by week and month by month had to endure the continued cold and the continual wet, the salt provisions, the endless toil, the boredom and misery of life in the blockading fleet. Even in the frigates, the eyes and claws of the blockaders, boredom had to be endured, the boredom of long periods with the hatches battened down, with the deck seams above dripping water on the men below, long nights and short days, broken sleep and yet not enough to do.

Even in the *Indefatigable* there was a feeling of restlessness in the air, and even a mere midshipman like Hornblower could be aware of it as he was looking over the men of his division before the captain's regular weekly inspection.

"What's the matter with your face, Styles?" he asked.

"Boils, sir. Awful bad."

On Styles' cheeks and lips there were half a dozen dabs of sticking plaster.

"Have you done anything about them?"

"Surgeon's mate, sir, 'e give me plaister for 'em, an' 'e says they'll soon come right, sir."

"Very well."

Now was there, or was there not, something strained about the expressions on the faces of the men on either side of Styles? Did they look like men smiling secretly to themselves? Laughing up their sleeves? Hornblower did not want to be an object of derision; it was bad for discipline—and it was worse for discipline if the men shared some secret unknown to their officers. He glanced sharply along the line again. Styles was standing like a block of wood, with no expression at all on his swarthy face; the black ringlets over his ears were properly combed, and no fault could be found with him. But Hornblower sensed that the recent conversation was a source of amusement to the rest of his division, and he did not like it.

After divisions he tackled Mr. Low, the surgeon, in the gun room.

"Boils?" said Low. "Of course the men have boils. Salt pork and split peas for nine weeks on end—what d'you expect but boils? Boils—gurry sores—blains—all the plagues of Egypt."

"On their faces?"

"That's one locality for boils. You'll find out others from your own personal experience."

"Does your mate attend to them?" persisted Hornblower.

"Of course."

"What's he like?"

"Muggridge?"

"Is that his name?"

"He's a good surgeon's mate. Get him to compound a black draught for you and you'll see. In fact, I'd prescribe one for you—you seem in a mighty bad temper, young man."

Mr. Low finished his glass of rum and pounded on the table for the steward. Hornblower realised that he was lucky to have found Low sober enough to give him even this much information, and turned away to go aloft so as to brood over the question in the solitude of the mizzen top. This was his new station in action; when the men were not at their quarters a man might find a little blessed solitude there—something hard to find in the crowded *Indefatigable*. Bundled up in his pea-jacket, Hornblower sat in the mizzen top; over his head the mizzen topmast drew erratic circles against the grey sky; beside him the topmast shrouds sang their high-pitched note in the blustering gale, and below him the life of the ship went on as she rolled and pitched, standing to the northward under close reefed topsails. At eight bells she would wear to the southward again on her incessant patrol. Until that time Hornblower was free to meditate on the boils on Styles' face and the covert grins on the faces of the other men of the division.

Two hands appeared on the stout wooden barricade surrounding the top, and as Hornblower looked up with annoyance at having his meditations interrupted, a head appeared above them. It was Finch, another man in Hornblower's division, who also had his station in action here in the mizzen top. He was a frail little man with wispy hair and pale blue eyes and a foolish smile, which lit up his face when, after betraying some disappointment at finding the mizzen top already occupied, he recognised Hornblower.

"Beg pardon, sir," he said. "I didn't know as how you was up here."

Finch was hanging on uncomfortably, back downwards, in the act of transferring himself from the futtock shrouds to the top, and each roll threatened to shake him loose.

"Oh, come here if you want to," said Hornblower, cursing himself for his softheartedness. A taut officer, he felt, would have told Finch to go back whence he came and not bother him.

"Thank 'ee, sir. Thank 'ee," said Finch, bringing his leg over the barricade and allowing the ship's roll to drop him into the top.

He crouched down to peer under the foot of the mizzen topsail forward to the mainmast head, and then turned back to smile disarmingly at Hornblower like a child caught in moderate mischief. Hornblower knew that Finch was a little weak in the head—the all-embracing press swept up idiots and landsmen to help man the fleet—although he was a trained seaman who could hand, reef, and steer. That smile betrayed him.

"It's better up here than down below, sir," said Finch, apologetically.

"You're right," said Hornblower with a disinterested intonation which would discourage conversation.

He turned away to ignore Finch, settled his back again comfortably, and allowed the steady swing of the top to mesmerise him into dreamy thought that might deal with his problem. Yet it was not easy, for Finch was as restless almost as a squirrel in a cage, peering forward, changing his position, and so continually breaking in on Hornblower's train of thought, wasting the minutes of his precious half hour of freedom.

"What the devil's the matter with you, Finch?" he rasped at last, patience quite exhausted.

"The Devil, sir?" said Finch. "It isn't the Devil. He's not up here, begging your pardon, sir."

That weak mysterious grin again, like a mischievous child. A great depth of secrets lay in those strange blue eyes. Finch peered under the topsail again; it was a gesture like a baby's playing peep-bo.

"There!" said Finch. "I saw Him that time, sir. God's come back to the maintop, sir."

"God?"

"Aye indeed, sir. Sometimes He's in the maintop. More often than not, sir. I saw Him that time, with His beard all a-blowing in the wind. 'Tis only from here that you can see Him, sir."

What could be said to a man with that sort of delusion? Hornblower racked his brains for an answer, and found none. Finch seemed to have forgotten his presence, and was playing peep-bo again under the foot of the mizzen topsail.

"There He is!" said Finch to himself. "There He is again! God's in the maintop, and the Devil's in the cable tier."

"Very appropriate," said Hornblower cynically, but to himself. He had no thought of laughing at Finch's delusions.

"The Devil's in the cable tier during the dogwatches," said Finch again to no one at all. "God stays in the maintop for ever."

"A curious timetable," was Hornblower's *sotto voce* comment.

From down on the deck below came the first stroke of eight bells, and at the same moment the pipes of the bosun's mates began to twitter, and the bellow of Waldron the bosun made itself heard.

"Turn out the watch below! All hands wear ship! All hands! All hands! You, master-at-arms, take the name of the last man up the hatchway. All hands!"

The interval of peace, short as it was, and broken by Finch's disturbing presence, was at an end. Hornblower dived over the barricade and gripped the futtock shrouds; not for him was the easy descent through the lubber's hole, not when the first lieutenant might see him and reprimand him for unseamanlike behaviour. Finch waited for him to quit the top, but even with this length start Hornblower was easily outpaced in the descent to the deck, for Finch, like the skilled seaman he was, ran down the shrouds as lightly as a monkey. Then the thought of Finch's curious illusions was temporarily submerged in the business of laying the ship on her new course.

But later in the day Hornblower's mind reverted inevitably to the odd things Finch had been saying. There could be no doubt that Finch firmly believed he saw what he said he saw. Both his words and his expression made that certain. He had spoken about God's beard—it was a pity that he had not spared a few words to describe the Devil in the cable tier. Horns, cloven hoof, and pitchfork? Hornblower wondered. And why was the Devil only loose in the cable tier during the dogwatches? Strange that he should keep to a timetable. Hornblower caught his breath as the sudden thought came to him that perhaps there might be some worldly explanation. The Devil might well be loose in the cable tier in a metaphorical fashion during the dogwatches. Devil's work might be going on there. Hornblower had to decide on what was his duty; and he had to decide further on what was expedient. He could report his suspicions to Eccles, the first lieutenant; but after a year of service Hornblower was under no illusions about what might happen to a junior midshipman who worried a first lieutenant with unfounded suspicions. It would be better to see for himself first, as far as that went. But he did not know what he would find—if he should find anything at all—and he did not know how he should deal with it if he found anything. Much worse than that, he did not know if he would be able to deal with it in officerlike fashion. He could make a fool of himself. He might mishandle whatever situation he found, and bring down obloquy and derision upon his head, and he might imperil the discipline of the ship—weaken the slender thread of allegiance that bound officers and men together, the discipline which kept three hundred men at the bidding of their captain suffering untold hardship without demur; which made them ready to face death at the word of command. When eight bells told the end of the afternoon watch and the beginning of the first dogwatch it was with trepidation that Hornblower went below to put a candle in a lantern and make his way forward to the cable tier.

It was dark down here, stuffy, odorous, and as the ship heaved and rolled he found himself stumbling over the various obstacles that impeded his progress. Yet forward there was a faint light, a murmur of voices. Hornblower choked down his fear that perhaps mutiny was being planned. He put his hand over the horn window of the lantern, so as to obscure its light, and crept forward. Two lanterns swung from the low deck beams, and crouching under them were a score or more of men—more than that, even—and the buzz of their talk came loudly but indistinguishably to Hornblower's ears. Then the buzz increased to a roar, and someone in the centre of the circle rose suddenly to as near his full height as the deck beams allowed. He was shaking himself violently from side to side for no apparent reason; his face was away from Hornblower, who saw with a gasp that his hands were tied behind him. The men roared again, like spectators at a prizefight, and the man with his hands tied swung round so that Hornblower could see his face. It was Styles, the man who suffered from boils; Hornblower knew him at once. But that was not what made the most impression on Hornblower. Clinging to the man's face, weird in the shifting meagre light, was a grey writhing shape, and it was to shake this off that Styles was flinging himself about so violently. It was a rat; Hornblower's stomach turned over with horror.

With a wild jerk of his head Styles broke the grip of the rat's teeth and flung the creature down, and then instantly plunged down on his knees, with his hands still bound behind him, to pursue it with his own teeth.

"Time!" roared a voice at that moment—the voice of Partridge, bosun's mate. Hornblower had been roused by it often enough to recognise it at once.

"Five dead," said another voice. "Pay all bets of evens or better."

Hornblower plunged forward. Part of the cable had been coiled down to make a rat pit ten feet across in which knelt Styles with dead and living rats about his knees. Partridge squatted beside the ring with a sandglass—used for timing the casting of the log—in front of him.

"Six dead," protested someone. "That un's dead."

"No, he ain't."

"'Is back's broken. 'E's a dead 'un."

"'E ain't a dead 'un," said Partridge.

The man who had protested looked up at that moment, and caught sight of Hornblower, and his words died away unspoken; at his silence the others followed his glance and stiffened into rigidity, and Hornblower stepped forward. He was still wondering what he should do; he was still fighting down the nausea excited by the horrible things he had seen. Desperately, he mastered his horror, and, thinking fast, took his stand on discipline.

"Who's in charge here?" he demanded.

He ran his eye round the circle. Petty officers and second-class warrant officers, mainly; bosun's mates, carpenter's mates. Muggridge, the surgeon's mate—his presence explained much. But his own position was not easy. A midshipman of scant service depended for his authority on board largely on the force of his own personality. He was only a warrant officer himself; when all was said and done a midshipman was much less important to the ship's economy—and was far more easily replaced—than, say, Washburn the cooper's mate over there, who knew all about the making and storage of the ship's water barrels.

"Who's in charge here?" he demanded again, and once more received no direct reply.

"We ain't on watch," said a voice in the background.

Hornblower by now had mastered his horror; his indignation still flared within him but he could appear outwardly calm.

"No, you're not on watch," he said coldly. "You're gambling."

Muggridge took up the defence at that.

"Gambling, Mr. Hornblower?" he said. "That's a very serious charge. Just a gentlemanly competition. You'll find it hard to sub–substantiate any charges of gambling."

Muggridge had been drinking, quite obviously, following perhaps the example of the head of his department. There was brandy to be got in the medical stores. A surge of wrath made Hornblower tremble; the effort necessary to keep himself standing stock still was almost too much for him. But the rise in internal pressure brought him inspiration.

"Mr. Muggridge," he said icily, "I advise you not to say too much. There are other charges possible, Mr. Muggridge. A member of His Majesty's forces can be charged with rendering himself unfit for service, Mr. Muggridge. And similarly there might be charges of aiding and abetting which might include *you*. I should consult the Articles of War if I were you, Mr. Muggridge. The punishment for such an offence is flogging round the fleet, I believe."

Hornblower pointed to Styles, with the blood streaming from his bitten face, and gave more force to his argument by the gesture. He had met the men's arguments with a more effective one along the same lines; they had taken up a legalistic defence and he had legalistically beaten it down. He had the upper hand now and could give vent to his moral indignation.

"I could bring charges against every one of you," he roared. "You could be court-martialled–disrated–flogged–every man Jack of you. By God, one more look like that from you, Partridge, and I'll do it. You'd all be in irons five minutes after I spoke to Mr. Eccles. I'll have no more of these filthy games. Let those rats loose, there, you, Oldroyd, and you, Lewis. Styles, get your face plastered up again. You, Partridge, take these men and coil this cable down properly again before Mr. Waldron sees it. I'll keep my eye on all of you in future. The next hint I have of misbehaviour and you'll all be at the gratings. I've said it and by God I mean it!"

Hornblower was surprised both at his own volubility and at his self-possession. He had not known himself capable of carrying off matters with such a high hand. He sought about in his mind for a final salvo with which to make his retirement dignified, and it came to him as he turned away so that he turned back to deliver it.

"After this I want to see you in the dogwatches skylarking on deck, not skulking in the cable tiers like a lot of Frenchmen."

That was the sort of speech to be expected of a pompous old captain, not a junior midshipman, but it served to give dignity to his retirement. There was a feverish buzz of voices as he left the group. Hornblower went up on deck, under the cheerless grey sky dark with premature night, to walk the deck to keep himself warm while the *Indefatigable* slashed her way to windward in the teeth of a roaring westerly, the spray flying in sheets over her bows, the straining seams leaking and her fabric groaning; the end of a day like all the preceding ones and the predecessor probably of innumerable more.

Yet the days passed, and with them came at last a break in the monotony. In the sombre dawn a hoarse bellow from the lookout turned every eye to windward, to where a dull blotch on the horizon marked the presence of a ship. The watch came running to the braces as the *Indefatigable* was laid as close to the wind as she would lie. Captain Pellew came on deck with a pea-jacket over his nightshirt, his wigless head comical in a pink nightcap; he trained his glass on the strange sail—a dozen glasses were pointing in that direction. Hornblower, looking through the glass reserved for the junior officer of the watch, saw the grey rectangle split into three, saw the three grow narrow, and then broaden again to coalesce into a single rectangle again.

"She's gone about," said Pellew. "Hands 'bout ship!"

Round came the *Indefatigable* on the other tack; the watch raced aloft to shake out a reef from the topsails while from the deck the officers looked up at the straining canvas to calculate the chances of the gale which howled round their ears splitting the sails or carrying away a spar. The *Indefatigable* lay over until it was hard to keep one's footing on the streaming deck; everyone without immediate duties clung to the weather rail and peered at the other ship.

"Fore and main topmasts exactly equal," said Lieutenant Bolton to Hornblower, his telescope to his eye. "Topsails white as milady's fingers. She's a Frenchie all right."

The sails of British ships were darkened with long service in all weathers; when a French ship escaped from harbour to run the blockade her spotless unweathered canvas disclosed her nationality without real need to take into consideration less obvious technical characteristics.

"We're weathering on her," said Hornblower; his eye was aching with staring through the glass, and his arms even were weary with holding the telescope to his eye, but in the excitement of the chase he could not relax.

"Not as much as I'd like," growled Bolton.

"Hands to the mainbrace!" roared Pellew at that moment.

It was a matter of the most vital concern to trim the sails so as to lie as close as possible to the wind; a hundred yards gained to windward would count as much as a mile gained in a stern chase. Pellew was looking up at the sails, back at the fleeting wake, across at the French ship, gauging the strength of the wind, estimating the strain on the rigging, doing everything that a lifetime of experience could suggest to close the gap between the two ships. Pellew's next order sent all hands to run out the guns on the weather side; that would in part counteract the heel and give the *Indefatigable* more grip upon the water.

"Now we're walking up to her," said Bolton with grudging optimism.

"Beat to quarters!" shouted Pellew.

The ship had been expecting that order. The roar of the marine bandsmen's drums echoed through the ship; the pipes twittered as the bosun's mates repeated the order, and the men ran in disciplined fashion to their duties. Hornblower, jumping for the weather mizzen shrouds, saw the eager grins on half a dozen faces—battle and the imminent possibility of death were a welcome change from the eternal monotony of the blockade. Up in the mizzen top he looked over his men. They were uncovering the locks of their muskets and looking to the priming; satisfied with their readiness for action Hornblower turned his attention to the swivel gun. He took the tarpaulin from the breech and the tompion from the muzzle, cast off the lashings which secured it, and saw that the swivel moved freely in the socket and the trunnions freely in the crotch. A jerk of the lanyard showed him that the lock was sparking well and there was no need for a new flint. Finch came climbing into the top with the canvas belt over his shoulder containing the charges for the gun; the bags of musket balls lay handy in a garland fixed to the barricade. Finch rammed home a cartridge down the short muzzle; Hornblower had ready a bag of balls to ram down onto it. Then he took a priming-quill and forced it down the touchhole, feeling sensitively to make sure the sharp point pierced the thin serge bag of the cartridge. Priming-quill and flintlock were necessary up here in the top, where no slow match or port-fire could be used with the danger of uncontrollable fire so great in the sails and the rigging. Yet musketry and swivel-gun fire from the tops were an important tactical consideration. With the ships laid yard-arm to yard-arm Hornblower's men could clear the hostile quarterdeck where centred the brains and control of the enemy.

"Stop that, Finch!" said Hornblower irritably; turning, he had caught sight of him peering up at the maintop and at this moment of tension Finch's delusions annoyed him.

"Beg your pardon, sir," said Finch, resuming his duties.

But a moment later Hornblower heard Finch whispering to himself.

"Mr. Bracegirdle's there," whispered Finch. "An' Oldroyd's there, an' all those others. But *He's* there too, so He is."

"Hands wear ship!" came the shouted order from the deck below.

The old *Indefatigable* was spinning round on her heel, the yards groaning as the braces swung them round. The French ship had made a bold attempt to rake her enemy as she clawed up to her, but Pellew's prompt handling defeated the plan. Now the ships were broadside to broadside, running free before the wind at long cannon shot.

"Just look at 'im!" roared Douglas, one of the musket men in the top. "Twenty guns a side. Looks brave enough, doesn't he?"

Standing beside Douglas, Hornblower could look down on the Frenchman's deck, her guns run out with the guns' crews clustering round them, officers in white breeches and blue coats walking up and down, the spray flying from her bows as she drove headlong before the wind.

"She'll look braver still when we take her into Plymouth Sound," said the seaman on the far side of Hornblower.

The *Indefatigable* was slightly the faster ship; an occasional touch of starboard helm was working her in closer to the enemy, into decisive range, without allowing the Frenchman to headreach upon her. Hornblower was impressed by the silence on both sides; he had always understood that the French were likely to open fire at long range and to squander ineffectively the first carefully loaded broadside.

"When's he goin' to fire?" asked Douglas, echoing Hornblower's thoughts.

"In his own good time," piped Finch.

The gap of tossing water between the two ships was growing narrower. Hornblower swung the swivel gun round and looked along the sights. He could aim well enough at the Frenchman's quarterdeck, but it was much too long a range for a bag of musket balls—in any case he dared not open fire until Pellew gave permission.

"Them's the men for us!" said Douglas, pointing to the Frenchman's mizzen top.

It looked as if there were soldiers up there, judging by the blue uniforms and the crossbelts; the French often eked out their scanty crews of trained seamen by shipping soldiers; in the British navy the marines were never employed aloft. The French soldiers saw the gesture and shook their fists, and a young officer among them drew his sword and brandished it over his head. With the ships parallel to each other like this the French mizzen top would be Hornblower's particular objective should he decide on trying to silence the firing there instead of sweeping the quarterdeck. He gazed curiously at the men it was his duty to kill. So interested was he that the bang of a cannon took him by surprise; before he could look down the rest of the Frenchman's broadside had gone off in straggling fashion, and a moment later the *Indefatigable* lurched as all her guns went off together. The wind blew the smoke forward, so that in the mizzen top they were not troubled by it at all. Hornblower's glance showed him dead men flung about on the *Indefatigable's* deck, dead men falling on the Frenchman's deck. Still the range was too great—very long musket shot, his eye told him.

"They're shootin' at us, sir," said Herbert.

"Let 'em," said Hornblower.

No musket fired from a heaving masthead at that range could possibly score a hit; that was obvious—so obvious that even Hornblower, madly excited as he was, could not help but be aware of it, and his certainty was apparent in his tone. It was interesting to see how the two calm words steadied the men. Down below the guns were roaring away continuously, and the ships were nearing each other fast.

"Open fire now, men!" said Hornblower. "Finch!"

He stared down the short length of the swivel gun. In the coarse V of the notch on the muzzle he could see the Frenchman's wheel, the two quartermasters standing behind it, the two officers beside it. He jerked the lanyard. A tenth of a second's delay, and then the gun roared out. He was conscious, before the smoke whirled round him, of the firing-quill, blown from the touchhole, flying past his temple; Finch was already sponging out the gun. The musket balls must have spread badly; only one of the helmsmen was down and someone else was already running to take his place. At that moment the whole top lurched frightfully; Hornblower felt it but he could not explain it. There was too much happening at once. The solid timbers under his feet jarred him as he stood—perhaps a shot had hit the mizzen mast. Finch was ramming in the cartridge; something struck the breech of the gun a heavy blow and left a bright splash of metal there—a musket bullet from the Frenchman's mizzen top. Hornblower tried to keep his head; he took out another sharpened quill and coaxed it down into the touchhole. It had to be done purposefully and yet gently; a quill broken off in the touchhole was likely to be a maddening nuisance. He felt the point of the quill pierce the cartridge; Finch rammed home the wad on top of the musket balls. A bullet struck the barricade beside him as Hornblower trained the gun down, but he gave it no thought. Surely the top was swaying more even than the heavy sea justified? No matter. He had a clear shot at the enemy's quarterdeck. He tugged at the lanyard. He saw men fall. He actually saw the spokes of the wheel spin round as it was left untended. Then the two ships came together with a shattering crash and his world dissolved into a chaos compared with which what had gone before was orderly.

The mast was falling. The top swung round in a dizzy arc so that only his fortunate grip on the swivel saved him from being flung out like a stone from a sling. It wheeled round. With the shrouds on one side shot away and two cannon balls in its heart the mast tottered and rolled. Then the tug of the mizzen stays inclined it forward, the tug of the other shrouds inclined it to starboard, and the wind in the mizzen topsail took charge when the back stays parted. The mast crashed forward; the topmast caught against the mainyard and the whole structure hung there before it could dissolve into its constituent parts. The severed butt-end of the mast must be resting on the deck for the moment; mast and topmast were still united at the cap and the trestle-trees into one continuous length, although why the topmast had not snapped at the cap was hard to say. With the lower end of the mast resting precariously on the deck, and the topmast resting against the mainyard, Hornblower and Finch still had a chance of life, but the ship's motion, another shot from the Frenchman, or the parting of the over-strained material could all end that chance. The mast could slip outwards, the topmast could break, the butt-end of the mast could slip along the deck—they had to save themselves if they could before any one of these imminent events occurred. The main topmast and everything above it was involved in the general ruin. It too had fallen and was dangling, sails, spars and ropes in one frightful tangle. The mizzen topsail had torn itself free.

Hornblower's eyes met Finch's; Finch and he were clinging to the swivel gun, and there was no one else in the steeply inclined top.

The starboard side mizzen topmast shrouds still survived; they, as well as the topmast, were resting across the mainyard, strained taut as fiddle strings, the mainyard tightening them just as the bridge tightens the strings of a fiddle. But along those shrouds lay the only way to safety—a sloping path from the peril of the top to the comparative safety of the mainyard.

The mast began to slip, to roll, out towards the end of the yard. Even if the mainyard held, the mizzen mast would soon fall into the sea alongside. All about them were thunderous noises—spars smashing, ropes parting; the guns were still bellowing and everyone below seemed to be yelling and screaming.

The top lurched again, frightfully. Two of the shrouds parted with the strain, with a noise clearly audible through the other din, and as they parted the mast twisted with a jerk, swinging round further the mizzen top, the swivel gun, and the two wretched beings who clung to it. Finch's staring blue eyes rolled with the movement of the top. Later Hornblower knew that the whole period of the fall of the mast was no longer than a few seconds, but at this time it seemed as if he had at least long minutes in which to think. Like Finch's, his eyes stared round him, saw the chance of safety.

"The mainyard!" he screamed.

Finch's face bore its foolish smile. Although instinct or training kept him gripping the swivel gun he seemingly had no fear, no desire to gain the safety of the mainyard.

"Finch, you fool!" yelled Hornblower.

He locked a desperate knee round the swivel so as to free a hand with which to gesticulate, but still Finch made no move.

"Jump, damn you!" raved Hornblower. "The shrouds—the yard. Jump!"

Finch only smiled.

"Jump and get to the maintop! Oh, Christ—!" Inspiration came in that frightful moment. "The maintop! God's there, Finch! Go along to God, quick!"

Those words penetrated into Finch's addled brain. He nodded with sublime unworldliness. Then he let go of the swivel and seemed to launch himself into the air like a frog. His body fell across the mizzen topmast shrouds and he began to scramble along them. The mast rolled again, so that when Hornblower launched himself at the shrouds it was a longer jump. Only his shoulders reached the outermost shroud. He swung off, clung, nearly lost his grip, but regained it as a counter-lurch of the leaning mast came to his assistance. Then he was scrambling along the shrouds, mad with panic. Here was the precious mainyard, and he threw himself across it, grappling its welcome solidity with his body, his feet feeling for the footrope. He was safe and steady on the yard just as the outward roll of the *Indefatigable* gave the balancing spars their final impetus, and the mizzen topmast parted company from the broken mizzen mast and the whole wreck fell down into the sea alongside. Hornblower shuffled along the yard, whither Finch had preceded him, to be received with rapture in the maintop by Midshipman Bracegirdle. Bracegirdle was not God, but as Hornblower leaned across the breastwork of the maintop he thought to himself that if he had not spoken about God being in the maintop Finch would never have made that leap.

"Thought we'd lost you," said Bracegirdle, helping him in and thumping him on the back. "Midshipman Hornblower, our flying angel."

Finch was in the top, too, smiling his fool's smile and surrounded by the crew of the top. Everything seemed mad and exhilarating. It was a shock to remember that they were in the midst of a battle, and yet the firing had ceased, and even the yelling had almost died away. He staggered to the side of the top—strange how difficult it was to walk—and looked over. Bracegirdle came with him. Foreshortened by the height he could make out a crowd of figures on the Frenchman's deck. Those check shirts must surely be worn by British sailors. Surely that was Eccles, the *Indefatigable's* first lieutenant, on the quarterdeck with a speaking trumpet.

"What has happened?" he asked Bracegirdle, bewildered.

"What has happened?" Bracegirdle stared for a moment before he understood. "We carried her by boarding. Eccles and the boarders were over the ship's side the moment we touched. Why, man, didn't you see?"

"No, I didn't see it," said Hornblower. He forced himself to joke. "Other matters demanded my attention at that moment."

He remembered how the mizzen top had lurched and swung, and he felt suddenly sick. But he did not want Bracegirdle to see it.

"I must go on deck and report," he said.

The descent of the main shrouds was a slow, ticklish business, for neither his hands nor his feet seemed to wish to go where he tried to place them. Even when he reached the deck he still felt insecure. Bolton was on the quarterdeck supervising the clearing away of the wreck of the mizzen mast. He gave a start of surprise as Hornblower approached.

"I thought you were overside with Davy Jones," he said. He glanced aloft. "You reached the mainyard in time?"

"Yes, sir."

"Excellent. I think you're born to be hanged, Hornblower." Bolton turned away to bellow at the men. "'Vast heaving, there! Clynes, get down into the chains with that tackle! Steady, now, or you'll lose it."

He watched the labours of the men for some moments before he turned back to Hornblower.

"No more trouble with the men for a couple of months," he said. "We'll work 'em 'till they drop, refitting. Prize crew will leave us shorthanded, to say nothing of our butcher's bill. It'll be a long time before they want something new. It'll be a long time for you, too, I fancy, Hornblower."

"Yes, sir," said Hornblower.

Six

HORNBLOWER
the Frogs, and the Lobsters

"They're coming," said Midshipman Kennedy.

Midshipman Hornblower's unmusical ear caught the raucous sounds of a military band, and soon, with a gleam of scarlet and white and gold, the head of the column came round the corner. The hot sunshine was reflected from the brass instruments; behind them the regimental colour flapped from its staff, borne proudly by an ensign with the colour guard round him. Two mounted officers rode behind the colour, and after them came the long red serpent of the half-battalion, the fixed bayonets flashing in the sun, while all the children of Plymouth, still not sated with military pomp, ran along with them.

The sailors standing ready on the quay looked at the soldiers marching up curiously, with something of pity and something of contempt mingled with their curiosity. The rigid drill, the heavy clothing, the iron discipline, the dull routine of the soldier were in sharp contrast with the far more flexible conditions in which the sailor lived. The sailors watched as the band ended with a flourish, and one of the mounted officers wheeled his horse to face the column. A shouted order turned every man to face the quay side, the movements being made so exactly together that five hundred boot-heels made a single sound. A huge sergeant-major, his sash gleaming on his chest, and the silver mounting of his cane winking in the sun, dressed the already perfect line. A third order brought down every musket-butt to earth.

"Unfix—bayonets!" roared the mounted officer, uttering the first words Hornblower had understood.

Hornblower positively goggled at the ensuing formalities, as the fuglemen strode their three paces forward, all exactly to time like marionettes worked by the same strings, turned their heads to look down the line, and gave the time for detaching the bayonets, for sheathing them, and for returning the muskets to the men's sides. The fuglemen fell back into their places, exactly to time again as far as Hornblower could see, but not exactly enough apparently, as the sergeant-major bellowed his discontent and brought the fuglemen out and sent them back again.

"I'd like to see him laying aloft on a stormy night," muttered Kennedy. "D'ye think he could take the main tops'l earring?"

"These Lobsters!" said Midshipman Bracegirdle.

The scarlet lines stood rigid, all five companies, the sergeants with their halberds indicating the intervals—from halberd to halberd the line of faces dipped down and then up again, with the men exactly sized off, the tallest men at the flanks and the shortest men in the centre of each company. Not a finger moved, not an eyebrow twitched. Down every back hung rigidly a powdered pigtail.

The mounted officer trotted down the line to where the naval party waited, and Lieutenant Bolton, in command, stepped forward with his hand to his hat brim.

"My men are ready to embark, sir," said the army officer. "The baggage will be here immediately."

"Aye aye, major," said Bolton—the army title and the navy reply in strange contrast.

"It would be better to address me as 'my lord,'" said the major.

"Aye aye, sir—my lord," replied Bolton, caught quite off his balance.

His Lordship, the Earl of Edrington, Major commanding this wing of the 43rd Foot, was a heavily built young man in his early twenties. He was a fine soldierly figure in his well-fitting uniform, and mounted on a magnificent charger, but he seemed a little young for his present responsible command. But the practice of the purchase of commissions was likely to put very young men in high command, and the army seemed satisfied with the system.

"The French auxiliaries have their orders to report here," went on Lord Edrington. "I suppose arrangements have been made for their transport as well?"

"Yes, my lord."

"Not one of the beggars can speak English, as far as I can make out. Have you got an officer to interpret?"

"Yes, sir. Mr. Hornblower!"

"Sir!"

"You will attend the embarkation of the French troops."

"Aye aye, sir."

More military music—Hornblower's tone-deaf ear distinguished it as making a thinner noise than the British infantry band—heralded the arrival of the Frenchmen farther down the quay by a side road, and Hornblower hastened there. This was the Royal, Christian, and Catholic French army, or a detachment of it at least—a battalion of the force raised by the *émigré* French nobles to fight against the Revolution. There was the white flag with the golden lilies at the head of the column, and a group of mounted officers to whom Hornblower touched his hat. One of them acknowledged his salute.

"The Marquis of Pouzauges, Brigadier General in the service of His Most Christian Majesty Louis XVII," said this individual in French by way of introduction. He wore a glittering white uniform with a blue ribbon across it.

Stumbling over the French words, Hornblower introduced himself as an aspirant of His Britannic Majesty's Marine, deputed to arrange the embarkation of French troops.

"Very good," said Pouzauges. "We are ready."

Hornblower looked down the French column. The men were standing in all attitudes, gazing about them. They were all well enough dressed, in blue uniforms which Hornblower guessed had been supplied by the British government, but the white crossbelts were already dirty, the metalwork tarnished, the arms dull. Yet doubtless they could fight.

"Those are the transports allotted to your men, sir," said Hornblower pointing. "The *Sophia* will take three hundred, and the *Dumbarton*—that one over there—will take two hundred and fifty. Here at the quay are the lighters to ferry the men out."

"Give the orders, M. de Moncoutant," said Pouzauges to one of the officers beside him.

The hired baggage carts had now come creaking up along the column, piled high with the men's kits, and the column broke into chattering swarms as the men hunted up their possessions. It was some time before the men were reassembled, each with his own kit-bag, and then there arose the question of detailing a fatigue party to deal with the regimental baggage; the men who were given the task yielded up their bags with obvious reluctance to their comrades, clearly in despair of ever seeing any of the contents again. Hornblower was still giving out information.

"All horses must go to the *Sophia*," he said. "She has accommodations for six chargers. The regimental baggage—"

He broke off short, for his eye had been caught by a singular jumble of apparatus lying in one of the carts.

"What is that, if you please?" he asked, curiosity overpowering him.

"That, sir," said Pouzauges, "is a guillotine."

"A guillotine?"

Hornblower had read much lately about this instrument. The Red Revolutionaries had set one up in Paris and kept it hard at work. The King of France, Louis XVI himself, had died under it. He did not expect to find one in the train of a counter-revolutionary army.

"Yes," said Pouzauges, "we take it with us to France. It is in my mind to give those anarchists a taste of their own medicine."

Hornblower did not have to make reply, fortunately, as a bellow from Bolton interrupted the conversation.

"What the hell's all this delay for, Mr. Hornblower? D'you want us to miss the tide?"

It was of course typical of life in any service that Hornblower should be reprimanded for the time wasted by the inefficiency of the French arrangements—that was the sort of thing he had already come to expect, and he had already learned that it was better to submit silently to reprimand than to offer excuses. He addressed himself again to the task of getting the French aboard their transports. It was a weary midshipman who at last reported himself to Bolton with his tally sheets and the news that the last Frenchman and horse and pieces of baggage were safely aboard, and he was greeted with the order to get his things together quickly and transfer them and himself to the *Sophia* where his services as interpreter were still needed.

The convoy dropped quickly down Plymouth Sound, rounded the Eddystone, and headed down channel, with H.M.S. *Indefatigable* flying her distinguishing pendant, the two gunbrigs which had been ordered to assist in convoying the expedition, and the four transports—a small enough force, it seemed to Hornblower, with which to attempt the overthrow of the French Republic. There were only eleven hundred infantry; the half-battalion of the 43rd and the weak battalion of Frenchmen (if they could be called that, seeing that many of them were soldiers of fortune of all nations) and although Hornblower had enough sense not to try to judge the Frenchmen as they lay in rows in the dark and stinking 'tween-decks in the agonies of seasickness he was puzzled that anyone could expect results from such a small force. His historical reading had told him of many small raids, in many wars, launched against the shores of France, and, although he knew that they had once been described by an opposition statesman as "breaking windows with guineas" he had been inclined to approve of them in principle, as bringing about a dissipation of the French strength—until now, when he found himself part of such an expedition.

So it was with relief that he heard from Pouzauges that the troops he had seen did not constitute the whole of the force to be employed—were indeed only a minor fraction of it. A little pale with seasickness, but manfully combating it, Pouzauges laid out a map on the cabin table and explained the plan.

"The Christian Army," explained Pouzauges, "will land here, at Quiberon. They sailed from Portsmouth—these English names are hard to pronounce—the day before we left Plymouth. There are five thousand men under the Baron de Charette. They will march on Vannes and Rennes."

"And what is your regiment to do?" asked Hornblower.

Pouzauges pointed to the map again.

"Here is the town of Muzillac," he said. "Twenty leagues from Quiberon. Here the main road from the south crosses the river Marais, where the tide ceases to flow. It is only a little river, as you see, but its banks are marshy, and the road passes it not only by a bridge but by a long causeway. The rebel armies are to the south, and on their northward march must come by Muzillac. We shall be there. We shall destroy the bridge and defend the crossing, delaying the rebels long enough to enable M. de Charette to raise all Brittany. He will soon have twenty thousand men in arms, the rebels will come back to their allegiance, and we shall march on Paris to restore His Most Christian Majesty to the throne."

So that was the plan. Hornblower was infected with the Frenchmen's enthusiasm. Certainly the road passed within ten miles of the coast, and there, in the broad estuary of the Vilaine, it should be possible to land a small force and seize Muzillac. There should be no difficulty about defending a causeway, such as Pouzauges described, for a day or two against even a large force. That would afford Charette every chance.

"My friend M. de Moncoutant here," went on Pouzauges, "is Lord of Muzillac. The people there will welcome him."

"Most of them will," said Moncoutant, his grey eyes narrowing. "Some will be sorry to see me. But I shall be glad of the encounter."

Western France, the Vendée and Brittany, had long been in a turmoil, and the population there, under the leadership of the nobility, had risen in arms more than once against the Paris government. But every rebellion had ended in defeat; the Royalist force now being convoyed to France was composed of the fragments of the defeated armies —a final cast of the dice, and a desperate one. Regarded in that light, the plan did not seem so sound.

It was a grey morning—a morning of grey sky and grey rocks—when the convoy rounded Belle Ile and stood in towards the estuary of the Vilaine river. Far to the northward were to be seen white topsails in Quiberon Bay—Hornblower, from the deck of the *Sophia,* saw signals pass back and forth from the *Indefatigable* as she reported her arrival to the senior officer of the main expedition there. It was a proof of the mobility and ubiquity of naval power that it could take advantage of the configuration of the land so that two blows could be struck almost in sight of each other from the sea yet separated by forty miles of roads on land. Hornblower raked the forbidding shore with his glass, re-read the orders for the captain of the *Sophia,* and stared again at the shore. He could distinguish the narrow mouth of the Marais river and the strip of mud where the troops were to land. The lead was going in the chains as the *Sophia* crept towards her allotted anchorage, and the ship was rolling uneasily; these waters, sheltered though they were, were a bedlam of conflicting currents that could make a choppy sea even in a calm. Then the anchor cable rumbled out through the hawsehole and the *Sophia* swung to the current while the crew set to work hoisting out the boats.

"France, dear beautiful France," said Pouzauges at Hornblower's side.

A hail came over the water from the *Indefatigable.*

"Mr. Hornblower!"

"Sir!" yelled Hornblower back through the captain's megaphone.

"You will go on shore with the French troops and stay with them until you receive further orders."

"Aye aye, sir."

So that was the way in which he was to set foot on foreign soil for the first time in his life.

Pouzauges' men were now pouring up from below; it was a slow and exasperating business getting them down the ship's side into the waiting boats. Hornblower wondered idly regarding what was happening on shore at this moment—without doubt mounted messengers were galloping north and south with the news of the arrival of the expedition, and soon the French Revolutionary generals would be parading their men and marching them hurriedly towards this place; it was well that the important strategic point that had to be seized was less than ten miles inland. He turned back to his duties; as soon as the men were ashore he would have to see that the baggage and reserve ammunition were landed, as well as the horses, now standing miserably in improvised stalls forward of the mainmast.

The first boats had left the ship's side; Hornblower watched the men stagger up the shore through mud and water, the French on the left and the red-coated British infantry on the right. There were some fishermen's cottages in sight up the beach, and Hornblower saw advance parties go forward to seize them; at least the landing had been effected without a single shot being fired. He came on shore with the ammunition, to find Bolton in charge of the beach.

"Get those ammunition boxes well above high water mark," said Bolton. "We can't send 'em forward until the Lobsters have found us some carts for 'em. And we'll need horses for those guns too."

At that moment Bolton's working party was engaged in manhandling two six-pounder guns in field carriages up the beach; they were to be manned by seamen and drawn by horses commandeered by the landing party, for it was in the old tradition that a British expeditionary force should always be thrown on shore dependent for military necessities on the countryside. Pouzauges and his staff were waiting impatiently for their chargers, and mounted them the moment they had been coaxed out of the boats onto the beach.

"Forward for France!" shouted Pouzauges, drawing his sword and raising the hilt to his lips.

Moncoutant and the others clattered forward to head the advancing infantry, while Pouzauges lingered to exchange a few words with Lord Edrington. The British infantry was drawn up in a rigid scarlet line; farther inland occasional red dots marked where the light company had been thrown forward as pickets. Hornblower could not hear the conversation, but he noticed that Bolton was drawn into it, and finally Bolton called him over.

"You must go forward with the Frogs, Hornblower," he said.

"I'll give you a horse," added Edrington. "Take that one—the roan. I've got to have someone I can trust along with them. Keep your eye on them and let me know the moment they get up to any monkey tricks—God knows what they'll do next."

"Here's the rest of your stores coming ashore," said Bolton. "I'll send 'em up as soon as you send some carts back to me. What the hell's *that*?"

"That's a portable guillotine, sir," said Hornblower. "Part of the French baggage."

All three turned and looked at Pouzauges, sitting his horse impatiently during this conversation which he did not understand. He knew what they were referring to, all the same.

"That's the first thing to be sent to Muzillac," he said to Hornblower. "Will you have the goodness to tell these gentlemen so?"

Hornblower translated.

"I'll send the guns and a load of ammunition first," said Bolton. "But I'll see he gets it soon. Now off you go."

Hornblower dubiously approached the roan horse. All he knew about riding he had learned in farmyards, but he got his foot up into the stirrup and climbed into the saddle, grabbing nervously at the reins as the animal started to move off. It seemed as far down to the ground from there as it did from the main topgallant yard. Pouzauges wheeled his horse about and started up the beach, and the roan followed its example, with Hornblower hanging on desperately, spattered by the mud thrown up by the French horse's heels.

From the fishing hamlet a muddy lane, bordered by green turf banks, led inland, and Pouzauges trotted smartly along it, Hornblower jolting behind him. They covered three or four miles before they overtook the rear of the French infantry, marching rapidly through the mud, and Pouzauges pulled his horse to a walk. When the column climbed a slight undulation they could see the white banner far ahead. Over the banks Hornblower could see rocky fields; out on the left there was a small farmhouse of grey stone. A blue-uniformed soldier was leading away a white horse pulling a cart, while two or three more soldiers were holding back the farmer's frantic wife. So the expeditionary force had secured some of its necessary transport. In another field a soldier was prodding a cow along with his bayonet—Hornblower could not imagine with what motive. Twice he heard distant musket shots to which no one seemed to pay any attention. Then, coming down the road, they encountered two soldiers leading bony horses towards the beach; the jests hurled at them by the marching column had set the men's faces in broad grins. But a little way farther on Hornblower saw a plough standing lonely in a little field, and a grey bundle lying near it. The bundle was a dead man.

Over on their right was the marshy river valley, and it was not long before Hornblower could see, far ahead, the bridge and the causeway which they had been sent to seize. The lane they were following came down a slight incline into the town, passing between a few grey cottages before emerging into the highroad along which there lay the town. There was a grey stone church, there was a building that could easily be identified as an inn and posting house with soldiers swarming round it, a slight broadening of the highroad, with an avenue of trees, which Hornblower assumed must be the central square of the town. A few faces peered from upper windows, but otherwise the houses were shut and there were no civilians to be seen except two women hastily shuttering their shops. Pouzauges reined up his horse in the square and began issuing orders. Already the horses were being led out of the post-house, and groups of men were bustling to and fro on seemingly urgent errands. In obedience to Pouzauges one officer called his men together —he had to expostulate and gesticulate before he succeeded—and started towards the bridge. Another party started along the highway in the opposite direction to guard against a possible surprise attack from there. A crowd of men squatted in the square devouring the bread that was brought out from one of the shops after its door had been beaten in, and two or three times civilians were dragged up to Pouzauges and at his orders were hurried away again to the town jail. The seizure of the town of Muzillac was complete.

Pouzauges seemed to think so, too, after an interval, for with a glance at Hornblower he turned his horse and trotted towards the causeway. The town ended before the road entered the marshes, and in a bit of waste ground beside the road the party sent out in this direction had already lighted a fire, and the men were gathered round it, toasting on their bayonets chunks of meat cut from a cow whose half-flayed corpse lay beside the fire. Farther on, where the causeway became the bridge over the river, a sentry sat sunning himself with his musket leaning against the parapet of the bridge at his back. Everything was peaceful enough. Pouzauges trotted as far as the crown of the bridge with Hornblower beside him, and looked over the country on the farther side. There was no sign of any enemy, and when they returned there was a mounted red-coated soldier waiting for them—Lord Edrington.

"I've come to see for myself," he said. "The position looks strong enough in all conscience here. Once you have the guns posted you should be able to hold this bridge until you can blow up the arch. But there's a ford, passable at low water, half a mile lower down. That is where I shall station myself—if we lose the ford they can turn the whole position and cut us off from the shore. Tell this gentleman—what's his name?—what I said."

Hornblower translated as well as he could, and stood by as interpreter while the two commanders pointed here and there and settled their respective duties.

"That's settled, then," said Edrington at length. "Don't forget, Mr. Hornblower, that I must be kept informed of every development."

He nodded to them and wheeled his horse and trotted off. As he left a cart approached from the direction of Muzillac, while behind it a loud clanking heralded the arrival of the two six-pounders, each drawn painfully by a couple of horses led by seamen. Sitting up on the front of the cart was Midshipman Bracegirdle, who saluted Hornblower with a broad grin.

"From quarterdeck to dung cart is but a step," he announced, swinging himself down. "From midshipman to captain of artillery."

He looked along the causeway and then around him.

"Put the guns over there and they'll sweep the whole length," suggested Hornblower.

"Exactly," said Bracegirdle.

Under his orders the guns were wheeled off the road and pointed along the causeway, and the dung cart was unloaded of its contents, a tarpaulin spread on the ground, the gunpowder cartridges laid on it and covered with another tarpaulin. The shot and the bags of grape were piled beside the guns, the seamen working with a will under the stimulus of their novel surroundings.

"Poverty brings strange bedfellows," said Bracegirdle. "And wars strange duties. Have you ever blown up a bridge?"

"Never," said Hornblower.

"Neither have I. Come, and let us do it. May I offer you a place in my carriage?"

Hornblower climbed up into the cart with Bracegirdle, and two seamen led the plodding horses along the causeway to the bridge. There they halted and looked down at the muddy water—running swiftly with the ebb—craning their heads over the parapet to look at the solid stone construction.

"It is the keystone of the arch which we should blow out," said Bracegirdle.

That was the proverbial recipe for the destruction of a bridge, but as Hornblower looked from the bridge to Bracegirdle and back again the idea did not seem easy to execute. Gunpowder exploded upwards and had to be held in on all sides—how was that to be done under the arch of the bridge?

"What about the pier?" he asked, tentatively.

"We can but look and see," said Bracegirdle and turned to the seaman by the cart. "Hannay, bring a rope."

They fastened the rope to the parapet and slid down it to a precarious foothold on the slippery ledge round the base of the pier, the river gurgling at their feet.

"That seems to be the solution," said Bracegirdle, crouching almost double under the arch.

Time slipped by fast as they made their preparations; a working party had to be brought from the guard of the bridge, picks and crowbars had to be found or extemporised, and some of the huge blocks with which the pier was built had to be picked out at the shoulder of the arch. Two kegs of gunpowder, lowered gingerly from above, had to be thrust into the holes so formed, a length of slow match put in at each bunghole, and led to the exterior while the kegs were tamped into their caves with all the stones and earth that could be crammed into them. It was almost twilight under the arch when the work was finished, the working party made laboriously to climb the rope up to the bridge, and Bracegirdle and Hornblower were left to look at each other again.

"I'll fire the fuses," said Bracegirdle. "You go next, sir."

It was not a matter for much argument. Bracegirdle was under orders to destroy the bridge, and Hornblower addressed himself to climbing up the rope while Bracegirdle took his tinderbox from his pocket. Once on the roadway of the bridge Hornblower sent away the cart and waited. It was only two or three minutes before Bracegirdle appeared, frantically climbing the rope and hurling himself over the parapet.

"Run!" was all that was said.

Together they scurried down the bridge and halted breathless to crouch by the abutment of the causeway. Then came a dull explosion, a tremor of the earth under their feet, and a cloud of smoke.

"Let's go and see," said Bracegirdle.

They retraced their steps towards where the bridge was still shrouded in smoke and dust.

"Only partly—" began Bracegirdle as they neared the scene and the dust cleared away.

And at that moment there was a second explosion which made them stagger as they stood. A lump of the roadbed hit the parapet beside them and burst like a shell, spattering them with fragments. There was a rumble and a clatter as the arch subsided into the river.

"That must have been the second keg going off," said Bracegirdle, wiping his face. "We should have remembered the fuses were likely to be of different lengths. Two promising careers might have ended suddenly if we had been any nearer."

"At any rate, the bridge is gone," said Hornblower.

"All's well that ends well," said Bracegirdle.

Seventy pounds of gunpowder had done their work. The bridge was cut clear across, leaving a ragged gap several feet wide, beyond which the roadway reached out toward the gap from the farther pier as a witness to the toughness of the mortar. Beneath their feet as they peered over they could see the river bed almost choked with lumps of stone.

"We'll need no more than an anchor watch tonight," said Bracegirdle.

Hornblower looked round to where the roan horse was tethered; he was tempted to return to Muzillac on foot, leading the animal, but shame forbade. He climbed with an effort into the saddle and headed the animal back up the road; ahead of him the sky was beginning to turn red with the approach of sunset.

He entered the main street of the town and rounded the slight bend to the central square, to see something that made him, without his own volition, tug at his reins and halt his horse. The square was full of people, townsfolk and soldiers, and in the centre of the square a tall narrow rectangle reached upwards towards the sky with a glittering blade at its upper end. The blade fell with a reverberating thump, and the little group of men round the base of the rectangle dragged something to one side and added it to the heap already there. The portable guillotine was at work.

Hornblower sat sick and horrified—this was worse than any flogging at the gratings. He was about to urge his horse forward when a strange sound caught his ear. A man was singing, loud and clear, and out from a building at the side of the square emerged a little procession. In front walked a big man with dark curly hair, wearing a white shirt and dark breeches. At either side and behind him walked soldiers. It was this man who was singing; the tune meant nothing to Hornblower, but he could hear the words distinctly—it was one of the verses of the French revolutionary song, echoes of which had penetrated even across the channel.

"Oh, sacred love of the Fatherland—" sang the man in the white shirt, and when the civilians in the square heard what he was singing, there was a rustle among them and they dropped to their knees, their heads bowed and their hands crossed upon their breasts.

The executioners were winding the blade up again, and the man in the white shirt followed its rise with his eyes while he still sang without a tremor in his voice. The blade reached the top, and the singing ceased at last as the executioners fell on the man with the white shirt and led him to the guillotine. Then the blade fell with another echoing crash.

It seemed that this was to be the last execution, for the soldiers began to push the civilians back towards their homes, and Hornblower urged his horse forward through the dissolving crowd. He was nearly thrown from his saddle when the animal plunged sideways, snorting furiously—it had scented the horrid heap that lay beside the guillotine. At the side of the square was a house with a balcony, and Hornblower looked up at it in time to see Pouzauges still standing there, wearing his white uniform and blue ribbon, his staff about him and his hands on the rail. There were sentries at the door, and to one of them Hornblower handed over his horse as he entered; Pouzauges was just descending the stairs.

"Good evening, sir," said Pouzauges with perfect courtesy. "I am glad you have found your way to headquarters. I trust it was without trouble? We are about to dine and will enjoy your company. You have your horse, I suppose? M. de Villers here will give orders for it to be looked after, I am sure."

It was all hard to believe. It was hard to believe that this polished gentleman had ordered the butchery that had just ended; it was hard to believe that the elegant young men with whom he sat at dinner were staking their lives on the overthrow of a barbarous but lusty young republic. But it was equally hard to believe, when he climbed into a four-poster bed that night, that he, Midshipman Horatio Hornblower, was in imminent deadly peril himself.

Outside in the street women wailed as the headless corpses, the harvest of the executions, were carried away, and he thought he would never sleep, but youth and fatigue had their way, and he slept for most of the night, although he awoke with the feeling that he had just been fighting off a nightmare. Everything was strange to him in the darkness, and it was several moments before he could account for the strangeness. He was in a bed and not—as he had spent the preceding three hundred nights—in a hammock; and the bed was steady as a rock instead of swaying about with the lively motion of a frigate. The stuffiness about him was the stuffiness of bed curtains, and not the stuffiness of the midshipmen's berth with its compound smell of stale humanity and stale bilgewater. He was on shore, in a house, in a bed, and everything about him was dead quiet, unnaturally so to a man accustomed to the innumerable noises of a wooden ship at sea.

Of course; he was in a house in the town of Muzillac in Brittany. He was sleeping in the headquarters of Brigadier General the Marquis de Pouzauges, commanding the French troops who constituted part of this expedition, which was itself part of a larger force invading Revolutionary France in the Royalist cause. Hornblower felt a quickening of the pulse, a faint sick feeling of insecurity, as he realised afresh that he was now in France, ten miles from the sea and the *Indefatigable* with only a rabble of Frenchmen—half of them mercenaries only nominally Frenchmen at that—around him to preserve him from death or captivity. He regretted his knowledge of French—if he had had none he would not be here, and good fortune might even have put him among the British half-battalion of the 43rd guarding the ford a mile away.

It was partly the thought of the British troops which roused him out of bed. It was his duty to see that liaison was kept up with them, and the situation might have changed while he slept. He drew aside the bed curtains and stepped down to the floor; as his legs took the weight of his body they protested furiously—all the riding he had done yesterday had left every muscle and joint aching so that he could hardly walk. But he hobbled in the darkness over to the window, found the latch of the shutters, and pushed them open. A three-quarter moon was shining down into the empty street of the town, and looking down he could see the three-cornered hat of the sentry posted outside, and the bayonet reflecting the moonlight. Returning from the window, he found his coat and his shoes and put them on, belted his cutlass about him, and then he crept downstairs as quietly as he could. In the room off the entrance hall a tallow dip guttered on the table, and beside it a French sergeant slept with his head on his arms, lightly, for he raised his head as Hornblower paused in the doorway. On the floor of the room the rest of the guard off duty were snoring stertorously, huddled together like pigs in a sty, their muskets stacked against the wall.

Hornblower nodded to the sergeant, opened the front door, and stepped out into the street. His lungs expanded gratefully as he breathed in the clean night air—morning air, rather, for there to the east the sky was assuming a lighter tinge—and the sentry, catching sight of the British naval officer, came clumsily to attention. In the square there still stood the gaunt harsh framework of the guillotine reaching up to the moonlit sky, and round it the black patch of the blood of its victims. Hornblower wondered who they were, who it could have been that the Royalists should seize and kill at such short notice, and he decided that they must have been petty officials of the Revolutionary government—the mayor and the customs officer and so on—if they were not merely men against whom the *émigrés* had cherished grudges since the days of the Revolution itself. It was a savage, merciless world, and at the moment he was very much alone in it, lonely, depressed, and unhappy.

He was distracted from these thoughts by the sergeant of the guard emerging from the door with a file of men; the sentry in the street was relieved, and the party went on round the house to relieve the others. Then across the street, he saw four drummers appear from another house, with a sergeant commanding them. They formed into a line, their drumsticks poised high before their faces, and then at a word from the sergeant, the eight drumsticks fell together with a crash, and the drummers proceeded to march slowly along the street beating out a jerky exhilarating rhythm. At the first corner, they stopped, and the drums rolled long and menacingly, and then they marched on again, beating out the previous rhythm. They were beating to arms, calling the men to their duties from their billets, and Hornblower, tone-deaf but highly sensitive to rhythm, thought it was fine music, real music. He turned back to headquarters with his depression fallen away from him. The sergeant of the guard came marching back with the relieved sentries; the first of the awakened soldiers were beginning to appear sleepily in the streets, and then, with a clatter of hoofs, a mounted messenger came riding up to headquarters, and the day was begun.

A pale young French officer read the note which the messenger brought, and politely handed it to Hornblower to read; he had to puzzle over it for a space—he was not accustomed to handwritten French—but its meaning became clear to him at length. It implied no new development; the main expeditionary force, landed yesterday at Quiberon, would move forward this morning on Vannes and Rennes while the subsidiary force to which Hornblower was attached must maintain its position at Muzillac guarding its flank. The Marquis de Pouzauges, immaculate in his white uniform and blue ribbon, appeared at that moment, read the note without comment, and turned to Hornblower with a polite invitation to breakfast.

They went back to the big kitchen with its copper cooking pans glittering on the walls, and a silent woman brought them coffee and bread.

She might be a patriotic Frenchwoman and an enthusiastic counter-revolutionary, but she showed no signs of it. Her feelings, of course, might easily have been influenced by the fact that this horde of men had taken over her house and were eating her food and sleeping in her rooms without payment. Maybe some of the horses and waggons seized for the use of the army were hers too—and maybe some of the people who had died under the guillotine last night were her friends. But she brought coffee, and the staff, standing about in the big kitchen with their spurs clinking, began to breakfast. Hornblower took his cup and a piece of bread—for four months before this his only bread had been ship's biscuit—and sipped at the stuff. He was not sure if he liked it; he had only tasted coffee three or four times before. But the second time he raised his cup to his lips, he did not sip; before he could do so, the distant boom of a cannon made him lower his cup and stand stock still. The cannon shot was repeated, and again, and then it was echoed by a sharper, nearer note—Midshipman Bracegirdle's six-pounders on the causeway.

In the kitchen there was instant stir and bustle. Somebody knocked a cup over and sent a river of black liquid swirling across the table. Somebody else managed to catch his spurs together so that he stumbled into somebody else's arms. Everyone seemed to be speaking at once. Hornblower was as excited as the rest of them; he wanted to rush out and see what was happening, but he thought at that moment of the disciplined calm which he had seen in H.M.S. *Indefatigable* as she went into action. He was not of this breed of Frenchmen, and to prove it he made himself put his cup to his lips again and drink calmly. Already most of the staff had dashed out of the kitchen shouting for their horses. It would take time to saddle up; he met Pouzauges' eye as the latter strode up and down the kitchen, and he drained his cup—a trifle too hot for comfort, but he felt it was a good gesture. There was bread to eat, and he made himself bite and chew and swallow, although he had no appetite; if he was to be in the field all day, he could not tell when he would get his next meal, and so he crammed a half loaf into his pocket.

The horses were being brought into the yard and saddled; the excitement had infected them, and they plunged and sidled about amid the curses of the officers. Pouzauges leapt up into his saddle and clattered away with the rest of the staff behind him, leaving behind only a single soldier holding Hornblower's roan. That was as it had better be—Hornblower knew that he would not keep his seat for half a minute if the horse took it into his head to plunge or rear. He walked slowly out to the animal, which was calmer now when the groom petted him, and climbed with infinite slowness and precaution into the saddle. With a pull at the bit he checked the brute's exuberance and walked it sedately into the street and towards the bridge in the wake of the galloping staff. It was better to make sure of arriving by keeping his horse down to a walk than to gallop and be thrown. The guns were still booming and he could see the puffs of smoke from Bracegirdle's six-pounders. On his left, the sun was rising in a clear sky.

At the bridge the situation seemed obvious enough. Where the arch had been blown up a few skirmishers on either side were firing at each other across the gap, and, at the far end of the causeway, across the Marais, a cloud of smoke revealed the presence of a hostile battery firing slowly and at extreme range. Beside the causeway on this side were Bracegirdle's two six-pounders, almost perfectly covered by a dip in the ground. Bracegirdle, with his cutlass belted round him, was standing between the guns which his party of seamen were working, and he waved his hand lightheartedly at Hornblower when he caught sight of him. A dark column of infantry appeared on the distant causeway. Bang—bang went Bracegirdle's guns. Hornblower's horse plunged at the noise, distracting him, but when he had time to look again, the column had disappeared. Then suddenly the causeway parapet near him flew into splinters; something hit the roadbed beside his horse's feet a tremendous blow and passed on with a roar—that was the closest so far in his life that a cannon shot had missed him. He lost a stirrup during the resultant struggle with his horse, and deemed it wiser, as soon as he regained moderate control, to dismount and lead the animal off the causeway towards the guns. Bracegirdle met him with a grin.

"No chance of their crossing here," he said. "At least, not if the Frogs stick to their work, and it looks as if they're willing to. The gap's within grapeshot range; they'll never bridge it. Can't think what they're burning powder for."

"Testing our strength, I suppose," said Hornblower, with an air of infinite military wisdom.

He would have been shaking with excitement if he had allowed his body to take charge. He did not know if he were being stiltedly unnatural, but even if he were that was better than to display excitement. There was something strangely pleasant, in a nightmare fashion, in standing here posing as a hardened veteran with cannon balls howling overhead; Bracegirdle seemed happy and smiling and quite master of himself, and Hornblower looked sharply at him, wondering if this were as much a pose as his own. He could not tell.

"Here they come again," said Bracegirdle. "Oh, only skirmishers."

A few scattered men were running out along the causeway to the bridge. At long musket range they fell to the ground and began spasmodic firing; already there were some dead men lying over there and the skirmishers took cover behind the corpses. On this side of the gap the skirmishers, better sheltered, fired back at them.

"They haven't a chance, here at any rate," said Bracegirdle. "And look there."

The main body of the Royalist force, summoned from the town, was marching up along the road. While they watched it, a cannon shot from the other side struck the head of the column and ploughed into it—Hornblower saw dead men flung this way and that, and the column wavered. Pouzauges came riding up and yelled orders, and the column, leaving its dead and wounded on the road, changed direction and took shelter in the marshy fields beside the causeway.

With nearly all the Royalist force assembled, it seemed indeed as if it would be utterly impossible for the Revolutionaries to force a crossing here.

"I'd better report on this to the Lobsters," said Hornblower.

"There was firing down that way at dawn," agreed Bracegirdle.

Skirting the wide marsh here ran a narrow path through the lush grass, leading to the ford which the 43rd were guarding. Hornblower led his horse onto the path before he mounted; he felt he would be more sure in that way of persuading the horse to take that direction. It was not long before he saw a dot of scarlet on the river-bank—pickets thrown out from the main body to watch against any unlikely attempt to cross the marshes and stream round the British flank. Then he saw the cottage that indicated the site of the ford; in the field beside it was a wide patch of scarlet indicating where the main body was waiting for developments. At this point the marsh narrowed where a ridge of slightly higher ground approached the water; a company of redcoats was drawn up here with Lord Edrington on horseback beside them. Hornblower rode up and made his report, somewhat jerkily as his horse moved restlessly under him.

"No serious attack, you say?" asked Edrington.

"No sign of one when I left, sir."

"Indeed?" Edrington stared across the river. "And here it's the same story. No attempt to cross the ford in force. Why should they show their hand and then not attack?"

"I thought they were burning powder unnecessarily, sir," said Hornblower.

"They're not fools," snapped Edrington, with another penetrating look across the river. "At any rate, there's no harm in assuming they are not."

He turned his horse and cantered back to the main body and gave an order to a captain who scrambled to his feet to receive it. The captain bellowed an order, and his company stood up and fell into line, rigid and motionless. Two further orders turned them to the right and marched them off in file, every man in step, every musket sloped at the same angle. Edrington watched them go.

"No harm in having a flank guard," he said.

The sound of a cannon across the water recalled them to the river; on the other side of the marsh a column of troops could be seen marching rapidly along the bank.

"That's the same column coming back, sir," said the company commander. "That or another just like it."

"Marching about and firing random shots," said Edrington. "Mr. Hornblower, have the *émigré* troops any flank guard out towards Quiberon?"

"Towards Quiberon, sir?" said Hornblower, taken aback.

"Damn it, can't you hear a plain question? Is there, or is there not?"

"I don't know, sir," confessed Hornblower, miserably.

There were five thousand *émigré* troops at Quiberon, and it seemed quite unnecessary to keep a guard out in that direction.

"Then present my compliments to the French *émigré* general, and suggest he post a strong detachment up the road, if he has not done so."

"Aye aye, sir."

Hornblower turned his horse's head back up the path towards the bridge. The sun was shining strongly now over the deserted fields. He could still hear the occasional thud of a cannon shot, but overhead a lark was singing in the blue sky. Then as he headed up the last low ridge towards Muzillac and the bridge he heard a sudden irregular outburst of firing; he fancied he heard screams and shouts, and what he saw, as he topped the rise, made him snatch at his reins and drag his horse to a halt. The fields before him were covered with fugitives in blue uniforms with white crossbelts, all running madly towards him. In among the fugitives were galloping horsemen, whirling sabres that flashed in the sunshine. Farther out to the left a whole column of horsemen were trotting fast across the fields, and farther back the sun glittered on lines of bayonets moving rapidly from the highroad towards the sea.

There could be no doubt of what had happened; during those sick seconds when he sat and stared, Hornblower realised the truth; the Revolutionaries had pushed in a force between Quiberon and Muzillac, and, keeping the *émigrés* occupied by demonstrations from across the river, had rushed down and brought off a complete surprise by this attack from an unexpected quarter. Heaven only knew what had happened at Quiberon—but this was no time to think about that. Hornblower dragged his horse's head round and kicked his heels into the brute's sides, urging him frantically back up the path towards the British. He bounced and rolled in his saddle, clinging on madly, consumed with fear lest he lose his seat and be captured by the pursuing French.

At the clatter of hoofs every eye turned towards him when he reached the British post. Edrington was there, standing with his horse's bridle over his arm.

"The French!" yelled Hornblower hoarsely, pointing back. "They're coming!"

"I expected nothing else," said Edrington.

He shouted an order before he put his foot in the stirrup to mount. The main body of the 43rd was standing in line by the time he was in the saddle. His adjutant went galloping off to recall the company from the water's edge.

"The French are in force, horse, foot, and guns, I suppose?" asked Edrington.

"Horse and foot at least, sir," gasped Hornblower, trying to keep his head clear. "I saw no guns."

"And the *émigrés* are running like rabbits?"

"Yes, sir."

"Here come the first of them."

Over the nearest ridge a few blue uniforms made their appearance, their wearers still running while stumbling with fatigue.

"I suppose we must cover their retreat, although they're not worth saving," said Edrington. "Look there!"

The company he had sent out as a flank guard was in sight on the crest of a slight slope: it was formed into a tiny square, red against the green, and as they watched they saw a mob of horsemen flood up the hill towards it and break into an eddy around it.

"Just as well I had them posted there," remarked Edrington calmly. "Ah, here comes Mayne's company."

The force from the ford came marching up. Harsh orders were shouted. Two companies wheeled round while the sergeant-major with his sabre and his silver-headed cane regulated the pace and the alignment as if the men were on the barrack square.

"I would suggest you stay by me, Mr. Hornblower," said Edrington.

He moved his horse up into the interval between the two columns, and Hornblower followed him dumbly. Another order, and the force began to march steadily across the valley, the sergeants calling the step and the sergeant-major watching the intervals. All round them now were fleeing *émigré* soldiers, most of them in the last stages of exhaustion—Hornblower noticed more than one of them fall down on the ground gasping and incapable of further movement. And then over the low slope to the right appeared a line of plumes, a line of sabres—a regiment of cavalry trotting rapidly forward. Hornblower saw the sabres lifted, saw the horses break into a gallop, heard the yells of the charging men. The redcoats around him halted; another shouted order, another slow, deliberate movement, and the half-battalion was in a square with the mounted officers in the centre and the colours waving over their heads. The charging horsemen were less than a hundred yards away. Some officer with a deep voice began giving orders, intoning them as if at some solemn ceremony. The first order brought the muskets from the men's shoulders, and the second was answered by a simultaneous click of opened priming pans. The third order brought the muskets to the present along one face of the square.

"Too high!" said the sergeant-major. "Lower, there, Number Seven."

The charging horsemen were only thirty yards away; Hornblower saw the leading men, their cloaks flying from their shoulders, leaning along their horses' necks with their sabres pointed forward at the full stretch of their arms.

"Fire!" said the deep voice.

In reply came a single sharp explosion as every musket went off at once. The smoke swirled round the square and disappeared. Where Hornblower had been looking, there were now a score of horses and men on the ground, some struggling in agony, some lying still. The cavalry regiment split like a torrent encountering a rock and hurtled harmlessly past the other faces of the square.

"Well enough," said Edrington.

The deep voice was intoning again; like marionettes all on the same string the company that had fired now reloaded, every man biting out his bullet at the same instant, every man ramming home his charge, every man spitting his bullet into his musket barrel with the same instantaneous inclination of the head. Edrington looked keenly at the cavalry collecting together in a disorderly mob down the valley.

"The Forty-Third will advance!" he ordered.

With solemn ritual the square opened up again into two columns and continued its interrupted march. The detached company came marching up to join them from out of a ring of dead men and horses. Someone raised a cheer.

"Silence in the ranks!" bellowed the sergeant-major. "Sergeant, take that man's name."

But Hornblower noticed how the sergeant-major was eyeing keenly the distance between the columns; it had to be maintained exactly so that a company wheeling back filled it to make the square.

"Here they come again," said Edrington.

The cavalry were forming for a new charge, but the square was ready for them. Now the horses were blown and the men were less enthusiastic. It was not a solid wall of horses that came down on them, but isolated groups, rushing first at one face and then at another, and pulling up or swerving aside as they reached the line of bayonets. The attacks were too feeble to meet with company volleys; at the word of command sections here and there gave fire to the more determined groups. Hornblower saw one man—an officer, judging by his gold lace—rein up before the bayonets and pull out a pistol. Before he could discharge it, half a dozen muskets went off together; the officer's face became a horrible bloody mask, and he and his horse fell together to the ground. Then all at once, the cavalry wheeled off, like starlings over a field, and the march could be resumed.

"No discipline about these Frogs, not on either side," said Edrington.

The march was headed for the sea, for the blessed shelter of the *Indefatigable*, but it seemed to Hornblower as if the pace were intolerably slow. The men were marching at the parade step, with agonising deliberation, while all round them and far ahead of them the fugitive *émigrés* poured in a broad stream towards safety. Looking back, Hornblower saw the fields full of marching columns—hurrying swarms, rather—of Revolutionary infantry in hot pursuit of them.

"Once let men run, and you can't do anything else with them," commented Edrington, following Hornblower's gaze.

Shouts and shots over to the flank caught their attention. Trotting over the fields, leaping wildly at the bumps, came a cart drawn by a lean horse. Someone in a seaman's frock and trousers was holding the reins; other seamen were visible over the sides firing muskets at the horsemen hovering about them. It was Bracegirdle with his dung cart; he might have lost his guns but he had saved his men. The pursuers dropped away as the cart neared the columns; Bracegirdle, standing up in the cart, caught sight of Hornblower on his horse and waved to him excitedly.

"Boadicea and her chariot!" he yelled.

"I'll thank you, sir," shouted Edrington with lungs of brass, "to go on and prepare for our embarkation."

"Aye aye, sir!"

The lean horse trotted on with the cart lurching after it and the grinning seamen clinging on to the sides. At the other flank appeared a swarm of infantry, a mad, gesticulating crowd, half running to cut off the 43rd's retreat. Edrington swept his glance round the fields.

"The Forty-Third will form line!" he shouted.

Like some ponderous machine, well oiled, the half-battalion fronted towards the swarm; the columns became lines, each man moving into his position like a brick laid on a wall.

"The Forty-Third will advance!"

The scarlet line swept forward, slowly, inexorably. The swarm hastened to meet it, officers to the front waving their swords and calling on their men to follow.

"Make ready!"

Every musket came down together; the priming pans clicked.

"Present!"

Up came the muskets, and the swarm hesitated before that fearful menace. Individuals tried to get back into the crowd to cover themselves from the volley with the bodies of their comrades.

"Fire!"

A crashing volley; Hornblower, looking over the heads of the British infantry from his point of vantage on horseback, saw the whole face of the swarm go down in swathes. Still the red line moved forward, at each deliberate step a shouted order brought a machinelike response as the men reloaded; five hundred mouths spat in five hundred bullets, five hundred right arms raised five hundred ramrods at once. When the muskets came to the present the red line was at the swathe of dead and wounded, for the swarm had withdrawn before the advance, and shrank back still further at the threat of the volley. The volley was fired; the advance went on. Another volley; another advance. Now the swarm was shredding away. Now men were running from it. Now every man had turned tail and fled from that frightful musketry. The hillside was black with fugitives as it had been when the *émigrés* were fleeing.

"Halt!"

The advance ceased; the line became a double column, and the retreat began again.

"Very creditable," remarked Edrington.

Hornblower's horse was trying jerkily to pick its way over a carpet of dead and wounded, and he was so busy keeping his seat, and his brain was in such a whirl, that he did not immediately realise that they had topped the last rise so that before them lay the glittering waters of the estuary. There were the ships riding at anchor, and there, blessed sight, were the boats swarming towards the shore. The strip of muddy beach was packed solid with *émigrés*. It was high time, for already the boldest of the Revolutionary infantry were hovering round the columns, taking long shots into them. Here and there a man fell.

"Close up!" snapped the sergeants, and the files marched on stolidly, leaving the wounded and dead behind them.

The adjutant's horse suddenly snorted and plunged, and then fell first to its knees, and, kicking, to its side, while the freckle-faced adjutant freed his feet from the stirrups and flung himself out of the saddle just in time to escape being pinned underneath.

"Are you hit, Stanley?" asked Edrington.

"No, my lord. All safe and sound," said the adjutant, brushing at his scarlet coat.

"You won't have to foot it far," said Edrington. "No need to throw out skirmishers to drive those fellows off. This is where we must make our stand."

He looked about him, at the fishermen's cottages above the beach, the panic-stricken *émigrés* at the water's edge, and the masses of Revolutionary infantry coming up in pursuit, leaving small enough time for preparation. Some of the redcoats poured into the cottages, appearing a moment later at the windows; it was fortunate that the fishing hamlet guarded one flank of the gap down to the beach while the other was guarded by a steep and inaccessible headland on whose summit a small block of redcoats established themselves. In the gap between the two points the remaining four companies formed a long line just sheltered by the crest of the beach.

The boats of the squadron were already loading with *émigrés* among the small breakers below. Hornblower heard the crack of a single pistol shot; he could guess that some officer down there was enforcing his orders in the only possible way to prevent the fear-driven men from pouring into the boats and swamping them. As if in answer came the roar of cannon on the other side. A battery of artillery had unlimbered just out of musket range and was firing at the British position, while all about it gathered the massed battalions of the Revolutionary infantry. The cannon balls howled close overhead.

"Let them fire away," said Edrington. "The longer the better."

The artillery could do little harm to the British in the fold of ground that protected them, and the Revolutionary commander must have realised that as well as the necessity for wasting no time. Over there the drums began to roll—a noise of indescribable menace—and then the columns surged forward. So close were they already that Hornblower could see the features of the officers in the lead, waving their hats and swords.

"Forty-Third, make ready!" said Edrington, and the priming pans clicked as one. "Seven paces forward—march!"

One—two—three—seven paces, painstakingly taken, took the line to the little crest.

"Present! Fire!"

A volley nothing could withstand. The columns halted, swayed, received another smashing volley, and another, and fell back in ruin.

"Excellent!" said Edrington.

The battery boomed again; a file of two redcoat soldiers was tossed back like dolls, to lie in a horrible bloody mass close beside Hornblower's horse's feet.

"Close up!" said a sergeant, and the men on either side had filled the gap.

"Forty-Third, seven paces back—march!"

The line was below the crest again, as the red-coated marionettes withdrew in steady time. Hornblower could not remember later whether it was twice or three times more that the Revolutionary masses came on again, each time to be dashed back by that disciplined musketry. But the sun was nearly setting in the ocean behind him when he looked back to see the beach almost cleared and Bracegirdle plodding up to them to report.

"I can spare one company now," said Edrington in reply but not taking his eyes off the French masses. "After they are on board, have every boat ready and waiting."

One company filed off; another attack was beaten back—after the preceding failures it was not pressed home with anything like the dash and fire of the earlier ones. Now the battery was turning its attention to the headland on the flank, and sending its balls among the redcoats there, while a battalion of French moved over to the attack at that point.

"That gives us time," said Edrington. "Captain Griffin, you can march the men off. Colour party, remain here."

Down the beach went the centre companies to the waiting boats, while the colours still waved to mark their old position, visible over the crest to the French. The company in the cottages came out, formed up, and marched down as well. Edrington trotted across to the foot of the little headland; he watched the French forming for the attack and the infantry wading out to the boats.

"Now, grenadiers!" he yelled, suddenly. "Run for it! Colour party!"

Down the steep seaward face of the headland came the last company, running, sliding, and stumbling. A musket, clumsily handled, went off unexpectedly. The last man came down the slope as the colour party reached the water's edge and began to climb into a boat with its precious burden. A wild yell went up from the French, and their whole mass came rushing towards the evacuated position.

"Now, sir," said Edrington, turning his horse seawards.

Hornblower fell from his saddle as his horse splashed into the shallows. He let go of the reins and plunged out, waist deep, shoulder deep, to where the longboat lay on its oars with its four-pounder gun in its bows and Bracegirdle beside it to haul him in. He looked up in time to see a curious incident: Edrington had reached the *Indefatigable's* gig, still holding his horse's reins. With the French pouring down the beach towards them, he turned and took a musket from the nearest soldier, pressed the muzzle to the horse's head, and fired. The horse fell in its death agony in the shallows; only Hornblower's roan remained as prize to the Revolutionaries.

"Back water!" said Bracegirdle, and the longboat backed away from the beach; Hornblower lay in the eyes of the boat feeling as if he had not the strength to move a limb, and the beach was covered with shouting, gesticulating Frenchmen, lit redly by the sunset.

"One moment," said Bracegirdle, reaching for the lanyard of the four-pounder, and tugging at it smartly.

The gun roared out in Hornblower's ear, and the charge cut a swathe of destruction on the beach.

"That was canister," said Bracegirdle. "Eighty four balls. Easy, port! Give way, starboard!"

The longboat turned, away from the beach and towards the welcoming ships. Hornblower looked back at the darkening coast of France. This was the end of an incident; his country's attempt to overturn the Revolution had met with a bloody repulse. Newspapers in Paris would exult; the *Gazette* in London would give the incident five cold lines. Clairvoyant, Hornblower could foresee that in a year's time, the world would hardly remember the incident. In twenty years, it would be entirely forgotten. Yet those headless corpses up there in Muzillac; those shattered redcoats; those Frenchmen caught in the four-pounder's blast of canister—they were all as dead as if it had been a day in which history had been changed. And he was just as weary. And in his pocket there was still the bread he had put there that morning and forgotten all about.

Seven

HORNBLOWER *and the Spanish Galleys*

THE OLD *Indefatigable* was lying at anchor in the Bay of Cadiz at the time when Spain made peace with France. Hornblower happened to be midshipman of the watch, and it was he who called the attention of Lieutenant Chadd to the approach of the eight-oared pinnace, with the red and yellow of Spain drooping at the stern. Chadd's glass made out gleam of gold on epaulette and cocked hat, and he bellowed the order for sideboys and marine guard to give the traditional honours to a captain in an allied service. Pellew, hurriedly warned, was at the gangway to meet his visitor, and it was at the gangway that the entire interview took place. The Spaniard, making a low bow with his hat across his stomach, offered a sealed envelope to the Englishman.

"Here, Mr. Hornblower," said Pellew, holding the letter unopened, "speak French to this fellow. Ask him to come below for a glass of wine."

But the Spaniard, with a further bow, declined the refreshment, and, with another bow, requested that Pellew open the letter immediately. Pellew broke the seal and read the contents, struggling with the French which he could read to a small extent although he could not speak it at all. He handed it to Hornblower.

"This means the Dagoes have made peace, doesn't it?"

Hornblower struggled through twelve lines of compliments addressed by His Excellency the Duke of Belchite (Grandee of the First Class, with eighteen other titles ending with Captain-General of Andalusia) to the Most Gallant Ship-Captain Sir Edward Pellew, Knight of the Bath. The second paragraph was short and contained only a brief intimation of peace. The third paragraph was as long as the first, and repeated its phraseology almost word for word in a ponderous farewell.

"That's all, sir," said Hornblower.

But the Spanish captain had a verbal message with which to supplement the written one.

"Please tell your captain," he said, in his lisping Spanish-French, "that now as a neutral power, Spain must enforce her rights. You have already been at anchor here for twenty four hours. Six hours from now—" The Spaniard took a gold watch from his pocket and glanced at it—"if you are within range of the batteries at Puntales there they will be given orders to fire on you."

Hornblower could only translate the brutal message without any attempt at softening it, and Pellew listened, white with anger despite his tan.

"Tell him—" he began, and then mastered his rage. "Damme if I'll let him see he has made me angry."

He put his hat across his stomach and bowed in as faithful an imitation of the Spaniard's courtliness as he could manage, before he turned to Hornblower.

"Tell him I have received his message with pleasure. Tell him I much regret that circumstances are separating him from me, and that I hope I shall always enjoy his personal friendship whatever the relations between our countries. Tell him—oh, you can tell him that sort of thing I want said, can't you, Hornblower? Let's see him over the side with dignity. Sideboys! Bosun's mates! Drummers!"

Hornblower poured out compliments to the best of his ability, and at every phrase the two captains exchanged bows, the Spaniard withdrawing a pace at each bow and Pellew following him up, not to be outdone in courtesy. The drums beat a ruffle, the marines presented arms, the pipes shrilled and twittered until the Spaniard's head had descended to the level of the maindeck, when Pellew stiffened up, clapped his hat on his head, and swung round on his first lieutenant.

"Mr. Eccles, I want to be under weigh within the hour, if you please."

Then he stamped down below to regain his equanimity in private.

Hands were aloft loosing sail ready to sheet home, while the clank of the capstan told how other men were heaving the cable short, and Hornblower was standing on the portside gangway with Mr. Wales the carpenter, looking over at the white houses of one of the most beautiful cities in Europe.

"I've been ashore there twicet," said Wales. "The wine's good—vino, they calls it—if you happens to like that kind o' muck. But don't you ever try that brandy, Mr. Hornblower. Poison, it is, rank poison. Hello! We're going to have an escort, I see."

Two long sharp prows had emerged from the inner bay, and were pointing towards the *Indefatigable*. Hornblower could not restrain himself from giving a cry of surprise as he followed Wales' gaze. The vessels approaching were galleys; along each side of them the oars were lifting and falling rhythmically, catching the sunlight as they feathered. The effect, as a hundred oars swung like one, was perfectly beautiful. Hornblower remembered a line in a Latin poem which he had translated as a schoolboy, and recalled his surprise when he discovered that to a Roman the "white wings" of a ship of war were her oars. Now the simile was plain; even a gull in flight, which Hornblower had always looked upon until now as displaying the perfection of motion, was not more beautiful than those galleys. They lay low in the water, immensely long for their beam. Neither the sails nor the lateen yards were set on the low raking masts. The bows blazed with gilding while the waters of the bay foamed round them as they headed into the teeth of the gentle breeze with the Spanish red and gold streaming aft from the masthead. Up—forward—down—went the oars with unchanging rhythm, the blades not varying an inch in their distance apart during the whole of the stroke. From the bows of each two long guns looked straight forward in the direction the galleys pointed.

"Twenty-four-pounders," said Wales. "If they catch you in a calm, they'll knock you to pieces. Lie off on your quarter where you can't bring a gun to bear and rake you till you strike. An' then God help you —better a Turkish prison than a Spanish one."

In a line-ahead that might have been drawn with a ruler and measured with a chain the galleys passed close along the port side of the *Indefatigable* and went ahead of her. As they passed, the roll of the drum and the call of the pipes summoned the crew of the *Indefatigable* to attention out of compliment to the flag and the commission pendant going by, while the galley's officers returned the salute.

"It don't seem right, somehow," muttered Wales under his breath, "to salute 'em like they was a frigate."

Level with the *Indefatigable's* bowsprit the leader backed her starboard-side oars, and spun like a top, despite her length and narrow beam, across the frigate's bows. The gentle wind blew straight to the frigate from the galley, and then from her consort as the latter followed; and a foul stench came back on the air and assailed Hornblower's nostrils, and not Hornblower's alone, clearly, for it brought forth cries of disgust from all the men on deck.

"They all stink like that," explained Wales. "Four men to the oar an' fifty oars. Two hundred galley slaves, that is. All chained to their benches. When you goes aboard one of them as a slave you're chained to your bench, an' you're never unchained until they drop you overside. Sometimes when the hands aren't busy they'll hose out the bilge, but that doesn't happen often, bein' Dagoes an' not many of 'em."

Hornblower as always sought exact information.

"How many, Mr. Wales?"

"Thirty, mebbe. Enough to hand the sails if they're making a passage. Or to man the guns—they strike the yards and sails, like now, before they goes into action, Mr. Hornblower," said Wales, pontifical as usual, and with that slight emphasis on the "Mister" inevitable when a warrant officer of sixty with no hope of further promotion addressed a warrant officer of eighteen (his nominal equal in rank) who might some day be an admiral. "So you see how it is. With no more than thirty of a crew an' two hundred slaves they daren't let 'em loose, not ever."

The galleys had turned again, and were now passing down the *Indefatigable's* starboard side. The beat of the oars had slowed very noticeably, and Hornblower had ample time to observe the vessel closely, the low forecastle and high poop with the gangway connecting them along the whole length of the galley; upon that gangway walked a man with a whip. The rowers were invisible below the bulwarks, the oars being worked through holes in the sides closed, as far as Hornblower could see, with sheets of leather round the oar-looms to keep out the sea. On the poop stood two men at the tiller and a small group of officers, their gold lace flashing in the sunshine. Save for the gold lace and the twenty-four-pounder bow chasers Hornblower was looking at exactly the same sort of vessel as the ancients used to fight their battles. Polybius and Thucydides wrote about galleys almost identical with these—for that matter it was not much more than two hundred years since the galleys had fought their last great battle at Lepanto against the Turks. But those battles had been fought with hundreds of galleys a side.

"How many do they have in commission now?" asked Hornblower.

"A dozen, mebbe—not that I knows for sure, o' course. Cartagena's their usual station, beyond the Gut."

Wales, as Hornblower understood, meant by this through the Strait of Gibraltar in the Mediterranean.

"Too frail for the Atlantic," Hornblower commented.

It was easy to deduce the reasons for the survival of this small number—the innate conservatism of the Spaniards would account for it to a large extent. Then there was the point that condemnation to the galleys was one way of disposing of criminals. And when all was said and done a galley might still be useful in a calm—merchant ships becalmed while trying to pass the Strait of Gibraltar might be snapped up by galleys pushing out from Cadiz or Cartagena. And at the very lowest estimate there might be some employment for galleys to tow vessels in and out of harbour with the wind unfavourable.

"Mr. Hornblower!" said Eccles. "My respects to the captain, and we're ready to get under weigh."

Hornblower dived below with his message.

"My compliments to Mr. Eccles," said Pellew, looking up from his desk, "and I'll be on deck immediately."

There was just enough of a southerly breeze to enable the *Indefatigable* to weather the point in safety. With her anchor catted she braced round her yards and began to steal seaward; in the disciplined stillness which prevailed the sound of the ripple of water under her cutwater was clearly to be heard—a musical note which told nothing, in its innocence, of the savagery and danger of the world of the sea into which she was entering. Creeping along under her topsail the *Indefatigable* made no more than three knots, and the galleys came surging past her again, oars beating their fastest rhythm, as if the galleys were boasting of their independence of the elements. Their gilt flashed in the sun as they overtook to windward, and once again their foul stench offended the nostrils of the men of the *Indefatigable*.

"I'd be obliged if they'd keep to leeward of us," muttered Pellew, watching them through his glass. "But I suppose that's not Spanish courtesy. Mr. Cutler!"

"Sir!" said the gunner.

"You may commence the salute."

"Aye aye, sir."

The forward carronade on the lee side roared out the first of its compliments, and the fort of Puntales began its reply. The sound of the salute rolled round the beautiful bay; nation was speaking to nation in all courtesy.

"The next time we hear those guns they'll be shotted, I fancy," said Pellew, gazing across at Puntales and the flag of Spain flying above it.

Indeed, the tide of war was turning against England. Nation after nation had retired from the contest against France, some worsted by arms, and some by the diplomacy of the vigorous young republic. To any thinking mind it was obvious that once the step from war to neutrality had been taken, the next step would be easy, from neutrality to war on the other side. Hornblower could foresee, close at hand, a time when all Europe would be arrayed in hostility to England, when she would be battling for her life against the rejuvenescent power of France and the malignity of the whole world.

"Set sail, please, Mr. Eccles," said Pellew.

Two hundred trained pairs of legs raced aloft; two hundred trained pairs of arms let loose the canvas, and the *Indefatigable* doubled her speed, heeling slightly to the gentle breeze. Now she was meeting the long Atlantic swell. So were the galleys; as the *Indefatigable* overtook them, Hornblower could see the leader put her nose into a long roller so that a cloud of spray broke over her forecastle. That was asking too much of such frail craft. Back went one bank of oars; forward went the other. The galleys rolled hideously for a moment in the trough of the sea before they completed their turn and headed back for the safe waters of Cadiz Bay. Someone forward in the *Indefatigable* began to boo, and the cry was instantly taken up through the ship. A storm of boos and whistles and catcalls pursued the galleys, the men momentarily quite out of hand while Pellew spluttered with rage on the quarterdeck and the petty officers strove in vain to take the names of the offenders. It was an ominous farewell to Spain.

Ominous indeed. It was not long before Captain Pellew gave the news to the ship that Spain had completed her change-over; with the treasure convoy safely in she had declared war against England; the revolutionary republic had won the alliance of the most decayed monarchy in Europe. British resources were now stretched to the utmost; there was another thousand miles of coast to watch, another fleet to blockade, another horde of privateers to guard against, and far fewer harbours in which to take refuge and from which to draw the fresh water and the meagre stores which enabled the hard-worked crews to remain at sea. It was then that friendship had to be cultivated with the half-savage Barbary States, and the insolence of the Deys and the Sultans had to be tolerated so that North Africa could provide the skinny bullocks and the barley grain to feed the British garrisons in the Mediterranean—all of them beleaguered on land—and the ships which kept open the way to them. Oran, Tetuán, Algiers wallowed in unwontedly honest prosperity with the influx of British gold.

It was a day of glassy calm in the Strait of Gibraltar. The sea was like a silver shield, the sky like a bowl of sapphire, with the mountains of Africa on the one hand, the mountains of Spain on the other as dark serrations on the horizon. It was not a comfortable situation for the *Indefatigable*, but that was not because of the blazing sun which softened the pitch in the deck seams. There is almost always a slight current setting inwards into the Mediterranean from the Atlantic, and the prevailing winds blow in the same direction. In a calm like this it was not unusual for a ship to be carried far through the Straits, past the Rock of Gibraltar, and then to have to beat for days and even weeks to make Gibraltar Bay. So that Pellew was not unnaturally anxious about his convoy of grain ships from Oran. Gibraltar had to be revictualled —Spain had already marched an army up for the siege—and he dared not risk being carried past his destination. His orders to his reluctant convoy had been enforced by flag and gun signals, for no shorthanded merchant ship relished the prospect of the labour Pellew wished to be executed. The *Indefatigable* no less than her convoy had lowered boats and the helpless ships were now all in tow. That was backbreaking, exhausting labour, the men at the oars tugging and straining, dragging the oar blades through the water, while the towlines tightened and bucked with superhuman perversity and the ships sheered freakishly from side to side. It was less than a mile an hour that the ships made in this fashion, at the cost of the complete exhaustion of the boats' crews, but at least it postponed the time when the Gibraltar current would carry them to leeward, and similarly gave more chance for the longed-for southerly wind—two hours of a southerly wind was all they wished for—to waft them up to the Mole.

Down in the *Indefatigable's* longboat and cutter the men tugging at their oars were so stupefied with their toil that they did not hear the commotion in the ship. They were just tugging and straining, under the pitiless sky, living through their two hours' spell of misery, but they were roused by the voice of the captain himself, hailing them from the forecastle.

"Mr. Bolton! Mr. Chadd! Cast off there, if you please. You'd better come and arm your men at once. Here come our friends from Cadiz."

Back on the quarterdeck, Pellew looked through his glass at the hazy horizon; he could make out from here by now what had first been reported from the masthead.

"They're heading straight for us," he said.

The two galleys were on their way from Cadiz; presumably a fast horseman from the lookout point at Tarifa had brought them the news of this golden opportunity, of the flat calm and the scattered and helpless convoy. This was the moment for galleys to justify their continued existence. They could capture and at least burn, although they could not hope to carry off, the unfortunate merchant ships while the *Inde-*

fatigable lay helpless hardly out of cannon's range. Pellew looked round at the two merchant ships and the three brigs; one of them was within half a mile of him and might be covered by his gunfire, but the others —a mile and a half, two miles away—had no such protection.

"Pistols and cutlasses, my lads!" he said to the men pouring up from overside. "Clap onto that stay tackle now. Smartly with that carronade, Mr. Cutler!"

The *Indefatigable* had been in too many expeditions where minutes counted to waste any time over these preparations. The boats' crews seized their arms, the six-pounder carronades were lowered into the bows of the cutter and longboat, and soon the boats, crowded with armed men, and provisioned against sudden emergency, were pulling away to meet the galleys.

"What the devil d'you think you're doing, Mr. Hornblower?"

Pellew had just caught sight of Hornblower in the act of swinging out of the jolly boat which was his special charge. He wondered what his midshipman thought he could achieve against a war-galley with a twelve-foot boat and a crew of six.

"We can pull to one of the convoy and reinforce the crew, sir," said Hornblower.

"Oh, very well then, carry on. I'll trust to your good sense even though that's a broken reed."

"Good on you, sir!" said Jackson ecstatically, as the jolly boat shoved off from the frigate. "Good on you! No one else wouldn't never have thought of that."

Jackson, the coxswain of the jolly boat, obviously thought that Hornblower had no intention of carrying out his suggestion to reinforce the crew of one of the merchant ships.

"Those stinking Dagoes," said stroke oar, between his teeth.

Hornblower was conscious of the presence in his crew of the same feeling of violent hostility toward the Spanish galleys as he felt within himself. In a fleeting moment of analysis, he attributed it to the circumstances in which they had first made the galley's acquaintance, as well as to the stench which the galleys trailed after them. He had never known this feeling of personal hatred before; when previously he had fought it had been as a servant of the King, not out of personal animosity. Yet here he was gripping the tiller under the scorching sky and leaning forward in his eagerness to be at actual grips with this enemy.

The longboat and cutter had a long start of them, and even though they were manned by crews who had already served a spell at the oars they were skimming over the water at such a speed that the jolly boat with all the advantage of the glassy-smooth water only caught slowly up to them. Overside the sea was of the bluest, deepest blue until the oar blades churned it white. Ahead of them the vessels of the convoy lay scattered where the sudden calm had caught them, and just beyond them Hornblower caught sight of the flash of oar blades as the galleys came sweeping down on their prey. Longboat and cutter were diverging in an endeavour to cover as many vessels as possible, and the gig was still far astern. There would hardly be time to board a ship even if Hornblower should wish to. He put the tiller over to incline his course after the cutter; one of the galleys at that moment abruptly made its appearance in the gap between two of the merchant ships. Hornblower saw the cutter swing round to point her six-pounder carronade at the advancing bows.

"Pull, you men! Pull!" he shrieked, mad with excitement.

He could not imagine what was going to happen, but he wanted to be in the fray. That six-pounder popgun was grossly inaccurate at any range longer than musket shot. It would serve to hurl a mass of grape into a crowd of men, but its ball would have small effect on the strengthened bows of a war galley.

"Pull!" shrieked Hornblower again. He was nearly up to them, wide on the cutter's quarter.

The carronade boomed out. Hornblower thought he saw the splinters fly from the galley's bow, but the shot had no more effect on deterring her than a peashooter could stop a charging bull. The galley turned a little, getting exactly into line, and then her oars' beat quickened. She was coming down to ram, like the Greeks at Salamis.

"Pull!" shrieked Hornblower.

Instinctively, he gave the tiller a touch to take the jolly boat out into a flanking position.

"Easy!"

The jolly boat's oars stilled, as their way carried them past the cutter. Hornblower could see Soames standing up in the sternsheets looking at the death which was cleaving the blue water towards him. Bow to bow the cutter might have stood a chance, but too late the cutter tried to evade the blow altogether. Hornblower saw her turn, presenting her vulnerable side to the galley's stem. That was all he could see, for the next moment the galley herself hid from him the final act of the tragedy. The jolly boat's starboard side oars only just cleared the galley's starboard oars as she swept by. Hornblower heard a shriek and a crash, saw the galley's forward motion almost cease at the collision. He was mad with the lust of fighting, quite insane, and his mind was working with the rapidity of insanity.

"Give way, port!" he yelled, and the jolly boat swung round under the galley's stern. "Give way all!"

The jolly boat leaped after the galley like a terrier after a bull.

"Grapple them, damn you, Jackson!"

Jackson shouted an oath in reply, as he leaped forward, seemingly hurdling the men at the oars without breaking their stroke. In the bows Jackson seized the boat's grapnel on its long line and flung it hard and true. It caught somewhere in the elaborate gilt rail on the galley's quarter. Jackson hauled on the line, the oars tugged madly in the effort to carry the jolly boat up to the galley's stern. At that moment Hornblower saw it, the sight which would long haunt his dreams—up from under the galley's stern came the shattered forepart of the cutter, still with men clinging to it who had survived the long passage under the whole length of the galley which had overrun them. There were straining faces, empurpled faces, faces already relaxing in death. But in a moment it was past and gone, and Hornblower felt the jerk transmitted through the line to the jolly boat as the galley leaped forward.

"I can't hold her!" shouted Jackson.

"Take a turn round the cleat, you fool!"

The galley was towing the jolly boat now, dragging her along at the end of a twenty-foot line close on her quarter, just clear of the arc of her rudder. The white water bubbled all around her, her bows were cocked up with the strain. It was a mad moment, as though they had harpooned a whale. Someone came running aft on the Spaniard's poop, knife in hand to cut the line.

"Shoot him, Jackson!" shrieked Hornblower again.

Jackson's pistol cracked, and the Spaniard fell to the deck out of sight—a good shot. Despite his fighting madness, despite the turmoil of rushing water and glaring sun, Hornblower tried to think out his next move. Inclination and commonsense alike told him that the best plan was to close with the enemy despite the odds.

"Pull up to them, there!" he shouted—everyone in the boat was shouting and yelling. The man in the bows of the jolly boat faced forward and took the grapnel line and began to haul in on it, but the speed of the boat through the water made any progress difficult, and after a yard or so had been gained the difficulty became insurmountable, for the grapnel was caught in the poop rail ten or eleven feet above water, and the angle of pull became progressively steeper as the jolly boat neared the stern of the galley. The boat's bow cocked higher out of the water than ever.

"Belay!" said Hornblower, and then, his voice rising again, "Out pistols, lads!"

A row of four or five swarthy faces had appeared at the stern of the galley. Muskets were pointing into the jolly boat, and there was a brief but furious exchange of shots. One man fell groaning into the bottom of the jolly boat, but the row of faces disappeared. Standing up precariously in the swaying sternsheets, Hornblower could still see nothing of the galley's poop deck save for the tops of two heads, belonging, it was clear, to the men at the tiller.

"Reload," he said to his men, remembering by a miracle to give the order. The ramrods went down the pistol barrels.

"Do that carefully if you ever want to see Pompey again," said Hornblower.

He was shaking with excitement and mad with the fury of fighting, and it was the automatic, drilled part of him which was giving these levelheaded orders. His higher faculties were quite negatived by his lust for blood. He was seeing things through a pink mist—that was how he remembered it when he looked back upon it later. There was a sudden crash of glass. Someone had thrust a musket barrel through the big stern window of the galley's after cabin. Luckily having thrust it through he had to recover himself to take aim. An irregular volley of pistols almost coincided with the report of the musket. Where the Spaniard's bullet went no one knew; but the Spaniard fell back from the window.

"By God! That's our way!" screamed Hornblower, and then, steadying himself, "Reload."

As the bullets were being spat into the barrels he stood up. His unused pistols were still in his belt; his cutlass was at his side.

"Come aft, here," he said to stroke oar; the jolly boat would stand no more weight in the bows than she had already. "And you, too."

Hornblower poised himself on the thwarts, eyeing the grapnel line and the cabin window.

"Bring 'em after me one at a time, Jackson," he said.

Then he braced himself and flung himself at the grapnel line. His feet grazed the water as the line sagged, but using all his clumsy strength his arms carried him upwards. Here was the shattered window at his side; he swung up his feet, kicked out a big remaining piece of the pane, and then shot his feet through and then the rest of himself. He came down on the deck of the cabin with a thud; it was dark in here compared with the blinding sun outside. As he got to his feet, he trod on something which gave out a cry of pain—the wounded Spaniard, evidently—and the hand with which he drew his cutlass was sticky with blood. Spanish blood. Rising, he hit his head a thunderous crash on the deck beams above, for the little cabin was very low, hardly more than five feet, and so severe was the blow that his senses almost left him. But before him was the cabin door and he reeled out through it, cutlass in hand. Over his head he heard a stamping of feet, and shots were fired behind him and above him—a further exchange, he presumed, between the jolly boat and the galley's stern rail. The cabin door opened into a low half-deck, and Hornblower reeled along it out into the sunshine again. He was on the tiny strip of maindeck at the break of the poop. Before him stretched the narrow gangway between the two sets of rowers; he could look down at these latter—two seas of bearded faces, mops of hair and lean sunburned bodies, swinging rhythmically back and forward to the beat of the oars.

That was all the impression he could form of them at the moment. At the far end of the gangway at the break of the forecastle stood the overseer with his whip; he was shouting words in rhythmic succession to the slaves—Spanish numbers, perhaps, to give them the time. There were three or four men on the forecastle; below them the half-doors through the forecastle bulkhead were hooked open, through which Hornblower could see the two big guns illuminated by the light through the port holes out of which they were run almost at the water level. The guns' crews were standing by the guns, but numerically they were far fewer than two twenty-four-pounders would demand. Hornblower remembered Wales' estimate of no more than thirty for a galley's crew. The men of one gun at least had been called aft to defend the poop against the jolly boat's attack.

A step behind him made him leap with anxiety and he swung round with his cutlass ready to meet Jackson stumbling out of the half-deck, cutlass in hand.

"Nigh on cracked my nut," said Jackson.

He was speaking thickly like a drunken man, and his words were chorused by further shots fired from the poop at the level of the top of their heads.

"Oldroyd's comin' next," said Jackson. "Franklin's dead."

On either side of them a companion ladder mounted to the poop deck. It seemed logical, mathematical, that they should each go up one but Hornblower thought better of it.

"Come along," he said, and headed for the starboard ladder, and, with Oldroyd putting in an appearance at that moment, he yelled to him to follow.

The hand ropes of the ladder were of twisted red and yellow cord —he even could notice that as he rushed up the ladder, pistol in one hand and cutlass in the other. After the first step, his eye was above deck level. There were more than a dozen men crowded on the tiny poop, but two were lying dead, and one was groaning with his back to the rail, and two stood by the tiller. The others were looking over the rail at the jolly boat. Hornblower was still insane with fighting madness. He must have leaped up the final two or three steps with a bound like a stag's, and he was screaming like a maniac as he flung himself at the Spaniards. His pistol went off apparently without his willing it, but the face of the man a yard away dissolved into bloody ruin, and Hornblower dropped the weapon and snatched the second, his thumb going to the hammer as he whirled his cutlass down with a crash on the sword which the next Spaniard raised as a feeble guard. He struck and struck and struck with a lunatic's strength. Here was Jackson beside him shouting hoarsely and striking out right and left.

"Kill 'em! Kill 'em!" shouted Jackson.

Hornblower saw Jackson's cutlass flash down on the head of the defenceless man at the tiller. Then out of the tail of his eye he saw another sword threaten him as he battered with his cutlass at the man before him, but his pistol saved him as he fired automatically again. Another pistol went off beside him—Oldroyd's, he supposed—and then the fight on the poop was over. By what miracle of ineptitude the Spaniards had allowed the attack to take them by surprise Hornblower never could discover. Perhaps they were ignorant of the wounding of the man in the cabin, and had relied on him to defend that route; perhaps it had never occurred to them that three men could be so utterly desperate as to attack a dozen; perhaps they never realised that three men had made the perilous passage of the grapnel line; perhaps—most probably—in the mad excitement of it all, they simply lost their heads, for five minutes could hardly have elapsed altogether from the time the jolly boat hooked on until the poop was cleared. Two or three Spaniards ran down the companion to the maindeck, and forward along the gangway between the rows of slaves. One was caught against the rail and made a gesture of surrender, but Jackson's hand was already at his throat. Jackson was a man of immense physical strength; he bent the Spaniard back over the rail, farther and farther, and then caught him by the thigh with his other hand and heaved him over. He fell with a shriek before Hornblower could interpose. The poop deck was covered with writhing men, like the bottom of a boat filled with flapping fish. One man was getting to his knees when Jackson and Oldroyd seized him. They swung him up to toss him over the rail.

"Stop that!" said Hornblower, and quite callously they dropped him again with a crash on the bloody planks.

Jackson and Oldroyd were like drunken men, unsteady on their feet, glazed of eye and stertorous of breath; Hornblower was just coming out of his insane fit. He stepped forward to the break of the poop, wiping the sweat out of his eyes while trying to wipe away the red mist that tinged his vision. Forward by the forecastle were gathered the rest of the Spaniards, a large group of them; as Hornblower came forward, one of them fired a musket at him but the ball went wide. Down below him the rowers were still swinging rhythmically, forward and back, forward and back, the hairy heads and the naked bodies moving in time to the oars; in time to the voice of the overseer, too, for the latter was still standing on the gangway (the rest of the Spaniards were clustered behind him) calling the time—"*Seis, siete, ocho.*"

"Stop!" bellowed Hornblower.

He walked to the starboard side to be in full view of the starboard-side rowers. He held up his hand and bellowed again. A hairy face or two was raised, but the oars still swung.

"*Uno, dos, tres,*" said the overseer.

Jackson appeared at Hornblower's elbow, and levelled a pistol to shoot the nearest rower.

"Oh, belay that!" said Hornblower testily. He knew he was sick of killings now. "Find my pistols and reload them."

He stood at the top of the companion like a man in a dream—in a nightmare. The galley slaves went on swinging and pulling; his dozen enemies were still clustered at the break of the forecastle thirty yards away; behind him the wounded Spaniards groaned away their lives. Another appeal to the rowers was as much ignored as the preceding ones. Oldroyd must have had the clearest head or have recovered himself quickest.

"I'll haul down his colours, sir, shall I?" he said.

Hornblower woke from his dream. On a staff above the taffrail fluttered the yellow and red.

"Yes, haul 'em down at once," he said.

Now his mind was clear, and now his horizon was no longer bounded by the narrow limits of the galley. He looked about him, over the blue, blue sea. There were the merchant ships; over there lay the *Indefatigable.* Behind him boiled the white wake of the galley—a curved wake. Not until that moment did he realise that he was in control of the tiller, and that for the last three minutes the galley had been cutting over the blue seas unsteered.

"Take the tiller, Oldroyd," he ordered.

Was that a galley disappearing into the hazy distance? It must be, and far in its wake was the longboat. And there, on the port bow, was the gig, resting on her oars—Hornblower could see little figures standing waving in bow and stern, and it dawned upon him that this was in acknowledgment of the hauling down of the Spanish colours. Another musket banged off forward, and the rail close at his hip was struck a tremendous blow which sent gilded splinters flying in the sunlight. But he had all his wits about him again, and he ran back over the dying men; at the after end of the poop he was out of sight of the gangway and safe from shot. He could still see the gig on the port bow.

"Starboard your helm, Oldroyd."

The galley turned slowly—her narrow length made her unhandy if the rudder were not assisted by the oars—but soon the bow was about to obscure the gig.

"Midships!"

Amazing that there, leaping in the white water that boiled under the galley's stern, was the jolly boat with one live man and two dead men still aboard.

"Where are the others, Bromley?" yelled Jackson.

Bromley pointed overside. They had been shot from the taffrail at the moment that Hornblower and the others were preparing to attack the poop.

"Why in hell don't you come aboard?"

Bromley took hold of his left arm with his right; the limb was clearly useless. There was no reinforcement to be obtained here, and yet full possession must be taken of the galley. Otherwise it was even conceivable that they would be carried off to Algeciras; even if they were masters of the rudder the man who controlled the oars dictated the course of the ship if he willed. There was only one course left to try.

Now that his fighting madness had ebbed away, Hornblower was in a sombre mood. He did not care what happened to him; hope and fear had alike deserted him, along with his previous exalted condition. It might be resignation that possessed him now. His mind, still calculating, told him that with only one thing left to do to achieve victory he must attempt it, and the flat, dead condition of his spirits enabled him to carry the attempt through like an automaton, unwavering and emotionless. He walked forward to the poop rail again; the Spaniards were still clustered at the far end of the gangway, with the overseer still giving the time to the oars. They looked up at him as he stood there. With the utmost care and attention he sheathed his cutlass, which he had held in his hand up to that moment. He noticed the blood on his coat and on his hands as he did so. Slowly, he settled the sheathed weapon at his side.

"My pistols, Jackson," he said.

Jackson handed him his pistols and with the same callous care, he thrust them into his belt. He turned back to Oldroyd, the Spaniards watching every movement fascinated.

"Stay by the tiller, Oldroyd. Jackson, follow me. Do nothing without my orders."

With the sun pouring down on his face, he strode down the companion ladder, walked to the gangway, and approached the Spaniards along it. On either side of him the hairy heads and naked bodies of the galley slaves still swung with the oars. He neared the Spaniards; swords and muskets and pistols were handled nervously, but every eye was on his face. Behind him Jackson coughed. Two yards only from the group, Hornblower halted and swept them with his glance. Then, with a gesture, he indicated the whole of the group except the overseer; and then pointed to the forecastle.

"Get for'rard, all of you," he said.

They stood staring at him, although they must have understood the gesture.

"Get for'rard," said Hornblower with a wave of his hand and a tap of his foot on the gangway.

There was only one man who seemed likely to demur actively, and Hornblower had it in mind to snatch a pistol from his belt and shoot him on the spot. But the pistol might misfire, the shot might rouse the Spaniards out of their fascinated dream. He stared the man down.

"Get for'rard, I say."

They began to move, they began to shamble off. Hornblower watched them go. Now his emotions were returning to him, and his heart was thumping madly in his chest so that it was hard to control himself. Yet he must not be precipitate. He had to wait until the others were well clear before he could address himself to the overseer.

"Stop those men," he said.

He glared into the overseer's eyes while pointing to the oarsmen; the overseer's lips moved, but he made no sound.

"Stop them," said Hornblower, and this time he put his hand to the butt of his pistol.

That sufficed. The overseer raised his voice in a high-pitched order, and the oars instantly ceased. Strange what sudden stillness possessed the ship with the cessation of the grinding of the oars in the holes. Now it was easy to hear the bubbling of the water round the galley as her way carried her forward. Hornblower turned back to hail Oldroyd.

"Oldroyd! Where away's the gig?"

"Close on the starboard bow, sir!"

"How close?"

"Two cables' lengths, sir. She's pulling for us now."

"Steer for her while you've steerage way."

"Aye aye, sir."

How long would it take the gig under oars to cover a quarter of a mile? Hornblower feared anticlimax, feared a sudden revulsion of feeling among the Spaniards at this late moment. Mere waiting might occasion it, and he must not stand merely idle. He could still hear the motion of the galley through the water, and he turned to Jackson.

"This ship carries her way well, Jackson, doesn't she?" he said, and he made himself laugh as he spoke, as if everything in the world were a matter of sublime certainty.

"Aye, sir, I suppose she does, sir," said the startled Jackson; he was fidgeting nervously with his pistols.

"And look at the man there," went on Hornblower, pointing to a galley slave. "Did you ever see such a beard in your life?"

"N–no, sir."

"Speak to me, you fool. Talk naturally."

"I–I dunno what to say, sir."

"You've no sense, damn you, Jackson. See the welt on that fellow's shoulder? He must have caught it from the overseer's whip not so long ago."

"Mebbe you're right, sir."

Hornblower was repressing his impatience and was about to make another speech when he heard a rasping thump alongside and a moment later the gig's crew was pouring over the bulwarks. The relief was inexpressible. Hornblower was about to relax completely when he remembered appearances. He stiffened himself up.

"Glad to see you aboard, sir," he said, as Lieutenant Chadd swung his legs over and dropped to the maindeck at the break of the forecastle.

"Glad to see *you,*" said Chadd, looking about him curiously.

"These men for'rard are prisoners, sir," said Hornblower. "It might be well to secure them. I think that is all that remains to be done."

Now he could not relax; it seemed to him as if he must remain strained and tense for ever. Strained and yet stupid, even when he heard the cheers of the hands in the *Indefatigable* as the galley came alongside her. Stupid and dull, making a stumbling report to Captain Pellew, forcing himself to remember to commend the bravery of Jackson and Oldroyd in the highest terms.

"The admiral will be pleased," said Pellew, looking at Hornblower keenly.

"I'm glad, sir," Hornblower heard himself say.

"Now that we've lost poor Soames," went on Pellew, "we shall need another watch-keeping officer. I have it in mind to give you an order as acting-lieutenant."

"Thank you, sir," said Hornblower, still stupid.

Soames had been a grey-haired officer of vast experience. He had sailed the seven seas, he had fought in a score of actions. But, faced with a new situation, he had not had the quickness of thought to keep his boat from under the ram of the galley. Soames was dead, and Acting-Lieutenant Hornblower would take his place. Fighting madness, sheer insanity, had won him this promise of promotion. Hornblower had never realised the black depths of lunacy into which he could sink. Like Soames, like all the rest of the crew of the *Indefatigable,* he had allowed himself to be carried away by his blind hatred for the galleys, and only good fortune had allowed him to live through it. That was something worth remembering.

Eight

HORNBLOWER
and the Examination for Lieutenant

H.M.S. *Indefatigable* was gliding into Gibraltar Bay, with Acting-Lieutenant Horatio Hornblower stiff and self-conscious on the quarter-deck beside Captain Pellew. He kept his telescope trained over toward Algeciras; it was a strange situation, this, that major naval bases of two hostile powers should be no more than six miles apart, and while approaching the harbour it was as well to keep close watch on Algeciras, for there was always the possibility that a squadron of Spaniards might push out suddenly to pounce on an unwary frigate coming in.

"Eight ships—nine ships with their yards crossed, sir," reported Hornblower.

"Thank you," answered Pellew. "Hands 'bout ship."

The *Indefatigable* tacked and headed in toward the Mole. Gibraltar Harbour was, as usual, crowded with shipping, for the whole naval effort of England in the Mediterranean was perforce based here. Pellew clewed up his topsails and put his helm over. Then the cable roared out and the *Indefatigable* swung at anchor.

"Call away my gig," ordered Pellew.

Pellew favoured dark blue and white as the colour scheme for his boat and its crew—dark blue shirts and white trousers for the men, with white hats with blue ribbons. The boat was of dark blue picked out with white, the oars had white looms and blue blades. The general effect was very smart indeed as the drive of the oars sent the gig skimming over the water to carry Pellew to pay his respects to the port admiral. It was not long after his return that a messenger came scurrying up to Hornblower.

"Captain's compliments, sir, and he'd like to see you in his cabin."

"Examine your conscience well," grinned Midshipman Bracegirdle. "What crimes have you committed?"

"I wish I knew," said Hornblower quite genuinely.

It is always a nervous moment going in to see the captain in reply to his summons. Hornblower swallowed as he approached the cabin door, and he had to brace himself a little to knock and enter. But there was nothing to be alarmed about; Pellew looked up with a smile from his desk.

"Ah, Mr. Hornblower, I hope you will consider this good news. There will be an examination for lieutenant tomorrow, in the *Santa Barbara* there. You are ready to take it, I hope?"

Hornblower was about to say, "I suppose so, sir," but checked himself. "Yes, sir," he said—Pellew hated slipshod answers.

"Very well, then. You report there at three P.M. with your certificates and journals."

"Aye aye, sir."

That was a very brief conversation for such an important subject. Hornblower had held Pellew's order as acting-lieutenant for two months now. Tomorrow he would take his examination. If he should pass, the admiral would confirm the order next day, and Hornblower would be a lieutenant with two months' seniority already. But if he should fail! That would mean he had been found unfit for lieutenant's rank. He would revert to midshipman, the two months' seniority would be lost, and it would be six months at least before he could try again. Eight months' seniority was a matter of enormous importance. It would affect all his subsequent career.

"Tell Mr. Bolton you have my permission to leave the ship tomorrow, and you may use one of the ship's boats."

"Thank you, sir."

"Good luck, Hornblower."

During the next twenty four hours Hornblower had not merely to try to read all through Norie's *Epitome of Navigation* again, and Clarke's *Complete Handbook of Seamanship,* but he had to see that his No. 1 uniform was spick-and-span. It cost his spirit ration to prevail on the warrant cook to allow the gunroom attendant to heat a flat-iron in the galley and iron out his neck handkerchief. Bracegirdle lent him a clean shirt, but there was a feverish moment when it was discovered that the gunroom's supply of shoe blacking had dried to a chip. Two midshipmen had to work it soft with lard, and the resultant compound, when applied to Hornblower's buckled shoes, was stubbornly resistant to taking a polish; only much labour with the gunroom's molting shoebrush and then with a soft cloth brought those shoes up to a condition of brightness worthy of an examination for lieutenant. And as for the cocked hat—the life of a cocked hat in the midshipman's berth is hard, and some of the dents could not be entirely eliminated.

"Take it off as soon as you can and keep it under your arm," advised Bracegirdle. "Maybe they won't see you come up the ship's side."

Everybody turned out to see Hornblower leave the ship, with his sword and his white breeches and his buckled shoes, his bundle of journals under his arm and his certificates of sobriety and good conduct in his pocket. The winter afternoon was already far advanced as he was rowed over to the *Santa Barbara* and went up the ship's side to report himself to the officer of the watch.

The *Santa Barbara* was a prison hulk, one of the prizes captured in Rodney's action off Cadiz in 1780 and kept rotting at her moorings, mastless, ever since, a storeship in time of peace and a prison in time of war. Red-coated soldiers, muskets loaded and bayonets fixed, guarded the gangways; on forecastle and quarterdeck were carronades, trained inboard and depressed to sweep the waist, wherein a few prisoners took the air, ragged and unhappy. As Hornblower came up the side he caught a whiff of the stench within, where two thousand prisoners were confined. Hornblower reported himself to the officer of the watch as come on board, and for what purpose.

"Whoever would have guessed it?" said the officer of the watch—an elderly lieutenant with white hair hanging down to his shoulders—running his eye over Hornblower's immaculate uniform and the portfolio under his arm. "Fifteen of your kind have already come on board, and —Holy Gemini, see there!"

Quite a flotilla of small craft was closing in on the *Santa Barbara.* Each boat held at least one cocked-hatted and white-breeched midshipman, and some held four or five.

"Every young gentleman in the Mediterranean Fleet is ambitious for an epaulette," said the lieutenant. "Just wait until the examining board sees how many there are of you! I wouldn't be in your shoes, young shaver, for something. Go aft, there, and wait in the port-side cabin."

It was already uncomfortably full; when Hornblower entered, fifteen pairs of eyes measured him up. There were officers of all ages from eighteen to forty, all in their No. 1's, all nervous—one or two of them had Norie's *Epitome* open on their laps and were anxiously reading passages about which they were doubtful. One little group was passing a bottle from hand to hand, presumably in an effort to keep up their courage. But no sooner had Hornblower entered than a stream of newcomers followed him. The cabin began to fill, and soon it was tightly packed. Half the forty men present found seats on the deck, and the others were forced to stand.

"Forty years back," said a loud voice somewhere, "my granddad marched with Clive to revenge the Black Hole of Calcutta. If he could have witnessed the fate of his posterity!"

"Have a drink," said another voice, "and to hell with care."

"Forty of us," commented a tall, thin, clerkly officer, counting heads. "How many of us will they pass, do you think? Five?"

"To hell with care," repeated the bibulous voice in the corner, and lifted itself in song. "Begone, dull care; I prithee be gone from me—"

"Cheese it, you fool!" rasped another voice. "Hark to that!"

The air was filled with the long-drawn twittering of the pipes of the bosun's mates, and someone on deck was shouting an order.

"A captain coming on board," remarked someone.

An officer had his eye at the crack of the door. "It's Dreadnought Foster," he reported.

"He's a tail twister if ever there was one," said a fat young officer seated comfortably with his back to the bulkhead.

Again the pipes twittered.

"Harvey, of the dockyard," reported the lookout.

The third captain followed immediately. "It's Black Charlie Hammond," said the lookout. "Looking as if he'd lost a guinea and found sixpence."

"Black Charlie?" exclaimed someone, scrambling to his feet in haste and pushing to the door. "Let's see! So it is! Then here is one young gentleman who will not stay for an answer. I know too well what that answer would be. 'Six months more at sea, sir, and damn your eyes for your impertinence in presenting yourself for examination in your present state of ignorance.' Black Charlie won't ever forget that I lost his pet poodle overside from the cutter in Port-o'-Spain when he was First of the *Pegasus*. Good-bye, gentlemen. Give my regards to the examining board."

With that he was gone, and they saw him explaining himself to the officer of the watch and hailing a shore boat to take him back to his ship. "One fewer of us, at least," said the clerkly officer—"What is it, my man?"

"The board's compliments, sir," said the marine messenger, "an' will the first young gentleman please to come along?"

There was a momentary hesitation; no one was anxious to be the first victim.

"The one nearest the door," said an elderly master's mate. "Will you volunteer, sir?"

"I'll be the Daniel," said the erstwhile lookout desperately. "Remember me in your prayers."

He pulled his coat smooth, twitched at his neckcloth and was gone, the remainder waiting in gloomy silence, relieved only by the glug-glug of the bottle as the bibulous midshipman took another swig. A full ten minutes passed before the candidate for promotion returned, making a brave effort to smile.

"Six months more at sea?" asked someone.

"No," was the unexpected answer. "Three!—I was told to send the next man. It had better be you."

"But what did they ask you?"

"They began by asking me to define a rhumb line—But don't keep them waiting, I advise you."

Some thirty officers had their textbooks open on the instant, to re-read about rhumb lines.

"You were there ten minutes," said the clerkly officer, looking at his watch. "Forty of us, ten minutes each—why, it'll be midnight before they reach the last of us. They'll never do it."

"They'll be hungry," said someone.

"Hungry for our blood," said another.

"Perhaps they'll try us in batches," suggested a third, "like the French tribunals."

Listening to them, Hornblower was reminded of French aristocrats jesting at the foot of the scaffold. Candidates departed and candidates returned, some gloomy, some smiling. The cabin was already far less crowded; Hornblower was able to secure sufficient deck space to seat himself, and he stretched out his legs with a nonchalant sigh of relief, and he no sooner emitted the sigh than he realised that it was a stage effect which he had put on for his own benefit. He was as nervous as he could be. The winter night was falling, and some good Samaritan on board sent in a couple of purser's dips to give a feeble illumination to the darkening cabin.

"They are passing one in three," said the clerkly officer, making ready for his turn. "May I be the third."

Hornblower got to his feet again when he left; it would be his turn next. He stepped out under the half-deck into the dark night and breathed the chill fresh air. A gentle breeze was blowing from the southward, cooled, presumably, by the snow-clad Atlas Mountains of Africa across the strait. There was neither moon nor stars. Here came the clerkly officer back again.

"Hurry," he said. "They're impatient."

Hornblower made his way past the sentry to the after cabin; it was brightly lit, so that he blinked as he entered, and stumbled over some obstruction. And it was only then that he remembered that he had not straightened his neckcloth and seen to it that his sword hung correctly at his side. He went on blinking in his nervousness at the three grim faces across the table.

"Well, sir?" said a stern voice. "Report yourself. We have no time to waste."

"H–Hornblower, sir. H–Horatio H–Hornblower. M–Midshipman–I mean Acting-Lieutenant, H.M.S. *Indefatigable*."

"Your certificates, please," said the right-hand face.

Hornblower handed them over, and as he waited for them to be examined, the left-hand face suddenly spoke. "You are close-hauled on the port tack, Mr. Hornblower, beating up-Channel with a nor'easterly wind blowing hard, with Dover bearing north two miles. Is that clear?"

"Yes, sir."

"Now the wind veers four points and takes you flat aback. What do you do, sir? What do you do?"

Hornblower's mind, if it was thinking about anything at all at that moment, was thinking about rhumb lines; this question took him as much aback as the situation it envisaged. His mouth opened and shut, but there was no word he could say.

"By now you're dismasted," said the middle face—a swarthy face; Hornblower was making the deduction that it must belong to Black Charlie Hammond. He could think about that even if he could not force his mind to think at all about his examination.

"Dismasted," said the left-hand face, with a smile like Nero enjoying a Christian's death agony. "With Dover cliffs under your lee. You are in serious trouble, Mr.—ah—Hornblower."

Serious indeed. Hornblower's mouth opened and shut again. His dulled mind heard, without paying special attention to it, the thud of a cannon shot somewhere not too far off. The board passed no remark on it either, but a moment later there came a series of further cannon shots which brought the three captains to their feet. Unceremoniously they rushed out of the cabin, sweeping out of the way the sentry at the door. Hornblower followed them; they arrived in the waist just in time to see a rocket soar up into the night sky and burst in a shower of red stars. It was the general alarm; over the water of the anchorage they could hear the drums rolling as all the ships present beat to quarters. On the port-side gangway the remainder of the candidates were clustered, speaking excitedly.

"See there!" said a voice.

Across half a mile of dark water a yellow light grew until the ship there was wrapped in flame. She had every sail set and was heading straight into the crowded anchorage.

"Fire ships!"

"Officer of the watch! Call my gig!" bellowed Foster.

A line of fire ships was running before the wind, straight at the crowd of anchored ships. The *Santa Barbara* was full of the wildest bustle as the seamen and marines came pouring on deck, and as captains and candidates shouted for boats to take them back to their ships. A line of orange flame lit up the water, followed at once by the roar of a broadside; some ship was firing her guns in the endeavour to sink a fire ship. Let one of those blazing hulls make contact with one of the anchored ships, even for a few seconds, and the fire would be transmitted to the dry, painted timber, to the tarred cordage, to the inflammable sails, so that nothing would put it out. To men in highly combustible ships filled with explosives, fire was the deadliest and most dreaded peril of the sea.

"You shore boat, there!" bellowed Hammond suddenly. "You shore boat! Come alongside! Come alongside, blast you!"

His eye had been quick to sight the pair-oar rowing by.

"Come alongside or I'll fire into you!" supplemented Foster. "Sentry, there, make ready to give them a shot!"

At the threat, the wherry turned and glided toward the mizzen chains.

"Here you are, gentlemen," said Hammond.

The three captains rushed to the mizzen chains and flung themselves down into the boat. Hornblower was at their heels. He knew there was small enough chance of a junior officer getting a boat to take him back to his ship, to which it was his bounden duty to go as soon as possible. After the captains had reached their destinations, he could use this boat to reach the *Indefatigable*. He threw himself off into the sternsheets as she pushed off, knocking the breath out of Captain Harvey, his sword scabbard clattering on the gunwale. But the three captains accepted his uninvited presence there without comment.

"Pull for the *Dreadnought,*" said Foster.

"Dammit, I'm the senior!" said Hammond. "Pull for *Calypso.*"

"*Calypso* it is," said Harvey. He had his hand on the tiller, heading the boat across the dark water.

"Pull! Oh, pull!" said Foster, in agony. There can be no mental torture like that of a captain whose ship is in peril and he not on board.

"There's one of them," said Harvey.

Just ahead, a small brig was bearing down on them under topsails; they could see the glow of the fire, and as they watched, the fire suddenly burst into roaring fury, wrapping the whole vessel in flames in a moment, like a set piece in a fireworks display. Flames spouted out of the holes in her sides and roared up through her hatchways. The very water around her glowed vivid red. They saw her halt in her career and begin to swing slowly around.

"She's across *Santa Barbara's* cable," said Foster.

"She's nearly clear," added Hammond. "God help 'em on board there. She'll be alongside her in a minute."

Hornblower thought of two thousand Spanish and French prisoners battened down below decks in the hulk.

"With a man at her wheel, she could be steered clear," said Foster. "We ought to do it!"

Then things happened rapidly. Harvey put the tiller over. "Pull away!" he roared at the boatmen.

The latter displayed an easily understood reluctance to row up to that fiery hull.

"Pull!" said Harvey.

He whipped out his sword from its scabbard, and the blade reflected the red fire as he thrust it menacingly at the stroke oar's throat. With a kind of sob, stroke tugged at his oar and the boat leaped forward.

"Lay us under her counter," said Foster. "I'll jump for it."

At last Hornblower found his tongue. "Let me go, sir. I'll handle her."

"Come with me, if you like," replied Foster. "It may need two of us."

His nickname of Dreadnought Foster may have had its origin in the name of his ship, but it was appropriate enough in all circumstances. Harvey swung the boat under the fire ship's stern; she was before the wind again now, and just gathering way, just heading down upon the *Santa Barbara.*

For a moment Hornblower was the nearest man in the boat to the brig and there was no time to be lost. He stood up on the thwart and jumped; his hands gripped something, and with a kick and a struggle he dragged his ungainly body up onto the deck. With the brig before the wind, the flames were blown forward; right aft here it was merely frightfully hot, but Hornblower's ears were filled with the roar of the flames and the crackling and banging of the burning wood. He stepped forward to the wheel and seized the spokes, the wheel was lashed with a loop of line and, as he cast this off and took hold of the wheel again, he could feel the rudder below him bite into the water. He flung his weight on the spoke and spun the wheel over. The brig was about to collide with the *Santa Barbara,* starboard bow to starboard bow, and the flames lit an anxious gesticulating crowd on the *Santa Barbara's* forecastle.

"Hard over!" roared Foster's voice in Hornblower's ear.

"Hard over it is!" said Hornblower, and the brig answered her wheel at that moment, her bow turned away, avoiding the collision.

An immense fountain of flame poured out from the hatchway abaft the mainmast, setting mast and rigging ablaze and at the same time a flaw of wind blew a wave of flame aft. Some instinct made Hornblower, while holding the wheel with one hand, snatch out his neckcloth with the other and bury his face in it. The flame whirled round him and was gone again. But the distraction had been dangerous; the brig had continued to turn under full helm, and now her stern was swinging in to bump against the *Santa Barbara's* bow. Hornblower desperately spun the wheel over the other way. The flames had driven Foster aft to the taffrail, but now he returned.

"Hard-a-lee!"

The brig was already responding. Her starboard quarter bumped the *Santa Barbara* in the waist, and then bumped clear.

"Midships!" shouted Foster.

At a distance of only two or three yards the fire ship passed on down the *Santa Barbara's* side; an anxious group ran along her gangways keeping up with her as she did so. On the quarterdeck another group stood by with a spar to boom the fire ship off; Hornblower saw them out of the tail of his eye as they went by. Now they were clear.

"There's the *Dauntless* on the port bow," said Foster. "Keep her clear."

"Aye aye, sir."

The din of the fire was tremendous; it could hardly be believed that on this little area of deck it was still possible to breathe and live. Hornblower felt the appalling heat on his hands and face. Both masts were immense pyramids of flame.

"Starboard a point," said Foster. "We'll lay her aground on the shoal by the Neutral Ground."

"Starboard a point," responded Hornblower.

He was being borne along on a wave of the highest exaltation; the roar of the fire was intoxicating, and he knew not a moment's fear. Then the whole deck only a yard or two forward of the wheel opened up in flame. Fire spouted out of the gaping seams and the heat was utterly unbearable, and the fire moved rapidly aft as the seams gaped progressively backward.

Hornblower felt for the loop of line to lash the wheel, but before he could do so the wheel spun idly under his hand, presumably as the tiller ropes below him were burned away, and at the same time the deck under his feet heaved and warped in the fire. He staggered back to the taffrail. Foster was there.

"Tiller ropes burned away, sir," reported Hornblower.

Flames roared up beside them. His coat sleeve was smouldering.

"Jump!" said Foster.

Hornblower felt Foster shoving him—everything was insane. He heaved himself over, gasped with fright as he hung in the air, and then felt the breath knocked out of his body as he hit the water. The water closed over him, and he knew panic as he struggled back to the surface. It was cold—the Mediterranean in December is cold. For the moment, the air in his clothes supported him, despite the weight of the sword at his side, but he could see nothing in the darkness, with his eyes still dazzled by the roaring flames. Somebody splashed beside him.

"They were following us in the boat to take us off," said Foster's voice. "Can you swim?"

"Yes, sir. Not very well."

"That might describe me," said Foster, and then he lifted his voice to hail, "Ahoy! Ahoy! Hammond! Harvey! Ahoy!"

He tried to raise himself as well as his voice, fell back with a splash, and splashed and splashed again, the water flowing into his mouth cutting short something he tried to say. Hornblower, beating the water with increasing feebleness, could still spare a thought—such were the vagaries of his wayward mind—for the interesting fact that even captains of such seniority were only mortal men after all. He tried to unbuckle his sword belt, failed, and sank deep with the effort, only just succeeding in struggling back to the surface. He gasped for breath, but in another attempt he managed to draw his sword half out of its scabbard, and as he struggled, it slid out the rest of the way by its own weight; yet he was not conscious of any noticeable relief.

It was then that he heard the splashing and grinding of oars, and loud voices, and he saw the dark shape of the approaching boat, and he uttered a spluttering cry. In a second or two the boat was up to them, and he was clutching the gunwale in panic.

They were lifting Foster in over the stern, and Hornblower knew he must keep still and make no effort to climb in, but it called for all his resolution to make himself hang quietly onto the side of the boat and wait his turn. He was interested in this overmastering fear, while he despised himself for it. It called for a conscious and serious effort of will power to make his hands alternately release their deathlike grip on the gunwale, so that the men in the boat could pass him round to the stern. Then they dragged him in and he fell face downward in the bottom of the boat, on the verge of fainting. Then somebody spoke in the boat, and Hornblower felt a cold shiver pass over his skin, and his feeble muscles tensed themselves, for the words spoken were Spanish —at any rate an unknown tongue, and Spanish presumably.

Somebody else answered in the same language. Hornblower tried to struggle up, and a restraining hand was laid on his shoulder. He rolled over, and with his eyes now accustomed to the darkness, he could see the three swarthy faces with the long black moustaches. These men were not Gibraltarians. On the instant he could guess who they were —the crew of one of the fire ships who had steered their craft in past the Mole, set fire to it, and made their escape in the boat. Foster was sitting doubled up, in the bottom of the boat, and now he lifted his face from his knees and stared round him.

"Who are these fellows?" he asked feebly—his struggle in the water had left him as weak as Hornblower.

"Spanish fire ship's crew, I fancy, sir," said Hornblower. "We're prisoners."

"Are we indeed!"

The knowledge galvanized him into activity just as it had Hornblower. He tried to get to his feet, and the Spaniard at the tiller thrust him down with a hand on his shoulder. Foster tried to put his hand away, and raised his voice in a feeble cry, but the man at the tiller was standing no nonsense. He brought out, in a lightning gesture, a knife from his belt. The light from the fire ship, burning itself harmlessly out on the shoal in the distance, ran redly along the blade, and Foster ceased to struggle. Men might call him Dreadnought Foster, but he could recognise the need for discretion.

"How are we heading?" he asked Hornblower, sufficiently quietly not to irritate their captors.

"North, sir. Maybe they're going to land on the Neutral Ground and make for the Line."

"That's their best chance," agreed Foster.

He turned his neck uncomfortably to look back up the harbour.

"Two other ships burning themselves out up there," he said. "There were three fire ships came in, I fancy."

"I saw three, sir."

"Then there's no damage done. But a bold endeavour. Whoever would have credited the Dons with making such an attempt?"

"They have learned about fire ships from us, perhaps, sir," suggested Hornblower.

"We may have 'nursed the pinion that impelled the steel,' you think?"

"It is possible, sir."

Foster was a cool enough customer, quoting poetry and discussing the naval situation while being carried off into captivity by a Spaniard who guarded him with a drawn knife. Cool might be a too accurate adjective; Hornblower was shivering in his wet clothes as the chill night air blew over him, and he felt weak and feeble after all the excitement and exertions of the day.

"Boat ahoy!" came a hail across the water; there was a dark nucleus in the night over there. The Spaniard in the sternsheets instantly dragged the tiller over, heading the boat directly away from it, while the two at the oars redoubled their exertions.

"Guard boat—" said Foster, but cut his explanation short at a further threat from the knife.

Of course there would be a boat rowing guard at this northern end of the anchorage; they might have thought of it.

"Boat ahoy!" came the hail again. "Lay on your oars or I'll fire into you!"

The Spaniard made no reply, and a second later came the flash and report of a musket shot. They heard nothing of the bullet, but the shot would put the fleet—toward which they were heading again—on the alert. But the Spaniards were going to play the game out to the end. They rowed doggedly on.

"Boat ahoy!"

This was another hail, from a boat right ahead of them. The Spaniards at the oars ceased their efforts in dismay, but a roar from the steersman set them instantly to work again. Hornblower could see the new boat almost directly ahead of them, and heard another hail from it as it rested on its oars. The Spaniard at the tiller shouted an order, and the stroke oar backed water and the boat turned sharply; another order, and both rowers tugged ahead again and the boat surged forward to ram. Should they succeed in overturning the intercepting boat, they might make their escape even now, while the pursuing boat stopped to pick up their friends.

Everything happened at once, with everyone shouting at the full pitch of his lungs, seemingly. There was the crash of the collision, both boats heeling wildly as the bow of the Spanish boat rode up over the British boat, but failed to overturn it. Someone fired a pistol, and the next moment the pursuing guard boat came dashing alongside, its crew leaping madly aboard them. Somebody flung himself on top of Hornblower, crushing the breath out of him and threatening to keep it out permanently with a hand on his throat. Hornblower heard Foster bellowing in protest, and a moment later his assailant released him, so that he could hear the midshipman of the guard boat apologising for this rough treatment of a post captain of the Royal Navy. Someone unmasked the guard boat's lantern, and by its light Foster revealed himself, bedraggled and battered. The light shone on their sullen prisoners.

"Boats ahoy!" came another hail, and yet another boat emerged from the darkness and pulled toward them.

"Cap'n Hammond, I believe!" hailed Foster, with an ominous rasp in his voice.

"Thank God!" they heard Hammond say, and the boat pulled into the faint circle of light.

"But no thanks to you," said Foster bitterly.

"After your fire ship cleared the *Santa Barbara* a puff of wind took you on faster than we could keep up with you," explained Harvey.

"We followed as fast as we could get these rock scorpions to row," added Hammond.

"And yet it called for Spaniards to save us from drowning," sneered Foster. The memory of his struggle in the water rankled, apparently. "I thought I could rely on two brother captains."

"What are you implying, sir?" snapped Hammond.

"I make no implications, but others may read implications into a simple statement of fact."

"I consider that an offensive remark, sir," said Harvey, "addressed to me equally with Captain Hammond."

"I congratulate you on your perspicacity, sir," replied Foster.

"I understand," said Harvey. "This is not a discussion we can pursue with these men present. I shall send a friend to wait on you."

"He will be welcome."

"Then I wish you a very good night, sir."

"And I, too, sir," said Hammond. "Give way there."

The boat pulled out of the circle of light, leaving an audience open-mouthed at this strange freak of human behaviour, that a man saved first from death and then from captivity should wantonly thrust himself into peril again. Foster looked after the boat for some seconds before speaking; perhaps he was already regretting his rather hysterical outburst.

"I shall have much to do before morning," he said, more to himself than to anyone near him, and then addressed himself to the midshipman of the guard boat. "You, sir, will take charge of these prisoners and convey me to my ship."

"Aye aye, sir."

"Is there anyone here who can speak their lingo? I would have it explained to them that I shall send them back to Cartagena under cartel, free without exchange. They saved our lives, and that is the least we can do in return." The final explanatory sentence was addressed to Hornblower.

"I think that is just, sir."

"And you, my fire-breathing friend. May I offer you my thanks? You did well. Should I live beyond tomorrow, I shall see that authority is informed of your actions."

"Thank you, sir." A question trembled on Hornblower's lips. It called for a little resolution to thrust it out, "And my examination, sir? My certificate?"

Foster shook his head. "That particular examining board will never reassemble, I fancy. You must wait your opportunity to go before another one."

"Aye aye, sir," said Hornblower, with despondency apparent in his tone.

"Now look'ee here, Mr. Hornblower," said Foster, turning upon him. "To the best of my recollection, you were flat aback, about to lose your spars and with Dover cliffs under your lee. In one more minute you would have been failed—it was the warning gun that saved you. Is not that so?"

"I suppose it is, sir."

"Then be thankful for small mercies. And even more thankful for big ones."

Nine
HORNBLOWER *and Noah's Ark*

Acting-Lieutenant Hornblower sat in the sternsheets of the longboat beside Mr. Tapling of the diplomatic service, with his feet among bags of gold. About him rose the steep shores of the Gulf of Oran, and ahead of him lay the city, white in the sunshine, like a mass of blocks of marble dumped by a careless hand upon the hillsides where they rose from the water. The oar blades, as the boat's crew pulled away rhythmically over the gentle swell, were biting into the clearest emerald green, and it was only a moment since they had left behind the bluest the Mediterranean could show.

"A pretty sight from here," said Tapling, gazing at the town they were approaching. "But closer inspection will show that the eye is deceived. And as for the nose! The stinks of the true believers have to be smelt to be believed. Lay her alongside the jetty there, Mr. Hornblower, beyond those xebecs."

"Aye aye, sir," said the coxswain, when Hornblower gave the order.

"There's a sentry on the water-front battery here," commented Tapling, looking about him keenly. "Not more than half asleep, either. And notice the guns in the two castles. Thirty-two-pounders, without a doubt. Stone shot piled in readiness. A stone shot flying into fragments on impact effects damage out of proportion to its size. And the walls seem sound enough. To seize Oran by a *coup de main* would not be easy, I am afraid. If His Nibs the Bey should choose to cut our throats and keep our gold it would be long before we were avenged, Mr. Hornblower."

"I don't think I should find any satisfaction in being avenged in any case, sir," said Hornblower.

"There's some truth in that. But doubtless His Nibs will spare us this time. The goose lays golden eggs—a boatload of gold every month must make a dazzling prospect for a pirate Bey in these days of convoys."

"Way 'nough," called the coxswain. "Oars!"

The longboat came gliding alongside the jetty and hooked on neatly. A few seated figures in the shade turned eyes at least, and in some cases even their heads as well, to look at the British boat's crew. A number of swarthy Moors appeared on the decks of the xebecs and gazed down at them, and one or two shouted remarks to them.

"No doubt they are describing the ancestry of the infidels," said Tapling. "Sticks and stones may break my bones, but names can never hurt me, especially when I do not understand them. Where's our man?"

He shaded his eyes to look along the water-front.

"No one in sight, sir, that looks like a Christian," said Hornblower.

"Our man's no Christian," said Tapling. "White, but no Christian. White by courtesy at that—a French-Arab-Levantine mixture. His Britannic Majesty's consul at Oran pro tem, and a Mussulman from expediency. Though there are very serious disadvantages about being a true believer. Who would want four wives at any time, especially when one pays for the doubtful privilege by abstaining from wine?"

Tapling stepped up onto the jetty and Hornblower followed him. The gentle swell that rolled up the Gulf broke soothingly below them, and the blinding heat of the noonday sun was reflected up into their faces from the stone blocks on which they stood. Far down the Gulf lay the two anchored ships—the storeship and H.M.S. *Indefatigable*—lovely on the bluest silver surface.

"And yet I would rather see Drury Lane on a Saturday night," said Tapling.

He turned back to look at the city wall, which guarded the place from seaborne attack. A narrow gate, flanked by bastions, opened onto the water-front. Sentries in red caftans were visible on the summit. In the deep shadow of the gate something was moving, but it was hard with eyes dazzled by the sun to see what it was. Then it emerged from the shadow as a little group coming towards them—a half-naked Negro leading a donkey, and on the back of the donkey, seated sideways far back towards the root of the tail, a vast figure in a blue robe.

"Shall we meet His Britannic Majesty's consul half-way?" asked Tapling. "No. Let him come to us."

The Negro halted the donkey, and the man on the donkey's back slid to the ground and came towards them—a mountainous man, waddling straddle-legged in his robe, his huge clay-coloured face topped by a white turban. A scanty black moustache and beard sprouted from his lips and chin.

"Your servant, Mr. Duras," said Tapling. "And may I present Acting-Lieutenant Horatio Hornblower, of the frigate *Indefatigable*?"

Mr. Duras nodded his perspiring head.

"Have you brought the money?" he asked, in guttural French; it took Hornblower a moment or two to adjust his mind to the language and his ear to Duras' intonation.

"Seven thousand golden guineas," replied Tapling, in reasonably good French.

"Good," said Duras, with a trace of relief. "Is it in the boat?"

"It is in the boat, and it stays in the boat at present," answered Tapling. "Do you remember the conditions agreed upon? Four hundred fat cattle, fifteen hundred *fanegas* of barley grain. When I see those in the lighters, and the lighters alongside the ships down the bay, then I hand over the money. Have you the stores ready?"

"Soon."

"As I expected. How long?"

"Soon—very soon."

Tapling made a grimace of resignation.

"Then we shall return to the ships. Tomorrow, perhaps, or the day after, we shall come back with the gold."

Alarm appeared on Duras' sweating face.

"No, do not do that," he said, hastily. "You do not know His Highness the Bey. He is changeable. If he knows the gold is here he will give orders for the cattle to be brought. Take the gold away, and he will not stir. And—and—he will be angry with me."

"*Ira principis mors est,*" said Tapling, and in response to Duras' blank look obliged by a translation. "The wrath of the prince means death. Is not that so?"

"Yes," said Duras, and he in turn said something in an unknown language, and stabbed at the air with his fingers in a peculiar gesture; and then translated, "May it not happen."

"Certainly we hope it may not happen," agreed Tapling with disarming cordiality. "The bowstring, the hook, even the bastinado are all unpleasant. It might be better if you went to the Bey and prevailed upon him to give the necessary orders for the grain and the cattle. Or we shall leave at nightfall."

Tapling glanced up at the sun to lay stress on the time limit.

"I shall go," said Duras, spreading his hands in a deprecatory gesture. "I shall go. But I beg of you, do not depart. Perhaps His Highness is busy in his harem. Then no one may disturb him. But I shall try.

The grain is here ready—it lies in the Kasbah there. It is only the cattle that have to be brought in. Please be patient. I implore you. His Highness is not accustomed to commerce, as you know, sir. Still less is he accustomed to commerce after the fashion of the Franks."

Duras wiped his streaming face with a corner of his robe.

"Pardon me," he said. "I do not feel well. But I shall go to His Highness. I shall go. Please wait for me."

"Until sunset," said Tapling implacably.

Duras called to his Negro attendant, who had been crouching huddled up under the donkey's belly to take advantage of the shade it cast. With an effort Duras hoisted his ponderous weight onto the donkey's hindquarters. He wiped his face again and looked at them with a trace of bewilderment.

"Wait for me," were the last words he said as the donkey was led away back into the city gate.

"He is afraid of the Bey," said Tapling watching him go. "I would rather face twenty Beys than Admiral Sir John Jervis in a tantrum. What will he do when he hears about this further delay, with the Fleet on short rations already? He'll have my guts for a necktie."

"One cannot expect punctuality of these people," said Hornblower with the easy philosophy of the man who does not bear the responsibility. But he thought of the British navy, without friends, without allies, maintaining desperately the blockade of a hostile Europe, in face of superior numbers, storms, disease, and now famine.

"Look at that!" said Tapling pointing suddenly.

It was a big grey rat which had made its appearance in the dry storm gutter that crossed the water-front here. Regardless of the bright sunshine it sat up and looked round at the world; even when Tapling stamped his foot it showed no great signs of alarm. When he stamped a second time it slowly turned to hide itself again in the drain, missed its footing so that it lay writhing for a moment at the mouth of the drain, and then regained its feet and disappeared into the darkness.

"An old rat, I suppose," said Tapling meditatively. "Senile, possibly. Even blind, it may be."

Hornblower cared nothing about rats, senile or otherwise. He took a step or two back in the direction of the longboat and the civilian officer conformed to his movements.

"Rig that mains'l so that it gives us some shade, Maxwell," said Hornblower. "We're here for the rest of the day."

"A great comfort," said Tapling, seating himself on a stone bollard beside the boat, "to be here in a heathen port. No need to worry in case any men run off. No need to worry about liquor. Only about bullocks and barley. And how to get a spark on this tinder."

He blew through the pipe that he took from his pocket, preparatory to filling it. The boat was shaded by the mainsail now, and the hands sat in the bows yarning in low tones, while the others made themselves as comfortable as possible in the sternsheets; the boat rolled peacefully in the tiny swell, the rhythmic sound as the fendoffs creaked between her gunwale and the jetty having a soothing effect while city and port dozed in the blazing afternoon heat. Yet it was not easy for a young man of Hornblower's active temperament to endure prolonged inaction. He climbed up on the jetty to stretch his legs, and paced up and down; a Moor in a white gown and turban came staggering in the sunshine along the water-front. His gait was unsteady, and he walked with his legs well apart to provide a firmer base for his swaying body.

"What was it you said, sir, about liquor being abhorred by the Moslems?" said Hornblower to Tapling down in the sternsheets.

"Not necessarily abhorred," replied Tapling, guardedly. "But anathematised, illegal, unlawful, and hard to obtain."

"Someone here has contrived to obtain some, sir," said Hornblower.

"Let me see," said Tapling, scrambling up; the hands, bored with waiting and interested as ever in liquor, landed from the bows to stare as well.

"That looks like a man who has drink taken," agreed Tapling.

"Three sheets in the wind, sir," said Maxwell, as the Moor staggered.

"And taken all aback," supplemented Tapling, as the Moor swerved wildly to one side in a semicircle.

At the end of the semicircle he fell with a crash on his face; his brown legs emerged from the robe a couple of times and were drawn in again, and he lay passive, his head on his arms, his turban fallen on the ground to reveal his shaven skull with a tassel of hair on the crown.

"Totally dismasted," said Hornblower.

"And hard aground," said Tapling.

But the Moor now lay oblivious of everything.

"And here's Duras," said Hornblower.

Out through the gate came the massive figure on the little donkey; another donkey bearing another portly figure followed, each donkey being led by a Negro slave, and after them came a dozen swarthy individuals whose muskets, and whose pretence at uniform, indicated that they were soldiers.

"The treasurer of His Highness," said Duras, by way of introduction when he and the other had dismounted. "Come to fetch the gold."

The portly Moor looked loftily upon them; Duras was still streaming with sweat in the hot sun.

"The gold is there," said Tapling, pointing. "In the sternsheets of the longboat. You will have a closer view of it when we have a closer view of the stores we are to buy."

Duras translated this speech into Arabic. There was a rapid interchange of sentences, before the treasurer apparently yielded. He turned and waved his arms back to the gate in what was evidently a prearranged signal. A dreary procession immediately emerged—a long line of men, all of them almost naked, white, black, and mulatto, each man staggering along under the burden of a sack of grain. Overseers with sticks walked with them.

"The money," said Duras, as a result of something said by the treasurer.

A word from Tapling set the hands to work lifting the heavy bags of gold onto the quay.

"With the corn on the jetty I will put the gold there too," said Tapling to Hornblower. "Keep your eye on it while I look at some of those sacks."

Tapling walked over to the slave gang. Here and there he opened a sack, looked into it, and inspected handfuls of the golden barley grain; other sacks he felt from the outside.

"No hope of looking over every sack in a hundred ton of barley," he remarked, strolling back again to Hornblower. "Much of it is sand, I expect. But that is the way of the heathen. The price is adjusted accordingly. Very well, effendi."

At a sign from Duras, and under the urgings of the overseers, the slaves burst into activity, trotting up to the quayside and dropping their sacks into the lighter which lay there. The first dozen men were organised into a working party to distribute the cargo evenly into the bottom of the lighter, while the others trotted off, their bodies gleaming with sweat, to fetch fresh loads. At the same time a couple of swarthy herdsmen came out through the gate driving a small herd of cattle.

"Scrubby little creatures," said Tapling, looking them over critically. "But that was allowed for in the price, too."

"The gold," said Duras.

In reply Tapling opened one of the bags at his feet, filled his hand with golden guineas, and let them cascade through his fingers into the bag again.

"Five hundred guineas there," he said. "Fourteen bags, as you see. They will be yours when the lighters are loaded and unmoored."

Duras wiped his face with a weary gesture. His knees seemed to be weak, and he leaned upon the patient donkey that stood behind him.

The cattle were being driven down a gangway into another lighter, and a second herd had now appeared and was waiting.

"Things move faster than you feared," said Hornblower.

"See how they drive the poor wretches," replied Tapling sententiously. "See! Things move fast when you have no concern for human flesh and blood."

A coloured slave had fallen to the ground under his burden. He lay there disregarding the blows rained on him by the sticks of the overseers. There was a small movement of his legs. Someone dragged him out of the way at last and the sacks continued to be carried to the lighter. The other lighter was filling fast with cattle, packed into a tight, bellowing mass in which no movement was possible.

"His Nibs is actually keeping his word," marvelled Tapling. "I'd 'a settled for the half, if I had been asked beforehand."

One of the herdsmen on the quay had sat down with his face in his hands; now he fell over limply on his side.

"Sir—" began Hornblower to Tapling, and the two men looked at each other with the same awful thought occurring to them at the same moment.

Duras began to say something; with one hand on the withers of the donkey and the other gesticulating in the air it seemed that he was making something of a speech, but there was no sense in the words he was roaring out in a hoarse voice. His face was swollen beyond its customary fatness and his expression was wildly distorted, while his cheeks were so suffused with blood as to look dark under his tan. Duras quitted his hold of the donkey and began to reel about in half circles, under the eyes of Moors and Englishmen. His voice died away to a whisper, his legs gave way under him, and he fell to his hands and knees and then to his face.

"That's the plague!" said Tapling. "The Black Death! I saw it in Smyrna in '96."

He and the other Englishmen had shrunk back on the one side, the soldiers and the treasurer on the other, leaving the palpitating body lying in the clear space between them.

"The plague, by St. Peter!" squealed one of the young sailors. He would have headed a rush to the longboat.

"Stand still, there!" roared Hornblower, scared of the plague but with the habits of discipline so deeply engrained in him by now that he checked the panic automatically.

"I was a fool not to have thought of it before," said Tapling. "That dying rat—that fellow over there who we thought was drunk. I should have known!"

The soldier who appeared to be the sergeant in command of the treasurer's escort was in explosive conversation with the chief of the overseers of the slaves, both of them staring and pointing at the dying Duras; the treasurer himself was clutching his robe about him and looking down at the wretched man at his feet in fascinated horror.

"Well, sir?" said Hornblower to Tapling. "What do we do?"

Hornblower was of the temperament that demands immediate action in face of a crisis.

"Do?" replied Tapling with a bitter smile. "We stay here and rot."

"Stay *here?*"

"The fleet will never have us back. Not until we have served three weeks of quarantine. Three weeks after the last case has occurred. Here in Oran."

"Nonsense!" said Hornblower, with all the respect due to his senior startled out of him. "No one would order that."

"Would they not? Have you ever seen an epidemic in a fleet?"

Hornblower had not, but he had heard enough about them—fleets where nine out of ten had died of putrid fevers. Crowded ships with twenty two inches of hammock space per man were ideal breeding places for epidemics. He realised that no captain, no admiral, would run that risk for the sake of a longboat's crew of twenty men.

The two xebecs against the jetty had suddenly cast off, and were working their way out of the harbour under sweeps.

"The plague can only have struck today," mused Hornblower, the habit of deduction strong in him despite his sick fear.

The cattle herders were abandoning their work, giving a wide berth to that one of their numbers who was lying on the quay. Up at the town gate it appeared that the guard was employed in driving people back into the town—apparently the rumour of plague had spread sufficiently therein to cause a panic, while the guard had just received orders not to allow the population to stream out into the surrounding country. There would be frightful things happening in the town soon.

The treasurer was climbing on his donkey; the crowd of grain-carrying slaves was melting away as the overseers fled.

"I must report this to the ship," said Hornblower; Tapling, as a civilian diplomatic officer, held no authority over him. The whole responsibility was Hornblower's. The longboat and the longboat's crew were Hornblower's command, entrusted to him by Captain Pellew whose authority derived from the King.

Amazing, how the panic was spreading. The treasurer was gone; Duras' Negro slave had ridden off on his late master's donkey; the soldiers had hastened off in a single group. The water-front was deserted now except for the dead and dying; along the water-front, presumably, at the foot of the wall, lay the way to the open country which all desired to seek. The Englishmen were standing alone, with the bags of gold at their feet.

"Plague spreads through the air," said Tapling. "Even the rats die of it. We have been here for hours. We were near enough to—that—" he nodded at the dying Duras—"to speak to him, to catch his breath. Which of us will be the first?"

"We'll see when the time comes," said Hornblower. It was his contrary nature to be sanguine in the face of depression; besides, he did not want the men to hear what Tapling was saying.

"And there's the Fleet!" said Tapling bitterly. "This lot—" he nodded at the deserted lighters, one almost full of cattle, the other almost full of grain sacks—"this lot would be a Godsend. The men are on two-thirds rations."

"Damn it, we can do something about it," said Hornblower. "Maxwell, put the gold back in the boat, and get that awning in."

The officer of the watch in H.M.S. *Indefatigable* saw the ship's longboat returning from the town. A slight breeze had swung the frigate and the *Caroline* (the transport brig) to their anchors, and the longboat, instead of running alongside, came up under the *Indefatigable's* stern to leeward.

"Mr. Christie!" hailed Hornblower, standing up in the bows of the longboat.

The officer of the watch came aft to the taffrail.

"What is it?" he demanded, puzzled.

"I must speak to the captain."

"Then come on board and speak to him. What the devil—?"

"Please ask the captain if I may speak to him."

Pellew appeared at the after cabin window; he could hardly have helped hearing the bellowed conversation.

"Yes, Mr. Hornblower?"

Hornblower told him the news.

"Keep to loo'ard, Mr. Hornblower."

"Yes, sir. But the stores—"

"What about them?"

Hornblower outlined the situation and made his request.

"It's not very regular," mused Pellew. "Besides—"

He did not want to shout aloud his thoughts that perhaps everyone in the longboat would be soon dead of plague.

"We'll be all right, sir. It's a week's rations for the squadron."

That was the point, the vital matter. Pellew had to balance the possible loss of a transport brig against the possible gain of supplies, immeasurably more important, which would enable the squadron to maintain its watch over the outlet to the Mediterranean. Looked at in that light Hornblower's suggestion had added force.

"Oh, very well, Mr. Hornblower. By the time you bring the stores out I'll have the crew transferred. I appoint you to the command of the *Caroline*."

"Thank you, sir."

"Mr. Tapling will continue as passenger with you."

"Very good, sir."

So when the crew of the longboat, toiling and sweating at the sweeps, brought the two lighters down the bay, they found the *Caroline* swinging deserted at her anchors, while a dozen curious telescopes from the *Indefatigable* watched the proceedings. Hornblower went up the brig's side with half a dozen hands.

"She's like a blooming Noah's Ark, sir," said Maxwell.

The comparison was apt; the *Caroline* was flush-decked, and the whole available deck area was divided by partitions into stalls for the cattle, while to enable the ship to be worked light gangways had been laid over the stalls into a practically continuous upper deck.

"An' all the animiles, sir," said another seaman.

"But Noah's animals walked in two by two," said Hornblower. "We're not so lucky. And we've got to get the grain on board first. Get those hatches unbattened."

In ordinary conditions a working party of two or three hundred men from the *Indefatigable* would have made short work of getting in the cargo from the lighters, but now it had to be done by the longboat's complement of eighteen. Luckily Pellew had had the forethought and kindness to have the ballast struck out of the holds, or they would have had to do that weary job first.

"Tail onto those tackles, men," said Hornblower.

Pellew saw the first bundle of grain sacks rise slowly into the air from the lighter, and swung over and down the *Caroline's* hatchway.

"He'll be all right," he decided. "Man the capstan and get under weigh, if you please, Mr. Bolton."

Hornblower, directing the work on the tackles, heard Pellew's voice come to him through the speaking trumpet.

"Good luck, Mr. Hornblower. Report in three weeks at Gibraltar."

"Very good, sir. Thank you, sir."

Hornblower turned back to find a seaman at his elbow knuckling his forehead.

"Beg pardon, sir. But can you hear those cattle bellerin', sir? 'Tis mortal hot, an' 'tis water they want, sir."

"Hell," said Hornblower.

He would never get the cattle on board before nightfall. He left a small party at work transferring cargo, and with the rest of the men he began to extemporise a method of watering the unfortunate cattle in the lighter. Half of *Caroline's* hold space was filled with water barrels and fodder, but it was an awkward business getting water down to the lighter with pump and hose, and the poor brutes down there surged about uncontrollably at the prospect of water. Hornblower saw the lighter heel and almost capsize; one of his men—luckily one who could swim—went hastily overboard from the lighter to avoid being crushed to death.

"Hell," said Hornblower, again, and that was by no means the last time.

Without any skilled advice he was having to learn the business of managing livestock at sea; each moment brought its lessons. A naval officer on active service indeed found himself engaged on strange duties. It was well after dark before Hornblower called a halt to the labours of his men, and it was before dawn that he roused them up to work again. It was still early in the morning that the last of the grain sacks was stowed away and Hornblower had to face the operation of swaying up the cattle from the lighter. After their night down there, with little water and less food, they were in no mood to be trifled with, but it was easier at first while they were crowded together. A bellyband was slipped round the nearest, the tackle hooked on, and the animal was swayed up, lowered to the deck through an opening in the gangways, and herded into one of the stalls with ease. The seamen, shouting and waving their shirts, thought it was great fun, but they were not sure when the next one, released from its bellyband, went on the rampage and chased them about the deck, threatening death with its horns, until it wandered into its stall where the bar could be promptly dropped to shut it in. Hornblower, looking at the sun rising rapidly in the east, did not think it fun at all.

And the emptier the lighter became, the more room the cattle had to rush about in it; to capture each one so as to put a bellyband on it was a desperate adventure. Nor were those half-wild bullocks soothed by the sight of their companions being successively hauled bellowing into the air over their heads. Before the day was half done Hornblower's men were as weary as if they had fought a battle, and there was not one of them who would not gladly have quitted this novel employment in exchange for some normal seaman's duty like going aloft to reef topsails on a stormy night. As soon as Hornblower had the notion of dividing the interior of the lighter up into sections with barricades of stout spars the work became easier, but it took time, and before it was done the cattle had already suffered a couple of casualties—weaker members of the herd crushed underfoot in the course of the wild rushes about the lighter.

And there was a distraction when a boat came out from the shore, with swarthy Moors at the oars and the treasurer in the stern. Hornblower left Tapling to negotiate—apparently the Bey at least had not been so frightened of the plague as to forget to ask for his money. All Hornblower insisted upon was that the boat should keep well to leeward, and the money was floated off to it headed up in an empty rum-puncheon. Night found not more than half the cattle in the stalls on board, with Hornblower worrying about feeding and watering them, and snatching at hints diplomatically won from those members of his crew who had had bucolic experience. But the earliest dawn saw him driving his men to work again, and deriving a momentary satisfaction from the sight of Tapling having to leap for his life to the gangway out of reach of a maddened bullock which was charging about the deck and refusing to enter a stall. And by the time the last animal was safely packed in Hornblower was faced with another problem—that of dealing with what one of the men elegantly termed "mucking out." Fodder—water—mucking out; that deckload of cattle seemed to promise enough work in itself to keep his eighteen men busy, without any thought of the needs of handling the ship.

But there were advantages about the men being kept busy, as Hornblower grimly decided; there had not been a single mention of plague since the work began. The anchorage where the *Caroline* lay was exposed to northeasterly winds, and it was necessary that he should take her out to sea before such a wind should blow. He mustered his men to divide them into watches; he was the only navigator, so that he had to appoint the coxswain and the under-coxswain, Jordan, as officers of the watch. Someone volunteered as cook, and Hornblower, running his eye over his assembled company, appointed Tapling as cook's mate. Tapling opened his mouth to protest, but there was that in Hornblower's expression which cut the protest short. There was no bosun no carpenter—no surgeon either, as Hornblower pointed out to himself gloomily. But on the other hand if the need for a doctor should arise it would, he hoped, be mercifully brief.

"Port watch, loose the jibs and main tops'l," ordered Hornblower. "Starboard watch, man the capstan."

So began that voyage of H.M. transport brig *Caroline* which became legendary (thanks to the highly coloured accounts retailed by the crew during innumerable dogwatches in later commissions) throughout the King's navy. The *Caroline* spent her three weeks of quarantine in homeless wanderings about the western Mediterranean. It was necessary that she should keep close up to the Straits, for fear lest the westerlies and the prevailing inward set of the current should take her out of reach of Gibraltar when the time came, so she beat about between the coasts of Spain and Africa trailing behind her a growing farmyard stench. The *Caroline* was a worn-out ship; with any sort of sea running she leaked like a sieve; and there were always hands at work on the pumps, either pumping her out or pumping seawater onto her deck to clean it or pumping up fresh water for the cattle.

Her top hamper made her almost unmanageable in a fresh breeze; her deck seams leaked, of course, when she worked, allowing a constant drip of unspeakable filth down below. The one consolation was in the supply of fresh meat—a commodity some of Hornblower's men had not tasted for three months. Hornblower recklessly sacrificed a bullock a day, for in that Mediterranean climate meat could not be kept sweet. So his men feasted on steaks and fresh tongues; there were plenty of men on board who had never in their whole lives before eaten a beef steak.

But fresh water was the trouble—it was a greater anxiety to Hornblower than ever it was to the average ship's captain, for the cattle were always thirsty; twice Hornblower had to land a raiding party at dawn on the coast of Spain, seize a fishing village, and fill his water casks in the local stream.

It was a dangerous adventure, and the second landing revealed the danger, for while the *Caroline* was trying to claw off the land again a Spanish *guarda-costa* lugger came gliding round the point with all sail set. Maxwell saw her first, but Hornblower saw her before he could report her presence.

"Very well, Maxwell," said Hornblower, trying to sound composed.

He turned his glass upon her. She was no more than three miles off, a trifle to windward, and the *Caroline* was embayed, cut off by the land from all chance of escape. The lugger could go three feet to her two, while the *Caroline's* clumsy superstructure prevented her from lying nearer than eight points to the wind. As Hornblower gazed, the accumulated irritation of the past seventeen days boiled over. He was furious with Fate for having thrust this ridiculous mission on him. He hated the *Caroline* and her clumsiness and her stinks and her cargo. He raged against the destiny which had caught him in this hopeless position.

"Hell!" said Hornblower, actually stamping his feet on the upper gangway in his anger. "Hell *and* damnation!"

He was dancing with rage, he observed with some curiosity. But with his fighting madness at the boil there was no chance of his yielding without a struggle, and his mental convulsions resulted in his producing a scheme for action. How many men of a crew did a Spanish *guarda-costa* carry? Twenty? That would be an outside figure—those luggers were only intended to act against petty smugglers. And with surprise on his side there was still a chance, despite the four eight-pounders that the lugger carried.

"Pistols and cutlasses, men," he said. "Jordan, choose two men and show yourselves up here. But the rest of you keep under cover. Hide yourselves. Yes, Mr. Tapling, you may serve with us. See that you are armed."

No one would expect resistance from a laden cattle transport; the Spaniards would expect to find on board a crew of a dozen at most, and not a disciplined force of twenty. The problem lay in luring the lugger within reach.

"Full and by," called Hornblower down to the helmsman below. "Be ready to jump, men. Maxwell, if a man shows himself before my order shoot him with your own hand. You hear me? That's an order, and you disobey me at your peril."

"Aye aye, sir," said Maxwell.

The lugger was romping up towards them; even in that light air there was a white wave under her sharp bows. Hornblower glanced up to make sure that the *Caroline* was displaying no colours. That made his plan legal under the laws of war. The report of a gun and a puff of smoke came from the lugger as she fired across the *Caroline's* bows.

"I'm going to heave-to, Jordan," said Hornblower. "Main tops'l braces. Helm-a-lee."

The *Caroline* came to the wind and lay there wallowing, a surrendered and helpless ship apparently, if ever there was one.

"Not a sound, men," said Hornblower.

The cattle bellowed mournfully. Here came the lugger, her crew plainly visible now. Hornblower could see an officer clinging to the mainshrouds ready to board, but no one else seemed to have a care in the world. Everyone seemed to be looking up at the clumsy superstructure and laughing at the farmyard noises issuing from it.

"Wait, men, wait," said Hornblower.

The lugger was coming alongside when Hornblower suddenly realised, with a hot flood of blood under his skin, that he himself was unarmed. He had told his men to take pistols and cutlasses; he had advised Tapling to arm himself, and yet he had clean forgotten about his own need for weapons. But it was too late now to try to remedy that. Someone in the lugger hailed in Spanish, and Hornblower spread his hands in a show of incomprehension. Now they were alongside.

"Come on, men!" shouted Hornblower.

He ran across the superstructure and with a gulp he flung himself across the gap at the officer in the shrouds. He gulped again as he went through the air; he fell with all his weight on the unfortunate man, clasped him round the shoulders, and fell with him to the deck. There were shouts and yells behind him as the *Caroline* spewed up her crew into the lugger. A rush of feet, a clatter and a clash. Hornblower got to his feet empty-handed. Maxwell was just striking down a man with his cutlass. Tapling was heading a rush forward into the bows, waving a cutlass and yelling like a madman. Then it was all over; the astonished Spaniards were unable to lift a hand in their own defence.

So it came about that on the twenty-second day of her quarantine the *Caroline* came into Gibraltar Bay with a captured *guarda-costa* lugger under her lee. A thick barnyard stench trailed with her, too, but at least, when Hornblower went on board the *Indefatigable* to make his report, he had a suitable reply ready for Mr. Midshipman Bracegirdle.

"Hullo, Noah, how are Shem and Ham?" asked Mr. Bracegirdle.

"Shem and Ham have taken a prize," said Hornblower. "I regret that Mr. Bracegirdle can't say the same."

But the chief commissary of the squadron, when Hornblower reported to him, had a comment to which even Hornblower was unable to make a reply.

"Do you mean to tell me, Mr. Hornblower," said the chief commissary, "that you allowed your men to eat fresh beef? A bullock a day for your eighteen men? There must have been plenty of ship's provisions on board. That was wanton extravagance, Mr. Hornblower. I'm surprised at you."

Ten

HORNBLOWER
the Duchess, and the Devil

Acting-Lieutenant Hornblower was bringing the sloop *Le Reve,* prize of H.M.S. *Indefatigable,* to anchor in Gibraltar Bay. He was nervous; if anyone had asked him if he thought that all the telescopes in the Mediterranean Fleet were trained upon him he would have laughed at the fantastic suggestion, but he felt as if they were. Nobody ever gauged more cautiously the strength of the gentle following breeze, or estimated more anxiously the distances between the big anchored ships of the line, or calculated more carefully the space *Le Reve* would need to swing at her anchor. Jackson, his petty officer, was standing forward awaiting the order to take in the jib, and he acted quickly at Hornblower's hail.

"Helm-a-lee," said Hornblower next, and *Le Reve* rounded into the wind. "Brail up!"

Le Reve crept forward, her momentum diminishing as the wind took her way off her.

"Let go!"

The cable growled a protest as the anchor took it out through the hawsehole—that welcome splash of the anchor, telling of the journey's end. Hornblower watched carefully while *Le Reve* took up on her cable, and then relaxed a little. He had brought the prize safely in. The commodore—Captain Sir Edward Pellew of H.M.S. *Indefatigable*—had clearly not yet returned, so that it was Hornblower's duty to report to the port admiral.

"Get the boat hoisted out," he ordered, and then, remembering his humanitarian duty, "And you can let the prisoners up on deck."

They had been battened down below for the last forty eight hours, because the fear of a recapture was the nightmare of every prizemaster. But here in the Bay with the Mediterranean Fleet all round that danger was at an end. Two hands at the oars of the gig sent her skimming over the water, and in ten minutes Hornblower was reporting his arrival to the admiral.

"You say she shows a fair turn of speed?" said the latter, looking over at the prize.

"Yes, sir. And she's handy enough," said Hornblower.

"I'll purchase her into the service. Never enough despatch vessels," mused the admiral.

Even with that hint it was a pleasant surprise to Hornblower when he received heavily sealed official orders, and opening them, read that "you are hereby requested and required—" to take H.M. sloop *Le Reve* under his command, and to proceed "with the utmost expedition" to Plymouth as soon as the despatches destined for England should be put in his charge. It was an independent command; it was a chance of seeing England again (it was three years since Hornblower had last set foot on the English shore) and it was a high professional compliment. But there was another letter, delivered at the same moment, which Hornblower read with less elation.

"Their Excellencies, Major-General Sir Hew and Lady Dalrymple, request the pleasure of Acting-Lieutenant Horatio Hornblower's company at dinner today, at three o'clock, at Government House."

It might be a pleasure to dine with the governor of Gibraltar and his lady, but it was only a mixed pleasure, at best, for an acting-lieutenant with a single sea-chest, faced with the need to dress himself suitably for such a function. Yet it was hardly possible for a young man to walk up to Government House from the landing slip without a thrill of excitement, especially as his friend Mr. Midshipman Bracegirdle, who came from a wealthy family and had a handsome allowance, had lent him a pair of the finest white stockings of China silk—Bracegirdle's calves were plump, and Hornblower's were skinny, but that difficulty had been artistically circumvented. Two small pads of oakum, some strips of sticking plaster from the surgeon's stores, and Hornblower now had a couple of legs of which no one need be ashamed. He could put his left leg forward to make his bow without any fear of wrinkles in his stockings, and sublimely conscious, as Bracegirdle said, of a leg of which any gentleman would be proud.

At Goverment House the usual polished and languid aide-de-camp took charge of Hornblower and led him forward. He made his bow to Sir Hew, a red-faced and fussy old gentleman, and to Lady Dalrymple, a red-faced and fussy old lady.

"Mr. Hornblower," said the latter, "I must present you—Your Grace, this is Mr. Hornblower, the new captain of *Le Reve*. Her Grace the Duchess of Wharfedale."

A duchess, no less! Hornblower poked forward his padded leg, pointed his toe, laid his hand on his heart and bowed with all the depth the tightness of his breeches allowed—he had still been growing when he bought them on joining the *Indefatigable*. Bold blue eyes, and a once beautiful middle-aged face.

"So this 'ere's the feller in question?" said the Duchess. "Matilda, my dear, are you going to hentrust me to a hinfant in harms?"

The startling vulgarity of the accent took Hornblower's breath away. He had been ready for almost anything except that a superbly dressed duchess should speak in the accent of Seven Dials. He raised his eyes to stare, while forgetting to straighten himself up, standing with his chin poked forward and his hand still on his heart.

"You look like a gander on a green," said the Duchess. "I hexpects you to 'iss hany moment."

She stuck her own chin out and swung it from side to side with her hands on her knees in a perfect imitation of a belligerent goose, apparently with so close a resemblance to Hornblower as well as to excite a roar of laughter from the other guests. Hornblower stood in blushing confusion.

"Don't be 'ard on the young feller," said the Duchess, coming to his defence and patting him on the shoulder. "'E's on'y young, an' thet's nothink to be ashamed of. Somethink to be prard of, for thet metter, to be trusted with a ship at thet hage."

It was lucky that the announcement of dinner came to save Hornblower from the further confusion into which this kindly remark had thrown him. Hornblower naturally found himself with the riff-raff, the tag-rag-and-bobtail of the middle of the table along with the other junior officers—Sir Hew sat at one end with the Duchess while Lady Dalrymple sat with a commodore at the other. Moreover there were not nearly as many women as men; that was only to be expected, as Gibraltar was, technically at least, a beleaguered fortress. So Hornblower had no woman on either side of him; at his right sat the young aide-de-camp who had first taken him in charge.

"Your health, Your Grace," said the commodore, looking down the length of the table and raising his glass.

"Thank'ee," replied the Duchess. "Just in time to save my life. I was wonderin' 'oo'd come to my rescue."

She raised her brimming glass to her lips and when she put it down again it was empty.

"A jolly boon companion you are going to have," said the aide-de-camp to Hornblower.

"How is she going to be my companion?" asked Hornblower, quite bewildered.

The aide-de-camp looked at him pityingly.

"So you have not been informed?" he asked. "As always the man most concerned is the last to know. When you sail with your despatches tomorrow you will have the honour of bearing Her Grace with you to England."

"God bless my soul," said Hornblower.

"Let's hope He does," said the aide-de-camp piously, nosing his wine. "Poor stuff this sweet Malaga is. Old Hare bought a job lot in '95, and every governor since then seems to think it's his duty to use it up."

"But who *is* she?" asked Hornblower.

"Her Grace the Duchess of Wharfedale," replied the aide-de-camp. "Did you not hear Lady Dalrymple's introduction?"

"But she doesn't talk like a duchess," protested Hornblower.

"No. The old Duke was in his dotage when he married her. She was an innkeeper's widow, so her friends say. You can imagine, if you like, what her enemies say."

"But what is she doing here?" went on Hornblower.

"She is on her way back to England. She was at Florence when the French marched in, I understand. She reached Leghorn, and bribed a coaster to bring her here. She asked Sir Hew to find her a passage, and Sir Hew asked the admiral—Sir Hew would ask anyone for anything on behalf of a duchess, even one said by her friends to be an innkeeper's widow."

"I see," said Hornblower.

There was a burst of merriment from the head of the table, and the Duchess was prodding the governor's scarlet-coated ribs with the handle of her knife, as if to make sure he saw the joke.

"Maybe you will not lack for mirth on your homeward voyage," said the aide-de-camp.

Just then a smoking sirloin of beef was put down in front of Hornblower, and all his other worries vanished before the necessity of carving it and remembering his manners. He took the carving knife and fork gingerly in his hands and glanced round at the company.

"May I help you to some of this beef, Your Grace? Madam? Sir? Well done or underdone, sir? A little of the brown fat?"

In the hot room the sweat ran down his face as he wrestled with the joint; he was fortunate that most of the guests desired helpings from the other removes so that he had little carving to do. He put a couple of haggled slices on his own plate as the simplest way of concealing the worst results of his own handiwork.

"Beef from Tetuán," sniffed the aide-de-camp. "Tough and stringy."

That was all very well for a governor's aide-de-camp—he could not guess how delicious was this food to a young naval officer fresh from beating about at sea in an overcrowded frigate. Even the thought of having to act as host to a duchess could not entirely spoil Hornblower's appetite. And the final dishes, the meringues and macaroons, the custards and the fruits, were ecstasy for a young man whose last pudding had been currant duff last Sunday.

"Those sweet things spoil a man's palate," said the aide-de-camp—much Hornblower cared.

They were drinking formal toasts now. Hornblower stood for the King and the royal family, and raised his glass for the Duchess.

"And now for the enemy," said Sir Hew, "may their treasure galleons try to cross the Atlantic."

"A supplement to that, Sir Hew," said the commodore at the other end, "may the Dons make up their minds to leave Cadiz."

There was a growl almost like wild animals from round the table. Most of the naval officers present were from Jervis' Mediterranean squadron which had beaten about in the Atlantic for the past several months hoping to catch the Spaniards should they come out. Jervis had to detach his ships to Gibraltar two at a time to replenish their stores, and these officers were from the two ships of the line present at the moment in Gibraltar.

"Johnny Jervis would say amen to that," said Sir Hew. "A bumper to the Dons then, gentlemen, and may they come out from Cadiz."

The ladies left them then, gathered together by Lady Dalrymple, and as soon as it was decently possible Hornblower made his excuses and slipped away, determined not to be heavy with wine the night before he sailed in independent command.

Maybe the prospect of the coming on board of the Duchess was a useful counter-irritant, and saved Hornblower from worrying too much about his first command. He was up before dawn—before even the brief Mediterranean twilight had begun—to see that his precious ship was in condition to face the sea, and the enemies who swarmed upon the sea. He had four popgun four-pounders to deal with those enemies, which meant that he was safe from no one; his was the weakest vessel at sea, for the smallest trading brig carried a more powerful armament. So that like all weak creatures his only safety lay in flight—Hornblower looked aloft in the half-light, where the sails would be set on which so much might depend. He went over the watch bill with his two watch-keeping officers, Midshipman Hunter and Master's Mate Winyatt, to make sure that every man of his crew of eleven knew his duty. Then all that remained was to put on his smartest seagoing uniform, try to eat breakfast, and wait for the Duchess.

She came early, fortunately; Their Excellencies had had to rise at a most unpleasant hour to see her off. Mr. Hunter reported the approach of the governor's launch with suppressed excitement.

"Thank you, Mr. Hunter," said Hornblower coldly—that was what the service demanded, even though not so many weeks before they had been playing follow-my-leader through the *Indefatigable's* rigging together.

The launch swirled alongside, and two neatly dressed seamen hooked on the ladder. *Le Reve* had such a small freeboard that boarding her presented no problem even for ladies. The governor stepped on board to the twittering of the only two pipes *Le Reve* could muster, and Lady Dalrymple followed him. Then came the Duchess, and the Duchess's companion; the latter was a younger woman, as beautiful as the Duchess must once have been. A couple of aides-de-camp followed, and by that time the minute deck of *Le Reve* was positively crowded, so that there was no room left to bring up the Duchess's baggage.

"Let us show you your quarters, Your Grace," said the governor.

Lady Dalrymple squawked her sympathy at sight of the minute cabin, which the two cots almost filled, and everyone's head, inevitably, bumped against the deck beam above.

"We shall live through it," said the Duchess, stoically, "an' that's more than many a man makin' a little trip to Tyburn could say."

One of the aides-de-camp produced a last minute packet of despatches and demanded Hornblower's signature on the receipt; the last farewells were said, and Sir Hew and Lady Dalrymple went down the side again to the twittering of the pipes.

"Man the windlass!" bellowed Hornblower the moment the launch's crew bent to their oars.

A few seconds' lusty work brought *Le Reve* up to her anchor.

"Anchor's aweigh, sir," reported Winyatt.

"Jib halliards!" shouted Hornblower. "Mains'l halliards!"

Le Reve came round before the wind as her sails were set and her rudder took a grip on the water. Everyone was so busy catting the anchor and setting sail that it was Hornblower himself who dipped his colours in salute as *Le Reve* crept out beyond the Mole before the gentle southeaster, and dipped her nose to the first of the big Atlantic rollers coming in through the Gut. Through the skylight beside him he heard a clatter and a wail, as something fell in the cabin with that first roll, but he could spare no attention for the woman below. He had the glass to his eye now, training it first on Algeciras and then upon Tarifa—some well-manned privateer or ship of war might easily dash out to snap up such a defenceless prey as *Le Reve*. He could not relax while the forenoon watch wore on. They rounded Cape Marroqui and he set a course for St. Vincent, and then the mountains of southern Spain began to sink below the horizon. Cape Trafalgar was just visible on the starboard bow when at last he shut the telescope and began to wonder about dinner; it was pleasant to be captain of his own ship and to be able to order dinner when he chose. His aching legs told him he had been on his feet too long—eleven continuous hours; if the future brought him many independent commands he would wear himself out by this sort of behaviour.

Down below he relaxed gratefully on the locker, and sent the cook to knock at the Duchess's cabin door to ask with his compliments if all was well; he heard the Duchess's sharp voice saying that they needed nothing, not even dinner. Hornblower philosophically shrugged his shoulders and ate his dinner with a young man's appetite. He went on deck again as night closed in upon them; Winyatt had the watch.

"It's coming up thick, sir," he said.

So it was. The sun was invisible on the horizon, engulfed in watery mist. It was the price he had to pay for a fair wind, he knew; in the winter months in these latitudes there was always likely to be fog where the cool land breeze reached the Atlantic.

"It'll be thicker still by morning," he said, gloomily, and revised his night orders, setting a course due west instead of west by north as he originally intended. He wanted to make certain of keeping clear of Cape St. Vincent in the event of fog.

That was one of those minute trifles which may affect a man's whole after life—Hornblower had plenty of time later to reflect on what might have happened had he not ordered that alteration of course. During the night he was often on deck, peering through the increasing mist, but at the time when the crisis came he was down below snatching a little sleep. What woke him was a seaman shaking his shoulder violently.

"Please, sir. Please, sir. Mr. Hunter sent me. Please, sir, won't you come on deck, he says, sir."

"I'll come," said Hornblower, blinking himself awake and rolling out of his cot.

The faintest beginnings of dawn were imparting some slight luminosity to the mist which was close about them. *Le Reve* was lurching over an ugly sea with barely enough wind behind her to give her steerage way. Hunter was standing with his back to the wheel in an attitude of tense anxiety.

"Listen!" he said, as Hornblower appeared.

He half-whispered the word, and in his excitement he omitted the "sir" which was due to his captain—and in his excitement Hornblower did not notice the omission. Hornblower listened. He heard the shipboard noises he could expect—the clattering of the blocks as *Le Reve* lurched, the sound of the sea at her bows. Then he heard other shipboard noises. There were other blocks clattering; the sea was breaking beneath other bows.

"There's a ship close alongside," said Hornblower.

"Yes, sir," said Hunter. "And after I sent below for you I heard an order given. And it was in Spanish—some foreign tongue, anyway."

The tenseness of fear was all about the little ship like the fog.

"Call all hands. Quietly," said Hornblower.

But as he gave the order he wondered if it would be any use. He could send his men to their stations, he could man and load his four-pounders, but if that ship out there in the fog was of any force greater than a merchant ship he was in deadly peril. Then he tried to comfort himself—perhaps the ship was some fat Spanish galleon bulging with treasure, and were he to board her boldly she would become his prize and make him rich for life.

"A 'appy Valentine's day to you," said a voice beside him, and he nearly jumped out of his skin with surprise. He had actually forgotten the presence of the Duchess on board.

"Stop that row!" he whispered furiously at her, and she pulled up abruptly in astonishment. She was bundled up in a cloak and hood against the damp air, and no further detail could be seen of her in the darkness and fog.

"May I hask—" she began.

"Shut up!" whispered Hornblower.

A harsh voice could be heard through the fog, other voices repeating the order, whistles being blown, much noise and bustle.

"That's Spanish, sir, isn't it?" whispered Hunter.

"Spanish for certain. Calling the watch. Listen!"

The two double-strokes of a ship's bell came to them across the water. Four bells in the morning watch. And instantly from all round them a dozen other bells could be heard, as if echoing the first.

"We're in the middle of a fleet, by God!" whispered Hunter.

"Big ships, too, sir," supplemented Winyatt who had joined them with the calling of all hands. "I could hear half a dozen different pipes when they called the watch."

"The Dons are out, then," said Hunter.

And the course I set has taken us into the midst of them, thought Hornblower bitterly. The coincidence was maddening, heartbreaking. But he forebore to waste breath over it. He even suppressed the frantic gibe that rose to his lips at the memory of Sir Hew's toast about the Spaniards coming out from Cadiz.

"They're setting more sail," was what he said. "Dagoes snug down at night, just like some fat Indiaman. They only set their t'gallants at daybreak."

All round them through the fog could be heard the whine of sheaves in blocks, the stamp-and-go of the men at the halliards, the sound of ropes thrown on decks, the chatter of a myriad voices.

"They make enough noise about it, blast 'em," said Hunter.

The tension under which he laboured was apparent as he stood straining to peer through the mist.

"Please God they're on a different course to us," said Winyatt, more sensibly. "Then we'll soon be through 'em."

"Not likely," said Hornblower.

Le Reve was running almost directly before what little wind there was; if the Spaniards were beating against it or had it on their beam they would be crossing her course at a considerable angle, so that the volume of sound from the nearest ship would have diminished or increased considerably in this time, and there was no indication of that whatever. It was far more likely that *Le Reve* had overhauled the Spanish fleet under its nightly short canvas and had sailed forward into the middle of it. It was a problem what to do next in that case, to shorten sail, or to heave-to, and let the Spaniards get ahead of them again, or to clap on sail to pass through. But the passage of the minutes brought clear proof that fleet and sloop were on practically the same course, as otherwise they could hardly fail to pass some ship close. As long as the mist held they were safest as they were.

But that was hardly to be expected with the coming of day.

"Can't we alter course, sir?" asked Winyatt.

"Wait," said Hornblower.

In the faint growing light he had seen shreds of denser mist blowing past them—a clear indication that they could not hope for continuous fog. At that moment they ran out of a fog bank into a clear patch of water.

"There she is, by God!" said Hunter.

Both officers and seamen began to move about in sudden panic.

"Stand still, damn you!" rasped Hornblower, his nervous tension releasing itself in the fierce monosyllables.

Less than a cable's length away a three-decked ship of the line was standing along parallel to them on their starboard side. Ahead and on the port side could be seen the outlines, still shadowy, of other battleships. Nothing could save them if they drew attention to themselves; all that could be done was to keep going as if they had as much right there as the ships of the line. It was possible that in the happy-go-lucky Spanish navy the officer of the watch over there did not know that no sloop like *Le Reve* was attached to the fleet—or even possibly by a miracle there *might* be one. *Le Reve* was French built and French rigged, after all. Side by side *Le Reve* and the battleship sailed over the lumpy sea. They were within point-blank range of fifty big guns, when one well aimed shot would sink them. Hunter was uttering filthy curses under his breath, but discipline had asserted itself; a telescope over there on the Spaniard's deck would not discover any suspicious bustle on board the sloop. Another shred of fog drifted past them, and then they were deep in a fresh fog bank.

"Thank God!" said Hunter, indifferent to the contrast between this present piety and his preceding blasphemy.

"Hands wear ship," said Hornblower. "Lay her on the port tack."

There was no need to tell the hands to do it quietly; they were as well aware of their danger as anyone. *Le Reve* silently rounded-to, the sheets were hauled in and coiled down without a sound; and the sloop, as close to the wind as she would lie, heeled to the small wind, meeting the lumpy waves with her port bow.

"We'll be crossing their course now," said Hornblower.

"Please God it'll be under their sterns and not their bows," said Winyatt.

There was the Duchess still in her cloak and hood, standing right aft as much out of the way as possible.

"Don't you think Your Grace had better go below?" asked Hornblower, making use by a great effort of the formal form of address.

"Oh no, *please,*" said the Duchess. "I couldn't bear it."

Hornblower shrugged his shoulders, and promptly forgot the Duchess's presence again as a new anxiety struck him. He dived below and came up again with the two big sealed envelopes of despatches. He took a belaying pin from the rail and began very carefully to tie the envelopes to the pin with a bit of line.

"Please," said the Duchess, "please, Mr. Hornblower, tell me what you are doing?"

"I want to make sure these will sink when I throw them overboard if we're captured," said Hornblower grimly.

"Then they'll be lost for good?"

"Better that than that the Spaniards should read 'em," said Hornblower with all the patience he could muster.

"I could look after them for you," said the Duchess. "Indeed I could."

Hornblower looked keenly at her.

"No," he said, "they might search your baggage. Probably they would."

"Baggage!" said the Duchess. "As if I'd put them in my baggage! I'll put them next my skin—they won't search *me* in any case. They'll never find 'em, not if I put 'em up my petticoats."

There was a brutal realism about those words that staggered Hornblower a little, but which also brought him to admit to himself that there was something in what the Duchess was saying.

"If they capture us—" said the Duchess, "I pray they won't but if they do—they'll never keep me prisoner. You know that. They'll send me to Lisbon or put me aboard a King's ship as soon as they can. Then the despatches will be delivered eventually. Late, but better late than never."

"That's so," mused Hornblower.

"I'll guard them like my life," said the Duchess. "I swear I'll never part from them. I'll tell no one I have them, not until I hand them to a King's Officer."

She met Hornblower's eyes with transparent honesty in her expression.

"Fog's thinning, sir," said Winyatt.

"Quick!" said the Duchess.

There was no time for further debate. Hornblower slipped the envelopes from their binding of rope and handed them over to her, and replaced the belaying pin in the rail.

"These damned French fashions," said the Duchess. "I was right when I said I'd put these letters up my petticoats. There's no room in my bosom."

Certainly the upper part of her gown was not at all capacious; the waist was close up under the armpits and the rest of the dress hung down from there quite straight in utter defiance of anatomy.

"Give me a yard of that rope, quick!" said the Duchess.

Winyatt cut her a length of the line with his knife and handed it to her. Already she was hauling at her petticoats; the appalled Hornblower saw a gleam of white thigh above her stocking tops before he tore his glance away. The fog was certainly thinning.

"You can look at me now," said the Duchess, but her petticoats only just fell in time as Hornblower looked round again. "They're inside my shift, next my skin as I promised. With these Directory fashions no one wears stays any more. So I tied the rope round my waist outside my shift. One envelope is flat against my chest and the other against my back. Would you suspect anything?"

She turned round for Hornblower's inspection.

"No, nothing shows," he said. "I must thank Your Grace."

"There is a certain thickening," said the Duchess, "but it does not matter what the Spaniards suspect as long as they do not suspect the truth."

Momentary cessation of the need for action brought some embarrassment to Hornblower. To discuss with a woman her shift and stays—or the absence of them—was a strange thing to do.

A watery sun, still nearly level, was breaking through the mist and shining in his eyes. The mainsail cast a watery shadow on the deck. With every second the sun was growing brighter.

"Here it comes," said Hunter.

The horizon ahead expanded rapidly, from a few yards to a hundred, from a hundred yards to half a mile. The sea was covered with ships. No less than six were in plain sight, four ships of the line and two big frigates, with the red-and-gold of Spain at their mastheads, and, what marked them even more obviously as Spaniards, huge wooden crosses hanging at their peaks.

"Wear ship again, Mr. Hunter," said Hornblower. "Back into the fog."

That was the one chance of safety. Those ships running down towards them were bound to ask questions, and they could not hope to avoid them all. *Le Reve* spun round on her heel, but the fog bank from which she had emerged was already attenuated, sucked up by the thirsty sun. They could see a drifting stretch of it ahead, but it was lazily rolling away from them at the same time as it was dwindling. The heavy sound of a cannon shot reached their ears, and close on their starboard quarter a ball threw up a fountain of water before plunging into the side of a wave just ahead. Hornblower looked round just in time to see the last of the puff of smoke from the bows of the frigate astern pursuing them.

"Starboard two points," he said to the helmsman, trying to gauge at one and the same moment the frigate's course, the direction of the wind, the bearing of the other ships, and that of the thin last nucleus of that wisp of fog.

"Starboard two points," said the helmsman.

"Fore and main sheets!" said Hunter.

Another shot, far astern this time but laid true for line; Hornblower suddenly remembered the Duchess.

"You must go below, Your Grace," he said, curtly.

"Oh, no, no, no!" burst out the Duchess with angry vehemence. "Please let me stay here. I can't go below to where that seasick maid of mine lies hoping to die. Not in that stinking box of a cabin."

There would be no safety in that cabin, Hornblower reflected—*Le Reve's* scantlings were too fragile to keep out any shot at all. Down below the waterline in the hold the women might be safe, but they would have to lie flat on top of beef barrels.

"Sail ahead!" screamed the lookout.

The mist there was parting and the outline of a ship of the line was emerging from it, less than a mile away and on almost the same course as *Le Reve's.* Thud—thud from the frigate astern. Those gunshots by now would have warned the whole Spanish fleet that something unusual was happening. The battleship ahead would know that the little sloop was being pursued. A ball tore through the air close by, with its usual terrifying noise. The ship ahead was awaiting their coming; Hornblower saw her topsails slowly turning.

"Hands to the sheets!" said Hornblower. "Mr. Hunter, jibe her over."

Le Reve came round again, heading for the lessening gap on the port side. The frigate astern turned to intercept. More jets of smoke from her bows. With an appalling noise a shot passed within a few feet of

Hornblower, so that the wind of it made him stagger. There was a hole in the mainsail.

"Your Grace," said Hornblower, "those aren't warning shots—"

It was the ship of the line which fired then, having succeeded in clearing away and manning some of her upper deck guns. It was as if the end of the world had come. One shot hit *Le Reve's* hull, and they felt the deck heave under their feet as a result, as if the little ship were disintegrating. But the mast was hit at the same moment, stays and shrouds parting, splinters raining all round. Mast, sails, boom, gaff and all went from above them over the side to windward. The wreckage dragged in the sea and turned the helpless wreck round with the last of her way. The little group aft stood momentarily dazed.

"Anybody hurt?" asked Hornblower, recovering himself.

"On'y a scratch, sir," said one voice.

It seemed a miracle that no one was killed.

"Carpenter's mate, sound the well," said Hornblower and then, recollecting himself. "No, damn it. Belay that order. If the Dons can save the ship, let 'em try."

Already the ship of the line whose salvo had done the damage was filling her topsails again and bearing away from them, while the frigate which had pursued them was running down on them fast. A wailing figure came scrambling out of the after hatchway. It was the Duchess's maid, so mad with terror that her seasickness was forgotten. The Duchess put a protective arm round her and tried to comfort her.

"Your Grace had better look to your baggage," said Hornblower. "No doubt you'll be leaving us shortly for other quarters with the Dons. I hope you will be more comfortable."

He was trying desperately hard to speak in a matter of fact way, as if nothing out of the ordinary were happening, as if he were not soon to be a prisoner of the Spaniards; but the Duchess saw the working of the usually firm mouth, and marked how the hands were tightly clenched.

"How can I tell you how sorry I am about this?" asked the Duchess, her voice soft with pity.

"That makes it the harder for me to bear," said Hornblower, and he even forced a smile.

The Spanish frigate was just rounding-to, a cable's length to windward.

"Please, sir," said Hunter.

"Well?"

"We can fight, sir. You give the word. Cold shot to drop in the boats when they try to board. We could beat 'em off once, perhaps."

Hornblower's tortured misery nearly made him snap out, "Don't be a fool," but he checked himself. He contented himself with pointing to the frigate. Twenty guns were glaring at them at far less than point-blank range. The very boat the frigate was hoisting out would be manned by at least twice as many men as *Le Reve* carried—she was no bigger than many a pleasure yacht. It was not odds of ten to one, or a hundred to one, but odds of ten thousand to one.

"I understand, sir," said Hunter.

Now the Spanish frigate's boat was in the water, about to shove off.

"A private word with you, please, Mr. Hornblower," said the Duchess suddenly.

Hunter and Winyatt heard what she said, and withdrew out of ear-shot.

"Yes, Your Grace?" said Hornblower.

The Duchess stood there, still with her arm round her weeping maid, looking straight at him.

"I'm no more of a Duchess than you are," she said.

"Good God!" said Hornblower. "Who—who are you, then?"

"Kitty Cobham."

The name meant a little to Hornblower, but only a little.

"You're too young for that name to have any memories for you, Mr. Hornblower, I see. It's five years since last I trod the boards."

That was it. Kitty Cobham the actress.

"I can't tell it all now," said the Duchess—the Spanish boat was dancing over the waves towards them. "But when the French marched into Florence that was only the last of my misfortunes. I was penniless when I escaped from them. Who would lift a finger for a onetime actress—one who had been betrayed and deserted? What was I to do? But a duchess—that was another story. Old Dalrymple at Gibraltar could not do enough for the Duchess of Wharfedale."

"Why did you choose that title?" asked Hornblower in spite of himself.

"I knew of her," said the Duchess with a shrug of the shoulders. "I knew her to be what I played her as. That was why I chose her—I always played character parts better than straight comedy. And not nearly so tedious in a long role."

"But my despatches!" said Hornblower in a sudden panic of realisation. "Give them back, quick."

"If you wish me to," said the Duchess. "But I can still be the Duchess when the Spaniards come. They will still set me free as speedily as they can. I'll guard those despatches better than my life—I swear it, I swear it! In less than a month I'll deliver them, if you trust me."

Hornblower looked at the pleading eyes. She might be a spy, ingeniously trying to preserve the despatches from being thrown overboard before the Spaniards took possession. But no spy could have hoped that *Le Reve* would run into the midst of the Spanish fleet.

"I made use of the bottle, I know," said the Duchess. "I drank. Yes, I did. But I stayed sober in Gibraltar, didn't I? And I won't touch a drop, not a drop, until I'm in England. I'll swear that, too. Please, sir—please. I beg of you. Let me do what I can for my country."

It was a strange decision for a man of nineteen to have to make—one who had never exchanged a word with an actress in his life before. A harsh voice overside told him that the Spanish boat was about to hook on.

"Keep them, then," said Hornblower. "Deliver them when you can."

He had not taken his eyes from her face. He was looking for a gleam of triumph in her expression. Had he seen anything of the sort he would have torn the despatches from her body at that moment. But all he saw was the natural look of pleasure, and it was then that he made up his mind to trust her—not before.

"Oh, thank you, sir," said the Duchess.

The Spanish boat had hooked on now, and a Spanish lieutenant was awkwardly trying to climb aboard. He arrived on the deck on his hands and knees, and Hornblower stepped over to receive him as he got to his feet. Captor and captive exchanged bows. Hornblower could not understand what the Spaniard said, but obviously they were formal sentences that he was using. The Spaniard caught sight of the two women aft and halted in surprise; Hornblower hastily made the presentation in what he hoped was Spanish.

"Señor el tenente Español," he said. *"Señora la Duquesa de Wharfedale."*

The title clearly had its effect; the lieutenant bowed profoundly, and his bow was received with the most lofty aloofness by the Duchess. Hornblower could be sure the despatches were safe. That was some alleviation of the misery of standing here on the deck of his waterlogged little ship, a prisoner of the Spaniards. As he waited he heard, from far to leeward, roll upon roll of thunder coming up against the wind. No thunder could endure that long. What he could hear must be the broadsides of ships in action—of fleets in action. Somewhere over there by Cape St. Vincent the British fleet must have caught the Spaniards at last. Fiercer and fiercer sounded the roll of the artillery. There was excitement among the Spaniards who had scrambled onto the deck of *Le Reve,* while Hornblower stood bareheaded waiting to be taken into captivity.

Captivity was a dreadful thing. Once the numbness had worn off Hornblower came to realise what a dreadful thing it was. Not even the news of the dreadful battering which the Spanish navy had received at St. Vincent could relieve the misery and despair of being a prisoner. It was not the physical conditions—ten square feet of floor space per man in an empty sail loft at Ferrol along with other captive warrant officers—for they were no worse than what a junior officer often had to put up with at sea. It was the loss of freedom, the fact of being a captive, that was so dreadful.

There was four months of it before the first letter came through to Hornblower; the Spanish government, inefficient in all ways, had the worst postal system in Europe. But here was the letter, addressed and re-addressed, now safely in his hands after he had practically snatched it from a stupid Spanish non-commissioned officer who had been puzzling over the strange name. Hornblower did not know the handwriting, and when he broke the seal and opened the letter the salutation made him think for a moment that he had opened someone else's letter.

"Darling Boy" it began. Now who on earth would call him that? He read on in a dream.

> Darling Boy—
>
> I hope it will give you happiness to hear that what you gave me has reached its destination. They told me, when I delivered it, that you are a prisoner, and my heart bleeds for you. And they told me too that they were pleased with you for what you had done. And one of those admirals is a shareholder in Drury Lane. Whoever would have thought of such a thing? But he smiled at me, and I smiled at him. I did not know he was a shareholder then, and I only smiled out of the kindness of my heart. And all that I told him about my dangers and perils with my precious burden were only histrionic exercises, I am afraid. Yet he believed me, and so struck was he by my smile and my adventures, that he demanded a part for me from Sherry, and behold, now I am playing second lead, usually a tragic mother, and receiving the acclaim of the groundlings. There are compensations in growing old, which I am discov-

ering too. And I have not tasted wine since I saw you last, nor shall I ever again. As one more reward my admiral promised me that he would forward this letter to you in the next cartel—an expression which no doubt means more to you than to me. I only hope that it reaches you in good time and brings you comfort in your affliction.

I pray nightly for you.
Ever your devoted friend,
Katharine Cobham

Comfort in his affliction? A little, perhaps. There was some comfort in knowing that the despatches had been delivered; there was some comfort in a secondhand report that Their Lordships were pleased with him. There was comfort even in knowing that the Duchess was re-established on the stage. But the sum total was nothing compared with his misery.

Here was a guard come to bring him to the Commandant, and beside the Commandant was the Irish renegade who served as interpreter. There were further papers on the Commandant's desk—it looked as if the same cartel which had brought in Kitty Cobham's note had brought in letters for the Commandant.

"Good afternoon, sir," said the Commandant, always polite, offering a chair.

"Good afternoon, sir, and many thanks," said Hornblower. He was learning Spanish slowly and painfully.

"You have been promoted," said the Irishman in English.

"W-what?" said Hornblower.

"Promoted," said the Irishman. "Here is the letter—'The Spanish authorities are informed that on account of his meritorious service the acting-commission of Mr. Horatio Hornblower, Midshipman and Acting-Lieutenant, has been confirmed. Their Lordships of the Admiralty express their confidence that Mr. Horatio Hornblower will be admitted immediately to the privileges of commissioned rank.' There you are, young man."

"My felicitations, sir," said the Commandant.

"Many thanks, sir," said Hornblower.

The Commandant was a kindly old gentleman with a pleasant smile for the awkward young man. He went on to say more, but Hornblower's Spanish was not equal to the technicalities he used, and Hornblower in despair looked at the interpreter.

"Now that you are a commissioned officer," said the latter, "you will be transferred to the quarters for captured officers."

"Thank you," said Hornblower.

"You will receive the half pay of your rank."

"Thank you."

"And your parole will be accepted. You will be at liberty to visit in the town and the neighbourhood for two hours each day on giving your parole."

"Thank you," said Hornblower.

Perhaps, during the long months which followed, it was some mitigation of his unhappiness that for two hours each day his parole gave him freedom; freedom to wander in the streets of the little town, to have a cup of chocolate or a glass of wine—providing he had any money—making polite and laborious conversation with Spanish soldiers or sailors or civilians. But it was better to spend his two hours wandering over the goat paths of the headland in the wind and the sun, in the companionship of the sea, which might alleviate the sick misery of captivity. There was slightly better food, slightly better quarters. And there was the knowledge that now he was a lieutenant, that he held the King's commission, that if ever, ever, the war should end and he should be set free he could starve on half pay—for with the end of the war there would be no employment for junior lieutenants. But he had earned his promotion. He had gained the approval of authority, that was something to think about on his solitary walks.

There came a day of southwesterly gales, with the wind shrieking in from across the Atlantic. Across three thousand miles of water it came, building up its strength unimpeded on its way, and heaping up the sea into racing mountain ridges which came crashing in upon the Spanish coast in thunder and spray. Hornblower stood on the headland above Ferrol Harbour, holding his worn greatcoat about him as he leaned forward into the wind to keep his footing. So powerful was the wind that it was difficult to breathe while facing it. If he turned his back he could breathe more easily, but then the wind blew his wild hair forward over his eyes, almost inverted his greatcoat over his head, and furthermore forced him into little tottering steps down the slope towards Ferrol whither he had no wish to return at present. For two hours he was alone and free, and those two hours were precious. He could breathe the Atlantic air, he could walk, he could do as he liked during that time. He could stare out to sea; it was not unusual to catch sight, from the headland, of some British ship of war which might be working slowly along the coast in the hope of snapping up a coasting vessel while keeping a watchful eye upon the Spanish naval activity. When such a ship went by during Hornblower's two hours of freedom, he would stand and gaze at it, as a man dying of thirst might gaze at a bucket of water held beyond his reach; he would note all the little details, the cut of the topsails and the style of the paint, while misery wrung his bowels. For this was the end of his second year as a prisoner of war. For twenty two months, for twenty two hours every day, he had been under lock and key, herded with five other junior lieutenants in a single room in the fortress of Ferrol. And today the wind roared by him, shouting in its outrageous freedom. He was facing into the wind; before him lay Corunna, its white houses resembling pieces of sugar scattered over the slopes. Between him and Corunna was all the open space of Corunna Bay, flogged white by the wind, and on his left hand was the narrow entrance to Ferrol Bay. On his right was the open Atlantic; from the foot of the low cliffs there the long wicked reef of the Dientes del Diablo—the Devil's Teeth—ran out to the northward, square across the path of the racing rollers driven by the wind. At half minute intervals the rollers would crash against the reef with an impact that shook even the solid headland on which Hornblower stood, and each roller dissolved into spray which was instantly whirled away by the wind to reveal again the long black tusks of the rocks.

Hornblower was not alone on the headland; a few yards away from him a Spanish militia artilleryman on lookout duty gazed with watery eyes through a telescope with which he continually swept the seaward horizon. When at war with England it was necessary to be vigilant; a fleet might suddenly appear over the horizon, to land a little army to capture Ferrol, and burn the dockyard installations and the ships. No hope of that today, thought Hornblower—there could be no landing of troops on that raging lee shore.

But all the same the sentry was undoubtedly staring very fixedly through his telescope right to windward; the sentry wiped his streaming eyes with his coat sleeve and stared again. Hornblower peered in the same direction, unable to see what it was that had attracted the sentry's attention. The sentry muttered something to himself, and then turned and ran clumsily down to the little stone guardhouse where sheltered the rest of the militia detachment stationed there to man the guns of the battery on the headland. He returned with the sergeant of the guard, who took the telescope and peered out to windward in the direction pointed out by the sentry. The two of them jabbered in their barbarous Gallego dialect; in two years of steady application Hornblower had mastered Galician as well as Castilian, but in that howling gale he could not intercept a word. Then finally, just as the sergeant nodded in agreement, Hornblower saw with his naked eyes what they were discussing. A pale grey square on the horizon above the grey sea—a ship's topsail. She must be running before the gale making for the shelter of Corunna or Ferrol.

It was a rash thing for a ship to do, because it would be no easy matter for her to round-to into Corunna Bay and anchor, and it would be even harder for her to hit off the narrow entrance to the Ferrol Inlet. A cautious captain would claw out to sea and heave-to with a generous amount of sea room until the wind should moderate. These Spanish captains, said Hornblower to himself, with a shrug of his shoulders; but naturally they would always wish to make harbour as quickly as possible when the Royal Navy was sweeping the seas. But the sergeant and the sentry were more excited than the appearance of a single ship would seem to justify. Hornblower could contain himself no longer, and edged up to the chattering pair, mentally framing his sentences in the unfamiliar tongue.

"Please, gentlemen," he said, and then started again, shouting against the wind. "Please, gentlemen, what is it that you see?"

The sergeant gave him a glance, and then, reaching some undiscoverable decision, handed over the telescope—Hornblower could hardly restrain himself from snatching it from his hands. With the telescope to his eye he could see far better; he could see a ship-rigged vessel, under close-reefed topsails (and that was much more sail than it was wise to carry) hurtling wildly towards them. And then a moment later he saw the other square of grey. Another topsail. Another ship. The fore topmast was noticeably shorter than the main topmast, and not only that, but the whole effect was familiar—she was a British ship of war, a British frigate, plunging along in hot pursuit of the other, which seemed most likely to be a Spanish privateer. It was a close chase; it would be a very near thing, whether the Spaniard would reach the protection of the shore batteries before the frigate overhauled her. He lowered the telescope to rest his eye, and instantly the sergeant snatched it from him. He had been watching the Englishman's face, and Hornblower's expression had told him what he wanted to know. Those two ships out there were behaving in such a way as to justify his rousing his officer and giving the alarm. Sergeant and sentry went running back to the guardhouse, and in a few moments the artillerymen were pouring out to man the batteries on the verge of the cliff. Soon enough came a mounted officer urging his horse up the path; a single glance through the telescope sufficed for him. He went clattering down to the battery and the next moment the boom of a gun from there alerted the rest of the defences. The flag of Spain rose up the flagstaff beside the battery, and Hornblower saw an answering flag rise up the flagstaff on San Anton, where another battery guarded Corunna Bay. All the guns of the harbour defences were now manned, and there would be no mercy shown to any English ship that came in range.

Pursuer and pursued had covered quite half the distance already towards Corunna. They were hull-up over the horizon now to Hornblower on the headland, who could see them plunging madly over the grey sea—Hornblower momentarily expected to see them carry away their topmasts or their sails blow from the bolt-ropes. The frigate was half a mile astern still, and she would have to be much closer than that to have any hope of hitting with her guns in that sea. Here came the Commandant and his staff, clattering on horseback up the path to see the climax of the drama; the Commandant caught sight of Hornblower, and doffed his hat with Spanish courtesy, while Hornblower, hatless, tried to bow with equal courtesy. Hornblower walked over to him with an urgent request—he had to lay his hand on the Spaniard's saddlebow and shout up into his face to be understood.

"My parole expires in ten minutes, sir," he yelled. "May I please extend it? May I please stay?"

"Yes, stay, señor," said the Commandant, generously.

Hornblower watched the chase, and at the same time observed closely the preparations for defence. He had given his parole, but no part of the gentlemanly code prevented him from taking note of all he could see. One day he might be free, and one day it might be useful to know all about the defences of Ferrol. Everyone else of the large group on the headland was watching the chase, and excitement rose higher as the ships came racing nearer. The English captain was keeping a hundred yards or more to seaward of the Spaniard, but he was quite unable to overhaul her—in fact it seemed to Hornblower as if the Spaniard were actually increasing his lead. But the English frigate being to seaward meant that escape in that direction was cut off. Any turn away from the land would reduce the Spaniard's lead to a negligible distance. If he did not get into Corunna Bay or Ferrol Inlet he was doomed.

Now he was level with the Corunna headland, and it was time to put his helm hard over and turn into the Bay and hope that his anchors would hold in the lee of the headland. But with a wind of that violence hurtling against cliffs and headlands strange things can happen. A flaw of wind coming out of the Bay must have caught her aback as she tried to round-to. Hornblower saw her stagger, saw her heel as the back-lash died away and the gale caught her again. She was laid over almost on her beam-ends and as she righted herself Hornblower saw a momentary gap open up in her main topsail. It was momentary because from the time the gap appeared the life of the topsail was momentary; the gap appeared and at once the sail vanished, blown into ribbons as soon as its continuity was impaired. With the loss of its balancing pressure the ship became unmanageable; the gale pressing against the fore topsail swung her round again before the wind like a weathervane. If there had been time to spare to set a fragment of sail farther aft she would have been saved, but in those enclosed waters there was no time to spare. At one moment she was about to round the Corunna headland; at the next she had lost the opportunity for ever.

There was still the chance that she might fetch the opening to the Ferrol Inlet; the wind was nearly fair for her to do that—nearly. Hornblower on the Ferrol headland was thinking along with the Spanish captain down there on the heaving deck. He saw him try to steady the ship so as to head for the narrow entrance, notorious among seamen for its difficulty. He saw him get her on her course, and for a few seconds as she flew across the mouth of the Bay it seemed as if the Spaniard would succeed, against all probability, in exactly hitting off the entrance to the inlet. Then the back-lash hit her again. Had she been quick on the helm she might still have been safe, but with her sail pressure so outbalanced she was bound to be slow in her response to her rudder. The shrieking wind blew her bows round, and it was instantly obvious, too, that she was doomed, but the Spanish captain played the game out to the last. He would not pile his ship up against the foot of the low cliffs. He put his helm hard over; with the aid of the wind rebounding from the cliffs he made a gallant attempt to clear the Ferrol headland altogether and give himself a chance to claw out to sea.

A gallant attempt, but doomed to failure as soon as begun; he actually cleared the headland, but the wind blew his bows round again, and, bows first, the ship plunged right at the long jagged line of the Devil's Teeth. Hornblower, the Commandant, and everyone, hurried across the headland to look down at the final act of the tragedy. With tremendous speed, driving straight before the wind, she raced at the reef. A roller picked her up as she neared it and seemed to increase her speed. Then she struck, and vanished from sight for a second as the roller burst into spray all about her. When the spray cleared she lay there transformed. Her three masts had all gone with the shock, and it was only a black hulk which emerged from the white foam. Her speed and the roller behind her had carried her almost over the reef—doubtless tearing her bottom out—and she hung by her stern, which stood out clear of the water, while her bows were just submerged in the comparatively still water in the lee of the reef.

There were men still alive on her. Hornblower could see them crouching for shelter under the break of her poop. Another Atlantic roller came surging up, and exploded on the Devil's Teeth, wrapping the wreck round with spray. But yet she emerged again, black against the creaming foam. She had cleared the reef sufficiently far to find shelter for most of her length in the lee of the thing that had destroyed her. Hornblower could see those living creatures crouching on her deck. They had a little longer to live—they might live five minutes, perhaps, if they were lucky. Five hours if they were not.

All round him the Spaniards were shouting maledictions. Women were weeping; some of the men were shaking their fists with rage at the British frigate, which, well satisfied with the destruction of her victim, had rounded-to in time and was now clawing out to sea again under storm canvas. It was horrible to see those poor devils down there die. If some larger wave than usual, bursting on the reef, did not lift the stern of the wreck clear so that she sank, she would still break up for the survivors to be whirled away with the fragments. And, if it took a long time for her to break up, the wretched men sheltering there would not be able to endure the constant beating of the cold spray upon them. Something should be done to save them, but no boat could round the headland and weather the Devil's Teeth to reach the wreck. That was so obvious as not to call for a second thought. But—Hornblower's thoughts began to race as he started to work on the alternatives. The Commandant on his horse was speaking vehemently to a Spanish naval officer, clearly on the same subject, and the naval officer was spreading his hands and saying that any attempt would be hopeless. And yet—For two years Hornblower had been a prisoner; all his pent-up restlessness was seeking an outlet, and after two years of the misery of confinement he did not care whether he lived or died. He went up to the Commandant and broke into the argument.

"Sir," he said, "let me try to save them. Perhaps from the little bay there—Perhaps some of the fishermen would come with me."

The Commandant looked at the officer and the officer shrugged his shoulders.

"What do you suggest, sir?" asked the Commandant of Hornblower.

"We might carry a boat across the headland from the dockyard," said Hornblower, struggling to word his ideas in Spanish, "but we must be quick—quick!"

He pointed to the wreck, and force was added to his words by the sight of a roller bursting over the Devil's Teeth.

"How would you carry a boat?" asked the Commandant.

To shout his plan in English against that wind would have been a strain; to do so in Spanish was beyond him.

"I can show you at the dockyard, sir," he yelled. "I cannot explain. But we must hurry!"

"You want to go to the dockyard, then?"

"Yes—oh yes."

"Mount behind me, sir," said the Commandant.

Awkwardly Hornblower scrambled up to a seat astride the horse's haunches and clutched at the Commandant's belt. He bumped frightfully as the animal wheeled round and trotted down the slope. All the idlers of the town and garrison ran beside them.

The dockyard at Ferrol was almost a phantom organisation, withered away like a tree deprived of its roots, thanks to the British blockade. Situated as it was at the most distant corner of Spain, connected with the interior by only the roughest of roads, it relied on receiving its supplies by sea, and any such reliance was likely with British cruisers off the coast to be disappointed. The last visit of Spanish ships of war had stripped the place of almost all its stores, and many of the dockyard hands had been pressed as seamen at the same time. But all that Hornblower needed was there, as he knew, thanks to his careful observation. He slid off the horse's hindquarters—miraculously avoiding an instinctive kick from the irritated animal—and collected his thoughts. He pointed to a low dray—a mere platform on wheels—which was used for carrying beef barrels and brandy kegs to the pier.

"Horses," he said, and a dozen willing hands set to work harnessing a team.

Beside the jetty floated half a dozen boats. There were tackle and shears, all the apparatus necessary for swinging heavy weights about. To put slings under a boat and swing her up was the work of only a minute or two. These Spaniards might be dilatory and lazy as a rule, but inspire them with the need for instant action, catch their enthusiasm, present them with a novel plan, and they would work like madmen—and some of them were skilled workmen, too. Oars, mast and sail (not that they would need the sail), rudder, tiller, and balers were all present. A group came running from a store shed with chocks for the boat, and, the moment these were set up on the dray, the dray was backed under the tackle and the boat lowered onto them.

"Empty barrels," said Hornblower. "Little ones—so."

A swarthy Galician fisherman grasped his intention at once, and amplified Hornblower's halting sentences with voluble explanation. A dozen empty water breakers, with their bungs driven well home, were brought, and the swarthy fishermen climbed on the dray and began to lash them under the thwarts. Properly secured, they would keep the boat afloat even were she filled to the gunwale with water.

"I want six men," shouted Hornblower, standing on the dray and looking round at the crowd. "Six fishermen who know little boats."

The swarthy fisherman lashing the breakers in the boat looked up from his task.

"I know whom we need, sir," he said.

He shouted a string of names, and half a dozen men came forward; burly, weather-beaten fellows, with the self-reliant look in their faces of men used to meeting difficulties. It was apparent that the swarthy Galician was their captain.

"Let us go, then," said Hornblower, but the Galician checked him.

Hornblower did not hear what he said, but some of the crowd nodded, turned away, and came hastening back staggering under a breaker of fresh water and a box that must contain biscuit. Hornblower was cross with himself for forgetting the possibility of their being blown out to sea. And the Commandant, still sitting his horse and watching these preparations with a keen eye, took note of these stores too.

"Remember, sir, that I have your parole," he said.

"You have my parole, sir," said Hornblower—for a few blessed moments he had actually forgotten that he was a prisoner.

The stores were safely put away into the sternsheets and the fishing boat captain caught Hornblower's eye and got a nod from him.

"Let us go," he roared to the crowd.

The iron-shod hoofs clashed on the cobbles and the dray lurched forward, with men leading the horses, men swarming alongside, and Hornblower and the captain riding on the dray like triumphing generals in a procession. They went through the dockyard gate, along the level main street of the little town, and turned up a steep lane which climbed the ridge constituting the backbone of the headland. The enthusiasm of the crowd was still lively; when the horses slowed as they breasted the slope a hundred men pushed at the back, strained at the sides, tugged at the traces to run the dray up the hillside. At the crest the lane became a track, but the dray still lurched and rumbled along. From the track diverged an even worse track, winding its way sideways down the slope through arbutus and myrtle towards the sandy cove which Hornblower had first had in mind—on fine days he had seen fishermen working a seine net on that beach, and he himself had taken note of it as a suitable place for a landing party should the Royal Navy ever plan a descent against Ferrol.

The wind was blowing as wildly as ever; it shrieked round Hornblower's ears. The sea as it came in view was chaotic with wave-crests, and then as they turned a shoulder of the slope they could see the line of the Devil's Teeth running out from the shore up there to windward, and still hanging precariously from their jagged fangs was the wreck, black against the seething foam. Somebody raised a shout at the sight, everybody heaved at the dray, so that the horses actually broke into a trot and the dray leaped and bounced over the obstructions in its way.

"Slowly," roared Hornblower. "Slowly!"

If they were to break an axle or smash a wheel at this moment the attempt would end in ludicrous failure. The Commandant on his horse enforced Hornblower's cries with loud orders of his own, and restrained the reckless enthusiasm of his people. More sedately the dray went on down the trail to the edge of the sandy beach. The wind picked up even the damp sand and flung it stinging into their faces, but only small waves broke here, for the beach was in a recess in the shoreline, the southwesterly wind was blowing a trifle off shore here, and up to windward the Devil's Teeth broke the force of the rollers as they raced along in a direction nearly parallel to the shoreline. The wheels plunged into the sand and the horses stopped at the water's edge. A score of willing hands unharnessed them and a hundred willing arms thrust the dray out into the water—all these things were easy with such vast manpower available. As the first wave broke over the floor of the dray the crew scrambled up and stood ready. There were rocks here, but mighty heaves by the militiamen and the dockyard workers waist deep in water forced the dray over them. The boat almost floated off its chocks, and the crew forced it clear and scrambled aboard, the wind beginning to swing her immediately. They grabbed for their oars and put their backs into half a dozen fierce strokes which brought her under command; the Galician captain had already laid a steering oar in the notch in the stern, with no attempt at shipping rudder and tiller. As he braced himself to steer he glanced at Hornblower, who tacitly left the job to him.

Hornblower, bent against the wind, was standing in the sternsheets planning a route through the rocks which would lead them to the wreck. The shore and the friendly beach were gone now, incredibly far away, and the boat was struggling out through a welter of water with the wind howling round her. In those jumbled waves her motion was senseless and she lurched in every direction successively. It was well that the boatmen were used to rowing in broken water so that their oars kept the boat under way, giving the captain the means by which, tugging fiercely at the steering oar, he could guide her through that maniacal confusion. Hornblower, planning his course, was able to guide the captain by his gestures, so that the captain could devote all the necessary attention to keeping the boat from being suddenly capsized by an unexpected wave. The wind howled, and the boat heaved and pitched as she met each lumpy wave, but yard by yard they were struggling up to the wreck. If there was any order in the waves at all, they were swinging round the outer end of the Devil's Teeth, so that the boat had to be carefully steered, turning to meet the waves with her bows and then turning back to gain precarious yards against the wind. Hornblower spared a glance for the men at the oars; at every second they were exerting their utmost strength. There could never be a moment's respite—tug and strain, tug and strain, until Hornblower wondered how human hearts and sinews could endure it.

But they were edging up towards the wreck. Hornblower, when the wind and spray allowed, could see the whole extent of her canted deck now. He could see human figures cowering under the break of the poop. He saw somebody there wave an arm to him. Next moment his attention was called away when a jagged monster suddenly leaped out of the sea twenty yards ahead. For a second he could not imagine what it was, and then it leaped clear again and he recognised it—the butt end of a broken mast. The mast was still anchored to the ship by a single surviving shroud attached to the upper end of the mast and to the ship, and the mast drifting down to leeward, was jerking and leaping on the waves as though some sea god below the surface was threatening them with his wrath. Hornblower called the steersman's attention to the menace and received a nod in return; the steersman's shouted "*Nombre de Dios*" was whirled away in the wind. They kept clear of the mast, and as they pulled up along it Hornblower could form a clearer notion of the speed of their progress now that he had a stationary object to help his judgment. He could see the painful inches gained at each frantic tug on the oars, and could see how the boat stopped dead or even went astern when the wilder gusts hit her, the oar blades pulling ineffectively through the water. Every inch of gain was only won at the cost of an infinity of labour.

Now they were past the mast, close to the submerged bows of the ship, and close enough to the Devil's Teeth to be deluged with spray as each wave burst on the farther side of the reef. There were inches of water washing back and forth in the bottom of the boat, but there was neither time nor opportunity to bale it out. This was the trickiest part of the whole effort, to get close enough alongside the wreck to be able to take off the survivors without stoving in the boat; there were wicked fangs of rock all about the after end of the wreck, while forward, although the forecastle was above the surface at times, the forward part of the waist was submerged. But the ship was canted a little over to port, towards them, which made the approach easier. When the water was at its lowest level, immediately before the next roller broke on the reef, Hornblower, standing up and craning his neck, could see no rocks beside the wreck in the middle part of the waist where the deck came down to water level. It was easy to direct the steersman towards that particular point, and then, as the boat moved in, to wave his arms and demand the attention of the little group under the break of the poop, and to point to the spot to which they were approaching. A wave burst upon the reef, broke over the stern of the wreck, and filled the boat almost full. She swung back and forth in the eddies, but the kegs kept her afloat and quick handling of the steering oar and lusty rowing kept her from being dashed against either the wreck or the rocks.

"Now!" shouted Hornblower—it did not matter that he spoke English at this decisive moment. The boat surged forward, while the survivors, releasing themselves from the lashings which had held them in their shelter, came slithering down the deck towards them. It was a little of a shock to see there were but four of them—twenty or thirty men must have been swept overboard when the ship hit the reef. The bows of the boat moved towards the wreck. At a shouted order from the steersman the oars fell still. One survivor braced himself and flung himself into the bows. A stroke of the oars, a tug at the steering oar, and the boat nosed forward again, and another survivor plunged into the boat. Then Hornblower, who had been watching the sea, saw the next breaker rear up over the reef. At his warning shout the boat backed away to safety—comparative safety—while the remaining survivors went scrambling back up the deck to the shelter of the poop. The wave burst and roared, the foam hissed and the spray rattled, and then they crept up to the wreck again. The third survivor poised himself for his leap, mistimed it, and fell into the sea, and no one ever saw him again. He was gone, sunk like a stone, crippled as he was with cold and exhaustion, but there was no time to spare for lamentation. The fourth survivor was waiting his chance and jumped at once, landing safely in the bows.

"Any more?" shouted Hornblower, and receiving a shake of the head in reply; they had saved three lives at the risk of eight.

"Let us go," said Hornblower, but the steersman needed no telling. Already he had allowed the wind to drift the boat away from the wreck, away from the rocks—away from the shore. An occasional strong pull at the oars sufficed to keep her bows to wind and wave. Hornblower looked down at the fainting survivors lying in the bottom of the boat with the water washing over them. He bent down and shook them into consciousness; he picked up the balers and forced them into their numb hands. They must keep active or die. It was astounding to find darkness closing about them, and it was urgent that they should decide on their next move immediately. The men at the oars were in no shape for any prolonged further rowing; if they tried to return to the sandy cove whence they had started they might be overtaken both by night and by exhaustion while still among the treacherous rocks off the shore there. Hornblower sat down beside the Galician captain, who laconically gave his views while vigilantly observing the waves racing down upon them.

"It is growing dark," said the captain, glancing round the sky. "Rocks. The men are tired."

"We had better not go back," said Hornblower.

"No."

"Then we must get out to sea."

Years of duty on blockade, of beating about off a lee shore, had ingrained into Hornblower the necessity for seeking sea room.

"Yes," said the captain, and he added something which Hornblower, thanks to the wind and his unfamiliarity with the language, was unable to catch. The captain roared the expression again, and accompanied his words with a vivid bit of pantomime with the one hand he could spare from the steering oar.

"A sea anchor," decided Hornblower to himself. "Quite right."

He looked back at the vanishing shore, and gauged the direction of the wind. It seemed to be backing a little southerly; the coast here trended away from them. They could ride to a sea anchor through the hours of darkness and run no risk of being cast ashore as long as these conditions persisted.

"Good," said Hornblower aloud.

He imitated the other's bit of pantomime and the captain gave him a glance of approval. At a bellow from him the two men forward took in their oars and set to work at constructing a sea anchor—merely a pair of oars attached to a long painter paid out over the bows. With this gale blowing the pressure of the wind on the boat set up enough drag on the float to keep their bows to the sea. Hornblower watched as the sea anchor began to take hold of the water.

"Good," he said again.

"Good," said the captain, taking in his steering oar.

Hornblower realised only now that he had been long exposed to a winter gale while wet to the skin. He was numb with cold, and he was shivering uncontrollably. At his feet one of the three survivors of the wreck was lying helpless; the other two had succeeded in baling out most of the water and as a result of their exertions were conscious and alert. The men who had been rowing sat drooping with weariness on their thwarts. The Galician captain was already down in the bottom of the boat lifting the helpless man in his arms. It was a common impulse of them all to huddle down into the bottom of the boat, beneath the thwarts, away from that shrieking wind.

So the night came down on them. Hornblower found himself welcoming the contact of other human bodies; he felt an arm round him and he put his arm round someone else. Around them a little water still surged about on the floorboards; above them the wind still shrieked and howled. The boat stood first on her head and then on her tail as the waves passed under them, and at the moment of climbing each crest she gave a shuddering jerk as she snubbed herself to the sea anchor. Every few seconds a new spat of spray whirled into the boat upon their shrinking bodies; it did not seem long before the accumulation of spray in the bottom of the boat made it necessary for them to disentangle themselves, and set about, groping in the darkness, the task of baling the water out again. Then they could huddle down again under the thwarts.

It was when they pulled themselves together for the third baling that in the middle of his nightmare of cold and exhaustion Hornblower was conscious that the body across which his arm lay was unnaturally stiff; the man the captain had been trying to revive had died as he lay there between the captain and Hornblower. The captain dragged the body away into the sternsheets in the darkness, and the night went on, cold wind and cold spray, jerk, pitch, and roll, sit up and bale and cower down and shudder. It was hideous torment; Hornblower could not trust himself to believe his eyes when he saw the first signs that the darkness was lessening. And then the grey dawn came gradually over the grey sea, and they were free to wonder what to do next. But as the light increased the problem was solved for them, for one of the fishermen, raising himself up in the boat, gave a hoarse cry, and pointed to the northern horizon, and there, almost hull-up, was a ship, hove-to under storm canvas. The captain took one glance at her—his eyesight must have been marvellous—and identified her.

"The English frigate," he said.

She must have made nearly the same amount of leeway hove-to as the boat did riding to her sea anchor.

"Signal to her," said Hornblower, and no one raised any objections.

The only white object available was Hornblower's shirt, and he took it off, shuddering in the cold, and they tied it to an oar and raised the oar in the mast-step. The captain saw Hornblower putting on his dripping coat over his bare ribs and in a single movement peeled off his thick blue jersey and offered it to him.

"Thank you, no," protested Hornblower, but the captain insisted; with a wide grin he pointed to the stiffened corpse lying in the sternsheets and announced he would replace the jersey with the dead man's clothing.

The argument was interrupted by a further cry from one of the fishermen. The frigate was coming to the wind; with treble-reefed fore and main topsails she was heading for them under the impulse of the lessening gale. Hornblower saw her running down on them; a glance in the other direction showed him the Galician mountains, faint on the southern horizon—warmth, freedom, and friendship on the one hand; solitude and captivity on the other. Under the lee of the frigate the boat bobbed and heaved fantastically; many inquisitive faces looked down on them. They were cold and cramped; the frigate dropped a boat and a couple of nimble seamen scrambled on board. A line was flung from the frigate, a whip lowered a breeches ring into the boat, and the English seamen helped the Spaniards one by one into the breeches and held them steady as they were swung up to the frigate's deck.

"I go last," said Hornblower when they turned to him. "I am a King's Officer."

"Good Lor' lumme," said the seamen.

"Send the body up, too," said Hornblower. "It can be given decent burial."

The stiff corpse was grotesque as it swayed through the air. The Galician captain tried to dispute with Hornblower the honor of going last, but Hornblower would not be argued with. Then finally the seamen helped him put his legs into the breeches, and secured him with a line round his waist. Up he soared, swaying dizzily with the roll of the ship; then they drew him in to the deck, lowering and shortening, until half a dozen strong arms took his weight and laid him gently on the deck.

"There you are, my hearty, safe and sound," said a bearded seaman.

"I am a King's Officer," said Hornblower. "Where's the officer of the watch?"

Wearing marvellous dry clothing, Hornblower found himself soon drinking hot rum-and-water in the cabin of Captain George Crome, of His Majesty's frigate *Syrtis*. Crome was a thin pale man with a depressed expression, but Hornblower knew of him as a first-rate officer.

"These Galicians make good seamen," said Crome. "I can't press them. But perhaps a few will volunteer sooner than go to a prison hulk."

"Sir," said Hornblower, and hesitated. It is ill for a junior lieutenant to argue with a post captain.

"Well?"

"Those men came to sea to save life. They are not liable to capture."

Crome's cold grey eyes became actively frosty—Hornblower was right about it being ill for a junior lieutenant to argue with a post captain.

"Are you telling me my duty, sir?" he asked.

"Good heavens no, sir," said Hornblower hastily. "It's a long time since I read the Admiralty Instructions and I expect my memory's at fault."

"Admiralty Instructions, eh?" said Crome, in a slightly different tone of voice.

"I expect I'm wrong, sir," said Hornblower, "but I seem to remember the same instruction applied to the other two—the survivors."

Even a post captain could only contravene Admiralty Instructions at his peril.

"I'll consider it," said Crome.

"I had the dead man sent on board, sir," went on Hornblower, "in the hope that perhaps you might give him proper burial. Those Galicians risked their lives to save him, sir, and I expect they'd be gratified."

"A Popish burial? I'll give orders to give 'em a free hand."

"Thank you, sir," said Hornblower.

"And now as regards yourself. You say you hold a commission as lieutenant. You can do duty in this ship until we meet the admiral again. Then he can decide. I haven't heard of the *Indefatigable* paying off, and legally you may still be borne on her books."

And that was when the Devil came to tempt Hornblower, as he took another sip of hot rum-and-water. The joy of being in a King's ship again was so keen as to be almost painful. To taste salt beef and biscuit again, and never again to taste beans and garbanzos. To have a ship's deck under his feet, to talk English. To be free—to be free! There was precious little chance of ever falling again into Spanish hands. Hornblower remembered with agonizing clarity the flat depression of captivity. All he had to do was not to say a word. He had only to keep silence for a day or two. But the Devil did not tempt him long, only until he had taken his next sip of rum-and-water. Then he thrust the Devil behind him and met Crome's eyes again.

"I'm sorry, sir," he said.

"What for?"

"I am here on parole. I gave my word before I left the beach."

"You did? That alters the case. You were within your rights, of course."

The giving of parole by captive British officers was so usual as to excite no comment.

"It was in the usual form, I suppose?" went on Crome. "That you would make no attempt to escape?"

"Yes, sir."

"Then what do you decide as a result?"

Of course Crome could not attempt to influence a gentleman's decision on a matter as personal as a parole.

"I must go back, sir," said Hornblower, "at the first opportunity."

He felt the sway of the ship, he looked round the homely cabin, and his heart was breaking.

"You can at least dine and sleep on board tonight," said Crome. "I'll not venture inshore again until the wind moderates. I'll send you to Corunna under a flag of truce when I can. And I'll see what the Instructions say about those prisoners."

It was a sunny morning when the sentry at Fort San Anton, in the harbour of Corunna, called his officers' attention to the fact that the British cruiser off the headland had hove-to out of gunshot and was lowering a boat. The sentry's responsibility ended there, and he could watch idly as his officer observed that the cutter, running smartly in under sail, was flying a white flag. She hove-to within musket shot, and it was a mild surprise to the sentry when in reply to the officer's hail someone rose up in the boat and replied in unmistakable Gallego dialect. Summoned alongside the landing ship, the cutter put ashore ten men and then headed out again to the frigate. Nine men were laughing and shouting; the tenth, the youngest, walked with a fixed expression on his face with never a sign of emotion—his expression did not change even when the others, with obvious affection, put their arms round his shoulders. No one ever troubled to explain to the sentry who the imperturbable young man was, and he was not very interested. After he had seen the group shipped off across Corunna Bay towards Ferrol he quite forgot the incident.

It was almost spring when a Spanish militia officer came into the barracks which served as a prison for officers in Ferrol.

"Señor Hornblower?" he asked—at least Hornblower, in the corner, knew that was what he was trying to say. He was used to the way Spaniards mutilated his name.

"Yes?" he said, rising.

"Would you please come with me? The Commandant has sent me for you, sir."

The Commandant was all smiles. He held a despatch in his hands.

"This, sir," he said, waving it at Hornblower, "is a personal order. It is countersigned by the Duke of Fuentesauco, Minister of Marine, but it is signed by the First Minister, Prince of the Peace and Duke of Alcudia."

"Yes, sir," said Hornblower.

He should have begun to hope at that moment, but there comes a time in a prisoner's life when he ceases to hope. He was more interested, even, in that strange title of Prince of the Peace which was now beginning to be heard in Spain.

"It says—'We, Carlos Leonardo Luis Manuel de Godoy y Boegas, First Minister of His Most Catholic Majesty, Prince of the Peace, Duke of Alcudia and Grandee of the First Class, Count of Alcudia, Knight of the Most Sacred Order of the Golden Fleece, Knight of the Holy Order of Santiago, Knight of the Most Distinguished Order of Calatrava, Captain General of His Most Catholic Majesty's forces by Land and Sea, Colonel General of the Guardia de Corps, Admiral of the Two Oceans, General of the cavalry, of the infantry, and of the artillery,'—in any event, sir, it is an order to me to take immediate steps to set you at liberty. I am to restore you under flag of truce to your fellow countrymen, in recognition of—'your courage and self-sacrifice in saving life at the peril of your own.'"

"Thank you, sir," said Hornblower.

Lieutenant Hornblower

ONE

Lieutenant William Bush came on board H.M.S. *Renown* as she lay at anchor in the Hamoaze and reported himself to the officer of the watch, who was a tall and rather gangling individual with hollow cheeks and a melancholy cast of countenance, whose uniform looked as if it had been put on in the dark and not readjusted since.

"Glad to have you aboard, sir," said the officer of the watch. "My name's Hornblower. The captain's ashore. First lieutenant went for'rard with the bosun ten minutes ago."

"Thank you," said Bush.

He looked keenly round him at the infinity of activities which were making the ship ready for a long period of service in distant waters.

"Hey there! You at the stay tackles! Handsomely! Handsomely! Belay!" Hornblower was bellowing this over Bush's shoulder. "Mr. Hobbs! Keep an eye on what your men are doing there!"

"Aye aye, sir," came a sulky reply.

"Mr. Hobbs! Lay aft here!"

A paunchy individual with a thick grey pigtail came rolling aft to where Hornblower stood with Bush at the gangway. He blinked up at Hornblower with the sun in his eyes; the sunlight lit up the sprouting grey beard on his tiers of chins.

"Mr. Hobbs!" said Hornblower. He spoke quietly, but there was an intensity of spirit underlying his words that surprised Bush. "That powder's got to come aboard before nightfall and you know it. So don't use that tone of voice when replying to an order. Answer cheerfully another time. How are you going to get the men to work if you sulk? Get for'rard and see to it."

Hornblower was leaning a little forward as he spoke; the hands which he clasped behind him served apparently to balance the jutting chin, but his attitude was negligent compared with the fierce intensity with which he spoke even though he was speaking in an undertone inaudible to all except the three of them.

"Aye aye, sir," said Hobbs, turning to go forward again.

Bush was making a mental note that this Hornblower was a firebrand when he met his glance and saw to his surprise a ghost of a twinkle in their melancholy depths. In a flash of insight he realised that this fierce young lieutenant was not fierce at all, and that the intensity with which he spoke was entirely assumed—it was almost as if Hornblower had been exercising himself in a foreign language.

"If they once start sulking you can't do anything with 'em," explained Hornblower, "and Hobbs is the worst of 'em—acting-gunner, and no good. Lazy as they make 'em."

"I see," said Bush.

The duplicity—play acting—of the young lieutenant aroused a momentary suspicion in Bush's mind. A man who could assume an appearance of wrath and abandon it again with so much facility was not to be trusted. Then, with an inevitable reaction, the twinkle in the brown eyes called up a responsive twinkle in Bush's frank blue eyes, and he felt a friendly impulse towards Hornblower, but Bush was innately cautious and checked the impulse at once, for there was a long voyage ahead of them and plenty of time for a more considered judgment. Meanwhile he was conscious of a keen scrutiny, and he could see that a question was imminent—and even Bush could guess what it would be. The next moment proved him right.

"What's the date of your commission?" asked Hornblower.

"July '96," said Bush.

"Thank you," said Hornblower in a flat tone that conveyed so little information that Bush had to ask the question in his turn.

"What's the date of yours?"

"August '97," said Hornblower. "You're senior to me. You're senior to Smith, too—January '97."

"Are you the junior lieutenant, then?"

"Yes," said Hornblower.

His tone did not reveal any disappointment that the newcomer had proved to be senior to him, but Bush could guess at it. Bush knew by very recent experience what it was to be the junior lieutenant in a ship of the line.

"You'll be third," went on Hornblower. "Smith fourth, and I'm fifth."

"I'll be third?" mused Bush, more to himself than to anyone else.

Every lieutenant could at least dream, even lieutenants like Bush with no imagination at all. Promotion was at least theoretically possible; from the caterpillar stage of lieutenant one might progress to the butterfly stage of captain, sometimes even without a chrysalis period as commander. Lieutenants undoubtedly were promoted on occasions; most of them, as was to be expected, being men who had friends at Court, or in Parliament, or who had been fortunate enough to attract the attention of an admiral and then lucky enough to be under that admiral's command at the moment when a vacancy occurred. Most of the captains on the list owed their promotion to one or other of such causes. But sometimes a lieutenant won his promotion through merit—through a combination of merit and good fortune, at least—and sometimes sheer blind chance brought it about. If a ship distinguished herself superlatively in some historic action the first lieutenant might be promoted (oddly enough, that promotion was considered a compliment to her captain) or if the captain should be killed in the action even a moderate success might result in a step for the senior surviving lieutenant who took his place. On the other hand some brilliant boat-action, some dashing exploit on shore, might win promotion for the lieutenant in command—the senior, of course. The chances were few enough in all conscience, but there were at least chances.

But of those few chances the great majority went to the senior lieutenant, to the first lieutenant; the chances of the junior lieutenant were doubly few. So that whenever a lieutenant dreamed of attaining the rank of captain, with its dignity and security and prize money, he soon found himself harking back to the consideration of his seniority as lieutenant. If this next commission of the *Renown's* took her away to some place where other lieutenants could not be sent on board by an admiral with favourites, there were only two lives between Bush and the position of first lieutenant with all its added chances of promotion. Naturally he thought about that; equally naturally he did not spare a thought for the fact that the man with whom he was conversing was divided by four lives from that same position.

"But still, it's the West Indies for us, anyway," said Hornblower philosophically. "Yellow fever. Ague. Hurricanes. Poisonous serpents. Bad water. Tropical heat. Putrid fever. And ten times more chances of action than with the Channel fleet."

"That's so," agreed Bush, appreciatively.

With only three and four years' seniority as lieutenants, respectively, the two young men (and with young men's confidence in their own immortality) could face the dangers of West Indian service with some complacence.

"Captain's coming off, sir," reported the midshipman of the watch hurriedly.

Hornblower whipped his telescope to eye and trained it on the approaching shore boat.

"Quite right," he said. "Run for'rard and tell Mr. Buckland. Bosun's mates! Sideboys! Lively, now!"

Captain Sawyer came up through the entry port, touched his hat to the quarterdeck, and looked suspiciously around him. The ship was in the condition of confusion to be expected when she was completing for foreign service, but that hardly justified the sidelong, shifty glances which Sawyer darted about him. He had a big face and a prominent hawk nose which he turned this way and that as he stood on the quarterdeck. He caught sight of Bush, who came forward and reported himself.

"You came aboard in my absence, did you?" asked Sawyer.

"Yes, sir," said Bush, a little surprised.

"Who told you I was on shore?"

"No one, sir."

"How did you guess it, then?"

"I didn't guess it, sir. I didn't know you were on shore until Mr. Hornblower told me."

"Mr. Hornblower? So you know each other already?"

"No, sir. I reported to him when I came on board."

"So that you could have a few private words without my knowledge?"

"No, sir."

Bush bit off the "of course not" which he was about to add. Brought up in a hard school, Bush had learned to utter no unnecessary words when dealing with a superior officer indulging in the touchiness superior officers might be expected to indulge in. Yet this particular touchiness seemed more unwarranted even than usual.

"I'll have you know I allow no one to conspire behind my back, Mr. —ah—Bush," said the captain.

"Aye aye, sir."

Bush met the captain's searching stare with the composure of innocence, but he was doing his best to keep his surprise out of his expression, too, and as he was no actor the struggle may have been evident.

"You wear your guilt on your face, Mr. Bush," said the captain. "I'll remember this."

With that he turned away and went below, and Bush, relaxing from his attitude of attention, turned to express his surprise to Hornblower. He was eager to ask questions about this extraordinary behaviour, but they died away on his lips when he saw that Hornblower's face was set in a wooden unresponsiveness. Puzzled and a little hurt, Bush was about to note Hornblower down as one of the captain's toadies—or as a madman as well—when he caught sight out of the tail of his eye of the captain's head reappearing above the deck. Sawyer must have swung round when at the foot of the companion and come up again simply for the purpose of catching his officers off their guard discussing him—and Hornblower knew more about his captain's habits than Bush did. Bush made an enormous effort to appear natural.

"Can I have a couple of hands to carry my sea-chest down?" he asked, hoping that the words did not sound nearly as stilted to the captain as they did to his own ears.

"Of course, Mr. Bush," said Hornblower, with a formidable formality. "See to it, if you please, Mr. James."

"Ha!" snorted the captain, and disappeared once more down the companion.

Hornblower flickered one eyebrow at Bush, but that was the only indication he gave, even then, of any recognition that the captain's actions were at all unusual, and Bush, as he followed his sea-chest down to his cabin, realised with dismay that this was a ship where no one ventured on any decisive expression of opinion. But the *Renown* was completing for sea, amid all the attendant bustle and confusion, and Bush was on board, legally one of her officers, and there was nothing he could do except reconcile himself philosophically to his fate. He would have to live through this commission, unless any of the possibilities catalogued by Hornblower in their first conversation should save him the trouble.

TWO

H.M.S. *Renown* was clawing her way southward under reefed topsails, a westerly wind laying her over as she thrashed along, heading for those latitudes where she would pick up the northeast trade wind and be able to run direct to her destination in the West Indies. The wind sang in the taut weather-rigging, and blustered round Bush's ears as he stood on the starboard side of the quarterdeck, balancing to the roll as the roaring wind sent one massive grey wave after another hurrying at the ship; the starboard bow received the wave first, beginning a leisurely climb, heaving the bowsprit up towards the sky, but before the pitch was in any way completed the ship began her roll, heaving slowly over, slowly, slowly, while the bowsprit rose still more steeply. And then as she still rolled the bows shook themselves free and began to slide down the far side of the wave, with the foam creaming round them; the bowsprit began the downward portion of its arc as the ship rose ponderously to an even heel again, and as she heeled a trifle into the wind with the send of the sea under her keel her stern rose while the last of the wave passed under it, her bows dipped, and she completed the corkscrew roll with the massive dignity to be expected of a ponderous fabric that carried five hundred tons of artillery on her decks. Pitch—roll—heave—roll; it was magnificent, rhythmic, majestic, and Bush, balancing on the deck with the practiced ease of ten years' experience, would have felt almost happy if the freshening of the wind did not bring with it the approaching necessity for another reef, which meant, in accordance with the ship's standing orders, that the captain should be informed.

Yet there were some minutes of grace left him, during which he could stand balancing on the deck and allow his mind to wander free. Not that Bush was conscious of any need for meditation—he would have smiled at such a suggestion were anyone to make it to him. But the last few days had passed in a whirl, from the moment when his orders had arrived and he had said good-bye to his mother and sisters (he had had three weeks with them after the *Conqueror* had paid off) and hurried to Plymouth, counting the money he had left in his pockets to make sure he could pay the post chaise charges. The *Renown* had been in all the flurry of completing for the West Indian station, and during the thirty six hours that elapsed before she sailed Bush had hardly had time to sit down, let alone sleep—his first good night's rest had come while the *Renown* clawed her way across the bay. Yet almost from the moment of his first arrival on board he had been harassed by the fantastic moods of the captain, now madly suspicious and again stupidly easygoing. Bush was not a man sensitive to atmosphere—he was a sturdy soul philosophically prepared to do his duty in any of the difficult conditions to be expected at sea—but he could not help but be conscious of the tenseness and fear that pervaded life in the *Renown*. He knew that he felt dissatisfied and worried, but he did not know that these were his own forms of tenseness and fear. In three days at sea he had hardly come to know a thing about his colleagues; he could vaguely guess that Buckland, the first lieutenant, was capable and steady, and that Roberts, the second, was kindly and easygoing. Hornblower seemed active and intelligent, Smith a trifle weak; but these deductions were really guesses. The wardroom officers—the lieutenants and the master and the surgeon and the purser—seemed to be secretive and very much inclined to maintain a strict reserve about themselves. Within wide limits this was right and proper—Bush was no frivolous chatterer himself—but the silence was carried to excess when conversation was limited to half a dozen words, all strictly professional. There was much that Bush could have learned speedily about the ship and her crew if the other officers had been prepared to share with him the results of their experience and observations during the year they had been on board but except for the single hint Bush had received from Hornblower when he came on board no one had uttered a word. If Bush had been given to Gothic flights of imagination he might have thought of himself as a ghost at sea with a company of ghosts, cut off from the world and from each other, ploughing across an endless sea to an unknown destination. As it was he could guess that the secretiveness of the wardroom was the result of the moods of the captain; and that brought him back abruptly to the thought that the wind was still freshening and a second reef was now necessary. He listened to the harping of the rigging, felt the heave of the deck under his feet, and shook his head regretfully. There was nothing for it.

"Mr. Wellard," he said to the volunteer beside him. "Go and tell the captain that I think another reef is necessary."

"Aye aye, sir."

It was only a few seconds before Wellard was back on deck again.

"Cap'n's coming himself, sir."

"Very good," said Bush.

He did not meet Wellard's eyes as he said the meaningless words; he did not want Wellard to see how he took the news, nor did he want to see any expression that Wellard's face might wear. Here came the captain, his shaggy long hair whipping in the wind and his hook nose turning this way and that as usual.

"You want to take in another reef, Mr. Bush?"

"Yes, sir," said Bush, and waited for the cutting remark that he expected. It was a pleasant surprise that none was forthcoming. The captain seemed almost genial.

"Very good, Mr. Bush. Call all hands."

The pipes shrilled along the decks.

"All hands! All hands! All hands to reef tops'ls. All hands!"

The men came pouring out; the cry of "all hands" brought out the officers from the wardroom and the cabins and the midshipmen's berth, hastening with their station-bills in their pockets to make sure that the reorganised crew were properly at their stations. The captain's orders pealed against the wind. Halliards and reef tackles were manned; the ship plunged and rolled over the grey sea under the grey sky so that a landsman might have wondered how a man could keep his footing on deck, far less venture aloft. Then in the midst of the evolution a young voice, soaring with excitement to a high treble, cut through the captain's orders.

"'Vast hauling there! 'Vast hauling!"

There was a piercing urgency about the order, and obediently the men ceased to pull. Then the captain bellowed from the poop.

"Who's that countermanding my orders?"

"It's me, sir—Wellard."

The young volunteer faced aft and screamed into the wind to make himself heard. From his station aft Bush saw the captain advance to the poop rail; Bush could see he was shaking with rage, the big nose pointing forward as though seeking a victim.

"You'll be sorry, Mr. Wellard. Oh yes, you'll be sorry."

Hornblower now made his appearance at Wellard's side. He was green with seasickness, as he had been ever since the *Renown* left Plymouth Sound.

"There's a reef point caught in the reef tackle block, sir—weather side," he hailed, and Bush, shifting his position, could see that this was so; if the men had continued to haul on the tackle, damage to the sail might easily have followed.

"What d'you mean by coming between me and a man who disobeys me?" shouted the captain. "It's useless to try to screen him."

"This is my station, sir," replied Hornblower. "Mr. Wellard was doing his duty."

"Conspiracy!" replied the captain. "You two are in collusion!"

In the face of such an impossible statement Hornblower could only stand still, his white face turned towards the captain.

"You go below, Mr. Wellard," roared the captain, when it was apparent that no reply would be forthcoming, "and you too, Mr. Hornblower. I'll deal with you in a few minutes. You hear me? Go below! I'll teach you to conspire."

It was a direct order, and had to be obeyed. Hornblower and Wellard walked slowly aft; it was obvious that Hornblower was rigidly refraining from exchanging a glance with the midshipman, lest a fresh accusation of conspiracy should be hurled at him. They went below while the captain watched them. As they disappeared down the companion the captain raised his big nose again.

"Send a hand to clear that reef tackle!" he ordered, in a tone as nearly normal as the wind permitted. "Haul away!"

The topsails had their second reef, and the men began to lay in off the yards. The captain stood by the poop rail looking over the ship as normal as any man could be expected to be.

"Wind's coming aft," he said to Buckland. "Aloft there! Send a hand to bear those backstays abreast the top-brim. Hands to the weather-braces. After guard! Haul in the weather main brace! Haul together, men! Well with the foreyard! Well with the main yard! Belay every inch of that!"

The orders were given sensibly and sanely, and the hands stood waiting for the watch below to be dismissed.

"Bosun's mate! My compliments to Mr. Lomax and I'll be glad to see him on deck."

Mr. Lomax was the purser, and the officers on the quarterdeck could hardly refrain from exchanging glances; it was hard to imagine any reason why the purser should be wanted on deck at this moment.

"You sent for me, sir?" said the purser, arriving short of breath on the quarterdeck.

"Yes, Mr. Lomax. The hands have been hauling in the weather main brace."

"Yes, sir?"

"Now we'll splice it."

"Sir?"

"You heard me. We'll splice the main brace. A tot of rum to every man. Aye, and to every boy."

"Sir?"

"You heard me. A tot of rum, I said. Do I have to give my orders twice? A tot of rum for every man. I'll give you five minutes, Mr. Lomax, and not a second longer."

The captain pulled out his watch and looked at it significantly.

"Aye aye, sir," said Lomax, which was all he could say. Yet he still stood for a second or two, looking first at the captain and then at the watch, until the big nose began to lift in his direction and the shaggy eyebrows began to come together. Then he turned and fled; if the unbelievable order had to be obeyed five minutes would not be long in which to collect his party together, unlock the spirit room, and bring up the spirits. The conversation between captain and purser could hardly have been overheard by more than half a dozen persons, but every hand had witnessed it, and the men were looking at each other unbelievingly, some with grins on their faces which Bush longed to wipe off.

"Bosun's mate! Run and tell Mr. Lomax two minutes have gone. Mr. Buckland! I'll have the hands aft here, if you please."

The men came trooping along the waist; it may have been merely Bush's overwrought imagination that made him think their manner slack and careless. The captain came forward to the quarterdeck rail, his face beaming in smiles that contrasted wildly with his scowls of a moment before.

"I know where loyalty's to be found, men," he shouted, "I've seen it. I see it now. I see your loyal hearts. I watch your unremitting labours. I've noticed them as I notice everything that goes on in this ship. Everything, I say. The traitors meet their deserts and the loyal hearts their reward. Give a cheer, you men."

The cheer was given, halfheartedly in some cases, with overexuberance in others. Lomax made his appearance at the main hatchway, four men with him each carrying a two-gallon anker.

"Just in time, Mr. Lomax. It would have gone hard with you if you had been late. See to it that the issue is made with none of the unfairness that goes on in some ships. Mr. Booth! Lay aft here."

The bulky bosun came hurrying on his short legs.

"You have your rattan with you, I hope?"

"Aye aye, sir."

Booth displayed his long silver-mounted cane, ringed at every two inches by a pronounced joint. The dilatory among the crew knew that cane well and not only the dilatory—at moments of excitement Mr. Booth was likely to make play with it on all within reach.

"Pick the two sturdiest of your mates. Justice will be executed."

Now the captain was neither beaming nor scowling. There was a smile on his heavy lips, but it might be a smile without significance as it was not re-echoed in his eyes.

"Follow me," said the captain to Booth and his mates, and he left the deck once more to Bush, who now had leisure to contemplate ruefully the disorganisation of the ship's routine and discipline occasioned by this strange whim.

When the spirits had been issued and drunk he could dismiss the watch below and set himself to drive the watch on deck to their duties again, slashing at their sulkiness and indifference with bitter words. And there was no pleasure now in standing on the heaving deck watching the corkscrew roll of the ship and the hurrying Atlantic waves, the trim of the sails and the handling of the wheel—Bush still was unaware that there was any pleasure to be found in these everyday matters, but he was vaguely aware that something had gone out of his life.

He saw Booth and his mates making their way forward again, and here came Wellard onto the quarterdeck.

"Reporting for duty, sir," he said.

The boy's face was white set in a strained rigidity, and Bush, looking keenly at him, saw that there was a hint of moisture in his eyes. He was walking stiffly, too, holding himself inflexibly; pride might be holding back his shoulders and holding up his head, but there was some other reason for his not bending at the hips.

"Very good, Mr. Wellard," said Bush.

He remembered those knots on Booth's cane. He had known injustice often enough. Not only boys but grown men were beaten without cause on occasions, and Bush had nodded sagely when it happened, thinking that contact with injustice in a world that was essentially unjust was part of everyone's education. And grown men smiled to each other when boys were beaten, agreeing that it did all parties good; boys had been beaten since history began, and it would be a bad day for the world if ever, inconceivably, boys should cease to be beaten. This was all very true, and yet in spite of it Bush felt sorry for Wellard. Fortunately there was something waiting to be done which might suit Wellard's mood and condition.

"Those sandglasses need to be run against each other, Mr. Wellard," said Bush, nodding over to the binnacle. "Run the minute glass against the half-hour glass as soon as they turn it at seven bells."

"Aye aye, sir."

"Mark off each minute on the slate unless you want to lose your reckoning," added Bush.

"Aye aye, sir."

It would be something to keep Wellard's mind off his troubles without calling for physical effort, watching the sand run out of the minute glass and turning it quickly, marking the slate and watching again. Bush had his doubts about that half-hour glass and it would be convenient to have both checked. Wellard walked stiffly over to the binnacle and made preparation to begin his observations.

Now here was the captain coming back again, the big nose pointing to one side and the other. But now the mood had changed again; the activity, the restlessness, had evaporated. He was like a man who had dined well. As etiquette dictated, Bush moved away from the weather rail when the captain appeared and the captain proceeded to pace slowly up and down the weather side of the quarterdeck, his steps accommodating themselves by long habit to the heave and pitch of the ship. Wellard took one glance and then devoted his whole attention to the matter of the sandglasses; seven bells had just struck and the half-hour glass had just been turned. For a short time the captain paced up and down. When he halted he studied the weather to windward, felt the wind on his cheek, looked attentively at the dogvane and up at the topsails to make sure that the yards were correctly trimmed, and came over and looked into the binnacle to check the course the helmsman was steering. It was all perfectly normal behaviour; any captain in any ship would do the same when he came on deck. Wellard was aware of the nearness of his captain and tried to give no sign of disquiet; he turned the minute glass and made another mark on the slate.

"Mr. Wellard at work?" said the captain.

His voice was thick and a little indistinct, the tone quite different from the anxiety-sharpened voice with which he had previously spoken. Wellard, his eyes on the sandglasses, paused before replying. Bush could guess that he was wondering what would be the safest, as well as the correct, thing to say.

"Aye aye, sir."

In the navy no one could go far wrong by saying that to a superior officer.

"Aye aye, sir," repeated the captain. "Mr. Wellard has learned better now perhaps than to conspire against his captain, against his lawful superior set in authority over him by the Act of His Most Gracious Majesty King George II?"

That was not an easy suggestion to answer. The last grains of sand were running out of the glass and Wellard waited for them; a "yes" or a "no" might be equally fatal.

"Mr. Wellard is sulky," said the captain. "Perhaps Mr. Wellard's mind is dwelling on what lies behind him. Behind him. 'By the waters of Babylon we sat down and wept.' But proud Mr. Wellard hardly wept. And he did not sit down at all. No, he would be careful not to sit down. The dishonourable part of him has paid the price of his dishonour. The grown man guilty of an honourable offence is flogged upon his back, but a boy, a nasty dirty-minded boy, is treated differently. Is not that so, Mr. Wellard?"

"Yes, sir," murmured Wellard. There was nothing else he could say, and an answer was necessary.

"Mr. Booth's cane was appropriate to the occasion. It did its work well. The malefactor bent over the gun could consider of his misdeeds."

Wellard inverted the glass again while the captain, apparently satisfied, took a couple of turns up and down the deck, to Bush's relief. But the captain checked himself in mid-stride beside Wellard and went on talking; his tone now was higher-pitched.

"So you chose to conspire against me?" he demanded. "You sought to hold me up to derision before the hands?"

"No, sir," said Wellard in sudden new alarm. "No sir, indeed not, sir."

"You and that cub Hornblower. *Mister* Hornblower. You plotted and you planned, so that my lawful authority should be set at nought."

"No, sir!"

"It is only the hands who are faithful to me in this ship where everyone else conspires against me. And cunningly you seek to undermine my influence over them. To make me a figure of fun in their sight. Confess it!"

"No, sir. I didn't, sir."

"Why attempt to deny it? It is plain, it is logical. Who was it who planned to catch that reef point in the reef tackle block?"

"No one, sir. It—"

"Then who was it that countermanded my orders? Who was it who put me to shame before both watches, with all hands on deck? It was a deep-laid plot. It shows every sign of it."

The captain's hands were behind his back, and he stood easily balancing on the deck with the wind flapping his coattails and blowing his hair forward over his cheeks, but Bush could see he was shaking with rage again—if it was not fear. Wellard turned the minute glass again and made a fresh mark on the slate.

"So you hide your face because of the guilt that is written on it?" blared the captain suddenly. "You pretend to be busy so as to deceive me. Hypocrisy!"

"I gave Mr. Wellard orders to test the glasses against each other, sir," said Bush.

He was intervening reluctantly, but to intervene was less painful than to stand by as a witness. The captain looked at him as if this was his first appearance on deck.

"You, Mr. Bush? You're sadly deceived if you believe there is any good in this young fellow. Unless—" the captain's expression was one of sudden suspicious fear—"unless you are part and parcel of this infamous affair. But you are not, are you, Mr. Bush? Not you. I have always thought better of you, Mr. Bush."

The expression of fear changed to one of ingratiating good fellowship.

"Yes, sir," said Bush.

"With the world against me I have always counted on you, Mr. Bush," said the captain, darting restless glances from under his eyebrows. "So you will rejoice when this embodiment of evil meets his deserts. We'll get the truth out of him."

Bush had the feeling that if he were a man of instant quickness of thought and readiness of tongue he would take advantage of this new attitude of the captain's to free Wellard from his peril; by posing as the captain's devoted companion in trouble and at the same time laughing off the thought of danger from any conspiracy, he might modify the captain's fears. So he felt, but he had no confidence in himself.

"He knows nothing, sir," he said, and he forced himself to grin. "He doesn't know the bobstay from the spanker-boom."

"You think so?" said the captain doubtfully, teetering on his heels with the roll of the ship. He seemed almost convinced, and then suddenly a new line of argument presented itself to him.

"No, Mr. Bush. You're too honest. I could see that the first moment I set eyes on you. You are ignorant of the depths of wickedness into which this world can sink. This lout has deceived you. Deceived you!"

The captain's voice rose again to a hoarse scream, and Wellard turned a white face towards Bush, lopsided with terror.

"Really, sir—" began Bush, still forcing a death's-head grin.

"No, no, no!" roared the captain. "Justice must be done! The truth must be brought to light! I'll have it out of him! Quartermaster! Quartermaster! Run for'rard and tell Mr. Booth to lay aft here. And his mates!"

The captain turned away and began to pace the deck as if to offer a safety valve to the pressure within him, but he turned back instantly.

"I'll have it out of him! Or he'll jump overboard! You hear me? Where's that bosun?"

"Mr. Wellard hasn't finished testing the glasses, sir," said Bush in one last feeble attempt to postpone the issue.

"Nor will he," said the captain.

Here came the bosun hurrying aft on his short legs, his two mates striding behind him.

"Mr. Booth!" said the captain; his mood had changed again and the mirthless smile was back on his lips. "Take that miscreant. Justice demands that he be dealt with further. Another dozen from your cane, properly applied. Another dozen, and he'll coo like a dove."

"Aye aye, sir," said the bosun, but he hesitated.

It was a momentary tableau; the captain with his flapping coat; the bosun looking appealingly at Bush and the burly bosun's mates standing like huge statues behind him; the helmsman apparently imperturbable while all this went on round him, handling the wheel and glancing up at the topsails; and the wretched boy beside the binnacle—all this under the grey sky, with the grey sea tossing about them and stretching as far as the pitiless horizon.

"Take him down to the maindeck, Mr. Booth," said the captain.

It was the utterly inevitable; behind the captain's words lay the authority of Parliament, the weight of ages-old tradition. There was nothing that could be done. Wellard's hands rested on the binnacle as though they would cling to it and as though he would have to be dragged away by force. But he dropped his hands to his sides and followed the bosun while the captain watched him, smiling.

It was a welcome distraction that came to Bush as the quartermaster reported "Ten minutes before eight bells, sir."

"Very good. Pipe the watch below."

Hornblower made his appearance on the quarterdeck and made his way towards Bush.

"You're not my relief," said Bush.

"Yes I am. Captain's orders."

Hornblower spoke without any expression—Bush was used to the ship's officers by now being as guarded as that, and he knew why it was. But his curiosity made him ask the question.

"Why?"

"I'm on watch and watch," said Hornblower stolidly. "Until further orders."

He looked at the horizon as he spoke, showing no sign of emotion.

"Hard luck," said Bush, and for a moment felt a twinge of doubt as to whether he had not ventured too far in offering such an expression of sympathy. But no one was within earshot.

"No wardroom liquor for me," went on Hornblower, "until further orders either. Neither my own nor anyone else's."

For some officers that would be a worse punishment than being put on watch and watch—four hours on duty and four hours off day and night—but Bush did not know enough about Hornblower's habits to judge whether this was the case with him. He was about to say "hard luck" again, when at that moment a wild cry of pain reached their ears, cutting its way through the whistling wind. A moment later it was repeated, with even greater intensity. Hornblower was looking out at the horizon and his expression did not change. Bush watched his face and decided not to pay attention to the cries.

"Hard luck," he said.

"It might be worse," said Hornblower.

THREE

It was Sunday morning. The *Renown* had caught the northeast trades and was plunging across the Atlantic at her best speed, with studding sails set on both sides, the roaring trades driving her along with a steady pitch and heave, her bluff bows now and then raising a smother of spray that supported momentary rainbows. The rigging was piping loud and clear, the treble and the tenor to the baritone and bass of the noises of the ship's fabric as she pitched—a symphony of the sea. A few clouds of startling white dotted the blue of the sky, and the sun shone down from among them, revivifying and rejuvenating, reflected in dancing facets from the imperial blue of the sea.

The ship was a thing of exquisite beauty in an exquisite setting, and her bluff bows and her rows of guns added something else to the picture. She was a magnificent fighting machine, the mistress of the waves over which she was sailing in solitary grandeur. Her very solitude told the story; with the fleets of her enemies cooped up in port, blockaded by vigilant squadrons eager to come to grips with them, the *Renown* could sail the seas in utter confidence that she had nothing to fear. No furtive blockade-runner could equal her in strength; nowhere at sea was there a hostile squadron which could face her in battle. She could flout the hostile coasts; with the enemy blockaded and helpless she could bring her ponderous might to bear in a blow struck wherever she might choose. At this moment she was heading to strike such a blow, perhaps, despatched across the ocean at the word of the Lords of the Admiralty.

And drawn up in ranks on her maindeck was the ship's company, the men whose endless task it was to keep this fabric at the highest efficiency, to repair the constant inroads made upon her material by sea and weather and the mere passage of time. The snow-white decks, the bright paint-work, the exact and orderly arrangement of the lines and ropes and spars, were proofs of the diligence of their work; and when the time should come for the *Renown* to deliver the ultimate argument regarding the sovereignty of the seas, it would be they who would man the guns—the *Renown* might be a magnificent fighting machine, but she was so only by virtue of the frail humans who handled her.

They, like the *Renown* herself, were only cogs in the greater machine which was the Royal Navy, and most of them, caught up in the time-honoured routine and discipline of the service, were content to be cogs, to wash decks and set up rigging, to point guns or to charge with cutlasses over hostile bulwarks, with little thought as to whether the ship's bows were headed north or south, whether it was Frenchman or Spaniard or Dutchman who received their charge. Today only the captain knew the mission upon which the Lords of the Admiralty—presumably in consultation with the Cabinet—had despatched the *Renown*. There had been the vague knowledge that she was headed for the West Indies, but whereabouts in that area, and what she was intended to do there was known only to one man in the seven hundred and forty on the *Renown's* decks.

Every possible man was drawn up on this Sunday morning on the maindeck, not merely the two watches, but every "idler" who had no place in the watches—the holders, who did their work so far below decks that for some of them it was literally true that they did not see the sun from one week's end to another, the cooper and his mates, the armourer and his mates, sail-maker and cook and stewards, all in their best clothes with the officers with their cocked hats and swords beside their divisions. Only the officer of the watch and his assistant warrant officer, the quartermasters at the wheel and the dozen hands necessary for lookouts and to handle the ship in a very sudden emergency were not included in the ranks that were drawn up in the waist at rigid attention, the lines swaying easily and simultaneously with the motion of the ship.

It was Sunday morning, and every hat was off, every head was bare as the ship's company listened to the words of the captain. But it was no church service; these bareheaded men were not worshipping their Maker. That could happen on three Sundays in every month, but on those Sundays there would not be quite such a strict inquisition throughout the ship to compel the attendance of every hand—and a tolerant Admiralty had lately decreed that Catholics and Jews and even Dissenters might be excused from attending church services. This was the fourth Sunday, when the worship of God was set aside in favour of a ceremonial more strict, more solemn, calling for the same clean shirts and bared heads, but not for the downcast eyes of the men in the ranks. Instead every man was looking to his front as he held his hat before him with the wind ruffling his hair; he was listening to laws as all-embracing as the Ten Commandments, to a code as rigid as Leviticus, because on the fourth Sunday of every month it was the captain's duty to read the Articles of War aloud to the ship's company, so that not even the illiterates could plead ignorance of them; a religious captain might squeeze in a brief church service as well, but the Articles of War had to be read.

The captain turned a page.

"Nineteenth Article," he read. "If any person in or belonging to the fleet shall make or endeavour to make any mutinous assembly upon any offence whatsoever, every person offending therein, and being convicted by the sentence of the court-martial, shall suffer death."

Bush, standing by his division, heard these words as he had heard them scores of times before. He had, in fact, heard them so often that he usually listened to them with inattention; the words of the previous eighteen articles had flowed past him practically without his hearing them. But he heard this Nineteenth Article distinctly; it was possible that the captain read it with special emphasis, and in addition Bush, raising his eyes in the blessed sunshine, caught sight of Hornblower, the officer of the watch, standing at the quarterdeck rail listening as well. And there was that word "death." It struck Bush's ear with special emphasis, as emphatic and as final as the sound of a stone dropped into a well, which was strange, for the other articles which the captain had read had used the word freely—death for holding back from danger, death for sleeping while on duty.

The captain went on reading.

"And if any person shall utter any words of sedition or mutiny he shall suffer death. . . .

"And if any officer, mariner, or soldier shall behave himself with contempt to his superior officer . . ."

Those words had a fuller meaning for Bush now, with Hornblower looking down at him; he felt a strange stirring within him. He looked at the captain, unkempt and seedy in his appearance, and went back in his memory through the events of the past few days; if ever a man had shown himself unfit for duty it was the captain, but he was maintained in his position of unlimited power by these Articles of War which he was reading. Bush glanced up at Hornblower again; he felt that he knew for certain what Hornblower was thinking about as he stood there by the quarterdeck rail, and it was strange to feel this sympathy with the ungainly angular young lieutenant with whom he had had such little contact.

"And if any officer, mariner, or soldier or other person in the fleet—" the captain had reached the Twenty-Second Article now—"shall presume to quarrel with any of his superior officers, or shall disobey any lawful command, every such person shall suffer death."

Bush had not realised before how the Articles of War harped on this subject. He had served contentedly under discipline, and had always philosophically assured himself that injustice or mismanagement could be lived through. He could see now very special reasons why they should be. And as if to clinch the argument, the captain was now reading the final Article of War, the one which filled in every gap.

"All other crimes committed by any person or persons in the fleet which are not mentioned in this Act . . ."

Bush remembered that article; by its aid an officer could accomplish the ruin of an inferior who was clever enough to escape being pinned down by any of the others.

The captain read the final solemn words and looked up from the page. The big nose turned like a gun being trained round as he looked at each officer in turn; his face with its unshaven cheeks bore an expression of coarse triumph. It was as if he had gained by this reading of the Articles reassurance regarding his fears. He inflated his chest; he seemed to rise on tiptoe to make his concluding speech.

"I'll have you all know that these Articles apply to my officers as much as to anyone else."

Those were words which Bush could hardly believe he had heard. It was incredible that a captain could say such a thing in his crew's hearing. If ever a speech was subversive of discipline it was this one. But the captain merely went on with routine.

"Carry on, Mr. Buckland."

"Aye aye, sir." Buckland took a pace forward in the grip of routine himself.

"On hats!"

Officers and men covered their heads now that the ceremonial was completed.

"Division officers, dismiss your divisions!"

The musicians of the marine band had been waiting for this moment. The drum sergeant waved his baton and the drumsticks crashed down on the side drums in a long roll. Piercing and sweet the fifes joined in —"The Irish Washerwoman," jerky and inspiriting. Smack—smack—smack; the marine soldiers brought their ordered muskets up to their shoulders. Whiting, the captain of marines, shouted the orders which sent the scarlet lines marching and countermarching in the sunshine over the limited area of the quarterdeck.

The captain had been standing by watching this orderly progress of the ship's routine. Now he raised his voice.

"Mr. Buckland!"

"Sir!"

The captain mounted a couple of steps of the quarterdeck ladder so that he might be clearly seen, and raised his voice so that as many as possible could hear his words.

"Rope yarn Sunday today."

"Aye aye, sir."

"And double rum for these good men."

"Aye aye, sir."

Buckland did his best to keep the discontent out of his voice. Coming on top of the captain's previous speech this was almost too much. A rope yarn Sunday meant that the men would spend the rest of the day in idleness. Double rum in that case most certainly meant fights and quarrels among the men. Bush, coming aft along the maindeck, was well aware of the disorder that was spreading among the crew, pampered by their captain. It was impossible to maintain discipline when every adverse report made by the officers was ignored by the captain. Bad characters and idlers were going unpunished; the willing hands were beginning to sulk while the unruly ones were growing openly restless. "These good men," the captain had said. The men knew well enough how bad their record had been during the last week. If the captain called them "good men" after that, worse still could be expected next week. And besides all this the men most certainly knew about the captain's treatment of his lieutenants, of the brutal reprimands dealt out to them, the savage punishments. "Today's wardroom joint is tomorrow's lower deck stew," said the proverb, meaning that whatever went on aft was soon being discussed in a garbled form forward; the men could not be expected to be obedient to officers whom they knew to be treated with contempt by the captain. Bush was worried as he mounted the quarterdeck.

The captain had gone in under the half-deck to his cabin; Buckland and Roberts were standing by the hammock nettings deep in conversation, and Bush joined them.

"These articles apply to my officers," said Buckland as he approached.

"Rope yarn Sunday and double rum," added Roberts. "All for these good men."

Buckland shot a furtive glance round the deck before he spoke next. It was pitiful to see the first lieutenant of a ship of the line taking precautions lest what he should say should be overheard. But Hornblower and Wellard were on the other side of the wheel. On the poop the master was assembling the midshipmen's navigation class with their sextants to take their noon sights.

"He's mad," said Buckland in as low a voice as the northeast trade wind would allow.

"We all know that," said Roberts.

Bush said nothing. He was too cautious to commit himself at present.

"Clive won't lift a finger," said Buckland. "He's a ninny if there ever was one."

Clive was the surgeon.

"Have you asked him?" asked Roberts.

"I tried to. But he wouldn't say a word. He's afraid."

"Don't move from where you are standing, gentlemen," broke in a loud harsh voice; the well-remembered voice of the captain, speaking apparently from the level of the deck on which they stood. All three officers started in surprise.

"Every sign of guilt," blared the voice. "Bear witness to it, Mr. Hobbs."

They looked round them. The skylight of the captain's fore cabin was open a couple of inches, and through the gap the captain was looking at them; they could see his eyes and his nose. He was a tall man and by standing on anything low, a book or a footstool, he could look from under the skylight over the coaming. Rigid, the officers waited while another pair of eyes appeared under the skylight beside the captain's. They belonged to Hobbs, the acting-gunner.

"Wait there until I come to you, gentlemen," said the captain with a sneer as he said the word "gentlemen." "Very good, Mr. Hobbs."

The two faces vanished from under the skylight, and the officers had hardly time to exchange despairing glances before the captain came striding up the ladder to them.

"A mutinous assembly, I believe," he said.

"No, sir," replied Buckland. Any word that was not a denial would be an admission of guilt, on a charge that could put a rope round his neck.

"Do you give me the lie on my own quarterdeck?" roared the captain. "I was right in suspecting my officers. Plotting. Whispering. Scheming. Planning. And now treating me with gross disrespect. I'll see that you regret this from this minute, Mr. Buckland."

"I intended no disrespect, sir," protested Buckland.

"You give me the lie again to my face! And you others stand by and abet him! You keep him in countenance! I thought better of you, Mr. Bush, until now."

Bush thought it wise to say nothing.

"Dumb insolence, eh?" said the captain. "Eager enough to talk when you think my eye isn't on you, all the same."

The captain glowered round the quarterdeck.

"And you, Mr. Hornblower," he said. "You did not see fit to report this assembly to me. Officer of the watch, indeed! And of course Wellard is in it too. That is only to be expected. But I fancy you will be in trouble with these gentlemen now, Mr. Wellard. You did not keep a sharp enough lookout for them. In fact you are in serious trouble now, Mr. Wellard, without a friend in the ship except for the gunner's daughter, whom you will be kissing again soon."

The captain stood towering on the quarterdeck with his gaze fixed on the unfortunate Wellard, who shrank visibly away from him. To kiss the gunner's daughter was to be bent over a gun and beaten.

"But later will still be sufficient time to deal with you, Mr. Wellard. The lieutenants first, as their lofty rank dictates."

The captain looked round at the lieutenants, fear and triumph strangely alternating in his expression.

"Mr. Hornblower is already on watch and watch," he said. "You others have enjoyed idleness in consequence, and Satan found mischief for your idle hands. Mr. Buckland does not keep a watch. The high and mighty and aspiring first lieutenant."

"Sir—" began Buckland, and then bit off the words which were about to follow. That word "aspiring" undoubtedly implied that he was scheming to gain command of the ship, but a court-martial would not read that meaning into it. Every officer was expected to be an aspiring officer and it would be no insult to say so.

"Sir!" jeered the captain. "Sir! So you have grace enough still to guard your tongue. Cunning, maybe. But you will not evade the consequences of your actions. Mr. Hornblower can stay on watch and watch. But these two gentlemen can report to you when every watch is called, and at two bells, at four bells, and at six bells in every watch. They are to be properly dressed when they report to you, and you are to be properly awake. Is that understood?"

Not one of the dumfounded trio could speak for a moment.

"Answer me!"

"Aye aye, sir," said Buckland.

"Aye aye, sir," said Bush and Roberts as the captain turned his eyes on them.

"Let there be no slackness in the execution of my orders," said the captain. "I shall have means of knowing if I am obeyed or not."

"Aye aye, sir," said Buckland.

The captain's sentence had condemned him, Bush, and Roberts to be roused and awakened every hour, day and night.

FOUR

IT WAS PITCH DARK down here, absolutely dark, not the tiniest glimmer of light at all. Out over the sea was the moonless night, and here it was three decks down, below the level of the sea's surface—through the oaken skin of the ship could be heard the rush of the water alongside, and the impact of the waves over which the ship rode; the fabric of the ship grumbled to itself with the alternating stresses of the pitch and the roll. Bush hung onto the steep ladder in the darkness and felt for foothold; finding it, he stepped off among the water barrels, and, crouching low, he began to make his way aft through the solid blackness. A rat squeaked and scurried past him, but rats were only to be expected down here in the hold, and Bush went on feeling his way aft unshaken. Out of the blackness before him, through the multitudinous murmurings of the ship, came a slight hiss, and Bush halted and hissed in reply. He was not self-conscious about these conspiratorial goings on. All precautions were necessary, for this was something very dangerous that he was doing.

"Bush!" whispered Buckland's voice.

"Yes."

"The others are here."

Ten minutes before, at two bells in the middle watch, Bush and Roberts had reported to Buckland in his cabin in obedience to the captain's order. A wink, a gesture, a whisper, and the appointment to meet here was made; it was an utterly fantastic state of affairs that the lieutenants of a King's ship should have to act in such a fashion for fear of spies and eavesdroppers, but it had been necessary. Then they had dispersed and by devious routes and different hatchways had made their way here. Hornblower, relieved by Smith on watch, had preceded them.

"We mustn't be here long," whispered Roberts.

Even by his whisper, even in the dark, one could guess at his nervousness. There could be no doubt about this being a mutinous assembly. They could all hang for what they were doing.

"Suppose we declare him unfit for command?" whispered Buckland. "Suppose we put him in irons?"

"We'd have to do it quick and sharp if we do it at all," whispered Hornblower. "He'll call on the hands and they might follow him. And then—"

There was no need for Hornblower to go on with that speech. Everyone who heard it formed a mental picture of corpses swaying at the yard-arms.

"Supposing we do it quick and sharp?" agreed Buckland. "Supposing we get him into irons?"

"Then we go on to Antigua," said Roberts.

"And a court-martial," said Bush, thinking as far ahead as that for the first time in this present crisis.

"Yes," whispered Buckland.

Into that flat monosyllable were packed various moods—inquiry and despair, desperation and doubt.

"That's the point," whispered Hornblower. "He'll give evidence. It'll sound different in court. We've been punished—watch and watch, no liquor. That could happen to anybody. It's no grounds for mutiny."

"But he's spoiling the hands."

"Double rum. Make and mend. It'll sound quite natural in court. It's not for us to criticise the captain's methods—so the court will think."

"But they'll see him."

"He's cunning. And he's no raving lunatic. He can talk—he can find reasons for everything. You've heard him. He'll be plausible."

"But he's held us up to contempt before the hands. He's set Hobbs to spy on us."

"That'll be a proof of how desperate his situation was, surrounded by us criminals. If we arrest him we're guilty until we've proved ourselves innocent. Any court's bound to be on the captain's side. Mutiny means hanging."

Hornblower was putting into words all the doubts that Bush felt in his bones and yet had been unable to express.

"That's right," whispered Bush.

"What about Wellard?" whispered Roberts. "Did you hear him scream the last time?"

"He's only a volunteer. Not even a midshipman. No friends. No family. What's the court going to say when they hear the captain had a boy beaten half a dozen times? They'll laugh. So would we if we didn't know. Do him good, we'd say, the same as it did the rest of us good."

A silence followed this statement of the obvious, broken in the end by Buckland whispering a succession of filthy oaths that could give small vent to his despair.

"He'll bring charges against us," whispered Roberts. "The minute we're in company with other ships. I know he will."

"Twenty two years I've held my commission," said Buckland. "Now he'll break me. He'll break you as well."

There would be no chance at all for officers charged before a court-martial by their captain with behaving with contempt towards him in a manner subversive of discipline. Every single one of them knew that. It gave an edge to their despair. Charges pressed by the captain with the insane venom and cunning he had displayed up to now might not even end in dismissal from the service—they might lead to the prison and the rope.

"Ten more days before we make Antigua," said Roberts. "If this wind holds fair—and it will."

"But we don't know we're destined for Antigua," said Hornblower. "That's only our guess. It might be weeks—it might be months."

"God help us!" said Buckland.

A slight clatter farther aft along the hold—a noise different from the noises of the working of the ship—made them all start. Bush clenched his hairy fists. But they were reassured by a voice calling softly to them.

"Mr. Buckland—Mr. Hornblower—sir!"

"Wellard, by God!" said Roberts.

They could hear Wellard scrambling towards them.

"The captain, sir!" said Wellard. "He's coming!"

"Holy God!"

"Which way?" snapped Hornblower.

"By the steerage hatchway. I got to the cockpit and came down from there. He was sending Hobbs—"

"Get for'rard, you three," said Hornblower, cutting into the explanation. "Get for'rard and scatter when you're on deck. Quick!"

Nobody stopped to think that Hornblower was giving orders to officers immensely his senior. Every instant of time was of vital importance, and not to be wasted in indecision, or in silly blasphemy. That was apparent as soon as he spoke. Bush turned with the others and plunged forward in the darkness, barking his shins painfully as he fell over unseen obstructions. Bush heard Hornblower say "Come along, Wellard" as he parted from them in his mad flight with the others beside him.

The cable tier—the ladder—and then the extraordinary safety of the lower gundeck. After the utter blackness of the hold there was enough light here for him to see fairly distinctly. Buckland and Roberts continued to ascend to the maindeck; Bush turned to make his way aft. The watch below had been in their hammocks long enough to be sound asleep; here to the noises of the ship was added the blended snoring of the sleepers as the close-hung rows of hammocks swayed with the motion of the ship in such a coincidence of timing as to appear like solid masses. Far down between the rows a light was approaching. It was a horn lantern with a lighted purser's dip inside it, and Hobbs the acting-gunner was carrying it, and two seamen were following him as he hurried along. There was an exchange of glances as Bush met the party. A momentary hesitation on Hobbs' part betrayed the fact that he would have greatly liked to ask Bush what he was doing on the lower gundeck, but that was something no acting warrant officer, even with the captain's favour behind him, could ask of a lieutenant. And there was annoyance in Hobbs' expression, too; obviously he was hurrying to secure all the exits from the hold, and was exasperated that Bush had escaped him. The seamen wore expressions of simple bewilderment at these goings on in the middle watch. Hobbs stood aside to let his superior pass, and Bush strode past him with no more than that one glance. It was extraordinary how much more confident he felt now that he was safely out of the hold and disassociated from any mutinous assembly. He decided to head for his cabin; it would not be long before four bells when by the captain's orders he had to report again to Buckland. The messenger sent by the officer of the watch to rouse him would find him lying on his cot. But as Bush went on and had progressed as far as the mainmast he arrived in the midst of a scene of bustle which he would most certainly have taken notice of if he had been innocent and which consequently he must (so he told himself) ask about now that he had seen it—he could not possibly walk by without a question or two. This was where the marines were berthed, and they were all of them out of their hammocks hastily equipping themselves—those who had their shirts and trousers on were putting on their crossbelts ready for action.

"What's all this?" demanded Bush, trying to make his voice sound as it would have sounded if he had no knowledge of anything irregular happening in the ship except this.

"Dunno, sir," said the private he addressed. "We was just told to turn out—muskets an' side arms and ball cartridge, sir."

A sergeant of marines looked out through the screen which divided the non-commissioned officers' bay from the rest of the deck.

"Captain's orders, sir," he said, and then with a roar at the men, "Come on! Slap it about, there!"

"Where's the captain, then?" asked Bush with all the innocence he could muster.

"Aft some 'eres, sir. 'E sent for the corpr'il's guard same time as we was told to turn out."

Four marine privates and a corporal supplied the sentry who stood day and night outside the captain's cabin. A single order was all that was needed to turn out the guard and provide the captain with at least a nucleus of armed and disciplined men ready for action.

"Very well, sergeant," said Bush, and he tried to look puzzled and to hurry naturally aft to find out what was going on. But he knew what fear was. He felt he would do anything rather than continue this walk to encounter whatever was awaiting him at the end of it. Whiting, the captain of marines, made his appearance, sleepy and unshaven, belting on his sword over his shirt.

"What in hell—?" he began, as he saw Bush.

"Don't ask *me!*" said Bush, striving after that natural appearance. So tense and desperate was he at that moment that his normally quiescent imagination was hard at work. He could imagine the prosecutor in the deceptive calm of a court-martial saying to Whiting, "Did Mr. Bush appear to be his usual self?" and it was frightfully necessary that Whiting should be able to answer, "Yes." Bush could even imagine the hairy touch of a rope round his neck. But next moment there was no more need for him to simulate surprise or ignorance. His reactions were genuine.

"Pass the word for the doctor," came the cry. "Pass the word, there."

And here came Wellard, white-faced, hurrying.

"Pass the word for the doctor. Call Dr. Clive."

"Who's hurt, Wellard?" asked Bush.

"The c–captain, sir."

Wellard looked distraught and shaken, but now Hornblower made his appearance behind him. Hornblower was pale, too, and breathing hard, but he seemed to have command of himself. The glance which he threw round him in the dim light of the lanterns passed over Bush without apparent recognition.

"Get Dr. Clive!" he snapped at one midshipman peering out from the midshipmen's berth, and then to another: "You, there. Run for the first lieutenant. Ask him to come below here. Run!"

Hornblower's glance took in Whiting and travelled forward to where the marines were snatching their muskets from the racks.

"Why are your men turning out, Captain Whiting?"

"Captain's orders."

"Then you can form them up. But I do not believe there is any emergency."

Only then did Hornblower's glance comprehend Bush.

"Oh, Mr. Bush. Will you take charge, sir, now that you're here? I've sent for the first lieutenant. The captain's hurt—badly hurt, I'm afraid, sir."

"But what's happened?" asked Bush.

"The captain's fallen down the hatchway, sir," said Hornblower.

In the dim light Hornblower's eyes stared straight into Bush's, but Bush could read no message in them. This after part of the lower gun-deck was crowded now, and Hornblower's definite statement, the first that had been made, raised a buzz of excitement. It was the sort of undisciplined noise that most easily roused Bush's wrath, and, perhaps fortunately, it brought a natural reaction from him.

"Silence, there!" he roared. "Get about your business."

When Bush glowered round at the excited crowd it fell silent.

"With your permission I'll go below again, sir," said Hornblower. "I must see after the captain."

"Very well, Mr. Hornblower," said Bush; the stereotyped phrase had been uttered so often before that it escaped sounding stilted.

"Come with me, Mr. Wellard," said Hornblower, and turned away.

Several new arrivals made their appearance as he did so—Buckland, his face white and strained, Roberts at his shoulder, Clive in his shirt and trousers walking sleepily from his cabin. All of them started a little at the sight of the marines forming line on the cumbered deck, their musket barrels glinting in the feeble light of the lanterns.

"Would you come at once, sir?" asked Hornblower, turning back at sight of Buckland.

"I'll come," said Buckland.

"What in the name of God is going on?" asked Clive.

"The captain's hurt," said Hornblower curtly. "Come at once. You'll need a light."

"The captain?" Clive blinked himself wider awake. "Where is he? Give me that lantern, you. Where are my mates? You, there, run and rouse my mates. They sling their hammocks in the sick bay."

So it was a procession of half a dozen that carried their lanterns down the ladder—the four lieutenants, Clive, and Wellard. While waiting at the head of the ladder Bush stole a side glance at Buckland; his face was working with anxiety. He would infinitely rather have been walking a shot-torn deck with grape flying round him. He rolled an inquiring eye at Bush, but with Clive within earshot Bush dared say no word—he knew no more than Buckland did, for that matter. There was no knowing what was awaiting them at the foot of the ladder—arrest, ruin, disgrace, perhaps death.

The faint light of a lantern revealed the scarlet tunic and white cross-belts of a marine, standing by the hatchway. He wore the chevrons of a corporal.

"Anything to report?" demanded Hornblower.

"No, sir. Nothink, sir."

"Captain's down there unconscious. There are two marines guarding him," said Hornblower to Clive, pointing down the hatchway, and Clive swung his bulk painfully onto the ladder and descended.

"Now, corporal," said Hornblower. "Tell the first lieutenant all you know about this."

The corporal stood stiffly at attention. With no fewer than four lieutenants eyeing him he was nervous, and he probably had a gloomy feeling based on his experience of the service that when there was trouble among the higher ranks it was likely to go ill with a mere corporal who was unfortunate enough to be involved, however innocently. He stood rigid, trying not to meet anybody's eye.

"Speak up, man," said Buckland, testily. He was nervous as well, but that was understandable in a first lieutenant whose captain had just met with a serious accident.

"I was corporal of the guard, sir. At two bells I relieved the sentry at the captain's door."

"Yes?"

"An'—an'—then I went to sleep again."

"Damn it," said Roberts. "Make your report."

"I was woke up, sir," went on the corporal, "by one of the gennelmen. Gunner, I think 'e is."

"Mr. Hobbs?"

"That may be 'is name, sir. 'E said, 'Cap'n's orders, and guard turn out.' So I turns out the guard, sir, an' there's the cap'n with Wade, the sentry I'd posted. 'E 'ad pistols in 'is 'ands, sir."

"Who—Wade?"

"No, sir, the cap'n, sir."

"What was his manner like?" demanded Hornblower.

"Well, sir—" the corporal did not want to offer any criticism of a captain, not even to a lieutenant.

"Belay that, then. Carry on."

"Cap'n says, sir, 'e says 'e says, sir, 'Follow me' an' then 'e says to the gennelman 'e says, 'Do your duty, Mr. Hobbs.' So Mr. Hobbs, 'e goes one way, sir, and we comes with the captain down 'ere, sir. 'There's mutiny brewing,' says the cap'n, 'black bloody mutiny. We've got to catch the mutineers. Catch 'em red 'anded,' says the cap'n."

The surgeon's head appeared in the hatchway.

"Give me another of those lanterns," he said.

"How's the captain?" demanded Buckland.

"Concussion and some fractures, I would say."

"Badly hurt?"

"No knowing yet. Where are my mates? Ah, there you are, Coleman. Splints and bandages, man, as quick as you can get 'em. And a carrying-plank and a canvas and lines. Run, man! You, Pierce, come on down and help me."

So the two surgeon's mates had hardly made their appearance than they were hurried away.

"Carry on, corporal," said Buckland.

"I dunno what I said, sir."

"The captain brought you down here."

"Yessir. 'E 'ad 'is pistols in 'is 'ands, sir, like I said, sir. 'E sent one file for'rard. 'Stop every bolt 'ol,' 'e says, an' 'e says 'You, corporal, take these two men down an' search.' 'E—'e was yellin', like. 'E 'ad 'is pistols in 'is 'ands."

The corporal looked anxiously at Buckland as he spoke.

"That's all right, corporal," said Buckland. "Just tell the truth."

The knowledge that the captain was unconscious and perhaps badly hurt had reassured him, just as it had reassured Bush.

"So I took the other file down the ladder, sir," said the corporal. "I went first with the lantern, seein' as 'ow I didn't 'ave no musket with me. We got down to the foot of the ladder in among those cases down there, sir. The cap'n, 'e was yellin' down the hatchway. ''Urry,' he says. ''Urry. Don't let 'em escape, 'Urry.' So we started climbin' for'rard over the stores, sir."

The corporal hesitated as he approached the climax of his story. He might possibly have been seeking a crude dramatic effect, but more likely he was still afraid of being entangled in circumstances that might damage him despite his innocence.

"What happened then?" demanded Buckland.

"Well, sir—"

Coleman reappeared at this moment, encumbered with various gear including a light six-foot plank he had been carrying on his shoulder. He looked to Buckland for permission to carry on, received a nod, laid the plank on the deck along with the canvas and lines, and disappeared with the rest down the ladder.

"Well?" said Buckland to the corporal.

"I dunno what 'appened, sir."

"Tell us what you know."

"I 'eard a yell, sir. An' a crash. I 'adn't 'ardly gone ten yards, sir. So I came back with the lantern."

"What did you find?"

"It was the cap'n, sir. Layin' there at the foot of the ladder. Like 'e was dead, sir. 'E'd fallen down the 'atchway, sir."

"What did you do?"

"I tried to turn 'im over, sir. 'Is face was all bloody-like. 'E was stunned, sir. I thought 'e might be dead but I could feel 'is 'eart."

"Yes?"

"I didn't know what I ought to do, sir. I didn't know nothink about this 'ere meeting, sir."

"But what *did* you do, in the end?"

"I left my two men with the cap'n, sir, an' I come up to give the alarm. I didn't know who to trust, sir."

There was irony in this situation—the corporal frightened lest he should be taken to task about a petty question as to whether he should have sent a messenger or come himself, while the four lieutenants eyeing him were in danger of hanging.

"Well?"

"I saw Mr. Hornblower, sir." The relief in the corporal's voice echoed the relief he must have felt at finding someone to take over his enormous responsibility. "'E was with young Mr. Wellard, I think 'is name is. Mr. Hornblower, 'e told me to stand guard 'ere, sir, after I told 'im about the cap'n."

"It sounds as if you did right, corporal," said Buckland, judicially.

"Thank 'ee, sir. Thank 'ee, sir."

Coleman came climbing up the ladder, and with another glance at Buckland for permission passed the gear he had left down to someone else under the hatchway. Then he descended again. Bush was looking at the corporal who, now his tale was told, was self-consciously awkward again under the concentrated gaze of four lieutenants.

"Now, corporal," said Hornblower, speaking unexpectedly and with deliberation. "You have no idea how the captain came to fall down the hatchway?"

"No, sir. Indeed I haven't, sir."

Hornblower shot one single glance at his colleagues, one and no more. The corporal's words and Hornblower's glance were vastly reassuring.

"He was excited, you say? Come on, man, speak up."

"Well, yessir." The corporal remembered his earlier unguarded statement, and then in a sudden flood of loquacity he went on. "'E was yellin' after us down the hatchway, sir. I expect 'e was leanin' over. 'E must 'ave been leanin' when the ship pitched, sir. 'E could catch 'is foot on the coamin' and fall 'ead first, sir."

"That's what must have happened," said Hornblower.

Clive came climbing up the ladder and stepped stiffly over the coaming.

"I'm going to sway him up now," he said. He looked at the four lieutenants and then put his hand in the bosom of his shirt and took out a pistol. "This was lying at the captain's side."

"I'll take charge of that," said Buckland.

"There ought to be another one down there, judging by what we've just heard," said Roberts, speaking for the first time. He spoke overloudly, too; excitement had worked on him, and his manner might appear suspicious to anyone with anything to suspect. Bush felt a twinge of annoyance and fear.

"I'll have 'em look for it after we've got the captain up," said Clive. He leaned over the hatchway and called down, "Come on up."

Coleman appeared first, climbing the ladder with a pair of lines in his hand, and after him a marine, clinging awkwardly to the ladder with one arm while the other supported a burden below him.

"Handsomely, handsomely, now," said Clive.

Coleman and the marine, emerging, drew the end of the plank up after them; swathed mummy-like in the canvas and bound to the plank was the body of the captain. That was the best way in which to mount ladders carrying a man with broken bones. Pierce, the other surgeon's mate, came climbing up next, holding the foot of the plank steady. The lieutenants clustered round to give a hand as the plank was hoisted over the coaming. In the light of the lanterns Bush could see the captain's face above the canvas. It was still and expressionless, what there was to be seen of it, for a white bandage concealed one eye and the nose. One temple was still stained with the traces of blood which the doctor had not entirely wiped away.

"Take him to his cabin," said Buckland.

That was the definitive order. This was an important moment. The captain being incapacitated, it was the first lieutenant's duty to take command, and those five words indicated that he had done so. In command, he could even give orders for dealing with the captain. But although this was a momentous step, it was one of routine; Buckland had assumed temporary command of the ship, during the captain's absences, a score of times before. Routine had carried him through this present crisis; the habits of thirty years of service in the navy, as midshipman and lieutenant, had enabled him to carry himself with his usual bearing towards his juniors, to act normally even though he did not know what dreadful fate awaited him at any moment in the immediate future.

And yet Bush, turning his eyes on him now that he had assumed command, was not too sure about the permanence of the effect of habit. Buckland was clearly a little shaken. That might be attributed to the natural reaction of an officer with responsibility thrust upon him in such startling circumstances. So an unsuspicious person—someone without knowledge of the hidden facts—might conclude. But Bush, with fear in his heart, wondering and despairing about what the captain would do when he recovered consciousness, could see that Buckland shared his fear. Chains—a court-martial—the hangman's rope; thoughts of these were unmanning Buckland. And the lives, certainly the whole futures, of the officers in the ship might depend on Buckland's actions.

"Pardon, sir," said Hornblower.

"Yes?" said Buckland, and then with an effort, "Yes, Mr. Hornblower?"

"Might I take the corporal's statement in writing now, while the facts are clear in his memory?"

"Very good, Mr. Hornblower."

"Thank you, sir," said Hornblower. There was nothing to be read in his expression at all, nothing except a respectful attention to duty. He turned to the corporal. "Report to me in my berth after you have reposted the sentry."

"Yessir."

The doctor and his party had already carried the captain away. Buckland was making no effort to move from the spot. It was as if he were paralysed.

"There's the matter of the captain's other pistol, sir," said Hornblower respectfully as ever.

"Oh yes." Buckland looked round him.

"Here's Wellard, sir."

"Oh yes. He'll do."

"Mr. Wellard," said Hornblower, "go down with a lantern and see if you can find the other pistol. Bring it to the first lieutenant on the quarterdeck."

"Aye aye, sir."

Wellard had recovered from most of his agitation; he had not taken his eyes from Hornblower for some time. Now he picked up the lantern and went down the ladder with it. What Hornblower had said about the quarterdeck penetrated into Buckland's mind, and he began to move off with the others following him. On the lower gundeck Captain Whiting saluted him.

"Any orders, sir?"

No doubt the word that the captain was incapacitated and that Buckland was in command had sped through the ship like wildfire. It took Buckland's numbed brain a second or two to function.

"No, Captain," he said at length, and then "Dismiss your men."

When they reached the quarterdeck the trade wind was still blowing briskly from over the starboard quarter, and the *Renown* was soaring along over the magic sea. Over their heads the great pyramids of sails were reaching up—up—up towards the uncounted stars; with the easy motion of the ship the mastheads were sweeping out great circles against the sky. On the port quarter a half-moon had just lifted itself out of the sea and hung, miraculously, above the horizon, sending a long glittering trail of silver towards the ship. The dark figures of the men on deck stood out plainly against the whitened planks.

Smith was officer of the watch. He came eagerly up to them as they came up the companionway. For the last hour and more he had been pacing about in a fever, hearing the noise and bustle down below, hearing the rumours which had coursed through the ship, and yet unable to leave his post to find out what was really going on.

"What's happened, sir?" he asked.

Smith had not been in the secret of the meeting of the other lieutenants. He had been less victimised by the captain, too. But he could not help being aware of the prevailing discontent; he must know that the captain was insane. Yet Buckland was not prepared for his question. He had not thought about how to tell the news, and he stood stock-still while Smith awaited his reply. In the end it was Hornblower who answered.

"The captain fell down the hold," he said; his tone was even and with no particular stress. "They've just carried him to his cabin unconscious."

"But how in God's name did he come to fall down the hold?" asked the bewildered Smith.

"He was looking for mutineers," said Hornblower, in that same even tone.

"I see," said Smith. "But—"

There he checked himself. That even tone of Hornblower's had warned him that this was a delicate subject; if he pursued it the question of the captain's sanity would arise, and he would be committed to an opinion on it. He did not want to ask any more questions in that case.

"Six bells, sir," reported the quartermaster to him.

"Very good," said Smith, automatically.

"I must take the marine corporal's deposition, sir," said Hornblower. "I come on watch at eight bells."

If Buckland were in command he could put an end to the ridiculous order that Hornblower should stand watch and watch, and that Bush and Roberts should report to him hourly. There was a moment's awkward pause. No one knew how long the captain would remain unconscious, nor in what condition he would regain consciousness. Wellard came running up to the quarterdeck.

"Here's the other pistol, sir," he said, handing it to Buckland, who took it, at the same time drawing its fellow from his pocket; he stood rather helplessly with them in his hands.

"Shall I relieve you of those, sir?" asked Hornblower, taking them. "And Wellard might be of help to me with the marine's deposition. Can I take him with me, sir?"

"Yes," said Buckland.

Hornblower turned to go below, followed by Wellard.

"Oh, Mr. Hornblower—" said Buckland.

"Sir?"

"Nothing," said Buckland, the inflection in his voice revealing the indecision under which he laboured.

"Pardon, sir, but I should take some rest if I were you," said Hornblower, standing at the head of the companionway. "You've had a tiring night."

Bush was in agreement with Hornblower; not that he cared at all whether Buckland had had a tiring night or not, but because if Buckland were to retire to his cabin there would be no chance of his betraying himself—and his associates—by an unguarded speech. Then it dawned upon Bush that this was just what Hornblower had in mind. And at the same time he was aware of regret at Hornblower's leaving them, and knew that Buckland felt the same regret. Hornblower was levelheaded, thinking fast whatever danger menaced him. It was his example which had given a natural appearance to the behaviour of all of them since the alarm down below. Perhaps Hornblower had a secret unshared with them; perhaps he knew more than they did about how the captain came to fall down the hold—Bush was puzzled and anxious about that—but if such was the case Hornblower had given no sign of it.

"When in God's name is that damned doctor going to report?" said Buckland, to no one in particular.

"Why don't you turn in, sir, until he does?" said Bush.

"I will." Buckland hesitated before he went on speaking. "You gentlemen had best continue to report to me every hour as the captain ordered."

"Aye aye, sir," said Bush and Roberts.

That meant, as Bush realised, that Buckland would take no chances; the captain must hear, when he should recover consciousness, that his orders had been carried out. Bush was anxious—desperate—as he went below to try to snatch half an hour's rest before he would next have to report. He could not hope to sleep. Through the slight partition that divided his cabin from the next he could hear a drone of voices as Hornblower took down the marine corporal's statement in writing.

FIVE

Breakfast was being served in the wardroom. It was a more silent and less cheerful meal even than breakfast there usually was. The master, the purser, the captain of marines, had said their conventional "good mornings" and had sat down to eat without further conversation. They had heard—as had everyone in the ship—that the captain was recovering consciousness.

Through the scuttles in the side of the ship came two long shafts of sunlight, illuminating the crowded little place, and swinging back and forward across the wardroom with the easy motion of the ship; the fresh, delightful air of the northeast trades came in through the hooked-open door. The coffee was hot; the biscuit, only three weeks on board, could not have been more than a month or two in store before that, because it had hardly any weevils in it. The wardroom cook had intelligently taken advantage of the good weather to fry the remains of last night's salt pork with some of the ship's dwindling store of onions. A breakfast of fried slivers of salt pork with onions, hot coffee and good biscuit, fresh air and sunshine and fair weather; the wardroom should have been a cheerful place. Instead there was brooding anxiety, apprehension, tense uneasiness. Bush looked across the table at Hornblower, drawn and pale and weary; there were many things Bush wanted to say to him but they had to remain unsaid, at least at present, while the shadow of the captain's madness darkened the sunlit ship.

Buckland came walking into the wardroom with the surgeon following him, and everyone looked up questioningly—practically everyone stood up to hear the news.

"He's conscious," said Buckland, and looked round at Clive for him to elaborate on that statement.

"Weak," said Clive.

Bush looked round at Hornblower, hoping that he would ask the questions that Bush wanted asked. Hornblower's face was set in a mask without expression. His glance was fixed penetratingly on Clive, but he did not open his mouth. It was Lomax the purser who asked the question in the end.

"Is he sensible?"

"Well—" said Clive, glancing sidelong at Buckland. Clearly the last thing Clive wanted to do was to commit himself definitely regarding the captain's sanity. "He's too weak at present to be sensible."

Lomax fortunately was inquisitive enough and bullheaded enough not to be deterred by Clive's reluctance.

"What about this concussion?" he asked. "What's it done to him?"

"The skull is intact," said Clive. "There are extensive scalp lacerations. The nose is broken. The clavicle—that's the collarbone—and a couple of ribs. He must have fallen headfirst down the hatchway, as might be expected if he tripped over the coaming."

"But how on earth did he come to do that?" asked Lomax.

"He has not said," answered Clive. "I think he does not remember."

"What?"

"That is a usual state of affairs," said Clive. "One might almost call it symptomatic. After a severe concussion the patient usually displays a lapse of memory, extending back to many hours before the injury."

Bush stole a glance at Hornblower again. His face was still expressionless, and Bush tried to follow his example, both in betraying no emotion and in leaving the questioning to others. And yet this was great, glorious, magnificent news which could not be too much elaborated on for Bush's taste.

"Where does he think he is?" went on Lomax.

"Oh, he knows he's in this ship," said Clive, cautiously.

Now Buckland turned upon Clive; Buckland was hollow-cheeked, unshaven, weary, but he had seen the captain in his berth, and he was in consequence a little more ready to force the issue.

"In your opinion is the captain fit for duty?" he demanded.

"Well—" said Clive again.

"Well?"

"Temporarily, perhaps not."

That was an unsatisfactory answer, but Buckland seemed to have exhausted all his resolution in extracting it. Hornblower raised a mask-like face and stared straight at Clive.

"You mean he is incapable at present of commanding this ship?"

The other officers murmured their concurrence in this demand for a quite definite statement, and Clive, looking round at the determined faces, had to yield.

"At present, yes."

"Then we all know where we stand," said Lomax, and there was satisfaction in his voice which was echoed by everyone in the wardroom except Clive and Buckland.

To deprive a captain of his command was a business of terrible, desperate importance. King and Parliament had combined to give Captain Sawyer command of the *Renown,* and to reverse their appointment savoured of treason, and anyone even remotely connected with the transaction might be tainted for the rest of his life with the unsavoury odour of insubordination and rebellion. Even the most junior master's mate in later years applying for some new appointment might be remembered as having been in the *Renown* when Sawyer was removed from his command and might have his application refused in consequence. It was necessary that there should be the appearance of the utmost legality in an affair which, under the strictest interpretation, could never be entirely legal.

"I have here Corporal Greenwood's statement, sir," said Hornblower, "signed with his mark and attested by Mr. Wellard and myself."

"Thank you," said Buckland, taking the paper; there was some slight hesitation in Buckland's gesture as though the document were a firecracker likely to go off unexpectedly. But only Bush, who was looking for it, could have noticed the hesitation. It was only a few hours since Buckland had been a fugitive in peril of his life, creeping through the bowels of the ship trying to avoid detection, and the names of Wellard and Greenwood, reminding him of this, were a shock to his ears. And like a demon conjured up by the saying of his name, Wellard appeared at that moment at the wardroom door.

"Mr. Roberts sent me down to ask for orders, sir," he said.

Roberts had the watch, and must be fretting with worry about what was going on below decks. Buckland stood in indecision.

"Both watches are on deck, sir," said Hornblower, deferentially.

Buckland looked an inquiry at him.

"You could tell this news to the hands, sir," went on Hornblower.

He was making a suggestion, unasked, to his superior officer, and so courting a snub. But his manner indicated the deepest respect, and nothing besides, but eagerness to save his superior all possible trouble.

"Thank you," said Buckland.

Anyone could read in his face the struggle that was going on within him; he was still shrinking from committing himself too deeply—as if he was not already committed!—and he was shrinking from the prospect of making a speech to the assembled hands, even while he realised the necessity of doing so. And the necessity grew greater the more he thought about it—rumours must be flying about the lower deck, where the crew, already unsettled by the captain's behaviour, must be growing more restive still in the prevailing uncertainty. A hard, definite statement must be made to them; it was vitally necessary. Yet the greater the necessity the greater the responsibility that Buckland bore, and he wavered obviously between these two frightening forces.

"All hands, sir?" prompted Hornblower, very softly.

"Yes," said Buckland, desperately taking the plunge.

"Very well, Mr. Wellard," said Hornblower.

Bush caught the look that Hornblower threw to Wellard with the words. There was a significance in it which might be interpreted as of a nature only to be expected when one junior officer was telling another to do something quickly before a senior could change his mind—that was how an uninitiated person would naturally interpret it—but to Bush, clairvoyant with fatigue and worry, there was some other significance in that glance. Wellard was pale and weak with fatigue and worry too; he was being reassured. Possibly he was being told that a secret was still safe.

"Aye aye, sir," said Wellard, and departed.

The pipes twittered through the ship.

"All hands! All hands!" roared the bosun's mates. "All hands fall in abaft the mainmast! All hands!"

Buckland went nervously up on deck, but he acquitted himself well enough at the moment of trial. In a harsh expressionless voice he told the assembled hands that the accident to the captain, which they all must have heard about, had rendered him incapable at present of continuing in command.

"But we'll all go on doing our duty," said Buckland, staring down at the level plain of upturned faces.

Bush, looking with him, picked out the grey head and paunchy figure of Hobbs, the acting-gunner, the captain's toady and informer. Things would be different for Mr. Hobbs in future—at least as long as the captain's disability endured. That was the point; as long as the captain's disability endured. Bush looked down at Hobbs and wondered how much he knew, how much he guessed—how much he would swear to at a court-martial. He tried to read the future in the fat old man's face, but his clairvoyance failed him. He could guess nothing.

When the hands were dismissed there was a moment of bustle and confusion, as the watches resumed their duties and the idlers streamed off below. It was there, in the noise and confusion of a crowd, that momentary privacy and freedom from observation could best be found. Bush intercepted Hornblower by the mizzenmast bitts and could ask the question that he had been wanting to ask for hours; the question on which so much depended.

"How did it happen?" asked Bush.

The bosun's mates were bellowing orders; the hands were scurrying hither and thither; all round the two of them was orderly confusion, a mass of people intent on their own business, while they stood face to face, isolated, with the beneficent sunshine streaming down on them, lighting up the set face which Hornblower turned towards his questioner.

"How did *what* happen, Mr. Bush?" said Hornblower.

"How did the captain fall down the hatchway?"

As soon as he had said the words Bush glanced back over his shoulder in sudden fright lest he should have been overheard. These might be hanging words. When he looked back Hornblower's face was quite expressionless.

"I think he must have overbalanced," he said, evenly, looking straight into Bush's eyes, and then he went on, "If you will excuse me, sir, I have some duties to attend to."

Later in the day every wardroom officer was introduced in turn to the captain's cabin to see with his own eyes what sort of wreck lay there. Bush saw only a feeble invalid, lying in the half-light of the cabin, the face almost covered with bandages, the fingers of one hand moving minutely, the other hand concealed in a sling.

"He's under an opiate," explained Clive in the wardroom. "I had to administer a heavy dose to enable me to try and set the fractured nose."

"I expect it was spread all over his face," said Lomax brutally. "It was big enough."

"The fracture was very extensive and comminuted," agreed Clive.

There were screams the next morning from the captain's cabin, screams of terror as well as of pain, and Clive and his mates emerged eventually sweating and worried. Clive went instantly to report confidentially to Buckland, but everyone in the ship had heard those screams or had been told about them by men who had; the surgeon's mates, questioned eagerly in the gunroom by the other warrant officers, could not maintain the monumental discretion that Clive aimed at in the wardroom. The wretched invalid was undoubtedly insane; he had fallen into a paroxysm of terror when they had attempted to examine the fractured nose, flinging himself about with a madman's strength so that, fearing damage to the other broken bones, they had had to swathe him in canvas as in a strait jacket, leaving only his left arm out. Laudanum and an extensive bleeding had reduced him to insensibility in the end, but later in the day when Bush saw him he was conscious again, a weeping, pitiful object, shrinking in fear from every face that he saw, persecuted by shadows, sobbing—it was a dreadful thing to see that burly man sobbing like a child—over his troubles, and trying to hide his face from a world which to his tortured mind held no friendship at all and only grim enmity.

"It frequently happens," said Clive pontifically—the longer the captain's illness lasted the more freely he would discuss it—"that an injury, a fall, or a burn, or a fracture, will completely unbalance a mind that previously was a little unstable."

"A little unstable!" said Lomax. "Did he turn out the marines in the middle watch to hunt for mutineers in the hold? Ask Mr. Hornblower here, ask Mr. Bush, if they thought he was a little unstable. He had Hornblower doing watch and watch, and Bush and Roberts and Buckland himself out of bed every hour day and night. He was as mad as a hatter even then."

It was extraordinary how freely tongues wagged now in the ship, now that there was no fear of reports being made to the captain.

"At least we can make seamen out of the crew now," said Carberry, the master, with a satisfaction in his voice that was echoed round the wardroom. Sail drill and gun drill, tautened discipline and hard work, were pulling together a crew that had fast been disintegrating. It was what Buckland obviously delighted in, what he had been itching to do from the moment they had left the Eddystone behind, and exercising the crew helped to lift his mind out of the other troubles that beset it.

For now there was a new responsibility, that all the wardroom discussed freely in Buckland's absence—Buckland was already fenced in by the solitude that surrounds the captain of a ship of war. This was Buckland's sole responsibility, and the wardroom could watch Buckland wrestling with it, as they would watch a prizefighter in the ring; there even were bets laid on the result, as to whether or not Buckland would take the final plunge, whether or not he would take the ultimate step that would proclaim himself as in command of the *Renown* and the captain as incurable.

Locked in the captain's desk were the captain's papers, and among those papers were the secret orders addressed to him by the Lords of the Admiralty. No other eyes than the captain's had seen those orders as yet; not a soul in the ship could make any guess at their contents. They might be merely routine orders, directing the *Renown* perhaps to join Admiral Bickerton's squadron; but also they might reveal some vital diplomatic secret of the kind that no mere lieutenant could be entrusted with. On the one hand Buckland could continue to head for Antigua, and there he could turn over his responsibilities to whoever was the senior officer. There might be some junior captain who could be transferred to the *Renown;* to read the orders and carry the ship off on whatever mission was allotted her. On the other hand Buckland could read the orders now; they might deal with some matter of the greatest urgency. Antigua was a convenient landfall for ships to make from England, but from a military point of view it was not so desirable, being considerably to leeward of most of the points of strategic importance.

If Buckland took the ship down to Antigua and then she had to beat back to windward he might be sharply rapped on the knuckles by My Lords of the Admiralty; yet if he read the secret orders on that account he might be reprimanded for his presumption. The wardroom could guess at his predicament and each individual officer could congratulate himself upon not being personally involved while wondering what Buckland would do about it.

Bush and Hornblower stood side by side on the poop, feet wide apart on the heaving deck, as they steadied themselves and looked through their sextants at the horizon. Through the darkened glass Bush could see the image of the sun reflected from the mirror. With infinite pains he moved the arm round, bringing the image down closer and closer to the horizon. The pitch of the ship over the long blue rollers troubled him, but he persevered, decided in the end that the image of the sun was just sitting on the horizon, and clamped the sextant. Then he could read and record the measurement. As a concession to newfangled prejudices, he decided to follow Hornblower's example and observe the altitude also from the opposite point of the horizon. He swung round and did so, and as he recorded his reading he tried to remember what he had to do about half the difference between the two readings. And the index error, and the "dip." He looked round to find that Hornblower had already finished his observation and was standing waiting for him.

"That's the greatest altitude I've ever measured," remarked Hornblower. "I've never been as far south as this before. What's your result?"

They compared readings.

"That's accurate enough," said Hornblower. "What's the difficulty?"

"Oh, I can shoot the sun," said Bush. "No trouble about that. It's the calculations that bother me—those damned corrections."

Hornblower raised an eyebrow for a moment. He was accustomed to taking his own observations each noon and making his own calculations of the ship's position, in order to keep himself in practice. He was aware of the mechanical difficulty of taking an accurate observation in a moving ship, but—although he knew of plenty of other instances—he still could not believe that any man could really find the subsequent mathematics difficult. They were so simple to him that when Bush had asked him if he could join him in their noontime exercise for the sake of improving himself he had taken it for granted that it was only the mechanics of using a sextant that troubled Bush. But he politely concealed his surprise.

"They're easy enough," he said, and then he added "sir." A wise officer, too, did not make too much display of his superior ability when speaking to his senior. He phrased his next speech carefully.

"If you were to come below with me, sir, you could check through my calculations."

Bush listened in patience to Hornblower's explanations. They made the problem perfectly clear for the moment—it was by a hurried last-minute reading up that Bush had been able to pass his examination for lieutenant, although it was seamanship and not navigation that got him through—but Bush knew by bitter experience that tomorrow it would be hazy again.

"Now we can plot the position," said Hornblower, bending over the chart.

Bush watched as Hornblower's capable fingers worked the parallel rulers across the chart; Hornblower had long bony hands with something of beauty about them, and it was actually fascinating to watch them doing work at which they were so supremely competent. The powerful fingers picked up the pencil and ruled a line.

"There's the point of interception," said Hornblower. "Now we can check against the dead reckoning."

Even Bush could follow the simple steps necessary to plot the ship's course by dead reckoning since noon yesterday. The pencil in the steady fingers made a tiny *x* on the chart.

"We're still being set to the s'uth'ard, you see," said Hornblower. "We're not far enough east yet for the Gulf Stream to set us to the nor'rard."

"Didn't you say you'd never navigated these waters before?" asked Bush.

"Yes."

"Then how—? Oh, I suppose you've been studying."

To Bush it was as strange that a man should read up beforehand and be prepared for conditions hitherto unknown as it was strange to Hornblower that a man should find trouble in mathematics.

"At any rate, there we are," said Hornblower, tapping the chart with the pencil.

"Yes," said Bush.

They both looked at the chart with the same thought in mind.

"What d'ye think Number One'll do?" asked Bush.

Buckland might be legally in command of the ship, but it was too early yet to speak of him as the captain—"the captain" was still that weeping figure swathed in canvas on the cot in the cabin.

"Can't tell," answered Hornblower, "but he makes up his mind now or never. We lose ground to loo'ard every day from now, you see."

"What'd *you* do?" Bush was curious about this junior lieutenant who had shown himself ready of resources and so guarded in speech.

"I'd read those orders," said Hornblower instantly. "I'd rather be in trouble for having done something than for not having done anything."

"I wonder," said Bush. On the other hand a definite action could be made the subject of a court-martial charge far more easily than the omission to do something; Bush felt this, but he had not the facility with words to express it easily.

"Those orders may detach us on independent service," went on Hornblower. "God, what a chance for Buckland!"

"Yes," said Bush.

The eagerness in Hornblower's expression was obvious. If ever a man yearned for an independent command and the consequent opportunity to distinguish himself it was Hornblower. Bush wondered faintly if he himself was as anxious to have the responsibility of the command of a ship of the line in troubled waters. He looked at Hornblower with an interest which he knew to be constantly increasing. Hornblower was a man always ready to adopt the bold course, a man who infinitely preferred action to inaction; widely read in his profession and yet a practical seaman, as Bush had already had plenty of opportunity to observe. A student yet a man of action; a fiery spirit and yet discreet—Bush remembered how tactfully he had acted during the crisis following the captain's injury and how dexterously he had handled Buckland.

And—and—what was the truth about that injury to the captain? Bush darted a more searching glance than ever at Hornblower as he followed up that train of thought. Bush's mind did not consciously frame the words "motive" and "opportunity" to itself—it was not that type of mind—but it felt its way along an obscure path of reasoning which might well have been signposted with those words. He wanted to ask again the question he had asked once before, but to do so would not merely invite but would merit a rebuff. Hornblower was established in a strong position and Bush could be sure that he would never abandon it through indiscretion or impatience. Bush looked at the lean eager face, at the long fingers drumming on the chart. It was not right or fit or proper that he should feel any admiration or even respect for Hornblower, who was not merely his junior in age by a couple of years—that did not matter—but was his junior as a lieutenant. The dates on their respective commissions really did matter; a junior was someone for whom it should be impossible to feel respect by the traditions of the service. Anything else would be unnatural, might even savour of the equalitarian French ideas which they were engaged in fighting. The thought of himself as infected with Red Revolutionary notions made Bush actually uneasy, and yet as he stirred uncomfortably in his chair he could not wholly discard those notions.

"I'll put these things away," said Hornblower, rising from his chair. "I'm exercising my lower deck guns' crews after the hands have had their dinner. And I have the first dogwatch after that."

SIX

THE LOWER DECK GUNS had been secured, and the sweating crews came pouring up on deck. Now that the *Renown* was as far south as 30° north latitude the lower gundeck, even with the ports open for artillery exercise, was a warm place, and hauling those guns in and running them out was warm work. Hornblower had kept the crews hard at it, one hundred and eighty men, who afterwards came pouring up into the sunshine and the fresh air of the trade wind to receive the good-humoured chaff of the rest of the crew who had not been working so hard but who knew perfectly well that their turn would come soon.

The guns' crews wiped their steaming foreheads and flung jests—jagged and unpolished like the flints in the soil from which they had sprung—back at their tormentors. It was exhilarating to an officer to see the high spirits of the men and to be aware of the good temper that prevailed; in the three days that had elapsed since the change in command the whole atmosphere of the ship had improved. Suspicion and fear had vanished; after a brief sulkiness the hands had found that exercise and regular work were stimulating and satisfactory.

Hornblower came aft, the sweat running down him, and touched his hat to Roberts, who was officer of the watch, where he stood chatting with Bush at the break of the poop. It was an unusual request that Hornblower made, and Roberts and Bush stared at him with surprise.

"But what about the deck, Mr. Hornblower?" asked Roberts.

"A hand can swab it off in two minutes, sir," replied Hornblower, wiping his face and looking at the blue sea overside with a longing that was obvious to the most casual glance. "I have fifteen minutes before I relieve you, sir—plenty of time."

"Oh, very well, Mr. Hornblower."

"Thank you, sir," said Hornblower, and he turned eagerly away with another touch of his hat, while Roberts and Bush exchanged glances which were as much amused as puzzled. They watched Hornblower give his orders.

"Captain of the waist! Captain of the waist, there!"

"Sir?"

"Get the wash-deck pump rigged at once."

"Rig the wash-deck pump, sir?"

"Yes. Four men for the handles. One for the hose. Jump to it, now. I'll be with you in two minutes."

"Aye aye, sir."

The captain of the waist set about obeying the strange order after a glance at the receding figure. Hornblower was as good as his word; it was only two minutes before he returned, but now he was naked except for a towel draped sketchily round him. This was all very strange.

"Give away," he said to the men at the pump handles.

They were dubious about all this, but they obeyed the order, and in alternate pairs they threw their weight upon the handles. Up—down, up—down; clank—clank. The seaman holding the hose felt it stir in his hands as the water from far overside came surging up along it, and next moment a clear stream of water came gushing out of it.

"Turn it on me," said Hornblower, casting his towel aside and standing naked in the sunshine. The hoseman hesitated.

"Hurry up, now!"

As dubiously as ever the hoseman obeyed orders, turning the jet upon his officer, who rotated first this way and then that as it splashed upon him; an amused crowd was gathering to watch.

"Pump, you sons of seacooks!" said Hornblower, and obediently the men at the pump handles, now grinning broadly, threw all their weight on the handles, with such enthusiasm that their feet left the deck as they hauled down upon them and the clear water came hurtling out through the hose with considerable force. Hornblower twirled round and round under the stinging impact, his face screwed up in painful ecstasy.

Buckland had been standing aft at the taffrail, lost in thought and gazing down at the ship's wake, but the clanking of the pump attracted his attention and he strolled forward to join Roberts and Bush and to look at the strange spectacle.

"Hornblower has some odd fancies," he remarked, but he smiled as he said it—a rather pathetic smile, for his face bore the marks of the anxieties he was going through.

"He seems to be enjoying himself, sir," said Bush.

Bush, looking at Hornblower revolving under the sparkling stream, was conscious of a prickling under his shirt in his heavy uniform coat, and actually had the feeling that it might be pleasurable to indulge in that sort of shower bath, however injurious it might be to the health.

"'Vast pumping!" yelled Hornblower. "Avast, there!"

The hands at the pumps ceased their labours, and the jet from the hose died away to a trickle, to nothing.

"Captain of the waist! Secure the pump. Get the deck swabbed."

"Aye aye, sir."

Hornblower grabbed his towel and came trotting back along the maindeck. He looked up at the group of officers with a grin which revealed his exhilaration and high spirits.

"Dunno if it's good for discipline," commented Roberts, as Hornblower disappeared, and then, with a tardy flash of insight, "I suppose it's all right."

"I suppose so," said Buckland. "Let's hope he doesn't get himself a fever, checking the perspiration like that."

"He showed no sign of one, sir," said Bush; lingering in Bush's mind's eye was the picture of Hornblower's grin. It blended with his memory of Hornblower's eager expression when they were discussing what Buckland had best do in the dilemma in which he found himself.

"Ten minutes to eight bells, sir," reported the quartermaster.

"Very well," said Roberts.

The wet patch on the deck was now almost dry; a faint steam rose from it as the sun, still fierce at four o'clock in the afternoon, beat on it.

"Call the watch," said Roberts.

Hornblower came running up to the quarterdeck with his telescope; he must have pulled on his clothes with the orderly rapidity that marked all his actions. He touched his hat to the quarterdeck and stood by to relieve Roberts.

"You feel refreshed after your bath?" asked Buckland.

"Yes, sir, thank you."

Bush looked at the pair of them, the elderly, worried first lieutenant and the young fifth lieutenant, the older man pathetically envying the youngster's youth. Bush was learning something about personalities. He would never be able to reduce the results of his observations to a tabular system, and it would never occur to him to do so, but he could learn without doing so; his experience and observations would blend with his native wit to govern his judgments, even if he were too self-conscious to philosophise over them. He was aware that naval officers (he knew almost nothing of mankind on land) could be divided into active individuals and passive individuals, into those eager for responsibility and action and into those content to wait until action was forced on them. Before that he had learned the simpler lesson that officers could be divided into the efficient and the blunderers, and also into the intelligent and the stupid—this last division was nearly the same as the one immediately preceding, but not quite. There were the officers who could be counted on to act quickly and correctly in an emergency. And those who could not—again the dividing line did not quite coincide with the preceding. And there were officers with discretion and officers with none, patient officers and impatient ones, officers with strong nerves and officers with weak nerves. In certain cases Bush's estimates had to contend with his prejudices—he was liable to be suspicious of brains and of originality of thought and of eagerness for activity, especially because in the absence of some of the other desirable qualities these things might be actual nuisances. The final and most striking difference Bush had observed during ten years of continuous warfare was that between the leaders and the led, but that again was a difference of which Bush was conscious without being able to express it in words, and especially not in words as succinct or as definite as these; but he was acutely aware of the difference even though he was not able to bring himself to define it.

But he had that difference at the back of his mind, all the same, as he looked at Buckland and Hornblower chattering together on the quarterdeck. The afternoon watch had ended, and the first dogwatch had begun, with Hornblower as officer of the watch. It was the traditional moment for relaxation; the heat of the day had passed, and the hands collected forward, some of them to gaze down at the dolphins leaping round the bows, while the officers who had been dozing during the afternoon in their cabins came up to the quarterdeck for air and paced up and down in little groups deep in conversation.

A ship of war manned for active service was the most crowded place in the world—more crowded than the most rundown tenement in Seven Dials—but long and hard experience had taught the inhabitants how to live even in those difficult conditions. Forward there were groups of men yarning, men skylarking; there were solitary men who had each pre-empted a square yard of deck for himself and sat, cross-legged, with tools and materials about them, doing scrimshaw work—delicate carvings on bone—or embroidery or whittling at models oblivious to the tumult about them. Similarly aft on the crowded quarterdeck the groups of officers strolled and chatted, avoiding the other groups without conscious effort.

It was in accordance with the traditions of the service that these groups left the windward side of the quarterdeck to Buckland as long as he was on deck; and Buckland seemed to be making a long stay this afternoon. He was deep in conversation with Hornblower, the two of them pacing up and down beside the quarterdeck carronades, eight yards forward, eight yards back again; long ago the navy had discovered that when the walking distance was so limited conversation must not be interrupted by the necessarily frequent turns. Every pair of officers turned inwards as they reached the limits of their walk, facing each other momentarily and continuing the conversation without a break, and walking with their hands clasped behind them as a result of the training they had all received as midshipmen not to put their hands in their pockets.

So walked Buckland and Hornblower, and curious glances were cast at them by the others, for even on this golden evening, with the blue-enamel sea overside and the sun sinking to starboard with the promise of a magnificent sunset, everyone was conscious that in the cabin just below their feet lay a wretched insane man, half swathed in a strait jacket; and Buckland had to make up his mind how to deal with him. Up and down, up and down walked Buckland and Hornblower. Hornblower seemed to be as deferential as ever, and Buckland seemed to be asking questions; but some of the replies he received must have been unexpected, for more than once Buckland stopped in the middle of a turn and stood facing Hornblower, apparently repeating his question, while Hornblower seemed to be standing his ground both literally and figuratively, sturdy and yet respectful, as Buckland stood with the sun illuminating his haggard features.

Perhaps it had been a fortunate chance that had made Hornblower decide to take a bath under the wash-deck pump—this conversation had its beginnings in that incident.

"Is that a council of war?" said Smith to Bush, looking across at the pair.

"Not likely," said Bush.

A first lieutenant would not deliberately ask the advice or even the opinion of one so junior. Yet—yet—it might be possible, starting with idle conversation about different matters.

"Don't tell me they're discussing Catholic Emancipation," said Lomax.

It was just possible, Bush realised guiltily, that they were discussing something else—that question as to how the captain had come to fall down the hatchway. Bush found himself automatically looking round the deck for Wellard when that thought occurred to him. Wellard was skylarking in the main rigging with the midshipmen and master's mates as if he had not a care in the world. But it could not be that question which Buckland and Hornblower were discussing. Their attitudes seemed to indicate that theories and not facts were the subject of the debate.

"Anyway, they've settled it," said Smith.

Hornblower was touching his hat to Buckland, and Buckland was turning to go below again. Several curious pairs of eyes looked across at Hornblower now that he was left solitary, and as he became conscious of their regard he strolled over to them.

"Affairs of state?" asked Lomax, asking the question which everyone wanted asked.

Hornblower met his gaze with a level glance.

"No," he said, and smiled.

"It certainly looked like matters of importance," said Smith.

"That depends on the definition," answered Hornblower.

He was still smiling, and his smile gave no clue at all regarding his thoughts. It would be rude to press him further; it was possible that he and Buckland had been discussing some private business. Nobody looking at him could guess.

"Come off those hammocks, there!" bellowed Hornblower; the skylarking midshipmen were breaking one of the rules of the ship, but it was a convenient moment to divert the conversation.

Three bells rang out; the first dogwatch was three-quarters completed.

"Mr. Roberts, sir!" suddenly called the sentry at the smokers' slow match by the hatchway. "Passing the word for Mr. Roberts!"

Roberts turned from the group.

"Who's passing the word for me?" he asked, although with the captain ill there could only be one man in the ship who could pass the word for the second lieutenant.

"Mr. Buckland, sir. Mr. Buckland passing the word for Mr. Roberts."

"Very well," said Roberts, hurrying down the companion.

The others exchanged glances. This might be the moment of decision. Yet on the other hand it might be only a routine matter. Hornblower took advantage of the distraction to turn away from the group and continue his walk on the weather side of the ship; he walked with his chin nearly down on his breast, his drooping head balanced by the hands behind his back. Bush thought he looked weary.

Now there came a fresh cry from below, repeated by the sentry at the hatchway.

"Mr. Clive! Passing the word for Mr. Clive. Mr. Buckland passing the word for Mr. Clive!"

"Oh ho!" said Lomax in significant tones, as the surgeon hurried down.

"Something happens," said Carberry the master.

Time went on without either the second lieutenant or the surgeon reappearing. Smith, under his arm the telescope that was the badge of his temporary office, touched his hat to Hornblower and prepared to relieve him as officer of the watch as the second dogwatch was called. In the east the sky was turning dark, and the sun was setting over the starboard quarter in a magnificent display of red and gold; from the ship towards the sun the surface of the sea was gilded and glittering, but close overside it was the richest purple. A flying fish broke the surface and went skimming along, leaving a transient, momentary furrow behind it like a groove in enamel.

"Look at that!" exclaimed Hornblower to Bush.

"A flying fish," said Bush, indifferently.

"Yes! There's another!"

Hornblower leaned over to get a better view.

"You'll see plenty of them before this voyage is over," said Bush.

"But I've never seen one before."

The play of expression on Hornblower's face was curious. One moment he was full of eager interest; the next he assumed an appearance of stolid indifference as a man might pull on a glove. His service at sea so far, varied though it might be, had been confined to European waters; years of dangerous activity on the French and Spanish coasts in a frigate, two years in the *Renown* in the Channel fleet, and he had been eagerly looking forward to the novelties he would encounter in tropical waters. But he was talking to a man to whom these things were no novelty, and who evinced no excitement at the sight of the first flying fish of the voyage. Hornblower was not going to be outdone in stolidity and self-control; if the wonders of the deep failed to move Bush they were not going to evoke any childish excitement in Hornblower, at least any apparent excitement if Hornblower could suppress it. He was a veteran, and he was not going to appear like a raw hand.

Bush looked up to see Roberts and Clive ascending the companionway in the gathering night, and turned eagerly towards them. Officers came from every part of the quarterdeck to hear what they had to say.

"Well, sir?" asked Lomax.

"He's done it," said Roberts.

"He's read the secret orders, sir?" asked Smith.

"As far as I know, yes."

"Oh!"

There was a pause before someone asked the inevitable silly question.

"What did they say?"

"They are secret orders," said Roberts, and now there was a touch of pomposity in his voice—it might be to compensate for his lack of knowledge, or it might be because Roberts was now growing more aware of the dignity of his position as second in command. "If Mr. Buckland had taken me into his confidence I still could not tell you."

"True enough," said Carberry.

"What did the captain do?" asked Lomax.

"Poor devil," said Clive. With all attention turned to him Clive grew expansive. "We might be fiends from the pit! You should have seen him cower away when we came in. Those morbid terrors grow more acute."

Clive awaited a request for further information, and even though none was forthcoming he went on with his story.

"We had to find the key to his desk. You would have thought we were going to cut his throat, judging by the way he wept and tried to hide. All the sorrows of the world—all the terrors of hell torment that wretched man."

"But you found the key?" persisted Lomax.

"We found it. And we opened his desk."

"And then?"

"Mr. Buckland found the orders. The usual linen envelope with the Admiralty seal. The envelope had been already opened."

"Naturally," said Lomax. "Well?"

"And now, I suppose," said Clive, conscious of the anticlimax, "I suppose he's reading them."

"And we are none the wiser."

There was a disappointed pause.

"Bless my soul!" said Carberry. "We've been at war since '93. Nearly ten years of it. D'ye still expect to know what lies in store for you? The West Indies today—Halifax tomorrow. We obey orders. Helm-a-lee—let go and haul. A bellyful of grape or champagne in a captured flagship. Who cares? We draw our four shilling a day, rain or shine."

"Mr. Carberry!" came the word from below. "Mr. Buckland passing the word for Mr. Carberry."

"Bless my soul!" said Carberry again.

"Now you can earn your four shilling a day," said Lomax.

The remark was addressed to his disappearing back, for Carberry was already hastening below.

"A change of course," said Smith. "I'll wager a week's pay on it."

"No takers," said Roberts.

It was the most likely new development of all, for Carberry the master was the officer charged with the navigation of the ship.

Already it was almost full night, dark enough to make the features of the speakers indistinct, although over to the westward there was still a red patch on the horizon, and a faint red trail over the black water towards the ship. The binnacle lights had been lit and the brighter stars were already visible in the dark sky, with the mastheads seeming to brush past them, with the motion of the ship, infinitely far over their heads. The ship's bell rang out, but the group showed no tendency to disperse. And then interest quickened. Here were Buckland and Carberry returning, ascending the companionway; the group drew on one side to clear them a passage.

"Officer of the watch!" said Buckland.

"Sir!" said Smith, coming forward in the darkness.

"We're altering course two points. Steer southwest."

"Aye aye, sir. Course southwest. Mr. Abbott, pipe the hands to the braces."

The *Renown* came round on her new course, with her sails trimmed to the wind which was now no more than a point on her port quarter. Carberry walked over to the binnacle and looked into it to make sure the helmsman was exactly obeying his orders.

"Another pull on the weather forebrace, there!" yelled Smith. "Belay!"

The bustle of the change of course died away.

"Course sou'west, sir," reported Smith.

"Very good, Mr. Smith," said Buckland by the rail.

"Pardon, sir," said Roberts, greatly daring, addressing him as he loomed in the darkness. "Can you tell us our mission, sir?"

"Not our mission. That is still secret, Mr. Roberts."

"Very good, sir."

"But I'll tell you where we're bound. Mr. Carberry knows already."

"Where, sir?"

"Santo Domingo. Scotchman's Bay."

There was a pause while this information was being digested.

"Santo Domingo," said someone, meditatively.

"Hispaniola," said Carberry, explanatorily.

"Hayti," said Hornblower.

"Santo Domingo—Hayti—Hispaniola," said Carberry. "Three names for the same island."

"Hayti!" exclaimed Roberts, some chord in his memory suddenly touched. "That's where the blacks are in rebellion."

"Yes," agreed Buckland.

Anyone could guess that Buckland was trying to say that word in as noncommittal a tone as possible; it might be because there was a difficult diplomatic situation with regard to the blacks, and it might be because fear of the captain was still a living force in the ship.

SEVEN

Lieutenant Buckland, in acting command of H.M.S. *Renown,* of seventy four guns, was on the quarterdeck of his ship peering through his telescope at the low mountains of Santo Domingo. The ship was rolling in a fashion unnatural and disturbing, for the long Atlantic swell, driven by the northeast trades, was passing under her keel while she lay hove-to to the final puffs of the land breeze which had blown since midnight and was now dying away as the fierce sun heated the island again. The *Renown* was actually wallowing, rolling her lower deck gunports under, first on one side and then on the other, for what little breeze there was was along the swell and did nothing to stiffen her as she lay with her mizzen topsail backed. She would lie right over on one side, until the gun tackles creaked with the strain of holding the guns in position, until it was hard to keep a foothold on the steep-sloping deck; she would lie there for a few harrowing seconds, and then slowly right herself, making no pause at all at the moment when she was upright and her deck horizontal, and continue, with a clattering of blocks and a rattle of gear, in a sickening swoop until she was as far over in the opposite direction, gun tackles creaking and unwary men slipping and sliding, and lie there unresponsive until the swell had rolled under her and she repeated her behaviour.

"For God's sake," said Hornblower, hanging on to a belaying pin in the mizzen fife rail to save himself from sliding down the deck into the scuppers, "can't he make up his mind?"

There was something in Hornblower's stare that made Bush look at him more closely.

"Seasick?" he asked, with curiosity.

"Who wouldn't be?" replied Hornblower. "How she rolls!"

Bush's cast-iron stomach had never given him the least qualm, but he was aware that less fortunate men suffered from seasickness even after weeks at sea, especially when subjected to a different kind of motion. This funereal rolling was nothing like the free action of the *Renown* under sail.

"Buckland has to see how the land lies," he said in an effort to cheer Hornblower up.

"How much more does he want to see?" grumbled Hornblower. "There's the Spanish colours flying on the fort up there. Everyone on shore knows now that a ship of the line is prowling about, and the Dons won't have to be very clever to guess that we're not here on a yachting trip. Now they've all the time they need to be ready to receive us."

"But what else could he do?"

"He could have come in in the dark with the sea breeze. Landing parties ready. Put them ashore at dawn. Storm the place before they knew there was any danger. Oh, God!"

The final exclamation had nothing to do with what went before. It was wrenched out of Hornblower by the commotion of his stomach. Despite his deep tan there was a sickly green colour in his cheeks.

"Hard luck," said Bush.

Buckland still stood trying to keep his telescope trained on the coast despite the rolling of the ship. This was Scotchman's Bay—the Bahia de Escocesa, as the Spanish charts had it. To the westward lay a shelving beach; the big rollers here broke far out and ran in creamy white up to the water's edge with diminishing force, but to the eastward the shore line rose in a line of tree-covered hills standing bluffly with their feet in blue water; the rollers burst against them in sheets of spray that climbed far up the cliffs before falling back in a smother of white. For thirty miles those hills ran beside the sea, almost due east and west; they constituted the Samaná peninsula, terminating in Samaná Point. According to the charts the peninsula was no more than ten miles wide; behind them, round Samaná Point, lay Samaná Bay, opening into the Mona Passage and a most convenient anchorage for privateers and small ships of war which could lie there, under the protection of the fort on the Samaná peninsula, ready to slip out and harass the West Indian convoys making use of the Mona Passage. The *Renown* had been given orders to clear out this raiders' lair before going down to leeward to Jamaica—everyone in the ship could guess that—but now that Buckland confronted the problem he was not at all sure how to solve it. His indecision was apparent to all the curious lookers-on who clustered on the *Renown's* deck.

The main topsail suddenly flapped like thunder, and the ship began to turn slowly head to sea; the land breeze was expiring, and the trade winds, blowing eternally across the Atlantic, were resuming their dominion. Buckland shut his telescope with relief. At least that was an excuse for postponing action.

"Mr. Roberts!"

"Sir!"

"Lay her on the port tack. Full and by!"

"Aye aye, sir."

The after guard came running to the mizzen braces, and the ship slowly paid off. Gradually the topsails caught the wind, and she began to lie over, gathering way as she did so. She met the next roller with her port bow, thrusting boldly into it in a burst of spray. The tautened weather-rigging began to sing a more cheerful note, blending with the music of her passage through the water. She was a live thing again, instead of rolling like a corpse in the trough. The roaring trade wind pressed her over, and she went surging along rising and swooping as if with pleasure, leaving a creamy wake behind her on the blue water while the sea roared under the bows.

"Better?" asked Bush of Hornblower.

"Better in one way," was the reply. Hornblower looked over at the distant hills of Santo Domingo. "I could wish we were going into action and not running away to think about it."

"What a fire-eater!" said Bush.

"A fire-eater? Me? Nothing like that—quite the opposite. I wish—oh, I wish for too much, I suppose."

There was no explaining some people, thought Bush, philosophically. He was content to bask in the sunshine now that its heat was tempered by the ship's passage through the wind. If action and danger lay in the future he could await it in stolid tranquility; and he certainly could congratulate himself that he did not have to carry Buckland's responsibility of carrying a ship of the line and seven hundred and twenty men into action. The prospect of action at least took one's mind off the horrid fact that confined below lay an insane captain.

At dinner in the wardroom he looked over at Hornblower, fidgety and nervous. Buckland had announced his intention of taking the bull by the horns the next morning, of rounding Samaná Point and forcing his way straight up the bay. It would not take many broadsides from the *Renown* to destroy any shipping that lay there at anchor. Bush thoroughly approved of the scheme. Wipe out the privateers, burn them, sink them, and then it would be time to decide what, if anything, should be done next. At the meeting in the wardroom when Buckland asked if any officer had any questions Smith had asked sensibly about the tides, and Carberry had given him the information; Roberts had asked a question or two about the situation on the south shore of the bay; but Hornblower at the foot of the table had kept his mouth shut, although looking with eager attention at each speaker in turn.

During the dogwatches Hornblower had paced the deck by himself, head bent in meditation; Bush noticed the fingers of the hands behind his back twisting and twining nervously, and he experienced a momentary doubt. Was it possible that this energetic young officer was lacking in physical courage? That phrase was not Bush's own—he had heard it used maliciously somewhere or other years ago. It was better to use it now than to tell himself outright that he suspected Hornblower might be a coward. Bush was not a man of large tolerance; if a man were a coward he wanted no more to do with him.

Half-way through next morning the pipes shrilled along the decks; the drums of the marines beat a rousing roll.

"Clear the decks for action! Hands to quarters! Clear for action!"

Bush came down to the lower gundeck which was his station for action; under his command was the whole deck and the seventeen twenty-four-pounders of the starboard battery, while Hornblower commanded under him those of the port side. The hands were already knocking down the screens and removing obstructions. A little group of the surgeon's crew came along the deck; they were carrying a strait-jacketed figure bound to a plank. Despite the jacket and the lashings it writhed feebly and wept pitifully—the captain being carried down to the safety of the cable tier while his cabin was cleared for action. A hand or two in the bustle found time to shake their heads over the unhappy figure, but Bush checked them soon enough. He wanted to be able to report the lower gundeck cleared for action with creditable speed.

Hornblower made his appearance, touched his hat to Bush, and stood by to supervise his guns. Most of this lower deck was in twilight, for the stout shafts of sunlight that came down the hatchways did little to illuminate the farther parts of the deck with its sombre red paint. Half a dozen ship's boys came along, each one carrying a bucket of sand, which they scattered in handfuls over the deck. Bush kept a sharp eye on them, because the guns' crews depended on that sand for firm foothold. The water buckets beside each gun were filled; they served a dual purpose, to dampen the swabs that cleaned out the guns and for immediate use against fire. Round the mainmast stood a ring of extra fire buckets; in tubs at either side of the ship smouldered the slow matches from which the gun captains could rekindle their linstocks when necessary. Fire and water. The marine sentries came clumping along the deck in their scarlet coats and white crossbelts, the tops of their shakos brushing the deck beams over their heads. Corporal Greenwood posted one at each hatchway, bayonet fixed and musket loaded. Their duty was to see that no unauthorised person ran down to take shelter in the safety of that part of the ship comfortably below waterline. Mr. Hobbs, the acting-gunner, with his mates and helpers made a momentary appearance on their way down to the magazine. They were all wearing list slippers to obviate any chance of setting off the loose powder which would be bound to be strewn about down there in the heat of action.

Soon the powder boys came running up, each with a charge for the guns. The breechings of the guns were cast off, and the crews stood by the tackles, waiting for the word to open the ports and run out the guns. Bush darted his glance along both sides. The gun captains were all at their posts. Ten men stood by every gun on the starboard side, five by every gun on the port side—maximum and minimum crews for twenty-four-pounders. It was Bush's responsibility to see to it that whichever battery came into action the guns were properly manned. If both sides had to be worked at once he had to make a fair division, and when the casualties began and guns were put out of service he had to redistribute the crews. The petty officers and warrant officers were reporting their subdivisions ready for action, and Bush turned to the midshipman beside him whose duty was to carry messages.

"Mr. Abbott, report the lower deck cleared for action. Ask if the guns should be run out."

"Aye aye, sir."

A moment before the ship had been full of noise and bustle, and now everything down here was still and quiet save for the creaking of the timbers; the ship was rising and swooping rhythmically over the sea—Bush as he stood by the mainmast was automatically swaying with the ship's motion. Young Abbott came running down the ladder again.

"Mr. Buckland's compliments, sir, and don't run the guns out yet."

"Very good."

Hornblower was standing farther aft, in line with the ringbolts of the train tackles; he had looked round to hear what message Abbott bore, and now he turned back again. He stood with his feet apart, and Bush saw him put one hand into the other, behind his back, and clasp it firmly. There was a rigidity about the set of his shoulders and in the way he held his head that might be significant of anything, eagerness for action or the reverse. A gun captain addressed a remark to Hornblower, and Bush watched him turn to answer it. Even in the half-light of the lower deck Bush could see there were signs of strain in his expression, and that smile might be forced. Oh well, decided Bush, as charitably as he could, men often looked like that before going into action.

Silently the ship sailed on; even Bush had his ears cocked trying to hear what was going on above him so as to draw deductions about the situation. Faintly down the hatchway came the call of a seaman.

"No bottom, sir. No bottom with this line."

So there was a man in the chains taking casts with the lead, and they must be drawing near the land; everyone down on the lower deck drew the same conclusion and started to remark about it to his neighbour.

"Silence, there!" snapped Bush.

Another cry from the leadsman, and then a bellowed order. Instantly the lower deck seemed to be filled solid with noise. The maindeck guns were being run out; in the confined space below every sound was multiplied and reverberated by the ship's timbers so that the gun-trucks rolling across the planking made a noise like thunder. Everyone looked to Bush for orders, but he stood steady; he had received none. Now a midshipman appeared descending the ladder.

"Mr. Buckland's compliments, sir, and please to run your guns out."

He had squealed his message without ever setting foot on deck, and everyone had heard it. There was an instant buzz round the deck, and excitable people began to reach for the gunports to open them.

"Still!" bellowed Bush. Guiltily all movement ceased.

"Up ports!"

The twilight of the lower deck changed to daylight as the ports opened; little rectangles of sunshine swayed about on the deck on the port side, broadening and narrowing with the motion of the ship.

"Run out!"

With the ports open the noise was not so great; the crews flung their weight on the tackles and the trucks roared as the guns thrust their muzzles out. Bush stepped to the nearest gun and stooped to peer out through the open port. There were the green hills of the island at extreme gunshot distance; here the cliffs were not nearly so abrupt, and there was a jungle-covered shelf at their feet.

"Hands wear ship!"

Bush could recognise Roberts' voice hailing from the quarterdeck. The deck under his feet steadied to the horizontal, and the distant hills seemed to swing with the vessel. The masts creaked as the yards came round. That must be Point Samaná which they were rounding. The motion of the ship had changed far more than would be the result of mere alteration of course. She was not only on an even keel but she was in quiet water, gliding along into the bay. Bush squatted down on his heels by the muzzle of a gun and peered at the shore. This was the south side of the peninsula at which he was looking, presenting a coastline toward the bay nearly as steep as the one on the seaward side. There was the fort on the crest and the Spanish flag waving over it. The excited midshipman came scuttling down the ladder like a squirrel.

"Sir! Sir! Will you try a ranging shot at the batteries when your guns bear?"

Bush ran a cold eye over him.

"Whose orders?" he asked.

"M–Mr. Buckland's, sir."

"Then say so. Very well. My respects to Mr. Buckland, and it will be a long time before my guns are within range."

"Aye aye, sir."

There was smoke rising from the fort, and not powder smoke either. Bush realised with something like a quiver of apprehension that probably it was smoke from a furnace for heating shot; soon the fort would be hurling red-hot shot at them, and Bush could see no chance of retaliation; he would never be able to elevate his guns sufficiently to reach the fort, while the fort, from its commanding position on the crest, could reach the ship easily enough. He straightened himself up and walked over to the port side to where Hornblower, in a similar attitude, was peering out beside a gun.

"There's a point running out here," said Hornblower. "See the shallows there? The channel must bend round them. And there's a battery on the point—look at the smoke. They're heating shot."

"I dare say," said Bush.

Soon they would be under a sharp crossfire. He hoped they would not be subjected to it for too long. He could hear orders being shouted on deck, and the masts creaked as the yards came round; they were working the *Renown* round the bend.

"The fort's opened fire, sir," reported the master's mate in charge of the forward guns on the starboard side.

"Very well, Mr. Purvis." He crossed over and looked out. "Did you see where the shot fell?"

"No, sir."

"They're firing on this side, too, sir," reported Hornblower.

"Very well."

Bush saw the fort spurting white cannon smoke. Then straight in the line between his eye and the fort, fifty yards from the side of the ship, a pillar of water rose up from the golden surface, and within the same instant of time something crashed into the side of the ship just above Bush's head. A ricochet had bounded from the surface and had lodged somewhere in the eighteen inches of oak that constituted the ship's side. Then followed a devil's tattoo of crashes; a well-aimed salvo was striking home.

"I might just reach the battery on this side now, sir," said Hornblower.

"Then try what you can do."

Now here was Buckland himself, hailing fretfully down the hatchway.

"Can't you open fire yet, Mr. Bush?"

"This minute, sir."

Hornblower was standing by the centre twenty-four-pounder. The gun captain slid the rolling handspike under the gun carriage, and heaved with all his weight. Two men at each side tackle tugged under his direction to point the gun true. With the elevating quoin quite free from the breech the gun was at its highest angle of elevation. The gun captain flipped up the iron apron over the touchhole, saw that the hole was filled with powder, and with a shout of "Stand clear" he thrust his smouldering linstock into it. The gun bellowed loud in the confined space; some of the smoke came drifting back through the port.

"Just below, sir," reported Hornblower standing at the next port. "When the guns are hot they'll reach it."

"Carry on, then."

"Open fire, first division!" yelled Hornblower.

The four foremost guns crashed out almost together.

"Second division!"

Bush could feel the deck heaving under him with the shock of the discharge and the recoil. Smoke came billowing back into the confined space; acrid, bitter, and the din was paralysing.

"Try again, men!" yelled Hornblower. "Division captains, see that you point true!"

There was a frightful crash close beside Bush and something

screamed past him to crash into the deck beam near his head. Something flying through an open gunport had struck a gun on its reinforced breech. Two men had fallen close beside it, one lying still and the other twisting and turning in agony. Bush was about to give an order regarding them when his attention was drawn to something more important. There was a deep gash in the deck beam by his head and from the depths of the gash smoke was curling. It was a red-hot shot that had struck the breech of the gun and had apparently flown into fragments. A large part—the largest part—had sunk deep into the beam and already the wood was smouldering.

"Fire buckets here!" roared Bush.

Ten pounds of red-hot glowing metal lodged in the dry timbers of the ship could start a blaze in a few seconds. At the same time there was a rush of feet overhead, the sound of gear being moved about, and then the clank-clank of pumps. So on the maindeck they were fighting fires too. Hornblower's guns were thundering on the port side, the guntrucks roaring over the planking. Hell was unchained, and the smoke of hell was eddying about him.

The masts creaked again with the swing of the yards; despite everything the ship had to be sailed up the tortuous channel. He peered out through a port, but his eye told him, as he forced himself to gauge the distance calmly, that the fort on the crest was still beyond range. No sense in wasting ammunition. He straightened himself and looked round the murky deck. There was something strange in the feel of the ship under his feet. He teetered on his toes to put his wild suspicions to the test. There was the slightest perceptible slope to the deck—a strange rigidity and permanence about it. Oh my God! Hornblower was looking round at him and made an urgent gesture downwards to confirm the awful thought. The *Renown* was aground. She must have run so smoothly and slowly up a mudbank as to lose her speed without any jerk perceptible. But she must have put her bows far up on the bank for the slope of the deck to be noticeable. There were more rending crashes as other shots from the shore struck home, a fresh hurrying and bustle as the fire parties ran to deal with the danger. Hard aground, and doomed to be slowly shot to pieces by those cursed forts, if the shots did not set them on fire to roast alive on the mudbank. Hornblower was beside him, his watch in his hand.

"Tide's still rising," he said. "It's an hour before high water. But I'm afraid we're pretty hard aground."

Bush could only look at him and swear, pouring out filth from his mouth as the only means of relieving his overwrought feelings.

"Steady there, Duff!" yelled Hornblower, looking away from him at a gun's crew gathered round their gun. "Swab that out properly! D'ye want your hands blown off when you load?"

By the time Hornblower looked round at Bush again the latter had regained his self-control.

"An hour to high water, you say?" he asked.

"Yes, sir. According to Carberry's calculations."

"God help us!"

"My shot's just reaching the battery on the point, sir. If I can keep the embrasures swept I'll slow their rate of fire even if I don't silence them."

Another crash as a shot struck home, and another.

"But the one across the channel's out of range."

"Yes," said Hornblower.

The powder boys were running through all the bustle with fresh charges for the guns. And here was the messenger-midshipman threading his way through them.

"Mr. Bush, sir! Will you please report to Mr. Buckland, sir? And we're aground, under fire, sir."

"Shut your mouth. I leave you in charge here, Mr. Hornblower."

"Aye aye, sir."

The sunlight on the quarterdeck was blinding. Buckland was standing hatless at the rail, trying to control the working of his features. There was a roar and a spluttering of steam as someone turned the jet of a hose on a fiery fragment lodged in the bulkhead. Dead men in the scuppers; wounded being carried off. A shot, or the splinters it had set flying, must have killed the man at the wheel so that the ship temporarily out of control had run aground.

"We have to kedge off," said Buckland.

"Aye aye, sir."

That meant putting out an anchor and heaving in on the cable with the capstan to haul the ship off the mud by main force. Bush looked round him to confirm what he had gathered regarding the ship's position from his restricted view below. Her bows were on the mud; she would have to be hauled off stern first. A shot howled close overhead, and Bush had to exert his self-control not to jump.

"You'll have to get a cable out aft through a stern port."

"Aye aye, sir."

"Roberts'll take the stream anchor off in the launch."

"Aye aye, sir."

The fact that Buckland omitted the formal "Mister" was significant of the strain he was undergoing and of the emergency of the occasion.

"I'll take the men from my guns, sir," said Bush.

"Very good."

Now was the time for discipline and training to assert themselves; the *Renown* was fortunate in having a crew more than half composed of seasoned men drilled in the blockade of Brest. At Plymouth she had only been filled up with pressed men. What had merely been a drill, an evolution, when the *Renown* was one of the Channel fleet, was now an operation on which the life of the ship depended, not something to be done perfunctorily in competition with the rest of the squadron. Bush gathered his guns' crews around him and set about the task of rousing out a cable and getting it aft to a port, while overhead Roberts' men were manning stay tackles and yard tackles to sway out the launch.

Down below the heat between the decks was greater even than above with the sun glaring down. The smoke from Hornblower's guns was eddying thick under the beams; Hornblower was holding his hat in his hand and wiping his streaming face with his handkerchief. He nodded as Bush appeared; there was no need for Bush to explain the duty on which he was engaged. With the guns still thundering and the smoke still eddying, powder boys still running with fresh charges and fire parties bustling with their buckets, Bush's men roused out the cable. The hundred fathoms of it weighed a trifle over a couple of tons; clear heads and skilled supervision were necessary to get the unwieldy cable laid out aft, but Bush was at his best doing work which called for single-minded attention to a single duty. He had it clear and faked down along the deck by the time the cutter was under the stern to receive the end, and then he watched the vast thing gradually snake out through the after port without a hitch. The launch came into his line of vision as he stood looking out, with the vast weight of the stream anchor dangling astern; it was a relief to know that the tricky business of getting the anchor into her had been successfully carried out. The second cutter carried the spring cable from the hawsehole. Roberts was in command; Bush heard him hail the cutter as the three boats drew off astern. There was a sudden jet of water among the boats; one or other, if not both, of the batteries ashore had shifted targets; a shot now into the launch would be a disaster, and one into a cutter would be a serious setback.

"Pardon, sir," said Hornblower's voice beside him, and Bush turned back from looking out over the glittering water.

"Well?"

"I could take some of the foremost guns and run 'em aft," said Hornblower. "Shifting the weight would help."

"So it would," agreed Bush; Hornblower's face was streaked and grimy with his exertions, as Bush noted while he considered if he had sufficient authority to give the order on his own responsibility. "Better get Buckland's permission. Ask him in my name if you like."

"Aye aye, sir."

These lower deck twenty-four-pounders weighed more than two tons each; the transfer of some from forward aft would be an important factor in getting the bows off the mudbank. Bush took another glance through the port. James, the midshipman in the first cutter, was turning to look back to check that the cable was out in exact line with the length of the ship. There would be a serious loss of tractive effort if there was an angle in the cable from anchor to capstan. Launch and cutter were coming together in preparation for dropping the anchor. All round them the water suddenly boiled to a salvo from the shore; the skipping jets of the ricochets showed that it was the fort on the hill that was firing at them—and making good practice for that extreme range. The sun caught an axe blade as it turned in the air in the sternsheets of the launch; Bush saw the momentary flash. They were letting the anchor drop from where it hung from the gallows in the stern. Thank God.

Hornblower's guns were still bellowing out, making the ship tremble with their recoil, and at the same time a splintering crash over his head told him that the other battery was still firing on the ship and still scoring hits. Everything was still going on at once; Hornblower had a gang of men at work dragging aft the foremost twenty-four-pounder on the starboard side—a ticklish job with the rolling handspike under the transom of the carriage. The trucks squealed horribly as the men struggled to turn the cumbersome thing and thread their way along the crowded deck. But Bush could spare Hornblower no more than a glance as he hurried up to the maindeck to see for himself what was happening at the capstan.

The men were already taking their places at the capstan bars under the supervision of Smith and Booth; the maindeck guns were being stripped of the last of their crews to supply enough hands. Naked to the waist, the men were spitting on their hands and testing their foothold—there was no need to tell them how serious the situation was; no need for Booth's knotted rattan.

"Heave away!" hailed Buckland from the quarterdeck.

"Heave away!" yelled Booth. "Heave, and wake the dead!"

The men flung their weight on the bars and the capstan came round, the pawls clanking rapidly as the capstan took up the slack. The boys with the nippers at the messenger had to hurry to keep pace. Then the intervals between the clanking of the pawls became longer as the capstan turned more slowly. More slowly; clank—clank—clank. Now the strain was coming; the bitts creaked as the cable tightened. Clank—clank. That was a new cable, and it could be expected to stretch a trifle.

The sudden howl of a shot—what wanton fate had directed it here of all places in the ship? Flying splinters and prostrate men; the shot had ploughed through the whole crowded mass. Red blood was pouring out, vivid in the sunshine; in understandable confusion the men drew away from the bloody wrecks.

"Stand to your posts!" yelled Smith. "You, boys! Get those men out of the way. Another capstan bar here! Smartly now!"

The ball which had wrought such fearful havoc had not spent all its force on human flesh; it had gone on to shatter the cheekpiece of a gun carriage and then to lodge in the ship's side. Nor had human blood quenched it; smoke was rising on the instant from where it rested. Bush himself seized a fire bucket and dashed its contents on the glowing ball; steam blended with the smoke and the water spat and sputtered. No single fire bucket could quench twenty four pounds of red-hot iron, but a fire party came running up to flood the smouldering menace.

The dead and the wounded had been dragged away and the men were at the capstan bars again.

"Heave!" shouted Booth. Clank—clank—clank. Slowly and more slowly still turned the capstan. Then it came to a dead stop while the bitts groaned under the strain.

"Heave! Heave!"

Clank! Then reluctantly, and after a long interval, clank! Then no more. The merciless sun beat down upon the men's straining backs; their horny feet sought for a grip against the cleats on the deck as they shoved and thrust against the bars. Bush went below again, leaving them straining away; he could, and did, send plenty of men up from the lower gundeck to treble-bank the capstan bars. There were men still hard at work in the smoky twilight hauling the last possible gun aft, but Hornblower was back among his guns supervising the pointing. Bush set his foot on the cable. It was not like a rope, but like a wooden spar, as rigid and unyielding. Then through the sole of his shoe Bush felt the slightest tremor, the very slightest; the men at the capstan were putting their reinforced strength against the bars. The clank of one more pawl gained reverberated along the ship's timbers; the cable shuddered a trifle more violently and then stiffened into total rigidity again. It did not creep over an eighth of an inch under Bush's foot, although he knew that at the capstan a hundred and fifty men were straining their hearts out at the bars. One of Hornblower's guns went off; Bush felt the jar of the recoil through the cable. Faintly down the hatchways came the shouts of encouragement from Smith and Booth at the capstan, but not an inch of gain could be noted at the cable. Hornblower came and touched his hat to Bush.

"D'you notice any movement when I fire a gun, sir?" As he asked the question he turned and waved to the captain of a midship gun which was loaded and run out. The gun captain brought the linstock down on the touchhole, and the gun roared out and came recoiling back through the smoke. Bush's foot on the cable recorded the effect.

"Only the jar—no—yes." Inspiration came to Bush. To the question he asked, Bush already knew the answer Hornblower would give. "What are you thinking of?"

"I could fire all my guns at once. That might break the suction, sir."

So it might, indeed. The *Renown* was lying on mud, which was clutching her in a firm grip. If she could be severely shaken while the hawser was maintained at full tension the grip might be broken.

"I think it's worth trying, by God," said Bush.

"Very good, sir. I'll have my guns loaded and ready in three minutes, sir." Hornblower turned to his battery and funnelled his hands round his mouth. "Cease fire! Cease fire, all!"

"I'll tell 'em at the capstan," said Bush.

"Very good, sir." Hornblower went on giving his orders. "Load and double-shot your guns. Prime and run out."

That was the last that Bush heard for the moment as he went up on the maindeck and made his suggestion to Smith, who nodded in instant agreement.

"'Vast heaving!" shouted Smith, and the sweating men at the bars eased their weary backs.

An explanation was necessary to Buckland on the quarterdeck; he saw the force of the argument. The unfortunate man, who was watching the failure of his first venture in independent command, and whose ship was in such deadly peril, was gripping at the rail and wringing it with his two hands as if he would twist it like a corkscrew. In the midst of all this there was a piece of desperately important news that Smith had to give.

"Roberts is dead," he said, out of the side of his mouth.

"No!"

"He's dead. A shot cut him in two in the launch."

"Good God!"

It was to Bush's credit that he felt sorrow at the death of Roberts before his mind recorded the fact that he was now first lieutenant of a ship of the line. But there was no time now to think of either sorrow or rejoicing, not with the *Renown* aground and under fire. Bush hailed down the hatchway.

"Below, there! Mr. Hornblower!"

"Sir!"

"Are your guns ready?"

"Another minute, sir."

"Better take the strain," said Bush to Smith, and then, louder, down the hatchway, "Await my order, Mr. Hornblower."

"Aye aye, sir."

The men settled themselves at the capstan bars again, braced their feet, and heaved.

"Heave!" shouted Booth. "Heave!"

The men might be pushing at the side of a church, so little movement did they get from the bars after the first inch.

"Heave!"

Bush left them and ran below. He set his foot on the rigid cable and nodded to Hornblower. The fifteen guns—two had been dragged aft from the port side—were run out and ready, the crews awaiting orders.

"Captains, take your linstocks!" shouted Hornblower. "All you others, stand clear! Now, I shall give you the words 'one, two, three.' At 'three' you touch your linstocks down. Understand?"

There was a buzz of agreement.

"All ready? All linstocks glowing?" The gun captains swung them about to get them as bright as possible. "Then one—two—three!"

Down came the linstocks on the touchholes, and almost simultaneously the guns roared out; even with the inevitable variation in the amounts of powder in the touchholes there was not a second between the first and the last of the fifteen explosions. Bush, his foot on the cable, felt the ship heave with the recoil—double-shotting the guns had increased the effect. The smoke came eddying into the sweltering heat, but Bush had no attention to give to it. The cable moved under his foot with the heave of the ship. Surely it was moving along. It was! He had to shift the position of his foot. The clank of a newly gained pawl on the windlass could be heard by everyone. Clank—clank. Someone in the smoke started a cheer and others took it up.

"Silence!" bellowed Hornblower.

Clank—clank—clank. Reluctant sounds; but the ship was moving. The cable was coming in slowly, like a mortally wounded monster. If only they could keep her on the move! Clank—clank—clank. The interval between the sounds was growing shorter—even Bush had to admit that to himself. The cable was coming in faster—faster.

"Take charge here, Mr. Hornblower," said Bush, and sprang for the maindeck. If the ship were free there would be urgent matters for the first lieutenant to attend to. The capstan pawls seemed almost to be playing a merry tune, so rapidly did they sound as the capstan turned.

Undoubtedly there was much to be attended to on deck. There were decisions which must be made at once. Bush touched his hat to Buckland.

"Any orders, sir?"

Buckland turned unhappy eyes on him.

"We've lost the flood," he said.

This must be the highest moment of the tide; if they were to touch ground again, kedging off would not be so simple an operation.

"Yes, sir," said Bush.

The decision could only lie with Buckland; no one else could share the responsibility. But it was terribly hard for a man to have to admit defeat in his very first command. Buckland looked as if for inspiration round the bay, where the red-and-gold flags of Spain flew above the banked-up powder smoke of the batteries—no inspiration could be found there.

"We can only get out with the land breeze," said Buckland.

"Yes, sir."

There was almost no longer for the land breeze to blow, either, thought Bush; Buckland knew it as well as he did. A shot from the fort on the hill struck into the main chains at that moment, with a jarring crash and a shower of splinters. They heard the call for the fire party, and with that Buckland reached the bitter decision.

"Heave in on the spring cable," he ordered. "Get her round, head to sea."

"Aye aye, sir."

Retreat—defeat; that was what that order meant. But defeat had to be faced; even with that order given there was much that had to be done to work the ship out of the imminent danger in which she lay. Bush turned to give the orders.

" 'Vast heaving at the capstan, there!"

The clanking ceased and the *Renown* rode free in the muddy, churned-up waters of the bay. To retreat she would have to turn tail, reverse herself in that confined space, and work her way out to sea. Fortunately the means were immediately available; by heaving in on the bow cable which had so far lain idle between hawsehole and anchor the ship could be brought short round.

"Cast off the stern cable messenger!"

The orders came quickly and easily; it was a routine piece of seamanship, even though it had to be carried out under the fire of red-hot shot. There were the boats still manned and afloat to drag the battered vessel out of harm's way if the precarious breeze should die away. Round came the *Renown's* bows under the pull of the bow cable as the capstan set to work upon it. Even though the wind was dying away to a sweltering calm it was possible, by hard work, to move the ship out of range of that accursed artillery. While the capstan was dragging the ship up to her anchor the necessity for keeping the ship on the move occurred to Bush. He touched his hat to Buckland again.

"Shall I warp her down the bay, sir?"

Buckland had been standing by the binnacle staring vacantly at the fort. It was not a question of physical cowardice—that was obvious—but the shock of defeat and the contemplation of the future had made the man temporarily incapable of logical thought. But Bush's question prodded him back into dealing with the current situation.

"Yes," said Buckland, and Bush turned away, happy to have something useful to do which he well knew how to do.

Another anchor had to be cockbilled at the port bow, another cable roused out. A hail to James, in command of the boats since Roberts' death, told him of the new evolution and called him under the bows for the anchor to be lowered down to the launch—the trickiest part of the whole business. Then the launch's crew bent to their oars and towed ahead, their boat crank with the ponderous weight that it bore dangling aft and with the cable paying out astern of it. Yard by yard, to the monotonous turning of the capstan, the *Renown* crept up to her first anchor, and when that cable was straight up and down the flutter of a signal warned James, now far ahead in the launch, to drop the anchor his boat carried and return for the stream anchor which was about to be hauled up. The stern cable, now of no more use, had to be unhitched and got in, the effort of the capstan transferred from one cable to the other, while the two cutters were given lines by which they could contribute their tiny effort to the general result, towing the ponderous ship and giving her the smallest conceivable amount of motion which yet was valuable when it was a matter of such urgency to withdraw the ship out of range.

Down below Hornblower was at work dragging forward the guns he had previously dragged aft; the rumble and squeal of the trucks over the planking was audible through the ship over the monotonous clanking of the capstan. Overhead blazed the pitiless sun, softening the pitch in the seams, while yard after painful yard, cable's length after cable's length, the ship crept on down the bay out of range of the red-hot shot, over the glittering still water; down the bay of Samaná until at last they were out of range, and could pause while the men drank a niggardly half-pint of warm odorous water before turning back to their labours. To bury the dead, to repair the damages, and to digest the realisation of defeat. Maybe to wonder if the captain's malign influence still persisted, mad and helpless though he was.

EIGHT

When the tropic night closed down upon the battered *Renown*, as she stood off the land under easy sail, just enough to stiffen her to ride easily over the Atlantic rollers that the trade wind, reinforced by the sea breeze, sent hurrying under her bows, Buckland sat anxiously discussing the situation with his new first lieutenant. Despite the breeze, the little cabin was like an oven; the two lanterns which hung from the deck beams to illuminate the chart on the table seemed to heat the room unbearably. Bush felt the perspiration prickling under his uniform, and his stock constricted his thick neck so that every now and again he put two fingers into it and tugged, without relief. It would have been the simplest matter in the world to take off his heavy uniform coat and unhook his stock, but it never crossed his mind that he should do so. Bodily discomfort was something that one bore without complaint in a hard world; habit and pride both helped.

"Then you think we should bear up for Jamaica?" asked Buckland.

"I wouldn't go as far as to advise it, sir," replied Bush, cautiously. The responsibility was Buckland's, entirely Buckland's, by the law of the navy, and Bush was a little irked at Buckland's trying to share it.

"But what else can we do?" asked Buckland. "What do you suggest?"

Bush remembered the plan of campaign Hornblower had sketched out to him, but he did not put it instantly forward; he had not weighed it sufficiently in his mind—he did not even know if he thought it practicable. Instead he temporised.

"If we head for Jamaica it'll be with our tails between our legs, sir," he said.

"That's perfectly true," agreed Buckland, with a helpless gesture. "There's the captain—"

"Yes," said Bush. "There's the captain."

If the *Renown* were to report to the admiral at Kingston with a resounding success to her record there might not be too diligent an inquiry into past events; but if she came limping in, defeated, battered, it would be far more likely that inquiry might be made into the reasons why her captain had been put under restraint, why Buckland had read the secret orders, why he had taken upon himself the responsibility of making the attack upon Samaná.

"It was young Hornblower who said the same thing to me," complained Buckland pettishly. "I wish I'd never listened to him."

"What did you ask him, sir?" asked Bush.

"Oh, I can't say that I asked him anything," replied Buckland, pettishly again. "We were yarning together on the quarterdeck one evening. It was his watch."

"I remember, sir," prompted Bush.

"We talked. The infernal little whippersnapper said just what you were saying—I don't remember how it started. But then it was a question of going to Antigua. Hornblower said that it would be better if we had the chance to achieve something before we faced an inquiry about the captain. He said it was my opportunity. So it was, I suppose. My great chance. But with Hornblower talking you'd think I was going to be posted captain tomorrow. And now—"

Buckland's gesture indicated how much chance he thought he had of ever being posted captain now.

Bush thought about the report Buckland would have to make; nine killed and twenty wounded; the *Renown's* attack ignominiously beaten off; Samaná Bay as safe a refuge for privateers as ever. He was glad he was not Buckland, but at the same time he realised that there was grave danger of his being tarred with the same brush. He was first lieutenant now, he was one of the officers who had acquiesced, if nothing more, in the displacement of Sawyer from command, and it would take a victory to invest him with any virtue at all in the eyes of his superiors.

"Damn it," said Buckland in pathetic self-defence. "We did our best. Anyone could run aground in that channel. It wasn't our fault that the helmsmen were killed. Nothing could get up the bay under that crossfire."

"Hornblower was suggesting a landing on the seaward side. In Scotchman's Bay, sir." Bush was speaking as cautiously as he could.

"Another of Hornblower's suggestions?" said Buckland.

"I think that's what he had in mind from the start, sir. A landing and a surprise attack."

Probably it was because the attempt had failed, but Bush now could see the unreason of taking a wooden ship into a situation where red-hot cannon balls could be fired into her.

"What do *you* think?"

"Well, sir—"

Bush was not sure enough about what he thought to be able to express himself with any clarity. But if they had failed once they might as well fail twice; as well be hanged for a sheep as for a lamb. Bush was a sturdy soul; it went against his grain to yield in face of difficulties, and he was irritated at the thought of a tame retreat after a single repulse. The difficulty was to devise an alternative plan of campaign. He tried to say all these things to Buckland, and was sufficiently carried away to be incautious.

"I see," said Buckland. In the light of the swaying lamps the play of the shadows on his face accentuated the struggle in his expression. He came to a sudden decision. "Let's hear what he has to say."

"Aye aye, sir. Smith has the watch. Hornblower has the middle—I expect he has turned in until he's called."

Buckland was as weary as anyone in the ship—wearier than most, it seemed likely. The thought of Hornblower stretched at ease in his cot while his superiors sat up fretting wrought Buckland up to a pitch of decision that he might not otherwise have reached, determining him to act at once instead of waiting till the morrow.

"Pass the word for him," he ordered.

Hornblower came into the cabin with commendable promptitude, his hair tousled and his clothes obviously hastily thrown on. He threw a nervous glance round the cabin as he entered; obviously he suffered from not unreasonable doubts as to why he had been summoned thus into the presence of his superiors.

"What plan is this I've been hearing about?" asked Buckland. "You had some suggestion for storming the fort, I understand, Mr. Hornblower."

Hornblower did not answer immediately; he was marshalling his arguments and reconsidering his first plan in the light of the new situation—Bush could see that it was hardly fair that Hornblower should be called upon to state his plan now that the *Renown* had made one attempt and had failed after sacrificing the initial advantage of surprise. But Bush could see that he was reordering his ideas.

"I thought a landing might have more chance, sir," he said. "But that was before the Dons knew there was a ship of the line in the neighbourhood."

"And now you don't think so?"

Buckland's tone was a mixture of relief and disappointment—relief that he might not have to reach any further decisions, and disappointment that some easy way of gaining success was not being put forward.

But Hornblower had had time now to sort out his ideas, and to think about times and distances. That showed in his face.

"I think something might well be tried, sir, as long as it was tried at once."

"At once?" This was night, the crew were weary, and Buckland's tone showed surprise at the suggestion of immediate activity. "You don't mean tonight?"

"Tonight might be the best time, sir. The Dons have seen us driven off with our tails between our legs—excuse me, sir, but that's how it'll look to them, at least. The last they saw of us was beating out of Samaná Bay at sunset. They'll be pleased with themselves. You know how they are, sir. An attack at dawn from another quarter, overland, would be the last thing they'd expect."

That sounded like sense to Bush, and he made a small approving noise, the most he would venture towards making a contribution to the debate.

"How would you make this attack, Mr. Hornblower?" asked Buckland.

Hornblower had his ideas in order now; the weariness disappeared and there was a glow of enthusiasm in his face.

"The wind's fair for Scotchman's Bay, sir. We could be back there in less than two hours—before midnight. By the time we arrive we can have the landing party told off and prepared. A hundred seamen and the marines. There's a good landing beach there—we saw it yesterday. The country inland must be marshy, before the hills of the peninsula start again, but we can land on the peninsula side of the marsh. I marked the place yesterday, sir."

"Well?"

Hornblower swallowed the realisation that it was possible for a man not to be able to continue from that point with a single leap of his imagination.

"The landing party can make their way up to the crest without difficulty, sir. There's no question of losing their way—the sea on one side and Samaná Bay on the other. They can move forward along the crest. At dawn they can rush the fort. What with the marsh and the cliffs the Dons'll keep a poor lookout on that side, I fancy, sir."

"You make it sound very easy, Mr. Hornblower. But—a hundred and eighty men?"

"Enough, I think, sir."

"What makes you think so?"

"There were six guns firing at us from the fort, sir. Ninety men at most—sixty more likely. Ammunition party; men to heat the furnaces. A hundred and fifty men altogether; perhaps as few as a hundred."

"But why should that be all they had?"

"The Dons have nothing to fear on that side of the island. They're holding out against the blacks, and the French, maybe, and the English in Jamaica. There's nothing to tempt the blacks to attack 'em across the marshes. It's south of Samaná Bay that the danger lies. The Dons'll have every man that can carry a musket on that side. That's where the cities are. That's where this fellow Toussaint, or whatever his name is, will be threatening 'em, sir."

The last word of this long speech came as a fortunate afterthought; Hornblower clearly was restraining himself from pointing out the obvious too didactically to his superior officer. And Bush could see Buckland squirm in discomfort at this casual mention of blacks and French. Those secret orders—which Bush had not been allowed to read—must lay down some drastic instructions regarding the complicated political situation in Santo Domingo, where the revolted slaves, the French, and the Spaniards (nominal allies though these last might be, elsewhere in the world) all contended for the mastery.

"We'll leave the blacks and the French out of this," said Buckland, confirming Bush's suspicions.

"Yes, sir. But the Dons won't," said Hornblower, not very abashed. "They're more afraid of the blacks than of us at present."

"So you think this attack might succeed?" asked Buckland, desperately changing the subject.

"I think it might, sir. But time's getting on."

Buckland sat looking at his two juniors in painful indecision, and Bush felt full sympathy for him. A second bloody repulse—possibly something even worse, the cutting off and capitulation of the entire landing party—would be Buckland's certain ruin.

"With the fort in our hands, sir," said Hornblower, "we can deal with the privateers up the bay. They could never use it as an anchorage again."

"That's true," agreed Buckland. It would be a neat and economical fulfilment of his orders; it would restore his credit.

The timbers of the ship creaked rhythmically as the *Renown* rode over the waves. The trade wind came blowing into the cabin, relieving it of some of its stuffiness, breathing cooler air on Bush's sweaty face.

"Damn it," said Buckland with sudden reckless decision. "Let's do it."

"Very good, sir," said Hornblower.

Bush had to restrain himself from saying something that would express his pleasure; Hornblower had used a neutral tone—too obvious pushing of Buckland along the path of action might have a reverse effect and goad him into reversing his decision even now.

And although this decision had been reached there was another one, almost equally important, which had to be reached at once.

"Who will be in command?" asked Buckland. It could only be a rhetorical question; nobody except Buckland could possibly supply the answer, and to Bush and Hornblower this was obvious. They could only wait.

"It'd be poor Roberts' duty if he had lived," said Buckland, and then he turned to look at Bush.

"Mr. Bush, you will take command."

"Aye aye, sir."

Bush got up from his chair and stood with his head bowed uneasily under the deck timbers above.

"Who do you want to take with you?"

Hornblower had been on his feet during the whole interview; now he shifted his weight self-consciously from one foot to the other.

"Do you require me any more, sir?" he said to Buckland.

Bush could not tell by looking at him what emotions were at work in him; he had the pose merely of a respectful, attentive officer. Bush thought about Smith, the remaining lieutenant in the ship. He thought about Whiting, the captain of marines, who would certainly have to take part in the landing. There were midshipmen and master's mates to be used as subordinate officers. He was going to be responsible for a risky and desperate operation of war—now it was his own credit, as well as Buckland's, that was at stake. Whom did he want at his side at this, one of the most important moments in his career? Another lieutenant, if he asked for one, would be second in command, might expect to have a voice in the decisions to be made.

"Do we need Mr. Hornblower any more, Mr. Bush?" asked Buckland.

Hornblower would be an active subordinate in command. A restless one, would be another way of expressing it. He would be apt to criticise, in thought at least. Bush did not think he cared to exercise command with Hornblower listening to his every order. This whole internal debate of Bush's did not take definite shape, with formal arguments pro and con; it was rather a conflict of prejudices and instincts, the result of years of experience, which Bush could never have expressed in words. He decided he needed neither Hornblower nor Smith at the moment before he looked again at Hornblower's face. Hornblower was trying to remain impassive; but Bush could see, with sympathetic insight, how desperately anxious he was to be invited to join in the expedition. Any officer would want to go, of course, would yearn to be given an opportunity to distinguish himself, but actuating Hornblower was some motive more urgent than this. Hornblower's hands were at his sides, in the "attention" position, but Bush noticed how the long fingers tapped against his thighs, restrained themselves, and then tapped again uncontrollably. It was not cool judgment that finally brought Bush to his decision, but something quite otherwise. It might be called kindliness; it might be called affection. He had grown fond of this volatile, versatile young man, and he had no doubts now as to his physical courage.

"I'd like Mr. Hornblower to come with me, sir," he said; it seemed almost without his volition that the words came from his mouth; a soft-hearted elder brother might have said much the same thing, burdening himself with the presence of a much younger brother out of kindness of heart when contemplating some pleasant day's activities.

And as he spoke he received a glance in return from Hornblower that stifled at birth any regrets he may have felt at allowing his sentiments to influence his judgment. There was so much of relief, so much of gratitude, in the way Hornblower looked at him that Bush experienced a kindly glow of magnanimity; he felt a bigger and better man for what he had done. Naturally he did not for a moment see anything incongruous about Hornblower's being grateful for a decision that would put him in peril of his life.

"Very well, Mr. Bush," said Buckland; typically, he wavered for a space after agreeing. "That will leave me with only one lieutenant."

"Carberry could take a watch, sir," replied Bush. "And there are several among the master's mates who are good watch-keeping officers."

It was as natural for Bush to argue down opposition once he had committed himself as it might be for a fish to snap at a lure.

"Very well," said Buckland again, almost with a sigh. "And what is it that's troubling you, Mr. Hornblower?"

"Nothing, sir."

"There was something you wanted to say. Out with it."

"Nothing important, sir. It can wait. But I was wondering about altering course, sir. We can head for Scotchman's Bay now and waste no time."

"I suppose we can." Buckland knew as well as any officer in the navy that the whims of wind and weather were unpredictable, and that action upon any decision at sea should in consequence never be delayed, but he was likely to forget it unless he were prodded. "Oh, very well. We'd better get her before the wind, then. What's the course?"

After the bustle of wearing the ship round had died away Buckland led the way back to his cabin and threw himself wearily into his chair again. He put on a whimsical air to conceal the anxiety which was now consuming him afresh.

"We've satisfied Mr. Hornblower for a moment," he said. "Now let's hear what you need, Mr. Bush."

The discussion regarding the proposed expedition proceeded along normal lines; the men to be employed, the equipment that was to be issued to them, the rendezvous that had to be arranged for next morning. Hornblower kept himself studiously in the background as these points were settled.

"Any suggestions, Mr. Hornblower?" asked Bush at length. Politeness, if not policy as well, dictated the question.

"Only one, sir. We might have with us some boat grapnels with lines attached. If we have to scale the walls they might be useful."

"That's so," agreed Bush. "Remember to see that they're issued."

"Aye aye, sir."

"Do you need a messenger, Mr. Hornblower?" asked Buckland.

"It might be better if I had one, sir."

"Anyone in particular?"

"I'd prefer to have Wellard, sir, if you've no objection. He's cool-headed and thinks quickly."

"Very well." Buckland looked hard at Hornblower at the mention of Wellard's name, but said nothing more on the subject for the moment.

"Anything else? No? Mr. Bush? All settled?"

"Yes, sir," said Bush.

Buckland drummed with his fingers on the table. The recent alteration of course had not been the decisive move; it did not commit him to anything. But the next order would. If the hands were roused out, arms issued to them, instructions given for a landing, he could hardly draw back. Another attempt; maybe another failure; maybe a disaster. It was not in his power to command success, while it was certainly in his power to obviate failure by simply not risking it. He looked up and met the gaze of his two subordinates turned on him remorselessly. No, it was too late now—he had been mistaken when he thought he could draw back. He could not.

"Then it only remains to issue the orders," he said. "Will you see to it, if you please?"

"Aye aye, sir," said Bush.

He and Hornblower were about to leave the cabin when Buckland asked the question he had wanted to ask for so long. It necessitated an abrupt change of subject, even though the curiosity that inspired the question had been reawakened by Hornblower's mention of Wellard. But Buckland, full of the virtuous glow of having reached a decision, felt emboldened to ask the question; it was a moment of exaltation in any case, and confidences were possible.

"By the way, Mr. Hornblower," he said, and Hornblower halted beside the door, "how did the captain come to fall down the hatchway?"

Bush saw the expressionless mask take the place of the eager look on Hornblower's face. The answer took a moment or two to come.

"I think he must have overbalanced, sir," said Hornblower, with the utmost respect and a complete absence of feeling in his voice. "The ship was lively that night, you remember, sir."

"I suppose she was," said Buckland; disappointment and perplexity were audible in his tone. He stared at Hornblower, but there was nothing to be gleaned from that face. "Oh, very well then. Carry on."

"Aye aye, sir."

NINE

THE SEA BREEZE had died away with the cooling of the land, and it was that breathless time of night when air pressures over island and ocean were evenly balanced. Not many miles out at sea the trade winds could blow, as they blew eternally, but here on the beach a humid calm prevailed. The long swell of the Atlantic broke momentarily at the first hint of shallows far out, but lived on, like some once vigorous man now feeble after an illness, to burst rhythmically in foam on the beach to the westward; here, where the limestone cliffs of the Samaná peninsula began, there was a sheltered corner where a small watercourse had worn a wide gully in the cliff, at the most easterly end of the wide beach. And sea and surf and beach seemed to be afire; in the dark night the phosphorescence of the water was vividly bright, heaving up with the surf, running up the beach with the breakers, and lighting up the oar blades as the launches pulled to shore. The boats seemed to be floating on fire which derived new life from their passage; each launch left a wake of fire behind it, with a vivid streak on either side where the oar blades had bitten into the water.

Both landing and ascent were easy at the foot of the gully; the launches nuzzled their bows into the sand and the landing party had only to climb out, thigh-deep in the water—thigh-deep in liquid fire—holding their weapons and cartridge boxes high to make sure they were not wetted. Even the experienced seamen in the party were impressed by the brightness of the phosphorescence; the raw hands were excited by it enough to raise a bubbling chatter which called for a sharp order to repress it. Bush was one of the earliest to climb out of his launch; he splashed ashore and stood on the unaccustomed solidity of the beach while the others followed him; the water streamed down out of his soggy trouser legs.

A dark figure appeared before him, coming from the direction of the other launch.

"My party is all ashore, sir," it reported.

"Very good, Mr. Hornblower."

"I'll start up the gully with the advanced guard then, sir?"

"Yes, Mr. Hornblower. Carry out your orders."

Bush was tense and excited, as far as his stoical training and phlegmatic temperament would allow him to be; he would have liked to plunge into action at once, but the careful scheme worked out in consultation with Hornblower did not allow it. He stood aside while his own party was being formed up and Hornblower called the other division to order.

"Starbowlines! Follow me closely. Every man is to keep in touch with the man ahead of him. Remember your muskets aren't loaded—it's no use snapping them if we meet an enemy. Cold steel for that. If any one of you is fool enough to load and fire he'll get four dozen at the gangway tomorrow. That I promise you. Woolton!"

"Sir!"

"Bring up the rear. Now follow me, you men, starting from the right of the line."

Hornblower's party filed off into the darkness. Already the marines were coming ashore, their scarlet tunics black against the phosphorescence. The white crossbelts were faintly visible side by side in a rigid two-deep line as they formed up, the noncommissioned officers snapping low-voiced orders at them. With his left hand still resting on his sword hilt Bush checked once more with his right hand that his pistols were in his belt and his cartridges in his pocket. A shadowy figure halted before him with a military click of the heels.

"All present and correct, sir. Ready to march off," said Whiting's voice.

"Thank you. We may as well start. Mr. Abbott!"

"Sir!"

"You have your orders. I'm leaving with the marine detachment now. Follow us."

"Aye aye, sir."

It was a long hard climb up the gully; the sand soon was replaced by rock, flat ledges of limestone, but even among the limestone there was a sturdy vegetation, fostered by the tropical rains which fell profusely on this northern face. Only in the bed of the watercourse itself, dry now with all the water having seeped into the limestone, was there a clear passage, if clear it could be called, for it was jagged and irregular, with steep ledges up which Bush had to heave himself. In a few minutes he was streaming with sweat, but he climbed on stubbornly. Behind him the marines followed clumsily, boots clashing, weapons and equipment clinking, so that anyone might think the noise would be heard a mile away. Someone slipped and swore.

"Keep a still tongue in yer 'ead!" snapped a corporal.

"Silence!" snarled Whiting over his shoulder.

Onward and upward; here and there the vegetation was lofty enough to cut off the faint light from the stars, and Bush had to grope his way along over the rock, his breath coming with difficulty, powerfully built man though he was. Fireflies showed here and there as he climbed; it was years since he had seen fireflies last, but he paid no attention to them now. They excited irrepressible comment among the marines following him, though; Bush felt a bitter rage against the uncontrolled louts who were imperilling everything—their own lives as well as the success of the expedition—by their silly comments.

"I'll deal with 'em, sir," said Whiting, and dropped back to let the column overtake him.

Higher up a squeaky voice, moderated as best its owner knew how, greeted him from the darkness ahead.

"Mr. Bush, sir?"

"Yes."

"This is Wellard, sir. Mr. Hornblower sent me back here to act as guide. There's grassland beginning just above here."

"Very well," said Bush.

He halted for a space, wiping his streaming face with his coat sleeve, while the column closed up behind him. It was not much farther to climb when he moved on again; Wellard led him past a clump of shadowy trees, and, sure enough, Bush felt grass under his feet, and he could walk more freely, uphill still, but only a gentle slope compared with the gully. There was a low challenge ahead of them.

"Friend," said Wellard. "This is Mr. Bush here."

"Glad to see you, sir," said another voice—Hornblower's.

Hornblower detached himself from the darkness and came forward to make his report.

"My party is formed up just ahead, sir. I've sent Saddler and two reliable men on as scouts."

"Very good," said Bush, and meant it.

The marine sergeant was reporting to Whiting.

"All present, sir, 'cept for Chapman, sir. 'E's sprained 'is ankle, or 'e says 'e 'as, sir. Left 'im be'ind back there, sir."

"Let your men rest, Captain Whiting," said Bush.

Life in the confines of a ship of the line was no sort of training for climbing cliffs in the tropics, especially as the day before had been exhausting. The marines lay down, some of them with groans of relief which drew the unmistakable reproof of savage kicks from the sergeant's toe.

"We're on the crest here, sir," said Hornblower. "You can see over into the bay from that side there."

"Three miles from the fort, d'ye think?"

Bush did not mean to ask a question, for he was in command, but Hornblower was so ready with his report that Bush could not help doing so.

"Perhaps. Less than four, anyway, sir. Dawn in four hours from now, and the moon rises in half an hour."

"Yes."

"There's some sort of track or path along the crest, sir, as you'd expect. It should lead to the fort."

"Yes."

Hornblower was a good subordinate, clearly. Bush realised now that there would naturally be a track along the crest of the peninsula—that would be the obvious thing—but the probability had not occurred to him until that moment.

"If you will permit me, sir," went on Hornblower, "I'll leave James in command of my party and push on ahead with Saddler and Wellard and see how the land lies."

"Very good, Mr. Hornblower."

Yet no sooner had Hornblower left than Bush felt a vague irritation. It seemed that Hornblower was taking too much on himself. Bush was not a man who would tolerate any infringement upon his authority. However, Bush was distracted from this train of thought by the arrival of the second division of seamen, who came sweating and gasping up to join the main body. With the memory of his own weariness when he arrived still fresh in his mind Bush allowed them a rest period before he should push on with his united force. Even in the darkness a cloud of insects had discovered the sweating force, and a host of them sang round Bush's ears and bit him viciously at every opportunity. The crew of the *Renown* had been long at sea and were tender and desirable in consequence. Bush slapped at himself and swore, and every man in his command did the same.

"Mr. Bush, sir?"

It was Hornblower back again.

"Yes?"

"It's a definite trail, sir. It crosses a gully just ahead, but it's not a serious obstacle."

"Thank you, Mr. Hornblower. We'll move forward. Start with your division, if you please."

"Aye aye, sir."

The advance began. The domed limestone top of the peninsula was covered with long grass, interspersed with occasional trees. Off the track walking was a little difficult on account of the toughness and irregularity of the bunches of high grass, but on the track it was comparatively easy. The men could move along it in something like a solid body, well closed up. Their eyes, thoroughly accustomed to the darkness, could see in the starlight enough to enable them to pick their way. The gully that Hornblower had reported was only a shallow depression with easily sloping sides and presented no difficulty.

Bush plodded on at the head of the marines with Whiting at his side, the darkness all about him like a warm blanket. There was a kind of dreamlike quality about the march, induced perhaps by the fact that Bush had not slept for twenty four hours and was stupid with the fatigues he had undergone during that period. The path was ascending gently—naturally, of course, since it was rising to the highest part of the peninsula where the fort was sited.

"Ah!" said Whiting suddenly.

The path had wandered to the right, away from the sea and towards the bay, and now they had crossed the backbone of the peninsula and opened up the view over the bay. On their right they could see clear down the bay to the sea, and there it was not quite dark, for above the horizon a little moonlight was struggling through the clouds that lay at the lower edge of the sky.

"Mr. Bush, sir?"

This was Wellard, his voice more under command this time.

"Here I am."

"Mr. Hornblower sent me back again, sir. There's another gully ahead, crossing the path. An' we've come across some cattle, sir. Asleep on the hill. We disturbed 'em, an' they're wandering about."

"Thank you, I understand," said Bush.

Bush had the lowest opinion of the ordinary man and the subordinary man who constituted the great bulk of his command. He knew perfectly well that if they were to blunder into cattle along this path they would think they were meeting the enemy. There would be excitement and noise, even if there was no shooting.

"Tell Mr. Hornblower I am going to halt for fifteen minutes."

"Aye aye, sir."

A rest and opportunity to close up the column were desirable for the weary men in any case, as long as there was time to spare. And during the rest the men could be personally and individually warned about the possibility of encountering cattle. Bush knew that merely to pass the word back down the column would be unsatisfactory, actually unsafe, with these tired and slow-witted men. He gave the order and the column came to a halt, of course with sleepy men bumping into the men in front of them with a clatter and a murmur that the whispered curses of the petty officers with difficulty suppressed. While the warning was being circulated among the men lying in the grass another trouble was reported to Bush by a petty officer.

"Seaman Black, sir. 'E's drunk."

"Drunk?"

"'E must 'ave 'ad sperrits in 'is canteen, sir. You can smell it on 'is breff. Dunno 'ow 'e got it, sir."

With a hundred and eighty seamen and marines under his command one man at least was likely to be drunk. The ability of the British sailor to get hold of liquor and his readiness to overindulge in it were part of his physical make-up, like his ears or his eyes.

"Where is he now?"

"'E made a noise, sir, so I clipped 'im on the ear'ole an' 'e's quiet now, sir."

There was much left untold in that brief sentence, as Bush could guess, but he had no reason to make further inquiry while he thought of what to do.

"Choose a steady seaman and leave him with Black when we go on."

"Aye aye, sir."

So the landing party was the weaker now by the loss of the services not only of the drunken Black but of the man who must be left behind to keep him out of mischief. But it was lucky that there were not more stragglers than there had been up to now.

As the column moved forward again Hornblower's unmistakable gangling figure showed up ahead, silhouetted against the faint moonlight. He fell into step beside Bush and made his report.

"I've sighted the fort, sir."

"You have?"

"Yes, sir. A mile ahead from here, or thereabouts, there's another gully. The fort's beyond that. You can see it against the moon. Maybe half a mile beyond, maybe less. I've left Wellard and Saddler at the gully with orders to halt the advance there."

"Thank you."

Bush plodded on over the uneven surface. Now despite his fatigue he was growing tense again, as the tiger having scented his prey braces his muscles for the spring. Bush was a fighting man, and the thought of action close ahead acted as a stimulant to him. Two hours to sunrise; time and to spare.

"Half a mile from the gully to the fort?" he asked.

"Less than that, I should say, sir."

"Very well. I'll halt there and wait for daylight."

"Yes, sir. May I go on to join my division?"

"You may, Mr. Hornblower."

Bush and Whiting were holding down the pace of the march to a slow methodical step, adapted to the capacity of the slowest and clumsiest man in the column; Bush at this moment was checking himself from lengthening his stride under the spur of the prospect of action. Hornblower went plunging ahead; Bush could see his awkward gait but found himself approving of his subordinate's overflowing energy. He began to discuss with Whiting plans for the final assault.

There was a petty officer waiting for them at the approach to the gully. Bush passed the word back for the column to be ready to halt, and then halted it. He went forward to reconnoitre; with Whiting and Hornblower beside him he stared forward at the square silhouette of the fort against the sky. It even seemed possible to see the dark line of the flagpole. Now his tenseness was eased; the scowl that had been on his face in the last stages of the advance had softened into an expression of good humour, which was wasted in the circumstances.

The arrangements were quickly made, the orders whispered back and forth, the final warnings given. It was the most dangerous moment so far, as the men had to be moved up into the gully and deployed ready for a rush. One whisper from Whiting called for more than a moment's cogitation from Bush.

"Shall I give permission for the men to load, sir?"

"No," answered Bush at length. "Cold steel."

It would be too much of a risk to allow all those muskets to be loaded in the dark. There would not only be the noise of the ramrods, but there was also the danger of some fool pulling a trigger. Hornblower went off to the left, Whiting with his marines to the right, and Bush lay down in the midst of his division in the centre. His legs ached with their unaccustomed exercise, and as he lay his head was inclined to swim with fatigue and lack of sleep. He roused himself and sat up so as to bring himself under control again. Except for his weariness he did not find the waiting period troublesome to him; years of life at sea with its uncounted eventless watches, and years of war with its endless periods of boredom, had inured him to waiting. Some of the seamen actually slept as they lay in the rocky gully; more than once Bush heard snores begin, abruptly cut off by the nudges of the snorers' neighbours.

Now there, at last, right ahead, beyond the fort—was the sky a little paler? Or was it merely that the moon had climbed above the cloud? All round about save there the sky was like purple velvet, still spangled with stars. But there—there—undoubtedly there was a pallor in the sky which had not been there before. Bush stirred and felt again at the uncomfortable pistols in his belt. They were at half-cock; he must remember to pull the hammers back. On the horizon there was a suspicion, the merest suggestion, of a redness mingled with the purple of the sky.

"Pass the word down the line," said Bush. "Prepare to attack."

He waited for the word to pass, but in less time than was possible for it to have reached the ends of the line there were sounds and disturbances in the gully. The damned fools who were always to be found in any body of men had started to rise as soon as the word had reached them, probably without even bothering to pass the word on themselves. But the example would be infectious, at least; beginning at the wings, and coming back to the centre where Bush was, a double ripple of men rising to their feet went along the line. Bush rose too. He drew his sword, balanced it in his hand, and when he was satisfied with his grip he drew a pistol with his left hand and pulled back the hammer. Over on the right there was a sudden clatter of metal; the marines were fixing their bayonets. Bush could see the faces now of the men to right and to left of him.

"Forward!" he said, and the line came surging up out of the gully. "Steady, there!"

He said the last words almost loudly; sooner or later the hotheads in the line would start to run, and later would be better than sooner. He wanted his men to reach the fort in a single wave, not in a succession of breathless individuals. Out on the left he heard Hornblower's voice saying "Steady" as well. The noise of the advance must reach the fort now, must attract the attention even of sleepy, careless Spanish sentries. Soon a sentry would call for his sergeant, the sergeant would come to see, would hesitate a moment, and then give the alarm. The fort bulked square in front of Bush, still shadowy black against the newly red sky; he simply could not restrain himself from quickening his step, and the line came hurrying forward along with him. Then someone raised a shout, and then the other hotheads shouted, and the whole line started to run, Bush running with them.

Like magic, they were at the edge of the ditch, a six-foot scarp, almost vertical, cut in the limestone.

"Come on!" shouted Bush.

Even with his sword and his pistol in his hands he was able to precipitate himself down the scarp, turning his back to the fort and clinging to the edge with his elbows before allowing himself to drop. The bottom of the dry ditch was slippery and irregular, but he plunged across it to the opposite scarp. Yelling men clustered along it, hauling themselves up.

"Give me a hoist!" shouted Bush to the men on either side of him, and they put their shoulders to his thighs and almost threw him up bodily. He found himself on his face, lying on the narrow shelf above the ditch at the foot of the ramparts. A few yards along a seaman was already trying to fling his grapnel up to the top. It came thundering down, missing Bush by no more than a yard, but the seaman without a glance at him snatched it back, poised himself again, and flung the grapnel up the ramparts. It caught, and the seaman, setting his feet against the ramparts and grasping the line with his hands, began to climb like a madman. Before he was half-way up another seaman had grabbed the line and started to scale the ramparts after him, and a yelling crowd of excited men gathered round contending for the next place. Farther along the foot of the ramparts another grapnel had caught and another crowd of yelling men were gathered about the line. Now there was musketry fire; a good many loud reports, and a whiff of powder smoke came to Bush's nostrils in sharp contrast with the pure night air that he had been breathing.

Round on the other face of the fort on his right the marines would be trying to burst in through the embrasures of the guns; Bush turned to his left to see what could be done there. Almost instantly he found his reward; here was the sally port into the fort—a wide wooden door bound with iron, sheltered in the angle of the small projecting bastion at the corner of the fort. Two idiots of seamen were firing their muskets up at the heads that were beginning to show above—not a thought for the door. The average seaman was not fit to be trusted with a musket.

Bush raised his voice so that it pealed like a trumpet above the din.

"Axemen here! Axemen! Axemen!"

There were still plenty of men down in the ditch who had not yet had time to scale the scarp; one of them, waving an axe, plunged through the crowd and began to climb up. But Silk, the immensely powerful bosun's mate who commanded a section of seamen in Bush's division, came running along the shelf and grabbed the axe. He began to hew at the door, with tremendous methodical blows, gathering his body together and then flinging the axehead into the wood with all the strength in his body. Another axeman arrived, elbowed Bush aside, and started to hack at the door as well, but he was neither as accomplished nor as powerful. The thunder of their blows resounded in the angle. The iron-barred wicket in the door opened, with a gleam of steel beyond the bars. Bush pointed his pistol and fired. Silk's axe drove clean through the door, and he wrenched the blade free; then, changing his aim, he began to swing the axe in a horizontal arc at the middle part of the door. Three mighty blows and he paused to direct the other axeman where to strike. Silk struck again and again; then he put down the axe, set his fingers in the jagged hole that had opened, his foot against the door, and with one frightful muscle-tearing effort he rent away a whole section of the door. There was a beam across the gap he had opened; Silk's axe crashed onto it and through it, and again. With a hoarse shout Silk plunged, axe in hand, through the jagged hole.

"Come along, men!" yelled Bush, at the top of his lungs, and plunged through after him.

This was the open courtyard of the fort. Bush stumbled over a dead man and looked up to see a group of men before him, in their shirts, or naked; coffee-coloured faces with long disordered moustaches; men with cutlasses and pistols. Silk flung himself upon them like a maniac, the axe swinging. A Spaniard fell under the axe; Bush saw a severed finger fall to the ground as the axe crashed through the Spaniard's ineffectual guard. Pistols banged and smoke eddied about as Bush rushed forward too. There were other men swarming after him. Bush's sword clashed against a cutlass and then the group turned and fled. Bush swung with his sword at a naked shoulder fleeing before him, and saw a red wound open in the flesh and heard the man scream. The man he was pursuing vanished somewhere, like a wraith, and Bush, hurrying on to find other enemies, met a red-coated marine, hatless, his hair wild and his eyes blazing, yelling like a fiend. Bush actually had to parry the bayonet thrust the marine made at him.

"Steady, you fool!" shouted Bush, only conscious after the words had passed his lips that they were spoken at the top of his voice.

There was a hint of recognition in the marine's mad eyes, and he turned aside, his bayonet at the charge, and rushed on. There were other marines in the background; they must have made their way in through the embrasures. They were all yelling, all drunk with fighting. And here was another rush of seamen, swarming down from the ramparts they had scaled. On the far side there were wooden buildings; his men were swarming round them and shots and screams were echoing from them. Those must be the barracks and storehouses, and the garrison must have fled there for shelter from the fury of the stormers.

Whiting appeared, his scarlet tunic filthy, his sword dangling from his wrist. His eyes were bleary and cloudy.

"Call 'em off," said Bush, grasping at his own sanity with a desperate effort.

It took Whiting a moment to recognise him and to understand the order.

"Yes, sir," he said.

A fresh flood of seamen came pouring into view beyond the buildings; Hornblower's division had found their way into the fort on the far side, evidently. Bush looked round him and called to a group of his own men who appeared at that moment.

"Follow me," he said, and pushed on.

A ramp with an easy slope led up the side of the ramparts. A dead man lay there, half-way up, but Bush gave the corpse no more attention than it deserved. At the top was the main battery, six huge guns pointing through the embrasures. And beyond was the sky, all bloody-red with the dawn. A third of the way up to the zenith reached the significant colour, but even while Bush halted to look at it a golden gleam of sun showed through the clouds on the horizon, and the red began to fade perceptibly; blue sky and white clouds and blazing golden sun took its place. That was the measure of the time the assault had taken; only the few minutes from earliest dawn to tropical sunrise. Bush stood and grasped this astonishing fact—it could have been late afternoon as far as his own sensations went.

Here from the gun platform the whole view of the bay opened up. There was the opposite shore; the shallows where the *Renown* had grounded (was it only yesterday?), the rolling country lifting immediately into the hills of that side, with the sharply defined shape of the other battery at the foot of the point. To the left the peninsula dropped sharply in a series of jagged headlands, stretching like fingers out into the blue, blue ocean; farther round still was the sapphire surface of Scotchman's Bay and there, with her backed mizzen topsail catching brilliantly the rising sun, lay the *Renown.* At that distance she looked like a lovely toy; Bush caught his breath at the sight of her, not because of the beauty of the scene but with relief. The sight of the ship, and the associated memories which the sight called up in his mind, brought his sanity flooding back; there were a thousand things to be done now.

Hornblower appeared up the other ramp; he looked like a scarecrow with his disordered clothes. He held sword in one hand and pistol in the other, just as did Bush. Beside him Wellard swung a cutlass singularly large for him, and at his heels were a score or more of seamen still under discipline, their muskets, with bayonets fixed, held before them ready for action.

"Morning, sir," said Hornblower. His battered cocked hat was still on his head for him to touch it, and he made a move to do so, checking himself at the realisation that his sword was in his hand.

"Good morning," said Bush, automatically.

"Congratulations, sir," said Hornblower. His face was white, and the smile on his lips was like the grin of a corpse. His beard sprouted over his lips and chin.

"Thank you," said Bush.

Hornblower pushed his pistol into his belt and then sheathed his sword.

"I've taken possession of all that side, sir," he went on, with a gesture behind him. "Shall I carry on?"

"Yes, carry on, Mr. Hornblower."

"Aye aye, sir."

This time Hornblower could touch his hat. He gave a rapid order posting a petty officer and men over the guns.

"You see, sir," said Hornblower, pointing, "a few got away."

Bush looked down the precipitous hillside that fell to the bay and could see a few figures down there.

"Not enough to trouble us," he said; his mind was just beginning to work smoothly now.

"No, sir. I've forty prisoners under guard at the main gate. I can see Whiting's collecting the rest. I'll go on now, sir, if I may."

"Very well, Mr. Hornblower."

Somebody at least had kept a clear head during the fury of the assault. Bush went on down the farther ramp. A petty officer and a couple of seamen stood there on guard; they came to attention as Bush appeared.

"What are you doing?" he asked.

"This yere's the magazine, zur," said the petty officer—Ambrose, captain of the foretop, who had never lost the broad Devon acquired in his childhood, despite his years in the navy. "We'm guarding of it."

"Mr. Hornblower's orders?"

"Iss, zur."

A forlorn party of prisoners squatted by the main gate. Hornblower had reported this presence of them. But there were guards he had said nothing about—a sentry at the well; guards at the gate; Woolton, the steadiest petty officer of them all, at a long wooden building beside the gate, and six men with him.

"What's your duty?" demanded Bush.

"Guarding the provision store, sir. There's liquor here."

"Very well."

If the madmen who had made the assault—that marine, for instance, whose bayonet thrust Bush had parried—had got at the liquor there would be no controlling them at all.

Abbott, the midshipman in subordinate command of Bush's own division, came hurrying up.

"What the hell d'ye think you've been doing?" demanded Bush, testily. "I've been without you since the attack began."

"Sorry, sir," apologised Abbott. Of course he had been carried away by the fury of the attack, but that was no excuse; certainly no excuse when one remembered young Wellard still at Hornblower's side and attending to his duties.

"Get ready to make the signal to the ship," ordered Bush. "You ought to have been ready to do that five minutes ago. Clear three guns. Who was it who was carrying the flag? Find him and bend it on over the Spanish colours. Jump to it, damn you."

Victory might be sweet, but it had no effect on Bush's temper, now that the reaction had set in. Bush had had no sleep and no breakfast, and even though perhaps only ten minutes had elapsed since the fort had been captured, his conscience nagged at him regarding those ten minutes; there were many things he ought to have done in that time.

It was a relief to turn away from the contemplation of his own shortcomings and to settle with Whiting regarding the safeguarding of the prisoners. They had all been fetched out of the barrack buildings by now; a hundred half-naked men, and at least a score of women, their hair streaming down their backs and their scanty clothing clutched about them. At a more peaceful moment Bush would have had an eye for those women, but as it was he merely felt irritated at the thought of an additional complication to deal with, and his eyes only took note of them as such.

Among the men there was a small sprinkling of Negroes and mulattoes, but most of them were Spaniards. Nearly all the dead men who lay here and there were fully clothed, in white uniforms with blue facings—they were the sentinels and the main guard who had paid the penalty for their lack of watchfulness.

"Who was in command?" asked Bush of Whiting.

"Can't tell, sir."

"Well, ask them, then."

Bush had command of no language at all save his own, and apparently neither had Whiting, judging by his unhappy glance.

"Please, sir—" this was Pierce, surgeon's mate, trying to attract his attention, "can I have a party to help carry the wounded into the shade?"

Before Bush could answer him Abbott was hailing from the gun platform.

"Guns clear, sir. May I draw powder charges from the magazines?"

And then before Bush could give permission here was young Wellard, trying to elbow Pierce on one side so as to command Bush's attention.

"Please, sir. Please, sir. Mr. Hornblower's respects, sir, an' could you please come up to the tower there, sir. Mr. Hornblower says it's urgent, sir."

Bush felt at that moment as if one more distraction would break his heart.

TEN

At each corner of the fort there was a small bastion built out, to give flanking fire along the walls, and on top of the southwest bastion stood a little watchtower which carried the flagstaff. Bush and Hornblower stood on the tower, the broad Atlantic behind them and before them the long gulf of the bay of Samaná. Over their heads waved two flags; the White Ensign above, the red and gold of Spain below. Out in the *Renown* they might not be able to make out the colours, but they would certainly see the two flags. And when having heard the three signal guns boom out they trained their telescopes on the fort they must have seen the flags slowly flutter down and rise again, dip and rise again. Three guns; two flags twice dipped. That was the signal that the fort was in English hands, and the *Renown* had seen it, for she had braced up her mizzen topsail and begun the long beat back along the coast of the peninsula.

Bush and Hornblower had with them the one telescope which a hasty search through the fort had brought to light; when one of them had it to his eye the other could hardly restrain his twitching fingers from snatching at it. At the moment Bush was looking through it, training it on the farther shore of the bay, and Hornblower was stabbing with an index finger at what he had been looking at a moment before.

"You see, sir?" he asked. "Farther up the bay than the battery. There's the town—Savaná, it's called. And beyond that there's the shipping. They'll up anchor any minute now."

"I see 'em," said Bush, the glass still at his eye. "Four small craft. No sail hoisted—hard to tell what they are."

"Easy enough to guess, though, sir."

"Yes, I suppose so," said Bush.

There would be no need for big men of war here, immediately adjacent to the Mona Passage. Half the Caribbean trade came up through here, passing within thirty miles of the bay of Samaná. Fast, handy craft, with a couple of long guns each and a large crew, could dash out and snap up prizes and retire to the protection of the bay, where the crossed fire of the batteries could be relied on to keep out enemies, as the events of yesterday had proved. The raiders would hardly have to spend a night at sea.

"They'll know by now we've got this fort," said Hornblower. "They'll guess that *Renown* will be coming round after 'em. They can sweep, and tow, and kedge. They'll be out of the bay before you can say Jack Robinson. And from Engano Point it's a fair wind for Martinique."

"Very likely," agreed Bush.

With a simultaneous thought they turned to look at the *Renown*. With her stern to them, her sails braced sharp on the starboard tack, she was making her way out to sea; it would be a long beat before she could go about in the certainty of being able to weather Cape Samaná. She looked lovely enough out there, with her white sails against the rich blue, but it would be hours before she could work round to stop the bolt hole. Bush turned back and considered the sheltered waters of the bay.

"Better man the guns and make ready for 'em," he said.

"Yes, sir," said Hornblower. He hesitated, "We won't have 'em under fire for long. They'll be shallow draught. They can hug the point over there closer than *Renown* could."

"But it won't take much to sink 'em, either," said Bush. "Oh, I see what you're after."

"Red-hot shot might make all the difference, sir," said Hornblower.

"Repay 'em in their own coin," said Bush, with a grin of satisfaction. Yesterday the *Renown* had endured the hellish fire of red-hot shot. To Bush the thought of roasting a few Dagoes was quite charming.

"That's right, sir," said Hornblower.

He was not grinning like Bush. There was a frown on his face; he was oppressed with the thought that the privateers might escape to continue their depredations elsewhere, and any means to reduce their chances should be used.

"But can you do it?" asked Bush suddenly. "D'ye know how to heat shot?"

"I'll find out, sir."

"I'll wager no man of ours knows how."

Shot could only be heated in a battery on land; a seagoing ship, constructed of inflammable material, could not run the risk of going into action with a flaming furnace inside her. The French, in the early days of the Revolutionary War, had made some disastrous experiments in the hope of finding a means of countering England's naval superiority, but after a few ships had set themselves on fire they had given up the attempt. Seagoing men now left the use of the heated weapon to shore-based garrison artillery.

"I'll try and find out for myself, sir," said Hornblower. "There's the furnace down there and all the gear."

Hornblower stood in the sunshine, already far too hot to be comfortable. His face was pale, dirty, and bearded, and in his expression eagerness and weariness were oddly at war.

"Have you had any breakfast yet?" asked Bush.

"No, sir." Hornblower looked straight at him. "Neither have you, sir."

"No," grinned Bush.

He had not been able to spare a moment for anything like that, with the whole defence of the fort to be organised. But he could bear fatigue and hunger and thirst, and he doubted if Hornblower could.

"I'll get a drink of water at the well, sir," said Hornblower.

As he said the words, and the full import came to him, a change in his expression was quite obvious. He ran the tip of his tongue over his lips; Bush could see that the lips were cracked and parched and that the tongue could do nothing to relieve them. The man had drunk nothing since he had landed twelve hours ago—twelve hours of desperate exertion in a tropical climate.

"See that you do, Mr. Hornblower," said Bush. "That's an order."

"Aye aye, sir."

Bush found the telescope leaving his hand and passing into Hornblower's.

"May I have another look, sir, before I go down? By George, I thought as much. That two-master's warping out, sir. Less than an hour before she's within range. I'll get the guns manned, sir. Take a look for yourself, sir."

He went darting down the stone stairs of the tower, having given back the telescope, but half-way down he paused.

"Don't forget your breakfast, sir," he said, his face upturned to Bush. "You've plenty of time for that."

Bush's glance through the telescope confirmed what Hornblower had said. At least one of the vessels up the bay was beginning to move. He turned and swept the rest of the land and water with a precautionary glance before handing the telescope to Abbott, who during all this conversation had been standing by, silent in the presence of his betters.

"Keep a sharp lookout," said Bush.

Down in the body of the fort Hornblower was already issuing rapid orders, and the men, roused to activity, were on the move. On the gun platform they were casting loose the remaining guns, and as Bush descended from the platform he saw Hornblower organising other working parties, snapping out orders with quick gestures. At the sight of Bush he turned guiltily and walked over to the well. A marine was winding up the bucket, and Hornblower seized it. He raised the bucket to his lips, leaning back to balance the weight; and he drank and drank, water slopping in quantities over his chest as he drank, water pouring over his face, until the bucket was empty, and then he put it down with a grin at Bush, his face still dripping water. The very sight of him was enough to make Bush, who had already had one drink from the well, feel consumed with thirst all over again.

By the time Bush had drunk there was the usual group of people clamouring for his attention, for orders and information, and by the time he had dealt with them there was smoke rising from the furnace in the corner of the courtyard, and a loud crackling from inside it. Bush walked over. A seaman, kneeling, was plying a pair of bellows; two other men were bringing wood from the pile against the ramparts. When the furnace door was opened the blast of heat that rose into Bush's face was enough to make him step back. Hornblower turned up with his hurried pace.

"How's the shot, Saddler?" he asked.

The petty officer picked up some rags, and, with them to shield his hands, laid hold of two long handles that projected from the far side of the furnace, balancing two projecting from the near side. When he drew them out it became apparent that all four handles were part of a large iron grating, the centre of which rested inside the furnace above the blazing fuel. Lying on the grating were rows of shot, still black in the sunshine. Saddler shifted his quid, gathered his saliva, and spat expertly on the nearest one. The spittle boiled off, but not with violence.

"Not very hot yet, sir," said Saddler.

"Us'll fry they devils," said the man with the bellows, unexpectedly; he looked up, as he crouched on his knees, with ecstasy in his face at the thought of burning his enemies alive.

Hornblower paid him no attention.

"Here, you bearer men," he said, "let's see what you can do."

Hornblower had been followed by a file of men, every pair carrying a piece of apparatus formed of two iron bars joined with iron crosspieces. The first pair approached. Saddler took a pair of tongs and gingerly worked a hot shot onto the bearer.

"Move on, you two," ordered Hornblower. "Next!"

When a shot lay on every bearer Hornblower led his men away.

"Now let's see you roll those into the guns," he said.

Bush followed, consumed with curiosity. The procession moved up the ramp to the gun platform, where now crews had been told off to every gun; the guns were run back with the muzzles well clear of the embrasures. Tubs of water stood by each pair of guns.

"Now, you rammers," said Hornblower, "are your dry wads in? Then in with your wet wads."

From the tubs the seamen brought out round flat disks of fibre, dripping with water.

"Two to a gun," said Hornblower.

The wet wads were thrust into the muzzles of the guns and then were forced down the bores with the club-ended ramrods.

"Ram 'em home," said Hornblower. "Now, bearers."

It was not such an easy thing to do, to put the ends of the bearing-stretchers at the muzzles of the guns and then to tilt so as to induce the hot shot to roll down into the bore.

"The Dons must've exercised with these guns better than we'd give 'em credit for," said Hornblower to Bush, "judging by the practice they made yesterday. Rammers!"

The ramrods thrust the shot home against the charges; there was a sharp sizzling noise as each hot shot rested against the wet wads.

"Run up!"

The guns' crews seized the tackles and heaved, and the ponderous guns rolled slowly forward to point their muzzles out through the embrasures.

"Aim for the point over there and fire!"

With handspikes under the rear axles the guns were traversed at the orders of the captains; the priming tubes were already in the touch-holes and each gun was fired as it bore. The sound of the explosions was very different here on a stone platform from when guns were fired in the confined spaces of a wooden ship. The slight wind blew the smoke sideways.

"Pretty fair!" said Hornblower, shading his eyes to watch the fall of the shot, and, turning to Bush, "That'll puzzle those gentlemen over there. They'll wonder what in the world we're firing at."

"How long," asked Bush, who had watched the whole process with a fascinated yet horrified interest, "before a hot shot burns through those wads and sets off the gun itself?"

"That is one of the things I do not know, sir," answered Hornblower with a grin. "It would not surprise me if we found out during the course of today."

"I dare say," said Bush, but Hornblower had swung round and was confronting a seaman who had come running up to the platform.

"What d'ye think you're doing?"

"Bringing a fresh charge, sir," said the man, surprised, indicating with a gesture the cartridge-container he carried.

"Then get back and wait for the order. Get back, all of you."

The ammunition carriers shrank back before his evident anger.

"Swab out!" ordered Hornblower to the guns' crews, and as the wetted sponges were thrust into the muzzles he turned to Bush again. "We can't be too careful, sir. We don't want any chance of live charges and red-hot shot coming together on this platform."

"Certainly not," agreed Bush.

He was both pleased and irritated that Hornblower should have dealt so efficiently with the organisation of the battery.

"Fresh charges!" yelled Hornblower, and the ammunition carriers he had previously sent back came trotting up the ramp again. "These are English cartridges, sir, I'll wager."

"Why do you say that?"

"West-Country serge, stitched and choked exactly like ours, sir. Out of English prizes, I fancy."

It was most probable; the Spanish forces which held this end of the island against the insurgents most likely depended on renewing their stores from English ships captured in the Mona Passage. Well, with good fortune they would take no more prizes—the implication, forcing itself on Bush's mind despite his many preoccupations, made him stir uneasily as he stood by the guns with his hands clasped behind him and the sun beating down on his face. The Dons would be in a bad way with their source of supplies cut off. They would not be able to hold out long against the rebellious blacks that hemmed them in here in the eastern end of Santo Domingo.

"Ram those wads handsomely, there, Cray," said Hornblower. "No powder in that bore, or we'll have 'Cray D.D.' in the ship's books."

There was a laugh at that; "D.D." in the ship's books meant "discharged, dead," but Bush was not paying attention. He had scrambled up the parapet and was staring out at the bay.

"They're standing down the bay," he said. "Stand by, Mr. Hornblower."

"Aye aye, sir."

Bush strained his sight to look at the four vessels creeping down the fairway. As he watched he saw the first one hoisting sail on both masts. Apparently she was taking advantage of a flaw of wind, blowing flukily in the confined and heated waters, to gain some of the desperately necessary distance towards the sea and safety.

"Mr. Abbott, bring down that glass!" shouted Hornblower.

As Abbott descended the steps Hornblower addressed a further comment to Bush.

"If they're making a bolt for it the moment they know we've got the fort it means they're not feeling too secure over there, sir."

"I suppose not."

"You might have expected 'em to try to recapture the fort one way or another. They could land a force up the peninsula and come down to attack us. I wonder why they're not trying that, sir? Why do they just upstick and run?"

"They're only Dagoes," said Bush. He refused to speculate further about the enemy's motives while action was imminent, and he grabbed the glass from Abbott's hands.

Through the telescope details were far plainer. Two large schooners with several guns a-side; a big lugger, and a vessel whose rig they still could not determine, as she was the farthest away and, with no sail set, was towing behind her boats out from the anchorage.

"It'll be long range, Mr. Hornblower," said Bush.

"Yes, sir. But they hit us with these same guns yesterday."

"Make sure of your aim. They won't be long under fire."

"Aye aye, sir."

The vessels were not coming down together. If they had done so they might stand a better chance, as the fort would only be able to fire on one at a time. But the panic feeling of every man for himself must have started them off as soon as each one separately could get under way—and perhaps the deep channel was too narrow for vessels in company. Now the leading schooner had taken in her sail again; the wind here, what there was of it, was foul for her when she turned to port along the channel. She had two boats out quickly enough to tow her; Bush's telescope could reveal every detail.

"Some time yet before she's in range, sir," said Hornblower. "I'll take a look at the furnace, with your permission."

"I'll come too," said Bush.

At the furnace the bellows were still being worked and the heat was tremendous—but it was far hotter when Saddler drew out the grating that carried the heated shot. Even in the sunshine they could see the glow of the spheres; as the heat rose from them the atmosphere above them wavered so that everything below was vague and distorted. It could be a scene in Hell. Saddler spat on the nearest cannon ball and the saliva leaped with an instant hiss from the smooth surface of the sphere, falling from it without contact to dance and leap on the grating under it until with a final hiss it vanished entirely. A second attempt by Saddler brought the same result.

"Hot enough, sir?" asked Saddler.

"Yes," said Hornblower.

Bush had often enough as a midshipman taken a smoothing-iron forward to the galley to heat it when there had been particular need to iron a shirt or a neckcloth; he remembered how he had made the same test of the temperature of the iron. It was a proof that the iron was dangerously hot to use when the spittle refused to make contact with it, but the shot was far hotter than that, infinitely hotter.

Saddler thrust the grating back into the furnace and wiped his streaming face with the rags that had shielded his hands.

"Stand by, you bearer men," said Hornblower. "You'll be busy enough soon."

With a glance at Bush for permission he was off again, back to the battery, hurrying with awkward galvanic strides. Bush followed more slowly; he was weary with all his exertions and it crossed his mind as he watched Hornblower hurrying up the ramp that Hornblower had probably been more active than he and was not blessed with nearly as powerful a physique. By the time he came up to him Hornblower was watching the leading schooner again.

"Her scantlings'll be weak," said Hornblower. "These twenty-four-pounders'll go clean through her most of the time, even at long range."

"Plunging shot," said Bush. "Maybe they'll go out through her bottom."

"Maybe so," said Hornblower, and then added "sir."

Even after all his years of service he was liable to forget that important monosyllable when he was thinking deeply.

"She's setting sail again!" said Bush. "They've got her head round."

"And the tows have cast off," added Hornblower. "Not long now."

He looked down the line of guns, all charged and primed, the quoins withdrawn so that they were at their highest elevation, the muzzles pointing upward as though awaiting the shot to be rolled into them. The schooner was moving perceptibly down the channel towards them.

Hornblower turned and walked down the row; behind his back one hand was twisting impatiently within the other; he came back and turned again, walking jerkily down the row—he seemed incapable of standing still, but when he caught Bush's eye on him he halted guiltily, forcing himself, with an obvious effort, to stand still like his superior officer. The schooner crept on, a full half-mile ahead of the next vessel.

"You might try a ranging shot," said Bush at length.

"Aye aye, sir," said Hornblower with instant agreement, like a river bursting through a broken dam. It seemed as if he had been compelling himself to wait until Bush should speak.

"Furnace, there!" hailed Hornblower. "Saddler! Send up one shot."

The bearers came plodding up the ramp, carrying carefully between them the glowing cannon ball. The bright redness of it was quite obvious—even the heat that it gave off was distinctly perceptible. The wet wads were rammed down the bore of the nearest gun, the shot bearer was hoisted up level with its muzzle, and, coaxed into motion with wad-hook and rammer, the fiery shot was rolled in. There was an instant hissing and spluttering of steam as the ball came into contact with the wet wads; Bush wondered again how long it would be before the wads were burned through and the charge set off; the recoil would make it decidedly uncomfortable for anyone who happened to be aiming the gun at that moment.

"Run up!" Hornblower was giving the orders; the gun's crew heaved at the tackles and the gun rumbled forward.

Hornblower took his place behind the gun and, squatting down, he squinted along it.

"Trail right!" Tackles and handspikes heaved the gun around. "A touch more! Steady! No, a touch left. Steady!"

Somewhat to Bush's relief Hornblower straightened himself and came from behind the gun. He leaped onto the parapet with his usual uncontrollable vigour and shaded his eyes; Bush at one side kept his telescope trained on the schooner.

"Fire!" said Hornblower.

The momentary hiss of the priming was drowned in the instant bellow of the gun. Bush saw the black line of the shot's path against the blue of the sky, reaching upward during the time it might take to draw a breath, sinking downward again; a strange sort of line, an inch long if he had to say its length, constantly renewing itself in front and constantly disappearing at its back end, and pointing straight at the schooner. It was still pointing at her, just above her—to that extent did the speed of the shot outpace the recording of retina and brain—when Bush saw the splash, right in line with the schooner's bows. He took his eye from the telescope as the splash disappeared, to find Hornblower looking at him.

"A cable's length short," he said, and Hornblower nodded agreement.

"We can open fire then, sir?" asked Hornblower.

"Yes, carry on, Mr. Hornblower."

The words were hardly out of his mouth before Hornblower was hailing again.

"Furnace, there! Five more shot!"

It took Bush a moment or two to see the point of that order. But clearly it was inadvisable to have hot shot and powder charges brought up on the platform at the same time; the gun that had been fired would have to remain unloaded until the other five had fired as well. Hornblower came down and stood at Bush's side again.

"I couldn't understand yesterday why they always fired salvos at us, sir," he said, "that reduced the rate of fire to the speed of the slowest gun. But I see now."

"So do I," said Bush.

"All your wet wads in?" demanded Hornblower of the guns' crews. "Certain? Carry on, then."

The shot were coaxed into the muzzles of the guns; they hissed and spluttered against the wads.

"Run up. Now take your aim. Make sure of it, captains."

The hissing and spluttering continued as the guns were trained.

"Fire when your gun bears!"

Hornblower was up on the parapet again; Bush could see perfectly well through embrasure of the idle gun. The five guns all fired within a second or two of each other; through Bush's telescope the sky was streaked by the passage of their shot.

"Sponge out!" said Hornblower and then, louder, "Six charges!"

He came down to Bush.

"One splash pretty close," said Bush.

"Two very short," said Hornblower, "and one far out on the right. I know who fired that one and I'll deal with him."

"One splash I didn't see," said Bush.

"Nor did I, sir. Clean over, perhaps. But possibly a hit."

The man with the charges came running up to the platform, and the eager crews seized them and rammed them home and the dry wads on top of the charges.

"Six shot!" shouted Hornblower to Saddler, and then, to the gun captains, "Prime. Put in your wet wads."

"She's altered course," said Bush. "The range can't have changed much."

"No, sir. Load and run up! Excuse me, sir."

He went hurrying off to take his stand by the left-hand gun, which presumably was the one which had been incorrectly laid previously. "Take your aim carefully," he called from his new position. "Fire when you're sure."

Bush saw him squat behind the left-hand gun, but he himself applied his attention to observing the results of the shooting.

The cycle repeated itself; the guns roared, the men came running with fresh charges, the red-hot shot were brought up. The guns were fired again before Hornblower came back to Bush's side.

"You're hitting, I think," said Bush. He turned back to look again through his glass. "I think—by God, yes! Smoke! Smoke!"

A faint black cloud was just visible between the schooner's masts. It thinned again, and Bush could not be perfectly sure. The nearest gun bellowed out, and a chance flaw of wind blew the powder smoke about them as they stood together, blotting out their view of the schooner.

"Confound it all!" said Bush, moving about restlessly in search of a better viewpoint.

The other guns went off almost simultaneously and added to the smoke.

"Bring up fresh charges!" yelled Hornblower with the smoke eddying round him. "See that you swab those guns out properly."

The smoke eddied away, revealing the schooner apparently unharmed, still creeping along the bay, and Bush cursed in his disappointment.

"The range is shortening and the guns are hot now," said Hornblower, and then, louder, "Gun captains! Get your quoins in!"

He hurried off to supervise the adjustment of the guns' elevation, and it was some seconds before he hailed again for hot shot to be brought up. In that time Bush noticed that the schooner's boats, which had been pulling in company with the schooner, were turning to run alongside her. That could mean that the schooner's captain was now sure that the flaws of wind would be sufficient to carry her round the point and safely to the mouth of the bay. The guns went off again in an irregular salvo, and Bush saw a trio of splashes rise from the water's surface close on the near side of the schooner.

"Fresh charges!" yelled Hornblower.

And then Bush saw the schooner swing round, presenting her stern to the battery and heading straight for the shallows of the further shore.

"What in hell—?" said Bush to himself.

Then he saw a sudden fountain of black smoke appear spouting from the schooner's deck, and while this sight was rejoicing him he saw the schooner's booms swing over as she took the ground. She was afire and had been deliberately run ashore. The smoke was dense about her hull, and while he held her in his telescope he saw her big white mainsail above the smoke suddenly disintegrate and disappear—the flames had caught it and whisked it away into nothing. He took the telescope from his eye and looked round for Hornblower, who was standing on the parapet again. Powder and smoke had grimed his face, already dark with the growth of his beard and his teeth showed strangely white as he grinned. The gunners were cheering, and the cheering was being echoed by the rest of the landing party in the fort.

Hornblower was gesticulating to make the gunners cease their noise so that he could be heard down in the fort as he countermanded his call for more shot.

"Belay that order, Saddler! Take those shot back, bearer men!"

He jumped down and approached Bush.

"That's done it," said the latter.

"The first one, anyway."

A great jet of smoke came from the burning wreck, reaching up and up from between her masts; the mainmast fell as they watched, and as it fell the report of the explosion came to their ears across the water; the fire had reached the schooner's powder store, and when the smoke cleared a little they could see that she now lay on the shore in two halves, blown asunder in the middle. The foremast still stood for a moment on the forward half, but it fell as they watched it; bows and stern were blazing fiercely, while the boats with the crews rowed away across the shallows.

"A nasty sight," said Hornblower, but Bush could see nothing unpleasant about the sight of an enemy burning. He was exulting.

"With half his men in the boats he didn't have enough hands to spare to fight the fires when we hit him," he said.

"Maybe a shot went through her deck and lodged in her hold," said Hornblower.

The tone of his voice made Bush look quickly at him, for he was speaking thickly and harshly like a drunken man; but he could not be drunk, although the dirty hairy face and bloodshot eyes might well have suggested it. The man was fatigued. Then the dull expression on Hornblower's face was replaced once more by a look of animation, and when he spoke his voice was natural again.

"Here comes the next," he said. "She must be nearly in range."

The second schooner, also with her boats in attendance, was coming down the channel, her sails set. Hornblower turned back to the guns.

"D'you see the next ship to aim at?" he called, and received a fierce roar of agreement, before he turned round to hail Saddler. "Bring up those shot, bearer men."

The procession of bearers with the glowing shot came up the ramp again—frightfully hot shot; the heat as each one went by, twenty four pounds of white-hot iron, was like the passage of a wave. The routine of rolling the fiendish things into the gun muzzles proceeded. There were some loud remarks from the men at the guns, and one of the shot fell with a thump on the stone floor of the battery, and lay there glowing. Two other guns were still not loaded.

"What's wrong there?" demanded Hornblower.

"Please, sir—"

Hornblower was already striding over to see for himself. From the muzzle of one of the three loaded guns there was a curl of steam; in all three there was a wild hissing as the hot shot rested on the wet wads.

"Run up, train, and fire," ordered Hornblower. "Now what's the matter with you others? Roll that thing out of the way."

"Shot won't fit, sir," said more than one voice as someone with a wad-hook awkwardly rolled the fallen shot up against the parapet. The bearers of the other two stood by, sweating. Anything Hornblower could say in reply was drowned for the moment by the roar of one of the guns—the men were still at the tackles, and the gun had gone off on its own volition as they ran it up. A man sat crying out with pain, for the carriage had recoiled over his foot and blood was already pouring from it onto the stone floor. The captains of the other two loaded guns made no pretence at training and aiming. The moment their guns were run up they shouted "Stand clear," and fired.

"Carry him down to Mr. Pierce," said Hornblower, indicating the injured man. "Now let's see about these shot."

Hornblower returned to Bush with a rueful look on his face, embarrassed and self-conscious.

"What's the trouble?" asked Bush.

"Those shot are too hot," explained Hornblower. "Damn it, I didn't think of that. They've half melted in the furnace and gone out of shape so that they won't fit the bore. What a fool I was not to think of that."

As his superior officer, Bush did not admit that he had not thought of it either. He said nothing.

"And the ones that hadn't gone out of shape were too hot anyway," went on Hornblower. "I'm the damnedest fool God ever made. Mad as a hatter. Did you see how that gun went off? The men'll be scared now and won't lay their guns properly—too anxious to fire it off before the recoil catches them. God, I'm a careless son of a swab."

"Easy, easy," said Bush, a prey to conflicting emotions.

Hornblower pounding his left hand with his right fist as he upbraided himself was a comic sight; Bush could not help laughing at him. And Bush knew perfectly well that Hornblower had done excellently so far, really excellently, to have mastered at a moment's notice so much of the technique of using red-hot shot. Moreover it must be confessed that Bush had experienced, during this expedition, more than one moment of pique at Hornblower's invariable bold assumption of responsibility; and the pique may even have been roused by a stronger motive, jealousy at Hornblower's good management—an unworthy motive, which Bush would disclaim with shocked surprise if he became aware of it. Yet it made the sight of Hornblower's present discomfiture all the more amusing at the moment.

"Don't take on so," said Bush with a grin.

"But it makes me wild to be such a—"

Hornblower cut the sentence off short. Bush could actually see him calling up his self-control and mastering himself, could see his annoyance at having been self-revelatory, could see the mask of the stoical and experienced fighting man put back into place to conceal the furious passions within.

"Would you take charge here, sir?" he said; it might be another person speaking. "I'll go and take a look at the furnace, if I may. They'll have to go easy with those bellows."

"Very good, Mr. Hornblower. Send the ammunition up and I'll direct the fire on the schooner."

"Aye aye, sir. I'll send up the last shot to go into the furnace. They won't be too hot yet, sir."

Hornblower went darting down the ramp while Bush moved behind the guns to direct the fire. The fresh charges came up and were rammed home, the wet wads went in on top of the dry wads, and then the bearers began to arrive with the shot.

"Steady, all of you," said Bush. "These won't be as hot as the last batch. Take your aim carefully."

But when Bush climbed onto the parapet and trained his telescope on the second schooner he could see that the schooner was changing her mind. She had brailed up her foresail and taken in her jibs; her boats were lying at an angle to her course, and were struggling, beetlelike, off her bows. They were pulling her round—she was going back up the bay and deciding not to run the gauntlet of the red-hot shot. There was the smouldering wreck of her consort to frighten her.

"She's turning tail!" said Bush loudly. "Hit her while you can, you men."

He saw the shot curving in the air, he saw the splashes in the water; he remembered how yesterday he had seen a ricochet shot from these very guns rebound from the water and strike the *Renown's* massive side—one of the splashes was dead true for line, and might well indicate a hit.

"Fresh charges!" he bellowed, turning to make himself heard down at the magazine. "Sponge out!"

But by the time the charges were in the guns the schooner had got her head right round, had reset her foresail, and was creeping back up the bay. Judging by the splashes of the last salvo she would be out of range before the next could be fired.

"Mr. Hornblower!"

"Sir!"

"'Vast sending any shot."

"Aye aye, sir."

When Hornblower came up again to the battery Bush pointed to the retreating schooner.

"He thought better of it, did he?" commented Hornblower. "Yes, and those other two have anchored, I should say."

His fingers were twitching for the one telescope again, and Bush handed it over.

"The other two aren't moving either," said Hornblower, and then he swung round and trained the telescope down the bay towards the sea. "*Renown's* gone about. She's caught the wind. Six miles? Seven miles? She'll be rounding the point in an hour."

It was Bush's turn to grab for the telescope. There was no mistaking the trim of those topsails. From the *Renown* he transferred his attention to the opposite shore of the bay. There was the other battery with the Spanish flag above it—the flag was now drooping, now flapping lazily in the light wind prevailing over the shore. He could make out no sign of activity whatever, and there was some finality in his gesture as he closed the telescope and looked at his second in command.

"Everything's quiet," he said. "Nothing to be done until *Renown* comes down."

"That is so," agreed Hornblower.

It was interesting to watch Hornblower's animation ebb away. Intense weariness was obvious in his face the moment he was off his guard.

"We can feed the men," said Bush, "and I'd like to have a look at the wounded. Those damned prisoners have to be sorted out— Whiting's got 'em all herded in the casemate, men and women, captains and drum boys. God knows what provisions there are here. We've got to see about that. Then we can set a watch, dismiss the watch below, and some of us can get some rest."

"So we can," said Hornblower; reminded of the necessary activities that still remained, he resumed his stolid expression. "Shall I go down and start attending to it, sir?"

ELEVEN

The sun at noontime was glaring down into the fort of Samaná. Within the walls the heat was pitilessly reflected inwards to a murderous concentration, so that even the corners which had shade were dreadfully hot. The sea breeze had not yet begun to blow, and from the flagstaff the White Ensign drooped spiritlessly, half covering the Spanish colours that drooped below it. Yet discipline still prevailed. On every bastion the lookouts stood in the blazing sun to guard against surprise. The marine sentries, with regular and measured step, were "walking their posts of duty in a smart and soldierly manner" in accordance with regulations, muskets sloped, scarlet tunics buttoned to the neck, crossbelts exactly in position. When one of them reached the end of his beat he would halt with a click of his heels, bring down his musket to the "order" position in three smart movements, and then, pushing his right hand forward and his left foot out, stand "at ease" until the heat and the flies drove him into motion again, when his heels would come together, the musket rise to his shoulder, and he would walk his beat once more. In the battery the guns' crews dozed on the unrelenting stone, the lucky men in the shade cast by the guns, the others in the narrow strip of shade at the foot of the parapet; but two men sat and kept themselves awake and every few minutes saw to it that the slow matches smouldering in the tubs were still alight, available to supply fire instantly if the guns had to be worked, whether to fire on ships in the bay or to beat off an attack by land. Out beyond Samaná Point H.M.S. *Renown* lay awaiting the first puffs of the sea breeze to come up the bay and get into touch with her landing party.

Beside the main storehouse Lieutenant Bush sat on a bench and tried to stay awake, cursing the heat, cursing his own kindness of heart that had led him to allow his junior officers to rest first while he assumed the responsibilities of officer on duty, envying the marines who lay asleep and snoring all about him. From time to time he stretched his legs, which were stiff and painful after all his exertions. He mopped his forehead and thought about loosening his neckcloth.

Round the corner came a hurried messenger.

"Mr. Bush, sir. Please sir, there's a boat puttin' off from the battery across the bay."

Bush rolled a stupefied eye at the messenger.

"Heading which way?"

"Straight towards us, sir. She's got a flag—a white flag, it looks like."

"I'll come and see. No peace for the wicked," said Bush, and he pulled himself to his feet, with all his joints complaining, and walked stiffly over to the ramp and up to the battery.

The petty officer of the watch was waiting there with the telescope, having descended from the lookout tower to meet him. Bush took the glass and looked through it. A six-oared boat, black against the blue of the bay, was pulling straight towards him, as the messenger had said. From the staff in the bow hung a flag, which might be white; there was no wind to extend it. But in the boat there were no more than ten people all told, so that there could be no immediate danger to the fort in any case. It was a long row across the glittering bay. Bush watched the boat heading steadily for the fort. The low cliffs which descended to meet the water on this side of Samaná peninsula sank in an easy gradient here in the neighbourhood of the fort; diagonally down the gradient ran a path to the landing stage, which could be swept—as Bush had already noted—by the fire of the last two guns at the right-hand end of the battery. But there was no need to man those guns, for this could not be an attack. And in confirmation a puff of wind blew out the flag in the boat. It was white.

Undeviating, the boat pulled for the landing stage and came alongside it. There was a flash of bright metal from the boat, and then in the heated air the notes of a trumpet call, high and clear, rose to strike against the ears of the garrison. Then two men climbed out of the boat onto the landing stage. They wore uniforms of blue and white, one of them with a sword at his side while the other carried the twinkling trumpet, which he set to his lips and blew again. Piercingly and sweet, the call echoed along the cliffs; the birds which had been drowsing in the heat came fluttering out with plaintive cries, disturbed as much by the trumpet call as they had been by the thunder of the artillery in the morning. The officer wearing the sword unrolled a white flag, and then he and the trumpeter set themselves to climb the steep path to the fort. This was a parley in accordance with the established etiquette of war. The pealing notes of the trumpet were proof that no surprise was intended; the white flag attested the pacific intentions of the bearer.

As Bush watched the slow ascent he meditated on what powers he had to conduct a negotiation with the enemy, and he thought dubiously about the difficulties that would be imposed on any negotiation by differences of language.

"Turn out the guard," he said to the petty officer, and then to the messenger, "My compliments to Mr. Hornblower, and ask him to come here as soon as he can."

The trumpet echoed up the path again; many of the sleepers in the fort were stirring at the sound, and it was a proof of the fatigue of the others that they went on sleeping. Down in the courtyard the tramp of feet and the sound of curt orders told how the marine guard was forming up. The white flag was almost at the edge of the ditch; the bearer halted, looking up at the parapets, while the trumpeter blew a last final call, the wild notes of the fanfare calling the last of the sleepers in the garrison to wakefulness.

"I'm here, sir," reported Hornblower.

The hat to which he raised his hand was lopsided, and he was like a scarecrow in his battered uniform. His face was clean, but it bore a plentiful growth of beard.

"Can you speak Spanish enough to deal with him?" asked Bush, indicating the Spanish officer with a jerk of his thumb.

"Well, sir—yes."

The last word was in a sense spoken against Hornblower's will. He would have liked to temporise, and then he had given the definite answer which any military situation demanded.

"Let's hear you, then."

"Aye aye, sir."

Hornblower stepped up on the parapet; the Spanish officer, looking up from the edge of the ditch, took off his hat at sight of him and bowed courteously; Hornblower did the same. There was a brief exchange of apparently polite phrases before Hornblower turned back to Bush.

"Are you going to admit him to the fort, sir?" he asked. "He says he has many negotiations to carry out."

"No," said Bush, without hesitation. "I don't want him spying round here."

Bush was not too sure about what the Spaniard could discover, but he was suspicious and cautious by temperament.

"Very good, sir."

"You'll have to go out to him, Mr. Hornblower. I'll cover you from here with the marines."

"Aye aye, sir."

With another exchange of courtesies Hornblower came down from the parapet and went down one ramp while the marine guard summoned by Bush marched up the other one. Bush, standing in an embrasure, saw the look on the Spaniard's face as the shakos and scarlet tunics and levelled muskets of the marines appeared in the other embrasures. Directly afterwards Hornblower appeared round the angle of the fort, having crossed the ditch by the narrow causeway from the main gate. Bush watched while once more hats were removed and Hornblower and the Spaniard exchanged bows, bobbing and scraping in a ludicrous Continental fashion. The Spaniard produced a paper, which he offered with a bow for Hornblower to read—his credentials, presumably. Hornblower glanced at them and handed them back. A gesture towards Bush on the parapet indicated his own credentials. Then Bush could see the Spaniard asking eager questions, and Hornblower answering them. He could tell by the way Hornblower was nodding his head that he was answering in the affirmative, and he felt dubious for a moment as to whether Hornblower might not be exceeding his authority. Yet the mere fact that he had to depend on someone else to conduct the negotiations did not irritate him; the thought that he himself might speak Spanish was utterly alien to him, and he was as reconciled to depending on an interpreter as he was to depending on cables to hoist anchors or on winds to carry him to his destination.

He watched the negotiations proceeding; observing closely he was aware when the subject under discussion changed. There was a moment when Hornblower pointed down the bay, and the Spaniard, turning, looked at the *Renown* just approaching the point. He looked long and searchingly before turning back to continue the discussion. He was a tall man, very thin, his coffee-coloured face divided by a thin black moustache. The sun beat down on the pair of them—the trumpeter had withdrawn out of earshot—for some time before Hornblower turned and looked up at Bush.

"I'll come in to report, sir, if I may," he hailed.

"Very well, Mr. Hornblower."

Bush went down to the courtyard to meet him; Hornblower touched his hat and waited to be asked before he began his report.

"He's Colonel Ortega," said Hornblower in reply to the "Well?" that Bush addressed to him. "His credentials are from Villanueva, the Captain-General, who must be just across the bay, sir."

"What does he want?" asked Bush, trying to assimilate this first rather indigestible piece of information.

"It was the prisoners he wanted to know about first, sir," said Hornblower, "the women especially."

"And you told him they weren't hurt?"

"Yes, sir. He was very anxious about them. I told him I would ask your permission for him to take the women back with him."

"I see," said Bush.

"I thought it would make matters easier here, sir. And he had a good deal that he wanted to say, and I thought that if I appeared agreeable he would speak more freely."

"Yes," said Bush.

"Then he wanted to know about the other prisoners, sir. The men. He wanted to know if any had been killed and when I said yes he asked which ones. I couldn't tell him that, sir—I didn't know. But I said I was sure you would supply him with a list; he said most of them had wives over there"—Hornblower pointed across the bay—"who were all anxious."

"I'll do that," said Bush.

"I thought he might take away the wounded as well as the women, sir. It would free our hands a little, and we can't give them proper treatment here."

"I must give that some thought first," said Bush.

"For that matter, sir, it might be possible to rid ourselves of all the prisoners. I fancy it would not be difficult to exact a promise from him in exchange that they would not serve again while *Renown* was in these waters."

"Sounds fishy to me," said Bush; he distrusted all foreigners.

"I think he'd keep his word, sir. He's a Spanish gentleman. Then we wouldn't have to guard them, or feed them, sir. And when we evacuate this place what are we going to do with them? Pack 'em on board *Renown*?"

A hundred prisoners in *Renown* would be an infernal nuisance, drinking twenty gallons of fresh water a day and having to be watched and guarded all the time. But Bush did not like to be rushed into making decisions, and he was not too sure that he cared to have Hornblower treating as obvious the points that he only arrived at after consideration.

"I'll have to think about that, too," said Bush.

"There was another thing that he only hinted at, sir. He wouldn't make any definite proposal, and I thought it better not to ask him."

"What was it?"

Hornblower paused before answering, and that in itself was a warning to Bush that something complicated was in the air.

"It's much more important than just a matter of prisoners, sir."

"Well?"

"It might be possible to arrange for a capitulation, sir."

"What do you mean by that?"

"A surrender, sir. An evacuation of all this end of the island by the Dons."

"My God!"

That was a startling suggestion. Bush's mind plodded along the paths it opened up. It would be an event of international importance; it might be a tremendous victory. Not just a paragraph in the *Gazette,* but a whole page. Perhaps rewards, distinction—even possibly promotion. And with that Bush's mind suddenly drew back in panic, as if the path it had been following ended in a precipice. The more important the event, the more closely it would be scrutinised, the more violent would be the criticism of those who disapproved. Here in Santo Domingo there was a complicated political situation; Bush knew it to be so, although he had never attempted to find out much about it, and certainly never to analyse it. He knew vaguely that French and Spanish interests clashed in the island, and that the Negro rebellion, now almost successful, was in opposition to both. He even knew, still more vaguely, that there was an anti-slavery movement in Parliament which persistently called attention to the state of affairs here. The thought of Parliament, of the Cabinet, of the King himself scrutinising his reports actually terrified Bush. The possible rewards that he had thought about shrank to nothing in comparison with the danger he ran. If he were to enter into a negotiation that embarrassed the government he would be offered up for instant sacrifice—not a hand would be raised to help a penniless and friendless lieutenant. He remembered Buckland's frightened manner when this question had been barely hinted at; the secret orders must be drastic in this regard.

"Don't lift a finger about that," said Bush. "Don't say a word."

"Aye aye, sir. Then if he brings the subject up I'm not to listen to him?"

"Well—" That might imply flinching away from duty. "It's a matter for Buckland to deal with, if any one."

"Yes, sir. I could suggest something, sir."

"And what's that?" Bush did not know whether to be irritated or pleased that Hornblower had one more suggestion to make. But he doubted his own ability to bargain or negotiate; he knew himself to be lacking in chicane and dissimulation.

"If you made an agreement about the prisoners, sir, it would take some time to carry out. There'd be the question of the parole. I could argue about the wording of it. Then it would take some time to ferry the prisoners over. You could insist that only one boat was at the landing stage at a time—that's an obvious precaution to take. It would give time for *Renown* to work up into the bay. She can anchor down there just out of range of the other battery, sir. Then the hole'll be stopped, and at the same time we'll still be in touch with the Dons so that Mr. Buckland can take charge of the negotiations if he wishes to."

"There's something in that notion," said Bush. Certainly it would relieve him of responsibility, and it was pleasant to think of spinning out time until the *Renown* was back, ready to add her ponderous weight in the struggle.

"So you authorise me to negotiate for the return of the prisoners on parole, sir?" asked Hornblower.

"Yes," said Bush, coming to a sudden decision. "But nothing else, mark you, Mr. Hornblower. Not if you value your commission."

"Aye aye, sir."

"And a temporary suspension of hostilities while they are being handed over, sir?"

"Yes," said Bush, reluctantly. It was a matter necessarily arising out of the previous one, but it had a suspicious sound to it, now that Hornblower had suggested the possibility of further negotiations.

So the day proceeded to wear into afternoon. A full hour was consumed in haggling over the wording of the parole under which the captured soldiers were to be released. It was two o'clock before agreement was reached, and later than that before Bush, standing by the main gate, watched the women troop out through it, carrying their bundles of belongings. The boat could not possibly carry them all; two trips had to be made with them before the male prisoners, starting with the wounded, could begin. To rejoice Bush's heart the *Renown* appeared at last round the point; with the sea breeze beginning to blow she came nobly up the bay.

And here came Hornblower again, clearly so weary that he could hardly drag one foot after another, to touch his hat to Bush.

"*Renown* knows nothing about the suspension of hostilities, sir," he said. "She'll see the boat crossing full of Spanish soldiers, an' she'll open fire as sure as a gun."

"How are we to let her know?"

"I've been discussing it with Ortega, sir. He'll lend us a boat and we can send a message down to her."

"I suppose we can."

Sleeplessness and exhaustion had given an edge to Bush's temper. This final suggestion, when Bush came to consider it, with his mind slowed by fatigue, was the last straw.

"You're taking altogether too much on yourself, Mr. Hornblower," he said. "Damn it, I'm in command here."

"Yes, sir," said Hornblower, standing at attention, while Bush gazed at him and tried to reassemble his thoughts after this spat of ill temper. There was no denying that *Renown* had to be informed; if she were to open fire it would be in direct violation of an agreement solemnly entered into, and to which he himself was a party.

"Oh, hell and damnation!" said Bush. "Have it your own way, then. Who are you going to send?"

"I could go myself, sir. Then I could tell Mr. Buckland everything necessary."

"You mean about—about—" Bush actually did not like to mention the dangerous subject.

"About the chance of further negotiations, sir," said Hornblower stolidly. "He has to know sooner or later. And while Ortega's still here—"

The implications were obvious enough, and the suggestion was sensible.

"All right. You'd better go, I suppose. And mark my words, Mr. Hornblower, you're to make it quite clear that I've authorised no negotiations of the sort you have in mind. Not a word. I've no responsibility. You understand?"

"Aye aye, sir."

TWELVE

THREE OFFICERS sat in what had been the commanding officer's room in Fort Samaná; in fact, seeing that Bush was now the commanding officer there, it could still be called the commanding officer's room. A bed with a mosquito net over it stood in one corner; at the other side of the room Buckland, Bush, and Hornblower sat in leather chairs. A lamp hanging from a beam overhead filled the room with its acrid smell, and lit up their sweating faces. It was hotter and stuffier even than it was in the ship, but at least here in the fort there was no brooding knowledge of a mad captain the other side of the bulkhead.

"I don't doubt for one moment," said Hornblower, "that when Villanueva sent Ortega here to open negotiations about the prisoners he also told him to put out a feeler regarding this evacuation."

"You can't be sure of that," said Buckland.

"Well, sir, put yourself in Ortega's position. Would you say a word about a subject of that importance if you weren't authorised to? If you weren't expressly ordered to, sir?"

"No, I wouldn't," said Buckland.

No one could doubt that who knew Buckland, and for him himself it was the most convincing argument.

"Then Villanueva had capitulation in mind as soon as he knew that we had captured this fort and that *Renown* would be able to anchor in the bay. You can see that must be so, sir."

"I suppose so," said Buckland, reluctantly.

"And if he's prepared to negotiate for a capitulation he must either be a poltroon or in serious danger, sir."

"Well—"

"It doesn't matter which is true, sir, whether his danger is real or imaginary, from the point of view of bargaining with him."

"You talk like a—like a sea lawyer," said Buckland. He was being forced by logic into taking a momentous decision, and he did not want to be, so that in his struggles against it he used one of the worst terms of opprobrium in his vocabulary.

"I'm sorry, sir," said Hornblower, "I meant no disrespect. I let my tongue run away with me. Of course it's for you to decide where your duty lies, sir."

Bush could see that that word "duty" had a stiffening effect on Buckland.

"Well, then, what d'you think lies behind all this?" asked Buckland. That might be intended as a temporising question, but it gave Hornblower permission to go on stating his views.

"Villanueva's been holding this end of the island against the insurgents for months now, sir. We don't know how much territory he holds, but we can guess that it's not much—only as far as the crest of those mountains across the bay, probably. Powder—lead—flints—shoes—he's probably in need of all of them."

"Judging by the prisoners we took, that's true, sir," interjected Bush. It would be hard to ascertain the motives that led him to make this contribution to the discussion; perhaps he was only interested in the truth for its own sake.

"Maybe it is," said Buckland.

"Now you've arrived, sir, and he's cut off from the sea. He doesn't know how long we can stay here. He doesn't know what your orders are."

Hornblower did not know either, commented Bush to himself, and Buckland stirred restlessly at the allusion.

"Never mind that," he said.

"He sees himself cut off, and his supplies dwindling. If this goes on he'll have to surrender. He would rather start negotiations now, while he can still hold out, while he has something to bargain with, than wait until the last moment and have to surrender unconditionally, sir."

"I see," said Buckland.

"And he'd rather surrender to us than to the blacks, sir," concluded Hornblower.

"Yes indeed," said Bush. Everyone had heard a little about the horrors of the servile rebellion which for eight years had deluged this land with blood and scorched it with fire. The three men were silent for a space as they thought about the implications of Hornblower's last remark.

"Oh, very well then," said Buckland at length. "Let's hear what this fellow has to say."

"Shall I bring him in here, sir? He's been waiting long enough. I can blindfold him."

"Do what you like," said Buckland with resignation.

A closer view, when the handkerchief had been removed, revealed Colonel Ortega as a younger man than he might have been thought at a distance. He was very slender, and he wore his threadbare uniform with some pretence at elegance. A muscle in his left cheek twitched continually. Buckland and Bush rose slowly to their feet to acknowledge the introductions Hornblower made.

"Colonel Ortega says he speaks no English," said Hornblower.

There was only the slightest extra stress on the word "says," and only the slightest lingering in the glance that Hornblower shot at his two superiors as he said it, but it conveyed a warning.

"Well, ask him what he wants," said Buckland.

The conversation in Spanish was formal; obviously all the opening remarks were cautious fencing as each speaker felt for the weaknesses in the other's position and sought to conceal his own. But even Bush was aware of the moment when the vague sentences ended and definite proposals began. Ortega was bearing himself as a man conferring a favour; Hornblower like someone who did not care whether a favour was conferred or not. In the end he turned to Buckland and spoke in English.

"He has terms for a capitulation pat enough," he said.

"Well?"

"Please don't let him guess what you think, sir. But he suggests a free passage for the garrison. Ships—men—civilians. Passports for the ships while on passage to a Spanish possession—Cuba or Puerto Rico, in other words, sir. In exchange he'll hand over everything intact. Military stores. The battery across the bay. Everything."

"But—" Buckland struggled wildly to keep himself from revealing his feelings.

"I haven't said anything to him worth mentioning, so far, sir," said Hornblower.

Ortega had been watching the byplay keenly enough, and now he spoke again to Hornblower, with his shoulders back and his head high. There was passion in his voice, but what was more at odds with the dignity of his bearing was a peculiar gesture with which he accentuated one of his remarks—a jerk of the hand which called up the picture of someone vomiting.

"He says otherwise he'll fight to the last," interposed Hornblower. "He says Spanish soldiers can be relied upon to die to the last man sooner than submit to dishonour. He says we can do no more to them than we've done already—that we've reached the end of our tether, in other words, sir. And that we daren't stay longer in the island to starve him out because of the yellow fever—the *vomito negro,* sir."

In the whirl of excitement of the last few days Bush had forgotten all about the possibility of yellow fever. He found that he was looking concerned at the mention of it, and he hurriedly tried to assume an appearance of indifference. A glance at Buckland showed his face going through exactly the same transitions.

"I see," said Buckland.

It was an appalling thought. If yellow fever were to strike it might within a week leave the *Renown* without enough men to work her sails.

Ortega broke into passionate speech again, and Hornblower translated.

"He says his troops have lived here all their lives. They won't get yellow jack as easily as our men, and many of them have already had it. He has had it himself, he says, sir."

Bush remembered the emphasis with which Ortega had tapped his breast.

"And the blacks believe us to be their enemies, because of what happened in Dominica, sir, so he says. He could make an alliance with them against us. They could send an army against us here in the fort tomorrow, then. But please don't look as if you believe him, sir."

"Damn it to hell," said Buckland, exasperated. Bush wondered vaguely what it was that had happened in Dominica. History—even contemporary history—was not one of his strong points.

Again Ortega spoke.

"He says that's his last word, sir. An honourable proposal and he won't abate a jot, so he says. You could send him away now that you've heard it all and say that you'll give him an answer in the morning."

"Very well."

There were ceremonious speeches still to be made. Ortega's bows were so polite that Buckland and Bush were constrained, though reluctantly, to stand and endeavour to return them. Hornblower tied the handkerchief round Ortega's eyes again and led him out.

"What do you think about it?" said Buckland to Bush.

"I'd like to think it over, sir," replied Bush.

Hornblower came in again while they were still considering the matter. He glanced at them both before addressing himself to Buckland.

"Will you be needing me again tonight, sir?"

"Oh damn it, you'd better stay. You know more about these Dagoes than we do. What do you think about it?"

"He made some good arguments, sir."

"I thought so too," said Buckland with apparent relief.

"Can't we turn the thumbscrews on them somehow, sir?" asked Bush. Even if he could not make suggestions himself, he was too cautious to agree readily to a bargain offered by a foreigner, even such a tempting one as this.

"We can bring the ship up the bay," said Buckland. "But the channel's tricky. You saw that yesterday."

Good God! it was still only yesterday that the *Renown* had tried to make her way in under the fire of red-hot shot. Buckland had had a day of comparative peace, so that the mention of yesterday did not appear as strange to him.

"We'll be still under the fire of the battery across the bay, even though we hold this one," said Buckland.

"We ought to be able to run past it, sir," protested Bush. "We can keep over to this side."

"And if we do run past? They've warped their ships right up the bay again. They draw six feet less of water than we do—and if they've got any sense they'll lighten 'em so as to warp 'em farther over the shallows. Nice fools we'll look if we come in an' then find 'em out of range, an' have to run out again under fire. That might stiffen 'em so that they wouldn't agree to the terms that fellow just offered."

Buckland was in a state of actual alarm at the thought of reporting two fruitless repulses.

"I can see that," said Bush, depressed.

"If we agree," said Buckland, warming to his subject, "the blacks'll take over all this end of the island. This bay can't be used by privateers then. The blacks'll have no ships, and couldn't man 'em if they had. We'll have executed our orders. Don't you agree, Mr. Hornblower?"

Bush transferred his gaze. Hornblower had looked weary in the morning, and he had had almost no rest during the day. His face was drawn and his eyes were rimmed with red.

"We might still be able to—to put the thumbscrews on 'em, sir," he said.

"How?"

"It'd be risky to take *Renown* into the upper end of the bay. But we might get at 'em from the peninsula here, all the same, sir, if you'd give the orders."

"God bless my soul!" said Bush, the exclamation jerked out of him.

"What orders?" asked Buckland.

"If we could mount a gun on the upper end of the peninsula we'd have the far end of the bay under fire, sir. We wouldn't need hot shot—we'd have all day to knock 'em to pieces however much they shifted their anchorage."

"So we would, by George," said Buckland. There was animation in his face. "Could you get one of these guns along there?"

"I've been thinking about it, sir, an' I'm afraid we couldn't. Not quickly, at least. Twenty-four-pounders. Two an' a half tons each. Garrison carriages. We've no horses. We couldn't move 'em with a hundred men over those gullies, four miles or more."

"Then what the hell's the use of talking about it?" demanded Buckland.

"We don't have to drag a gun from here, sir," said Hornblower. "We could use one from the ship. One of those long nine-pounders we've got mounted as bow chasers. Those long guns have a range pretty nearly as good as these twenty-fours, sir."

"But how do we get it there?"

Bush had a glimmering of the answer even before Hornblower replied.

"Send it round in the launch, sir, with tackle and cables, near to where we landed yesterday. The cliff's steep there. And there are big trees to attach the cables to. We could sway a gun up easy enough. Those nine-pounders only weigh a ton."

"I know that," said Buckland, sharply.

It was one thing to make unexpected suggestions, but it was quite another to tell a veteran officer facts with which he was well acquainted.

"Yes, of course, sir. But with a nine-pounder at the top of the cliff it wouldn't be so difficult to move it across the neck of land until we had the upper bay under our fire. We wouldn't have to cross any gullies. Half a mile—uphill, but not too steep, sir—and it would be done."

"And what d'you think would happen then?"

"We'd have those ships under fire, sir. Only a nine-pounder, I know, but they're not built to take punishment. We could batter 'em into wrecks in twelve hours' steady fire. Less than that, perhaps. An' I suppose we could heat the shot if we wanted to, but we wouldn't have to. All we'd have to do would be to open fire, I think, sir."

"Why?"

"The Dons wouldn't risk those ships, sir. Ortega spoke very big about making an alliance with the blacks, but that was only talking big, sir.

Give the blacks a chance an' they'll cut every white throat they can. An' I don't blame 'em—excuse me, sir."

"Well?"

"Those ships are the Dons' only way of escape. If they see they're going to be destroyed they'll be frightened. It would mean surrendering to the blacks—that or being killed to the last man. And woman, sir. They'd rather surrender to us."

"So they would, by jingo," said Bush.

"They'd climb down, d'ye think?"

"Yes—I mean I think so, sir. You could name your own terms, then. Unconditional surrender for the soldiers."

"It's what we said at the start," said Bush. "They'd rather surrender to us than to the blacks, if they have to."

"You could allow some conditions to salve their pride, sir," said Hornblower. "Agree that the women are to be conveyed to Cuba or Puerto Rico if they wish. But nothing important. Those ships would be our prizes, sir."

"Prizes, by George!" said Buckland.

Prizes meant prize money, and as commanding officer he would have the lion's share of it. Not only that—and perhaps the money was the smallest consideration—but prizes escorted triumphantly into port were much more impressive than ships sunk out of sight of the eyes of authority. And unconditional surrender had a ring of finality about it, proof that the victory gained could not be more complete.

"What do you say, Mr. Bush?" asked Buckland.

"I think it might be worth trying, sir," said Bush.

He was fatalistic now about Hornblower. Exasperation over his activity and ingenuity had died of surfeit. There was something of resignation about Bush's attitude, but there was something of admiration too. Bush was a generous soul, and there was not a mean motive in him. Hornblower's careful handling of his superior had not been lost on him, and Bush was decently envious of the tact that had been necessary. Bush realistically admitted to himself that even though he had fretted at the prospect of agreeing to Ortega's terms he had not been able to think of a way to modify them, while Hornblower had. Hornblower was a very brilliant young officer, Bush decided; he himself made no pretence at brilliance, and now he had taken the last step and had overcome his suspicions of brilliance. He made himself abandon his caution and commit himself to a definite opinion.

"I think Mr. Hornblower deserves every credit," he said.

"Of course," said Buckland—but the slight hint of surprise in his voice seemed to indicate that he did not really believe it; and he changed the subject without pursuing it further. "We'll start tomorrow—I'll get both launches out as soon as the hands've had breakfast. By noon—now what's the matter with you, Mr. Hornblower?"

"Well, sir—"

"Come on. Out with it."

"Ortega comes back tomorrow morning to hear our terms again, sir. I suppose he'll get up at dawn or not long after. He'll have a bite of breakfast. Then he'll have a few words with Villanueva. Then he'll row across the bay. He might be here at eight bells. Later than that, probably, a little—"

"Who cares when Ortega has his breakfast? What's all this rigmarole for?"

"Ortega gets here at two bells in the forenoon. If he finds we haven't wasted a minute; if I can tell him that you've rejected his terms absolutely, sir, and not only that, if we can show him the gun mounted, and say we'll open fire in an hour if they don't surrender without conditions, he'll be much more impressed."

"That's true, sir," said Bush.

"Otherwise it won't be so easy, sir. You'll either have to temporise again while the gun's being got into position, or you'll have to use threats. I'll have to say to him *if* you don't agree then we'll start hoisting a gun up. In either case you'll be allowing him time, sir. He might think of some other way out of it. The weather might turn dirty—there might even be a hurricane get up. But if he's sure we'll stand no nonsense, sir—"

"That's the way to treat 'em," said Bush.

"But even if we start at dawn—" said Buckland, and having progressed so far in his speech he realised the alternative. "You mean we can get to work now?"

"We have all night before us, sir. You could have the launches hoisted out and the gun swayed down into one of them. Slings and cables and some sort of carrying cradle prepared. Hands told off—"

"And start at dawn!"

"At dawn the boats can be round the peninsula waiting for daylight, sir. You could send some hands with a hundred fathoms of line up from the ship to here. They can start off along the path before daylight. That'd save time."

"So it would, by George!" said Bush; he had no trouble in visualising the problems of seamanship involved in hoisting a gun up the face of a cliff.

"We're shorthanded already in the ship," said Buckland. "I'll have to turn up both watches."

"That won't hurt 'em, sir," said Bush. He had already been two nights without sleep and was now contemplating a third.

"Who shall I send? I'll want a responsible officer in charge. A good seaman at that."

"I'll go if you like, sir," said Hornblower.

"No. You'll have to be here to deal with Ortega. If I send Smith I'll have no lieutenant left on board."

"Maybe you could send me, sir," said Bush. "That is, if you were to leave Mr. Hornblower in command here."

"Um—" said Buckland. "Oh well, I don't see anything else to do. Can I trust you, Mr. Hornblower?"

"I'll do my best, sir."

"Let me see—" said Buckland.

"I could go back to the ship with you in your gig, sir," said Bush. "Then there'd be no time wasted."

This prodding of a senior officer into action was something new to Bush, but he was learning the art fast. The fact that the three of them had not long ago been fellow conspirators made it easier; and once the ice was broken, as soon as Buckland had once admitted his juniors to give him counsel and advice, it became easier with repetition.

"Yes, I suppose you'd better," said Buckland, and Bush promptly rose to his feet, so that Buckland could hardly help doing the same.

Bush ran his eye over Hornblower's battered form.

"Now look you here, Mr. Hornblower," he said. "You take some sleep. You need it."

"I relieve Whiting as officer on duty at midnight, sir," said Hornblower, "and I have to go the rounds."

"Maybe that's true. You'll still have two hours before midnight. Turn in until then. And have Whiting relieve you at eight bells again."

"Aye aye, sir."

At the very thought of abandoning himself to the sleep for which he yearned Hornblower swayed with fatigue.

"You could make that an order, sir," suggested Bush to Buckland.

"What's that? Oh yes, get a rest while you can, Mr. Hornblower."

"Aye aye, sir."

Bush picked his way down the steep path to the landing stage at

Buckland's heels, and took his seat beside him in the sternsheets of the gig.

"I can't make that fellow Hornblower out," said Buckland a little peevishly on one occasion as they rowed back to the anchored *Renown.*

"He's a good officer, sir," answered Bush, but he spoke a little absently. Already in his mind he was tackling the problem of hoisting a long nine-pounder up a cliff, and he was sorting out mentally the necessary equipment, and planning the necessary orders. Two heavy anchors —not merely boat grapnels—to anchor the buoy solidly. The thwarts of the launch had better be shored up to bear the weight of the gun. Travelling blocks. Slings—for the final hoist it might be safer to suspend the gun by its cascabel and trunnions.

Bush was not of the mental type that takes pleasure in theoretical exercises. To plan a campaign; to put himself mentally in the position of the enemy and think along alien lines; to devise unexpected expedients; all this was beyond his capacity. But to deal with a definite concrete problem, a simple matter of ropes and tackles and breaking strains, pure seamanship—he had a lifetime of experience to reinforce his natural bent in that direction.

THIRTEEN

"TAKE THE STRAIN," said Bush, standing on the cliff's edge and looking far, far down to where the launch floated moored to the buoy and with an anchor astern to keep her steady. Black against the Atlantic blue two ropes came down from over his head, curving slightly but almost vertical, down to the buoy. A poet might have seen something dramatic and beautiful in those spider lines cleaving the air, but Bush merely saw a couple of ropes, and the white flag down in the launch signalling that all was clear for hoisting. The blocks creaked as the men pulled in on the slack.

"Now, handsomely," said Bush. This work was too important to be delegated to Mr. Midshipman James, standing beside him. "Hoist away. Handsomely."

The creaking took on a different tone as the weight came on the blocks. The curves of the ropes altered, appeared almost deformed, as the gun began to rise from its cradle on the thwarts. The shallow, lovely catenaries changed to a harsher, more angular figure. Bush had his telescope to his eye and could see the gun stir and move, and slowly—that was what Bush meant by "handsomely" in the language of the sea—it began to upend itself, to dangle from the traveller, to rise clear of the launch; hanging, just as Bush had visualised it, from the slings through its cascabel and round its trunnions. It was safe enough—if those slings were to give way or to slip, the gun would crash through the bottom of the launch. The line about its muzzle restrained it from swinging too violently.

"Hoist away," said Bush again, and the traveller began to mount the rope with the gun pendant below it. This was the next ticklish moment, when the pull came most transversely. But everything held fast.

"Hoist away."

Now the gun was mounting up the rope. Beyond the launch's stern it dipped, with the stretching of the cable and the straightening of the curve, until its muzzle was almost in the sea. But the hoisting proceeded steadily, and it rose clear of the water, up, up, up. The sheaves hummed rhythmically in the blocks as the hands hove on the line. The sun shone on the men from its level position in the glowing east, stretching out their shadows and those of the trees to incredible lengths over the irregular plateau.

"Easy, there!" said Bush. "Belay!"

The gun had reached the cliff edge.

"Move that cat's cradle over this way a couple of feet. Now, sway in. Lower. Good. Cast off those lines."

The gun lay, eight feet of dull bronze, upon the cat's cradle that had been spread to receive it. This was a small area of stout rope-netting, from which diverged, knotted thickly to the central portion, a score or more of individual lines, each laid out separately on the ground.

"We'll get that on its way first. Take a line, each of you marines."

The thirty red-coated marines that Hornblower had sent along from the fort moved up to the cat's cradle. Their noncommissioned officers pushed them into position, and Bush checked to see that each man was there.

"Take hold."

It was better to go to a little trouble and see that everything was correctly balanced at the start rather than risk that the unwieldy lump of metal should roll off the cat's cradle and should have to be laboriously manoeuvred back into position.

"Now, all of you together when I give the word. Lift!"

The gun rose a foot from the ground as every man exerted himself.

"March! Belay that, sergeant."

The sergeant had begun to call the step, but on this irregular ground with every man supporting eighty pounds of weight it was better that they should not try to keep step.

"Halt! Lower!"

The gun had moved twenty yards towards the position Bush had selected for it.

"Carry on, sergeant. Keep 'em moving. Not too fast."

Marines were only dumb animals, not even machines, and were liable to tire. It was better to be conservative with their strength. But while they laboured at carrying the gun the necessary half-mile up to the crest the seamen could work at hauling up the rest of the stores from the launches. Nothing would be as difficult as the gun. The gun carriage was a featherweight by comparison; even the nets, each holding twenty nine-pound cannon balls, were easy to handle. Rammers, sponges, and wad-hooks, two of each in case of accidents; wads; and now the powder charges. With only two and a half pounds of powder in each they seemed tiny compared with the eight-pound charges Bush had grown accustomed to on the lower gundeck. Last of all came the heavy timbers destined to form a smooth floor upon which the gun could be worked. They were awkward things to carry, but with each timber on the shoulders of four men they could be carried up the gentle slope fast enough, overtaking the unfortunate marines, who, streaming with sweat, were lifting and carrying, lifting and carrying, on their way up.

Bush stood for a moment at the cliff edge checking over the stores with James' assistance. Linstocks and slow match; primers and quills; barricoes of water; handspikes, hammers, and nails; everything necessary, he decided—not merely his professional reputation but his self-respect depended on his having omitted nothing. He waved his flag, and received an answer from the launches. The second launch cast off her mooring line, and then, hauling up her anchor, she went off with her consort to pull back round Point Samaná to rejoin *Renown*—in the ship they would be most desperately shorthanded until the launches' crews should come on board again. From the trees to which it was secured, over Bush's head, the rope hung down to the buoy, neglected unless it should be needed again; Bush hardly spared it a glance. Now he was free to walk up to the crest and prepare for action; a glance at the sun assured him that it was less than three hours since sunrise even now.

He organised the final carrying party and started up to the crest. When he reached it the bay opened below him. He put his glass to his eye; the three vessels were lying at anchor within easy cannon shot of where he stood, and when he swung the glass to his left he could just make out, far, far away, the two specks which were the flags flying over the fort—the swell of the land hid the body of the building from his sight. He closed the glass and applied himself to the selection of a level piece of ground on which to lay the timbers for the platform. Already the men with the lightest loads were around him, chattering and pointing excitedly until with a growl he silenced them.

The hammers thumped upon the nails as the crosspieces were nailed into position on the timbers. No sooner had they ceased than the gun carriage was swung up onto it by the lusty efforts of half a dozen men. They attached the tackles and saw to it that the gun-trucks ran easily before chocking them. The marines came staggering up, sweating and gasping under their monstrous burden. Now was the moment for the trickiest piece of work in the morning's programme; Bush distributed his steadiest men round the carrying ropes, a reliable petty officer on either side to watch that accurate balance was maintained.

"Lift and carry."

The gun lay beside the carriage on the platform.

"Lift. Lift. Higher. Not high enough. Lift, you men!"

There were gasps and grunts as the men struggled to raise the gun.

"Keep her at that! Back away, starboard side! Go with 'em, port side. Lift! Bring the bows round now. Steady!"

The gun in its cat's cradle hung precariously over the carriage as Bush lined it up.

"Now, back towards me! Steady! Lower! Slowly, damn you! Steady! For'rard a little! Now lower again!"

The gun sank down towards its position on the carriage. It rested there, the trunnions not quite in their holes, the breech not quite in position on the bed.

"Hold it! Berry! Chapman! Handspikes under those trunnions! Ease her along!"

With something of a jar the ton of metal subsided into its place on the carriage, trunnions home into their holes and breech settled upon the bed. A couple of hands set to work untying the knots that would free the cat's cradle from under the gun, but Berry, gunner's mate, had already snapped the capsquares down upon the trunnions, and the gun was now a gun, a vital fighting weapon and not an inanimate ingot of metal. The shot were being piled at the edge of the platform.

"Lay those charges out back there!" said Bush, pointing.

No one in his senses allowed unprotected explosives nearer a gun than was necessary. Berry was kneeling on the platform, bent over the flint and steel with which he was working, to catch a spark upon the tinder with which to ignite the slow match. Bush wiped away the sweat that streamed over his face and neck; even though he had not taken actual physical part in the carrying and heaving he felt the effect of his exertions. He looked at the sun again to judge the time; this was no moment for resting upon his labours.

"Gun's crew fall in!" he ordered. "Load and run up!"

He applied his eye to the telescope.

"Aim for the schooner," he said. "Take a careful aim."

The gun-trucks squealed as the handspikes trained the gun round.

"Gun laid, sir," reported the gun captain.

"Then fire!"

The gun banged out sharp and clear, a higher-pitched report than the deafening thunderous roar of the massive twenty-four-pounders. That report would resound round the bay. Even if the shot missed its mark this time, the men down in those ships would know that the next, or the next, would strike. Looking up at the high shore through hastily trained telescopes they would see the powder smoke slowly drifting along the verge of the cliff, and would recognise their doom. Over on the southern shore Villanueva would have his attention called to it, and would know that escape was finally cut off for the men under his command and the women under his protection. Yet all the same, Bush, gazing through the telescope, could mark no fall of the shot.

"Load and fire again. Make sure of your aim."

While they loaded Bush turned his telescope upon the flags over the fort, until the gun captain's cry told him that loading was completed. The gun banged out, and Bush thought he saw the fleeting black line of the course of the shot.

"You're firing over her. Put the quoins in and reduce the elevation. Try again!"

He looked again at the flags. They were very slowly descending, down out of his sight. Now they rose once more, very slowly, fluttered for a moment at the head of the flagstaff, and sank again. The next time they rose they remained steady. That was the preconcerted signal. Dipping the colours twice meant that the gun had been heard in the fort and all was well. It was Bush's duty now to complete ten rounds of firing, slowly. Bush watched each round carefully; it seemed likely that the schooner was being hit. Those flying nine-pound balls of iron were crashing through the frail upper works, smashing and destroying, casting up showers of splinters.

At the eighth round something screamed through the air like a banshee two yards over Bush's head, a whirling irregular scream which died away abruptly behind his back.

"What the hell was that?" demanded Bush.

"The gun's unbushed, sir," said Berry.

"God—" Bush poured out a torrent of blasphemy, uncontrolled, almost hysterical. This was the climax of days and nights of strain and labour, the bitterest blow that could be imagined, with success almost within their grasp and now snatched away. He swore frightfully, and then came back to his senses; it would not be good for the men to know that their officer was as disappointed as Bush knew himself to be. His curses died away when he restrained himself, and he walked forward to look at the gun.

The damage was plain. The touchhole in the breech of a gun, especially a bronze gun, was always a weak point. At each round some small part of the explosion vented itself through the hole, the blast of hot gas and unconsumed powder grains eroding the edges of the hole, enlarging it until the loss of force became severe enough to impair the efficiency of the gun. Then the gun had to be "bushed"; a tapering plug, with a hole pierced through its length and a flange round its base, had to be forced into the touchhole from inside the gun, small end first. The hole in the plug served as the new touchhole, and the explosions of the gun served to drive the plug more and more thoroughly home, until the plug itself began to erode and to weaken, forcing itself up through the touchhole while the flange burned away in the fierce heat of the explosions until at last it would blow itself clean out, as it had done now.

Bush looked at the huge hole in the breech, a full inch wide; if the gun were to be fired in that condition half the powder charge would blow out through it. The range would be halved at best, and every subsequent round would enlarge the hole further.

"D'ye have a new vent-fitting?" he demanded.

"Well, sir—" Berry began to go slowly through his pockets, rummaging through their manifold contents while gazing absently at the sky and while Bush fumed with impatience. "Yes, sir."

Berry produced, seemingly at the eleventh hour, the cast-iron plug that meant so much.

"Lucky for you," said Bush, grimly. "Get it fitted and don't waste any more time."

"Aye aye, sir. I'll have to file it to size, sir. Then I'll have to put it in place."

"Start work and stop talking. Mr. James!"

"Sir!"

"Run to the fort." Bush took a few steps away from the gun as he spoke, so as to get out of earshot of the men. "Tell Mr. Hornblower that the gun's unbushed. It'll be an hour before we can open fire again. Tell him I'll fire three shots when the gun's ready, and ask him to acknowledge them as before."

"Aye aye, sir."

At the last moment Bush remembered something.

"Mr. James! Don't make your report in anyone's hearing. Don't let that Spanish fellow, what's-his-name, hear about this. Not if you want to be kind to your backside."

"Aye aye, sir."

"Run!"

That would be a very long hot run for Mr. James; Bush watched him go and then turned back to the gun. Berry had selected a file from his roll of tools and was sitting on the rear step of the gun scraping away at the plug. Bush sat on the edge of the platform; the irritation at the disablement of the gun was overlaid by his satisfaction with himself as a diplomat. He was pleased at having remembered to warn James against letting Ortega into the secret. The men were chattering and beginning to skylark about; a few minutes more and they would be scattering all over the peninsula. Bush lifted his head and barked at them.

"Silence, there! Sergeant!"

"Sir?"

"Post four sentries. Give 'em beats on all four sides. No one to pass that line on any account whatever."

"Yessir."

"Let the rest of your men sit down. You gun's crew! Sit there and don't chatter like Portugee bumboat men."

The sun was very hot, and the rasp-rasp-rasp of Berry's file was, if anything, soothing. Bush had hardly ceased speaking when fatigue and sleeplessness demanded their due; his eyes closed and his chin sank on his breast. In one second he was asleep; in three he was awake again, with the world whirling round him as he recovered himself from falling over. He blinked at the unreal world; the blink prolonged itself into sleep, and again he caught himself up, on the point of keeling over. Bush felt that he would give anything at all, in this world or the next, to sink quietly onto his side and allow sleep to overwhelm him. He fought down the temptation; he was the only officer present and there might be an instant emergency. Straightening his back, he glowered at the world, and then even with his back straight he went to sleep again. There was only one thing to do. He rose to his feet, with his weary joints protesting, and began to pace up and down beside the gun platform, up and down in the sunshine, with the sweat pouring off him, while the gun's crew quickly subsided into the sleep he envied them—they lay like pigs in a sty, at all angles—and while Berry's file went whit-whit-whit on the vent-fitting. The minutes dragged by and the sun mounted higher and higher. Berry paused in his work to gauge the fitting against the touchhole, and then went on filing; he paused again to clean his file, and each time Bush looked sharply at him, only to be disappointed, and to go back to thinking how much he wanted to go to sleep.

"I have it to size now, sir," said Berry at last.

"Then fit it, damn you," said Bush. "You gun's crew, wake up, there! Rise and shine! Wake up, there!"

While Bush kicked the snoring men awake Berry had produced a length of twine from his pocket. With a slowness that Bush found maddening he proceeded to tie one end into a loop and then drop the loop in through the touchhole. Then he took the wad-hook, and, walking round to the muzzle of the gun and squatting down, he proceeded to push the hook up the eight-foot length of the bore and try to catch the loop on it. Over and over again he twisted the hook and withdrew it a little with no corresponding reaction on the part of the twine hanging from the touchhole, but at last he made his catch. As he brought the hook out the twine slid down into the hole, and when the wad-hook was withdrawn from the muzzle the loop was hanging on it. Still with intense deliberation Berry calmly proceeded to undo the loop and pass the end of the twine through the hole in the vent-fitting, and then secure the end to a little toggle which he also took from his pocket. He dropped the vent-fitting into the muzzle and walked round to the breech again, and pulled in on the twine, the vent-fitting rattling down the bore until it leaped up to its position under the touchhole with a sharp tap that every ear heard. Even so it was only after some minutes of fumbling and adjustment that Berry had the vent-fitting placed to his satisfaction with its small end in the hole, and he gestured to the gun captain to hold it steady with the twine. Now he took the rammer and thrust it with infinite care up the muzzle, feeling sensitively with it and pressing down upon the handle when he had it exactly placed. Another gesture from Berry, and a seaman brought a hammer and struck down upon the handle which Berry held firm. At each blow the vent-fitting showed more clearly down in the touchhole, rising an eighth of an inch at a time until it was firmly jammed.

"Ready?" asked Bush as Berry waved the seaman away.

"Not quite, sir."

Berry withdrew the rammer and walked slowly round to the breech again. He looked down at the vent-fitting with his head first on one side and then on the other, like a terrier at a rathole. He seemed to be satisfied, and yet he walked back again to the muzzle and took up the wad-hook. Bush glared round the horizon to ease his impatience; over towards where the fort lay a tiny figure was visible coming towards them. Bush clapped a telescope to his eye. It was a white-trousered individual, now running, now walking, and apparently waving his arm as though to attract attention. It might be Wellard; Bush was nearly sure it was. Meanwhile Berry had caught the twine again with the wad-hook and drawn it out again. He cut the toggle free from the twine with a stroke of his sheath knife and dropped it in his pocket, and then, once more as if he had all the time in the world, he returned to the breech and wound up his twine.

"Two rounds with one-third charges ought to do it now, sir," he announced. "That'll seat—"

"It can wait a few minutes longer," said Bush, interrupting him with a short-tempered delight in showing this self-satisfied skilled worker that his decisions need not all be treated like gospel.

Wellard was in clear sight of them all now, running and walking and stumbling over the irregular surface. He reached the gun gasping for breath, sweat running down his face.

"Please, sir—" he began. Bush was about to blare at him for his disrespectful approach but Wellard anticipated him. He twitched his coat into position, settled his absurd little hat on his head, and stepped forward with all the stiff precision his gasping lungs would allow.

"Mr. Hornblower's respects, sir," he said, raising his hand to his hat brim.

"Well, Mr. Wellard?"

"Please will you not reopen fire, sir."

Wellard's chest was heaving, and that was all he could say between two gasps. The sweat running down into his eyes made him blink, but he manfully stood to attention ignoring it.

"And why not, pray, Mr. Wellard?"

Even Bush could guess at the answer, but asked the question because the child deserved to be taken seriously.

"The Dons have agreed to a capitulation, sir."

"Good! Those ships there?"

"They'll be our prizes, sir."

"Hurray!" yelled Berry, his arms in the air.

Five hundred pounds for Buckland, five shillings for Berry, but prize money was something to cheer about in any case. And this was a victory, the destruction of a nest of privateers, the capture of a Spanish regiment, security for convoys going through the Mona Passage. It had only needed the mounting of the gun to search the anchorage to bring the Dons to their senses.

"Very good, Mr. Wellard, thank you," said Bush.

So Wellard could step back and wipe the sweat out of his eyes, and Bush could wonder what item in the terms of the capitulation would be likely to rob him of his next night's rest.

FOURTEEN

Bush stood on the quarterdeck of the *Renown* at Buckland's side with his telescope trained on the fort.

"The party's leaving there now, sir," he said, and then, after an interval, "the boat's putting off from the landing stage."

The *Renown* swung at her anchor in the mouth of the Gulf of Samaná, and close beside her rode her three prizes. All four ships were jammed with the prisoners who had surrendered themselves, and sails were ready to loose the moment the *Renown* should give the signal.

"The boat's well clear now," said Bush. "I wonder—ah!"

The fort on the crest had burst into a great fountain of smoke, within which could be made out flying fragments of masonry. A moment later came the crash of the explosion. Two tons of gunpowder, ignited by the slow match left burning by the demolition party, did the work. Ramparts and bastions, tower and platform, all were dashed into ruins. Already at the foot of the steep slope to the water lay what was left of the guns, trunnions blasted off, muzzles split, and touchholes spiked; the insurgents when they came to take over the place would have no means to re-establish the defences of the bay—the other battery on the point across the water had already been blown up.

"It looks as if the damage is complete enough, sir," said Bush.

"Yes," said Buckland, his eye to his telescope observing the ruins as they began to show through the smoke and dust. "We'll get under way as soon as the boat's hoisted in, if you please."

"Aye aye, sir," said Bush.

With the boat lowered onto its chocks the hands went to the capstan and hauled the ship laboriously up to her anchor; the sails were loosed as the anchor rose clear. The main topsail aback gave her a trifle of sternway, and then, with the wheel hard over and hands at the headsail sheets, she came round. The topsails, braced up, caught the wind as the quartermaster at the wheel spun the spokes over hastily, and now she was under full command, moving easily through the water, heeling a little to the wind, the sea swinging under her cutwater, heading out close-hauled to weather Engano Point. Somebody forward began to cheer, and in a moment the entire crew was yelling lustily as the *Renown* left the scene of her victory. The prizes were getting under way at the same time, and the prize crews on board echoed the cheering. Bush's telescope could pick out Hornblower on the deck of *La Gaditana*, the big ship-rigged prize, waving his hat to the *Renown*.

"I'll see that everything is secure below, sir," said Bush.

There were marine sentries beside the midshipmen's berth, bayonets fixed and muskets loaded. From within, as Bush listened, there was a wild babble of voices. Fifty women were cramped into that space, and almost as many children. That was bad, but it was necessary to confine them while the ship got under way. Later on they could be allowed on deck, in batches perhaps, for air and exercise. The hatchways in the lower gundeck were closed by gratings, and every hatchway was guarded by a sentry. Up through the gratings rose the smell of humanity; there were four hundred Spanish soldiers confined down there in conditions not much better than prevailed in a slave ship. It was only since dawn that they had been down there, and already there was this stench. For the men, as for the women, there would have to be arrangements made to allow them to take the air in batches. It meant endless trouble and precaution; Bush had already gone to considerable trouble to organise a system by which the prisoners should be supplied with food and drink. But every water butt was full, two boatloads of yams had been brought on board from the shore, and, given the steady breeze that could be expected, the run to Kingston would be completed in less than a week. Then their troubles would be ended and the prisoners handed over to the military authorities—probably the prisoners would be as relieved as Bush would be.

On deck again Bush looked over at the green hills of Santo Domingo out on the starboard beam as, close-hauled, the *Renown* coasted along them; on that side too, under her lee as his orders had dictated, Hornblower had the three prizes under easy sail. Even with this brisk seven-knot breeze blowing and the *Renown* with all sail set those three vessels had the heels of her if they cared to show them; privateers depended both for catching their prey and evading their enemies on the ability to work fast to the windward and Hornblower could soon have left the *Renown* far behind if he were not under orders to keep within sight and to leeward so that the *Renown* could run down to him and protect him if an enemy should appear. The prize crews were small enough in all conscience, and just as in the *Renown* Hornblower had all the prisoners he could guard battened down below.

Bush touched his hat to Buckland as the latter came onto the quarterdeck.

"I'll start bringing the prisoners up if I may, sir," he said.

"Do as you think proper, if you please, Mr. Bush."

The quarterdeck for the women, the maindeck for the men. It was hard to make them understand that they had to take turns; those of the women who were brought on deck seemed to fancy that they were going to be permanently separated from those kept below, and there was lamentation and expostulation which accorded ill with the dignified routine which should be observed on the quarterdeck of a ship of the line. And the children knew no discipline whatever, and ran shrieking about in all directions while harassed seamen tried to bring them back to their mothers. And other seamen had to be detailed to bring the prisoners their food and water; Bush, tackling each aggravating problem as it arose, began to think that life as first lieutenant in a ship of the line (which he had once believed to be a paradise too wonderful for him to aspire to) was not worth the living.

There were thirty officers crammed into the steerage, from the elegant Villanueva down to the second mate of *La Gaditana;* they were almost as much trouble to Bush as all the other prisoners combined, for they took the air on the poop, from which point of vantage they endeavoured to hold conversations with their wives on the quarterdeck, while they had to be fed from the wardroom stores, which were rapidly depleted by the large Spanish appetites. Bush found himself looking forward more and more eagerly to their arrival at Kingston, and he had neither time nor inclination to brood over what might be their reception there, which was probably just as well, for while he could hope for commendation for the part he had played in the attack on Santo Domingo he could also fear the result of an inquiry into the circumstances which had deprived Captain Sawyer of his command.

Day by day the wind held fair; day by day the *Renown* surged along over the blue Caribbean with the prizes to leeward on the port bow; the prisoners, even the women, began to recover from their seasickness, and feeding them and guarding them became more and more matters of routine making less demand on everyone. They sighted Cape Beata to the northward and could haul their port tacks on board and lay a course direct for Kingston, but save for that they hardly had to handle a sail, for the wind blew steady and the hourly heaving of the log recorded eight knots with almost monotonous regularity. The sun rose splendidly behind them each morning; and each evening the bowsprit pointed into a flaming sunset. In the daytime the sun blazed down upon the ship save for the brief intervals when sharp rainstorms blotted out sun and sea; at night the ship rose and swooped with the following sea under a canopy of stars.

It was a dark lovely night when Bush completed his evening rounds and went in to report to Buckland. The sentries were posted; the watch below was asleep with all lights out; the watch on deck had taken in the royals as a precaution against a rain squall striking the ship without warning in the darkness; the course was east by north, and Mr. Carberry had the watch, and the convoy was in sight a mile on the port bow. The guard over the captain in his cabin was at his post. All this Bush recounted to Buckland in the time-honoured fashion of the navy, and Buckland listened to it with the navy's time-honoured patience.

"Thank you, Mr. Bush."

"Thank you, sir. Good night, sir."

"Good night, Mr. Bush."

Bush's cabin opened on the half-deck; it was hot and stuffy with the heat of the tropics, but Bush did not care. He had six clear hours in which to sleep, seeing that he was going to take the morning watch, and he was not the man to waste any of that. He threw off his outer clothes, and standing in his shirt he cast a final look round his cabin before putting out the light. Shoes and trousers were on the sea-chest ready to be put on at a moment's notice in the event of an emergency. Sword and pistols were in their beckets against the bulkhead. All was well. The messenger who would come to call him would bring a lamp, so, using his hand to deflect his breath, he blew out the light. Then he dropped upon the cot, lying on his back with his arms and legs spread wide so as to allow the sweat every chance to evaporate, and he closed his eyes. Thanks to his blessed stolidity of temperament he was soon asleep. At midnight he awoke long enough to hear the watches called, and to tell himself blissfully that there was no need to awake, and he had not sweated enough to make his position on the cot uncomfortable.

Later he awoke again, and looked up into the darkness with uncomprehending eyes as his ears told him all was not well. There were loud cries, there was a rush of feet overhead. Perhaps a fluky rain squall had taken the ship aback. But those were the wrong noises. Were some of those cries cries of pain? Was that the scream of a woman? Were those infernal women squabbling with each other again? Now there was another rush of feet, and wild shouting, which brought Bush off his cot in a flash. He tore open his cabin door, and as he did so he heard the bang of a musket which left him in no doubt as to what was happening. He turned back and grabbed for sword and pistol, and by the time he was outside his cabin door again the ship was full of a yelling tumult. It was as if the hatchways were the entrances to Hell, and pouring up through them were the infernal powers, screaming with triumph in the dimly lit recesses of the ship.

As he emerged the sentry under the lantern fired his musket, lantern and musket flash illuminating a wave of humanity pouring upon the sentry and instantly submerging him; Bush caught a glimpse of a woman leading the wave, a handsome mulatto woman, wife to one of the privateer officers, now screaming with open mouth and staring eyes as she led the rush. Bush levelled his pistol and fired, but they were up to him in an instant. He backed into his narrow doorway. Hands grabbed his sword blade, and he tore it through their grip; he struck wildly with his empty pistol, he kicked out with his bare feet to free himself from the hands that grabbed at him. Thrusting overhand with his sword he stabbed again and again into the mass of bodies pressing against him. Twice his head struck against the deck beams above but he did not feel the blows. Then the flood had washed past him. There were shouts and screams and blows farther along, but he himself had been passed by, save by the groaning men who wallowed at his feet—his bare feet slipping in the hot blood that poured over them.

His first thought was for Buckland, but a single glance aft assured him that by himself he stood no chance of being of any aid to him, and in that case his post was on the quarterdeck, and he ran out, sword in hand, to make his way there. At the foot of the companion ladder there was another whirl of yelling Spaniards; above there were shouts and cries as the after guard fought it out. Forward there was other fighting going on; the stars were shining on white-shirted groups that fought and struggled with savage desperation. Unknown to himself he was yelling with the rest; a band of men turned upon him as he approached, and he felt the heavy blow of a belaying pin against his sword blade. But Bush inflamed with fighting madness was an enemy to be feared; his immense strength was allied to a lightfooted quickness. He struck and parried, leaping over the cumbered deck. He knew nothing, and during those mad minutes he thought of nothing save to fight against these enemies, to reconquer the ship by the strength of his single arm. Then he regained some of his sanity at the moment when he struck down one of the group against whom he was fighting. He must rally the crew, set an example, concentrate his men into a cohesive body. He raised his voice in a bellow.

"Renowns! Renowns! Here, Renowns! Come on!"

There was a fresh swirl in the mad confusion on the maindeck. There was a searing pain across his shoulder blade; instinctively he turned and his left hand seized a throat and he had a moment in which to brace himself and exert all his strength, with a wrench and a heave flinging the man onto the deck.

"Renowns!" he yelled again.

There was a rush of feet as a body of men rallied round him.

"Come on!"

But the charge that he led was met by a wall of men advancing forward against him from aft. Bush and his little group were swept back, across the deck, jammed against the bulwarks. Somebody shouted something in Spanish in front of him, and there was an eddy in the ring; then a musket flashed and banged. The flash lit up the swarthy faces that ringed them round, lit up the bayonet on the muzzle of the musket, and the man beside Bush gave a sharp cry and fell to the deck; Bush could feel him flapping and struggling against his feet. Someone at least had a firearm—taken from an arms rack or from a marine—and had managed to reload it. They would be shot to pieces where they stood, if they were to stand.

"Come on!" yelled Bush again, and sprang forward.

But the disheartened little group behind him did not stir, and Bush gave back from the rigid ring. Another musket flashed and banged, and another man fell. Someone raised his voice and called to them in Spanish. Bush could not understand the words, but he could guess it was a demand for surrender.

"I'll see you damned first!" he said.

He was almost weeping with rage. The thought of his magnificent ship falling into alien hands was appalling now that the realisation of the possibility arose in his mind. A ship of the line captured and carried off into some Cuban port—what would England say? What would the navy say? He did not want to live to find out. He was a desperate man who wanted to die.

This time it was with no intelligible appeal to his men that he sprang forward, but with a wild animal cry; he was insane with fury, a fighting lunatic and with a lunatic's strength. He burst through the ring of his enemies, slashing and smiting, but he was the only one who succeeded; he was out onto the clear deck while the struggle went on behind him.

But the madness ebbed away. He found himself leaning—hiding himself, it might almost be said—beside one of the maindeck eighteen-pounders, forgotten for the moment, his sword still in his hand, trying with a slow brain to take stock of his situation. Mental pictures moved slowly across his mind's eye. He could not doubt that some members of the ship's company had risked the ship for the sake of their lust. There had been no bargaining; none of the women had sold themselves in exchange for a betrayal. But he could guess that the women had seemed complacent, that some of the guards had neglected their duty to take advantage of such an opportunity. Then there would be a slow seepage of prisoners out of confinement, probably the officers from out of the midshipmen's berth, and then the sudden well-planned uprising. A torrent of prisoners pouring up, the sentries overwhelmed, the arms seized; the watch below, asleep in their hammocks and incapable of resistance, driven like sheep in a mass forward, herded into a crowd against the bulkhead and restrained there by an armed party while other parties secured the officers aft, and, surging onto the maindeck, captured or slew every man there. All about the ship now there must still be little groups of seamen and marines still free like himself, but weaponless and demoralised; with the coming of daylight the Spaniards would reorganise themselves and would hunt through the ship and destroy any further resistance piecemeal, group by group. It was unbelievable that such a thing could have happened, and yet it had. Four hundred disciplined and desperate men, reckless of their lives and guided by brave officers, might achieve much.

There were orders—Spanish orders—being shouted about the deck now. The ship had come up into the wind all aback when the quartermasters at the wheel had been overwhelmed, and she was wallowing in the trough of the waves, now coming up, now falling off again, with the canvas overhead all flapping and thundering. There were Spanish sea officers—those of the prizes—on board. They would be able to bring the ship under control in a few minutes. Even with a crew of landsmen they would be able to brace the yards, man the wheel, and set a course close-hauled up the Jamaica Channel. Beyond, only a long day's run, lay Santiago. Now there was the faintest, tiniest light in the sky. Morning—the awful morning—was about to break. Bush took a fresh grip of his sword hilt; his head was swimming and he passed his forearm over his face to wipe away the cobwebs that seemed to be gathering over his eyes.

And then, pale but silhouetted against the sky on the other side of the ship, he saw the topsail of another vessel moving slowly forward along the ship's side; masts, yards, rigging; another topsail slowly turning. There were wild shouts and yells from the *Renown*, a grinding crash as the two ships came together. An agonising pause, like the moment before a roller breaks upon the shore. And then up over the bulwarks of the *Renown* appeared the heads and shoulders of men; the shakos of marines, the cold glitter of bayonets and cutlasses. There was Hornblower, hatless, swinging his leg over and leaping down to the deck, sword in hand, the others leaping with him on either hand. Weak and faint as he was, Bush still could think clearly enough to realise that Hornblower must have collected the prize crews from all three vessels before running alongside in *La Gaditana;* by Bush's calculation he could have brought thirty seamen and thirty marines to this attack. But while one part of Bush's brain could think with this clarity and logic the other part of it seemed to be hampered and clogged so that what went on before his eyes moved with nightmare slowness. It might have been a slow-order drill, as the boarding party climbed down on the deck. Everything was changed and unreal. The shouts of the Spaniards might have been the shrill cries of little children at play. Bush saw the muskets levelled and fired, but the irregular volley sounded in his ears no louder than popguns. The charge was sweeping the deck; Bush tried to spring forward to join with it but his legs strangely would not move. He found himself lying on the deck and his arms had no strength when he tried to lift himself up.

He saw the ferocious bloody battle that was waged, a fight as wild and as irregular as the one that had preceded it, when little groups of men seemed to appear from nowhere and fling themselves into the struggle, sometimes on this side and sometimes on that. Now came another surge of men, nearly naked seamen with Silk at their head; Silk was swinging the rammer of a gun, a vast unwieldy weapon with which he struck out right and left at the Spaniards who broke before him. Another swirl and eddy in the fight; a Spanish soldier trying to run, limping, with a wounded thigh, and a British seaman with a boarding pike in pursuit, stabbing the wretched man under the ribs and leaving him moving feebly in the blood that poured from him.

Now the maindeck was clear save for the corpses that lay heaped upon it, although below decks he could hear the fight going on, shots and screams and crashes. It all seemed to die away. This weakness was not exactly pleasant. To allow himself to put his head down on his arm and forget his responsibilities might seem tempting, but just over the horizon of his conscious mind there were hideous nightmare things waiting to spring out on him, of which he was frightened, but it made him weaker still to struggle against them. But his head was down on his arm, and it was a tremendous effort to lift it again; later it was a worse effort still, but he tried to force himself to make it, to rise and deal with all the things that must be done. Now there was a hard voice speaking, painful to his ears.

"This 'ere's Mr. Bush, sir. 'Ere 'e is!"

Hands were lifting his head. The sunshine was agonising as it poured into his eyes, and he closed his eyelids tight to keep it out.

"Bush! Bush!" That was Hornblower's voice, pleading and tender. "Bush, please, speak to me."

Two gentle hands were holding his face between them. Bush could just separate his eyelids sufficiently to see Hornblower bending over him, but to speak called for more strength than he possessed. He could only shake his head a little, smiling because of the sense of comfort and security conveyed by Hornblower's hands.

FIFTEEN

"Mr. Hornblower's respects, sir," said the messenger, putting his head inside Bush's cabin after knocking on the door. "The admiral's flag is flying off Mosquito Point, an' we're just goin' to fire the salute, sir."

"Very good," said Bush.

Lying on his cot he had followed in his mind's eye all that had been going on in the ship. She was on the port tack at the moment and had clewed up all sail save topsails and jib. They must be inside Gun Key, then. He heard Hornblower's voice hailing.

"Lee braces, there! Hands wear ship."

He heard the grumble of the tiller ropes as the wheel was put over; they must be rounding Port Royal Point. The *Renown* rose to a level keel—she had been heeling very slightly—and then lay over to port, so little that, lying on his cot, Bush could hardly feel it. Then came the bang of the first saluting gun; despite the kindly warning that Hornblower had sent down Bush was taken sufficiently by surprise to start a little at the sound. He was as weak and nervous as a kitten, he told himself. At five-second intervals the salute went on, while Bush resettled himself in bed. Movement was not very easy, even allowing for his weakness, on account of all the stitches that closed the numerous cuts and gashes on his body. He was sewn together like a crazy quilt; and any movement was painful.

The ship fell oddly quiet again when the salute was over—he was nearly sure it had been fifteen guns; Lambert presumably had been promoted to vice-admiral. They must be gliding northward up Port Royal Bay; Bush tried to remember how Salt Pond Hill looked, and the mountains in the background—what were they called? Liguanea, or something like that—he could never tackle these Dago names. They called it the Long Mountain behind Rock Fort.

"Tops'l sheets!" came Hornblower's voice from above. "Tops'l clew lines."

The ship must be gliding slowly to her anchorage.

"Helm-a-lee!"

Turning into the wind would take her way off her.

"Silence, there in the waist!"

Bush could imagine how the hands would be excited and chattering at coming into harbour—the old hands would be telling the new ones about the grog shops and the unholy entertainments that Kingston, just up the channel, provided for seamen.

"Let go!"

That rumble and vibration; no sailor, not even one as matter-of-fact as Bush, could hear the sound of the cable roaring through the hawse-hole without a certain amount of emotion. And this was a moment of very mixed and violent emotions. This was no homecoming; it might be the end of an incident, but it would be most certainly the beginning of a new series of incidents. The immediate future held the likelihood of calamity. Not the risk of death or wounds; Bush would have welcomed that as an alternative to the ordeal that lay ahead. Even in his weak state he could still feel the tension mount in his body as his mind tried to foresee the future. He would like to move about, at least fidget and wriggle if he could not walk, in an endeavour to ease that tension, but he could not even fidget while fifty-three stitches held together the half-closed gashes on his body. There would most certainly be an inquiry into the doings on board H.M.S. *Renown*, and there was a possibility of a court-martial—of a whole series of court-martials—as a result.

Captain Sawyer was dead. Someone among the Spaniards, drunk with blood lust, at the time when the prisoners had tried to retake the ship, had struck down the wretched lunatic when they had burst into the cabin where he was confined. Hell had no fire hot enough for the man—or woman—who could do such a thing, even though it might be looked upon as a merciful release for the poor soul which had cowered before imagined terrors for so long. It was a strange irony that at the moment while a merciless hand had cut the madman's throat some among the free prisoners had spared Buckland, had taken him prisoner as he lay in his cot and bound him with his bedding so that he lay helpless while the battle for his ship was being fought out to its bloody end. Buckland would have much to explain to a court of inquiry.

Bush heard the pipes of the bosun's mates and strained his ears to hear the orders given.

"Gig's crew away! Hands to lower the gig!"

Buckland would of course be going off at once to report to the admiral, and just as Bush came to that conclusion Buckland came into the cabin. Naturally he was dressed with the utmost care, in spotless white trousers and his best uniform coat. He was smoothly shaved, and the formal regularity of his neckcloth was the best proof of the anxious attention he had given to it. He carried his cocked hat in his hand as he stooped under the deck beams, and his sword hung from his hip. But he could not speak immediately; he could only stand and stare at Bush. Usually his cheeks were somewhat pudgy, but this morning they were hollow with care; the staring eyes were glassy, and the lips were twitching. A man on his way to the gallows might look like that.

"You're going to make your report, sir?" asked Bush, after waiting for his superior to speak first.

"Yes," said Buckland.

Beside his cocked hat he held in his hand the sealed reports over which he had been labouring. Bush had been called in to help him compose the first, the anxious one regarding the displacement of Captain Sawyer from command; and his own personal report was embodied in the second one, redolent with conscious virtue, telling of the capitulation of the Spanish forces in Santo Domingo. But the third one, with its account of the uprising of the prisoners on board, and its confession that Buckland had been taken prisoner asleep in bed, had been written without Bush's help.

"I wish to God I was dead," said Buckland.

"Don't say that, sir," said Bush, as cheerfully as his own apprehensions and his weak state would allow.

"I wish I was," repeated Buckland.

"Your gig's alongside, sir," said Hornblower's voice. "And the prizes are just anchoring astern of us."

Buckland turned his dead-fish eyes towards him; Hornblower was not quite as neat in appearance, but he had clearly gone to some pains with his uniform.

"Thank you," said Buckland, and then, after a pause, he asked his question explosively. "Tell me, Mr. Hornblower—this is the last chance —how did the captain come to fall down the hatchway?"

"I am quite unable to tell you, sir," said Hornblower.

There was no hint whatever to be gleaned from his expressionless face or from the words he used.

"Now, Mr. Hornblower," said Buckland, nervously tapping the reports in his hand. "I'm treating you well. You'll find I've given you all the praise I could in these reports. I've given you full credit for what you did at Santo Domingo, and for boarding the ship when the prisoners rose. Full credit, Mr. Hornblower. Won't you—won't you—?"

"I really cannot add anything to what you already know, sir," said Hornblower.

"But what am I going to say when they start asking me?" said Buckland.

"Just say the truth, sir, that the captain was found under the hatchway and that no inquiry could establish any other indication than that he fell by accident."

"I wish I knew," said Buckland.

"You know all that will ever be known, sir. Your pardon, sir," Hornblower extended his hand and picked a thread of oakum from off Buckland's lapel before he went on speaking, "the admiral will be overjoyed at hearing that we've wiped out the Dons at Samaná, sir. He's probably been worrying himself grey-haired over convoys in the Mona Passage. And we've brought three prizes in. He'll have his one-eighth of their value. You can't believe he'll resent that, can you, sir?"

"I suppose not," said Buckland.

"He'll have seen the prizes coming in with us—everyone in the flagship's looking at them now and wondering about them. He'll be expecting good news. He'll be in no mood to ask questions this morning, sir. Except perhaps to ask you if you'll take Madeira or sherry."

For the life of him Bush could not guess whether Hornblower's smile was natural or not, but he was a witness of the infusion of new spirits into Buckland.

"But later on—" said Buckland.

"Later on's another day, sir. We can be sure of one thing, though—admirals don't like to be kept waiting, sir."

"I suppose I'd better go," said Buckland.

Hornblower returned to Bush's cabin after having supervised the departure of the gig. This time his smile was clearly not forced; it played whimsically about the corners of his mouth.

"I don't see anything to laugh at," said Bush.

He tried to ease his position under the sheet that covered him. Now that the ship was stationary and the nearby land interfered with the free course of the wind the ship was much warmer already; the sun was shining down mercilessly, almost vertically over the deck that lay hardly more than a yard above Bush's upturned face.

"You're quite right, sir," said Hornblower, stooping over him and adjusting the sheet. "There's nothing to laugh at."

"Then take that damned grin off your face," said Bush, petulantly.

Excitement and the heat were working on his weakness to make his head swim again.

"Aye aye, sir. Is there anything else I can do?"

"No," said Bush.

"Very good, sir. I'll attend to my other duties, then."

Alone in his cabin Bush rather regretted Hornblower's absence. As far as his weakness would permit, he would have liked to discuss the immediate future; he lay and thought about it, muzzy-mindedly, while the sweat soaked the bandages that swathed him. But there could be no logical order in his thoughts. He swore feebly to himself; listening, he tried to guess what was going on in the ship with hardly more success than when he had tried to guess the future. He closed his eyes to sleep, and he opened them again when he started wondering about how Buckland was progressing in his interview with Admiral Lambert.

A lob-lolly boy—sick berth attendant—came in with a tray that bore a jug and a glass. He poured out a glassful of liquid and with an arm supporting Bush's neck he held it to Bush's lips. At the touch of the cool liquid, and as its refreshing scent reached his nose, Bush suddenly realised he was horribly thirsty, and he drank eagerly, draining the glass.

"What's that?" he asked.

"Lemonade, sir, with Mr. Hornblower's respects."

"Mr. Hornblower?"

"Yes, sir. There's a bumboat alongside an' Mr. Hornblower bought some lemons an' told me to squeeze 'em for you."

"My thanks to Mr. Hornblower."

"Aye aye, sir. Another glass, sir?"

"Yes."

That was better. Later on there were a whole succession of noises which he found hard to explain to himself, the tramp of booted feet on the deck, shouted orders, oars and more oars rowing alongside. Then there were steps outside his cabin door and Clive the surgeon entered, ushering in a stranger, a skinny, white-haired man with twinkling blue eyes.

"I'm Sankey, surgeon of the naval hospital ashore," he announced, "I've come to take you where you'll be more comfortable."

"I don't want to leave the ship," said Bush.

"In the service," said Sankey with professional cheerfulness, "you should have learned that it is the rule always to have to do what you don't want to do."

He turned back the sheet and contemplated Bush's bandaged form.

"Pardon this liberty," he said, still hatefully cheerful, "but I have to sign a receipt for you—I trust you've never signed a receipt for ship's stores without examining into their condition, lieutenant."

"Damn you to hell!" said Bush.

"A nasty temper," said Sankey with a glance at Clive. "I fear you have not prescribed a sufficiency of opening medicine."

He laid hands on Bush, and with Clive's assistance dexterously twitched him over so that he lay face downward.

"The Dagoes seem to have done a crude job of carving you, sir," went on Sankey, addressing Bush's defenceless back. "Nine wounds, I understand."

"And fifty-three stitches," added Clive.

"That will look well in the *Gazette*," said Sankey with a giggle, and proceeded to extemporise a quotation: "Lieutenant—ah—Bush received no fewer than nine wounds in the course of his heroic defence, but I am happy to state that he is rapidly recovering from them."

Bush tried to turn his head so as to snarl out an appropriate reply, but his neck was one of the sorest parts of him and he could only growl unintelligibly, and he was not turned onto his back again until his growls had died down.

"And now we'll whisk our little cupid away," said Sankey. "Come in, you stretcher men."

Carried out onto the maindeck Bush found the sunlight blinding, and Sankey stooped to draw the sheet over his eyes.

"Belay that!" said Bush, as he realised his intention, and there was enough of the old bellow in his voice to cause Sankey to pause. "I want to see!"

The explanation of the trampling and bustle on the deck was plain now. Across the waist was drawn up a guard of one of the West Indian regiments, bayonets fixed and every man at attention. The Spanish prisoners were being brought up through the hatchways for despatch to the shore in the lighters alongside. Bush recognised Ortega, limping along with a man on either side to support him; one trouserleg had been cut off and his thigh was bandaged, and the bandage and the other trouserleg were black with dried blood.

"A cutthroat crew, to be sure," said Sankey. "And now, if you have feasted your eyes on them long enough, we can sway you down into the boat."

Hornblower came hurrying down from the quarterdeck and went down on his knee beside the stretcher.

"Are you all right, sir?" he asked anxiously.

"Yes, thank'ee," said Bush.

"I'll have your gear packed and sent ashore after you, sir."

"Thank you."

"Careful with those slings," snapped Hornblower, as the tackles were being attached to the stretcher.

"Sir! Sir!" Midshipman James was dancing about at Hornblower's elbow, anxious for his attention. "Boat's heading for us with a captain aboard."

That was news demanding instant consideration.

"Good-bye, sir," said Hornblower. "Best of luck, sir. See you soon."

He turned away, and Bush felt no ill will at this brief farewell, for a captain coming on board had to be received with the correct compliments. Moreover, Bush himself was desperately anxious to know the business that brought this captain on board.

"Hoist away!" ordered Sankey.

"Avast!" said Bush, and in reply to Sankey's look of inquiry, "let's wait a minute."

"I have no objection myself to knowing what is going on," said Sankey.

The calls of the bosun's mates shrilled along the deck. The sideboys came running; the military guard wheeled to face the entry port; the marines formed up beside them. Up through the entry port came the captain, his gold lace flaming in the sunshine. Hornblower touched his hat.

"You are Mr. Hornblower, at present the senior lieutenant on board this ship?"

"Yes, sir. Lieutenant Horatio Hornblower, at your service."

"My name is Cogshill," said the captain and he produced a paper which he proceeded to unfold and read aloud. "Orders from Sir Richard Lambert, Vice Admiral of the Blue, Knight of the Bath, Commanding His Majesty's ships and vessels on the Jamaica station, to Captain James Edward Cogshill, of His Majesty's ship *Buckler*. You are hereby requested and required to repair immediately on board of His Majesty's ship *Renown* now lying in Port Royal Bay and to take command pro tempore of the aforesaid ship *Renown*."

Cogshill folded his paper again. The assumption of command, even temporarily, of a king's ship was a solemn act, only to be performed with the correct ceremonial. No orders that Cogshill might give on board would be legal until he had read aloud the authority by which he gave them. Now he had "read himself in," and now he held the enormous powers of a captain on board—he could make and unmake warrant officers, he could order imprisonment or the lash, by virtue of the delegation of power from the King in Council down through the Lords of the Admiralty and Sir Richard Lambert.

"Welcome on board, sir," said Hornblower, touching his hat again.

"Very interesting," said Sankey, when Bush had been swayed down into the hospital boat alongside and Sankey had taken his seat beside the stretcher. "Take charge, coxs'n. I knew Cogshill was a favourite of the admiral's. Promotion to a ship of the line from a twenty-eight-gun frigate is a long step for our friend James Edward. Sir Richard has wasted no time."

"The orders said it was only—only temporary," said Bush, not quite able to bring out the words "pro tempore" with any aplomb.

"Time enough to make out the permanent orders in due form," said Sankey. "It is from this moment that Cogshill's pay is increased from ten shillings to two pounds a day."

The Negro oarsmen of the hospital boat were bending to their work, sending the launch skimming over the glittering water, and Sankey turned his head to look at the squadron lying at anchor in the distance —a three-decker and a couple of frigates.

"That's the *Buckler,*" he said, pointing. "Lucky for Cogshill his ship was in here at this moment. There'll be plenty of promotion in the admiral's gift now. You lost two lieutenants in the *Renown*?"

"Yes," said Bush. Roberts had been cut in two by a shot from Samaná during the first attack, and Smith had been killed at the post of duty defending the quarterdeck when the prisoners rose.

"A captain and two lieutenants," said Sankey meditatively. "Sawyer had been insane for some time, I understand?"

"Yes."

"And yet they killed him?"

"Yes."

"A chapter of accidents. It might have been better for your first lieutenant if he had met the same fate."

Bush did not make any reply to that remark, even though the same thought had occurred to him. Buckland had been taken prisoner in his bed, and he would never be able to live that down.

"I think," said Sankey judicially, "he will never be able to look for promotion. Unfortunate for him, seeing that he could otherwise have expected it as a result of your successes in Santo Domingo, on which so far I have not congratulated you, sir. My felicitations."

"Thank you," said Bush.

"A resounding success. Now it will be interesting to see what use Sir Richard—may his name be ever revered—will make of all these vacancies. Cogshill to the *Renown*. That seems certain. Then a commander must be promoted to the *Buckler*. The ineffable joy of post rank! There are four commanders on this station—I wonder which of them will enter through the pearly gates? You have been on this station before, I believe, sir?"

"Not for three years," said Bush.

"Then you can hardly be expected to be up to date regarding the relative standing of the officers here in Sir Richard's esteem. Then a lieutenant will be made commander. No doubt about who that will be."

Sankey spared Bush a glance, and Bush asked the question which was expected of him.

"Who?"

"Dutton. First lieutenant of the flagship. Are you acquainted with him?"

"I think so. Lanky fellow with a scar on his cheek?"

"Yes. Sir Richard believes that the sun rises and sets on him. And I believe that Lieutenant Dutton—Commander as he soon will be—is of the same opinion."

Bush had no comment to make, and he would not have made one if he had. Surgeon Sankey was quite obviously a scatterbrained old gossip, and quite capable of repeating any remarks made to him. He merely nodded—as much of a nod as his sore neck and his recumbent position allowed—and waited for Sankey to continue his monologue.

"So Dutton will be a commander. That'll mean vacancies for three lieutenants. Sir Richard will be able to gladden the hearts of three of his friends by promoting their sons from midshipmen. Assuming, that is to say, that Sir Richard has as many as three friends."

"Oars! Bowman!" said the coxswain of the launch; they were rounding the tip of the jetty. The boat ran gently alongside and was secured; Sankey climbed out and supervised the lifting of the stretcher. With steady steps the Negro bearers began to carry the stretcher up the road towards the hospital while the heat of the island closed round Bush like the warm water in a bath.

"Let me see," said Sankey, falling into step beside the stretcher. "We had just promoted three midshipmen to lieutenant. So among the warrant ranks there will be three vacancies. But let me see—I fancy you had casualties in the *Renown*?"

"Plenty," said Bush.

Midshipmen and master's mates had given their lives in defence of their ship.

"Of course. That was only to be expected. So there will be many more than three vacancies. So the hearts of the supernumeraries, of the volunteers, of all those unfortunates serving without pay in the hope of eventual preferment, will be gladdened by numerous appointments. From the limbo of nothingness to the inferno of warrant rank. The path of glory—I do not have to asperse your knowledge of literature by reminding you of what the poet said."

Bush had no idea what the poet said, but he was not going to admit it.

"And now we are arrived," said Sankey. "I will attend you to your cabin."

Inside the building the darkness left Bush almost blind for a space after the dazzling sunshine. There were whitewashed corridors; there was a long twilit ward divided by screens into minute rooms. He suddenly realised that he was quite exhausted, that all he wanted to do was to close his eyes and rest. The final lifting of him from the stretcher to the bed and the settling of him there seemed almost more than he could bear. He had no attention to spare for Sankey's final chatter. When the mosquito net was at last drawn round his bed and he was left alone he felt as if he were at the summit of a long sleek green wave, down which he went gliding, gliding, endlessly gliding. It was almost a pleasant sensation, but not quite.

When he reached the foot of the wave he had to struggle up it again, recovering his strength, through a night and a day and another night, and during that time he came to learn about the life in the hospital—the sounds, the groans, that came from other patients behind other screens, the not-quite-muffled howls of lunatic patients at the far end of the whitewashed corridor; morning and evening rounds; by the end of his second day there he had begun to listen with appetite for the noises that presaged the bringing in of his meals.

"You are a fortunate man," remarked Sankey, examining his stitched-up body. "These are all incised wounds. Not a single deep puncture. It's contrary to all my professional experience. Usually the Dagoes can be relied upon to use their knives in a more effective manner. Just look at this cut here."

The cut in question ran from Bush's shoulder to his spine, so that Sankey could not literally mean what he had just said.

"Eight inches long at least," went on Sankey. "Yet not more than two inches deep, even though, as I suspect, the scapula is notched. Four inches with the point would have been far more effective. This other cut here seems to be the only one that indicates any ambition to plumb the arterial depths. Clearly the man who wielded the knife here intended to stab. But it was a stab from above downwards, and the jagged beginning of it shows how the point was turned by the ribs down which the knife slid, severing a few fibres of latissimus dorsi but tailing off at the end into a mere superficial laceration. The effort of a tyro. Turn over, please. Remember, Mr. Bush, if ever you use a knife, to give an upward inclination to the point. The human ribs lie open to welcome an upward thrust; before a downward thrust they overlap and forbid all entrance, and the descending knife, as in this case, bounds in vain from one rib to the next, knocking for admission at each in turn and being refused."

"I'm glad of that," said Bush. "Ouch!"

"And every cut is healing well," said Sankey. "No sign of mortification."

Bush suddenly realised that Sankey was moving his nose about close to his body; it was by its smell that gangrene first became apparent.

"A good clean cut," said Sankey, "rapidly sutured and bound up in its own blood, can be expected to heal by first intention more often than not. Many times more often than not. And these are mostly clean cuts, haggled, as I said, only a little here and there. Bend this knee if you please. Your honourable scars, Mr. Bush, will in the course of a few years become almost unnoticeable. Thin lines of white whose criss-cross pattern will be hardly a blemish on your classic torso."

"Good," said Bush; he was not quite sure what his torso was, but he was not going to ask Sankey to explain all these anatomical terms.

This morning Sankey had hardly left him before he returned with a visitor.

"Captain Cogshill to inspect you," he said. "Here he is, sir."

Cogshill looked down at Bush upon the bed.

"Doctor Sankey gives me the good news that you are recovering rapidly," he said.

"I think I am, sir."

"The admiral has ordered a court of inquiry, and I am nominated a member of the court. Naturally your evidence will be required, Mr. Bush, and it is my duty to ascertain how soon you will be able to give it."

Bush felt a little wave of apprehension ripple over him. A court of inquiry was only a shade less terrifying than the court-martial to which it might lead. Even with a conscience absolutely clear Bush would rather—far rather—handle a ship on a lee shore in a gale than face questions and have to give answers, submit his motives to analysis and misconstruction, and struggle against the entanglements of legal forms. But it was medicine that had to be swallowed, and the sensible thing was to hold his nose and gulp it down however nauseating.

"I'm ready at any time, sir."

"Tomorrow I shall take out the sutures, sir," interposed Sankey. "You will observe that Mr. Bush is still weak. He was entirely exsanguinated by his wounds."

"What do you mean by that?"

"I mean he was drained of his blood. And the ordeal of taking out the sutures—"

"The stitches, do you mean?"

"The stitches, sir. The ordeal of removing them may momentarily retard Mr. Bush's recovery of his strength. But if the court will indulge him with a chair when he gives his evidence—"

"That can certainly be granted."

"Then in three days from now he can answer any necessary questions."

"Next Friday, then?"

"Yes, sir. That is the earliest. I could wish it would be later."

"To assemble a court on this station," explained Cogshill with his cold courtesy, "is not easy, when every ship is away on necessary duty so much of the time. Next Friday will be convenient."

"Yes, sir," said Sankey.

It was some sort of gratification to Bush, who had endured so much of Sankey's chatter, to see him almost subdued in his manner when addressing someone as eminent as a captain.

"Very well, then," said Cogshill. He bowed to Bush. "I wish you the quickest of recoveries."

"Thank you, sir," said Bush.

Even lying on his back he could not check the instinctive attempt to return the bow, but his wounds hurt him when he started to double up in the middle and prevented him from appearing ridiculous. With Cogshill gone Bush had time to worry about the future; the fear of it haunted him a little even while he ate his dinner, but the lob-lolly boy who came to take away the remains ushered in another visitor, the sight of whom drove away the black thoughts. It was Hornblower, standing at the door with a basket in his hand, and Bush's face lit up at the sight of him.

"How are you, sir?" asked Hornblower.

They shook hands, each reflecting the pleasure of the other's greeting.

"All the better for seeing you," said Bush, and meant it.

"This is my first chance of coming ashore," said Hornblower. "You can guess that I've been kept busy."

Bush could guess easily enough; it was no trouble to him to visualise all the duties that had been heaped on Hornblower, the necessity to complete *Renown* again with powder and shot, food and water, to clean up the ship after the prisoners had been removed, to eradicate the traces of the recent fighting, to attend to the formalities connected with the disposal of the prizes, the wounded, the sick, and the effects of the dead. And Bush was eager to hear the details, as a housewife might be when illness had removed her from the supervision of her household. He plied Hornblower with questions, and the technical discussion that ensued prevented Hornblower for some time from indicating the basket he had brought.

"Pawpaws," he said. "Mangoes. A pineapple. That's only the second pineapple I've ever seen."

"Thank you. Very kind of you," said Bush. But it was utterly beyond possibility that he could give the least hint of the feelings that the gift evoked in him, that after lying lonely for these days in the hospital he should find that someone cared about him—that in any case someone should give him so much as a thought. The words he spoke were limping and quite inadequate, and only a sensitive and sympathetic mind could guess at the feelings which the words concealed rather than expressed. But he was saved from further embarrassment by Hornblower abruptly introducing a new subject.

"The admiral's taking the *Gaditana* into the navy," he announced.

"Is he, by George!"

"Yes. Eighteen guns—six-pounders and nines. She'll rate as a sloop of war."

"So he'll have to promote a commander for her."

"Yes."

"By George!" said Bush again.

Some lucky lieutenant would get that important step. It might have been Buckland—it still might be, if no weight were given to the consideration that he had been captured asleep in bed.

"Lambert's renaming her the *Retribution*," said Hornblower.

"Not a bad name, either."

"No."

There was silence for a moment; each of them was reliving, from his own point of view, those awful minutes while the *Renown* was being recaptured, while the Spaniards who tried to fight it out were slaughtered without mercy.

"You know about the court of inquiry, I suppose?" asked Bush; it was a logical step from his last train of thought.

"Yes. How did you know about it?"

"Cogshill's just been in here to warn me that I'll have to give evidence."

"I see."

There followed silence more pregnant than the last as they thought about the ordeal ahead. Hornblower deliberately broke it.

"I was going to tell you," he said, "that I had to reeve new tiller lines in *Renown*. Both of them were frayed—there's too much wear there. I think they're led round too sharp an angle."

That provoked a technical discussion which Hornblower encouraged until it was time for him to leave.

SIXTEEN

The court of inquiry was not nearly as awe-inspiring as a court-martial. There was no gun fired, no court-martial flag hoisted; the captains who constituted the board wore their everyday uniforms, and the witnesses were not required to give their evidence under oath; Bush had forgotten about this last fact until he was called into the court.

"Please take a seat, Mr. Bush," said the president. "I understand you are still weak from your wounds."

Bush hobbled across to the chair indicated and was just able to reach it in time to sit down. The great cabin of the *Renown*—here, where Captain Sawyer had lain quivering and weeping with fear—was sweltering hot. The president had the logbook and journal in front of him, and he held in his hand what Bush recognised to be his own report regarding the attack on Samaná, which he had addressed to Buckland.

"This report of yours does you credit, Mr. Bush," said the president. "It appears that you stormed this fort with no more than six casualties, although it was constructed with a ditch, parapets, and ramparts in regular style, and defended by a garrison of seventy men, and armed with twenty-four-pounders."

"We took them by surprise, sir," said Bush.

"It is that which is to your credit."

The surprise of the garrison of Samaná could not have been greater than Bush's own surprise at this reception; he was expecting something far more unpleasant and inquisitorial. A glance across at Buckland, who had been called in before him, was not quite so reassuring; Buckland was pale and unhappy. But there was something he must say before the thought of Buckland should distract him.

"The credit should be given to Lieutenant Hornblower, sir," he said. "It was his plan."

"So you very handsomely say in your report. I may as well say at once that it is the opinion of this court that all the circumstances regarding the attack on Samaná and the subsequent capitulation are in accordance with the best traditions of the service."

"Thank you, sir."

"Now we come to the next matter. The attempt of the prisoners to capture the *Renown.* You were by this time acting as first lieutenant of the ship, Mr. Bush?"

"Yes, sir."

Step by step Bush was taken through the events of that night. He was responsible under Buckland for the arrangements made for guarding and feeding the prisoners. There were fifty women, wives of the prisoners, under guard in the midshipmen's berth. Yes, it was difficult to supervise them as closely as the men. Yes, he had gone his rounds after pipedown, yes, he had heard a disturbance. And so on.

"And you were found lying among the dead, unconscious from your wounds?"

"Yes, sir."

"Thank you, Mr. Bush."

A fresh-faced young captain at the end of the table asked a question. "And all this time Captain Sawyer was confined to his cabin, until he was murdered?"

The president interposed.

"Captain Hibbert, Mr. Buckland has already enlightened us regarding Captain Sawyer's indisposition."

There was annoyance in the glance that the president of the court turned upon Captain Hibbert, and light suddenly dawned upon Bush. Sawyer had a wife, children, friends, who would not desire that any attention should be called to the fact that he had died insane. The president of the court was probably acting under explicit orders to hush that part of the business up. He would welcome questions about it no more than Bush himself would, now that Sawyer was dead in his country's cause. Buckland could not have been very closely examined about it, either. His unhappy look must be due to having to describe his inglorious part in the attempt on the *Renown.*

"I don't expect any of you gentlemen wish to ask Mr. Bush any more questions?" asked the president of the court in such a way that questions could not possibly have been asked. "Call Lieutenant Hornblower."

Hornblower made his bow to the court; he was wearing that impassive expression which Bush knew by now to conceal an internal turbulence. He was asked as few questions on Samaná as Bush had been.

"It has been suggested," said the president, "that this attack on the fort, and the hoisting up of the gun to search the bay, were on your initiative?"

"I can't think why that suggestion was made, sir. Mr. Buckland bore the entire responsibility."

"I won't press you further about that, Mr. Hornblower, then. I think we all understand. Now, let us hear about your recapture of the *Renown*. What first attracted your attention?"

It called for steady questioning to get the story out of Hornblower. He had heard a couple of musket shots, which had worried him, and then he saw the *Renown* come up into the wind which made him certain something was seriously wrong. So he had collected his prize crews together and laid the *Renown* on board.

"Were you not afraid of losing the prizes, Mr. Hornblower?"

"Better to lose the prizes than the ship, sir. Besides—"

"Besides what, Mr. Hornblower?"

"I had every sheet and halliard cut in the prizes before we left them, sir. It took them some time to reeve new ones, so it was easy to recapture them."

"You seem to have thought of everything, Mr. Hornblower," said the president, and there was a buzz of approval through the court. "And you seem to have made a very prompt counterattack on the *Renown*. You did not wait to ascertain the extent of the danger? Yet for all you knew the attempt to take the ship might have already failed."

"In that case no harm was done except the disabling of the rigging of the prizes, sir. But if the ship had actually fallen into the hands of the prisoners it was essential that an attack should be directed on her before any defence could be organised."

"We understand. Thank you, Mr. Hornblower."

The inquiry was nearly over. Carberry was still too ill with his wounds to be able to give evidence; Whiting of the marines was dead. The court conferred only a moment before announcing its findings.

"It is the opinion of this court," announced the president, "that strict inquiry should be made among the Spanish prisoners to determine who it was that murdered Captain Sawyer, and that the murderer, if still alive, should be brought to justice. And as the result of our examination of the surviving officers of H.M.S. *Renown* it is our opinion that no further action is necessary."

That meant there would be no court-martial. Bush found himself grinning with relief as he sought to meet Hornblower's eye, but when he succeeded his smile met with a cold reception. Bush tried to shut off his smile and look like a man of such clear conscience that it was no relief to be told that he would not be court-martialled. And a glance at Buckland changed his elation to a feeling of pity. The man was desperately unhappy; his professional ambitions had come to an abrupt end. After the capitulation of Samaná he must have cherished hope, for with that considerable achievement to his credit, and his captain unfit for service, there was every possibility that he would receive the vital promotion to commander at least, possibly even to captain. The fact that he had been surprised in bed meant an end to all that. He would always be remembered for it, and the fact would remain in people's minds when the circumstances were forgotten. He was doomed to remain an ageing first lieutenant.

Bush remembered guiltily that it was only by good fortune that he himself had awakened in time. His wounds might be painful, but they had served an invaluable purpose in diverting attention from his own responsibility; he had fought until he had fallen unconscious, and perhaps that was to his credit, but Buckland would have done the same had the opportunity been granted him. But Buckland was damned, while he himself had come through the ordeal at least no worse off than he had been before. Bush felt the illogicality of it all, although he would have been hard pressed if he had to put it into words. And in any case logical thinking on the subject of reputation and promotion was not easy, because during all these years Bush had become more and more imbued with the knowledge that the service was a hard and ungrateful one, in which fortune was even more capricious than in other walks of life. Good luck came and went in the navy as unpredictably as death chose its victims when a broadside swept a crowded deck. Bush was fatalistic and resigned about that, and it was not a state of mind conducive to penetrating thought.

"Ah, Mr. Bush," said Captain Cogshill, "it's a pleasure to see you on your feet. I hope you will remain on board to have dinner with me. I hope to secure the presence of the other lieutenants."

"With much pleasure, sir," said Bush. Every lieutenant said that in reply to his captain's invitation.

"In fifteen minutes' time, then? Excellent."

The captains who had constituted the court of inquiry were leaving the ship, in strict order of seniority, and the calls of the bosun's mates echoed along the deck as each one left, a careless hand to a hat brim in acknowledgment of the compliments bestowed. Down from the entry port went each in turn, gold lace, epaulettes, and all, these blessed individuals who had achieved the ultimate beatitude of post rank, and the smart gigs pulled away towards the anchored ships.

"You're dining on board, sir?" said Hornblower to Bush.

"Yes."

On the deck of their own ship the "sir" came quite naturally, as naturally as it had been dropped when Hornblower had been visiting his friend in the hospital ashore. Hornblower turned to touch his hat to Buckland.

"May I leave the deck to Hart, sir? I'm invited to dine in the cabin."

"Very well, Mr. Hornblower." Buckland forced a smile. "We'll have two new lieutenants soon, and you'll cease to be the junior."

"I shan't be sorry, sir."

These men who had been through so much together were grasping eagerly at trivialities to keep the conversation going for fear lest more serious matters should lift their ugly heads.

"Time for us to go along," said Buckland.

Captain Cogshill was a courtly host. There were flowers in the great cabin now; they must have been kept hidden away in his sleeping cabin while the inquiry was being held so as not to detract from the formality of the proceedings. And the cabin windows were wide open, and a wind scoop brought into the cabin what little air was moving.

"That is a land crab salad before you, Mr. Hornblower. Coconut-fed land crab. Some prefer it to dairy-fed pork. Perhaps you will serve it to those who would care for some?"

The steward brought in a vast smoking joint which he put on the table.

"A saddle of fresh lamb," said the captain. "Sheep do badly in these islands and I fear this may not be fit to eat. But perhaps you will at least try it. Mr. Buckland, will you carve? You see, gentlemen, I still have some real potatoes left—one grows weary of yams. Mr. Hornblower, will you take wine?"

"With pleasure, sir."

"And Mr. Bush—to your speedy recovery, sir."

Bush drained his glass thirstily. Sankey had warned him, when he left the hospital, that overindulgence in spirituous liquors might result in inflammation of his wounds, but there was pleasure in pouring the wine down his throat and feeling the grateful warmth it brought to his stomach. The dinner proceeded.

"You gentlemen who have served on this station before must be acquainted with this," said the captain, contemplating a steaming dish that had been laid before him. "A West Indian pepper pot—not as good as one finds in Trinidad, I fear. Mr. Hornblower, will you make your first essay? Come in!"

The last words were in response to a knock on the cabin door. A smartly dressed midshipman entered. His beautiful uniform, his elegant bearing, marked him as one of that class of naval officer in receipt of a comfortable allowance from home, or even of substantial means of his own. Some sprig of the nobility, doubtless, serving his legal time until favouritism and interest should whisk him up the ladder of promotion.

"I'm sent by the admiral, sir," he announced.

Of course; Bush, his perceptions comfortably sensitised with wine, could see at once that with those clothes and that manner he must be on the admiral's staff.

"And what's your message?" asked Cogshill.

"The admiral's compliments, sir, and he'd like Mr. Hornblower's presence on board the flagship as soon as is convenient."

"And dinner not half-way finished," commented Cogshill, looking at Hornblower. But an admiral's request for something as soon as convenient meant immediately, convenient or not. Very likely it was a matter of no importance, either.

"I'd better leave, sir, if I may," said Hornblower. He glanced at Buckland. "May I have a boat, sir?"

"Pardon me, sir," interposed the midshipman. "The admiral said that the boat which brought me would serve to convey you to the flagship."

"That settles it," said Cogshill. "You'd better go, Mr. Hornblower. We'll save some of this pepper pot for you against your return."

"Thank you, sir," said Hornblower, rising.

As soon as he had left, the captain asked the inevitable question.

"What in the world does the admiral want with Hornblower?"

He looked round the table and received no verbal reply. There was a strained look on Buckland's face, however, as Bush saw. It seemed as if in his misery Buckland was clairvoyant.

"Well, we'll know in time," said Cogshill. "The wine's beside you, Mr. Buckland. Don't let it stagnate."

Dinner went on. The pepper pot rasped on Bush's palate and inflamed his stomach, making the wine doubly grateful when he drank it. When the cheese was removed, and the cloth with it, the steward brought in fruit and nuts in silver dishes.

"Port," said Captain Cogshill. "'79. A good year. About this brandy I know little, as one might expect in these times."

Brandy could only come from France, smuggled, presumably, and as a result of trading with the enemy.

"But here," went on the captain, "is some excellent Dutch geneva—I bought it at the prize sale after we took St. Eustatius. And here is another Dutch liquor—it comes from Curaçao, and if the orange flavour is not too sickly for your palates you might find it pleasant. Swedish schnapps, fiery but excellent, I fancy—that was after we captured Saba. The wise man does not mix grain and grape, so they say, but I understand schnapps is made from potatoes, and so does not come under the ban. Mr. Buckland?"

"Schnapps for me," said Buckland a little thickly.

"Mr. Bush?"

"I'll drink along with you, sir."

That was the easiest way of deciding.

"Then let us make it brandy. Gentlemen, may Boney grow bonier than ever."

They drank the toast, and the brandy went down to warm Bush's interior to a really comfortable pitch. He was feeling happy and relaxed, and two toasts later he was feeling better than he had felt since the *Renown* left Plymouth.

"Come in!" said the captain.

The door opened slowly, and Hornblower stood framed in the opening. There was the old look of strain in his face; Bush could see it even though Hornblower's figure seemed to waver a little before his eyes—the way objects appeared over the rack of red-hot cannon balls at Samaná—and although Hornblower's countenance seemed to be a little fuzzy round the edges.

"Come in, come in, man," said the captain. "The toasts are just beginning. Sit in your old place. Brandy for heroes, as Johnson said in his wisdom. Mr. Bush!"

"V–victorious war. O–oceans of gore. P–prizes galore. B–b–beauty ashore. Hic," said Bush, inordinately proud of himself that he had remembered that toast and had it ready when called upon.

"Drink fair, Mr. Hornblower," said the captain, "we have a start of you already. A stern chase is a long chase."

Hornblower put his glass to his lips again.

"Mr. Buckland!"

"Jollity and—jollity and—jollity and—and—and—mirth," said Buckland, managing to get the last word out at last. His face was as red as a beetroot and seemed to Bush's heated imagination to fill the entire cabin like the setting sun; most amusing.

"You've come back from the admiral, Mr. Hornblower," said the captain with sudden recollection.

"Yes, sir."

The curt reply seemed out of place in the general atmosphere of good-will; Bush was distinctly conscious of it, and of the pause which followed.

"Is all well?" asked the captain at length, apologetic about prying into someone else's business and yet led to do so by the silence.

"Yes, sir." Hornblower was turning his glass round and round on the table between long nervous fingers, every finger a foot long, it seemed to Bush. "He has made me commander into *Retribution.*"

The words were spoken quietly, but they had the impact of pistol shots in the silence of the room.

"God bless my soul!" said the captain. "Then that's our new toast. To the new commander, and a cheer for him too!"

Bush cheered lustily and downed his brandy.

"Good old Hornblower!" he said. "Good old Hornblower!"

To him it was really excellent news; he leaned over and patted Hornblower's shoulder. He knew his face was one big smile, and he put his head on one side and his shoulder on the table so that Hornblower should get the full benefit of it.

Buckland put his glass down on the table with a sharp tap.

"Damn you!" he said. "Damn you! Damn you to Hell!"

"Easy there!" said the captain hastily. "Let's fill the glasses. A brimmer there, Mr. Buckland. Now, our country! Noble England! Queen of the waves!"

Buckland's anger was drowned in the fresh flood of liquor, yet later in the session his sorrows overcame him and he sat at the table weeping quietly, with the tears running down his cheeks; but Bush was too happy to allow Buckland's misery to affect him. He always remembered that afternoon as one of the most successful dinners he had ever attended. He could also remember Hornblower's smile at the end of dinner.

"We can't send you back to the hospital today," said Hornblower. "You'd better sleep in your own cot tonight. Let me take you there."

That was very agreeable; Bush put both arms round Hornblower's shoulders and walked with dragging feet. It did not matter that his feet dragged and his legs would not function while he had this support; Hornblower was the best man in the world and Bush could announce it by singing "For He's a Jolly Good Fellow" while lurching along the alleyway. And Hornblower lowered him onto the heaving cot and grinned down at him as he clung to the edges of the cot; Bush was a little astonished that the ship should sway like this while at anchor.

SEVENTEEN

THAT WAS HOW Hornblower came to leave the *Renown.* The coveted promotion was in his grasp, and he was busy enough commissioning the *Retribution,* making her ready for sea, and organising the scratch crew which was drafted into her. Bush saw something of him during this time, and could congratulate him soberly on the epaulette which, worn on his left shoulder, marked him as a commander, one of those gilded individuals for whom bosun's mates piped the side and who could look forward with confidence to eventual promotion to captain. Bush called him "sir," and even when he said it for the first time the expression did not seem unnatural.

Bush had learned something during the past few weeks which his service during the years had not called to his attention. Those years had been passed at sea, among the perils of the sea, amid the ever-changing conditions of wind and weather, deep water and shoal. In the ships of the line in which he had served there had only been minutes of battle for every week at sea, and he had gradually become fixed in the idea that seamanship was the one requisite for a naval officer. To be master of the countless details of managing a wooden sailing ship; not only to be able to handle her under sail, but to be conversant with all the petty but important trifles regarding cordage and cables, pumps and salt pork, dry rot and the Articles of War; that was what was necessary. But he knew now of other qualities equally necessary; a bold and yet thoughtful initiative, moral as well as physical courage, tactful handling both of superiors and of subordinates, ingenuity and quickness of thought. A fighting navy needed to fight, and needed fighting men to lead it.

Yet even though this realisation reconciled him to Hornblower's promotion, there was irony in the fact that he was plunged back immediately into petty detail of the most undignified sort. For now he had to wage war on the insect world and not on mankind; the Spanish prisoners in the six days they had been on board had infected the ship with all the parasites they had brought with them. Fleas, lice, and bedbugs swarmed everywhere, and in the congenial environment of a wooden ship in the tropics full of men they flourished exceedingly. Heads had to be cropped and bedding baked; and in a desperate attempt to wall in the bedbugs woodwork had to be repainted—a success of a day or two flattered only to deceive, for after each interval the pests showed up again. Even the cockroaches and the rats that had always been in the ship seemed to multiply and become omnipresent.

It was perhaps an unfortunate coincidence that the height of his exasperation with this state of affairs coincided with the payment of prize money for the captures at Samaná. A hundred pounds to spend, a couple of days' leave granted by Captain Cogshill, and Hornblower at a loose end at the same time—those two days were a lurid period, during which Hornblower and Bush contrived to spend each of them a hundred pounds in the dubious delights of Kingston. Two wild days and two wild nights, and then Bush went back on board the *Renown*, shaken and limp, only too glad to get out to sea and recover. And when he returned from this first cruise under Cogshill's command Hornblower came to say good-bye.

"I'm sailing with the land breeze tomorrow morning," he said.

"Whither bound, sir?"

"England," said Hornblower.

Bush could not restrain a whistle at the news. There were men in the squadron who had not seen England for ten years.

"I'll be back again," said Hornblower. "A convoy to the Downs. Despatches for the Commissioners. Pick up the replies and a convoy out again. The usual round."

For a sloop of war it was indeed the usual round. The *Retribution* with her eighteen guns and disciplined crew could fight almost any privateer afloat; with her speed and handiness she could cover a convoy more effectively than the ship of the line or even the frigates that accompanied the larger convoys to give solid protection.

"You'll get your commission confirmed, sir," said Bush, with a glance at Hornblower's epaulette.

"I hope so," said Hornblower.

Confirmation of a commission bestowed by a commander-in-chief on a foreign station was a mere formality.

"That is," said Hornblower, "if they don't make peace."

"No chance of that, sir," said Bush, and it was clear from Hornblower's grin that he, too, thought there was no possibility of peace either, despite the hints in the two-months-old newspapers that came out from England to the effect that negotiations were possible. With Bonaparte in supreme power in France, restless, ambitious, and unscrupulous, and with none of the points settled that were in dispute between the two countries, no fighting man could believe that the negotiations could result even in an armistice, and certainly not in a permanent peace.

"Good luck in any case, sir," said Bush, and there was no mere formality about those words.

They shook hands and parted; it says much for Bush's feelings towards Hornblower that in the grey dawn next morning he rolled out of his cot and went up on deck to watch the *Retribution*, ghostlike under her topsails, and with the lead going in the chains, steal out round the point, wafted along by the land breeze. Bush watched her go; life in the service meant many partings. Meanwhile there was war to be waged against bedbugs.

Eleven weeks later the squadron was in the Mona Passage, beating against the trade winds. Lambert had brought them out here with the usual double objective of every admiral, to exercise his ships and to see an important convoy through the most dangerous part of its voyage. The hills of Santo Domingo were out of sight at the moment over the westerly horizon, but Mona was in sight ahead, table-topped and, from this point of view, an unrelieved oblong in outline; over on the port bow lay Mona's little sister Monita, exhibiting a strong family resemblance.

The lookout frigate ahead sent up a signal.

"You're too slow, Mr. Truscott," bellowed Bush at the signal midshipman, as was right and proper.

"Sail in sight, bearing northeast," read the signal midshipman, glass to eye.

That might be anything, from the advanced guard of a French squadron broken out from Brest to a wandering trader.

The signal came down and was almost instantly replaced.

"Friendly sail in sight bearing northeast," read Truscott.

A squall came down and blotted out the horizon. The *Renown* had to pay off momentarily before its impact. The rain rattled on the deck as the ship lay over, and then the wind abruptly moderated, the sun came out again, and the squall was past. Bush busied himself with the task of regaining station, of laying the *Renown* her exact two cables' length astern of her next ahead. She was last in the line of three, and the flagship was the first. Now the strange sail was well over the horizon. She was a sloop of war as the telescope showed at once; Bush thought for a moment that she might be the *Retribution*, returned after a very quick double passage, but it only took a second glance to make sure she was not. Truscott read her number and referred to the list.

"*Clara*, sloop of war: Captain Ford," he announced.

Clara had sailed for England with despatches three weeks before *Retribution*, Bush knew.

"*Clara* to Flag," went on Truscott. "Have despatches."

She was nearing fast. Up the flagship's halliards soared a string of black balls which broke into flags at the top.

"All ships," read Truscott, with excitement evident in his voice, for this meant that *Renown* would have orders to obey. "Heave-to."

"Main tops'l braces!" yelled Bush. "Mr. Abbott! My respects to the captain and the squadron's heaving-to."

The squadron came to the wind and lay heaving easily over the rollers. Bush watched *Clara's* boat dancing over the waves towards the flagship.

"Keep the hands at the braces, Mr. Bush," said Captain Cogshill. "I expect we'll fill again as soon as the despatches are delivered."

But Cogshill was wrong. Bush watched through his glass the officer from the *Clara* go up the flagship's side, but the minutes passed and the flagship still lay hove-to, the squadron still pitched on the waves. Now a new string of black balls went up the flagship's halliards.

"All ships," read Truscott. "Captains repair on board the flagship."

"Gig's crew away!" roared Bush.

It must be important, or at least unusual, news for the admiral to wish to communicate it to the captains immediately and in person. Bush walked the quarterdeck with Buckland while they waited. The French fleet might be out; the Northern Alliance might be growing restive again. The King's illness might have returned. It might be anything; they could be certain only that it was not nothing. The minutes passed and lengthened into half-hours; it could hardly be bad news—if it were, Lambert would not be wasting precious time like this, with the whole squadron going off slowly to leeward. Then at last the wind brought to their ears, over the blue water, the high-pitched sound of the pipes of the bosun's mates in the flagship. Bush clapped his glass to his eye.

"First one's coming off," he said.

Gig after gig left the flagship's side, and now they could see the *Renown's* gig with her captain in the sternsheets. Buckland went to meet him as he came up the side. Cogshill touched his hat; he was looking a little dazed.

"It's peace," he said.

The wind brought them the sound of cheering from the flagship—the announcement must have been made to the ship's company on board, and it was the sound of that cheering that gave any reality at all to the news the captain brought.

"Peace, sir?" asked Buckland.

"Yes, peace. Preliminaries are signed. The ambassadors meet in France next month to settle the terms, but it's peace. All hostilities are at an end—they are to cease in every part of the world on the arrival of this news."

"Peace!" said Bush.

For nine years the world had been convulsed with war; ships had burned and men had bled from Manila to Panama, west about and east about. It was hard to believe that he was living now in a world where men did not fire cannons at each other on sight. Cogshill's next remark had a bearing on this last thought.

"National ships of the French, Batavian, and Italian Republics will be saluted with the honours due to foreign ships of war," he said.

Buckland whistled at that, as well he might. It meant that England had recognised the existence of the red republics against which she had fought for so long. Yesterday it had been almost treason to speak the word "republic." Now a captain could use it casually in an official statement.

"And what happens to us, sir?" asked Buckland.

"That's what we must wait to hear," said Cogshill. "But the navy is to be reduced to peacetime establishment. That means that nine ships out of ten will be paid off."

"Holy Moses!" said Bush.

Now the next ship ahead was cheering, the sound coming shrilly through the air.

"Call the hands," said Cogshill. "They must be told."

The ship's company of the *Renown* rejoiced to hear the news. They cheered as wildly as did the crews of the other ships. For them it meant the approaching end of savage discipline and incredible hardship. Freedom, liberty, a return to their homes. Bush looked down at the sea of ecstatic faces and wondered what the news implied for him. Freedom and liberty, possibly; but they meant life on a lieutenant's half pay. That was something he had never experienced; in his earliest youth he had entered the navy as a midshipman—the peacetime navy which he could hardly remember—and during the nine years of the war he had only known two short intervals of leave. He was not too sure that he cared for the novel prospects that the future held out to him.

He glanced up at the flagship and turned to bellow at the signal midshipman.

"Mr. Truscott! Don't you see that signal? Attend to your duties, or it will be the worse for you, peace or no peace."

The wretched Truscott put his glass to his eye.

"All ships," he read. "Form line on the larboard tack."

Bush glanced at the captain for permission to proceed.

"Hands to the braces, there!" yelled Bush. "Fill that main tops'l. Smarter than that, you lubbers! Full and by, quartermaster. Mr. Cope, haven't you eyes in your head? Take another pull at that weather-brace! God bless my soul! Easy there! Belay!"

"All ships," read Truscott with his telescope, as the *Renown* gathered way and settled in the wake of her next ahead, "tack in succession."

"Stand by to go about!" yelled Bush.

He noted the progress of the next ahead, and then spared time to berate the watch for its dilatoriness in going to its stations for tacking ship.

"You slow-footed slobs! I'll have some of you dancing at the gratings before long!"

The next ahead had tacked by now, and the *Renown* was advancing into the white water she had left behind.

"Ready about!" shouted Bush. "Headsail sheets! Helm-a-lee!"

The *Renown* came ponderously about and filled on the starboard tack.

"Course sou'west by west," said Truscott, reading the next signal.

Southwest by west. The admiral must be heading back for Port Royal. He could guess that was the first step towards the reduction of the fleet to its peacetime establishment. The sun was warm and delightful, and the *Renown*, steadying before the wind, was roaring along over the blue Caribbean. She was keeping her station well; there was no need to shiver the mizzen topsail yet. This was a good life. He could not make himself believe that it was coming to an end. He tried to think of a winter's day in England, with nothing to do. No ship to handle. Half pay—his sisters had half his pay as it was, which would mean there would be nothing for him, as well as nothing to do. A cold winter's day. No, he simply could not imagine it, and he left off trying.

EIGHTEEN

It was a cold winter's day in Portsmouth; a black frost, and there was a penetrating east wind blowing down the street as Bush came out of the dockyard gates. He turned up the collar of his pea-jacket over his muffler and crammed his hands into his pockets, and he bowed his head into the wind as he strode forward into it, his eyes watering, his nose running, while that east wind seemed to find its way between his ribs, making the scars that covered them ache anew. He would not allow himself to look up at the Keppel's Head as he went past it. In there, he knew, there would be warmth and good company. The fortunate officers with prize money to spend; the incredibly fortunate officers who had found themselves appointments in the peacetime navy—they would be in there yarning and taking wine with each other. He could not afford wine. He thought longingly for a moment about a tankard of beer, but he rejected the idea immediately, although the temptation was strong. He had a month's half pay in his pocket—he was on his way back from the Clerk of the Cheque from whom he had drawn it—but that had to last four and a half weeks and he knew he could not afford it.

He had tried of course for a billet in the merchant service, as mate, but that was as hopeless a prospect at present as obtaining an appointment as lieutenant. Having started life as a midshipman and spent all his adult life in the fighting service he did not know enough about bills of lading or cargo stowage. The merchant service looked on the navy with genial contempt, and said the latter always had a hundred men available to do a job the merchantman had to do with six. And with every ship that was paid off a fresh batch of master's mates, trained for the merchant service and pressed from it, sought jobs in their old profession, heightening the competition every month.

Someone came out from a side street just in front of him and turned into the wind ahead of him—a naval officer. That gangling walk; those shoulders bent into the wind; he could not help but recognise Hornblower.

"Sir! Sir!" he called, and Hornblower turned.

There was a momentary irritation in his expression but it vanished the moment he recognised Bush.

"It's good to see you," he said, his hand held out.

"Good to see *you,* sir," said Bush.

"Don't call me 'sir,'" said Hornblower.

"No, sir? What—why—?"

Hornblower had no greatcoat on; and his left shoulder was bare of the epaulette he should have worn as a commander. Bush's eyes went to it automatically. He could see the old pinholes in the material which showed where the epaulette had once been fastened.

"I'm not a commander," said Hornblower. "They didn't confirm my appointment."

"Good God!"

Hornblower's face was unnaturally white—Bush was accustomed to seeing it deeply tanned—and his cheeks were hollow, but his expression was set in the old unrevealing cast that Bush remembered so well.

"Preliminaries of peace were signed the day I took *Retribution* into Plymouth," said Hornblower.

"What infernal luck!" said Bush.

Lieutenants waited all their lives for the fortunate combination of circumstances that might bring them promotion, and most of them waited in vain. It was more than likely now Hornblower would wait in vain for the rest of his life.

"Have you applied for an appointment as lieutenant?" asked Bush.

"Yes. And I suppose you have?" replied Hornblower.

"Yes."

There was no need to say more than that on that subject. The peacetime navy employed one-tenth of the lieutenants who were employed in wartime; to receive an appointment one had to be of vast seniority or else have powerful friends.

"I spent a month in London," said Hornblower. "There was always a crowd round the Admiralty and the Navy Office."

"I expect so," said Bush.

The wind came shrieking round the corner.

"God, but it's cold!" said Bush.

His mind toyed with the thought of various ways to continue the conversation in shelter. If they went to the Keppel's Head now it would mean paying for two pints of beer, and Hornblower would have to pay for the same.

"I'm going into the Long Rooms just here," said Hornblower. "Come in with me—or are you busy?"

"No, I'm not busy," said Bush, doubtfully, "but—"

"Oh, it's all right," said Hornblower. "Come on."

There was reassurance in the confident way in which Hornblower spoke about the Long Rooms. Bush only knew of them by reputation. They were frequented by officers of the navy and the army with money to spare. Bush had heard much about the high stakes that were indulged in at play there, and about the elegance of the refreshments offered by the proprietor. If Hornblower could speak thus casually about the Long Rooms he could not be as desperately hard up as he seemed to be. They crossed the street and Hornblower held open the door and ushered him through. It was a long oak-panelled room; the gloom of the outer day was made cheerful here by the light of candles, and a magnificent fire flamed on the hearth. In the centre several card tables with chairs round them stood ready for play; the ends of the room were furnished as comfortable lounges. A servant in a green baize apron was making the room tidy, and came to take their hats and Bush's coat as they entered.

"Good morning, sir," he said.

"Good morning, Jenkins," said Hornblower.

He walked with unconcealed haste over to the fire and stood before it warming himself. Bush saw that his teeth were chattering.

"A bad day to be out without your pea-jacket," he said.

"Yes," said Hornblower.

He clipped that affirmative a little short, so that in a minute degree it failed to be an indifferent, flat agreement. It was that which caused Bush to realise that it was not eccentricity or absent-mindedness that had brought Hornblower out into a black frost without his greatcoat. Bush looked at Hornblower sharply, and he might even have asked a tactless question if he had not been forestalled by the opening of an inner door beside them. A short, plump, but exceedingly elegant gentleman came in; he was dressed in the height of fashion, save that he wore his hair long, tied back and with powder in the style of the last generation. This made his age hard to guess. He looked at the pair of them with keen dark eyes.

"Good morning, Marquis," said Hornblower. "It is a pleasure to present—M. le Marquis de Sainte-Croix—Lieutenant Bush."

The Marquis bowed gracefully, and Bush endeavoured to imitate him. But for all that graceful bow, Bush was quite aware of the considering eyes running over him. A lieutenant looking over a likely hand, or a farmer looking at a pig at a fair, might have worn the same expression. Bush guessed that the Marquis was making a mental estimate as to how much Bush might be good for at the card tables, and suddenly became acutely conscious of his shabby uniform. Apparently the Marquis reached the same conclusion as Bush did, but he began a conversation nevertheless.

"A bitter wind," he said.

"Yes," said Bush.

"It will be rough in the Channel," went on the Marquis, politely raising a professional topic.

"Indeed it will," agreed Bush.

"And no ships will come in from the westward."

"You can be sure of that."

The Marquis spoke excellent English. He turned to Hornblower.

"Have you seen Mr. Truelove lately?" he asked.

"No," said Hornblower. "But I met Mr. Wilson."

Truelove and Wilson were names familiar to Bush; they were the most famous prize agents in England—a quarter of the navy at least employed that firm to dispose of their captures for them. The Marquis turned back to Bush.

"I hope you have been fortunate in the matter of prize money, Mr. Bush?" he said.

"No such luck," said Bush. His hundred pounds had gone in a two days' debauch at Kingston.

"The sums they handle are fabulous, nothing less than fabulous. I understand the ship's company of the *Caradoc* will share seventy thousand pounds when they come in."

"Very likely," said Bush. He had heard of the captures the *Caradoc* had made in the Bay of Biscay.

"But while this wind persists they must wait before enjoying their good fortune, poor fellows. They were not paid off on the conclusion of peace, but were ordered to Malta to assist in relieving the garrison. Now they are expected back daily."

For an immigrant civilian the Marquis displayed a laudable interest in the affairs of the service. And he was consistently polite, as his next speech showed.

"I trust you will consider yourself at home here, Mr. Bush," he said. "Now I hope you will pardon me, as I have much business to attend to."

He withdrew through the curtained door, leaving Bush and Hornblower looking at each other.

"A queer customer," said Bush.

"Not so queer when you come to know him," said Hornblower.

The fire had warmed him by now, and there was a little colour in his cheeks.

"What do you *do* here?" asked Bush, curiosity finally overcoming his politeness.

"I play whist," said Hornblower.

"Whist?"

All that Bush knew about whist was that it was a slow game favoured by intellectuals. When Bush gambled he preferred something with a greater element of chance and which did not make any demand on his thoughts.

"A good many men from the services drop in here for whist," said Hornblower. "I'm always glad to make a fourth."

"But I'd heard—"

Bush had heard of all sorts of other games being played in the Long Rooms; hazard, vingt-et-un, even roulette.

"The games for high stakes are played in there," said Hornblower, pointing to the curtained door. "I stay here."

"Wise man," said Bush. But he was quite sure there was some further information that was being withheld from him. And he was not actuated by simple curiosity. The affection and the interest that he felt towards Hornblower drove him into further questioning.

"Do you win?" he asked.

"Frequently," said Hornblower. "Enough to live."

"But you have your half pay?" went on Bush.

Hornblower yielded in face of this persistence.

"No," he said. "I'm not entitled."

"Not entitled?" Bush's voice rose a semitone. "But you're a permanent lieutenant."

"Yes. But I was a temporary commander. I drew three months' full pay for that rank before the Admiralty refused to confirm."

"And then they put you under stoppages?"

"Yes. Until I've repaid the excess." Hornblower smiled; a nearly natural smile. "I've lived through two months of it. Only five more and I'll be back on half pay."

"Holy Peter!" said Bush.

Half pay was bad enough; it meant a life of constant care and economy, but one could live. Hornblower had nothing at all. Bush knew now why Hornblower had no greatcoat. He felt a sudden wave of anger. A recollection rose in his mind, as clear to his inward eye as this pleasant room was to his outward one. He remembered Hornblower swinging himself down, sword in hand, onto the deck of the *Renown*, plunging into a battle against odds which could only result in either death or victory. Hornblower, who had planned and worked endlessly to ensure success—even in that last conflict—and then had flung his life upon the board as a final stake; and today Hornblower was standing with chattering teeth trying to warm himself beside a fire by the charity of a frog-eating gambling hall keeper with the look of a dancing master.

"It's a hellish outrage," said Bush, and then he made his offer. He offered his money, even though he knew as he offered it that it meant most certainly that he would go hungry, and that his sisters, if not exactly hungry, would hardly have enough to eat. But Hornblower shook his head.

"Thank you," he said, "I'll never forget that. But I can't accept it. You know that I couldn't. But I'll never cease to be grateful to you. I'm grateful in another way, too. You've brightened the world for me by saying that."

Even in the face of Hornblower's refusal Bush repeated his offer, and tried to press it, but Hornblower was firm in his refusal. Perhaps it was because Bush looked so downcast that Hornblower gave him some further information in the hope of cheering him up.

"Things aren't as bad as they seem," he said. "You don't understand that I'm in receipt of regular pay—a permanent salarium from our friend the Marquis."

"I didn't know that," said Bush.

"Half a guinea a week," explained Hornblower. "Ten shillings and sixpence every Saturday morning, rain or shine."

"And what do you have to do for it?" Bush's half pay was more than twice that sum.

"I only have to play whist," explained Hornblower. "Only that. From twelve midday until two in the morning I'm here to play whist with any three that need a fourth."

"I see," said Bush.

"The Marquis in his generosity also makes me free of these rooms. I have no subscription to pay. No table money. And I can keep my winnings."

"And pay your losses?"

Hornblower shrugged.

"Naturally. But the losses do not come as often as one might think. The reason's simple enough. The whist players who find it hard to obtain partners, and who are cold-shouldered by the others, are naturally the bad players. Strangely anxious to play, even so. And when the Marquis happens to be in here and Major Jones and Admiral Smith and Mr. Robinson are seeking a fourth while everyone seems strangely preoccupied he catches my eye—the sort of reproving look a wife might throw at a husband talking too loud at a dinner—and I rise to my feet and offer to be the fourth. It is odd they are flattered to play with Hornblower, as often it costs them money."

"I see," said Bush again, and he remembered Hornblower standing by the furnace in Fort Samaná organising the firing of red-hot shot at the Spanish privateers.

"The life is not entirely one of beer and skittles, naturally," went on Hornblower; with the dam once broken he could not restrain his loquacity. "After the fourth hour or so it becomes irksome to play with bad players. When I go to Hell I don't doubt that my punishment will be always to partner players who pay no attention to my discards. But then on the other hand I frequently play a rubber or two with the good players. There are moments when I feel I would rather lose to a good player than win from a bad one."

"That's just the point," said Bush, harking back to an old theme. "How about the losses?"

Bush's experiences of gambling had mostly been of losses, and in this hardheaded moment he could remember the times when he had been weak.

"I can deal with them," said Hornblower. He touched his breast pocket. "I keep ten pounds here. My *corps de réserve,* you understand. I can always endure a run of losses in consequence. Should that reserve be depleted, then sacrifices have to be made to build it up again."

The sacrifices being skipped meals, thought Bush grimly. He looked so woebegone that Hornblower offered further comfort.

"But five more months," he said, "and I'll be on half pay again. And before that—who knows? Some captain may take me off the beach."

"That's true," said Bush.

It was true insofar as the possibility existed. Sometimes ships were recommissioned. A captain might be in need of a lieutenant; a captain might invite Hornblower to fill the vacancy. But every captain was besieged by friends seeking appointments, and in any event the Admiralty was also besieged by lieutenants of great seniority—or lieutenants with powerful friends—and captains were most likely to listen to recommendations of high authority.

The door opened and a group of men came in.

"It's high time for customers to arrive," said Hornblower, with a grin at Bush. "Stay and meet my friends."

The red coats of the army, the blue coats of the navy, the bottle-green and snuff-coloured coats of civilians; Bush and Hornblower made room for them before the fire after the introductions were made, and the coat-tails were parted as their wearers lined up before the flames. But the exclamations about the cold, and the polite conversation, died away rapidly.

"Whist?" asked one of the newcomers tentatively.

"Not for me. Not for us," said another, the leader of the redcoats. "The Twenty-Ninth Foot has other fish to fry. We've a permanent engagement with our friend the Marquis in the next room. Come on, Major, let's see if we can call a main right this time."

"Then will you make a four, Mr. Hornblower? How about your friend Mr. Bush?"

"I don't play," said Bush.

"With pleasure," said Hornblower. "You will excuse me, Mr. Bush, I know. There is the new number of the *Naval Chronicle* on the table there. There's a *Gazette* letter on the last page which might perhaps hold your interest for a while. And there is another item you might think important, too."

Bush could guess what the letter was even before he picked the periodical up, but when he found the place there was the same feeling of pleased shock to see his name in print there, as keen as the first time he saw it: "I have the honour to be, etc., Wm. Bush."

The *Naval Chronicle* in these days of peace found it hard, apparently, to obtain sufficient matter to fill its pages, and gave much space to the reprinting of these despatches. "Copy of a letter from Vice-Admiral Sir Richard Lambert to Evan Nepean, Esq., Secretary to the Lords Commissioners of the Admiralty." That was only Lambert's covering letter enclosing the reports. Here was the first one—it was with a strange internal sensation that he remembered helping Buckland with the writing of it, as the *Renown* ran westerly along the coast of Santo Domingo the day before the prisoners broke out. It was Buckland's report on the fighting at Samaná. To Bush the most important line was "in the handsomest manner—under the direction of Lieutenant William Bush, the senior officer, whose report I enclose." And here was his very own literary work, as enclosed by Buckland.

H.M.S. Renown, *off Santo Domingo. January 9th, 1802*

SIR,

I have the honour to inform you . . .

Bush relived those days of a year ago as he re-read his own words; those words which he had composed with so much labour even though he had referred, during the writing of them, to other reports written by other men so as to get the phrasing right.

. . . I cannot end this report without a reference to the gallant conduct and most helpful suggestions of Lieutenant Horatio Hornblower, who was my second in command on this occasion, and to whom in great part the success of the expedition is due.

There was Hornblower now, playing cards with a post captain and two contractors.

Bush turned back through the pages of the *Naval Chronicle*. Here was the Plymouth letter, a daily account of the doings in the port during the last month.

"Orders came down this day for the following ships to be paid off. . . ." "Came in from Gibraltar *La Diana*, 44, and the *Tamar*, 38, to be paid off as soon as they go up the harbour and to be laid up." "Sailed the *Caesar*, 80, for Portsmouth, to be paid off." And here was an item just as significant, or even more so: "Yesterday there was a large sale of serviceable stores landed from the different men of war." The navy was growing smaller every day, and with every ship that was paid off another batch of lieutenants would be looking for billets. And here was an item—"This afternoon a fishing boat turning out of Catwater jibed and overset, by which accident two industrious fishermen with large families were drowned." This was the *Naval Chronicle*, whose pages had once bulged with the news of the Nile and of Camperdown; now it told of accidents to industrious fishermen. Bush was too interested in his own concerns to feel any sympathy towards their large families.

There was another drowning as a final item; a name—a combination of names—caught Bush's attention so that he read the paragraph with a quickened pulse.

Last night the jolly boat of His Majesty's cutter *Rapid*, in the Revenue service, while returning in the fog from delivering a message on shore, was swept by the ebb tide athwart the hawse of a merchantman anchored off Fisher's Nose, and capsized. Two seamen and Mr. Henry Wellard, Midshipman, were drowned. Mr. Wellard was a most promising young man recently appointed to the *Rapid*, having served as a volunteer in His Majesty's ship *Renown*.

Bush read the passage and pondered over it. He thought it important to the extent that he read the remainder of the *Naval Chronicle* without taking in any of it; and it was with surprise that he realised he would have to leave quickly in order to catch the carrier's waggon back to Chichester.

A good many people were coming into the Rooms now; the door was continually opening to admit them. Some of them were naval officers with whom he had a nodding acquaintance. All of them made straight for the fire for warmth before beginning to play. And Hornblower was on his feet now; apparently the rubber was finished, and Bush took the opportunity to catch his eye and give an indication that he wished to leave. Hornblower came over to him. It was with regret that they shook hands.

"When do we meet again?" asked Hornblower.

"I come in each month to draw my half pay," said Bush. "I usually spend the night because of the carrier's waggon. Perhaps we could dine—?"

"You can always find me here," said Hornblower. "But—do you have a regular place to stay?"

"I stay where it's convenient," replied Bush.

They both of them knew that meant that he stayed where it was cheap.

"I lodge in Highbury Street. I'll write the address down." Hornblower turned to a desk in the corner and wrote on a sheet of paper which he handed to Bush. "Would you care to share my room when next you come? My landlady is a sharp one. No doubt she will make a charge for a cot for you, but even so—"

"It'll save money," said Bush, putting the paper in his pocket; his grin as he spoke masked the sentiment in his next words. "And I'll see more of you."

"By George, yes," said Hornblower. Words were not adequate.

Jenkins had come sidling up and was holding Bush's greatcoat for him to put on. There was that in Jenkins' manner which told Bush that gentlemen when helped into their coats at the Long Rooms presented

Jenkins with a shilling. Bush decided at first that he would be eternally damned before he parted with a shilling, and then he changed his mind. Maybe Hornblower would give Jenkins a shilling if he did not. He felt in his pocket and handed the coin over.

"Thank you, sir," said Jenkins.

With Jenkins out of earshot again Bush lingered, wondering how to frame his question.

"That was hard luck on young Wellard," he said, tentatively.

"Yes," said Hornblower.

"D'you think," went on Bush, plunging desperately, "he had anything to do with the captain's falling down the hatchway?"

"I couldn't give an opinion," answered Hornblower. "I didn't know enough about it."

"But—" began Bush, and checked himself again; he knew by the look on Hornblower's face that it was no use asking further questions.

The Marquis had come into the room and was looking round in unobtrusive inspection. Bush saw him take note of the several men who were not playing, and of Hornblower standing in idle gossip by the door. Bush saw the meaning glance which he directed at Hornblower, and fell into sudden panic.

"Good-bye," he said, hastily.

The black northeast wind that greeted him in the street was no more cruel than the rest of the world.

NINETEEN

IT WAS A SHORT, HARD-FACED WOMAN who opened the door in reply to Bush's knock, and she looked at Bush even harder when he asked for Lieutenant Hornblower.

"Top of the house," she said, at last, and left Bush to find his way up.

There could be no doubt about Hornblower's pleasure at seeing him. His face was lit with a smile and he drew Bush into the room while shaking his hand. It was an attic, with a steeply sloping ceiling; it contained a bed and a night table and a single wooden chair, but, as far as Bush's cursory glance could discover, nothing else at all.

"And how is it with you?" asked Bush, seating himself in the proffered chair, while Hornblower sat on the bed.

"Well enough," replied Hornblower—but was there, or was there not, a guilty pause before that answer? In any case the pause was covered up by the quick counterquestion. "And with you?"

"So-so," said Bush.

They talked indifferently for a space, with Hornblower asking questions about the Chichester cottage that Bush lived in with his sisters.

"We must see about your bed for tonight," said Hornblower at the first pause. "I'll go down and give Mrs. Mason a hail."

"I'd better come too," said Bush.

Mrs. Mason lived in a hard world, quite obviously; she turned the proposition over in her mind for several seconds before she agreed to it.

"A shilling for the bed," she said. "Can't wash the sheets for less than that with soap as it is."

"Very good," said Bush.

He saw Mrs. Mason's hand held out, and he put the shilling into it; no one could be in any doubt about Mrs. Mason's determination to be paid in advance by any friend of Hornblower's. Hornblower had dived for his pocket when he caught sight of the gesture, but Bush was too quick for him.

"And you'll be talking till all hours," said Mrs. Mason. "Mind you don't disturb my other gentlemen. And douse the light while you talk, too, or you'll be burning a shilling's worth of tallow."

"Of course," said Hornblower.

"Maria! Maria!" called Mrs. Mason.

A young woman—no, a woman not quite young—came up the stairs from the depths of the house at the call.

"Yes, Mother?"

Maria listened to Mrs. Mason's instructions for making up a truckle bed in Mr. Hornblower's room.

"Yes, Mother," she said.

"Not teaching today, Maria?" asked Hornblower pleasantly.

"No, sir." The smile that lit her plain face showed her keen pleasure at being addressed.

"Oak-Apple Day? No, not yet. It's not the King's Birthday. Then why this holiday?"

"Mumps, sir," said Maria. "They all have mumps, except Johnnie Bristow."

"That agrees with everything I've heard about Johnnie Bristow," said Hornblower.

"Yes, sir," said Maria. She smiled again, clearly pleased not only that Hornblower should jest with her but also because he remembered what she had told him about the school.

Back in the attic again Hornblower and Bush resumed their conversation, this time on a more serious plane. The state of Europe occupied their attention.

"This man Bonaparte," said Bush. "He's a restless cove."

"That's the right word for him," agreed Hornblower.

"Isn't he satisfied? Back in '96 when I was in the old *Superb* in the Mediterranean—that was when I was commissioned lieutenant—he was just a general. I can remember hearing his name for the first time, when we were blockading Toulon. Then he went to Egypt. Now he's First Consul—isn't that what he calls himself?"

"Yes. But he's Napoleon now, not Bonaparte any more. First Consul for life."

"Funny sort of name. Not what I'd choose for myself."

"Lieutenant Napoleon Bush," said Hornblower. "It wouldn't sound well."

They laughed together at the ridiculous combination.

"The *Morning Chronicle* says he's going a step farther," went on Hornblower. "There's talk that he's going to call himself Emperor."

"Emperor!"

Even Bush could catch the connotations of that title, with its claims to universal pre-eminence.

"I suppose he's mad?" asked Bush.

"If he is, he's the most dangerous madman in Europe."

"I don't trust him over this Malta business. I don't trust him an inch," said Bush, emphatically. "You mark my words, we'll have to fight him again in the end. Teach him a lesson he won't forget. It'll come sooner or later—we can't go on like this."

"I think you're quite right," said Hornblower. "And sooner rather than later."

"Then—" said Bush.

He could not talk and think at the same time, not when his thoughts were as tumultuous as the ones this conclusion called up; war with France meant the re-expansion of the navy; the threat of invasion and the needs of convoy would mean the commissioning of every small craft that could float and carry a gun. It would mean the end of half pay for him; it would mean walking a deck again and handling a ship under sail. And it would mean hardship again, danger, anxiety, monotony—all the concomitants of war. These thoughts rushed into his brain with so much velocity, and in such a continuous stream, that they made a sort of whirlpool of his mind, in which the good and the bad circled after each other, each in turn chasing the other out of his attention.

"War's a foul business," said Hornblower, solemnly. "Remember the things you've seen."

"I suppose you're right," said Bush; there was no need to particularise. But it was an unexpected remark, all the same. Hornblower grinned and relieved the tension.

"Well," he said, "Boney can call himself Emperor if he likes. I have to earn my half guinea at the Long Rooms."

Bush was about to take this opportunity to ask Hornblower how he was profiting there, but he was interrupted by a rumble outside the door and a knock.

"Here comes your bed," said Hornblower, walking over to open the door.

Maria came trundling the thing in. She smiled at them.

"Over here or over there?" she asked.

Hornblower looked at Bush.

"It doesn't matter," said Bush.

"I'll put it against the wall, then."

"Let me help," said Hornblower.

"Oh no, sir. Please sir, I can do it."

The attention fluttered her—and Bush could see that with her sturdy figure she was in no need of help. To cover her confusion she began to thump at the bedding, putting the pillows into the pillowslips.

"I trust you have already had the mumps, Maria?" said Hornblower.

"Oh yes, sir. I had them as a child, on both sides."

The exercise and her agitation between them had brought the colour into her cheeks. With blunt but capable hands she spread the sheet. Then she paused as another implication of Hornblower's inquiry occurred to her.

"You've no need to worry, sir. I shan't give them to you if you haven't had them."

"I wasn't thinking about that," said Hornblower, simply.

"Oh, sir," said Maria, twitching the sheet into mathematical smoothness. She spread the blankets before she looked up again. "Are you going out directly, sir?"

"Yes. I ought to have left already."

"Let me take that coat of yours for a minute, sir. I can sponge it and freshen it up."

"Oh, I wouldn't have you go to that trouble, Maria."

"It wouldn't be any trouble, sir. Of course not. Please let me, sir. It looks—"

"It looks the worse for wear," said Hornblower, glancing down at it. "There's no cure for old age that's yet been discovered."

"Please let me take it, sir. There's some spirits of hartshorn downstairs. It will make quite a difference. Really it will."

"But—"

"Oh, please, sir."

Hornblower reluctantly put up his hand and undid a button.

"I'll only be a minute with it," said Maria, hastening to him. Her hands were extended to the other buttons, but a sweep of Hornblower's quick nervous fingers had anticipated her. He pulled off his coat and she took it out of his hands.

"You've mended that shirt yourself," she said, accusingly.

"Yes, I have."

Hornblower was a little embarrassed at the revelation of the worn garment. Maria studied the patch.

"I would have done that for you if you'd asked me, sir."

"And a good deal better, no doubt."

"Oh, I wasn't saying that, sir. But it isn't fit that you should patch your own shirts."

"Whose should I patch, then?"

Maria giggled.

"You're too quick with your tongue for me," she said. "Now, just wait here and talk to the lieutenant while I sponge this."

She darted out of the room and they heard her footsteps hurrying down the stairs, while Hornblower looked half-ruefully at Bush.

"There's a strange pleasure," he said, "in knowing that there's a human being who cares whether I'm alive or dead. Why that should give pleasure is a question to be debated by the philosophic mind."

"I suppose so," said Bush.

He had sisters who devoted all their attention to him whenever it was possible, and he was used to it. At home he took their ministrations for granted. He heard the church clock strike the half-hour, and it recalled his thoughts to the further business of the day.

"You're going to the Long Rooms now?" he asked.

"Yes. And you, I suppose, want to go to the dockyard? The monthly visit to the Clerk of the Cheque?"

"Yes."

"We can walk together as far as the Rooms, if you care to. As soon as our friend Maria returns my coat to me."

"That's what I was thinking," said Bush.

It was not long before Maria came knocking at the door again.

"It's done," she said, holding out the coat. "It's nice and fresh now."

But something seemed to have gone out of her. She seemed a little frightened, a little apprehensive.

"What's the matter, Maria?" asked Hornblower, quick to feel the change of attitude.

"Nothing. Of course there's nothing the matter with me," said Maria, defensively, and then she changed the subject. "Put your coat on now, or you'll be late."

Walking along Highbury Street Bush asked the question he had had in mind for some time, regarding whether Hornblower had experienced good fortune lately at the Rooms. Hornblower looked at him oddly.

"Not as good as it might be," he said.

"Bad?"

"Bad enough. My opponents' aces lie behind my kings, ready for instant regicide. And my opponents' kings lie behind my aces, so that when they venture out from the security of the hand they survive all perils and take the trick. In the long run the chances right themselves mathematically. But the periods when they are unbalanced in the wrong direction can be distressing."

"I see," said Bush, although he was not too sure that he did; but one thing he did know, and that was that Hornblower had been losing. And he knew Hornblower well enough by now to know that when he talked in an airy fashion as he was doing now he was more anxious than he cared to admit.

They had reached the Long Rooms, and paused at the door.

"You'll call in for me on your way back?" asked Hornblower. "There's an eating house in Broad Street with a fourpenny ordinary. Sixpence with pudding. Would you care to try it?"

"Yes, indeed. Thank you. Good luck," said Bush, and he paused before continuing. "Be careful."

"I shall be careful," said Hornblower, and went in through the door.

The weather was in marked contrast with what had prevailed during Bush's last visit. Then there had been a black frost and an east wind; today there was a hint of spring in the air. As Bush walked along the Hard the harbour entrance revealed itself to him on his left, its muddy water sparkling in the clear light. A flush-decked sloop was coming out with the ebb, the gentle puffs of wind from the northwest just giving her steerage way. Despatches for Halifax, perhaps. Money to pay the Gibraltar garrison. Or maybe a reinforcement for the revenue cutters that were finding so much difficulty in dealing with the peacetime wave of smuggling. Whatever it was, there were fortunate officers on board, with an appointment, with three years' employment ahead of them, with a deck under their feet and a wardroom in which to dine. Lucky devils. Bush acknowledged the salute of the porter at the gate and went into the yard.

He emerged into the late afternoon and made his way back to the Long Rooms. Hornblower was at a table near the corner and looked up to smile at him, the candlelight illuminating his face. Bush found himself the latest *Naval Chronicle* and settled himself to read it. Beside him a group of army and navy officers argued in low tones regarding the difficulties of living in the same world as Bonaparte. Malta and Genoa, Santo Domingo and Miquelet, came up in the conversation.

"Mark my words," said one of them, thumping his hand with his fist, "we'll be at war with him again soon enough."

There was a murmur of agreement.

"It'll be war to the knife," supplemented another. "If once he drives us to extremity, we shall never rest until Mr. Napoleon Bonaparte is hanging to the nearest tree."

The others agreed to that with a fierce roar, like wild beasts.

"Gentlemen," said one of the players at Hornblower's table, looking round over his shoulder. "Could you find it convenient to continue your discussion at the far end of the room? This end is dedicated to the most scientific and difficult of all games."

The words were uttered in a pleasant high tenor, but it was obvious that the speaker had every expectation of being instantly obeyed.

"Very good, my lord," said one of the naval officers.

That made Bush look more closely, and he recognised the speaker, although it was six years since he had seen him last. It was Admiral Lord Parry, who had been made a lord after Camperdown; now he was one of the commissioners of the navy, one of the people who could make or break a naval officer. The mop of snow-white curls that ringed the bald spot on the top of his head, his smooth old man's face, his mild speech, accorded ill with the nickname of "Old Bloodybones" which had been given him by the lower deck far back in the American War. Hornblower was moving in very high society. Bush watched Lord Parry extend a skinny white hand and cut the cards to Hornblower. It was obvious from his colouring that Parry, like Hornblower, had not been to sea for a long time. Hornblower dealt and the game proceeded in its paralysing stillness; the cards made hardly a sound as they fell on the green cloth, and each trick was picked up and laid down almost silently, with only the slightest click. The line of tricks in front of Parry grew like a snake, silent as a snake gliding over a rock, like a snake it closed on itself and then lengthened again, and then the hand was finished and the cards swept together.

"Small slam," said Parry as the players attended to their markers, and that was all that was said. The two tiny words sounded as clearly and as briefly in the silence as two bells in the middle watch. Hornblower cut the cards and the next deal began in the same mystic silence. Bush could not see the fascination of it. He would prefer a game in which he could roar at his losses and exult over his winnings; and preferably one in which the turn of a single card, and not of the whole fifty two, would decide who had won and who had lost. No, he was wrong. There was undoubtedly a fascination about it, a poisonous fascination. Opium? No. This silent game was like the quiet interplay of duelling swords as compared with the crash of cutlass blades, and it was as deadly. A small-sword through the lungs killed as effectively as—more effectively than—the sweep of a cutlass.

"A short rubber," commented Parry; the silence was over, and the cards lay in disorder on the table.

"Yes, my lord," said Hornblower.

Bush, taking note of everything with the keen observation of anxiety, saw Hornblower put his hand to his breast pocket—the pocket that he had indicated as holding his reserve—and take out a little fold of one-pound notes. When he had made his payment Bush could see that what he returned to his pocket was only a single note.

"You encountered the worst of good fortune," said Parry, pocketing his winnings. "On the two occasions when you dealt, the trump that you turned up proved to be the only one that you held. I cannot remember another occasion when the dealer has held a singleton trump twice running."

"In a long enough period of play, my lord," said Hornblower, "every possible combination of cards can be expected."

He spoke with a polite indifference that for a moment almost gave Bush heart to believe his losses were not serious, until he remembered the single note that had been put back into Hornblower's breast pocket.

"But it is rare to see such a run of ill luck," said Parry. "And yet you play an excellent game, Mr.—Mr.—please forgive me, but your name escaped me at the moment of introduction."

"Hornblower," said Hornblower.

"Ah, yes, of course. For some reason the name is familiar to me."

Bush glanced quickly at Hornblower. There never was such a perfect moment for reminding a Lord Commissioner about the fact that his promotion to commander had not been confirmed.

"When I was a midshipman, my lord," said Hornblower, "I was seasick while at anchor in Spithead on board the old *Justinian*. I believe the story is still told."

"That doesn't seem to be the connection I remember," answered Parry. "But we have been diverted from what I was going to say. I was about to express regret that I cannot give you your immediate revenge, although I should be most glad to have the opportunity of studying your play of the cards again."

"You are very kind, my lord," said Hornblower, and Bush writhed—he had been writhing ever since Hornblower had given the go-by to that golden opportunity. This last speech had a flavour of amused bitterness that Bush feared would be evident to the admiral. But fortunately Parry did not know Hornblower as well as Bush did.

"Most unfortunately," said Parry, "I am due to dine with Admiral Lambert."

This time the coincidence startled Hornblower into being human. "Admiral Lambert, my lord?"

"Yes. You know him?"

"I had the honour of serving under him on the Jamaica station. This is Mr. Bush, who commanded the storming party from the *Renown* that compelled the capitulation of Santo Domingo."

"Glad to see you, Mr. Bush," said Parry, and it was only just evident that if he was glad he was not overjoyed. A commissioner might well find embarrassment at an encounter with an unemployed lieutenant with a distinguished record. Parry lost no time in turning back to Hornblower.

"It was in my mind," he said, "to try to persuade Admiral Lambert to return here with me after dinner so that I could offer you your revenge. Would we find you here if we did?"

"I am most honoured, my lord," said Hornblower with a bow, but Bush noted the uncontrollable flutter of his fingers towards his almost empty breast pocket.

"Then would you be kind enough to accept a semi-engagement? On account of Admiral Lambert I can make no promise, except that I will do my best to persuade him."

"I'm dining with Mr. Bush, my lord. But I would be the last to stand in the way."

"Then we may take it as being settled as near as may be?"

"Yes, my lord."

Parry withdrew then, ushered out by his flag lieutenant who had been one of the whist four, with all the dignity and pomp that might be expected of a peer, an admiral, and a commissioner, and he left Hornblower grinning at Bush.

"D'you think it's time for us to dine too?" he asked.

"I think so," said Bush.

The eating house in Broad Street was run, as might almost have been expected, by a wooden-legged sailor. He had a pert son to assist him, who stood by when they sat at a scrubbed oaken table on oaken benches, their feet in the sawdust, and ordered their dinner.

"Ale?" asked the boy.

"No. No ale," said Hornblower.

The pert boy's manner gave some indication of what he thought about gentlemen of the navy who ate the fourpenny ordinary and drank nothing with it. He dumped the loaded plates in front of them; boiled mutton—not very much mutton—potatoes and carrots and parsnips and barley and a dab of pease pudding, all swimming in pale gravy.

"It keeps away hunger," said Hornblower.

It might indeed do that, but apparently Hornblower had not kept hunger away lately. He began to eat his food with elaborate unconcern, but with each mouthful his appetite increased and his restraint decreased. In an extraordinarily short time his plate was empty; he mopped it clean with his bread and ate the bread. Bush was not a slow eater, but he was taken a little aback when he looked up and saw that Hornblower had finished every mouthful while his own plate was still half full. Hornblower laughed nervously.

"Eating alone gives one bad habits," he said—and the best proof of his embarrassment was the lameness of his explanation.

He was aware of that, as soon as he had spoken, and he tried to carry it off by leaning back on his bench in a superior fashion; and to show how much at ease he was he thrust his hands into the side pockets of his coat. As he did so his whole expression changed. He lost some of the little colour there was in his cheeks. There was utter consternation in his expression—there was even fear. Bush took instant alarm; he thought Hornblower must have had a seizure, and it was only after that first thought that he connected Hornblower's changed appearance with his gesture of putting his hands in his pockets. But a man who had found a snake in his pocket would hardly wear that look of horror.

"What's the matter?" asked Bush. "What in God's name—?"

Hornblower slowly drew his right hand out of his pocket. He kept it closed for a moment round what it held, and then he opened it, slowly, reluctantly, like a man fearful of his destiny. Harmless enough; it was a silver coin—a half crown.

"That's nothing to take on about," said Bush, quite puzzled. "I wouldn't even mind finding a half crown in my pocket."

"But—but—" stammered Hornblower, and Bush began to realise some of the implications.

"It wasn't there this morning," said Hornblower, and then he smiled the old bitter smile. "I know too well what money I have in my pockets."

"I suppose you do," agreed Bush; but even now, with his mind going back through the events of the morning, and making the obvious deductions, he could not understand quite why Hornblower should be so worried. "That wench put it there?"

"Yes. Maria," said Hornblower. "It must have been her. That's why she took my coat to sponge it."

"She's a good soul," said Bush.

"Oh God!" said Hornblower. "But I can't—I can't—"

"Why not?" asked Bush, and he really thought that question unanswerable.

"No," said Hornblower. "It's—it's—I wish she hadn't done it. The poor girl—"

" 'Poor girl' be blowed!" said Bush. "She's only trying to do you a good turn."

Hornblower looked at him for a long time without speaking, and then he made a little hopeless gesture, as though despairing of ever making Bush see the matter from his point of view.

"You can look like that if you like," said Bush, steadily, determined to stick to his guns. "But there's no need to act as if the French had landed just because a girl slips half a crown into your pocket."

"But don't you see—" began Hornblower, and then he finally abandoned all attempt at explanation. Under Bush's puzzled gaze he mastered himself. The unhappiness left his face, and he assumed his old inscrutable look—it was as if he had shut down the vizor of a helmet over his face.

"Very well," he said. "We'll make the most of it, by God!"

Then he rapped on the table.

"Boy!"

"Yessir."

"We'll have a pint of wine. Let someone run and fetch it at once. A pint of wine—port wine."

"Yessir."

"And what's the pudding today?"

"Currant duff, sir."

"Good. We'll have some. Both of us. And let's have a saucer of jam to spread on it."

"Yessir."

"And we'll need cheese before our wine. Is there any cheese in the house, or must you send out for some?"

"There's some in the house, sir."

"Then put it on the table."

"Yessir."

Now was it not, thought Bush, exactly what might be expected of Hornblower that he should push away the half of his huge slice of currant duff unfinished? And he only had a nibble of cheese, hardly enough to clear his palate. He raised his glass, and Bush followed his example.

"To a lovely lady," said Hornblower.

They drank, and now there was an irresponsible twinkle in Hornblower's eyes that worried Bush even while he told himself that he was tired of Hornblower's tantrums. He decided to change the subject, and he prided himself on the tactful way in which he did so.

"To a fortunate evening," he said, raising his glass in his turn.

"A timely toast," said Hornblower.

"You can afford to play?" asked Bush.

"Naturally."

"You can stand another run of bad luck?"

"I can afford to lose one rubber," answered Hornblower.

"Oh."

"But on the other hand if I win the first I can afford to lose the next two. And if I win the first and second I can afford to lose the next three. And so on."

"Oh."

That did not sound too hopeful; and Hornblower's gleaming eyes looking at him from his wooden countenance were positively disturbing. Bush shifted uneasily in his seat and changed the conversation again.

"They're putting the *Hastings* into commission again," he said. "Had you heard?"

"Yes. Peacetime establishment—three lieutenants, and all three selected two months back."

"I was afraid that was so."

"But our chance will come," said Hornblower. "Here's to it."

"D'you think Parry will bring Lambert to the Long Rooms?" asked Bush when he took the glass from his lips.

"I have no doubt about it," said Hornblower.

Now he was restless again.

"I must be back there soon," he said. "Parry might hurry Lambert through his dinner."

"My guess is that he would," said Bush, preparing to rise.

"There's no necessity for you to come back with me if you don't care to," said Hornblower. "You might find it wearisome to sit idle there."

"I wouldn't miss it for worlds," said Bush.

TWENTY

The long rooms were full with the evening crowd. At nearly every table in the outer room there were earnest parties playing serious games, while through the curtained door that opened into the inner room came a continuous murmur that indicated that play in there was exciting and noisy. But for Bush standing restlessly by the fire, occasionally exchanging absent-minded remarks with the people who came and went, there was only one point of interest, and that was the candle-lit table near the wall where Hornblower was playing in very exalted society. His companions were the two admirals and a colonel of infantry, the latter a bulky man with a face almost as red as his coat, whom Parry had brought with him along with Admiral Lambert. The flag lieutenant who had previously partnered Parry was now relegated to the role of onlooker, and stood beside Bush, and occasionally made incomprehensible remarks about the play. The Marquis had looked in more than once. Bush had observed his glance to rest upon the table with something of approval. No matter if there were others who wanted to play; no matter if the rules of the rooms gave any visitor the right to join a table at the conclusion of a rubber; a party that included two flag officers and a field officer could do as it pleased.

Hornblower had won the first rubber to Bush's enormous relief, although actually he had not been able to follow the details of the play and the score well enough to know that such was the case until the cards were swept up and payments made. He saw Hornblower tuck away some money into that breast pocket.

"It would be pleasant," said Admiral Parry, "if we could restore the old currency, would it not? If the country could dispense with these dirty notes and go back again to our good old golden guineas?"

"Indeed it would," said the colonel.

"The longshore sharks," said Lambert, "meet every ship that comes in from abroad. Twenty three and sixpence they offer for every guinea, so you can be sure they are worth more than that."

Parry took something from his pocket and laid it on the table.

"Boney has restored the French currency, you see," he said. "They call this a napoleon, now that he is First Consul for life. A twenty-franc piece—a louis d'or, as we used to say."

"Napoleon, First Consul," said the colonel, looking at the coin with curiosity, and then he turned it over. "French Republic."

"The 'republic' is mere hypocrisy, of course," said Parry. "There never was a worse tyranny since the days of Nero."

"We'll show him up," said Lambert.

"Amen to that," said Parry, and then he put the coin away again. "But we are delaying the business of the evening. I fear that is my fault. Let us cut again. Ah, I partner you this time, colonel. Would you care to sit opposite me? I omitted to thank you, Mr. Hornblower, for your excellent partnership."

"You are too kind, my lord," said Hornblower, taking the chair at the admiral's right.

The next rubber began and progressed silently to its close.

"I am glad to see that the cards have decided to be kind to you, Mr. Hornblower," said Parry, "even though our honours have reduced your winnings. Fifteen shillings, I believe?"

"Thank you," said Hornblower, taking the money.

Bush remembered what Hornblower had said about being able to afford to lose three rubbers if he won the first two.

"Damned small stakes in my opinion, my lord," said the colonel. "Must we play as low as this?"

"That is for the company to decide," replied Parry. "I myself have no objection. Half a crown instead of a shilling? Let us ask Mr. Hornblower?"

Bush turned to look at Hornblower with renewed anxiety.

"As you will, my lord," said Hornblower, with the most elaborate indifference.

"Sir Richard?"

"I don't mind at all," said Lambert.

"Half a crown a trick, then," said Parry. "Waiter, fresh cards, if you please."

Bush had hurriedly to revise his estimate of the amount of losses Hornblower could endure. With the stakes nearly trebled it would be bad if he lost a single rubber.

"You and I again, Mr. Hornblower," said Parry, observing the cut. "You wish to retain your present seat?"

"I am indifferent, my lord."

"I am not," said Parry. "Nor am I yet so old as to decline to change my seat in accordance with the run of the cards. Our philosophers have not yet decided that it is a mere vulgar superstition."

He heaved himself out of his chair and moved opposite Hornblower, and play began again, with Bush watching more anxiously even than at the start. He watched each side in turn take the odd trick, and then three times running he saw Hornblower lay the majority of tricks in front of him. During the next couple of hands he lost count of the score, but finally he was relieved to see only two tricks before the colonel when the rubber ended.

"Excellent," said Parry, "a profitable rubber, Mr. Hornblower. I'm glad you decided to trump my knave of hearts. It must have been a difficult decision for you, but it was undoubtedly the right one."

"It deprived me of a lead I could well have used," said Lambert. "The opposition was indeed formidable, colonel."

"Yes," agreed the colonel, not quite as good-temperedly. "And twice I held hands with neither an ace nor a king, which helped the opposition to be formidable. Can you give me change, Mr. Hornblower?"

There was a five-pound note among the money that the colonel handed over to Hornblower, and it went into the breast pocket of his coat.

"At least, colonel," said Parry, when they cut again, "you have Mr. Hornblower as your partner this time."

As the rubber proceeded Bush was aware that the flag lieutenant beside him was watching with greater and greater interest.

"By the odd trick, by George!" said he when the last cards were played.

"That was a close shave, partner," said the colonel, his good humour clearly restored. "I hoped you held that queen, but I couldn't be sure."

"Fortune was with us, sir," said Hornblower.

The flag lieutenant glanced at Bush; it seemed as if the flag lieutenant was of opinion that the colonel should have been in no doubt, from the previous play, that Hornblower held the queen. Now that Bush's attention was drawn to it, he decided that Hornblower must have thought just the same—the slightest inflection in his voice implied it—but was sensibly not saying so.

"I lose a rubber at five pounds ten and win one at fifteen shillings," said the colonel, receiving his winnings from Lambert. "Who'd like to increase the stakes again?"

To the credit of the two admirals they both glanced at Hornblower without replying.

"As you gentlemen wish," said Hornblower.

"In that case I'm quite agreeable," said Parry.

"Five shillings a trick, then," said the colonel. "That makes the game worth playing."

"The game is always worth playing," protested Parry.

"Of course, my lord," said the colonel, but without suggesting that they should revert to the previous stakes.

Now the stakes were really serious; by Bush's calculation a really disastrous rubber might cost Hornblower twenty pounds, and his further calculation told him that Hornblower could hardly have more than twenty pounds tucked away in his breast pocket. It was a relief to him when Hornblower and Lambert won the next rubber easily.

"This is a most enjoyable evening," said Lambert, and he smiled with a glance down at the fistful of the colonel's money he was holding, "nor am I referring to any monetary gains."

"Instructive as well as amusing," said Parry, paying out to Hornblower.

Play proceeded, silently as ever, the silence only broken by the brief interchanges of remarks between rubbers. Now that he could afford it, fortunately, Hornblower lost a rubber, but it was a cheap one, and he immediately won another profitable one. His gains mounted steadily with hardly a setback. It was growing late, and Bush was feeling weary, but the players showed few signs of fatigue, and the flag lieutenant stayed on with the limitless patience he must have acquired during his present appointment, philosophic and fatalistic since he could not possibly do anything to accelerate his admiral's decision to go to bed. The other players drifted away from the room; later still the curtained door opened and the gamblers from the inner room came streaming out, some noisy, some silent, and the Marquis made his appearance, silent and unruffled, to watch the final rubbers with unobtrusive interest, seeing to it that the candles were snuffed and fresh ones brought, and new cards ready on demand. It was Parry who first glanced at the clock.

"Half past three," he said. "Perhaps you gentlemen—?"

"Too late to go to bed now, my lord," said the colonel. "Sir Richard and I have to be up early, as you know."

"My orders are all given," said Lambert.

"So are mine," said the colonel.

Bush was stupid with long late hours spent in a stuffy atmosphere, but he thought he noticed an admonitory glance from Parry, directed at the two speakers. He wondered idly what orders Lambert and the colonel would have given, and still more idly why they should be orders that Parry did not wish to be mentioned. There seemed to be just the slightest trace of hurry, just the slightest hint of a desire to change the subject, in Parry's manner when he spoke.

"Very well, then, we can play another rubber, if Mr. Hornblower has no objection?"

"None at all, my lord."

Hornblower was imperturbable; if he had noticed anything remarkable about the recent interchange he gave no sign of it. Probably he was weary, though—Bush was led to suspect that by his very imperturbability. Bush knew by now that Hornblower worked as hard to conceal his human weaknesses as some men worked to conceal ignoble birth.

Hornblower had the colonel as partner, and no one could be in the room without being aware that this final rubber was being played in an atmosphere of even fiercer competition than its predecessors. Not a word was spoken between the hands; the score was marked, the tricks swept up, the other pack proffered and cut in deadly silence. Each hand was desperately close, too. In nearly every case it was only a single trick that divided the victors and the vanquished, so that the rubber dragged on and on with painful slowness. Then a hand finished amid a climax of tension. The flag lieutenant and the Marquis had kept count of the score, and when Lambert took the last trick they uttered audible sighs, and the colonel was so moved that he broke the silence at last.

"Neck and neck, by God!" he said. "This next hand must settle it."

But he was properly rebuked by the stony silence with which his remark was received. Parry merely took the cards from the colonel's right side and passed them over to Hornblower to cut. Then Parry dealt, and turned up the king of diamonds as trump, and the colonel led. Trick succeeded trick. For a space, after losing a single trick, Lambert and Parry carried all before them. Six tricks lay before Parry, and only one before Hornblower. The colonel's remark about being neck and neck was fresh in Bush's ears. One more trick out of the next six would give the rubber to the two admirals. Five to one was long odds, and Bush uncomfortably resigned himself to his friend losing this final rubber. Then the colonel took a trick and the game was still alive. Hornblower took the next trick, so that there was still hope. Hornblower led the ace of diamonds, and before it could be played to he laid down his other three cards to claim the rest of the tricks; the queen and knave of diamonds lay conspicuously on the table.

"Rubber!" exclaimed the colonel, "we've won it, partner! I thought all was lost."

Parry was ruefully contemplating his fallen king.

"I agree that you had to lead your ace, Mr. Hornblower," he said, "but I would be enchanted to know why you were so certain that my king was unguarded. There were two other diamonds unaccounted for. Would it be asking too much of you to reveal the secret?"

Hornblower raised his eyebrows in some slight surprise at a question whose answer was so obvious.

"You were marked with the king, my lord," he said, "but it was the rest of your hand which was significant, for you were also marked with holding three clubs. With only four cards in your hand the king could not be guarded."

"A perfect explanation," said Parry, "it only goes to confirm me in my conviction that you are an excellent whist player, Mr. Hornblower."

"Thank you, my lord."

Parry's quizzical smile had a great deal of friendship in it. If Hornblower's previous behaviour had not already won Parry's regard, this last coup certainly had.

"I'll bear your name in mind, Mr. Hornblower," he said. "Sir Richard has already told me the reason why it was familiar to me. It was regrettable that the policy of immediate economy imposed on the Admiralty by the Cabinet should have resulted in your commission as commander not being confirmed."

"I thought I was the only one who regretted it, my lord."

Bush winced again when he heard the words; this was the time for Hornblower to ingratiate himself with those in authority, not to offend them with unconcealed bitterness. This meeting with Parry was a stroke of good fortune that any half-pay naval officer would give two fingers for. Bush was reassured, however, by a glance at the speakers. Hornblower was smiling with infectious lightheartedness, and Parry was smiling back at him. Either the implied bitterness had escaped Parry's notice or it had only existed in Bush's mind.

"I was actually forgetting that I owe you a further thirty five shillings," said Parry, with a start of recollection. "Forgive me. There, I think that settles my monied indebtedness; I am still in your debt for a valuable experience."

It was a thick wad of money that Hornblower put back in his pocket.

"I trust you will keep a sharp lookout for footpads on your way back, Mr. Hornblower," said Parry with a glance.

"Mr. Bush will be walking home with me, my lord. It would be a valiant footpad that would face him."

"No need to worry about footpads tonight," interposed the colonel. "Not tonight."

The colonel wore a significant grin; the others displayed a momentary disapproval of what apparently was an indiscretion, but the disapproval faded out again when the colonel waved a hand at the clock.

"Our orders go into force at four, my lord," said Lambert.

"And now it is half past. Excellent."

The flag lieutenant came in at that moment; he had slipped out when the last card was played.

"The carriage is at the door, my lord," he said.

"Thank you. I wish you gentlemen a good evening, then."

They all walked to the door together; there was the carriage in the street, and the two admirals, the colonel, and the flag lieutenant mounted into it. Hornblower and Bush watched it drive away.

"Now what the devil are those orders that come into force at four?" asked Bush. The earliest dawn was showing over the rooftops.

"God knows," said Hornblower.

They headed for the corner of Highbury Street.

"How much did you win?"

"It was over forty pounds—it must be about forty five pounds," said Hornblower.

"A good night's work."

"Yes. The chances usually right themselves in time." There was something flat and listless in Hornblower's tone as he spoke. He took several more strides before he burst out into speech again with a vigour that was in odd contrast. "I wish to God it had happened last week. Yesterday, even."

"But why?"

"That girl. That poor girl."

"God bless my soul!" said Bush. He had forgotten all about the fact that Maria had slipped half a crown into Hornblower's pocket and he was surprised that Hornblower had not forgotten as well. "Why trouble your head about her?"

"I don't know," said Hornblower, and then he took two more strides. "But I do."

Bush had no time to meditate over this curious avowal, for he heard a sound that made him grasp Hornblower's elbow with sudden excitement.

"Listen!"

Ahead of them, along the silent street, a heavy military tread could be heard. It was approaching. The faint light shone on white crossbelts and brass buttons. It was a military patrol, muskets at the slope, a sergeant marching beside it, his chevrons and his half-pike revealing his rank.

"Now, what the deuce—?" said Bush.

"Halt!" said the sergeant to his men, and then to the other two, "May I ask you two gennelmen who you are?"

"We are naval officers," said Bush.

The lantern the sergeant carried was not really necessary to reveal them. The sergeant came to attention.

"Thank you, sir," he said.

"What are you doing with this patrol, sergeant?" asked Bush.

"I have my orders, sir," replied the sergeant. "Begging your pardon, sir. By the left, quick—march!"

The patrol strode forward, and the sergeant clapped his hand to his half-pike in salute as he passed on.

"What in the name of all that's holy?" wondered Bush. "Boney can't have made a surprise landing. Every bell would be ringing if that were so. You'd think the press gang was out, a real hot press. But it can't be."

"Look there!" said Hornblower.

Another party of men was marching along the street, but not in red coats, not with the military stiffness of the soldiers. Checked shirts and blue trousers; a midshipman marching at the head, white patches on his collar and his dirk at his side.

"The press gang for certain!" exclaimed Bush. "Look at the bludgeons!"

Every seaman carried a club in his hand.

"Midshipman!" said Hornblower, sharply. "What's all this?"

The midshipman halted at the tone of command and the sight of the uniforms.

"Orders, sir," he began, and then, realising that with the growing daylight he need no longer preserve secrecy, especially to naval men, he went on. "Press gang, sir. We've orders to press every seaman we find. The patrols are out on every road."

"So I believe. But what's the press for?"

"Dunno, sir. Orders, sir."

That was sufficient answer, maybe.

"Very good. Carry on."

"The press, by jingo!" said Bush. "Something's happening."

"I expect you're right," said Hornblower.

They had turned into Highbury Street now, and were making their way along to Mrs. Mason's house.

"There's the first results," said Hornblower.

They stood on the doorstep to watch them go by, a hundred men at least, escorted along by a score of seamen with staves, a midshipman in command. Some of the pressed men were bewildered and silent; some were talking volubly—the noise they were making was rousing the street. Every man among them had at least one hand in a trouser pocket; those who were not gesticulating had both hands in their pockets.

"It's like old times," said Bush with a grin. "They've cut their waistbands."

With their waistbands cut it was necessary for them to keep a hand in a trouser pocket, as otherwise their trousers would fall down. No one could run away when handicapped in this fashion.

"A likely-looking lot of prime seamen," said Bush, running a professional eye over them.

"Hard luck on them, all the same," said Hornblower.

"Hard luck?" said Bush in surprise.

Was the ox unlucky when it was turned into beef? Or for that matter was the guinea unlucky when it changed hands? This was life; for a merchant seaman to find himself a sailor of the King was as natural a thing as for his hair to turn grey if he should live so long. And the only way to secure him was to surprise him in the night, rouse him out of bed, snatch him from the grog shop and the brothel, converting him in a single second from a free man earning his livelihood in his own way into a pressed man who could not take a step on shore of his own free will without risking being flogged round the fleet. Bush could no more sympathise with the pressed man than he could sympathise with the night being replaced by day.

Hornblower was still looking at the press gang and the recruits.

"It may be war," he said, slowly.

"War!" said Bush.

"We'll know when the mail comes in," said Hornblower. "Parry could have told us last night, I fancy."

"But—war!" said Bush.

The crowd went on down the street towards the dockyard, its noise dwindling with the increasing distance, and Hornblower turned towards the street door, taking the ponderous key out of his pocket. When they entered the house they saw Maria standing at the foot of the staircase, a candlestick with an unlighted candle in her hand. She wore a long coat over her nightclothes; she had put on her mobcap hastily, for a couple of curling papers showed under its edge.

"You're safe!" she said.

"Of course we're safe, Maria," said Hornblower. "What do you think could happen to us?"

"There was all that noise in the street," said Maria. "I looked out. Was it the press gang?"

"That's just what it was," said Bush.

"Is it—is it war?"

"That's what it may be."

"Oh!" Maria's face revealed her distress. "Oh!"

Her eyes searched their faces.

"No need to worry, Miss Maria," said Bush. "It'll be many a long year before Boney brings his flat-bottoms up Spithead."

"It's not that," said Maria. Now she was looking only at Hornblower. In a flash she had forgotten Bush's existence.

"You'll be going away!" she said.

"I shall have my duty to do if I am called upon, Maria," said Hornblower.

Now a grim figure appeared climbing the stairs from the basement—Mrs. Mason; she had no mobcap on so that her curl papers were all visible.

"You'll disturb my other gentlemen with all this noise," she said.

"Mother, they think it's going to be war," said Maria.

"And not a bad thing perhaps if it means some people will pay what they owe."

"I'll do that this minute," said Hornblower hotly. "What's my reckoning, Mrs. Mason?"

"Oh please, please—" said Maria interposing.

"You just shut your mouth, miss," snapped Mrs. Mason. "It's only because of you that I've let this young spark run on."

"Mother!"

" 'I'll pay my reckoning,' he says, like a lord. And not a shirt in his chest. His chest'd be at the pawnbroker's too if I hadn't nobbled it."

"I said I'd pay my reckoning and I mean it, Mrs. Mason," said Hornblower with enormous dignity.

"Let's see the colour of your money, then," stipulated Mrs. Mason, not in the least convinced. "Twenty seven and six."

Hornblower brought a fistful of silver out of his trouser pocket. But there was not enough there, and he had to extract a note from his breast pocket, revealing as he did so that there were many more.

"So!" said Mrs. Mason. She looked down at the money in her hand as if it were fairy gold, and opposing emotions waged war in her expression.

"I think I might give you a week's warning, too," said Hornblower, harshly.

"Oh no!" said Maria.

"That's a nice room you have upstairs," said Mrs. Mason. "You wouldn't be leaving me just on account of a few words."

"Don't leave us, Mr. Hornblower," said Maria.

If ever there was a man completely at a loss it was Hornblower. After a glance at him Bush found it hard not to grin. The man who could keep a cool head when playing for high stakes with admirals—the man who fired the broadside that shook the *Renown* off the mud when under the fire of red-hot shot—was helpless when confronted by a couple of women. It would be a picturesque gesture to pay his reckoning—if necessary to pay an extra week's rent in lieu of warning—and to shake the dust of the place from his feet. But on the other hand he had been allowed credit here, and it would be a poor return for that consideration to leave the moment he could pay. But to stay on in a house that knew his secrets was an irksome prospect too. The dignified Hornblower who was ashamed of ever appearing human would hardly feel at home among people who knew that he had been human enough to be in debt. Bush was aware of all these problems as they confronted Hornblower, of the kindly feelings and the embittered ones. And Bush could be fond of him even while he laughed at him, and could respect him even while he knew of his weaknesses.

"When did you gennelmen have supper?" asked Mrs. Mason.

"I don't think we did," answered Hornblower, with a side glance at Bush.

"You must be hungry, then, if you was up all night. Let me cook you a nice breakfast. A couple of thick chops for each of you. Now how about that?"

"By George!" said Hornblower.

"You go on up," said Mrs. Mason. "I'll send the girl up with hot water an' you can shave. Then when you come down there'll be a nice breakfast ready for you. Maria, run and make the fire up."

Up in the attic Hornblower looked whimsically at Bush.

"That bed you paid a shilling for is still virgin," he said. "You haven't had a wink of sleep all night and it's my fault. Please forgive me."

"It's not the first night I haven't slept," said Bush. He had not slept on the night they stormed Samaná; many were the occasions in foul weather when he had kept the deck for twenty four hours continuously. And after a month of living with his sisters in the Chichester cottage, of nothing to do except to weed the garden, of trying to sleep for twelve hours a night for that very reason, the variety of excitement he had gone through had been actually pleasant. He sat down on the bed while Hornblower paced the floor.

"You'll have plenty more if it's war," Hornblower said, and Bush shrugged his shoulders.

A thump on the door announced the arrival of the maid of all work of the house, a can of hot water in each hand. Her ragged dress was too large for her—handed down presumably from Mrs. Mason or from Maria—and her hair was tousled, but she, too, turned wide eyes on Hornblower as she brought in the hot water. Those wide eyes were too big for her skinny face, and they followed Hornblower as he moved about the room, and never had a glance for Bush. It was plain that Hornblower was as much the hero of this fourteen-year-old foundling as he was of Maria.

"Thank you, Susie," said Hornblower, and Susie dropped an angular curtsey before she scuttled from the room with one last glance round the door as she left.

Hornblower waved a hand at the washhand stand and the hot water.

"You first," said Bush.

Hornblower peeled off his coat and his shirt and addressed himself to the business of shaving. The razor blade rasped on his bristly cheeks; he turned his face this way and that so as to apply the edge. Neither of them felt any need for conversation, and it was practically in silence that Hornblower washed himself, poured the wash water into the slop pail, and stood aside for Bush to shave himself.

"Make the most of it," said Hornblower. "A pint of fresh twice a week for shaving'll be all you'll get if you have your wish."

"Who cares?" said Bush.

He shaved, restropped his razor with care, and put it back into his roll of toilet articles. The scars that seamed his ribs gleamed pale as he moved. When he had finished dressing he glanced at Hornblower.

"Chops," said Hornblower. "Thick chops. Come on."

There were several places laid at the table in the dining room opening out of the hall, but nobody else was present; apparently it was not the breakfast hour of Mrs. Mason's other gentlemen.

"Only a minute, sir," said Susie, showing up in the doorway for a moment before hurrying down into the kitchen.

She came staggering back laden with a tray; Hornblower pushed back his chair and was about to help her, but she checked him with a scandalised squeak and managed to put the tray safely on the side table without accident.

"I can serve you, sir," she said.

She scuttled back and forward between the two tables like the boys running with the nippers when the cable was being hove in. Coffee-pot and toast, butter and jam, sugar and milk, cruet and hot plates and finally a wide dish which she laid before Hornblower; she took off the cover and there was a noble dish of chops whose delightful scent, hitherto pent up, filled the room.

"Ah," said Hornblower, taking up a spoon and fork to serve. "Have you had your breakfast, Susie?"

"Me, sir? No, sir. Not yet, sir."

Hornblower paused, spoon and fork in hand, looking from the chops to Susie and back again. Then he put down the spoon and thrust his right hand into his trouser pocket.

"There's no way in which you can have one of these chops?" he said.

"Me, sir? Of course not, sir."

"Now here's half a crown."

"Half a crown, sir!"

That was more than a day's wages for a labourer.

"I want a promise from you, Susie."

"Sir—sir—!"

Susie's hands were behind her.

"Take this, and promise me that the first chance that comes your way, the moment Mrs. Mason lets you out, you'll buy yourself something to eat. Fill that wretched little belly of yours. Faggots and pease pudding, pig's trotters, all the things you like. Promise me."

"But sir—"

Half a crown, the prospect of unlimited food, were things that could not be real.

"Oh, take it," said Hornblower testily.

"Yes, sir."

Susie clasped the coin in her skinny hand.

"Don't forget I have your promise."

"Yes, sir, please sir, thank you, sir."

"Now put it away and clear out quick."

"Yes, sir."

She fled out of the room and Hornblower began once more to serve the chops.

"I'll be able to enjoy my breakfast now," said Hornblower self-consciously.

"No doubt," said Bush; he buttered himself a piece of toast, dabbed mustard on his plate—to eat mustard with mutton marked him as a sailor, but he did it without a thought. With good food in front of him there was no need for thought, and he ate in silence. It was only when Hornblower spoke again that Bush realised that Hornblower had been construing the silence as accusatory of something.

"Half a crown," said Hornblower, defensively, "may mean many things to many people. Yesterday—"

"You're quite right," said Bush, filling in the gap as politeness dictated, and then he looked up and realised that it was not because he had no more to say that Hornblower had left the sentence uncompleted.

Maria was standing framed in the dining room door; her bonnet, gloves, and shawl indicated that she was about to go out, presumably to early marketing since the school where she taught was temporarily closed.

"I—I looked in to see that you had everything you wanted," she said. The hesitation in her speech seemed to indicate that she had heard Hornblower's last words, but it was not certain.

"Thank you. Delightful," mumbled Hornblower.

"Please don't get up," said Maria, hastily and with a hint of hostility, as Hornblower and Bush began to rise. Her eyes were wet.

A knocking on the street door relieved the tension, and Maria fled to answer it. From the dining room they heard a masculine voice, and Maria reappeared, a corporal of marines towering behind her dumpy form.

"Lieutenant Hornblower?" he asked.

"That's me."

"From the admiral, sir."

The corporal held out a letter and a folded newspaper. There was a maddening delay while a pencil was found for Hornblower to sign the receipt. Then the corporal took his leave with a clicking of heels and Hornblower stood with the letter in one hand and the newspaper in the other.

"Oh, open it—please open it," said Maria.

Hornblower tore the wafer and unfolded the sheet. He read the note, and then re-read it, nodding his head as if the note confirmed some preconceived theory.

"You see that sometimes it is profitable to play whist," he said, "in more ways than one."

He handed the note over to Bush; his smile was a little lopsided.

SIR [read Bush]:

It is with pleasure that I take this opportunity of informing you in advance of any official notification that your promotion to Commander is now confirmed and that you will be shortly appointed to the Command of a Sloop of War.

"By God, sir!" said Bush. "Congratulations. For the second time, sir. It's only what you deserve, as I said before."

"Thank you," said Hornblower. "Finish reading it."

The arrival at this moment of the Mail Coach with the London newspapers [said the second paragraph] enables me to send you the information regarding the changed situation without being unnecessarily prolix in this letter. You will gather from what you read in the accompanying copy of the *Sun* the reasons why conditions of military secrecy should prevail during our very pleasant evening, so that I need not apologise for not having enlightened you, while I remain,

Your obedient servant,

PARRY

By the time Bush had finished the letter Hornblower had opened the newspaper at the relevant passage, which he pointed out to Bush.

Message from HIS MAJESTY

House of Commons, March 8, 1803

The CHANCELLOR OF THE EXCHEQUER brought down the following message from His Majesty:

"His Majesty thinks it necessary to acquaint the House of Commons, that, as very considerable military preparations are carrying on in the ports of France and Holland, he has judged it expedient to adopt additional measures of precaution for the security of his dominions.

George R."

That was all Bush needed to read. Boney's fleet of flat-bottomed boats, and his army of invasion mustered along the Channel coast, were being met by the appropriate and necessary countermove. Last night's press gang measures, planned and carried out with a secrecy for which Bush could feel nothing except wholehearted approval (he had led too many press gangs not to know how completely seamen made themselves scarce at the first hint of a press) would provide the crews for the ships necessary to secure England's safety. There were ships in plenty, laid up in every harbour in England; and officers—Bush knew very well how many officers were available. With the fleet manned and at sea England could laugh at the treacherous attack Boney had planned.

"They've done the right thing for once, by God!" said Bush, slapping the newspaper.

"But what is it?" asked Maria.

She had been standing silent, watching the two men, her glance shifting from one to the other in an endeavour to read their expressions. Bush remembered that she had winced at his outburst of congratulation.

"It'll be war next week," said Hornblower. "Boney won't endure a bold answer."

"Oh," said Maria. "But you—what about you?"

"I'm made commander," said Hornblower. "I'm going to be appointed to a sloop of war."

"Oh," said Maria again.

There was a second or two of agonised effort at self-control, and then she broke down. Her head drooped farther and farther, until she put her gloved hands to her face, turning away from the two men so that they only saw her shoulders with the shawl across them, shaking with sobs.

"Maria," said Hornblower gently. "Please, Maria, please don't."

Maria turned and presented a slobbered face to him, unevenly framed in the bonnet which had been pushed askew.

"I'll n-n-never see you again," sobbed Maria. "I've been so happy with the m-m-mumps at school, I thought I'd m-m-make your bed and do your room. And n-now this happens!"

"But Maria," said Hornblower, his hands flapped helplessly. "I've my duty to do."

"I wish I was d–dead! Indeed I wish I was dead!" said Maria and the tears poured down her cheeks to drip upon her shawl; they streamed from eyes which had a fixed look of despair, while the wide mouth was shapeless.

This was something Bush could not endure. He liked pretty, saucy women. What he was looking at now jarred on him unbearably—perhaps it rasped his aesthetic sensibility, unlikely though it might seem that Bush should have such a thing. Perhaps he was merely irritated by the spectacle of uncontrolled hysteria, but if that was the case he was irritated beyond all bearing. He felt that if he had to put up with Maria's waterworks for another minute he would break a blood vessel.

"Let's get out of here," he said to Hornblower.

In reply he received a look of surprise. It had not occurred to Hornblower that he might run away from a situation for which his temperament necessarily made him feel responsible. Bush knew perfectly well that, given time, Maria would recover. He knew that women who wished themselves dead one day could be as lively as crickets the next day after another man had chucked them under the chin. In any case he did not see why he and Hornblower should concern themselves about something which was entirely Maria's fault.

"Oh!" said Maria; she stumbled forward and supported herself with her hands upon the table with its cooling coffee-pot and its congealing half-consumed chops. She lifted her head and wailed again.

"Oh, for God's sake—" said Bush in disgust. He turned to Hornblower. "Come along."

By the time Bush was on the staircase he realised that Hornblower had not followed him, would not follow him. And Bush did not go back to fetch him. Even though Bush was not the man to desert a comrade in peril; even though he would gladly take his place in a boat launching out through the most dreadful surf to rescue men in danger; even though he would stand shoulder to shoulder with Hornblower and be hewn to pieces with him by an overwhelming enemy; for all this he would not go back to save Hornblower. If Hornblower was going to be foolish Bush felt he could not stop him. And he salved his conscience by telling himself that perhaps Hornblower would not be foolish.

Up in the attic Bush set about rolling up his nightshirt with his toilet things. The methodical checking over of his razor and comb and brushes, seeing that nothing was left behind, soothed his irritated nerves. The prospect of immediate employment and immediate action revealed itself to him in all its delightful certainty, breaking through the evaporating clouds of his irritation. He began to hum to himself tunelessly. It would be sensible to call in again at the dockyard—he might even look in at the Keppel's Head to discuss the morning's amazing news; both courses would be advisable if he wanted to secure for himself quickly a new appointment. Hat in hand he tucked his neat package under his arm and cast a final glance round the room to make sure that he had left nothing, and he was still humming as he closed the attic door behind him. On the staircase, about to step down into the hall, he stood for a moment with one foot suspended, not in doubt as to whether he should go into the dining room, but arranging in his mind what he should say when he went in.

Maria had dried her tears. She was standing there smiling, although her bonnet was still askew. Hornblower was smiling too; it might be with relief that Maria had left off weeping. He looked round at Bush's entrance, and his face revealed surprise at the sight of Bush's hat and bundle.

"I'm getting under way," said Bush. "I have to thank you for your hospitality, sir."

"But—" said Hornblower, "you don't have to go just yet, do you?"

There was that "sir" again in Bush's speech. They had been through so much together, and they knew so much about each other. Now war was coming again, and Hornblower was Bush's superior officer. Bush explained what he wanted to do before taking the carrier's cart back to Chichester, and Hornblower nodded.

"Pack your chest," he said. "It won't be long before you need it."

Bush cleared his throat in preparation for the formal words he was going to use.

"I didn't express my congratulations properly," he said portentously, "I wanted to say that I don't believe the Admiralty could have made a better choice out of the whole list of lieutenants when they selected you for promotion, sir."

"You're too kind," said Hornblower.

"I'm sure Mr. Bush is quite right," said Maria.

She gazed up at Hornblower with adoration shining in her face, and he looked down at her with infinite kindness. And already there was something a little proprietorial about the adoration, and perhaps there was something wistful about the kindness.

Hornblower and the Atropos

ONE

HAVING CLIMBED up through the locks, the canal boat was now winding over the pleasant Cotswold country. Hornblower was bubbling with good spirits, on his way to take up a new command, seeing new sights, travelling in an entirely new way, at a moment when the entirely unpredictable English weather had decided to stage a clear sunny day in the middle of December. This was a delightful way of travelling, despite the cold.

"Your pardon for a moment, ma'am," said Hornblower.

Maria, with the sleeping little Horatio in her arms, gave a sigh at her husband's restlessness and shifted her knees to allow him passage, and he rose under the restricted height of the first-class cabin and stepped out through the forward door into the open bow of the passage boat. Here he could stand on his sea-chest and look round him. She was a queer craft, fully seventy feet long and, judging by eye as he looked aft, he would think hardly five feet in beam—the same proportions as had the crazy dugout canoes he had seen in use in the West Indies. Her draught must be less than a foot; that was clear as she tore along behind the cantering horses at a speed that must certainly be all of eight knots—nine miles an hour he told himself, hurriedly, for that was the way they measured speeds here inland.

The passage boat was making her way from Gloucester to London along the Thames and Severn Canal; going far more smoothly than the stage coach, it was very nearly as fast and decidedly cheaper, at a penny a mile, even in the first class. He and Maria with the child were the only first-class passengers, and the boatman when Hornblower had paid the fares had cocked an eye at Maria's condition and had said that by rights they ought to pay two children's fares instead of one. Maria had snorted with disdain at such vulgarity, while the onlookers chuckled.

Standing on his sea-chest, Hornblower could look over the canal banks, at the grey stone boundary walls and the grey stone farms. The rhythmic sound of the hoofs of the cantering tow horses accentuated the smoothness of the travel; the boat itself made hardly a sound as she slid along over the surface of the water—Hornblower noticed that the boatmen had the trick of lifting the bows, by a sudden acceleration, onto the crest of the bow raised by her passage, and retaining them there. This reduced turbulence in the canal to a minimum; it was only when he looked aft that he could see, far back, the reeds at the banks bowing and straightening again long after they had gone by. It was this trick that made the fantastic speed possible. The cantering horses maintained their nine miles an hour, being changed every half hour. There were two towlines, attached to timber heads at bow and stern; one boatman rode as postillion on the rear horse, controlling the lead horse with shouts and the cracking of his whip. In the stern sat the other boatman, surly and with one hand missing and replaced by a hook; with the other he held the tiller and steered the boat round the curves with a skill that Hornblower admired.

A sudden ringing of the horses' hoofs on stone warned Hornblower just in time. The horses were dashing, without any slackening of pace, under a low bridge, where the tow path, cramped between the water and the arch, gave them barely room to pass. The mounted boatman buried his face in his horse's mane to pass under; Hornblower had just time to leap down from his sea-chest and seat himself as the bridge hurried over him. Hornblower heard the helmsman's loud laugh at his momentary discomfiture.

"You learn to move fast in a canal boat, Captain," the steersman called to him from his place by the tiller. "Two dozen for the last man off the yard! None o' that here on Cotswold, Captain, but a broken head for *you* if you don't look lively."

"Don't let that fellow be so rude to you, Horatio," said Maria from the cabin. "Can't you stop him?"

"Not so easy, dear," replied Hornblower. "It's he who's captain of this craft, and I'm only a passenger."

"Well, if you can't stop him, come in here where he can't be rude to you."

"Yes, my dear, in a minute."

Hornblower chose to risk the jeers of the boatman rather than miss looking round him; this was the best opportunity he had had of watching the working of the canals which in the last thirty years had changed the economic face of England. And not far ahead was Sapperton Tunnel, the engineering marvel of the age, the greatest achievement of the new science. He certainly wanted to see that. Let the steersman laugh his head off if he wanted to. He must be an old sailor, discharged as disabled by the loss of his hand. It must be a wonderful experience for him to have a naval captain under his command.

The grey stone tower of a lock-house showed ahead, with the minute figure of the lock-keeper opening the gates. A yell from the postillion-boatman checked the speed of the horses; the boat glided on, its speed diminishing greatly as the bows slid off the bow wave. As the boat entered the lock the one-handed steersman leaped ashore with a line which he flipped dexterously round a bollard; a smart tug or two took most of the way off the boat, and the boatman, running forward, secured the line to another bollard.

"Heave us that line, Captain," he cried, and Hornblower obediently threw up the bow line for him to secure forward. The law of the sea applied equally in inland waters—the ship first and personal dignity a long way second.

Already the lock-keeper was closing the gates behind them and the lock-keeper's wife was opening the paddles of the upper gate, the water swirling in. The lower gates closed with a crash with the mounting pressure, and the boat rose with the gurgling water. The horses were changed in a twinkling; the postillion scrambled into his saddle, and proceeded to tilt a black bottle against his lips during the remaining few seconds while the lock filled. The steersman was casting off the lines—Hornblower took the bow line from him—and the lock-keeper's wife was thrusting at one upper gate while the lock-keeper, running up from the lower gate, thrust at the other. The postillion yelled and cracked his whip, the boat sprang forward while the helmsman leaped to his place astern, and they were off again with not a second wasted. Assuredly this canal traffic was a miracle of modernity, and it was gratifying to be on board the very fastest of the canal boats, the *Queen Charlotte,* that took priority over all other traffic. On her bow she carried a glittering scythe-blade as the proud symbol of her superior importance. It would sever the towline of any approaching boat which did not drop her line quickly enough to let her through. The two score of farmers' wives and wenches who sat aft in the second class with their chickens and ducks and eggs and butter were all of them travelling as much as twenty miles to market, in the confident expectation of returning the same day. Quite astonishing.

Here, as they climbed to the summit level, lock succeeded lock at frequent intervals, and at each the postillion held his black bottle to his lips, and his yells to his horses became more raucous and his whip-cracking more continuous. Hornblower obediently handed the bow line at each lock, despite Maria's urgings to the contrary.

"My dear," said Hornblower, "we save time if I do."

"But it isn't right," said Maria. "He knows you're a captain in the navy."

"He knows it too well," said Hornblower with a lopsided smile. "And after all I have a command to take up."

"As if it couldn't wait!" said Maria with a sniff.

It was hard to make Maria understand that to a captain his command was all in all, that he wished to lose not an hour, not a minute, in his journey to assume command of his sloop of war in London River; he was yearning to see what *Atropos* was like, with the mingled hope and apprehension that might be expected of an Oriental bridegroom affianced to a veiled bride—that was not a simile that it would be wise to mention to Maria, though.

Now they were gliding down the summit level of the canal; the cutting was growing deeper and deeper, so that the echo of the sound of the horses' hoofs came ringing from the rocky banks. Round the shallow curve must surely be Sapperton Tunnel.

"Hold hard, Charlie!" suddenly yelled the steersman. A moment later he sprang to the after towline and tried to cast it off from the timber head, and there was wild confusion. Shouts and yells on the tow path, horses whinnying, hoofs clattering. Hornblower caught a glimpse of the lead horse leaping frantically up the steep slope of the cutting—just ahead of them was the castellated but gloomy mouth of the tunnel and there was no other way for the horse to turn. The *Queen Charlotte* lurched hideously against the bank to the accompaniment of screams from the second-class cabin; for a moment Hornblower was sure she would capsize. She righted herself and came to a stop as the towlines slackened; the frantic struggles of the second horse, entangled in two towlines, ended as it kicked itself free. The steersman had scrambled onto the tow path and had dropped the after line over a bollard.

"A pretty kettle o' fish," he said.

Another man had shown up, running down the bank from the top whence spare horses looked down at them, whinnying. He held the heads of the *Queen Charlotte's* horses, and near his feet lay Charlie, the boatman-postillion, his face a mask of blood.

"Get ye back in there!" bellowed the steersman to the women who were all scrambling out of the second-class cabin. "All's well. Get ye back! Once let them loose on the country," he added to Hornblower, "and they'd be harder to catch than their own chickens."

"What is it, Horatio?" asked Maria, standing at the door of the first-class cabin with the baby in her arms.

"Nothing to alarm yourself about, my dear," said Hornblower. "Compose yourself. This is no time for agitation."

He turned and looked at the one-handed steersman, who bent down to examine Charlie; taking a hold of the breast of his coat with his steel hook he hauled up, but Charlie's head only hung back helplessly, the blood running over his cheeks.

"Not much use out of Charlie," said the steersman, letting him drop with a thump. As Hornblower stooped to look he could catch the reek of gin three feet from the bleeding mouth. Half stunned and half drunk —more than half of both for that matter.

"We've the tunnel to leg through," said the steersman. "Who's up at the Tunnel House?"

"Ne'er a soul," replied the man with the horses. "The trade all went through in the early morning."

The steersman whistled.

"You'll have to come wi' us," he said.

"Not I," said the horseholder. "I've sixteen horses—eighteen with these two. I can't leave 'em."

The steersman swore a couple of astonishing oaths—astonishing even to Hornblower, who had heard many in his time.

"What d'you mean by 'legging' through the tunnel?" Hornblower asked.

The steersman pointed with his hook at the black forbidding tunnel mouth in the castellated entrance.

"No tow path through the tunnel, o' course, Captain," he said. "So we leaves our horses here an' we legs through. We puts a pair o' 'wings' on the bows—sort o' catheads, in a way. Charlie lies on one an' I lies on the other, wi' our heads inboard an' our feet agin the tunnel wall. Then we sort o' walks, and we gets the boat along that way, and we picks up another pair o' horses at the south end."

"I see," said Hornblower.

"I'll souse this sot wi' a couple o' buckets o' water," said the steersman. "Mebbe it'll bring him round."

"Maybe," said Hornblower.

But buckets of water made no difference to the unconscious Charlie, who was clearly concussed. The slow blood flowed again after his battered face had been washed clean. The steersman produced another couple of oaths.

"The other trade'll be coming up arter you," said the horseholder. "'Nother couple o' hours, mebbe."

All he received in reply was a further series of oaths.

"We have to have daylight to run the Thames staunches," said the steersman. "Two hours? We'll only just get there by daylight if we go now."

He looked round him, at the silent canal cut and tunnel mouth, at the chattering women in the boat and the few doddering old gaffers along with them.

"Twelve hours late, we'll be," he concluded, morosely.

A day late in taking up his command, thought Hornblower.

"Damn it," he said, "I'll help you leg through."

"Good on ye, sir," said the steersman, significantly dropping the equalitarian "captain" for the "sir" he had carefully eschewed so far. "D'ye think you can?"

"Likely enough," said Hornblower.

"Let's fit those wings," said the steersman, with sudden decision.

They were small platforms, projecting out from either bow.

"Horatio," asked Maria, "whatever are you doing?"

That was just what Maria *would* ask. Hornblower was tempted to make use of the rejoinder he had heard used once in the *Renown*, to the effect that he was getting milk from a male ostrich, but he checked himself.

"Just helping the boatman, dear," he said patiently.

"You don't think enough of your position," said Maria.

Hornblower was by now a sufficiently experienced married man to realise the advantages of allowing his wife to say what she liked as long as he could continue to do as he liked. With the wings fitted he and the steersman on board, and the horseholder on the bank, took their places along the side of the *Queen Charlotte*. A strong united shove sent the boat gliding into the cut, heading for the tunnel.

"Keep 'er goin', sir," said the steersman, scrambling forward to the port-side wing. It was obvious that it would be far easier to maintain gentle way on the boat than to progress in fits and starts of alternate stopping and moving. Hornblower hurried to the starboard-side wing and laid himself down on it as the bows of the boat crept into the dark tunnel. Lying on his right side, with his head inboard, he felt his feet come into contact with the brick lining of the tunnel. He pressed with his feet, and then by a simple backward walking motion he urged the boat along.

"Hold hard, sir," said the steersman—his head was just beside Hornblower's—"there's two miles an' more to go."

A tunnel two miles long, driven through the solid rock of the Cotswolds! No wonder it was the marvel of the age. The Romans with all their aqueducts had achieved nothing to compare with this. Farther and farther into the tunnel they went, into darkness that increased in intensity, until it was frightfully, astonishingly dark, with the eye recording nothing at all, strain as it might. At their entrance into the tunnel the women had chattered and laughed, and had shouted to hear the echoes in the tunnel.

"Silly lot o' hens," muttered the steersman.

Now they fell silent, oppressed by the darkness, all except Maria.

"I trust you remember you have your good clothes on, Horatio," she said.

"Yes, dear," said Hornblower, happy in the knowledge that she could not possibly see him.

It was not a very dignified thing he was doing, and not at all comfortable. After a few minutes he was acutely aware of the hardness of the platform on which he was lying; nor was it long before his legs began to protest against the effort demanded of them. He tried to shift his position a little, to bring other muscles into play and other areas of himself into contact with the platform, but he learned fast enough that it had to be done with tact and timing, so as not to disturb the smooth rhythm of the propulsion of the boat—the steersman beside him grunted a brief protest as Hornblower missed a thrust with his right leg and the boat baulked a little.

"Keep 'er goin', sir," he repeated.

So they went on through the darkness, in the strangest sort of mesmeric nightmare, suspended in utter blackness, utterly silent, for their speed was not sufficient to raise a ripple round the *Queen Charlotte's* bows. Hornblower went on thrusting with his feet, urging his aching legs into further efforts; he could tell by the sensations conveyed through the soles of his shoes that the tunnel was no longer brick-lined—his feet pressed against naked rock, rough and irregular as the tunnellers' picks and gunpowder had left it. That made his present employment more difficult.

He became aware of a slight noise in the distance—a low muttering sound, at first so feeble that when he first took note of it he realised that he had been hearing it already for some time. It gradually increased in volume as the boat crept along, until it was a loud roaring; he had no idea what it could be, but as the steersman beside him seemed unconcerned he decided not to ask about it.

"Easy a minute, sir," said the steersman, and Hornblower, wondering, rested his aching legs, while the steersman, still recumbent, fumbled and tugged beside him. Next moment he had dragged a tarpaulin completely over both of them, except for their feet protruding from under the edges. It was no darker under the tarpaulin than outside it, but it was considerably stuffier.

"Carry on, sir," said the steersman, and Hornblower recommenced pushing with his feet against the wall, the roaring he had heard before somewhat muffled by the tarpaulin. A trickle of water vollied loudly on the tarpaulin, and then another, and he suddenly understood what the roaring was.

"Here it comes," said the steersman under the tarpaulin.

An underground spring here broke through the roof of the tunnel and tumbled roaring into the canal. The water fell down on them in deafening cataracts. It thundered upon the roofs of the cabins, quite drowning the cries of the women within. The weight of its impact pressed the tarpaulin upon him. Then the torrent eased, fell away to trickles, and then they were past it.

"Only one more o' those," said the steersman in the stuffy darkness beside him. "It's better arter a dry summer."

"Are you wet, Horatio?" asked Maria's voice.

"No, dear," said Hornblower, the simple negative having the desired cushioning effect and smothering further expostulation.

Actually his feet were wet, but after eleven years at sea that was not a new experience; he was much more concerned with the weariness of his legs. It seemed an age before the next trickling of water and the steersman's "Here it comes" heralded the next deluge. They crawled on beyond it, and the steersman, with a grunt of relief, dragged the tarpaulin from off them. And with its removal Hornblower twisting his neck suddenly saw something far ahead. His eyes were by now accustomed to the darkness, and in that massive darkness, incredibly far away, there was something to be seen, a minute something, the size apparently of a grain of sand. It was the farther mouth of the tunnel. He worked away with his legs with renewed vitality. The tunnel opening grew in size, from a grain of sand to a pea; it assumed the crescentic shape to be expected of it; it grew larger still, and with its growth the light increased in the tunnel by infinitesimal gradations, until Hornblower could see the dark surface of the water, the irregularities of the tunnel roof. Now the tunnel was brick-lined again, and progress was easier—and seemed easier still.

"Easy all," said the steersman with a final thrust.

It seemed unbelievable to Hornblower that he did not have to work his legs any more, that he was emerging into daylight, that no more underground springs would cascade upon him as he lay suffocating under a tarpaulin. The boat slowly slid out of the tunnel's mouth, and despite its slow progress, and despite the fact that outside the sun shone with only wintry brilliance, he was quite blinded for a while. The chatter of the passengers rose into a roar almost comparable with the sound of the underground spring upon the tarpaulin. Hornblower sat up and blinked round him. There was a horseholder on the tow path with a pair of horses; he caught the line the steersman tossed to him and between them they drew the boat to the bank. Many of the passengers were leaving at this point, and they began to swarm out at once with their packages and their chickens. Others were waiting to board.

"Horatio," said Maria, coming out of the first-class cabin; little Horatio was awake now and was whimpering a little.

"Yes, my dear?"

Hornblower was conscious of Maria's eyes taking in the disorder of his clothes. He knew that Maria would scold him, brush him down, treat him with the same maternal possessiveness as she treated his son, and he knew that at the moment he did not want to be possessed.

"One moment, dear, if you will pardon me," he said, and stepped nimbly out onto the tow path, joining himself to the conversation of the steersman and the horseholder.

"Ne'er a man here," said the latter. "An' you won't find one before Oxford, that I'll warrant you."

In reply the steersman said much the same things as he had said to the other horseholder.

"That's how it is, an' all," said the horseholder philosophically. "You'll have to wait for the trade."

"No spare men here?" asked Hornblower.

"None, sir," said the steersman, and then, after a moment's hesitation, "I suppose, sir, you wouldn't care to drive a pair o' horses?"

"Not I," answered Hornblower hastily—he was taken sufficiently by surprise by the question to make no attempt to disguise his dismay at the thought of driving two horses in the manner of the injured Charlie;

then he saw how to recover his dignity and keep himself safe from Maria's ministrations, and he added, "But I'll take the tiller."

"O' course you could, sir," answered the steersman. "Not the first time you've handled a tiller. Not by a long chalk. An' I'll drive the nags, me an' my jury fist an' all."

He glanced down at the steel hook that replaced his missing hand.

"Very well," said Hornblower.

"I'm grateful to you, sir, that I am," said the steersman, and to emphasize his sincerity he swore a couple more oaths. "I've a contract on this here v'yage—that's two chests o' tea for'rard there, first o' the China crop for Lunnon delivery. You'll save me pounds, sir, an' my good name as well. Grateful I am, by—"

He emphasized his sincerity again.

"That's all right," said Hornblower. "The sooner we start the sooner we arrive. What's your name?"

"Jenkins, sir. Tom Jenkins," the steersman—now to be the postillion—tugged at his forelock, "main topman in the old *Superb,* Cap'n Keates, sir."

"Very well, Jenkins. Let's start."

The horseholder tended to the business of attaching the horses' towlines, and while Jenkins cast off the bow line, Hornblower cast off the stern one and stood by with a single turn round the bollard; Jenkins climbed nimbly into the saddle and draped the reins about his hook.

"But, Horatio," said Maria, "whatever are you thinking about?"

"About arriving in London, my dear," said Hornblower, and at that moment the whip cracked and the towlines tightened.

Hornblower had to spring for the sternsheets, line in hand, and he had to grab for the tiller. Maybe Maria was still expostulating, but if she were Hornblower was already far too busy to hear anything she said. It was impressive how quickly the *Queen Charlotte* picked up speed as the horses, suddenly breaking into a trot, pulled her bows up onto her bow wave. From a trot they changed to a canter, and the speed seemed fantastic—far faster, to Hornblower's heated imagination, now that he was at the helm instead of being a mere irresponsible passenger. The banks were flying by; fortunately in this deep cut of the summit level the channel was straight at first, for the steering was not perfectly simple. The two towlines, one at the bow and one at the stern, held the boat parallel to the bank with the smallest use of the rudder—an economic employment of force that appealed to Hornblower's mathematical mind, but which made the feel of the boat a little unnatural as he tentatively tried the tiller.

He looked forward at the approaching bend with some apprehension, and as they neared it he darted his eyes from bank to bank to make sure he was holding in mid-channel. And round the bend, almost upon them, was a bridge—another of these infernal canal bridges, built for economy, with the tow path bulging out under the arch, so that it was hard to sight for the centre of the greatly narrowed channel. Maria was certainly saying something to him, and little Horatio was undoubtedly yelling like a fury, but this was no moment to spare them either a glance or a thought. He steadied the boat round the bend. The hoofs of the lead horse were already ringing on the cobbles under the bridge. God! He was over too far. He tugged the tiller across. Too far the other way! He pushed the tiller back, straightening the boat on her course even as her bows entered the narrows. She turned, very nearly fast enough—her starboard quarter, just where he stood, hit with a solid thump against the elbow of the brick-faced canal side, but she had a thick rope rubbing strake there—presumably to meet situations of this sort—which cushioned the shock; it was not violent enough to throw the passengers off their benches in the cabin, although it nearly threw Hornblower, crouching low under the arch, onto his face. No time to think, not even though little Horatio had apparently been bumped by the shock and was now screaming even more wildly in the bows; the canal was curving back again and he had to guide the *Queen Charlotte* round the bend.

Crack—crack—crack—crack—that was Jenkins with his whip—was not the speed already great enough for him? Round the bend, coming towards them, there was another canal boat, creeping peacefully along towed by a single horse. Hornblower realised that Jenkins' four whip cracks were a signal, demanding a clear passage. He hoped most sincerely and fervently that one would be granted, as the canal boat hastened down upon the barge.

The bargee at the tow horse's head brought the beast to a standstill, edging him over into the hedge beside the tow path; the bargee's wife put her tiller over and the barge swerved majestically, with her residual way, towards the reeds that lined the opposite bank; so between horse and barge the tow rope sank to the ground on the tow path, and into the water in a deep bight. Over the tow rope cantered Jenkins' horses, and Hornblower headed the passage boat for the narrow space between the barge and the tow path. He could guess that the water beside the path was shallow; it was necessary to steer the passage boat to shave the barge as closely as possible, and in any case the bargee's wife, accustomed to encountering skilled steersmen, had only left him the minimum of room. Hornblower was in a fair way towards panic as the passage boat dashed forward.

Starboard—meet her. Port—meet her. He was giving these orders to himself, as he might to his coxswain; like a streak of lightning through the dark confusion of his mind flashed the thought that although he might give the orders he could not trust his clumsy limbs to execute them with the precision of a skilled helmsman. Into the gap now; the stern was still swinging and at the last moment he got the tiller over to check her. The barge seemed to flash by; out of the tail of his eye he was dimly aware of the bargee's wife's greeting, changing to surprise as she noted that the *Queen Charlotte* was being steered by a man quite unknown to her. Faintly to his ear came the sound of what she said, but he could distinguish no word—he had no attention to spare for compliments.

They were through, in that flash, and he could breathe again, he could smile, he could grin; all was well in a marvellous world, steering a passage boat at nine miles an hour along the Thames and Severn Canal. But that was another yell from Jenkins; he was checking his horses, and there was the grey tower of a lock-house ahead. The gates were open, the lock-keeper standing by them. Hornblower steered for them, greatly helped by the *Queen Charlotte's* abrupt reduction in speed as her bow wave passed ahead of her. Hornblower grabbed for the stern rope, leaped for the bank, and miraculously kept his footing. The bollard was ten feet ahead; he ran forward and dropped a loop over it and took the strain. The ideal method was to take nearly all the way off the boat, let her creep into the lock, and stop her fully at the next bollard, but it was too much to hope that he could at his first attempt execute all this exactly. He let the line slip through his hands, watching the boat's progress, and then took too sudden a pull at it. Line and bollard creaked; the *Queen Charlotte* swung her bows across the lock to bump them against the further side, and she lay there half in and half out, helpless, so that the lock-keeper's wife had to run along from the farther gates, lean over, shove the bows clear while seizing the bow line, and, with the line over her sturdy shoulder, haul the boat the final dozen yards into the lock—a clear waste of a couple of minutes. Nor was this all, for, as they had now passed the summit level, this was a downward lock, and Hornblower had not readied his mind for this transition. He was taken by surprise when the *Queen Charlotte* subsided abruptly, with the opening of the gate paddles, along with the emptying water, and he had only just time to slack away the stern line, or else the boat might have been left hanging on it.

"Ee, man, you know little about boats," said the lock-keeper's wife, and Hornblower's ears burned with embarrassment. He thought of the examination he had passed in navigation and seamanship; he thought of how often he had tacked a monstrous ship of the line in heavy weather. That experience was not of much use to him here in inland Gloucestershire—or perhaps it was Oxfordshire by now—and in any case the lock was empty, the gates opening, the towlines tightening, and he had to leap down six feet or more in a hurry into the already moving stern, remembering to take the stern line down with him. He managed it, clumsily as ever, and he heard the lock-keeper's wife's hearty laugh as he glided on below her; and she said something more, too, but he could pay no attention to it, as he had to grab for the tiller and steer the hurrying boat out under the bridge. And when he had first paid for their passages he had pictured to himself the leisurely life of the canal boatman!

And, heavens and earth! Here was Maria beside him, having made her way aft.

"How can you let these people be so insolent to you, dear?" she was asking. "Why don't you tell them who you are?"

"My dear—" began Hornblower, and then stopped.

If Maria could not see the incongruity of a naval captain mishandling a canal boat it was hopeless to argue. Besides, he had no attention to spare for her, not with those cantering horses whisking the *Queen Charlotte* along like this.

"And this all seems very unnecessary, dear," went on Maria. "Why should you demean yourself like this? Is there all this need for haste?"

Hornblower took the boat round a bend—he congratulated himself that he was getting the feel of the tiller now.

"Why don't you answer me?" went on Maria. "And I have our dinner waiting for us, and little Horatio—"

She was like the voice of conscience—for that matter, that was exactly what she was.

"Maria!" snapped Hornblower. "Get for'rard! Get for'rard, I say. Go back to the cabin."

"But, my dear—"

"Get for'rard!"

Hornblower roared this out—here was another barge approaching and he could spare no time for the niceties of married life.

"You are very heartless," said Maria. "And in my condition, too."

Heartless, maybe, but certainly preoccupied. Hornblower pulled the tiller over, and Maria put her handkerchief to her eyes and flounced—as much of a flounce as was possible to her as she was—back into the cabin again. The *Queen Charlotte* shot neatly down the gap between the barge and the tow path, and Hornblower could actually spare enough attention to acknowledge with a wave of his hand the greeting of the bargee's wife. He had time, too, now, for a prick of conscience about his treatment of Maria, but only a momentary one. He still had to steer the boat.

TWO

THERE WAS STILL PLENTY of daylight when they came out into the Thames valley, and Hornblower, looking down to starboard, could see the infant river—not such an infant at its winter level—running below. Every turn and every lock brought the canal nearer to the stream, and at last they reached Inglesham, with Lechlade church steeple in view ahead, and the junction with the river. At Inglesham lock Jenkins left his horses and came back to speak to Hornblower.

"There's three staunches on the river next that we have to run, sir," he said.

Hornblower had no idea what a staunch was, and he very much wanted to know before he had to "run" them, but at the same time he did not want to admit ignorance. Jenkins may have been tactful enough to sense his difficulty; at least he gave an explanation.

"They're dams across the river, sir," he told Hornblower. "At this time o' year, with plenty of water, some o' the paddles are kept out for good, at the tow path end o' the staunch. There's a fall o' five or six feet."

"Five or six feet?" repeated Hornblower, startled.

"Yes, sir. 'Bout that much. But it isn't a real fall, if you know what I mean, sir. Steep, but no more."

"And we have to run down it?"

"Yes, sir. It's easy enough, sir—at the top, leastways."

"And at the bottom?"

"There's an eddy there, sir, like as you'd expect. But if you hold her straight, sir, the nags'll take you through."

"I'll hold her straight," said Hornblower.

"O' course you will, sir."

"But what the devil do they have these staunches on the river for?"

"They keeps back the water for the mills—an' the navigation, sir."

"But why don't they have locks?"

Jenkins spread his hand and his hook in a gesture of ignorance.

"Dunno, sir. There's locks from Oxford down. These 'ere staunches are a plague. Takes six horses to get the old *Queen Charlotte* up 'em, sometimes."

Hornblower's thinking about the subject had not yet progressed as far as wondering about how the staunches were passed upriver; and he was a little annoyed with himself at not having raised the point. But he managed to nod sagely at the information.

"I daresay," he said. "Well, it doesn't concern us this voyage."

"No, sir," said Jenkins. He pointed down the canal. "The first 'un is half a mile below Lechlade Bridge, there. It's well over on the port side. You can't miss it, sir."

Hornblower hoped he was right about that. He took his place in the stern and seized the tiller with a bold attempt to conceal his misgivings, and he waved to the lock-keeper as the boat moved rapidly out of the lock—he was adept enough by now to be able to spare attention for that even with a gate to negotiate. They shot out onto the surface of the young river; there was plenty of current running in their direction—Hornblower noted the eddy at the point—but the speed of the horses gave them plenty of steerage-way.

Lechlade Bridge just ahead of them—the staunch was half a mile beyond, Jenkins said. Although the air was distinctly cold now Hornblower was conscious that his palms, as they rested on the tiller, were distinctly damp. To him now it appeared a wildly reckless thing to do, to attempt to shoot the staunch inexperienced as he was. He would prefer—infinitely prefer—not to try. But he had to steer through the arch of the bridge—the horses splashed fetlock deep there—and then it was too late to do anything about his change of mind. There was the line of the staunch across the stream, the gap in it plainly visible on the port side. Beyond the staunch the surface of the river was not visible because of the drop, but above the gap the water headed down in a steep sleek slope, higher at the sides than in the middle; the fragments which floated on the surface were all hurrying towards it, like people in a public hall all pressing towards a single exit. Hornblower steered for the centre of the gap, choking a little with excitement; he could feel the altered trim of the boat as her bows sank and her stern rose on the slope. Now they were flying down, down. Below, the smooth slope narrowed down to a point, beyond which and on each side was the turbulent water of the eddy. He still had steerage-way enough to steer down the point; as he felt the boat answer the helm he was momentarily tempted to follow up the mathematical line of thought presented by that situation, but he had neither time nor really the inclination. The bows hit the turbulent water with a jar and a splash; the boat lurched in the eddy, but next moment the towlines plucked them forward again.

Two seconds' careful steering and they were through the eddy and gliding over a smooth surface once more, foam-streaked but smooth, and Hornblower was laughing out loud. It had been simple, but so exhilarating that it did not occur to him to condemn himself for his earlier misgivings. Jenkins looked back, turning in his saddle, and waved his whip, and Hornblower waved back.

"Horatio, you *must* come and have your dinner!" said Maria. "And you have left me alone all day."

"Not long before we reach Oxford now, dear," said Hornblower—he was just able to conceal the fact that he had temporarily, until then, forgotten the existence of his wife and child.

"Horatio—"

"In a little while, dear," said Hornblower.

The winter evening was closing round them, the light mellowing while it faded over ploughland and meadow, over the pollard willows knee-deep in the stream, over the farmhouses and cottages. It was all very lovely; Hornblower had the feeling that he did not want this moment ever to end. This was happiness, as his earlier feelings of well-being changed to something more peaceful, just as the surface of the river had changed below the eddy. Soon he would be back in another life again, plunged once more into a world of cruelty and war—the world he had left behind in the tidewater of the Severn and would meet again in the tidewater of the Thames. It was symbolic that it should be here in the centre of England, at the midpoint of his journey, that he should reach this momentary summit of happiness. The cattle in the fields, the rooks in the trees—were they part of this happiness? Possibly, but not certainly. The happiness came from within him, and depended on even more transitory factors than those. Hornblower breathed the evening air as though it were divine poetry and then he noticed Jenkins waving to him from his saddle and pointing with his whip, and the moment was over, lost for ever.

That was the next staunch at which Jenkins was pointing. Hornblower steered boldly for it, without a moment of nervousness; he steadied the boat on her course above it, felt the heave and sudden acceleration as she topped the slope, and grinned with delight as she shot down it, hit the eddy below, and emerged as before after a brief period of indecision. Onward, down the river, through the gathering night. Bridges; another staunch—Hornblower was glad it was the last; there had been much point to what Jenkins had said about needing daylight in which to run them—villages, churches. Now it was quite dark, and he was cold and weary. The next time Maria came aft to him he could address her sympathetically, and even share her indignation that Oxford was so far away. Jenkins had lighted candle-lanterns; one hung on the collar of the lead horse and the other from the cantle of the saddle of the horse he rode. Hornblower, in the sternsheets of the *Queen Charlotte,* saw the specks of light dancing on the tow path—they gave him an indication of the turns the river was making, and just enabled him to steer a safe course, although twice his heart was in his mouth as the side of the boat brushed against the reeds at the river-bank. It was quite dark when Hornblower felt the boat slow up suddenly with the easing of the towlines, and in response to Jenkins' quiet hail he steered the boat towards a lantern-lit landing stage; ready hands took the lines and moored the boat, and the passengers began to swarm out.

"Captain—sir?" said Jenkins.

That was not the way he had used the word "captain" at their first acquaintance. Then it had been with an equalitarian gibe; now he was using the formula and the intonation that would be used by any member of a ship's company addressing his captain.

"Yes?" said Hornblower.

"This is Oxford, sir, and the relief is here."

In the wavering lantern light Hornblower could see the two men indicated.

"So now I can have my dinner?" he asked, with gentle irony.

"That you can, sir, an' it's sorry I am that you have had to wait for it. Sir, I'm your debtor. Sir—"

"Oh, that's all right, Jenkins," said Hornblower testily. "I had my own reasons for wishing to get to London."

"Thank'ee, sir, and—"

"How far to London now?"

"A hunderd miles to Brentford, sir, by the river. You'll be there at the first light. How'll the tide be then, Jem?"

"Just at the flood," said the member of the relief crew holding the whip. "You can take water there, sir, an' be at Whitehall Steps in an hour."

"Thank you," said Hornblower. "I'll say good-bye to you, then, Jenkins."

"Good-bye, sir, and thank'ee agen for a true gennelman."

Maria was standing by the bows of the boat, and even in the dim light Hornblower thought he could detect reproach in her attitude. But it was not immediately apparent in her words.

"I've found you a hot supper, Horatio," was what she said.

"By jingo!" said Hornblower.

Standing on the quay were a few boys and young women come to sell food to the river travellers. The one who caught Hornblower's eye was a sturdy lad with a keg, clearly containing beer, on a barrow, and Hornblower realised that he was consumed with thirst even more acutely than with hunger.

"That's what I want," he said. "Give me a quart."

"On'y pints, sir," said the boy.

"Two pints then, you lubber."

He emptied the first wooden piggin without an effort, without even taking breath, and started on the second, before he remembered his manners. He had honestly been so consumed with thirst that he had forgotten them completely.

"How about you, dear?" he asked Maria.

"I think I'd like half a pint," said Maria—Hornblower could have guessed at her reply beforehand; Maria would think it was a sign of a lady to drink beer only by the half pint.

"On'y pints, sir," said the boy again.

"Well, give the lady a pint and I'll finish it," said Hornblower, his second piggin two-thirds empty.

"All aboard!" called the new steersman. "All aboard!"

"That'll be a shilling, sir," said the boy.

"Eightpence a quart for this beer!" marvelled Maria.

"Cheap at the price," said Hornblower. "Here, boy."

Out of sheer lightness of heart he gave the boy a half crown, and the boy spun it in the air delightedly before putting it in his pocket. Hornblower took the piggin from Maria's hand and drained it and tossed it to the boy.

"All aboard!"

Hornblower stepped down into the boat and elaborately handed Maria down too. He was taken a little aback to find that the *Queen Charlotte* had acquired some more first-class passengers either here or farther back along their route. There were two or three men and half a dozen women sitting in the cabin lit by the light of a lamp; little Horatio was asleep in one corner. Maria was fluttered; she wanted to speak about domestic subjects, but was self-conscious about it in the presence of strangers. She whispered what she had to say, while her hands now and then gesticulated towards the stony-faced strangers to indicate how much more she would have said if there were no fellow passengers.

"That was two and six you gave the boy, dear," she said. "Why did you do it?"

"Just lunacy, my dear, lunacy," said Hornblower, speaking lightheartedly but not so far from the truth.

Maria sighed as she looked at this unpredictable husband of hers who could throw away eighteenpence and talk about lunacy in the hearing of strangers without dropping his voice.

"And here's the supper I bought," said Maria, "while you were talking to the men. I hope it's still hot. You've not had a bite all day, and by now the bread and meat I brought for dinner will be stale."

"I'll eat whatever there is, and more," said Hornblower, with more than a quart of beer inside his otherwise empty stomach.

Maria indicated the two wooden platters awaiting them on the bench beside little Horatio.

"I got out our spoons and forks," explained Maria. "We leave the platters on board here."

"Excellent," said Hornblower.

There were two sausages on each platter, embedded in masses of pease pudding, still steaming. Hornblower sat down with his platter on his lap and began to eat. Those were beef sausages, naturally, if they were not mutton or possibly goat or horse, and they apparently were made from the purest gristle. The skins were as tough as their contents. Hornblower stole a sideways glance at Maria, eating with apparent contentment. He had hurt her feelings several times today and he could not bear to do it again; otherwise he would have pitched those sausages over the side into the river where possibly the fish could deal with them. But as it was he made a valiant effort to eat them. By the time he had started the second he decided it was beyond him. He made his handkerchief ready in his left hand.

"We'll be at the first lock any moment," he said to Maria, with a gesture of his right hand calling her attention to the dark window. Maria tried to peer out, and Hornblower flipped the second sausage into his handkerchief and stuffed it into his side pocket. He caught the eye of the elderly man sitting nearly opposite him across the narrow cabin. This individual had been sitting muffled up in greatcoat and scarf, his hat pressed down low on his forehead, grouchily keeping watch from under his eyebrows at every movement the Hornblowers had made. Hornblower gave him an elaborate wink in reply to the astonishment which replaced the grouchy old gentleman's bad-tempered curiosity. It was not a conspiratorial wink, nor did Hornblower attempt the hopeless task of trying to pretend that he stuffed hot greasy sausages into his pocket every day of his life; the wink simply dared the old gentleman to comment on or even think about the remarkable act. He applied himself to finishing off the pease pudding.

"You eat so fast, dear," said Maria. "It cannot be good for your stomach."

She herself was struggling desperately with her own sausages.

"I'm hungry enough to eat a horse," said Hornblower. "Now I'll start on our dinner, stale or not."

"I am delighted," said Maria. "Let me—"

"No, dear. Sit still. I'll look after myself."

Hornblower took the food parcel and opened it.

"Quite excellent," he said, with his mouth full of bread and meat.

At every moment he was making amends to Maria for his cavalier treatment of her during the day. The larger the meals he ate, the more appetite he evinced, the better Maria was pleased. A little gesture like helping himself to his own dinner gratified her absurdly. He could give her so much happiness; he could hurt her so easily.

"I regret having seen so little of you during the day, dear," he said. "It was my loss. But if I had not helped with the working of the boat we should still be at Sapperton Tunnel."

"Yes, dear," said Maria.

"I would have liked to point out the scenery to you as we passed it," went on Hornblower, battling with the self-contempt that his hypocrisy was arousing. "I trust you enjoyed it even so?"

"Not nearly as much as if you had been with me, dear," said Maria, but gratified beyond all measure. She darted glances at the other women in the cabin to detect the envy they must feel on account of her having such a wonderful husband.

"The boy was good?" asked Hornblower. "He ate his pap?"

"Every bit of it," answered Maria proudly, looking down at the sleeping child. "He was inclined to whimper at times, but now he is sleeping happily."

"If it had been two years from now that we made this journey," said Hornblower, "how interested he would have been! He would have helped with the lines, and I could have taught him to hold the tiller."

Now he was not being hypocritical at all.

"He showed a lively interest even now," said Maria.

"And what about his little sister?" asked Hornblower. "Did she behave well?"

"Horatio!" said Maria, a little scandalised.

"I hope not badly, dear," said Hornblower, smiling away her embarrassment.

"No, excellently," admitted Maria.

They were gliding into a lock; Hornblower heard the rattle of the paddles being let down behind them.

"You made very little progress with your sausages, dear," he said. "Let me dispose of them while you tackle some of this bread and meat, which is really delicious."

"But, dear—"

"I insist."

He took Maria's platter and his own, and stepped out into the bows of the boat in the darkness. It was the work of a moment to give the platters a quick rinse overside, the work of another moment to drop overside the sausage from his pocket; and he returned with the dripping platters to a Maria both scandalised and delighted at the condescension of her husband in thus doing menial work.

"Too dark to enjoy any scenery," he said—already the boat was moving out of the lock—"Maria, my dear, when you have completed your supper I will endeavour to make you as comfortable as is possible for the night."

He bent over the sleeping child while Maria repacked the remains of the supper.

"Now, my dear."

"Horatio, really you should not. Horatio, please, I beg of you—"

"No need for a hat at this time of night. Let's have it off. Now there's plenty of room for you on the bench. Put your feet up here. No need for shoes either. Not a word, now. Now a pillow for your head. The bag will make a good foundation. Comfortable like that? Now, the coat over you to keep you warm. There, now sleep well, my dear."

Maria was carried away by his masterful attentions so that she could not protest. She had lain still for a full two minutes before she opened her eyes again to ask what he was doing for his own comfort.

"I shall be supremely comfortable, my dear. I'm an old campaigner. Now close those eyes again, and sleep in peace, my dear."

Hornblower was by no means supremely comfortable, although he had often spent worse nights, in open boats, for instance. With Maria and the child lying on the thinly cushioned bench he had necessarily to sit upright, as the other passengers were doing. What with the lamp and the breathing of all those people in the cramped little cabin the air was stuffy; his legs were cramped, the small of his back ached, and the part on which he sat protested against bearing his weight unrelieved. But it was only one night to live through, after all. He crammed his hands into his pockets and settled himself again, while the boat went on down the river through the darkness, stopping at intervals at the locks, bumping gently against the walls, gliding forward again. He knew nothing, naturally, of the river between Oxford and London, so he could not guess where they were at any time. But they were heading downstream and towards his new command.

Lucky he was to have a command, he told himself. Not a frigate, but a sloop so big—twenty two guns—as to justify having a captain and not a commander. It was the best that could be hoped for, for the man who a month ago was the six hundred and first captain out of the six hundred and two on the list. Apparently Caldecott, the previous captain of the *Atropos,* had broken down in health while fitting her out at Deptford, which accounted for his unexpected summons thither to replace him. And the orders had no sooner reached him than the news of Nelson's victory at Trafalgar had arrived in England. Since that time no one had had a thought save for Nelson and Trafalgar. The country was wild with delight at the destruction of Villeneuve's fleet, and in the depths of sorrow at Nelson's death. Nelson—Trafalgar—Nelson—Trafalgar—no column in a newspaper, no momentary gossip with a stranger, but contained those names. The country had been lavish with its rewards. A state funeral was promised for Nelson; for the navy there were peerages and knighthoods and promotions. With the re-creation of the rank of Admiral of the Red, twenty new admirals had been promoted from the top of the captains' list; two captains had fallen at Trafalgar, and two more had died; so that Hornblower was now the five hundred and seventy seventh captain in seniority. But at the same time promotion had been lavish among the commanders and lieutenants. There were forty one new captains on the list—there was something gratifying in the thought that now he was senior to forty two captains. But it meant that now there were six hundred and nineteen captains seeking employment, and even in the vast Royal Navy there were not enough vacancies for all those. A hundred at least—more likely a hundred and fifty—would be on half pay awaiting employment. That was as it should be, one might think. That proportion not only made allowance for sickness and old age among the captains, but also made it unnecessary to employ those who had been proved to be inefficient.

Unless the inefficient had friends in high places—then it would be the friendless, and the unfortunate who languished on half pay. Hornblower knew himself to be friendless, and even though he had just been congratulating himself on his good fortune he always thought himself ultimately doomed to misfortune. He was on his way to take over a ship that someone else had fitted out, with officers and men he knew nothing of; those facts were sufficient basis on which his gloomy pessimism could build itself.

Maria sighed and turned herself on the bench; Hornblower crept down to her to rearrange the heavy coat over her body.

THREE

AT BRENTFORD, in the early light of the winter's morning, it was cold and damp and gloomy. Little Horatio whimpered ceaselessly; Maria was uncomfortable and weary, as she stood beside Hornblower while her trunk and Hornblower's two sea-chests were being hoisted out of the boat.

"Is it far to Deptford, my dear?" she asked.

"Far enough," said Hornblower; between Brentford and Deptford lay the whole extent of London and much more besides, while the river on which they were to travel wound sinuously in wide curves, backwards and forwards. And they had arrived late, and the tide would barely serve.

The wherrymen were soliciting for his custom.

"Boat, sir? Sculls, sir? Oars, sir?"

"Oars," said Hornblower.

It cost twice as much for a wherry rowed by two oarsmen as for one rowed by a single man with sculls, but with the ebbing tide it was worth it. Hornblower helped Maria and the baby down into the sternsheets and looked on while the baggage was handed down.

"Right, Bill. Give way," said stroke-oar, and the wherry shot away from the slip out onto the grey river.

"Ooh," said Maria, a little afraid.

The oars ground in the rowlocks, the boat danced on the choppy water.

"They say the old King's fair 'mazed, sir, at Lord Nelson's death," said stroke, with a jerk of his hand towards Kew, across the river. "That's where he lives, sir. In the Palace there."

"Yes," said Hornblower; in no mood to discuss the King or Lord Nelson or anyone else.

The wind was brisk and westerly; had it been easterly the river would have been far more choppy, and their progress would be delayed, so there was something at least to be said in favour of this grey world.

"Easy, 'Arry," said bow, and the wherry began to round the bend.

"Hush, baby. Don't you like the nasty boat?" said Maria to little Horatio, who was making it plain that Maria had guessed at the truth of the matter.

"Nipper's cold, likely," volunteered stroke.

"I think he is," agreed Maria.

The boatman and Maria fell into conversation, to Hornblower's relief; he could immerse himself in his thoughts then, in his hopes and his apprehensions—the latter predominating—about his ship that awaited him down-river. It would only be an hour or two before he would go on board. Ship, officers, and crew were all unknown to him.

"The Dook lives there, ma'am," said the boatman, through little Horatio's yells, "an' you can see the Bishop's Palace through the trees."

This was Maria's first visit to London; it was convenient that they should have a loquacious boatman.

"See the pretty houses," said Maria, dancing the baby in her arms. "Look at the pretty boats."

The houses were getting thicker and thicker; they shot bridge after bridge, and the boat traffic on the river was growing dense, and suddenly Hornblower became aware they were at London's edge.

"Westminster, ma'am," said the boatman. "I used to ply on the ferry here until they built the bridge. A ha'penny toll took the bread out of the mouths of many an honest boatman then."

"I should think so, indeed," said Maria, sympathetically. By now she had forgotten the dignity of her position as a captain's wife.

"White'all Steps, ma'am, and that 'ere's the Strand."

Hornblower had taken boat to Whitehall Steps often, during those bitter days of half pay when he was soliciting employment from the Admiralty.

"Saint Paul's, ma'am."

Now they were really within the City of London. Hornblower could smell the smoke of the coal fires.

"Easy, 'Arry," said bow again, looking back over his shoulder. Boats, lighters, and barges covered the surface of the river, and there was London Bridge ahead of them.

"Give way, 'ard," said bow, and the two oarsmen pulled desperately through a gap in the traffic above the bridge. Through the narrow arches the tide ran fast; the river was piled up above the constriction of the bridge. They shot down through the narrow opening.

"Goodness!" said Maria.

And here was the greatest port in the world; ships at anchor, ships discharging cargo, with only the narrowest channel down the centre.

North-country collier brigs, Ramsgate trawlers, coasters, grain ships, with the grey Tower looking down on them.

"The Pool's always a rare sight, ma'am," said stroke. "Even wi' the war an' all."

All this busy shipping was the best proof that Bonaparte across the water was losing his war against England. England could never be conquered while the navy dominated the sea, strangling the Continental powers while allowing free passage to British commerce.

Below the Pool lay a ship of war, idly at anchor, topmasts sent down, hands at work on stages overside painting. At her bows was a crude figurehead of a draped female painted in red and white; in her clumsily carved hands she carried a large pair of gilded shears, and it was those which told Hornblower what the ship was, before he could count the eleven gunports aside, before they passed under her stern and he could read her name, *Atropos*. He choked down his excitement as he stared at her, taking note of her trim and her lines, of the petty officer of the anchor watch—of everything that in that piercing moment he could possibly observe.

"*Atropos*, twenty two," said stroke-oar, noting Hornblower's interest.

"My husband is captain of her," said Maria proudly.

"Indeed, sir?" answered stroke, with a new respect that must have been gratifying to Maria.

Already the boat was swinging round; there was Deptford Creek and Deptford Hard.

"Easy!" said bow. "Give way again. Easy!"

The boat rasped against the shore, and the journey from Gloucester was over. No, not over, decided Hornblower preparing to disembark. There was now all the tedious business before them of getting a lodging, taking their baggage there, and settling Maria in before he could get to his ship. Life was a succession of pills that had to be swallowed. He paid the boatman under Maria's watchful eye; fortunately a riverside lounger came to solicit custom, and produced a barrow on which he piled the luggage. Hornblower took Maria's arm and helped her up the slippery Hard as she carried the baby.

"Glad I'll be," said Maria, "to take these shoes off. And the sooner little Horatio is changed the better. There, there, darling."

Only the briefest walk, luckily, took them to the George. A plump landlady received them, running a sympathetic eye over Maria's condition. She took them up to a room while a maid under her vigorous urgings sped to get hot water and towels.

"There, my poppet," said the landlady to little Horatio.

"Ooh," said Maria, sitting down on the bed and already beginning to take off her shoes.

Hornblower was standing by the door waiting for his sea-chests to be brought up.

"When are you expecting, ma'am?" asked the landlady.

It seemed not a moment before she and Maria were discussing midwives and the rising cost of living—the latter subject introduced by Maria's determination to chaffer over the price of the room. The potman and the riverside lounger carried the baggage up and put it down on the floor of the room, interrupting the discussion. Hornblower took out his keys and knelt eagerly at his chest.

"Horatio, dear," said Maria, "we're speaking to you."

"Eh—what?" asked Hornblower absently over his shoulder.

"Something hot, sir, while breakfast is preparing?" asked the landlady. "Rum punch? A dish o' tea?"

"Not for me, thank you," said Hornblower.

He had his chest open by now and was unpacking it feverishly.

"Cannot that wait until we've had breakfast, dear?" asked Maria. "Then I could do it for you."

"I fear not, ma'am," said Hornblower, still on his knees.

"Your best shirts! You're crumpling them," protested Maria.

Hornblower was dragging out his uniform coat from beneath them. He laid the coat on the other chest and searched for his epaulette.

"You're going to your ship!" exclaimed Maria.

"Of course, my dear," said Hornblower.

The landlady was out of the room and conversation could run more freely.

"But you must have your breakfast first!" expostulated Maria.

Hornblower made himself see reason.

"Five minutes for breakfast, then, after I've shaved," he said.

He laid out his coat on the bed, with a frown at its creases, and he unlatched the japanned box which held his cocked hat. He threw off the coat he was wearing and undid, feverishly, his neckcloth and stock. Little Horatio decided at that moment to protest again against a heartless world, and Hornblower unrolled his housewife and took out his razor and addressed himself to shaving while Maria attended to the baby.

"I'll take Horatio down for his bread and milk, dear," said Maria.

"Yes, dear," said Hornblower through the lather.

The mirror caught Maria's reflection, and he forced himself back into the world again. She was standing pathetically looking at him, and he put down his razor, and took up the towel and wiped the lather from his mouth.

"Not a kiss since yesterday!" he said. "Maria, darling, don't you think you've been neglecting me?"

She came to his outheld arms; her eyes were wet, but the gentleness of his voice and the lightness of his tone brought a smile to her lips despite her tears.

"I thought I was the neglected one," she whispered.

She kissed him eagerly, possessively, her hands at his shoulders, holding him to her swollen body.

"I have been thinking about my duty," he said to her, "to the exclusion of the other things I should have thought about. Can you forgive me, dearest?"

"Forgive!" The smile and the tears were both more evident as she spoke. "Don't say that, darling. Do what you will—I'm yours, I'm yours."

Hornblower felt a wave of real tenderness rise within him as he kissed her again; the happiness, the whole life, of a human creature depended on his patience and his tact. His wiping off of the lather had not been very effective; there were smears of it on Maria's face.

"Sweetness," he said, "that makes you my very dearest possession."

And while he kissed her he thought of *Atropos* riding to her anchor out there in the river, and despised himself as a hypocritical unfaithful lover. But his concealment of his impatience brought its reward, for when little Horatio began to wail again it was Maria who drew back first.

"The poor lamb!" she said, and quitted Hornblower's arms to go and attend to him. She looked up at her husband from where she bent over the child, and smiled at him. "I must see that both of these men of mine are fed."

There was something Hornblower had to say, but it called for tact, and he fumbled in his mind before he found the right way to say it.

"Dearest," he said. "I do not mind if the whole world knows I have just kissed you, but I fear lest you would be ashamed."

"Goodness!" said Maria, grasping his meaning and hurrying to the mirror to wipe off the smears of lather. Then she snatched up the baby. "I'll see that your breakfast is ready when you come down."

She smiled at him with so much happiness in her face, and she blew him a kiss before she left the room. Hornblower turned again to renew the lather and prepare himself for going on board. His mind was full of his ship, his wife, his child, and the child to be. The fleeting happiness of yesterday was forgotten; perhaps, not being aware that he was unhappy now, he could be deemed happy today as well, but he was not a man with a gift for happiness.

With breakfast finished at last he took boat again at the Hard to go the short distance to his ship; as he sat in the sternsheets he settled his cocked hat with its gold loop and button, and he let his cloak hang loose to reveal the epaulette on his right shoulder that marked him as a captain of less than three years' seniority. He momentarily tapped his pocket to make sure that his orders were in it, and then sat upright in the boat with all the dignity he could muster. He could imagine what was happening in *Atropos*—the master's mate of the watch catching sight of the cocked hat and the epaulette, the messenger scurrying to tell the first lieutenant, the call for sideboys and bosun's mates, the wave of nervousness and curiosity that would pass over the ship at the news that the new captain was about to come on board. The thought of it made him smile despite his own nervousness and curiosity.

"Boat ahoy!" came the hail from the ship.

The boatman gave an inquiring glance at Hornblower, received a nod in return, and turned to hail back with a pair of lungs of leather.

"*Atropos!*"

That was positive assurance to the ship that this was her captain approaching.

"Lay her alongside," said Hornblower.

Atropos sat low in the water, flush-decked; the mizzen chains were within easy reach of Hornblower where he stood. The boatman coughed decorously.

"Did you remember my fare, sir?" he asked, and Hornblower had to find coppers to pay him.

Then he went up the ship's side, refusing, as far as his self-control would allow, to let the incident fluster him. He tried to conceal his excitement as he reached the deck amid the twittering of the pipes, with his hand to his hatbrim in salute, but he was not capable of seeing with clarity the faces that awaited him there.

"John Jones, first lieutenant," said a voice. "Welcome aboard, sir."

Then there were other names, other faces as vague as the names. Hornblower checked himself from swallowing in his excitement for fear lest it should be noticed. He went to some pains to speak in a tone of exactly the right pitch.

"Call the ship's company, Mr. Jones, if you please."

"All hands! All hands!"

The cry went through the ship while the pipes twittered and squealed again. There was a rush of feet, a bustling and a subdued murmur. Now there was a sea of faces before him in the waist, but he was still too excited to observe them in detail.

"Ship's company assembled, sir."

Hornblower touched his hat in reply—he had to assume that Jones had touched his hat to him, for he was not aware of it—and took out his orders and began to read.

"Orders from the Commissioners for executing the office of Lord High Admiral of Great Britain and Ireland, addressed to Captain Horatio Hornblower of His Majesty's Navy. You are hereby required—"

He read them through to the end, folded them, and returned them to his pocket. Now he was legally captain of the *Atropos*, holding a position of which only a court-martial—or an Act of Parliament—could deprive him. And from this moment his half pay ceased and he would begin to draw the pay of a captain of a Sixth-Rate. Was it significant that it was from this moment the mists began to clear from before his eyes? Jones was a lantern-jawed man, his close-shaven beard showing blue through his tan. Hornblower met his eyes.

"Dismiss the ship's company, Mr. Jones."

"Aye aye, sir."

This might have been the moment for a speech, Hornblower knew. It was even customary to make one. But he had prepared nothing to say; and he told himself it was better to say nothing. He had it in mind that he would give a first impression of someone cold and hard and efficient and unsentimental. He turned to the waiting group of lieutenants; now he could distinguish their features, recognise that they were distinct individuals, these men whom he would have to trust and use for years in the future; but their names had escaped him completely. He had really heard nothing of them in those excited seconds after arriving on the quarterdeck.

"Thank you, gentlemen," he said to them. "We shall know each other better soon, I do not doubt."

There was a touching of hats and a general turning away of them all except Jones.

"There's an Admiralty letter waiting for you, sir," said the latter.

An Admiralty letter! Orders! The key to the future, which would reveal what was to be their fate—the words which might despatch him and the *Atropos* to China or Greenland or Brazil. Hornblower felt his excitement surge up again—it had hardly subsided in any case. Once more he checked himself from swallowing.

"Thank you, Mr. Jones. I'll read it as soon as I have leisure."

"Would you care to come below, sir?"

"Thank you."

The captain's quarters in the *Atropos* were as minute as Hornblower had expected: the smallest possible day-cabin and night-cabin. They were so small that they were not bulkheaded off from one another; a curtain was supposed to be hung between them, but there was no curtain. There was nothing at all—no cot, no desk, no chair, nothing. Apparently Caldecott had made a clean sweep of all his belongings when he left the ship. There was nothing surprising about that, but it was inconvenient. The cabin was dark and stuffy, but as the ship was newly out of dry dock she had not yet acquired all the manifold smells which would impregnate her later.

"Where are these orders?" demanded Hornblower, brusque with his suppressed excitement.

"In my desk, sir. I'll fetch 'em at once."

It could not be too quickly for Hornblower, who stood under the little skylight awaiting Jones' return. He took the sealed package into his hand and stood holding it for a moment. This was an instant of transition. The journey of the last twenty four hours had been a longer period, but of the same kind—an interval between one kind of activity and another. The next few seconds would eventually transform the *Atropos* from an idle ship in the Thames to an active ship at sea, lookouts at the mastheads, guns ready for action, peril and adventure and death only just over the horizon if not alongside. Hornblower broke the seal—the foul anchor of the Admiralty, the most inappropriate emblem conceivable for a nation that ruled the sea. Looking up, he met Jones' eyes, as the first lieutenant waited anxiously to hear what their fate was to be. Hornblower knew now that he should have sent Jones away before breaking the seal, but it was too late now. Hornblower read the opening lines—he could have announced beforehand what would be the first six words, or even the first twelve.

> You are hereby requested and required, immediately upon receipt of these orders—

This was the moment; Hornblower savoured it for one half of one second.

—to wait upon Henry Pallender, Esq., Blue Mantle Pursuivant at Arms, at the College of Heralds—

"God bless my soul!" said Hornblower.

"What is it, sir?" asked Jones.

"I don't know yet," answered Hornblower.

—there to consult with him upon the arrangements to be made for the funeral Procession by water of the late Vice Admiral Lord Viscount Nelson.

"So that's it," said Hornblower.

"It's *what,* sir?" asked Jones, but Hornblower could not spare the time at present to enlighten him.

You will take upon yourself, by the authority of these orders, the command of all officers, seamen, and Royal Marines to be engaged in the Procession aforesaid, likewise of all vessels, boats, and barges belonging to the Cities of London and Westminster and to the City Companies. You will issue all the orders necessary for the Procession to be conducted in a seamanlike manner. You will, by your consultations with Henry Pallender, Esq., aforesaid, ascertain the requirements of Ceremonial and Precedence, but you are hereby charged, upon your peril, to pay strict attention to conditions of Tide and Weather so that not only may Ceremonial be observed, but also that no Danger or Damage may be incurred by the boats, barges, and vessels aforesaid, nor by their Crews and Passengers.

"Please, sir. *Please,* sir," said Jones.

Hornblower's thoughts came back into the little cabin.

"These are orders for me personally," he said. "Oh—very well, you can read them if you wish to."

Jones read them with moving lips and finally looked up at Hornblower with a bewildered expression.

"So the ship stays here, sir?" he asked.

"She certainly does. She is from this moment the flagship of the funeral procession," said Hornblower. "I shall need a boat and boat's crew at once. Oh yes, pen and paper to send a message to my wife."

"Aye aye, sir."

"See there's a good petty officer in the boat. She'll be waiting a good deal ashore."

"Aye aye, sir. We're having men run every day."

Of course desertion could be a very serious problem in a ship anchored here in the river, within swimming distance of shore and innumerable boats plying about, with the whole City of London close at hand into which a deserter might disappear. And there could be the question of liquor being surreptitiously sold on board from shore boats. And Hornblower had been on board for a full ten minutes and he was no wiser about the things he most wanted to know—about how *Atropos* was manned and officered, what she lacked, what was her material condition—than he had been yesterday. But all the problems with which he was so anxious to deal must for the moment be shelved, to be dealt with at intervals when this new strange duty permitted. The mere question of the furnishing of his cabin might demand more attention than he could spare at present. Hornblower knew from the newspaper he had read yesterday that Nelson's body was at the Nore, awaiting a fair wind before being brought up to Greenwich. Time was pressing, and there were orders in hundreds to be written, he did not doubt.

And so the moment of transition was over. If he had been allowed a thousand guesses as to what his orders would contain, he would never have thought of this particular duty. He could laugh about it if it were not so serious. He could laugh in any case, and he did. After a moment's glance of surprise Mr. Jones decided that he should laugh too, and did so, obsequiously.

FOUR

"BLACK BREECHES?" asked Hornblower, startled.

"Of course. Black breeches and stockings, and mourning bands," said Mr. Pallender solemnly.

He was an aged man, and although the top of his head was bald he wore the remainder of his white hair long, clubbed at the nape of his neck in a thick short queue tied with black ribbon. He had pale blue eyes, rheumy with age, and a thin pointed nose which in the chill of the room bore a small drop at its reddish tip—perhaps always bore one.

Hornblower made a note on the sheet of paper before him regarding the black breeches and stockings and mourning bands. He also made a mental note that he would have to obtain these things for himself as well, and he wondered where the money was coming from to do it.

"It would be best," went on Mr. Pallender, "if the procession were to pass through the City at midday. Then the populace will have plenty of time to assemble, and the apprentices can do a morning's work."

"I can't promise that," said Hornblower. "It depends on the tide."

"The tide, Captain Hornblower? You must realise that this is a ceremonial in which the Court—His Majesty himself—is deeply interested."

"But it has to depend on the tide all the same," said Hornblower. "And even on the winds too."

"Indeed? His Majesty will be most provoked if his ideas are scouted."

"I see," said Hornblower.

He thought of remarking that although His Majesty ruled the waves he had no more control over the tides than had his illustrious predecessor King Canute, but he thought better of it. Mr. Pallender was not the type to appreciate jokes about the limitations of the royal power. Instead Hornblower decided to imitate Mr. Pallender's solemnity.

"Since the actual day of the ceremonial hasn't yet been decided upon," he said, "it might be possible to choose such a day as the tide serves best."

"I suppose so," conceded Mr. Pallender.

Hornblower made a note of the necessity of immediately consulting the tide-tables.

"The Lord Mayor," said Mr. Pallender, "will not be present in person, but his representative will."

"I understand."

There would be some small relief in not being responsible for the person of the Lord Mayor, but not much, seeing that the eight most senior admirals in the navy were going to be present, and were going to be his responsibility.

"Are you sure you won't try a little of this brandy?" asked Mr. Pallender, giving the decanter a little push.

"No, thank you."

Hornblower had no desire at all to drink brandy at this time of day; but now he knew what gave Mr. Pallender's nose that reddish tip. Mr. Pallender sipped appreciatively before going on.

"Now as regards the minute guns—"

Along the processional route apparently there were fifteen points at which minute guns were to be fired, and His Majesty would be listening to see that they were properly timed. Hornblower covered more paper with notes. There would be thirty eight boats and barges in the procession, to be assembled in the tricky tideway at Greenwich, marshalled in order, brought up to Whitehall Steps, and dispersed again after delivering over the body to a naval guard of honour assembled there which would escort it to the Admiralty to lie there for the night before the final procession to St. Paul's.

"Can you tell me, sir," asked Hornblower, "what kind of vessel these ceremonial barges are?"

He regretted the question as soon as he asked it; Mr. Pallender showed surprise that any man should not be familiar with ceremonial barges, but as for knowing how handy they were in choppy water, or even how many oars aside they rowed, that was of course more than could be expected of Mr. Pallender. Hornblower realised that the sooner he took one over, and rowed it over the course of the procession in the appropriate tidal conditions, timing every stage, the better. He went on adding to his pages of notes while Mr. Pallender went on with what to him was most important—the order of precedence of the boats; how the whole College of Heralds would be present, including Norroy King of Arms and himself, Blue Mantle Pursuivant; the royal dukes and the admirals; the formalities to be observed at the embarkation and the landing; the Chief Mourner and the trainbearer, the pallbearers and the Family of the Deceased.

"Thank you, sir," said Hornblower at last, gathering up his notes. "I will begin these preparations at once."

"Greatly obliged, I'm sure, sir," said Mr. Pallender, as Hornblower took his leave.

This was an operation as elaborate as Abercrombie's landing on the Egyptian coast—and in the Mediterranean there were no tides to complicate arrangements. Thirty eight boats with their crews and oarsmen; guards of honour; mourners and officials; there would be a thousand officers and men at least under Hornblower's command. And Hornblower's heart sank a little when he was able to take one of the barges from the hands of the workmen who were attaching the insignia to it in Deptford Yard, and conduct his own trials with it. It was a vast clumsy vessel, not much smaller and no more manageable than a cargo lighter. Forward in the open bows she pulled twelve oars; from midships aft she was covered with a vast canopy of solid construction, exposing an enormous area to the wind. The barge allotted to the conveyance of the Body (Mr. Pallender had made that capital letter quite obvious in their discussion) was being so covered with plumes that she would catch the wind like a frigate's mainsail. There must be lusty oarsmen detailed to the task of rowing that barge along—and it would be best to have as nearly complete a relief available as possible, hidden away under the canopy. But as she would head the procession, with the other boats taking station upon her, he must be careful not to overdo that. He must time everything exactly—up with the flood tide, arriving at Whitehall Steps precisely at slack water so that the complicated manoeuvres there could be carried out with the minimum of risk, and then back with the ebb, dispersing barges and crews along the route as convenient.

"My dear," said Maria to him, in their bedroom at the George, "I fear I have little of your attention at present."

"Your pardon, dear?" said Hornblower, looking round from the table at which he was writing. He was deep in plans for issuing a solid breakfast to a thousand men who would have small chance of eating again all day.

"I was telling you that I spoke to the midwife today. She seems a worthy woman. She will hold herself free from tomorrow. As she lives only in the next street there is no need for her to take up residence here until the time comes, which is fortunate—you know how little money we have, Horatio."

"Yes, dear," said Hornblower. "Have those black breeches of mine been delivered yet?"

It was a perfectly natural step from Maria's approaching confinement to Hornblower's black breeches, via the question of money, but Maria resented her husband's apparent heartlessness.

"Do you care more for your breeches than for your child?" she asked, "or for me?"

"Dearest," answered Hornblower. He had to put down his pen and rise from his chair to comfort her. "I have much on my mind. I can't tell you how much I regret it at this moment."

This was the very devil. The eyes not only of London but of all England would be on that procession. He would never be forgiven if there was any blunder. But he had to take Maria's hands in his and reassure her.

"You, my dear," he said, smiling into her eyes, "are my all in all. There is nothing in my world as important as you are."

"I wish I could be sure," said Maria.

He kissed the hands he held.

"What can I say to make you sure?" he asked. "That I love you?"

"That would be pleasant enough," said Maria.

"I love you, dear," he said, but he had not had a smile from her as yet, and he went on, "I love you more dearly even than my new black breeches."

"Oh!" said Maria.

He had to labour the point to make sure that she understood he was both joking and tender.

"More dearly than a thousand pair of black breeches," he said. "Could any man say more?"

She was smiling now, and she took her hands from his and laid them on his shoulders.

"Is that a compliment for me to treasure always?" she asked.

"It will always be true, my dear," he said.

"You are the kindest of husbands," she said, and the break in her voice showed that she meant it.

"With the sweetest of wives," he answered. "And now may I go on with my work?"

"Of course, darling. Of course. I fear I am selfish. But—but—darling, I love you so. I love you so!"

"There, there," said Hornblower patting her shoulder. Perhaps he felt as strongly over this business as Maria did, but he had much else to feel strongly about. And if he mismanaged these ceremonial arrangements the child to come might go on short commons with him on half pay for life. And Nelson's body was at this very moment lying in state at Greenwich, and the day after tomorrow was the date fixed for the procession, with the tide beginning to flood at eleven, and there was still much to be done. He was glad to get back to the writing of his orders. He was glad to go back on board *Atropos* and plunge into business there.

"Mr. Jones, I'd be glad if you'd call the midshipmen and master's mates. I need half a dozen who can write a fair round hand."

The cabin of the *Atropos* took on the appearance of a schoolroom, with the midshipmen sitting on mess stools at improvised tables, with inkwells and pens, copying out Hornblower's drafts of the orders, and Hornblower going from one to another, like a squirrel in a cage, answering questions.

"Please, sir, I can't read this word."

"Please, sir, do I start a new paragraph here?"

It was one way of finding out something of the junior officers, of distinguishing them as individuals out of what had been so far a formless mass of officers; there were the ones who appealed for help at every turn, and the ones who could make deductions from the context; there were the stupid ones who wrote orders that made nonsense.

"Damn it, man," said Hornblower, "would anyone out of Bedlam say a thing like that—far less write it?"

"That's what it looked like, sir," said the midshipman stubbornly.

"God help us all!" said Hornblower in despair.

But that was the man who wrote a very clear hand; Hornblower put him onto the task of writing the beginnings of each letter:

H.M.S. *Atropos* at Deptford
January 6th 1806

SIR,

By virtue of the powers entrusted to me by the Lords Commissioners of the Admiralty—

Other men could carry on from there, with a saving of time. The ninety different written orders with their duplicates were written at last, and distributed by midnight; crews and petty officers had been found from various sources for every boat that was to take part in the procession, rations allotted to them, their place in the line clearly stated —"You will take the seventeenth position, immediately after the barge of the Commander-in-chief at the Nore and immediately preceding that of the Worshipful Company of Fishmongers."

The final arrangements were made with Mr. Pallender at two in the morning of the day of the procession, and Hornblower, yawning, could think of nothing else to be done. Yes, there was a final change to be made.

"Mr. Horrocks, you will come with me with the Body in the first barge. Mr. Smiley, you'll command the second with the Chief Mourner."

Horrocks was the stupidest of the midshipmen and Smiley the brightest—it had been natural to reserve the latter for himself, but now he realised how stupid Horrocks was, and how necessary it was to keep him under his own eye.

"Aye aye, sir."

Hornblower fancied Smiley looked pleased at thus escaping from the direct supervision of his captain, and he pricked that bubble.

"You'll have nine admirals and four captains as passengers, Mr. Smiley," he said. "Including Admiral of the Fleet Sir Peter Parker and Lord St. Vincent."

Smiley did not look nearly as pleased at that.

"Mr. Jones, have the longboat with the hands at Greenwich Pier at six o'clock, if you please."

"Aye aye, sir."

"And call away the gig for me now."

"Aye aye, sir."

"I'll be at the George until five. Send any messages there."

"Aye aye, sir."

He still had a personal life; Maria was very near her time now.

On deck there was a brisk westerly wind harping in the rigging, gusty, Hornblower noted. The barges would call for careful handling unless it dropped considerably. He stepped down into the gig.

"Make for Deptford Hard," he ordered the coxswain, and clasped his coat close tightly round him, for the cabin of the *Atropos* had been hot with lamps and candles and many people. He walked up the Hard and knocked at the door of the George; from the window at the side there was a faint light showing and the window of their room above was illuminated. The door opened to reveal the landlady.

"Oh, it's you, sir. I thought it was the midwife. I've just sent Davie for her. Your good lady—"

"Let me by," said Hornblower.

Maria was walking about the bedroom in her dressing gown; two candles illuminated the room, and the shadows of the bed-tester and the other furniture moved in sinister fashion as Hornblower opened the door.

"Darling!" said Maria.

Hornblower came towards her, his hands held out.

"I hope all is well with you, dear," he said.

"I think so. I—I hope so. It has only just begun," said Maria.

They kissed.

"Darling," said Maria. "How good of you to come here. I—I was hoping I should see you again before—before—my time came."

"Not good of me," said Hornblower. "I came because I wanted to come. I wanted to see you."

"But you are so busy. Today is the day of the procession, is it not?"

"Yes," said Hornblower.

"And our child will be born today. A little girl, dear? Or another little boy?"

"We'll know soon," said Hornblower. He knew which Maria wanted. "Whichever it is we'll love her—or him."

"That we shall," said Maria.

The last syllable was jerked out of her more forcibly than necessary, and Maria's face took on an expression of preoccupation.

"How is it, dearest?" asked Hornblower, concerned.

"Only a pain," said Maria, smiling—forcing a smile, as Hornblower well knew. "They are not coming close together yet."

"I wish I could help," said Hornblower, in the manner of uncounted millions of fathers.

"You have helped by coming to me, my darling," said Maria.

A bustle outside the door and a knock heralded the entrance of the midwife and the landlady.

"Well, well," said the midwife. "So it has begun, has it?"

Hornblower looked her over carefully. She was not neat—no one could be expected to be in those conditions—but she was at least sober, and her gap-toothed smile was kindly.

"I'll have a look at you, ma'am," said the midwife, and then, with a sidelong glance, "gentleman will retire."

Maria looked at him. She was trying so hard to appear unconcerned.

"I'll see you again, dear," said Hornblower, trying equally hard.

Outside the bedroom the landlady was cordial in her offers of hospitality.

"How about a go of brandy, sir? Or a glass o' rum, hot?"

"No, thank you," said Hornblower.

"The young gennelman's sleeping in with one o' the maids now," explained the landlady. "He didn't cry, no, not a sound, when we carried him in. A fine little fellow he is, sir."

"Yes," said Hornblower. He could smile at the thought of his little son.

"You'd better come into the coffee-room, sir," said the landlady. "There's still what's left of the fire there."

"Thank you," said Hornblower, with a glance at his watch. God, how time was passing!

"Your good lady will be all right," said the landlady maternally. "It'll be a boy, as sure as fate. I can tell by the way she was carrying."

"Perhaps you'll be right," said Hornblower, and he looked at his watch again. He really must start preparations for the day.

"Now see here, please," he said, and then he paused, as he made his mind clear itself of its preoccupation with Maria, and of its deadly fatigue. He began to list the things he needed from the bedroom upstairs, ticking them off on his fingers as he told them to the landlady. The black breeches and stockings, the epaulette and the best cocked hat, the sword and the mourning band.

"I'll get 'em, sir. You can dress in here—no one won't disturb you, not at this time o' night."

She came back later with her arms full of the things Hornblower had asked for.

"A marvel that I should forget this was the day of the Funeral, sir," she said. "No one hasn't talked o' nothing else along the river not for the last week. There's your things, sir."

She looked closely at Hornblower in the candlelight.

"You'd better shave, sir," she went on. "You can use my husband's razor if yours is in the ship."

One mention of maternity, it seemed, turned all women into mothers.

"Very well," said Hornblower.

Later he was dressed and looking at his watch again.

"I must leave now," he said. "Will you find out if I can see my wife?"

"I'll tell you now you can't, sir," said the landlady. "Not if you can hear what I can hear."

Much of what Hornblower felt must have shown in his expression, for the landlady went on—

"It'll all be over in a hower, sir: whyn't you wait a bit?"

"Wait?" repeated Hornblower, looking at his watch again. "No, I can't do that. I'll have to go."

The landlady lighted the candle of his lantern at that on the coffee-room mantel.

"Lord a mercy," she said. "You look just the picture. But it's cold out."

She fastened the button of his coat close at his neck.

"Can't have you catching cold. There! Don't you worry, now."

Good advice, thought Hornblower, walking down the slope towards the river again, but as difficult to act upon as most good advice. He saw the light of the gig at the water's edge, and a sudden movement of shadowy figures there. The gig's crew must have appointed one of its members to keep watch for his lantern, while the others snatched what sleep they could in the exceedingly uncomfortable spaces of the gig. But however uncomfortable they were, they were better off than he was. He felt he could sleep on the bobstay of the *Atropos* if only he had the chance. He got into the gig.

"Down river," he ordered the coxswain.

At Greenwich Pier it was still dark, no sign as yet of the late January dawn. And the wind was blowing steadily from the west, downstream. It would probably freshen as the day went on. A loud challenge halted him as he walked down the pier.

"Friend," said Hornblower, opening his cloak for his lantern to show his uniform.

"Advance and give the countersign!"

"The Immortal Memory," said Hornblower—he had chosen that countersign himself; one detail out of a thousand details of the day before.

"Pass, friend. All's well," said the sentry.

He was a private in the Blackheath Militia; during the time the Body had been lying in state at Greenwich there had had to be guards posted at all points to prevent the public from straying into the areas where they were not wanted. The Hospital was lighted up; there was already bustle and excitement there.

"The Governor's dressing now, sir," said a wooden-legged lieutenant. "We're expecting the quality at eight."

"Yes," said Hornblower. "I know."

It was he who had drawn up the timetable; the national, naval, and civic dignitaries were to come by road from London, to accompany the Body back by water. And here was the Body, in its coffin, the trestles on which it lay concealed by flags and trophies and heraldic insignia. And here came the Governor, limping with his rheumatism, his bald head shining in the lamplight.

"Morning, Hornblower."

"Good morning, sir."

"Everything settled?"

"Yes, sir. But the wind's blowing very fresh from the west. It'll hold back the flood."

"I feared as much."

"It will delay the boats, too, of course, sir."

"Of course."

"In that case, sir, I'd be obliged if you would do all you can to see that the Mourners leave in time. There'll be little to spare, sir."

"I'll do my best, Hornblower. But you can't hurry an Admiral of the Fleet. You can't hurry Lord St. Vincent. You can't hurry a Lord Mayor —not even his representative."

"It will be difficult, I know, sir."

"I'll do my best, Hornblower. But they have to have their bite of breakfast."

The Governor gestured towards the next room, where, under the supervision of the wooden-legged lieutenant, seamen with black scarves round their necks were laying out a meal. There were cold pies, there were hams, there were cold roasts of beef being assembled on the buffet; silver was being set out on the dazzling white cloth. At the smaller buffet a trusted petty officer was setting out decanters and bottles.

"A bite and a glass of something?" asked the Governor.

Hornblower looked, as always, at his watch.

"Thank you, sir. I've three minutes to spare."

It was gratifying to have a meal when he expected to have none; it was gratifying to gulp down slices of ham which otherwise would have gone down the throat of an Admiral of the Fleet. He washed the ham down with a glass of water, to the ill-concealed amazement of the petty officer at the wine buffet.

"Thank you, sir," he said to the Governor. "I must take my leave now."

"Good-bye, Hornblower. Good luck."

At the pier now it was almost dawn—light enough to satisfy the Mohammedan definition of being able to distinguish a black thread from a white. And the river was alive now with boats. From upstream the wind carried down the sound of the splash of oars and sharp naval commands. Here was the *Atropos*' longboat, with Smiley and Horrocks in the stern; here were the boats from the guardship and the receiving ship; measured tread on the pier heralded the arrival of another contingent of seamen. The day was beginning in earnest.

Really in earnest. The thirty eight boats had to be manned and arranged in their correct order, stretching a mile downstream. There were the fools who had mislaid their orders, and the fools who could not understand theirs. Hornblower dashed up and down the line in the gig, that watch of his continually in and out of his pocket. To complicate matters, the grog sellers, anticipating a good day's business, were already out and rowing along the line, and they obviously had effected some surreptitious sales. There were red faces and foolish grins to be seen. The ebb was still running strongly, with the wind behind it. Horrocks, in the state barge that was to carry the Body, completely misjudged his distances as he tried to come alongside. The clumsy great boat, swept round by the wind, borne by the tide, hit the pier on her starboard quarter with a resounding crash. Hornblower on the pier opened his mouth to swear, and then shut it again. If he were to swear at every mishap he would be voiceless soon. It was enough to dart a glance at the unhappy Horrocks. The big rawboned lout wilted under it; and then turned to rave at the oarsmen.

These ceremonial barges were heartbreaking boats to manage, admittedly. Their twelve oars hardly sufficed to control their more than forty feet of length, and the windage of the huge cabin aft was enormous. Hornblower left Horrocks struggling to get into his station, and stepped down into his gig again. They flew downstream; they toiled up. Everything seemed to be in order. Hornblower, looking over the side from the pier when he landed again, thought he could detect a slacking of the ebb. Late, but good enough. High and clear from the Hospital came the notes of a trumpet. Tone-deaf as he was, the notes meant nothing to him. But the sound itself was sufficient. The militia were forming up along the road from the Hospital to the pier, and here came the dignitaries in solemn procession, walking two by two, the least important leading. The boats came to the pier to receive them, in inverted order of numbers—how hard that had been for Hornblower to impress upon the petty officers commanding!—and dropped back again downstream to wait, reversing their order. Even now there was a boat or two out of correct order, but this was not a moment for trifles. The dignitaries on the pier were hustled into even inappropriate boats without a chance of protesting. More and more important were the dignitaries advancing onto the pier—here were the Heralds and Pursuivants, Mr. Pallender among them. And here at last was the Chief Mourner, Admiral of the Fleet Sir Peter Parker, with Blackwood bearing his train, and eight other admirals with—as the drillbook stated—melancholy aspects; perhaps their aspects would be melancholy even without the drillbook. Hornblower saw them down into their boat, all of them. The tide had turned, and already the flow was apparent. Minutes would be precious now.

The shattering boom of a gun from not far away made Hornblower start, and he hoped nobody would notice it. That was the first of the minute guns, that would boom on from now until the Body reached its next temporary resting place at the Admiralty. For Hornblower it was the signal that the Body had started from the Hospital. He handed Sir Peter Parker into the barge. A loud order from the militia colonel, and the troops reversed their arms and rested on them—Hornblower had seen them doing that drill every available minute during the last two days. He reversed his own sword with as much military precision as he could manage—a couple of days ago Maria, coming into the bedroom at the George, had caught him practising the drill, and had laughed immoderately. The mourners' barge had shoved off, and Horrocks was gingerly bringing his up to the pier. Hornblower watched from under his eyebrows, but now that the wind was against the tide it was not such a difficult operation. The band approached; all tunes were dreary to Hornblower, but he gathered that the one they were playing was drearier than most. They wheeled to the right at the base of the pier, and the seamen drawing the gun carriage, stepping short, with bowed heads, came into view behind them. Hornblower thought of the long line of boats struggling to keep position all down the reach, and wished they would step out, although he knew such a wish was nonsense. The monotonous booming of the minute gun marked the passage of valuable time. Up to the pier's end came the carriage. It was a tricky business to transfer the coffin from the gun carriage to the top of the state barge; Hornblower caught some of the words whispered, savagely, by the petty officer supervising the operation, and tried not to smile at their incongruity. But the coffin was put safely in place, and quickly lashed into position, and while the wreaths and flags were being arranged to conceal the lashings Hornblower advanced to the barge. He had to make himself step short, with his back bowed and the melancholy aspect on his face, his reversed sword under his right arm, and he strove to maintain the attitude while making the wide stride from the pier onto the stern of the barge behind the canopy.

"Shove off!" he ordered, out of the side of his mouth. The minute guns bellowed a farewell to them as the barge left the pier, the oarblades dragging through the water before she gathered way. Horrocks beside him put the tiller over, and they headed out for midstream. Before they straightened on their course Hornblower, his head still bowed, was able to steal a sideways glance downstream at the waiting procession. All seemed to be well; the boats were bunched in places, crowded in others, with the effort of maintaining station in difficult weather conditions, but once everyone was under way it would be easier.

"Slow at first," he growled to Horrocks, and Horrocks translated the order to the rowers; it was necessary to give the boats time to take up station.

Hornblower wanted to look at his watch. Moreover, he realised that he would have to keep his eye continually on his watch, and he certainly could not be pulling it out of his pocket every minute. The foot of the coffin was there by his face. With a quick movement he hauled out both watch and chain, and hung them on the end handle, the watch dangling conveniently before his nose. All was well; they were four minutes late, but they still had a full eleven minutes in reserve.

"Lengthen the stroke," he growled to Horrocks.

Now they were rounding the bend. The shipping here was crowded with spectators, so was the shore, even as far from London as this. The *Atropos* had her yards manned by the remnant of her crew, as Hornblower had ordered. He could see that out of the tail of his eye; and, as they approached, the clear sharp bang of her aftermost nine-pounder took up the tale of minute guns from the one at Greenwich. All well, still. Of all the ungrateful duties a naval officer ever had to perform, this one must be the worst. However perfect the performance, would he receive any credit? Of course not. Nobody—not even the Admiralty—would stop to think how much thought and labour were necessary to arrange the greatest water procession London had ever seen, on one of the trickiest possible tideways. And if anything went wrong there were hundreds of thousands of pairs of eyes ready to observe it, and hundreds of thousands of pairs of lips ready to open in condemnation.

"Sir! Sir!"

The curtains at the after end of the cabin had parted; an anxious seaman's face was peering out, from where the reserve rowers lay concealed; so anxious was the speaker that he put out his hand to twitch at Hornblower's black breeches to call attention to himself.

"What is it?"

"Sir! We've sprung a leak!"

My God! The news chimed in with his thoughts with perfectly devilish accuracy of timing.

"How bad?"

"Dunno, sir. But it's up over the floorboards. That's 'ow we know. Must be making pretty fast, sir."

That must have been when Horrocks allowed the barge to crash against the pier. A plank started. Up over the floorboards already? They would never get to Whitehall Steps in time, then. God, if they were to sink here in the middle of the river! Never, never, *never*, would England forgive the man who allowed Nelson's coffin to sink, unceremoniously, in Thames mud beside the Isle of Dogs. Get in to shore and effect repairs? With the whole procession behind them—God, what confusion there would be! And without any doubt at all they would miss the tide, and disappoint the waiting thousands, to say nothing of His Majesty. And tomorrow was the final ceremony, when the Body would be carried from the Admiralty to St. Paul's—dukes, peers, the royal family, thousands of troops, hundreds of thousands of people were to take part in or to watch the ceremonies. To sink would be disaster. To stop would be disaster. No; he could get into shore and effect repairs, causing today's ceremony to be abandoned. But then they could get the Body up to the Admiralty tonight, enabling tomorrow's funeral to be carried out. It would ruin him professionally, but it was the safest half measure. No, no, no! To hell with half measures.

"Mr. Horrocks!"

"Sir!"

"I'll take the tiller. Get down in there. Wait, you fool, and listen to me. Get those floorboards up and deal with that leak. Keep bailing—use hats or anything else. Find that leak and stop it if you can—use one of the men's shirts. Wait. Don't let all the world see you bailing. Pitch the water out here, past my legs. Understand?"

"Er—yes, sir."

"Give me the tiller, then. Get below. And if you fail I'll have the hide off you, if it's the last thing I do on earth. Get below."

Horrocks dived down through the curtains, while Hornblower took the tiller and shifted his position so as to see forward past the coffin. He had to let his sword drop, and of course had had to abandon his melancholy aspect, but that was no hardship. The westerly wind was blowing half a gale now, right in their teeth; against the tide it was raising a decided chop on the water—spray was flying from the bows and now and then the oarblades raised fountains. Perhaps it was a fitting homecoming for the dead hero whose corpse lay just before him. As they came to the bend a fresher gust set them sagging off to leeward, the wind acting powerfully on all the top hamper in the stern.

"Put your backs into it!" shouted Hornblower to the rowers, throwing much of his dignity to the wind, although he was the leading figure in the procession.

The rowers clenched their teeth, snarling with the effort as they tugged at the oars, dragging the obstinate barge by main force forward. Here the wind, acting directly against the tide, was raising some quite respectable rollers, and the barge plunged over them, bows up, bows down, stagger, and heave, like a fishing smack in a gale at sea, lurching and plunging; it was hard to stand upright on her, harder to hold her on her course. And surely—surely—Hornblower was conscious of the water on board cascading forward and back as she plunged. With the ponderous coffin stowed so high up he was nervous about the stability of the absurd craft. Inch by inch they struggled round the bend, and once round it the massed shipping on the north side gave them a lee.

"Haven't you got those floorboards up, Mr. Horrocks?" said Hornblower, trying to hurl the words down into the cabin without stooping in the sight of the crowds.

He heard a splintering crash at that moment, and Horrocks' face emerged between the curtains.

"They were all nailed down tight here," he said. "I had to prise 'em up. We're down by the stern an' we'd have to bail from here anyways."

What with the coffin and the auxiliary rowers they would, of course, be down by the stern.

"How much water?"

"Nigh on a foot, I should say, sir."

"Bail like hell!"

Horrocks' nose had hardly been withdrawn from between the curtains when a hatful of water shot out past Hornblower's legs, and was followed by another and another and another. A good deal of it soused Hornblower's new black breeches. He cursed but he could not complain. That was Bermondsey on the Surrey shore; Hornblower glanced at his watch dangling from the coffin. They were dropping very slightly behind time, thanks to this wind. Not dangerously, though. They were not nearly in as much danger of missing the tide as they were of sinking in mid-river. Hornblower shifted position miserably in his soaking breeches and glanced back. The procession was keeping station well enough; he could see about half of it, for the centre of it was just now fighting round the bend he had already negotiated. Ahead lay another bend, this time to starboard. They would have a head-wind there again.

So indeed they had. Once more they plunged and staggered over the rollers. There was one moment when the barge put her bows down and shipped a mass of water over them—as much must have come in as Horrocks had been able by now to bail out. Hornblower cursed again, forgetting all about the melancholy aspect he should maintain. He could hear and feel the water rolling about in her as she plunged. But the hatfuls of water were still flying out from between the curtains, past —and onto—Hornblower's legs. Hornblower did not worry now about the effect on the crowd of the sight of the funeral barge bailing out; any seamen among the crowd, seeing that rough water, would appreciate the necessity for it without making allowance for a leak. They fought their way round the bend; for a few desperate moments it seemed as if they were making no progress at all, with the oarblades dragging through the water. But the gust was succeeded by a momentary lull and they went on again.

"Can't you plug that leak, Mr. Horrocks?"

"'Tain't easy, sir," said Horrocks, putting his nose out again. "There's a whole plank stove in. The treenails at the ends are on'y just holding, sir. If I plug too hard—"

"Oh, very well. Get on with the bailing again."

Make for the shore? Over there, beside the Tower? That would be a convenient place. No, damn it! Never! Bail, bail, bail. Steer a course that gave them the utmost advantage from the flood and from the lee afforded by the shipping—that calculation was a tricky one, something to occupy his mind. If he could spare a moment to look round he could see the thousands of spectators massed along the shores. If he could spare a moment—God, he had forgotten all about Maria! He had left her in labour. Perhaps—most likely—the child was born by now. Perhaps—perhaps—no, that did not bear thinking about.

London Bridge, with its narrow arches and the wicked swirls and eddies beyond. He knew by the trials he had made two days before that the oars were too wide for the arches. Careful timing was necessary; fortunately the bridge itself broke most of the force of the wind. He brought the tiller over and steadied the barge as best he could on a course direct for the arch's centre.

"Now, pull!" he bellowed to the oarsmen; the barge swept forward, carried by the tide and the renewed efforts of the oarsmen. "In oars!"

Fortunately they did it smartly. They shot into the arch, and there the wind was waiting for them, shrieking through the gap, but their way took them forward. Hornblower measured their progress with his eye. The bows lurched and began to swing in the eddy beyond, but they were just clear enough even though he himself was still under the arch.

"Pull!" he yelled—under the bridge he had no fear of being seen behaving without dignity.

Out came the oars. They groaned in their rowlocks. The eddy was turning her—the oars were dragging her forward—now the rudder could bite again. Through—with the eddies left behind.

The water was still cascading out through the curtains, still soaking his dripping breeches, but despite the rate at which they were bailing he did not like the feel of the barge at all. She was sluggish, lazy. The leak must be gaining on them, and they were nearing the danger point.

"Keep pulling!" he shouted to the rowers; glancing back he saw the second barge, with the Chief Mourners, emerging from the bridge. Round the bend to sight the churches in the Strand—never did shipwrecked mariner sight a sail with more pleasure.

"Water's nearly up to the thwarts, sir," said Horrocks.

"Bail, damn you!"

Somerset House, and one more bend, a shallow one, to Whitehall Steps. Hornblower knew what orders he had given for the procession —orders drawn up in consultation with Mr. Pallender. Here the funeral barge was to draw towards the Surrey bank, allowing the next six barges in turn to come alongside the Steps and disembark their passengers. When the passengers had formed up in proper order, and not until then, the funeral barge was to come alongside for the coffin to be disembarked with proper ceremony. But not with water up to the thwarts—not with the barge sinking under his feet. He turned and looked back to where Smiley was standing in the sternsheets of the second barge. His head was bowed as the instructions stated, but fortunately the coxswain at the tiller noticed, and nudged Smiley to call his attention. Hornblower put up his hand with a gesture to stop; he accentuated the signal by gesturing as though pushing back. He had to repeat the signal before Smiley understood and nodded in reply. Hornblower ported his helm and the barge came sluggishly round, creeping across the river. Round farther—no, with that wind, and with the flood slacking off, it would be better to come alongside bows upstream. Hornblower steadied the tiller, judging his distances, and the barge crept towards the steps.

"Easy all!"

Thank God, they were alongside! There was a Herald at Arms, tabard and all, standing there with the naval officer in command of the escort.

"Sir!" protested the Herald, as vehemently as his melancholy aspect allowed. "You're out of your order—you—"

"Shut your mouth!" growled Hornblower, and then, to the naval officer, "Get this coffin ashore, quick!"

They got it ashore as quickly as dignity would permit; Hornblower, standing beside them, head bowed, sword reversed again, heaved a genuine sigh of relief as he saw, from under his lowered brows, the barge rise perceptibly in the water when freed from the ponderous weight of the coffin. Still with his head bowed he snapped his orders.

"Mr. Horrocks! Take the barge over to the jetty there. Quick! Get a tarpaulin, put it overside and plug that leak. Get her bailed out. Give way, now."

The barge drew away from the Steps; Hornblower could see that Horrocks had not exaggerated when he said the water was up to the thwarts. Smiley, intelligently, was now bringing the Mourners' barge up to the Steps, and Hornblower, remembering to step short, moved out of the way. One by one they landed, Sir Peter Parker with Blackwood bearing his train, Cornwallis, St. Vincent. St. Vincent, labouring on his gouty feet, his shoulders hunched as well as his head bent, could hardly wait to growl his complaints, out of the corner of his mouth as he went up the Steps.

"What the devil, Hornblower?" he demanded. "Don't you read your own orders?"

Hornblower took a few steps—stepping slow and short—alongside him.

"We sprung a leak, sir—I mean, my lord," he said, out of the corner of his mouth in turn. "We were nigh on sinking. No time to spare."

"Ha!" said St. Vincent. "Oh, very well then. Make a report to that effect."

"Thank you, my lord," said Hornblower.

He halted again, head bowed, sword reversed, and allowed the other mourners to flow on past him. This was extemporised ceremonial, but it worked. Hornblower tried to stand like a statue, although no statue he had ever seen was clothed in breeches streaming with wet. He had to repress a start when he remembered again about Maria. He wished he knew. And then he had more difficulty in repressing another start. His watch! That was still dangling on the coffin, now being put into the waiting hearse. Oh well, he could do nothing about that at the moment. And nothing about Maria. He went on standing in his icy breeches.

FIVE

The sentry at the Admiralty was worried but adamant.

"Pardon, sir, but them's my orders. No one to pass, not even a admiral, sir."

"Where's the petty officer of the guard?" demanded Hornblower.

The petty officer was a little more inclined to listen to reason.

"It's our orders, sir," he said, however. "I daren't, sir. You understand, sir."

No naval petty officer gladly said "No" to a post captain, even one of less than three years' seniority.

Hornblower recognised a cock-hatted lieutenant passing in the background.

"Bracegirdle!" he hailed.

Bracegirdle had been a midshipman along with him in the old *Indefatigable,* and had shared more than one wild adventure with him. Now he was wearing a lieutenant's uniform with the aiguillettes of a staff appointment.

"How are you, sir?" he asked, coming forward.

They shook hands and looked each other over, as men will, meeting after years of war. Hornblower told about his watch, and asked permission to be allowed in to get it. Bracegirdle whistled sympathetically.

"That's bad," he said. "If it was anyone but old Jervie I'd risk it. But that's his own personal order. I've no desire to beg my bread in the gutter for the rest of my days."

Jervie was Admiral Lord St. Vincent, recently become First Lord of the Admiralty again, and once Sir John Jervis whose disciplinary principles were talked of with bated breath throughout the navy.

"You're his flag lieutenant?" asked Hornblower.

"That's what I am," said Bracegirdle. "There are easier appointments. I'd exchange for the command of a powder hulk in Hell. But I only have to wait for that. By the time I've gone through my period of servitude with Jervie that'll be the only command they'll offer me."

"Then I can say good-bye to my watch," said Hornblower.

"Without even a farewell kiss," said Bracegirdle. "But in after years when you visit the crypt of St. Paul's you will be able to look at the hero's tomb with the satisfaction of knowing that your watch is in there along with him."

"Your humour is frequently misplaced, Mr. Bracegirdle," replied Hornblower, quite exasperated, "and you seem to have forgotten that the difference in rank between us should invite a more respectful attitude on the part of a junior officer."

Hornblower was tired and irritated; even as he said the words he was annoyed with himself for saying them. He was fond of Bracegirdle, and there was still the bond of perils shared with him, and the memory of lighthearted banter in the days when they were both midshipmen. It was not good manners, so to speak, to make use of his superior rank (which only good fortune had brought him) to wound Bracegirdle's feelings—as undoubtedly he had, and merely to soothe his own. Bracegirdle brought himself stiffly to attention.

"I beg your pardon, sir," he said. "I allowed my tongue to run away with me. I hope you will overlook the offence, sir."

The two officers eyed each other for a moment before Bracegirdle unbent again.

"I haven't said yet how sorry I am about your watch, sir," he said. "I'm genuinely sorry on your account. Really sorry, sir."

Hornblower was about to make a pacific reply, when another figure appeared behind Bracegirdle, huge and ungainly, still in gold-laced full dress, and peering from under vast white eyebrows at the two officers. It was St. Vincent; Hornblower touched his hat and the gesture informed Bracegirdle that his superior was behind him.

"What's the young man so sorry about, Hornblower?" asked St. Vincent.

Hornblower explained as briefly as he could, with hardly a stumble this time over saying "my lord."

"I'm glad to see Mr. Bracegirdle was carrying out my orders," said St. Vincent. "We'd have the Admiralty chockablock with sightseers in a moment otherwise. But you have my personal permission, Captain Hornblower, to pass the sentries."

"Thank you, my lord. I am most grateful."

St. Vincent was about to hobble on his way when he checked himself and looked more acutely than ever at Hornblower.

"Have you been presented to His Majesty yet, young Hornblower?"

"No, sir—my lord."

"You should be. Every officer should show his respect to his King. I'll take you myself."

Hornblower thought about his wife, about the new baby, about his ship at Deptford, about his wet uniform which would have to be pressed into incredible smartness before he could show it at Court. He thought about the rich, and the great, and the powerful, who frequented courts, and knew he would be out of place there and would be unhappy every minute he was compelled to appear there. It might be possible to make an excuse. But—but it would be a new adventure. The distasteful aspects about which he had been thinking were really so many challenges, which he felt spurred to meet.

"Thank you, my lord," he said, searching in his mind for the words appropriate to the subject, "I should be most honoured, most deeply obliged."

"Settled, then. Today's Monday, isn't it? Levee's on Wednesday. I'll take you in my coach. Be here at nine."

"Aye aye, sir—my lord."

"Pass Captain Hornblower through, Mr. Bracegirdle," said St. Vincent, and hobbled on his way.

Bracegirdle led Hornblower through to where the coffin stood on its trestles, and there, sure enough, the watch still hung on the end handle. Hornblower unhooked it with relief and followed Bracegirdle out again. Then he stood and offered his hand to Bracegirdle in farewell; as they clasped hands Bracegirdle's expression was one of hesitant inquiry.

"Two bells in the forenoon watch the day after tomorrow, then, sir," he said; there was the faintest accent on the "forenoon."

"Yes, I'll see you then," said Hornblower.

His other responsibilities were crowding in upon him, and he turned and hurried back to Whitehall Steps. But as he walked, with his mind busily engaged in planning his activities for the next two days, that slight stress came back into his mind. Bracegirdle had relieved him of one small extra worry—by tomorrow at the latest he would have been in painful doubt as to whether his appointment with St. Vincent had been for the morning or the evening.

At the Steps the ebb was already running full; there were broad strips of mud visible on either side of the river. Over at the Lambeth jetty the funeral barge could be seen with Horrocks and his men completing their task of getting a tarpaulin over the bottom of the boat. The other boats which had taken part in the procession were clustered here, there, and everywhere, and it was with pleasure that Hornblower saw his own gig clinging to the steps below him. He climbed down into it, picked up his speaking trumpet, and plunged into the business of dispersing the craft in accordance with the scheme he had laid down in his previous orders. The wind was blowing as briskly as ever, but, now that the tide had turned, the water was more smooth, and the only new difficulty he encountered was the great number of small craft that now were pulling about the river, bearing sightseers to a closer inspection of the ceremonial vessels.

Aldermen and City Companies, Heralds at Arms and admirals, had all landed and gone home to their respective dinners, and the January darkness had hardly closed in before Hornblower dismissed the last of his charges at Greenwich and, getting back into his gig, was able with relief to give the order to pull for Deptford Hard. He climbed wearily up to the George, cold and hungry and fatigued. That busy day seemed to stretch back in his memory for a week at least—except that he had left Maria in labour only that morning.

He came walking into the George, and the first face that he caught sight of was the landlord's—a shadowy figure with whom he was scarcely acquainted, in this house where the landlady assumed all the responsibility.

"How's my wife?" demanded Hornblower.

The landlord blinked.

"I don't rightly know, sir," he said, and Hornblower turned away from him impatiently and ran up the stairs. He hesitated at the bedroom door, with his hand on the handle; his heart was beating fast. Then he heard a murmur of voices within and opened the door. There was Maria in bed, lying back on the pillows, and the midwife moving about by the window. The light of a candle faintly illuminated Maria's face.

"Horry!" said Maria; the glad surprise in her voice accounted for her use of the diminutive.

Hornblower took her hand.

"All well, dearest?" he asked.

"Yes," said Maria.

She held up her lips to be kissed, but even before the kiss was completed she was turning her eyes towards the wicker basket which stood on a small table beside the bed.

"It's a little girl, darling," she said. "Our little girl."

"And a fine little baby, too," added the midwife.

Hornblower walked round the bed and peered into the basket. The blanket there concealed a diminutive figure—Hornblower, grown accustomed to playing with little Horatio, had forgotten how tiny a thing was a newborn baby—and a minute red face, a sort of caricature of humanity, was visible on the little pillow. He gazed down upon it; the little lips opened and emitted a squall, faint and high-pitched, so that little Horatio's remembered cries were lusty bellows by comparison.

"She's beautiful," said Hornblower, gallantly, while the squalling continued and two minute clenched fists appeared above the edge of the blanket.

"Our little Maria," said Maria. "I'm sure her hair is going to curl."

"Now, now," said the midwife, not in reproof of this extravagant prophecy but because Maria was trying to lift herself in bed to gaze at the child.

"She has only to grow up like her mother," said Hornblower, "to be the best daughter I could wish for."

Maria rewarded him with a smile as she sank back on the pillow again.

"Little Horatio's downstairs," she said. "He has seen his sister."

"And what did he think of her?"

"He cried when she did," said Maria.

"I had better see how he is," suggested Hornblower.

"Please do," said Maria, but she extended her hand to him again, and Hornblower bent and kissed it.

The room was very warm with a fire burning briskly in the grate, and it smelt of sickness, oppressive to Hornblower's lungs after the keen January air that had filled them all day.

"I am happy beyond all measure to see you so well, dear," said Hornblower, taking his leave.

Downstairs as he stood hesitating in the hall the landlady popped her head out from the kitchen.

"The young gennelman's in here, sir," she said, "if you don't mind stepping in."

Little Horatio was sitting up in a highchair. His face lit up with a smile as he caught sight of his father—the most flattering experience Hornblower had ever known—and he bounced up and down in his chair and waved the crust he held in his fist.

"There! See him smile 'cause his daddy's come home!" said the landlady; then she hesitated before she put forward a suggestion which she knew to verge on the extravagant. "His bedtime's coming soon, sir. Would you care to play with him until then, sir?"

"Yes," said Hornblower.

"There, baby!" said the landlady. "Daddy's going to play with you. Oops-a-daisy, then. The bar parlour's empty now, sir. This way, sir. Emily, bring a candle for the captain."

Little Horatio was in two minds, once he found himself on the parlour floor, as to which of two methods of progression was most satisfactory to a man almost a year old. On hands and knees he could make prodigious speed, and in any direction he chose. But on the other hand he could pull himself upright by clinging to the leg of a chair, and the radiant expression on his face when he did so was proof of the satisfaction this afforded him. Then, having let go of the chair, provided he had already been successful in the monstrous effort necessary to turn away from it, he could manage to take a step towards his father; he was then compelled to stop and sway perilously on widely separated feet before taking another step, and it was rarely that he could accomplish a step before sitting down on the floor with something of a bump. And was it possible that the monosyllable he said so frequently—"Da" it sounded like—was an attempt to say "Daddy"?

This was happiness again, fleeting, transient, to have his little son tottering towards him with a beaming smile.

"Come to Daddy," said Hornblower, hands outstretched.

Then the smile would turn to a mischievous grin, and down on his hands and knees went young Horatio, galloping like lightning across the room, and gurgling with delirious joy when his father came running after him to seize him and swing him into the air. Simple and delightful pleasure; and then as Hornblower held the kicking gurgling baby up at arm's length he had a fleeting recollection of the moment when he himself had hung suspended in the mizzen rigging on that occasion when the *Indefatigable's* mizzenmast fell when he was in command of the top. This child would know peril and danger—and fear, in later years. He would not let the thought cloud his happiness. He lowered the baby down and then held him at arm's length again—a most successful performance, judging by the gurgles it elicited.

The landlady came in, knocking at the door.

"That's a big man," she said, and Hornblower forced himself not to feel self-conscious at being caught enjoying the company of his own child.

"Dunno what come over me, sir," went on the landlady. "I clear forgot to ask if you wanted supper."

"Supper?" said Hornblower. The last time he had eaten was in the Painted Hall at Greenwich.

"Bacon an' eggs?" asked the landlady. "A bite o' cold beef?"

"Both, if you please," said Hornblower.

"Three shakes of a duck's tail an' you'll have 'em," said the landlady. "You keep that young feller busy while I get it."

"I ought to go back to Mrs. Hornblower."

"She'll do for another ten minutes without you," said the landlady, briskly.

The smell of bacon and eggs when they came was heavenly. Hornblower could sit down with appetite while Emily bore little Horatio off to bed. And after bacon and eggs, cold beef and pickled onions, and a flagon of beer—another simple pleasure, that of eating his fill and more, the knowledge that he was eating too much serving as a sauce to him who kept himself almost invariably within bounds and who looked upon overindulgence usually with suspicion and contempt. With his duty carried out successfully today he had for once no care for the morrow, not even when the day after tomorrow would see him engaged in the rather frightening experience of attending the King's levee. And Maria had come safely through her ordeal, and he had a little daughter who would be as adorable as his little son. Then he sneezed three times running.

SIX

"WHITEHALL STEPS," said Hornblower, stepping down into his gig at Deptford Hard.

It was convenient having his gig for use here; it was faster than a wherryman's boat and it cost him nothing.

"Give way!" said the coxswain.

Of course it was raining. The westerly wind still blew and bore with it today flurries of heavy rain, which hissed down on the surface of the river, roared on the tarpaulins of the wretched boat's crew, and rattled loudly on the sou'-wester which Hornblower wore on his head while he sheltered his cocked hat under his boat cloak. He sniffled lamentably. He had the worst cold he had ever experienced, and he needed to use his handkerchief. But that meant bringing a hand out from under his cloak, and he would not do that—with the boat cloak spread round him like a tent as he sat in the sternsheets, and with the sou'-wester on top, he could hope to keep himself reasonably dry as far as Whitehall if he did not disturb the arrangement. He preferred to sniff.

Up the river, through the rain; under London Bridge, round the bends he had come to know so well during the last few days. He cowered in misery under his boat cloak, shuddering. He was sure he had never felt so ill in his life before. He ought to be in bed, with hot bricks at his feet and hot rum and water at his side, but on the day when the First Lord was going to take him to the Court of St. James's he could not possibly plead illness, not even though the shivers ran up and down his spine and his legs felt too weak to carry him.

The Steps were slippery where the tide had receded from them; in his weak state he could hardly keep his footing as he climbed them. At the top, with the rain still beating down, he put his appearance to rights as well as he could. He rolled up the sou'-wester and put it in the pocket of his cloak, put on his cocked hat, and hurried, bending forward into the driving rain, the hundred and fifty yards to the Admiralty. Even in the short time that took him his stockings were splashed and wet, and the brim of his cocked hat was filled with water. He was glad to stand before the fire in the Captain's Room while he waited until Bracegirdle came in with the announcement that His Lordship was ready for him.

"Morning, Hornblower," said St. Vincent, standing under the portico.

"Good morning, my lord."

"No use waiting for a smooth," growled St. Vincent, looking up at the rain and eyeing the distance between him and his coach. "Come on."

He hobbled manfully forward. Hornblower and Bracegirdle advanced with him. They had no cloaks on—Hornblower had left his at the Admiralty—and had to wait in the rain while St. Vincent walked to the coach and with infinite slowness hauled himself into it. Hornblower followed him and Bracegirdle squeezed in after him, perching on the turn-down seat in front. The coach rumbled forward over the cobbles, with a vibration from the iron-rimmed wheels that found an echo in the shudders that were still playing up and down Hornblower's spine.

"All nonsense, of course, having to use a coach to St. James's from the Admiralty," growled St. Vincent. "I used to walk a full three miles on my quarterdeck in the old *Orion*."

Hornblower sniffed again, miserably. He could not even congratulate himself on the fact that as he felt so ill he knew almost no qualms about this new experience which was awaiting him, because, stupefied by his cold, he was unable even to indulge in his habitual self-analysis.

"I read your report last night, Hornblower," went on St. Vincent. "Satisfactory."

"Thank you, my lord." He braced himself into appearing intelligent. "And did the funeral at Saint Paul's go off well yesterday?"

"Well enough."

The coach rumbled down the Mall.

"Here we are," said St. Vincent. "You'll come back with me, I suppose, Hornblower? I don't intend to stay long. Nine in the morning and I haven't done a third of my day's work yet."

"Thank you, my lord. I'll take station on you, then."

The coach door opened, and Bracegirdle nimbly stepped out to help his chief down the steps. Hornblower followed; now his heart was beating faster. There were red uniforms, blue and gold uniforms, blue and silver uniforms, in evidence everywhere; many of the men were in powder. One powdered wig—the dark eyes below it were in startling contrast—detached itself and approached St. Vincent. The uniform was black and silver; the polished facets of the silver-hilted sword caught and reflected the light at a myriad points.

"Good morning, my lord."

"Morning, Catterick. Here's my protégé, Captain Horatio Hornblower."

Catterick's keen dark eyes took in every detail of Hornblower's appearance in one sweeping glance, coat, breeches, stockings, sword, but his expression did not change. One might gather he was used to the appearance of shabby naval officers at levees.

"His lordship is presenting you, I understand, Captain. You accompany him into the Presence Chamber."

Hornblower nodded; he was wondering how much was implied by that word "protégé." His hat was in his hand, and he made haste to cram it under his arm as the others did.

"Follow me, then," said St. Vincent.

Up the stairs; uniformed men on guard on the landings; another black and silver uniform at the head of the stairs; a further brief exchange of sentences; powdered footmen massed about the doorway; announcements made in a superb speaking voice, restrained but penetrating.

"Admiral the Right Honourable Earl St. Vincent. Captain Horatio Hornblower. Lieutenant Anthony Bracegirdle."

The Presence Chamber was a mass of colour. Every possible uniform was represented there. The scarlet of the infantry; light cavalry in all the colours of the rainbow, befrogged and befurred, cloaks swinging, sabres trailing; heavy cavalry in jack boots up to the thigh; foreign uniforms of white and green; St. Vincent carried his vast bulk through them all, like a battleship among yachts. And there was the King, seated in a thronelike chair with a lofty back; it was an odd surprise to see him, in his little tiewig, looking so exactly like his pictures. Behind him stood a semicircle of men wearing ribbons and stars, blue ribbons, red ribbons, green ribbons, over the left shoulder and over the right; Knights of the Garter, of the Bath, of St. Patrick, these must be, the great men of the land. St. Vincent was bending himself in clumsy obeisance to the King.

"Glad to see you, my lord, glad to see you," said the latter. "Haven't had a moment since Monday. Glad all went well."

"Thank you, Sir. May I present the officer responsible for the naval ceremonial?"

"You may."

The King turned his eyes on Hornblower; light blue eyes, prominent, but kindly.

"Captain Horatio Hornblower," said St. Vincent, and Hornblower did his best to bow, as his French *émigré* dancing teacher had tried to teach him ten years before, left foot forward, hand over his heart. He did not know how far down to bend; he did not know how long to stay there when he had bent. But he came up again at last, with something of the sensation of breaking the surface of the water after a deep dive.

"What ship, sir? What ship?" asked the King.

"*Atropos,* twenty two, Your Majesty."

Sleepless during the previous night, Hornblower had imagined that question might be put to him, and so the answer came fast enough.

"Where is she now?"

"Deptford, Your Majesty."

"But you go to sea soon?"

"I—I—" Hornblower could not answer that question, but St. Vincent spoke up for him.

"Very shortly, Sir," he said.

"I see," said the King. "I see."

He put up his hand and stroked his forehead with a gesture of infinite weariness before recalling himself to the business in hand.

"My great-nephew," he said, "Prince Ernst—did I speak to you about him, my lord?"

"You did, Sir," answered St. Vincent.

"Do you think Captain Hornblower would be a suitable officer for the duty?"

"Why yes, Sir. Quite suitable."

"Less than three years' seniority," mused the King, his eyes resting on Hornblower's epaulette. "But still. Harmond!"

"Your Majesty."

A glittering figure with ribbon and star came gliding forward from the semicircle.

"Present Captain Hornblower to His Serene Highness."

"Yes, Your Majesty."

There was a smile in the pale blue eyes.

"Thank you, Captain," said the King. "Do your duty as you have done it, and your conscience will always be clear."

"Yes, Your Majesty," said Hornblower.

St. Vincent was bowing again; Hornblower bowed. He was aware of the fact that he must not turn his back upon the King—that was almost the sum of his knowledge of court ceremonial—and he found it not so difficult to withdraw. Already there was a line formed of people waiting their turn to reach the royal presence, and he sidled away from them in St. Vincent's wake.

"This way, if you please," said Harmond, directing their course to the farther side of the room. "Wait a moment."

"His Majesty's service makes strange bedfellows sometimes," said St. Vincent as they waited. "I hardly expected you would be saddled with this, Hornblower."

"I—I have not yet understood," said Hornblower.

"Oh, the Prince is—"

"This way, if you please," said Harmond, appearing again.

He led them towards a diminutive figure who awaited them with composure. A young man—no, only a boy—wearing an outlandish uniform of gold and green, a short gold-hilted sword at his side, orders on his breast, and two more hanging from his neck. Behind him towered a burly figure in a more moderate version of the same uniform, swarthy, with fat pendulous cheeks. The boy himself was handsome, with fair hair falling in ringlets about his ears, frank blue eyes, and a nose slightly turned upwards. The burly figure stepped forward, intercepting the approach of the group to the boy. Harmond and he exchanged glances.

"Presentations should be made to me first," said the burly figure; he spoke thickly, in what Hornblower guessed to be a German accent.

"And why, sir?" asked Harmond.

"By the fundamental law of Seitz-Bunau only the High Chamberlain can make presentations to His Serene Highness."

"Yes?"

"And I, sir, am the High Chamberlain. As you know."

"Very well, sir," said Harmond with resignation. "Then may I have the honour to present—Admiral the Right Honourable Earl St. Vincent; Captain Horatio Hornblower; Lieutenant Anthony Bracegirdle."

Hornblower was about to bow, but out of the tail of his eye he caught sight of St. Vincent still holding himself ponderously erect, and he restrained himself.

"To whom have I the honour of being presented?" asked St. Vincent, coldly. It appeared as if St. Vincent entertained some prejudice against Germans.

"Doctor Eisenbeiss," said Harmond.

"His Excellency the Baron von Eisenbeiss, High Chamberlain and Secretary of State to His Serene Highness the Prince of Seitz-Bunau," said the burly man, in further explanation. "It is with much pleasure that I make your acquaintance."

He stood meeting St. Vincent's eyes for a moment, and then he bowed; St. Vincent bowed only after Eisenbeiss had begun to bow; Hornblower and Bracegirdle followed his example. All four of them straightened up at the same moment.

"And now," said Eisenbeiss, "I have the honour to present—"

He turned to the Prince and continued his speech in German, apparently repeating his first words and then mentioning the names in turn. The little Prince gave a half bow at each name, but as St. Vincent bowed low—nearly as low as he had bowed to the King—Hornblower did likewise. Then the Prince spoke in German to Eisenbeiss.

"His Serene Highness says," translated the latter, "that he is delighted to make the acquaintance of officers of His Majesty's Navy, because it is His Highness's will that he should make war against the French tyrant in their company."

"Tell His Serene Highness," said St. Vincent, "that we are all delighted, too."

The translation was made, and the Prince produced a smile for each of them. Then there was an uncomfortable moment as they looked at each other. Finally Eisenbeiss said something again to the Prince, received a reply, and then turned to the group.

"His Serene Highness," he announced, "says that he will not detain you longer."

"Hm'ph," said St. Vincent, but he bent himself once more in the middle, as did the others, and then they withdrew themselves, backwards and sideways, from out of His Serene Highness's presence.

"Damned upstart whippersnapper," mumbled St. Vincent to himself, and then added, "At any rate, our duty's done. We can leave. Follow me over to that door."

Down below loud bawling by a footman in the courtyard brought up the Earl's coach again, and they climbed in, Hornblower utterly dazed by reason of his cold, the excitement he had been through, and his puzzlement about the incident in which he had taken part.

"Well, that's your midshipman, Hornblower," said St. Vincent. His voice was so like the rumbling of the iron tires over the cobbles that Hornblower was not sure that he had heard aright—especially as what St. Vincent had said was so strange.

"I beg your pardon, my lord?"

"I've no doubt you heard me. I said that's your midshipman—the Prince of Seitz-Bunau."

"But who is he, my lord?"

"One of those German princes. Boney chased him out of his principality last year, on his way to Austerlitz. Country's brimful of German princes chased out by Boney. The point is that this one's the King's great-nephew, as you heard."

"And he's to be one of my midshipmen?"

"That is so. He's young enough to learn sense, not like most of 'em. Most of 'em go in the army. On the staff, God help the staff. But now the navy's fashionable—first time since the Dutch Wars. We've been winning battles, and God knows the soldiers haven't. So all the ne'er-do-well young lords join the navy nowadays instead of the light dragoons. It was His Majesty's own idea that this young fellow should do the same."

"I understand, my lord."

"It won't do him any harm. *Atropos* won't be any palace, of course."

"That's what I was thinking, my lord. The midshipmen's berth in *Atropos*—"

"You have to put him there, all the same. Not much room in a flush-decked sloop. If it were a ship of the line he might berth by himself, but if it's to be *Atropos* he'll have to take what comes. And it won't be caviar and venison, either. I'll send you orders on the subject, of course."

"Aye aye, my lord."

The coach was grinding to a stop at the Admiralty; someone opened the door, and St. Vincent began to heave himself out of his seat. Hornblower followed him in under the portico.

"I'll bid you good-bye, then, Hornblower," said St. Vincent, offering his hand.

"Good-bye, my lord."

St. Vincent stood looking at him from under his eyebrows.

"The navy has two duties, Hornblower," he said. "We all know what one is—to fight the French and give Boney what for."

"Yes, my lord?"

"The other we don't think about so much. We have to see that when we go we leave behind us a navy which is as good as the one in which we served. You've less than three years' seniority now, Hornblower, but you'll find you'll grow older. It'll seem you've hardly had time to look round before you'll have forty three years' seniority, like me. It goes fast enough, I assure you. Perhaps then you'll be taking another young officer to present him at the Palace."

"Er—yes, my lord."

"Choose carefully, Hornblower, if it ever becomes your duty. One can make mistakes. But let them be honest mistakes."

"Yes, my lord."

"That's all."

The old man turned away without another word, leaving Hornblower with Bracegirdle under the portico.

"Jervie's in a melting mood," said Bracegirdle.

"So it seems."

"I think he wanted to say he had his eye on you, sir."

"But he had an anchor out to windward all the same," said Hornblower, thinking of what St. Vincent had said about the chance of one's making mistakes.

"Jervie never forgives, sir," said Bracegirdle, seriously.

"Well—"

Twelve years of service in the navy had gone far to make Hornblower, on occasions, fatalist enough to be able to shrug off that sort of peril—at least until it was past.

"I'll take my boat cloak, if you please," he said, "and I'll say good-bye, and thank you."

"A glass of something? A cup of tea? A mouthful to eat, sir?"

"No, thank you, I'd better shove off."

Maria was waiting for him at Deptford, longing to hear about his visit to Court and his presentation to the King. Maria had been wildly excited when Hornblower had told her what he was going to do. The thought that he was going to meet the Lord's anointed face to face was almost too much for her—the midwife had come forward with a warning that all this excitement might bring on a fever. And he had not merely been presented to the King, but the King had actually spoken to him, had discussed his professional career with him. Besides, he was to have a real prince as a midshipman on board his ship—a dispossessed prince, admittedly, but to counterbalance that was the fact that the Prince was a great-nephew of the King, related by blood to the royal family. That would delight Maria as much as his presentation at Court.

She would want to know all about it, who was there (Hornblower found himself wishing he had been able to identify a single one of the figures who had stood behind the throne) and what everyone was wearing—that would be easier, as there had been no women present, of course, at the levee, and practically everyone had been in uniform. He would have to be careful in his account, as it was possible to hurt Maria's feelings. Hornblower himself fought for his country; it might be better said that he fought for the ideals of liberty and decency against the unprincipled tyrant who ruled across the Channel; the hackneyed phrase "for King and Country" hardly expressed his feelings at all. If he was ready to lay down his life for his King that really had no reference to the kindly pop-eyed old gentleman with whom he had been speaking this morning; it meant that he was ready to die for the system of liberty and order that the old gentleman represented. But to Maria the King was representative of something other than liberty and order; he had received the blessing of the Church; he was somebody to be spoken about with awe. To turn one's back on the King was to Hornblower a breach of good manners, something damaging, in some degree, to the conventions which held the country together in the face of its imminent peril; but to Maria it would be something very close to sacrilege. He would have to be careful not to speak too lightly of the old gentleman.

And yet (the gig was carrying him through the Pool now, under the walls of the Tower) Hornblower had to admit it to himself that Maria's views about his service in the navy were not on as lofty a plane as his own. To Maria it was a gentlemanly trade; it gave her a certain social status to which she otherwise would not have attained, and it put food into the mouth of her precious child—children, now that little Maria was born. But self-sacrifice for a cause; the incurring of danger beyond the dictates of duty; honour; glory—these were conceptions that Maria cared little about. She was in fact rather inclined to turn up her nose at them as purely masculine notions, part of an elaborate game or ritual devised by men to make them feel superior to and different from women whose self-respect and sublime certainty of superiority needed no such puerile bolstering.

It was a surprise to Hornblower to find that the gig was now passing the *Atropos* as she lay at the edge of the stream. He should have been all eyes to see that all was well with her and that the officer of the watch had been on the alert to detect the gig as she came down the river; as it was, Hornblower merely had time to acknowledge the salute of Lieutenant Jones as the gig left the ship behind. There was Deptford Dock, and beside it the enormous activities of the Victualling Yard. From a sailing barge lying beside the jetty a gang of men were at work driving a herd of pigs up into the yard, destined for slaughter and salting down to feed the navy.

"Eyes in the boat, there!" growled the coxswain.

One of the gig's crew had made a *sotto voce* joke about those pigs, evidently. It was hard to believe, even with this evidence before their eyes, that the unrecognisable, wooden-hard chunks of matter that were issued from the brine barrels to the men at sea really came from decent respectable animals like those there. Hornblower's sympathies were with his men.

The coxswain was putting his tiller over to bring the gig up to Deptford Hard. Hornblower disembarked, to walk up to the George, to where his family was awaiting him. He would sit by Maria's bed and tell her about the pageantry of the Court of St. James's. He would hold his little daughter in his arms; he would play with his little son. It might well be for the very last time; at any moment his orders would come, and he would take *Atropos* to sea. Battle, storm, shipwreck, disease—what were the chances that he would never come back again? And if ever he did, the squalling baby he was leaving behind would be a trim little miss playing with her dolls; little Horatio would be at least starting with slate and pencil writing his letters and figures; he might be beginning to decline *mensa* and learning the Greek alphabet. And he himself? He hoped he would be able to say he had done his duty; he hoped that those weaknesses of which he was so conscious would not prevent him from achieving something of which his children might be proud.

SEVEN

So it was to be the Mediterranean. Hornblower sat in his canvas chair in his cabin in *Atropos*, re-reading the orders which had come for him.

Sir,

I am commanded by the Lords Commissioners of the Admiralty—

He was to prepare himself with the utmost diligence ready to proceed to Gibraltar, and there he was to call for orders which the Vice Admiral Commanding in the Mediterranean might send to him there. In the event that no such orders should be forthcoming, he was to ascertain where the vice admiral was likely to be found, and to proceed with the same diligence to put himself under the vice admiral's orders.

That must be Cuthbert Collingwood—Lord Collingwood, now that he had received his peerage after Trafalgar. The fleet that had won the battle there—or such ships of it as were still seaworthy—had been sent into the Mediterranean after the battle, he knew. The destruction of the French and Spanish fleets outside Cadiz had definitely established British command of the Atlantic, so now the navy was carrying its ponderous weight into the Mediterranean to head off there any moves that Bonaparte might make now that Austerlitz had given him command of Continental Europe. Austerlitz—Trafalgar. The French army—and the Royal Navy. The one might be balanced against the other. There was no corner of Europe whither French troops might not march—as long as there was land for them to march on; there was no corner of the sea where British ships might not bring their influence to bear—as long as there was water in which they could float. In the landlocked Mediterranean with its peninsulas and islands sea power could best confront land power. The bloody and seemingly endless conflict between tyranny and liberty would be fought out there. He would play his part in it. The Secretary to the Lords Commissioners signed himself "your obedient humble servant," but before he did so he went on to say that Their Lordships rested assured that *Atropos* was ready for immediate departure, so that on receipt of final orders and of the last-minute despatches which would be entrusted to her she would be able to leave at once. Hornblower and his ship, in other words, were being put on notice of instant readiness.

Hornblower felt a slight feeling of apprehension, a sensation of goose-flesh at the back of his neck. He did not believe that his ship was prepared in all respects to leave at a moment's notice.

Hornblower lifted up his voice in a call to the sentry outside his door.

"Pass the word for Mr. Jones."

He heard the cry repeated in the 'tween-decks like an echo, as he sat on with the orders in his hands. It was only a few moments before Mr. Jones came in hastily, and it was only when he arrived that Hornblower realised that he had not prepared himself to give the necessary orders and make the necessary inquiries. As a result Hornblower found himself compelled to look Jones over without speaking. His mind was sorting out his thoughts without reacting at all to the reports his eyes were making to it, but Hornblower's steady stare discomposed the unfortunate Jones, who put his hand up nervously to his face. Hornblower saw a dab of dry lather in front of Jones' right ear, and as the lieutenant's gesture recalled him to himself he noticed something more; one lantern cheek was smooth and well shaved, while the other bristled with a fair growth of black beard.

"Pardon, sir," said Jones, "but your call caught me half shaved, and I judged it best to come at once."

"Very well, Mr. Jones," said Hornblower; he was not sorry that Jones had something to explain away while he himself was not ready with the definite orders that a good officer should be able to issue.

Under that embarrassing stare Jones had to speak again.

"Did you want me, sir?"

"Yes," said Hornblower. "We are under orders for the Mediterranean."

"Indeed, sir?" Mr. Jones' remarks did not make any great contribution to the progress of the conversation.

"I want your report on how soon we can be ready for sea."

"Oh, sir—"

Jones put his hand up to his face again; perhaps it was as long as it was because of his habit of pulling at his chin.

"Are stores and water complete?"

"Well, sir, you see—"

"You mean they are not?"

"N—no, sir. Not altogether."

Hornblower was about to ask for an explanation, but changed his approach at the last second.

"I won't ask why at present. How short are we?"

"Well, sir—" The wretched Jones entered into a hurried statement. They were twenty tons of water short. Bread, spirits, meat—

"You mean that with the Victualling Yard only across the river you have not kept the ship complete with stores?"

"Well, sir—" Jones tried to explain that he had not thought it necessary to draw supplies from day to day. "There was plenty of other work for the hands, sir, fitting out."

"Watch bills? Station bills?"

These were the lists that allocated the hands to their duties and quarters in the ship.

"We're twenty topmen short, sir," said Jones pitifully.

"All the more reason to make the most of what we have."

"Yes, sir, of course, sir." Jones sought desperately in his mind for excuses for himself. "Some of our beef, sir—it—it isn't fit to eat."

"Worse than usual?"

"Yes, sir. Must be some of an old batch. Real bad, some of it."

"In which tier?"

"I'll ask the purser, sir."

"You mean you don't know?"

"No, sir—yes, sir."

Hornblower fell into deep thought again, but as once more he did not take his eyes from Jones' face that did not help the delinquent first lieutenant to recover his equanimity. Actually Hornblower was condemning himself. During the few days he had held command of the *Atropos* he had been hard at work on the details of Nelson's funeral, and then he had been preoccupied with his own family affairs, but all that was no excuse. The captain of a ship should be aware at every moment of the state of his command. He was savagely angry with himself. He hardly knew his officers' names; he could not even estimate what sort of fight *Atropos* could put up—and yet he would not have to go very far down the river to find his ship likely to be in action.

"What about the gunner's stores?" he asked. "Powder? Shot? Wads? Cartridges?"

"I'll send for the gunner, sir, shall I?" asked Jones. He was desperate at all this revelation of his own inadequacies.

"I'll see 'em all in a minute," said Hornblower. "Purser, gunner, bosun, cooper, master's mate."

These were the subordinate heads of department responsible through the first lieutenant to the captain for the proper functioning of the ship.

"Aye aye, sir."

"What the devil's that noise?" asked Hornblower pettishly. For some minutes now there had been some sort of altercation on the quarter-deck over their heads. Strange voices were making themselves heard through the skylight.

"Shall I find out, sir?" asked Jones eagerly, hoping for some distraction. But as he spoke there was a knock at the cabin door.

"This'll tell us," said Hornblower. "Come in!"

Midshipman Horrocks opened the door.

"Mr. Still's respects, sir, an' there are some gentlemen come on board with an Admiralty letter for you, sir."

"Ask them to come here."

It could only be trouble of one sort or another, Hornblower decided, as he waited. One more distraction at a moment when he was about to be desperately busy. Horrocks ushered in two figures, one large and one diminutive, wearing glittering uniforms of green and gold—Hornblower had last seen them only yesterday at the Court of St. James's, the German princeling and his bear-leader. Hornblower rose to his feet, and Eisenbeiss stepped forward with an elaborate bow, to which Hornblower replied with a curt nod.

"Well, sir?"

Eisenbeiss ceremoniously handed over a letter; a glance showed Hornblower that it was addressed to him. He opened it carefully and read it.

> You are hereby requested and required to receive into your ship His Serene Highness Ernst Prince of Seitz-Bunau, who has been rated as midshipman in His Majesty's Navy. You will employ your diligence in instructing His Serene Highness in his new profession as well as in continuing his education in readiness for the day which under Providence may not be far distant when His Serene Highness will again assume the government of his hereditary dominions. You will also receive into your ship His Excellency the Baron Otto von Eisenbeiss, Chamberlain and First Secretary of State to His Serene Highness. His Excellency was until recently practicing as a surgeon, and he has received from the Navy Office a warrant as such in His Majesty's Navy. You will make use of His Excellency's services, therefore, as Surgeon in your ship while, as far as naval

discipline and the Articles of War allow, he continues to act as Chamberlain to His Serene Highness.

"I see," he said. He looked at the odd pair in their resplendent uniforms. "Welcome aboard, Your Highness."

The prince nodded and smiled, clearly without understanding.

Hornblower sat down again, and Eisenbeiss began to speak at once, his thick German accent stressing his grievances.

"I must protest, sir," he said.

"Well?" said Hornblower, in a tone that might well have conveyed a warning.

"His Serene Highness is not being treated with proper respect. When we reached your ship I sent my footman on board to announce us so that His Highness could be received with royal honours. They were absolutely refused, sir. The man on the deck there—I presume he is an officer—said he had no instructions. It was only when I showed him that letter, sir, that he allowed us to come on board at all."

"Quite right. He had no instructions."

"I trust you will make amends, then. And may I remind you that you are sitting in the presence of royalty?"

"You call me 'sir,'" snapped Hornblower. "And you will address me as my subordinate should."

Eisenbeiss jerked himself upright in his indignation, so that his head came with a shattering crash against the deck beam above; this checked his flow of words and enabled Hornblower to continue.

"As officers in the King's service you should have worn the King's uniform. You have your dunnage with you?"

Eisenbeiss was still too stunned to answer, even if he understood the word, and Horrocks spoke for him.

"Please, sir, it's in the boat alongside. Chests and chests of it."

"Thank you, Mr. Horrocks. Now, Doctor, I understand you have the necessary professional qualifications to act as surgeon in this ship. That is so?"

Eisenbeiss still strove to retain his dignity.

"As Secretary of State I am addressed as 'Your Excellency,'" he said.

"But as surgeon in this ship you are addressed as 'Doctor.' And that is the last time I shall overlook the omission of the word 'sir.' Now. Your qualifications?"

"I am a surgeon—sir."

The last word came out with a jerk as Hornblower's eyebrows rose.

"You have been in practice recently?"

"Until a few months ago—sir. I was surgeon to the Court of Seitz-Bunau. But now I am—"

"Now you are surgeon in H.M.S. *Atropos,* and we can leave off the farce of your being Secretary of State."

"Sir—"

"Silence, if you please, Doctor. Mr. Horrocks!"

"Sir!"

"My compliments to Mr. Still. I'll have these two gentlemen's baggage swayed up. They are to make immediate selection of their necessities to the extent of one sea-chest each. You will be able to help them in their choice. The remainder is to leave the ship within ten minutes by the boat in which it came. Is that quite clear, Mr. Horrocks?"

"Aye aye, sir. If you please, sir, there's a couple of footmen with the baggage."

"Footmen?"

"Yes, sir, in uniforms like these." Horrocks indicated the green and gold of the Germans.

"That's two more hands, then. Read 'em in and send 'em for'rard."

The navy could always use more men, and a couple of fat well-fed footmen would make useful hands in time to come.

"But, sir—" said Eisenbeiss.

"Speak when you're spoken to, Doctor. Now, Mr. Horrocks, you will take the Prince and settle him into the midshipmen's berth. I'll introduce you. Mr. Midshipman Horrocks—er, Mr. Midshipman Prince."

Horrocks automatically offered his hand, and the Prince as automatically took it, displaying no immediate change at the contamination of a human touch. He smiled shyly, without understanding.

"And my compliments to the master's mate, too, Mr. Horrocks. Ask him to be good enough to show the doctor where he berths for'rard."

"Aye aye, sir."

"Now, Doctor, in half an hour I wish to see you both in the King's uniform. You can take up your duties then. There will be a court of inquiry opened at that time, consisting of the first lieutenant, the purser, and yourself, to decide whether certain hogsheads of beef are fit for human consumption. You will be secretary of that court and I want your written report by noon. Go with Mr. Horrocks now."

Eisenbeiss hesitated a moment under Hornblower's sharp glance before he turned to leave the cabin, but at the curtain his indignation overcame him again.

"I shall write to the Prime Minister, sir," he said. "He shall hear about this treatment of His Majesty's Allies."

"Yes, Doctor. If you contravene the Mutiny Act you'll swing at the yard-arm. Now, Mr. Jones, with regard to these station and quarter bills."

As Hornblower turned to Jones to re-enter into the business of getting *Atropos* ready for sea he was conscious of feeling some contempt for himself. He could browbeat a silly German doctor effectively enough; he could flatter himself that he had dealt adequately with what might have been a difficult though petty situation. But that was nothing to be proud of, when he had to realise that with regard to his real duties he had been found wanting. He had wasted precious hours. During the last two days he had twice played with his little son; he had sat by his wife's bedside and held his little daughter in his arms, when really he should have been on board here looking after his ship. It was no excuse that it was Jones' duty to have attended to the matters under consideration; it had been Hornblower's duty to see that Jones had attended to them. A naval officer should not have a wife or children—this present situation was the proof of that trite saying. Hornblower found himself setting his mouth hard as he came to that conclusion. There were still eight hours of daylight left today. He began an orderly planning of those eight hours. There were the matters that would call for his own personal activity, like appealing to the superintendent of the dockyard; there were the matters he could safely leave to his subordinates. There was work that could be done on one side of the ship, leaving the other side clear; there was work that would demand the services of skilled seamen, and work that landsmen could do. There were some jobs that could not be started until other jobs were finished. If he was not careful some of his officers would have to be in two places at once, there would be confusion, delay, ridiculous disorder. But with good planning it could be done.

Purser and gunner, bosun and cooper, each in turn was summoned to the after cabin. To each was allotted his tasks; to each was grudgingly conceded a proportion of the men that each demanded. Soon the pipes were shrilling through the ship.

"Launch's crew away!"

Soon the launch was pulling across the river, full of the empty barrels the cooper and his mates had made ready, to begin ferrying over the twenty tons of water necessary to complete the ship's requirements. A dozen men went scurrying up the shrouds and out along the yards under the urging of the bosun; yard-arm tackles and stay tackles had to be readied for the day's work.

"Mr. Jones! I am leaving the ship now. Have that report on the beef ready for me by the time I return from the dockyard."

Hornblower became aware of two figures on the quarterdeck trying to attract his attention. They were the Prince and the doctor. He ran his eye over their uniforms, the white collar patches of the midshipman and the plain coat of the surgeon.

"They'll do," he said; "your duties are awaiting you, Doctor. Mr. Horrocks! Keep Mr. Prince under your lee for today. Call away my gig."

The captain superintendent of the dockyard listened to Hornblower's request with the indifference acquired during years of listening to requests from urgent officers.

"I've the men ready to send for the shot, sir. Port side's clear for the powder hulk to come alongside—slack water in half an hour, sir. I can send men to man her too if necessary. It's only four tons that I need. Half an hour with the hulk."

"You say you're ready now?"

"Yes, sir."

The captain superintendent looked across at the *Atropos* lying in the stream.

"Very well. I hope what you say is quite correct, Captain, for your sake. You can start warping the hulk alongside—I warn you I want her back at her moorings in an hour."

"Thank you, sir."

Back in the *Atropos* the cry went round the ship.

"Hands to the capstan! Waisters! Sailmakers! Lob-lolly boys!"

The inmost recesses of the ship were cleared of men to man the capstan bars—any pair of arms, any stout back, would serve for that purpose. A drum went roaring along the deck.

"All lights out!"

The cook and his mates dumped the galley fire overside and went reluctantly to man the yard-arm and stay tackles. The powder hulk came creeping alongside. She had stout sheers and wide hatchways, efficient equipment for the rapid transfer of explosives. Four tons of powder, eighty kegs of one hundredweight each, came climbing out of the hulk's holds to be swayed down the hatchways of the *Atropos*, while down below the gunner and his mates and a sweating working party toiled in near-darkness—barefooted to avoid all chance of friction or sparks—to range the kegs about the magazines. Some day *Atropos* might be fighting for her life, and her life would depend on the proper arrangement of those kegs down below so that the demands of the guns on deck might be met.

The members of the court of inquiry, fresh from their investigation of the defective beef barrels, made their appearance on deck again.

"Mr. Jones, show the doctor how to make his report in due form." Then to the purser, "Mr. Carslake, I want to be able to sign your indents as soon as that report is ready."

One final look round the deck, and Hornblower could dive below, take pen and ink and paper, and devote himself single-mindedly to composing a suitable covering letter to the Victualling Yard (worded with the right urgency and tactfully coaxing the authorities there into agreement without annoying them by too certain assumption of acquiescence) beginning: "Sir, I have the honour to enclose—" and concluding—"in the best interests of His Majesty's service, Your Obedient Servant—."

Then he could come on deck again to see how the work was progressing and fume for a space before Jones and Carslake appeared with the documents they had been preparing. Amid the confusion and din he had to clear his head again to read them with care before signing them with a bold "H. Hornblower, Captain."

"Mr. Carslake, you can take my gig over to the Victualling Yard. Mr. Jones, I expect the Yard will need hands to man their lighter. See to that, if you please."

A moment to spare now to observe the hands at work, to settle his cocked hat square on his head, to clasp his hands behind him, to walk slowly forward, doing his best to look quite cool and imperturbable, as if all this wild activity were the most natural thing in the world.

"Avast heaving there on that stay tackle. Belay!"

The powder keg hung suspended just over the deck. Hornblower forced himself to speak coldly, without excitement. A stave of the keg had started a trifle. There was a minute trail of powder grains on the deck; more were dribbling very slowly out.

"Sway that keg back into the hulk. You, bosun's mate, get a wet mop and swill that powder off the deck."

An accident could have fired that powder easily. The flash would pass in either direction; four tons of powder in *Atropos,* forty, perhaps in the hulk—what would have happened to the massed shipping in the Pool in that event? The men were eyeing him; this would be a suitable moment to encourage them with their work.

"Greenwich Hospital is over there, men," said Hornblower, pointing down-river to the graceful outlines of Wren's building. "Some of us will wind up there in the end, I expect, but we don't want to be blown straight there today."

A feeble enough joke, perhaps, but it raised a grin or two all the same. "Carry on."

Hornblower continued his stroll forward, the imperturbable captain who was nevertheless human enough to crack a joke. It was the same sort of acting that he used towards Maria when she seemed likely to be in a difficult mood.

Here was the lighter with the shot, coming along the starboard side. Hornblower looked down into it. Nine-pounder balls for the four long guns, two forward and two aft; twelve-pounder balls for the eighteen carronades that constituted the ship's main armament. The twenty tons of iron made a pathetically small mass lying in the bottom of the lighter, when regarded with the eye of a man who had served in a ship of the line; the old *Renown* would have discharged that weight of shot in a couple of hours' fighting. But this dead weight was a very considerable proportion of the load *Atropos* had to carry. Half of it would be distributed fairly evenly along the ship in the shot-garlands; where he decided to stow the other ten tons would make all the difference to *Atropos,* could add a knot to her speed or reduce it by a knot, could make her stiff in a breeze or crank, handy, or awkward under sail. He could not reach a decision about that until the rest of the stores were on board and he had had an opportunity of observing her trim. Hornblower ran a keen eye over the nets in which the shot were to be swayed up at the starboard fore yard-arm, and went back through his mind in search of the data stored away there regarding the breaking strain of Manila line—this, he could tell, had been several years in service.

"Sixteen rounds to the load," he called down into the lighter. "No more."

"Aye aye, sir."

It was typical of Hornblower's mind that it should spend a moment or two thinking about the effect that would be produced if one of those nets was to give way; the shot would pour down into the lighter again; falling from the height of the yard-arm they could go clear through the bottom of the lighter; with all that dead weight on board the lighter would sink like a stone, there on the edge of the fairway, to be an intolerable nuisance to London's shipping until divers had painfully cleared the sunken wreck of the shot, and camels had lifted the wreck clear of the channel. The vast shipping of the Port of London could be seriously impeded as a result of a momentary inattention regarding the condition of a cargo net.

Jones was hastening across the deck to touch his hat to him.

"The last of the powder's just coming aboard, sir."

"Thank you, Mr. Jones. Have the hulk warped back to her moorings. Mr. Owen can send the powder boys here to put the shot in the garlands as they come on board."

"Aye aye, sir."

And the gig was coming back across the river with Carslake sitting in the stern.

"Well, Mr. Carslake, how did the Victualling Yard receive those indents?"

"They've accepted them, sir. They'll have the stores on the quayside tomorrow morning."

"Tomorrow? Didn't you listen to my orders, Mr. Carslake? I don't want to have to put a black mark against your name. Mr. Jones! I'm going over to the Victualling Yard. Come back with me, Mr. Carslake."

The Victualling Yard was a department of the Navy Office, not of the Admiralty. The officials there had to be approached differently from those of the dockyard. One might almost think the two organisations were rivals, instead of working to a common patriotic end against a deadly enemy.

"I can bring my own men to do the work," said Hornblower. "You needn't use your own gangs at all."

"M'm," said the victualling superintendent.

"I'll move everything to the quayside myself, besides lightering it over."

"M'm," said the victualling superintendent again, a trifle more receptively.

"I would be most deeply obliged to you," went on Hornblower. "You need only instruct one of your clerks to point out the stores to the officer in command of my working party. Everything else will be attended to. I beg of you, sir."

It was highly gratifying to a Navy Office official to have a captain, metaphorically, on his knees to him, in this fashion. Equally gratifying was the thought that the navy would do all the work, with a great saving of time-tallies to the Victualling Yard. Hornblower could see the satisfaction in the fellow's fat face. He wanted to wipe it off with his fist, but he kept himself humble. It did him no harm, and by this means he was bending the fellow to his will as surely as if he was using threats.

"There's the matter of those stores you have condemned," said the superintendent.

"My court of inquiry was in due form," said Hornblower.

"Yes," said the superintendent thoughtfully.

"Of course I can return you the hogsheads," suggested Hornblower. "I was intending to do so, as soon as I had emptied the beef over into the tide."

"No, please do not go to that trouble. Return me the full hogsheads."

The working of the minds of these government Jacks-in-office was beyond normal understanding. Hornblower could not believe—although it was just possible—that the superintendent had any personal financial interest in the matter of those condemned stores. But the fact that the condemnation had taken place presumably was a blot on his record, or on the record of the yard. If the hogsheads were returned to them no mention of the condemnation need be made officially, and presumably they could be palmed off again on some other ship—some ship that might go to sea without the opportunity of sampling the stuff first. Sailors fighting for their country might starve as long as the Victualling Yard's records were unsmirched.

"I'll return the full hogsheads gladly, sir," said Hornblower. "I'll send them over to you in the lighter that brings the other stores over."

"That might do very well," said the superintendent.

"I am delighted, and, as I said, intensely obliged to you, sir. I'll have my launch over here with a working party in ten minutes."

Hornblower bowed with all the unction he could command; this was not the moment to spoil the ship for a ha'p'orth of tar. He bowed himself out before the discussion could be reopened. But the superintendent's last words were—

"Remember to return those hogsheads, Captain."

The powder hulk had been warped back to her moorings; the other ordnance stores that were being taken on board seemed trifling in appearance, bundles of wads, and bales of empty serge cartridges, a couple of sheaves of flexible rammers, spare gun-trucks, reels of slow match—the multifarious accessories necessary to keep twenty two guns in action. Hornblower sent off Midshipman Smiley with the working party promised to the Victualling Yard.

"Now I'll have those condemned hogsheads got up on deck, Mr. Carslake. I must keep my promise to return them."

"Aye aye, sir," said Carslake.

Carslake was a bull-headed, youngish man with expressionless pale blue eyes. Those eyes were even more expressionless than usual. He had been a witness of the interview between Hornblower and the superintendent, and he did not allow his feelings to show. Hornblower could not guess whether Carslake as a purser thoroughly approved of saving the stores to be fobbed off on another ship or whether as a sailor certain to endure privations at sea he despised Hornblower's weakness in agreeing to the superintendent's demands.

"I'll mark 'em before I return 'em," said Hornblower.

He had thought of paint when he had been so accommodating towards the superintendent, but was not quite happy in his mind about it, for turpentine would remove paint fast enough. A better idea occurred to him, marvellously, at that very moment.

"Have the cook relight the fire in the galley," he ordered. "I'll have—I'll have a couple of iron musket ramrods heated in the fire. Get them from the armourer, if you please."

"Aye aye, sir. If you please, sir, it's long past the hands' dinnertime."

"When I've time for my own dinner the hands can have theirs," said Hornblower.

He was glad that the deck was crowded so that those words of his could be overheard, for he had had the question of the men's dinnertime in his mind for some time although he was quite resolved not to waste a moment over it.

The first of the condemned hogsheads came creaking and swaying up from the hold and was lowered to the deck. Hornblower looked round him; there was Horrocks with the young Prince, quite bewildered with all the continuous bustle, trailing after him.

"You'll do, Mr. Horrocks. Come here," said Hornblower. He took the chalk from beside the slate at the binnacle; and wrote with it, in large letters diagonally round the hogshead, the word "CONDEMNED." "There are two irons heating in the galley fire. You and Mr. Prince can spend your time branding these hogsheads. Trace out those letters on every one. Understand?"

"Er—yes, sir."

"Good and deep, so there is no chance of planing it off. Look sharp about it."

"Aye aye, sir."

The next lighter for the dockyard was alongside now, at the port side recently vacated by the powder hulk. It was full of bosun's stores, cordage, canvas, paint; and a weary party of men were at work swaying the bundles up. There seemed no end to this business of getting *Atropos* fully equipped for sea. Hornblower himself felt as leg-weary as a foundered horse, and he stiffened himself up to conceal his fatigue. But as he looked across the river he could see the Victualling Yard's lighter already emerging from the Creek. Smiley had his men at work on the sweeps, straining to row the ponderous thing across the ebbing tide. From the quarterdeck he could see the lighter was crammed with the hogsheads and kegs and biscuit bags. Soon *Atropos* would be full-gorged. And the acrid smell of the red-hot irons burning into the brine-soaked staves of the condemned hogsheads came to his nostrils. No ship would ever accept those stores. It was a queer duty for a Serene Highness to be employed upon. How had those orders read? "You will employ your diligence in instructing His Serene Highness in his new profession." Well, perhaps it was not a bad introduction to the methods of fighting men and civilian employees.

Later—ever so much later, it seemed—Mr. Jones came up and touched his hat.

"The last of the stores are on board, sir," he said. "Mr. Smiley's just returning the Victualling Yard's lighter."

"Thank you, Mr. Jones. Call away my gig, please."

Hornblower stepped down into the boat conscious of many weary eyes on him. The winter afternoon was dissolving in a cold and gloomy drizzle as a small rain was beginning to fall. Hornblower had himself rowed round his ship at a convenient distance to observe her trim. He looked at her from ahead, from broadside on, from astern. In his mind's eye he was visualising her underwater lines. He looked up at the spread of her lower yards; the wind would be pressing against the canvas there, and he worked out the balance of the forces involved, wind against lateral resistance, rudder versus headsails. He had to consider sea-worthiness and handiness as well as speed. He climbed back on deck to where Jones was awaiting him.

"I want her more down by the head," he announced. "I'll have those beef casks at the for'rard end of the tier, and the shot for'rard of the magazine. Get the hands to work, if you please."

Once more the pipes shrilled through the ship as the hands began to move the stores ranged upon the deck. It was with anxiety that Hornblower's return was awaited from his next pull round the ship.

"She'll do for the present," said Hornblower.

It was not a casual decision, no stage-effect. The moment *Atropos* should clear the land she would be in danger, she might find herself in instant action. She was only a little ship; even a well-found privateer might give her a hard battle. To overtake in pursuit, to escape in flight; to handle quickly when manoeuvring for position in action; to claw off to windward should she be caught on a lee shore; she must be capable of all this, and she must be capable of it today, for tomorrow, even tomorrow, might be too late. The lives of his crew, his own life, his professional reputation, could hang on that decision.

"You can strike everything below now, Mr. Jones."

Slowly the littered decks began to clear, while the rain grew heavier and the night began to close in round the little ship. The tiers of great casks, down against the skin of the ship, were squeezed and wedged into position; the contents of the hold had to be jammed into a solid mass, for once at sea *Atropos* would roll and pitch, and nothing must budge, nothing must shift, lest the fabric of the ship be damaged or even perhaps the ship might be rolled completely over by the movement of an avalanche of her cargo. The navy still thought of Sir Edward Berry as the officer who, when captain of Nelson's own *Vanguard*, allowed the masts of his ship to be rolled clean out of her in a moderate gale of wind off Sardinia.

Hornblower stood aft by the taffrail while the rain streamed down on him. He had not gone below; this might be part of the penance he was inflicting on himself for not having sufficiently supervised the management of his ship.

"The decks are cleared, sir," said Jones, looming up in the wet darkness before him.

"Very well, Mr. Jones. When everything is swabbed down the men can have their dinners."

The little cabin down below was cold and dark and cheerless. Two canvas chairs and a trestle table stood in the day-cabin; in the night-cabin there was nothing at all. The oil lamp shone gloomily over the bare planks of the deck under his feet. Hornblower could call for his gig again; it would whisk him fast enough half a mile downstream to Deptford Hard, and there at the George were his wife and his children. There would be a roaring fire of sea coal, a spluttering beefsteak with cabbage, a feather bed with the sheets made almost too hot to bear by the application of a warming pan. His chilled body and aching legs yearned inexpressibly for that care and warmth. But in his present mood he would have none of them. Instead he dined, shivering, off ship's fare hastily laid out for him on the trestle table. He had a hammock slung for himself in the night-cabin, and he climbed into it and wrapped himself in clammy blankets. He had not lain in a hammock since he was a midshipman, and his spine had grown unused to the necessary curvature. He was too numb, both mentally and physically, to feel any glow of conscious virtue.

EIGHT

Fog in the Downs, cold, dense, and impenetrable over the surface of the sea. There was no breath of air to set it stirring; overside the surface of the sea, just visible when Hornblower looked down at it from the deck, was black and glassy. Only close against the side could be detected the faintest of ripples, showing how the tide was coursing beside the ship as she lay anchored in the Downs. Condensing on the rigging overhead, the fog dripped in melancholy fashion onto the deck about him, an occasional drop landing with a dull impact on his cocked hat; the heavy frieze pea-jacket that he wore looked as if it were frosted with the moisture that hung upon it. Yet it was not freezing weather, although Hornblower felt chilled through and through inside his layers of clothing as he turned back from his gloomy contemplation of the sea.

"Now, Mr. Jones," he said, "we'll start again. We'll have topmasts and yards struck—all top hamper down and stowed away. Order 'out pipes,' if you please."

"Aye aye, sir," said Jones.

The hands had already spent half the morning at sail drill; Hornblower was taking advantage of the fogbound calm to exercise his ship's company. With so many landsmen on board, with officers unfamiliar with their divisions, this fog actually could be used to advantage; the ship could be made more of a working, fighting unit during this interval of grace before proceeding down-Channel. Hornblower put his cold hand inside his coat and brought out his watch; as if the gesture had called forth the sound, five bells rang out sharply from beside the binnacle, and from the thick fog surrounding them came the sound of other bells—there were many ships anchored in the Downs all about them, so many that it was some minutes before the last sound died away; the sandglasses on board the ships were by no means in agreement.

While the bells were still sounding Hornblower took note of the position of the minute hand of his watch and nodded to Jones. Instantly came a roar of orders; the men, already called to attention after their brief stand-easy, came pouring aft with their petty officers urging them on. Watch in hand, Hornblower stood back by the taffrail. From where he stood only the lower part of the main rigging was visible; the foremast was completely hidden in fog. The hands went hurrying up the ratlines, Hornblower watching keenly to see what proportion of them were vague about their stations and duties. He could have wished that he could see all that was going on—but then if there had been no fog there would have been no sail drill, and *Atropos* would have been making the best of her way down-Channel. Here was the Prince, hurried along by Horrocks with a hand at his shoulder.

"Come on," said Horrocks, leaping at the ratlines.

The Prince sprang up beside him. Hornblower could see the bewildered expression on the boy's face. He had small enough idea of what he was doing. He would learn, no doubt—he was learning much even from the fact that the blood royal, the King's great-nephew, could be shoved about by the plebeian hand of a midshipman.

Hornblower got out of the way as the mizzen topsail came swaying down. A yelping master's mate came running up with a small pack of waisters at his heels; they fell upon the ponderous roll and dragged it to the side. The mizzenmast hands were working faster than the mainmast, apparently—the main topsail was not lowered yet. Jones, his head drawn back so that his Adam's apple protruded apparently by inches, was bellowing the next orders to the masthead. A shout from above answered him. Down the ratlines came a flood of men again.

"Let go! Haul! Lower away!"

The mizzen topsail yard turned in a solemn arc and made its slow descent down the mast. There was an exasperating delay while the mainstay tackle was applied—organisation at this point was exceedingly poor—but at last the yard was down and lying along the booms beside its fellows. The complicated and difficult business of striking the topmasts followed.

"An hour and a quarter, Mr. Jones. More nearly an hour and twenty minutes. Far too long. Half an hour—half an hour with five minutes' grace; that's the longest you should ever take."

"Yes, sir," said Jones. There was nothing else he could say.

As Hornblower was eyeing him before giving his next orders a faint dull thud came to his ears, sounding flatly through the fog. A musket shot? A pistol shot? That was certainly what it sounded like, but with the fog changing the quality of all the sounds he could not be sure. Even if it were a shot, fired in one of the numerous invisible ships round about, there might be endless innocent explanations of it; and it might not be a shot. A hatch cover dropped on a deck—a grating being pushed into place—it could be anything.

The hands were grouped about the deck, looming vaguely in the fog, awaiting further orders. Hornblower guessed that they were sweating despite the cold. This was the way to get that London beer out of them, but he did not want to drive them too hard.

"Five minutes stand-easy," said Hornblower. "And, Mr. Jones, you had better station a good petty officer at that mainstay tackle."

"Aye aye, sir."

Hornblower turned away to give Jones an opportunity to arrange his reorganisation. He set himself to walk the deck to bring some life back into his cold body; his watch was still in his hand through sheer forgetfulness to replace it in his pocket. He ended his walk at the ship's side, glancing over into the black water. Now what was that floating down beside the ship? Something long and black; when Hornblower first caught sight of it it had bumped one end against the ship's side under the main chains, and, as he watched, it swung solemnly round, drawn by the tide, and came down towards him. It was an oar. Curiosity overcame him. In a crowded anchorage like this there was nothing very surprising about a floating oar, but still—

"Here, quartermaster," said Hornblower. "Get down into the mizzen chains with a line to catch that oar."

It was only an oar; Hornblower looked it over as the quartermaster held it for his inspection. The leather button was fairly well worn—it was by no means a new oar. On the other hand, judging by the fact that the leather was not entirely soaked through, it had not long been in the water, minutes rather than days, obviously. There was the number "27" burned into the loom, and it was that which caused Hornblower to look more sharply. The 7 bore a crossbar. No Englishman ever wrote a 7 with a crossbar. But everyone on the Continent did; there were Danes and Swedes and Norwegians, Russians and Prussians, at sea, either neutrals in the war or allies of England. Yet a Frenchman or a Dutchman, one of England's enemies, would also write a 7 in that way.

And there had certainly been something that sounded like a shot. A floating oar and a musket shot made a combination that would be hard to explain. Now if they had been connected in causation! Hornblower still had his watch in his hand. That shot—if it was a shot—had made itself heard just before he gave the order for stand-easy, seven or eight minutes ago. The tide was running at a good two knots. If the shot had caused the oar to be dropped into the water it must have been fired a quarter of a mile or so—two cables' length—upstream. The quartermaster still holding the oar was looking at him curiously, and Jones was waiting, with the men poised for action, for his next orders. Hornblower was tempted to pay no more attention to the incident.

But he was a King's officer, and it was his duty to make inquiry into the unexplainable at sea. He hesitated in inward debate; the fog was horribly thick. If he sent a boat to investigate it would probably lose itself; Hornblower had had much experience of making his way by boat in a fog-ridden anchorage. Then he could go himself. Hornblower felt a qualm at the thought of blundering about trying to find his way in the fog—he could make a fool of himself so easily in the eyes of his crew. Yet on the other hand that was not likely to be as exasperating as fuming on board waiting for a dilatory boat to return.

"Mr. Jones," he said, "call away my gig."

"Aye aye, sir," said Jones, the astonishment in his voice hardly concealed at all.

Hornblower walked to the binnacle and took a careful reading of how the ship's head lay. It was the most careful reading he could possibly take, not because his comfort or his safety was involved but because his personal dignity depended on getting that reading right. North by east half east. As the ship lay riding to her anchor bows to the tide he could be sure that the oar had come down from that direction.

"I want a good boat compass in the gig, Mr. Jones, if you please."

"Aye aye, sir."

Hornblower hesitated before that last and final order, which would commit him to a public admission that he thought there was a chance of something serious awaiting him in the fog. But not to give the order would be to strain at a gnat and swallow a camel. If that had really been a musket shot that he had heard there was a possibility of action; there was a likelihood that at least a show of force would be necessary.

"Pistols and cutlasses for the gig's crew, Mr. Jones, if you please."

"Aye aye, sir," said Jones, as if nothing could astonish him again.

Hornblower turned back as he was about to step down into the boat.

"I shall start timing you from this moment, Mr. Jones. Try to get those tops'l yards across in half an hour from now—I'll be back before then."

"Aye aye, sir."

The ship broke into a roar of activity as Hornblower took his place in the sternsheets of the gig.

"I'll take the tiller," he said to the coxswain. "Give way."

He steered the gig along the *Atropos* from stern to bow. He took one last look up at her bows, at her bowsprit and bobstay, and then the fog swallowed them up. The gig was instantly in a world of its own, constricted about by the walls of mist. The sounds of activity on board the ship died rapidly away.

"Pull steady!" growled Hornblower to the man at the oars. That little boat compass would be swinging about chasing its tail in ten seconds if he allowed the gig to keep anything except an exactly straight course. North by east half east.

"Seventeen," said Hornblower to himself. "Eighteen. Nineteen."

He was counting the strokes of the oars; it was a rough way of estimating the progress made. At seven feet to the stroke less than two hundred strokes meant a quarter of a mile. But there was the speed of the tide to be allowed for. It would be nearer five hundred strokes —all very vague, but every possible precaution must be taken on a foolish expedition like this.

"Seventy four, seventy five," said Hornblower, his eyes glued to the compass.

Even with the brisk tide running, the surface of the sea was a glassy flat calm; the oarblades, lifting from the water at the completion of each stroke, left whirlpools circling on the surface.

"Two hundred," said Hornblower, suppressing a momentary fear that he had miscounted and that it was really three hundred.

The oars groaned on monotonously in the rowlocks.

"Keep your eyes ahead," said Hornblower to the coxswain. "Tell me the moment you see anything. Two sixty four."

It seemed only yesterday that he had sat in the sternsheets of the jolly boat of the *Indefatigable*, rowing up the estuary of the Gironde to cut out the *Papillon*. But that was more than ten years ago. Three hundred. Three hundred and fifty.

"Sir," said the coxswain, tersely.

Hornblower looked forward. Ahead, a trifle on the port bow, there was the slightest thickening in the fog, the slightest looming of something solid there.

"Easy all!" said Hornblower, and the boat continued to glide over the surface; he put the tiller over slightly so as to approach whatever it was more directly. But the boat's way died away before they were near enough to distinguish any details, and at Hornblower's command the men began to row again. Distantly came a low hail out of the fog, apparently called forth by the renewal of the sound of the oars.

"Boat ahoy!"

At least the hail was in English. By now there was visible the vague outline of a large brig; from the heaviness of her spars and fast lines she looked like one of the West India packets.

"What brig's that?" hailed Hornblower in reply.

"*Amelia Jane* of London, thirty seven days out from Barbados."

That was a direct confirmation of Hornblower's first impression. But that voice? It did not sound quite English, somehow. There were foreign captains in the British merchant service, plenty of them, but hardly likely to be in command of a West India packet.

"Easy," said Hornblower to the rowers. The gig glided silently on over the water. He could see no sign of anything wrong.

"Keep your distance," said the voice from the brig.

There was nothing suspicious about the words. Any ship at anchor hardly more than twenty miles from the coast of France was fully entitled to be wary of strangers approaching in a fog. But that word sounded more like "deestance" all the same. Hornblower put his helm over to pass under the brig's stern. Several heads were now apparent at the brig's side; they moved round the stern in time with the gig. There was the brig's name, sure enough. "*Amelia Jane*, London." Then Hornblower caught sight of something else; it was a large boat lying under the brig's port quarter from the main chains. There might be a hundred possible explanations of that, but it was a suspicious circumstance.

"Brig ahoy!" he hailed. "I'm coming aboard."

"Keep off!" said the voice in reply.

Some of the heads at the brig's side developed shoulders, and three or four muskets were pointed at the gig.

"I am a King's officer," said Hornblower.

He stood up in the sternsheets and unbuttoned his pea-jacket so that his uniform was visible. The central figure at the brig's side, the man who had been speaking, looked for a long moment and then spread his hands in a gesture of despair.

"Yes," he said.

Hornblower went up the brig's side as briskly as his chilled limbs would permit. As he stood on the deck he felt a trifle self-conscious at being unarmed, for facing him were more than a dozen men, hostility in their bearing, and some of them with muskets in their hands. But the gig's crew had followed him onto the deck and closed up behind him, handling their cutlasses and pistols.

"Cap'n, sir!" It was the voice from overside of one of the two men left down in the gig. "Please, sir, there's a dead man in the boat here."

Hornblower turned away to look over. A dead man certainly lay there, doubled up in the bottom of the boat. That accounted for the floating oar, then. And for the shot, of course. The man had been killed by a bullet from the brig at the moment the boat was laid alongside; the brig had been taken by boarding. Hornblower looked back towards the group on the deck.

"Frenchmen?" he asked.

"Yes, sir."

The fellow was a man of sense. He had not attempted a hopeless resistance when his coup had been discovered. Although he had fifteen men at his back and there were only eight altogether in the gig he had realised that the presence of a King's ship in the immediate vicinity made his final capture a certainty.

"Where's the crew?" asked Hornblower.

The Frenchman pointed forward, and at a gesture from Hornblower one of his men ran to release the brig's crew from their confinement in the forecastle, half a dozen Negro hands and a couple of officers.

"Much obliged to you, mister," said the captain, coming forward.

"I'm Captain Hornblower of His Majesty's ship *Atropos,*" said Hornblower.

"I beg your pardon, Captain." He was an elderly man, his white hair and blue eyes in marked contrast with his mahogany tan. "You've saved my ship."

"Yes," said Hornblower, "you had better disarm those men."

"Gladly, sir. See to it, Jack."

The other officer, presumably the mate, walked aft to take muskets and swords from the unresisting Frenchmen.

"They came out of the fog and laid me alongside before I was aware, almost, sir," went on the captain. "A King's ship took my four best hands when we was off the Start, or I'd have made a better account of them. I only got one crack at them as it was."

"It was that crack that brought me here," said Hornblower shortly. "Where did they come from?"

"Now that's just what I was asking myself," said the captain. "Not from France in that boat, they couldn't have come."

They turned their gaze inquiringly upon the dejected group of Frenchmen. It was a question of considerable importance. The Frenchmen must have come from a ship, and that ship must be anchored somewhere amid the crowded vessels in the Downs. And at that rate she must be disguised as a British vessel or a neutral, coming in with the others before the wind dropped and the fog closed down. There had been plenty of similar incidents during the war. It was an easy way to snap up a prize. But it meant that somewhere close at hand there was a wolf in sheep's clothing, a disguised French privateer, probably crammed with men—she might have made more than one prize. In the bustle and confusion that would ensue when a breeze should get up, with everyone anxious to up anchor and away, she could count on being able to make her escape along with her prizes.

"When the fog closed down," said the captain, "the nearest vessel to us was a Ramsgate trawler. She anchored at the same time as we did. I doubt if it could be her."

It was a matter of so much importance that Hornblower could not keep still. He turned and paced the deck for a space, his mind working rapidly. Yet his mind was not completely made up when he turned back and gave his first order in execution of the vague plan. He did not know if he would have the resolution to go through with it.

"Leadbitter," he said to the coxswain.

"Sir!"

"Tie those men's hands behind them."

"Sir?"

"You heard what I said."

To bind prisoners was almost a violation of the laws of war. When Leadbitter approached to carry out his orders the Frenchmen showed evident resentment. A buzz of voices arose.

"You can't do this, sir," said their spokesman. "We have—"

"Shut your mouth!" snapped Hornblower.

Even having to give that order put him in a bad temper, and his bad temper was made worse by his doubts about himself. Now that the Frenchmen were disarmed they could offer no resistance in face of the drawn pistols of the British sailors. With loud protests they had to submit, as Leadbitter went from man to man tying their wrists behind their backs. Hornblower was hating himself for the part he had to play, even while his calculating mind told him that he had a fair chance of success. He had to pose as a bloodthirsty man, delighting in the taking of human life, without mercy in his soul, gratified by the sight of the death struggles of a fellow human. Such men did exist, he knew. There were gloomy tyrants in the King's service. In the past ten years of war at sea there had been some outrages, a few, on both sides. These Frenchmen did not know him for what he really was, nor did the West India crew. Nor for that matter his own men. Their acquaintance had been so short that they had no reason to believe him not to have homicidal tendencies, so that their behaviour would not weaken the impression he wished to convey. He turned to one of his men.

"Run aloft," he said. "Reeve a whip through the block at the main yard-arm."

That portended a hanging. The man looked at him with a momentary unbelief, but the scowl on Hornblower's face sent him scurrying up the ratlines. Then Hornblower strode to where the wretched Frenchmen were standing bound; their glance shifted from the man at the yard-arm to Hornblower's grim face, and their anxious chattering died away.

"You are pirates," said Hornblower, speaking slowly and distinctly. "I am going to hang you."

In case the English-speaking Frenchman's vocabulary did not include the word "hang" he pointed significantly to the man at the yard-arm. They could all understand that. They remained silent for a second or two, and then several of them began to speak at once in torrential French which Hornblower could not well follow, and then the leader, having pulled himself together, began his protest in English.

"We are not pirates," he said.

"I think you are," said Hornblower.

"We are privateersmen," said the Frenchman.

"Pirates," said Hornblower.

The talk among the Frenchmen rose to a fresh height; Hornblower's French was good enough for him to make out that the leader was translating his curt words to his companions, and they were urging him to explain more fully their position.

"I assure you, sir," said the wretched man, striving to be eloquent in a strange language, "we are privateersmen and not pirates."

Hornblower regarded him with a stony countenance, and without answering turned away to give further orders.

"Leadbitter," he said. "I'll have a hangman's noose on the end of that line."

Then he turned back to the Frenchmen.

"Who do you say you are then?" he asked. He tried to utter the words as indifferently as he could.

"We are from the privateer *Vengeance* of Dunkirk, sir. I am Jacques Lebon, prizemaster."

Privateers usually went to sea with several extra officers, who could be put into prizes to navigate them back to a French port without impairing the fighting efficiency of the privateer, which could continue her cruise. These officers were usually selected for their ability to speak English and for their knowledge of English seagoing ways, and they bore the title of "prizemaster." Hornblower turned back to observe the noose now dangling significantly from the yard-arm, and then addressed the prizemaster.

"You have no papers," he said.

He forced his lips into a sneer as he spoke; to the wretched men studying every line in his face his expression appeared quite unnatural, as indeed it was. And Hornblower was gambling a little when he said what he did. If the prizemaster had been able to produce any papers the whole line of attack would have to be altered; but it was not much of a gamble. Hornblower was certain when he spoke that if Lebon had had papers in his pocket he would have already mentioned them, asking someone to dive into his pocket for them. That would be the first reaction of any Frenchman whose identity had been put in question.

"No," said Lebon, crestfallen. It was hardly likely that he would have, when engaged on an ordinary operation of war.

"Then you hang," said Hornblower. "All of you. One by one."

The laugh he forced himself to produce sounded positively inhuman, horrible. Anyone hearing it would be justified in thinking that he was inspired by the anticipated pleasure of watching the death struggles of a dozen men. The white-haired captain of the *Amelia Jane* could not bear the prospect, and came forward to enter into the discussion.

"Sir," he said, "what are you going to do?"

"I am going to attend to my own business, sir," said Hornblower, striving to throw into his voice all the harshness he had ever heard employed by all the insolent officers he had met during his service. "May I ask you to be kind enough to do the same?"

"But you can't be meaning to hang the poor devils," went on the captain.

"But that is what I do mean."

"But not in my ship, sir—not now—not without trial."

"In your ship, sir, which you allowed to be captured. And now. Pirates taken red-handed can be hanged instantly, as you know, sir. And that is what I shall do."

It was a stroke of good fortune that the captain should have entered into the discussion. His appearance of sick dismay and the tone of his protests were convincingly genuine—they would never have been so if he had been admitted previously to a planned scheme. Hornblower's attitude towards him was brutal, but it was for the good of the cause.

"Sir," persisted the captain, "I'm sure they're only privateersmen—"

"Please refrain from interfering with a King's officer in the execution of his duty. You two men, there, come here."

The two of the crew of the gig that he indicated approached obediently. Probably they had seen hangings before, along with every kind of brutality in a brutal service. But the imminent certainty of taking personal part in a hanging obviously impressed them. There was some reluctance visible in their expressions, but the hard discipline of the service would make certain they would obey the orders of this one man, unarmed and outnumbered.

Hornblower looked along the line of faces. Momentarily he felt a horrid sickness in his stomach as it occurred to him to wonder how he would be feeling if he really was selecting a victim.

"I'll have that one first," he said, pointing.

The bull-throated swarthy man whom he indicated paled and shuddered; backing away he tried to shelter himself among his fellows. They were all speaking at once, jerking their arms frantically against the bonds that secured their wrists behind them.

"Sir!" said Lebon. "Please—I beg of you—I implore—"

Hornblower condescended to spare him a glance, and Lebon went on in a wild struggle against the difficulties of language and the handicap of not being free to gesticulate.

"We are privateersmen. We fight for the Empire, for France." Now he was on his knees, his face lifted. As he could not use his hands he was actually nuzzling with his mouth against the skirts of Hornblower's pea-jacket. "We surrendered. We did not fight. We caused no death."

"Take this man away from me," said Hornblower, withdrawing out of reach.

But Lebon on his knees followed him over the deck, nuzzling and pleading.

"Captain," said the English captain, interceding once again. "Can't you at least wait and land 'em for trial? If they're pirates it'll be proved quick enough."

"I want to see 'em dangling," said Hornblower, searching feverishly in his mind for the most impressive thing he could say.

The two English seamen, taking advantage of the volume of protest, had paused in the execution of their orders. Hornblower looked up at the noose, dangling dimly but horribly in the fog.

"I don't believe for one single moment," went on Hornblower, "that these men are what they say they are. Just a band of thieves, pirates. Leadbitter, put four men on that line. I'll give the word when they are to walk away with it."

"Sir," said Lebon. "I assure you, word of honour, we are from the privateer *Vengeance*."

"Bah!" replied Hornblower. "Where is she?"

"Over there," said Lebon. He could not point with his hands; he pointed with his chin, over the port bow of the anchored *Amelia Jane*. It was not a very definite indication, but it was a considerable help, even that much.

"Did you see any vessel over there before the fog closed down, captain?" demanded Hornblower, turning to the English captain.

"Only the Ramsgate trawler," he said, reluctantly.

"That is our ship!" said Lebon. "That is the *Vengeance!* She was a Dunkirk trawler—we—we made her look like that."

So that was it. A Dunkirk trawler. Her fish holds could be crammed full of men. A slight alteration of gear, an "R" painted on her mainsail, a suitable name painted on her stern and then she could wander about the narrow seas without question, snapping up prizes almost at will.

"Where did you say she lay?" demanded Hornblower.

"There—oh!"

Lebon checked himself as he realised how much information he was giving away.

"I can hazard a good guess as to how she bears from us," interposed the English captain. "I saw—oh!"

He broke off exactly as Lebon had done, but from surprise. He was staring at Hornblower. It was like the denouement scene in some silly farce. The lost heir was at last revealed. The idea of now accepting the admiration of his unwitting fellow players, of modestly admitting that he was not the monster of ferocity he had pretended to be, irritated Hornblower beyond all bearing. All his instincts and good taste rose against the trite and the obvious. Now that he had acquired the information he had sought he could please himself as long as he acted instantly on that information. The scowl he wished to retain rested the more easily on his features with this revulsion of feeling.

"I'd be sorry to miss a hanging," he said, half to himself, and he allowed his eye to wander again from the dangling noose to the shrinking group of Frenchmen who were still ignorant of what had just happened. "If that thick neck were stretched a little—"

He broke off and took a brief turn up and down the deck, eyed by every man who stood on it.

"Very well," he said, halting. "It's against my better judgment, but I'll wait before I hang these men. What was the approximate bearing of that trawler when she anchored, Captain?"

"It was at slack water," began the captain, making his calculations. "We were just beginning to swing. I should say—"

The captain was obviously a man of sober judgment and keen observation. Hornblower listened to what he had to say.

"Very well," said Hornblower when he had finished. "Leadbitter, I'll leave you on board with two men. Keep an eye on these prisoners and see they don't retake the brig. I'm returning to the ship now. Wait here for further orders."

He went down into his gig; the captain accompanying him to the ship's side was clearly and gratifyingly puzzled. It was almost beyond his belief that Hornblower could be the demoniac monster that he had appeared to be, and if he were it was strange good fortune that his ferocity should have obtained, by pure chance, the information that the prisoners had just given him. Yet on the other hand it was almost beyond his belief that if Hornblower had employed a clever ruse to gain the information he should refuse to enjoy the plaudits of his audience and not to bask in their surprise and admiration. Either notion was puzzling. That was well. Let him be puzzled. Let them all be puzzled—although it seemed as if the sobered hands pulling at the oars of the gig were not at all puzzled. Unheeding of all that had been at stake they were clearly convinced that their captain had shown himself in his true colours, and was a man who would sooner see a man's death agonies than eat his dinner. Let 'em think so. It would do no harm. Hornblower could spare them no thought in any case, with all his attention glued upon the compass card. It would be ludicrous—it would be horribly comic—if after all this he were to miss *Atropos* on his way back to her, if he were to blunder about in the fog for hours looking for his own ship. The reciprocal of north by east half east was south by west half west, and he kept the gig rigidly on that course. With what still remained of the ebb tide behind them it would only be a few seconds before they ought to sight *Atropos*. It was a very great comfort when they did.

Mr. Jones received Hornblower at the ship's side. A glance had told him that the gig's crew was two men and a coxswain short. It was hard to think of any explanation of that, and Mr. Jones was bursting with curiosity. He could not help but wonder what his captain had been doing, out there in the fog. His curiosity even overcame his apprehension at the sight of the scowl which Hornblower still wore—now that he was back in his ship Hornblower was beginning to feel much more strongly the qualms that should have influenced him regarding what Their Lordships might think of his absence from his ship. He ignored Jones' questions.

"You got those tops'l yards across, I see, Mr. Jones."

"Yes, sir. I sent the hands to dinner when you didn't come back, sir. I thought—"

"They'll have five minutes to finish their dinners. No longer. Mr. Jones, if you were in command of two boats sent to capture a hostile vessel at anchor in this fog, how would you set about it? What orders would you give?"

"Well, sir, I'd—I'd—"

Mr. Jones was not a man of quickness of thought or rapid adaptability to a new situation. He hummed and he hawed. But there were very few officers in the navy who had not been on at least one cutting-out and boarding operation. He knew well enough what he should do, and it slowly became apparent.

"Very well, Mr. Jones. You will now hoist out the longboat and the launch. You will man them and see that the boats' crews are fully armed. You will proceed north by east half east—fix that in your mind, Mr. Jones, north by east half east—from this ship for a quarter of a mile. There you will find a West India brig, the *Amelia Jane*. She has just been recaptured from a French prize crew, and my coxswain is on board with two men. From her you will take a new departure. There's a French privateer, the *Vengeance*. She's a Dunkirk trawler disguised as a Ramsgate trawler. She is probably heavily manned—at least fifty of a crew left—and she is anchored approximately three cables' lengths approximately northwest of the *Amelia Jane*. You will capture her, by surprise if possible. Mr. Still will be in command of the second boat. I will listen while you give him his instructions. That will save repetition. Mr. Still!"

The despatch that Hornblower wrote that evening and entrusted to the *Amelia Jane* for delivery to the Admiralty was couched in the usual navy phraseology.

SIR,

I have the honour to report to you for the information of Their Lordships that this day while anchored in dense fog in the Downs I became aware that it seemed likely that some disturbance was taking place near at hand. On investigating I had the good fortune to recapture the brig *Amelia Jane,* homeward bound from Barbados, which was in possession of a French prize crew. From information gained from the prisoners I was able to send my first lieutenant, Mr. Jones, with the boats of H.M. ship under my command, to attack the French private ship of war *Vengeance* of Dunkirk. She was handsomely carried by Mr. Jones and his officers and men, including Mr. Still, second lieutenant, Messrs. Horrocks and Smiley, and His Serene Highness the Prince of Seitz-Bunau, midshipmen, after a brief action in which our loss was two men slightly wounded while the French Captain, Monsieur Ducos, met with a severe wound while trying to rally his crew. The *Vengeance* proved to be a French trawler masquerading as an English fishing boat. Including the prize crew she carried a crew of seventy one officers and men, and she was armed with one four-pounder carronade concealed under her net.

I have the honour to remain,

Your obed't servant,

H. HORNBLOWER, CAPTAIN

Before sealing it Hornblower read through this report with a lopsided smile on his face. He wondered if anyone would ever read between the lines of that bald narrative, how much anyone would guess, how much anyone would deduce. The fog, the cold, the wet; the revolting scene on the deck of the *Amelia Jane;* the interplay of emotion; could anyone ever guess at all the truth? And there was no doubt that his gig's crew was already spreading round the ship horrible reports about his lust for blood. There was some kind of sardonic satisfaction to be derived from that, too. A knock at the door. Could he never be undisturbed?

"Come in," he called.

It was Jones. His glance took in the quill in Hornblower's fingers, and the inkwell and papers on the table before him.

"Your pardon, sir," he said. "I hope I don't come too late."

"What is it?" asked Hornblower; he had little sympathy for Jones and his undetermined manners.

"If you are going to send a report to the Admiralty, sir—and I suppose you are, sir—"

"Yes, of course I am."

"I don't know if you're going to mention my name, sir—I don't want to ask if you are, sir—I don't want to presume—"

If Jones was soliciting a special mention of himself in the Admiralty letter he would get none at all.

"What is it you're saying to me, Mr. Jones?"

"It's only that my name's a common one, sir. John Jones, sir. There are twelve John Joneses in the lieutenants' list, sir. I didn't know if you knew, sir, but I am John Jones the Ninth. That's how I'm known at the Admiralty, sir. If you didn't say that, perhaps—"

"Very well, Mr. Jones. I understand. You can rely on me to see that justice is done."

"Thank you, sir."

With Jones out of the way Hornblower sighed a little, looked at his report, and drew a fresh sheet towards him. There was no chance of inserting "the Ninth" legibly after the mention of Jones' name. The only thing to do was to take a fresh sheet and write it all over again. An odd occupation for a bloodthirsty tyrant.

NINE

Hornblower watched with a keen eye his crew at work as they took in sail while *Atropos* came gliding into Gibraltar Bay. He could call them well-drilled now. The long beat down the Channel, the battles with the Biscay gales, had made a correlated team of them. There was no confusion and only the minimum number of orders. The men came hurrying off the yards; he saw two figures swing themselves onto the main backstays and come sliding down all the way from the masthead, disdaining to use the shrouds and ratlines. They reached the deck simultaneously and stood grinning at each other for a moment—clearly they had been engaged in a race. One was Smiley, the midshipman of the maintop. The other, His Serene Highness the Prince of Seitz-Bunau. That boy had improved beyond all expectation. If ever he should sit on his throne again in his princely German capital he would have strange memories to recall.

But this was not the time for a captain to let his attention wander.

"Let go, Mr. Jones!" he hailed, and the anchor fell, dragging the grumbling hawser out through the hawsehole; Hornblower watched while *Atropos* took up her cable and then rode to her anchor. She was in her assigned berth; Hornblower looked up at the towering Rock and over at the Spanish shore. Nothing seemed to have changed since the last time—so many years ago—that he had come sailing into Gibraltar Bay. The sun was shining down on him, and it was good to feel this Mediterranean sun again, even though there was little warmth in it during this bleak winter weather.

"Call away my gig, if you please, Mr. Jones."

Hornblower ran below to gird on his sword and to take the better of his two cocked hats out of its tin case so as to make himself as presentable as possible when he went ashore to pay his official calls. There was a very decided thrill in the thought that soon he would be reading the orders that would carry him forward into the next phase of his adventures—adventures possibly; more probably the mere dreariness of beating about on eternal blockade duty outside a French port.

Yet in Collingwood's orders to him, when he came to read them, there was a paragraph which left him wondering what his fate was to be.

> You will take into your ship Mr. William McCullum, of the Honourable East India Company's Service, together with his native assistants, and you will give them passage when, in obedience to the first paragraph of these orders, you come to join me.

Mr. McCullum was awaiting him in the Governor's anteroom. He was a burly, heavy-set man in his early thirties, blue-eyed and with a thick mat of black hair.

"Captain Horatio Hornblower?" There was a roll to the "r's" which betrayed the county of his origin.

"Mr. McCullum?"

"Of the Company's Service."

The two men eyed each other.

"You are to take passage in my ship?"

"Aye."

The fellow carried himself with an air of vast independence. Yet judging by the scantiness of the silver lace on his uniform, and by the fact that he wore no sword, he was not of a very lofty position in the Company's hierarchy.

"Who are these native assistants of yours?"

"Three Sinhalese divers."

"Sinhalese?"

Hornblower said the word with caution. He had never heard it before, at least pronounced in that way. He suspected that it meant something to do with Ceylon, but he was not going to make a display of his ignorance.

"Pearl divers from Ceylon," said McCullum.

So he had guessed right. But he could not imagine for one moment why Collingwood, at grips with the French in the Mediterranean, should need Ceylonese pearl divers.

"And what is your official position, Mr. McCullum?"

"I am wreck-master and salvage director of the Coromandel Coast."

That went far to explain the man's ostentatious lack of deference. He was one of those experts whose skill made them too valuable to be trifled with. He might have drifted out to India as a cabin boy or apprentice; presumably he had been treated like a menial while young, but he had learned a trade so well as now to be indispensable and in a position to repay the slights he had endured earlier. The more the gold lace he was addressing the brusquer was likely to be his manner.

"Very well, Mr. McCullum. I shall be sailing immediately and I shall be glad if you will come on board with your assistants at the earliest possible moment. Within an hour. Do you have any equipment with you to be shipped?"

"Very little besides my chests and the divers' bundles. They are ready, along with the food for them."

"Food?"

"The poor bodies—" McCullum narrowed the vowel sound until the word sounded like "puir"—"are benighted heathen, followers of Buddha. They well-nigh died on the voyage here, never having known what it was to have a full belly before. A scrap of vegetable, a drop of oil, a bit of fish for a relish. That's what they're used to living on."

Oil? Vegetables? Ships of war could hardly be expected to supply such things.

"I've a puncheon of Spanish olive oil for them," explained McCullum. "They've taken kindly to it although it's far removed from their buffalo butter. Lentils and onions and carrots. Give them salt beef and they'll die, and that would be poor business after shipping them all round the Cape of Good Hope."

The statement was made with apparent callousness, but Hornblower suspected that the manner concealed some consideration for his unfortunate subordinates so far from their homes. He began to like McCullum a little better.

"I'll give orders for them to be well looked after," he said.

"Thank you." That was the first shade of politeness that had crept into McCullum's speech. "The poor devils have been perishing of cold here on the Rock. That makes them homesick, like, a long way they are from home, too."

"Why have they been sent here in any case?" asked Hornblower. That question had been striving for utterance for some time; he had not asked it because it would have given McCullum too good an opportunity to snub him.

"Because they can dive in sixteen and a half fathoms," said McCullum, staring straight at him.

It was not quite a snub; Hornblower was aware that he owed the modification to his promise that they would be well treated. He would not risk another question despite his consuming curiosity. He was completely puzzled as to why the Mediterranean Fleet should need divers who could go down through a hundred feet of water. He contented himself with ending the interview with an offer to send a boat for McCullum and his men.

The Ceylonese when they made their appearance on the deck of the *Atropos* were of an appearance to excite pity. They held their white cotton clothes close about them against the cold; the keen air that blew down from the snow-clad Spanish mountains set them shivering. They were thin frail-looking men, and they looked about them with no curiosity but with only a dull resignation in their dark eyes. They were of a deep brown colour, so as to excite the interests of the hands who gathered to stare. They spared no glances for the white men, but conversed briefly with each other in high piping musical voices.

"Give them the warmest corner of the 'tween-decks, Mr. Jones," said Hornblower. "See that they are comfortable. Consult with Mr. McCullum regarding anything they may need. Allow me to present Mr. McCullum—Mr. Jones. I would be greatly obliged if you will extend to Mr. McCullum the hospitality of the wardroom."

Hornblower had to phrase it that way. The wardroom theoretically was a voluntary association of officers, who could make their own choice as to what members they might admit. But it would be a bold set of officers who decided to exclude a wardroom guest recommended by their captain, as Jones and Hornblower both knew.

"You must provide a cot for Mr. McCullum, too, Mr. Jones, if you please. You can decide for yourself where you will put it."

It was comforting to be able to say that. Hornblower knew perfectly well—and so did Jones, as his slightly dismayed expression revealed—that in a twenty-two-gun sloop there was not a square foot of deck space to spare. Everyone was already overcrowded, and McCullum's presence would add seriously to the overcrowding. But it was Jones who would have to find a way round the difficulty.

"Aye aye, sir," said Jones; the interval that elapsed before he said it was the best indication of the involved train of thought he had been following out.

"Excellent," said Hornblower. "You can attend to it after we're under way. No more time to waste, Mr. Jones."

Minutes were always valuable. The wind might always shift, or drop. An hour wasted now might mean the loss of a week. Hornblower was in a fever to get his ship clear of the Gut and into the wider waters of the Mediterranean, where he would have sea room in which to beat against a head-wind should a Levanter come blowing out of the east. Before his mind's eye he had a picture of the western Mediterranean; the northwesterly blowing at present could carry him quickly along the southern coast of Spain, past the dangerous shoal of Alboran, until at Cape de Gata the Spanish coast trended away boldly to the northward. Once there he would be less restricted; until Cape de Gata was left behind he could not be happy. There was also—Hornblower could not deny it—his own personal desire to be up and doing, to find out what was awaiting him in the future, to put himself at least in the possible path of adventure. It was fortunate that his duty and his inclination should coincide in this way; one of the few small bits of good fortune, he told himself with amused grimness, that he had experienced since he had made his original choice of the career of a naval officer.

But at least he had come into Gibraltar Bay after dawn and he was leaving before nightfall. He could not be accused of wasting any time. They had rounded the Rock; Hornblower looked into the binnacle and up at the commission pendant blowing out from the masthead.

"Full and bye," he ordered.

"Full and bye, sir," echoed the quartermaster at the wheel.

A keen gust of wind came blowing down out of the Sierra de Ronda, laying the *Atropos* over as the trimmed yards braced the sails to catch it. Over she lay; a short steep wave came after them, the remnants of an Atlantic roller that had survived its passage through the Gut. *Atropos* lifted her stern to it, heaving jerkily in this unnatural opposition of wind and wave. Spray burst under her counter, and spray burst round her bows as she plunged. She plunged again in the choppy sea. She was only a little ship, the smallest three-master vessel in the service, the smallest that could merit a captain to command her. The lofty frigates, the massive seventy fours, could condescend to her. Hornblower looked round him at the wintry Mediterranean, at the fresh clouds obscuring the sinking sun. The waves could toss his ship about, the winds could heel her over, but standing there, braced on the quarterdeck, he was master of them. Exaltation surged within him as his ship hurried forward into the unknown.

The exaltation even remained when he quitted the deck and descended into the cabin. Here the prospect was cheerless in the extreme. He had mortified his flesh after he had come on board his ship at Deptford. His conscience had nagged at him for the scanty hours he had wasted with his wife and children; and he had never left his ship again for a moment after he had reported her ready for sea. No farewell to Maria lying in childbed, no last parting from little Horatio and little

Maria. And no purchase of cabin equipment. The furniture about him was what the ship's carpenter had made for him—canvas chairs, a rough-and-ready table, a cot whose frame was strung with cordage to support a coarse canvas mattress stuffed with straw. A canvas pillow, straw-filled, to support his head; coarse navy blankets to cover his skinny body. There was no carpet on the deck under his feet; the light came from a swinging and odorous ship's lantern. A shelf with a hole in it supported a tin washbasin; on the bulkhead above it hung the scrap of polished-steel mirror from Hornblower's meagre canvas dressing-roll. The most substantial articles present were the two sea-chests in the corners; apart from them a monk's cell could hardly have been more bare.

But there was no self-pity in Hornblower's mind as he crouched under the low deck beams unhooking his stock preparatory to going to bed. He expected little from this world, and he could lead an inner life of the mind that could render him oblivious to discomfort. And he had saved a good deal of money by not furnishing his cabin, money which would pay the midwife's fee, the long bill at the George, and the fare for the carrier's cart which would convey Maria and the children to lodge with her mother at Southsea. He was thinking about them—they must be well on their way now—as he drew the clammy blankets over himself and rested his cheek on the rough pillow. Then he had to forget Maria and the children as he reminded himself that as the *Atropos'* junction with the fleet was so imminent he must exercise the midshipmen and the signal ratings in signalling. He must devote a good many hours to that, and there would not be much time to spare, for the creaking of the timbers, the heave of the ship, told him that the wind was holding steady.

The wind continued to hold fair. It was at noon on the sixth day that the lookout hailed the deck.

"Sail ho! Dead to loo'ard."

"Bear down on her, Mr. Jones, if you please. Mr. Smiley! Take a glass and see what you make of her."

This was the second of the rendezvous which Collingwood had named in his orders. Yesterday's had been barren, off Cape Carbomara. Not a sail had been sighted since leaving Gibraltar. Collingwood's frigates had swept the sea clear of French and Spanish shipping, and the British Levant convoy was not due for another month. And no one could guess what was going on in Italy at this moment.

"Captain, sir! She's a frigate. One of ours."

"Very well. Signal midshipman! Be ready with the private signal and our number."

Thank Heaven for all the signalling exercise he had been giving during the last few days.

"Captain, sir! I can see mastheads beyond her. Looks like a fleet."

"Very well, Mr. Jones, I'll have the gunner make ready to salute the flag, if you please."

"Aye aye, sir."

There was the Mediterranean Fleet, a score of ships of the line, moving slowly in two columns over the blue sea under a blue sky.

"Frigate's *Maenad,* twenty eight, sir."

"Very well."

Reaching out like the tentacles of a sea monster, the scouting frigates lay far ahead of the main body of the fleet, four of them, with a fifth far to windward, whence most likely would appear ships hostile or friendly. The air was clear; Hornblower on the quarterdeck with his glass to his eye could see the double column of topsails of ships of the line, close-hauled, every ship exactly the same distance astern of her predecessor. He could see the vice admiral's flag at the foremast of the leader of the weather line.

"Mr. Carslake! Have the mail bags ready for sending off."

"Aye aye, sir."

His own packet of despatches for Collingwood was handy in his cabin.

"Signal midshipman! Can't you see the flagship's making a signal?"

"Yes, sir, but the flags are blowing straight away from us. I can't make them out."

"What do you think the repeating frigate's for? Use your eyes."

"General signal, sir. Number Forty one. That is 'tack,' sir."

"Very well."

As *Atropos* had not yet officially joined the Mediterranean squadron a general signal could not apply to her. Down came the signal from the flagship's yard-arm; that was the executive moment. Round came the flagship's yards; round came the yards of the scouting frigates, and of the leader of the lee column. One by one, at precise intervals, the succeeding ships in the columns came round in order; Hornblower could see the momentary backing and filling of the mizzen topsails which maintained the ships so exactly spaced. It was significant that the drill was being carried out under all plain sail, and not merely under the "fighting sails." There was something thrilling in the sight of this perfection of drill; but at the same time something a little disturbing. Hornblower found himself wondering, with a qualm of doubt, if he would be able to maintain *Atropos* so exactly in station now that the time had come to join the fleet.

The manoeuvre was completed now; on its new tack the fleet was steadily plunging forward over the blue sea. There was more bunting fluttering at the flagship's yard-arm.

"General signal, sir. 'Hands to dinner.'"

"Very well."

Hornblower felt a bubbling of excitement within him as he stood and watched. The next signal would surely be for him.

"Our number, sir! Flag to *Atropos*. Take station to windward of me at two cables' lengths."

"Very well. Acknowledge."

There were eyes turned upon him everywhere on deck. This was the moment of trial. He had to come down past the screening frigates, cross ahead of what was now the weather column, and come to the wind at the right moment and at the right distance. And the whole fleet would be watching the little ship. First he had to estimate how far the flagship would progress towards his starboard hand while he was running down to her. But there was nothing for it but to try; there was some faint comfort in being an officer in a fighting service where an order was something that must be obeyed.

"Quartermaster! Port a little. Meet her. Steady as you go! Keep her at that! Mr. Jones!"

"Aye aye, sir."

No need for an order to Jones. He was more anxious—at least more apparently anxious—than Hornblower was. He had the hands at the braces trimming the yards already. Hornblower looked up at yards and commission pendant to assure himself that the bracing was exact. They had left the *Maenad* behind already; here they were passing *Amphion*, one of the central frigates in the screen. Hornblower could see her lying over as she thrashed to windward, the spray flying from her bows. He turned back to look at the flagship, nearly hull up, at least two of her three rows of checkered gunports visible.

"Port a little! Steady!"

He resented having to give that additional order; he wished he could have headed straight for his station with no alteration of course. The leading ship—she wore a rear admiral's flag—of the weather column was now nearly on his port beam. Four cables' length was the distance between the two columns, but as his station was to windward of the flagship, nearly on her starboard beam, he would be by no means between the two ships, nor equidistant from them. He juggled in his mind with the scalene triangle that could be drawn connecting *Atropos* with the two flagships.

"Mr. Jones! Clue up the mizzen tops'l." Now *Atropos* would have a reserve of speed that he could call for if necessary. He was glad that he had subjected his crew to ceaseless sail drill ever since leaving Deptford. "Stand by the mizzen tops'l sheets."

The reduction in the after sail would make *Atropos* a little slower in coming to the wind; he must bear it in mind. They were fast approaching their station. His eye darted from one column of ships to the other; he could see all the starboard sides of one and all the port sides of the other. It might be useful to take sextant angles, but he would rather trust his eye in a trigonometrical problem as uncomplicated as this. His judgment told him this must be the moment. The bows were pointing at the flagship's jib-boom.

"Port your helm," he ordered. Perhaps he was wrong. Perhaps the little ship's response would be delayed. Perhaps—he had to keep his voice steady. "Bring her to the wind."

The wheel spun over. There was a nervous second or two. Then he felt the heel of the ship alter under his feet; and he saw the flagship come round on *Atropos'* port beam, and he knew *Atropos* was turning.

"Steady!"

The yards were braced up; strong arms were hauling on the tacks. A moment or two while *Atropos* regained the small amount of way she had lost through her turn; but even making allowance for that he could see that the flagship was slowly head-reaching on her.

"Mr. Jones! Sheet home the mizzen tops'l."

With the mizzen topsail drawing full they would head-reach in turn upon the flagship.

"Keep the hands at the braces there!"

Occasionally spilling the wind from the mizzen topsail would enable *Atropos* to keep her speed equal to the flagship's. Hornblower felt the wind on his neck; he looked up at the pendant and at the flagship. He was exactly to windward of her, and there were two cables' lengths between them.

"Mr. Jones! You may begin the salute."

Fifteen guns for a vice admiral, a minute and a quarter to fire them. That might be long enough for him to regain his composure, and for his heart to resume its normal rate of beating. Now they were part of the Mediterranean Fleet, the tiniest, most insignificant part of it. Hornblower looked down the massive lines of ships ploughing along behind them, three-deckers, two-deckers, ships of a hundred guns and ships of seventy four, the ships which had fought at Trafalgar, the roar of whose cannon had dashed from Bonaparte's lips the heady cup of world domination. On the invisibly distant Mediterranean shores that encompassed them armies might march, kings might be set up and kings might be pulled down; but it was these ships which in the end would decide the destiny of the world, as long as the men who sailed them retained their skill, as long as they remained ready to endure danger and hardship, as long as the government at home remained resolute and unafraid.

"Our number, sir! Flag to *Atropos*. 'Welcome.'"

"Reply to Flag. 'Respectful greetings.'"

Eager hands worked vigorously on the signal halliards.

"Signal '*Atropos* to Flag. Have aboard despatches and letters for fleet.'"

"Flagship acknowledges, sir."

"Flagship's signalling again," announced Still; from a point of vantage on the weather side he could see through his glass enough of the flagship's quarterdeck, despite the fact that she was heeling away from him, to make out that signal ratings were bending fresh flags on the halliards. The dark lumps soared up to the flagship's yard-arm and broke into gaily coloured bunting.

"General signal. 'Heave-to on the starboard tack.'"

"Acknowledge, Mr. Jones! Clue up the courses."

Hornblower watched the hands at the clue-garnets and buntlines, the hands at the tacks and sheets.

"Signal's down, sir."

Hornblower had already seen the first movement of descent.

"Back the mizzen tops'l. Let her come up."

Atropos rode easily, just meeting the waves with her bow, as the sharp struggle with the wind changed to yielding acquiescence, like a girl's resistance coming to an end in her lover's arms. But this was no time for that sort of sentimental simile—here was another long signal from the flagship.

"General signal. 'Send to—' our number, sir—'for letters.'"

"Mr. Carslake! Have those mailbags on deck at once. You'll have a boat from every ship in the fleet alongside."

It was at least a month—it might well be two—since any letters had reached the fleet from England. Not a newspaper, not a word. Possibly some of the ships present had not yet seen the accounts in the press of the victory they had won at Trafalgar four months before. *Atropos* had brought a respite from the dreadful isolation in which a fleet at sea habitually lived. Boats would be hastening as fast as sail or oar could drive them to collect the pitifully lean mailbags.

Another signal.

"Our number, sir. 'Flag to *Atropos*. Come and report.'"

"Call away my gig."

He was wearing the shabbier of his two coats. There was just time, when he ran below to get the packets of despatches, to change his coat, to pass a comb through his hair, and twitch his neckcloth into position. He was back on deck just as his gig touched the water. Lusty work at the oars carried him round to the flagship. A chair dangled at her side, now almost lipped as a wave rose at it, now high above the water as the wave passed on. He had to watch carefully for his chance; as it was there was an uncomfortable moment when he hung by his arms as the gig went away from under him. But he managed to seat himself, and he felt the chair soar swiftly upwards as the hands above hauled on the tackle. The pipes shrilled as his head reached the level of the maindeck and the chair was swung in. He stepped aboard with his hand to the brim of his hat.

The deck was as white as paper, as white as the gloves and the shirts of the sideboys. Gold leaf gleamed in the sun, the most elaborate Turks' heads adorned the ropework. The King's own yacht could not be smarter than the quarterdeck of the *Ocean*—that was what could be done in the flagship of a victorious admiral. It was as well to remember that Collingwood's previous flagship, the *Royal Sovereign*, had been pounded into a mastless hulk, with four hundred dead and wounded on board her, at Trafalgar. The lieutenant of the watch, his telescope quite dazzling with polished brass and pipe-clayed twine, wore spotless and unwrinkled white trousers; the buttons on his well-fitting coat winked in the sunshine. It occurred to Hornblower that to be always as smart as that, in a ship additionally crowded by the presence of an admiral and his staff, could be by no means easy. Service in a flagship might be the quick way to promotion, but there were many crumpled petals in the bed of roses. The flag captain, Rotherham—Hornblower knew his name, it had appeared in a hundred newspaper accounts of Trafalgar—and the flag lieutenant were equally smart as they made him welcome.

"His Lordship is awaiting you below, sir," said the flag lieutenant. "Will you come this way?"

Collingwood shook hands with him in the great cabin below. He was a large man, stoop-shouldered, with a pleasant smile. He eagerly took the packets Hornblower offered him, glancing at the superscriptions. One he kept in his hands, the others he gave to his secretary. He remembered his manners as he was about to break the seal.

"Please sit down, Captain. Harkness, a glass of Madeira for Captain Hornblower. Or there is some Marsala that I can recommend, sir. Please forgive me for a moment. You will understand when I tell you these are letters from my wife."

It was an upholstered chair in which Hornblower sat; under his feet was a thick carpet; there were a couple of pictures in gilt frames on the bulkheads; silver lamps hung by silver chains from the deck beams. Looking round him while Collingwood eagerly skimmed through his letters Hornblower thought of all this being hurriedly bundled away when the *Ocean* cleared for action. But what held his attention most was two long boxes against the great stern windows. They were filled with earth and were planted with flowers—hyacinths and daffodils, blooming and lovely. The scent of the hyacinths reached Hornblower's nostrils where he sat. There was something fantastically charming about them here at sea.

"I've been successful with my bulbs this year," said Collingwood, putting his letters in his pocket and following Hornblower's glance. He walked over and tilted up a daffodil bloom with sensitive fingers, looking down into its open face. "They are beautiful, aren't they? Soon the daffodils will be flowering in England—sometime perhaps I'll see them again. Meanwhile these help to keep me contented. It is three years since I last set foot on land."

Commanders-in-chief might win peerages and pensions, but their children, too, grew up without knowing their fathers. And Collingwood had walked shot-torn decks in a hundred fights; but Hornblower, looking at the wistful smile, thought of other things than battles—thirty thousand turbulent seamen to be kept disciplined and efficient, court-martial findings to be confirmed, the eternal problems of provisions and water, convoys and blockade.

"You will give me the pleasure of your company at dinner, Captain?" asked Collingwood.

"I should be honoured, my lord."

It was gratifying to bring that phrase out pat like that, with hardly more than the least feeling of embarrassment.

"That is excellent. You will be able to tell me all the gossip of home. I fear there will be no other opportunity for some time, as *Atropos* will not be staying with the fleet."

"Indeed, my lord?"

This was a moment of high excitement, when the future was about to be revealed to him. But of course the excitement must not be allowed to appear; only the guarded interest of a self-contained captain ready for anything.

"I fear so—not that you young captains with your saucy little ships want to stay tied to a fleet's apron strings."

Collingwood was smiling again, but there was something in the words that started a new train of thought in Hornblower's mind. Of course, Collingwood had watched the advent of the newest recruit to his fleet with a keen eye. Hornblower suddenly realised that if *Atropos* had been clumsy in taking up station, or dilatory in answering signals, his reception here might not have been so pleasant. He might be standing at attention at this moment submitting with a tight-shut mouth to a dressing down exemplary in its drastic quality. The thought caused a little prickling of gooseflesh at the back of his neck. It reduced his reply to a not very coherent mumble.

"You have this man McCullum and his natives on board?" asked Collingwood.

"Yes, my lord."

Only a little self-restraint was necessary to refrain from asking what the mission would be; Collingwood would tell him.

"You are not acquainted with the Levant?"

"No, my lord."

So it was to be the Levant, among the Turks and the Greeks and the Syrians.

"You soon will be, Captain. After taking my despatches to Malta you will convey Mr. McCullum to Marmorice Bay and assist him in his operations there."

Marmorice Bay? That was on the coast of Asia Minor. The fleet and transports which had attacked Egypt some years ago had rendezvoused there. It was a far cry from Deptford.

"Aye aye, my lord," said Hornblower.

"I understand you have no sailing master in *Atropos*."

"No, my lord. Two master's mates."

"In Malta you will have a sailing master assigned to you. George Turner; he is familiar with Turkish waters and he was with the fleet in Marmorice. He took the bearings when *Speedwell* sank."

Speedwell? Hornblower raked back in his memory. She was the transport which had capsized and sunk at her anchors in a sudden gale of wind in Marmorice Bay.

"Yes, my lord."

"She had on board the military chest of the expeditionary force. I don't expect you knew that."

"No indeed, my lord."

"A very considerable sum in gold and silver coin for the pay and subsistence of the troops—a quarter of a million sterling. She sank in water far deeper than any diver in the service could reach. But as no one knew what our gallant allies the Turks might contrive by way of salvage with infinite leisure, it was decided to keep the loss secret. And for once a secret remained a secret."

"Yes, my lord."

Certainly it was not common knowledge that a quarter of a million in coin lay at the bottom of Marmorice Bay.

"So the government had to send to India for divers who could reach those depths."

"I see, my lord."

"Now it will be your duty to go to Marmorice Bay and with the assistance of McCullum and Turner to recover that treasure."

"Aye aye, my lord."

No imagination could ever compass the possible range of duties of a naval officer. But it was satisfactory that the words he had just uttered were the only ones a naval officer could say in such circumstances.

"You will have to be careful in your dealings with our friend the Turk. He will be curious about your presence in Marmorice, and when he ascertains the object of your visit he may raise objections. You will have to conduct yourself according to the circumstances of the moment."

"Aye aye, my lord."

"You will not find all this in your orders, Captain. But you must understand that the Cabinet has no wish for complications with the Turks. Yet at the same time a quarter of a million sterling in cash would be a godsend to the government today—or any day. The money is badly needed, but no offence should be offered to the Turks."

It was necessary to steer clear of Scylla and yet not fall into Charybdis, said Hornblower to himself.

"I think I understand, my lord."

"Fortunately it is an unfrequented coast. The Turks maintain very small forces, either military or naval, in the locality. That does not mean that you should attempt to carry off matters with a high hand."

Not in *Atropos* with eleven popguns a side, thought Hornblower, and then he mentally withdrew the sneer. He understood what Collingwood meant.

"No, my lord."

"Very well then, Captain, thank you."

The secretary at Collingwood's elbow had a pile of opened despatches in his hand, and was clearly waiting for a break in the conversation to give him an opportunity to intervene, and the flag lieutenant was hovering in the background. Both of them moved in at once.

"Dinner will be in half an hour, my lord," said the flag lieutenant.

"These are the urgent letters, my lord," said the secretary.

Hornblower rose to his feet in some embarrassment.

"Perhaps, Captain, you would enjoy a turn on the quarterdeck, eh?" asked Collingwood. "Flags here would keep you company, I'm sure."

When a vice admiral made suggestions to a captain and a flag lieutenant he did not have to wait long before they were acted upon. But out on the quarterdeck, pacing up and down making polite conversation, Hornblower could have wished that Collingwood had not been so thoughtful as to provide him with company. He had a great deal to think about.

TEN

Malta; Ricasoli Point on the one hand and Fort St. Elmo returning the salute on the other, and the Grand Harbour opening up between them; Valletta with its palaces on the promontory; gaily painted small craft everywhere; a fresh northeasterly wind blowing. That wind—the "gregale," the sailing directions called it—did not allow Hornblower any leisure at present for sightseeing. In confined waters a sailing ship before the wind always seemed pigheadedly determined to maintain her speed however much her canvas was reduced, even under bare poles. It called for accurate timing to round-to at the right moment, to take her way off her, to clue up, and drop anchor at the right moment.

Nor would there be any leisure for Hornblower, it appeared, during the few hours that he would be here. He could combine his official calls with his personal delivery of the despatches entrusted to him, which would save a good deal of time, but that saving was immediately eaten up—as the fat kine of Pharaoh's dream were eaten up by the lean kine—by the demands on his attention, and, just as the lean kine were no fatter after their meal, so he was just as busy even when his planning had saved that much time. It would be quarter-day, or as near to it as made no matter, by the time letters from Malta would reach England, so that now he could draw against his pay. Not to any great extent, of course—there were Maria and the children to be considered—but enough to provide himself with a few luxuries in this island where bread was dear and luxuries cheap. Oranges and olives and fresh vegetables—the bumboats were already awaiting permission to come alongside.

McCullum, with his salvage operations in mind, was anxious for an indent to be made for supplies he considered necessary. He wanted a mile of half-inch line and a quarter mile of slow match—a fantastic demand, to Hornblower's mind, but McCullum knew more about his business than he did, presumably—and five hundred feet of leather "fuse-hose," which was something Hornblower had hardly heard of. Hornblower signed the indent wondering vaguely whether the Navy Office would surcharge him with it, and turned away to face the inevitable fact that every officer in the ship wished to go ashore and was presenting irrefutable reasons to Jones in favour of his so doing. If *Atropos* had been on fire they could not be more passionately anxious to be out of her.

And here was another complication: a note from His Excellency the Governor. Would Captain Hornblower and one of his officers dine at the Palace this afternoon? It would be impossible to refuse, so no time need be wasted on debate regarding that point—His Excellency was just as anxious as any ordinary mortal to hear the gossip from England and to see a new face—while there was equally no debate regarding which officer he should take with him. His Excellency would never forgive him if he heard who had been on board *Atropos* and he had not been afforded the opportunity of seating royalty at his table.

"Pass the word for Mr. Prince," said Hornblower, "and the doctor."

It would be necessary to have the doctor to interpret to the Prince exactly what was going to happen; the boy had learned a good deal of English during his month on board, but the vocabulary of the gunroom was hardly inclusive enough to permit of discussions of viceregal etiquette. The Prince came in a little breathless, still twitching his uniform into some kind of order; Eisenbeiss was breathing hard too—he had to come the whole length of the ship and through a narrow hatchway.

"Please explain to His Serene Highness," said Hornblower, "that he is coming ashore with me to dine with the Governor."

Eisenbeiss spoke in German, and the boy gave his mechanical little bow. The use of German evoked the manners of royalty from under the new veneer of a British midshipman.

"His Serene Highness is to wear his court dress?" asked Eisenbeiss.

"No," said Hornblower, "his uniform. And if ever I see him again with his shoes as badly brushed as those are I'll take the cane to him."

"Sir—" said Eisenbeiss, but words failed him. The thought of the cane being applied to his Prince struck him dumb; fortunately, perhaps.

"So that I am to wear this uniform too, sir?" asked Eisenbeiss.

"I fear you have not been invited, Doctor," said Hornblower.

"But I am First Chamberlain to His Serene Highness, sir," exploded Eisenbeiss. "This will be a visit of ceremony, and it is a fundamental law of Seitz-Bunau that I make all presentations."

Hornblower kept his temper.

"And I represent His Britannic Majesty," he said.

"Surely His Britannic Majesty cannot wish that his ally should not be treated with the honours due to his royal position? As Secretary of State it is my duty to make an official protest."

"Yes," said Hornblower. He put out his hand and bent the Prince's head forward. "You might be better employed seeing that His Serene Highness washes behind his ears."

"Sir! Sir!" said Eisenbeiss.

"Be ready and properly dressed in half an hour, if you please, Mr. Prince."

Dinner at the Palace ran the dreary course it might be expected to take. It was fortunate that, on being received by the Governor's aide-de-camp, Hornblower was able to shuffle onto his shoulders the burden of the difficult decision regarding the presentations—Hornblower could not guess whether His Serene Highness should be presented to His Excellency or vice versa, and he was a little amused to note Her Excellency's hurried asides when she heard the quality of her second guest; the seating arrangements for dinner needed hasty revision. So Hornblower found himself between two dull women, one of them with red hands and the other with a chronic sniff. He struggled to make polite conversation, and he was careful with his wine glass, contriving merely to sip when the others drank deep.

The Governor drank to His Serene Highness the Prince of Seitz-Bunau, and the Prince, with the most perfect aplomb, drank to His Majesty the King of Great Britain; presumably those were the first words of English he had ever learned, long before he had learned to shout "Vast heaving" or "Come on, you no-sailors, you." When the ladies had withdrawn, Hornblower listened to His Excellency's comments about Bonaparte's threatening invasion of southern Italy, and about the chances of preserving Sicily from his clutches; and a decent interval after returning to the drawing room he caught the Prince's eye. The Prince smiled back at him and rose to his feet. It was odd to watch him receiving the bows of the men and the curtseys of the ladies with the assurance of ingrained habit. Tomorrow the boy would be in the gun-room mess again—Hornblower wondered whether he was able yet to stand up for his rights there and make sure he received no more than his fair share of gristle when the meat was served.

The gig whisked them across the Grand Harbour from the Governor's steps to the ship's side, and Hornblower came onto the quarterdeck with the bosun's mates' pipes to welcome him. He was conscious even before he had taken his hand from his hatbrim that there was something wrong. He looked round him at the ship illuminated by the wild sunset the gregale had brought with it. There was no trouble with the hands, judging by their attitudes as they stood crowded forward. The three Ceylonese divers were there in their accustomed isolation by the knight-heads. But the officers grouped aft wore an apprehensive look; Hornblower's eyes moved from face to face, from Jones to Still, the two lieutenants, to Carslake, the purser, and to Silver, the master's mate of the watch. It was Jones as senior officer who came forward to report.

"If you please, sir—"

"What is it, Mr. Jones?"

"If you please, sir, there has been a duel."

No one could ever guess what would be the next burden to be laid on a captain's shoulders. It might be an outbreak of plague, or the discovery of dry rot in the ship's timbers. And Jones' manner implied not merely that there had been a duel, but that someone had been hurt in it.

"Who fought?" demanded Hornblower.

"The doctor and Mr. McCullum, sir."

Well, somewhere they could pick up another doctor, and if the worst came to the worst they could manage without one at all.

"What happened?"

"Mr. McCullum was shot through the lungs, sir."

God! That was something entirely different, something of vital importance. A bullet through the lungs meant death almost for certain, and what was he to do with McCullum dead? McCullum had been sent for all the way from India. It would take a year and a half to get someone out from there to replace him. No ordinary man with salvage experience would do—it had to be someone who knew how to use the Ceylonese divers. Hornblower wondered with sick despair whether a man had ever been so plagued as he was. He had to swallow before he could speak again.

"Where is he now?"

"Mr. McCullum, sir? He's in the hands of the garrison surgeon in the hospital ashore."

"He's still alive?"

Jones spread despairing hands.

"Yes, sir. He was alive half an hour ago."

"Where's the doctor?"

"Down below in his berth, sir."

"I'll see him. No, wait. I'll send for him when I want him."

He wanted to think; he needed time and leisure to decide what was to be done. It was his instinct to walk the deck; that was how he could work off the high internal pressure of his emotions. It was only incidentally that the rhythmic exercise brought his thoughts into orderly sequence. And this little deck was crowded with idle officers—his cabin down below was of course quite useless. That was the moment when Jones came forward with something else to bother him.

"Mr. Turner's come aboard, sir."

Mr. Turner? Turner? That was the sailing master with experience of Turkish waters whom Collingwood had detailed specially to service in *Atropos.* He came from behind Jones as the words were said, a wizened old man with a letter in his hand, presumably the orders which had brought him on board.

"Welcome aboard, Mr. Turner," said Hornblower, forcing himself into cordiality while wondering whether he would ever make use of Turner's services.

"Your servant, sir," said Turner with old-fashioned politeness.

"Mr. Jones, see that Mr. Turner's comfortable."

"Aye aye, sir."

That was the only reply Jones could make, however hard of execution the order might be. But clearly Jones meditated some supplementary remark; it could be that he was going to suggest putting Turner into McCullum's quarters. Hornblower could not bear the thought of having to listen to anything of the sort while he had yet to reach a decision. It was the final irritation that roused him to the pitch of acting with the arbitrariness of a captain of the old school.

"Get below, all of you!" he snapped. "I want this deck clear."

They looked at him as if they had not heard him aright, and he knew they had.

"Get below, if you please," he said, and the "if you please" did nothing to soften the harshness of his request. "Master's mate of the watch, see that this deck is kept clear, and keep out of my way yourself."

They went below—this was an order from the captain who (according to the reports of his gig's crew) had barely been diverted from hanging a dozen French prisoners for no other reason than a desire to see their death struggles. So he had the quarterdeck to himself, on which to stride up and down, from taffrail to mizzenmast and back again, in the fast fading twilight. He walked rapidly, turning with a jerk at each end, irritation and worry goading him on.

He had to reach a decision. The obvious thing to do was to report to Collingwood and await further orders. But how long would it be before any vessel left Malta with letters for Collingwood, and how long would it be before another returned? A month altogether, probably.

No captain worth his salt would keep *Atropos* lying idle in Grand Harbour for a month. He could guess what Collingwood would think of a man who evaded responsibility like that. He could take *Atropos* and seek out Collingwood himself, but the same objections applied. And how would he appear in Collingwood's eyes if he were to arrive off Toulon or Leghorn or wherever the chances of war might have summoned Collingwood, at the moment when he was supposed to be two thousand miles away? No. No. It would never do. At least he had reduced two apparent possibilities to impossibilities.

Then he must proceed with his orders as if nothing had happened to McCullum. That meant he must undertake the salvage operations himself, and he knew nothing about the subject. A wave of fury passed over him as his mind dwelt on the inconvenience and loss occasioned by the duel. The idiotic Eisenbeiss and the bad-tempered McCullum. They had no business incommoding England in her struggle with Bonaparte merely to satisfy their own ridiculous passions. He himself had borne with Eisenbeiss' elephantine nonsense. Why could not McCullum have done the same? And in any event why could not McCullum have held his pistol straighter and killed the ridiculous doctor instead of getting killed himself? But that sort of rhetorical question did not get him any further with his own urgent problems; he must not think along those lines. Moreover, with a grinding feeling of guilt another consideration crept in. He should have been aware of bad blood between the people in his ship. He remembered the lighthearted way in which he had put on Jones' shoulders the responsibility for accommodating McCullum in his crowded little ship. In the wardroom the doctor and McCullum had probably got on each other's nerves; there could be no doubt about that—and presumably ashore, over wine in some tavern, the enmity had flared up and brought about the duel. He should have known about the possibility and nipped it in the bud. Hornblower scourged himself spiritually for his remissness. He experienced bitter self-contempt at that moment. Perhaps he was unfit to be captain of one of His Majesty's ships.

The thought brought about an even greater internal upheaval. He could not bear it. He must prove to himself that there was no truth in it, or he must break himself in the attempt. He must carry through that salvage operation by his own efforts if necessary. He must. He *must*.

So that was the decision. He had only to reach it for the emotion to die down within him, to leave him thinking feverishly but clearly. He must of course do everything possible to ensure success, omit nothing that could help. McCullum had indented for "leather fuse-hose"; that was some indication of how the salvage problem was to be approached. And McCullum was not yet dead, as far as he knew. He might—no, it was hardly possible. No one ever survived a bullet through the lungs. And yet—

"Mr. Nash!"

"Sir!" said the master's mate of the watch, coming at the run.

"My gig. I'm going over to the hospital."

There was still just a little light in the sky, but overside the water was black as ink, reflecting in long irregular lines the lights that showed in Valletta. The oars ground rhythmically in the rowlocks. Hornblower restrained himself from urging the men to pull harder. They could never have rowed fast enough to satisfy the pressing need for instant action that seethed inside him.

The garrison officers were still at mess, sitting over their wine, and the mess sergeant at Hornblower's request went in and fetched out the surgeon. He was a youngish man, and fortunately still sober. He stood with the candlelight on his face and listened attentively to Hornblower's questions.

"The bullet hit him in the right armpit," said the surgeon. "One would expect that, as he would be standing with his shoulder turned to his opponent and his arm raised. The actual wound was on the posterior margin of the armpit, towards the back, in other words, and on the level of the fifth rib."

The heart was on the level of the fifth rib, as Hornblower knew, and the expression had an ominous sound.

"I suppose the bullet did not go right through?" he asked.

"No," replied the surgeon. "It is very rare for a pistol bullet if it touches bone to go through the body, even at twelve paces. The powder charge is only one drachm. Naturally the bullet is still there, presumably within the chest cavity."

"So he is unlikely to live?"

"Very unlikely, sir. It is a surprise he has lived so long. The haemoptysis—the spitting of blood, you understand, sir—has been extremely slight. Most chest wounds die of internal bleeding within an hour or two, but in this case the lung can hardly have been touched. There is considerable contusion under the right scapula—that is the shoulder blade—indicating that the bullet terminated its course there."

"Close to the heart?"

"Close to the heart, sir. But it can have touched none of the great vessels there, most surprisingly, or he would have been dead within a few seconds."

"Then why do you think he will not live?"

The doctor shook his head.

"Once an opening has been made in the chest cavity, sir, there is little chance, and with the bullet still inside the chance is negligible. It will certainly have carried fragments of clothing in with it. We may expect internal mortification, a general gathering of malignant humours, and eventual death within a few days."

"You could not probe for the bullet?"

"Within the chest wall? My dear sir!"

"What action have you taken, then?"

"I have bound up the wound of entry to put an end to the bleeding there. I have strapped up the chest to ensure that the jagged ends of the broken ribs do no more damage to the lungs. I took two ounces of blood from the left basilar vein, and I administered an opiate."

"An opiate? So he is not conscious now?"

"Certainly not."

Hornblower felt hardly wiser than he had done when Jones first told him the news.

"You say he may live a few days? How many?"

"I know nothing about the patient's constitution, sir. But he is a powerful man in the prime of life. It might be as much as a week. It might even be more. But on the other hand if events take a bad turn he might be dead tomorrow."

"But if it is several days? Will he retain his senses during that time?"

"Likely enough. When he ceases to it is a sign of the approaching end. Then we can expect fever, restlessness, delirium, and death."

Several days of consciousness were possible, therefore. And the faintest, remotest chance that McCullum would live after all.

"Supposing I took him to sea with me? Would that help? Or hinder?"

"You would have to ensure his immobility on account of the fractured ribs. But at sea he might perhaps even live longer. There are the usual Mediterranean agues in this island. And in addition there is an endemic low fever. My hospital is full of such cases."

Now this was a piece of information that really helped in coming to a decision.

"Thank you, Doctor," said Hornblower, and he took his decision. Then it was only a matter of minutes to make the arrangements with the surgeon and to take his leave. The gig took him back through the darkness, over the black water, to where *Atropos'* riding light showed faintly.

"Pass the word for the doctor to come to my cabin at once," was Hornblower's reply to the salute of the officer of the watch.

Eisenbeiss came slowly in. There was something of apprehension and something of bravado in his manner. He was prepared to defend himself against the storm he was certain was about to descend on him. What he did not expect was the reception he actually experienced. He approached the table behind which Hornblower was seated and stood sullen, meeting Hornblower's eyes with the guilty defiance of a man who had just taken another human's life.

"Mr. McCullum," began Hornblower, and the doctor's thick lips showed a trace of a sneer, "is being sent on board here tonight. He is still alive."

"On board here?" repeated the doctor, surprised into a change of attitude.

"You address me as 'sir.' Yes, I am having him sent over from the hospital. My orders to you are to make every preparation for his reception."

The doctor's response was unintelligible German, but there could be no doubt it was an ejaculation of astonishment.

"Your answer to me is 'aye aye, sir,'" snapped Hornblower, his pent-up emotion and strain almost making him tremble as he sat at the table. He could not prevent his fist from clenching, but he just managed to refrain from allowing it to pound the table. The intensity of his feelings must have had their effect telepathically.

"Aye aye, sir," said the doctor grudgingly.

"Mr. McCullum's life is extremely valuable, Doctor. Much more valuable than yours."

The doctor could only mumble in reply to that.

"It is your duty to keep him alive."

Hornblower's fist unclenched now, and he could make his points slowly, one by one, accentuating each with the slow tap of the tip of a lean forefinger on the table.

"You are to do all you can for him. If there is anything special that you require for the purpose you are to inform me and I shall endeavour to obtain it for you. His life is to be saved, or, if not, it is to be prolonged as far as possible. I would recommend you to establish an hospital for him abaft Number Six carronade on the starboard side, where the motion of the ship will be least felt, and where it will be possible to rig a shelter for him from the weather. You will apply to Mr. Jones for that. The ship's pigs can be taken for'rard where they will not discommode him."

Hornblower's pause and glance called forth an "aye aye, sir" from the doctor's lips like a cork from out of a bottle, so that Hornblower could proceed.

"We sail at dawn tomorrow," he went on. "Mr. McCullum is to live until we reach our destination, and until long after, long enough for him to execute the duty which has brought him from India. That is quite clear to you?"

"Yes, sir," answered the doctor, although his puzzled expression proved that there was something about the orders which he could not explain to himself.

"You had better keep him alive," continued Hornblower. "You had certainly better. If he dies I can try you for murder under the ordinary laws of England. Don't look at me like that. I am speaking the truth. The common law knows nothing about duels. I can hang you, Doctor."

The doctor was a shade paler, and his big hands tried to express what his paralysed tongue would not.

"But simply hanging you would be too good for you, Doctor," said Hornblower. "I can do more than that, and I shall. You have a fat fleshy back. The cat would sink deeply into it. You've seen men flogged—you saw two flogged last week. You heard them scream. You will scream at the gratings too, Doctor. That I promise you."

"No!" said the doctor. "You can't—"

"You address me as 'sir,' and you do not contradict me. You heard my promise? I shall carry it out. I can, and I shall."

In a ship detached far from superior authority there was nothing a captain might not do, and the doctor knew it. And with Hornblower's grim face before him and those remorseless eyes staring into his the doctor could not doubt the possibility. Hornblower was trying to keep his expression set hard, and to pay no attention to the internal calculations that persisted in maintaining themselves inside him. There might be terrible trouble if the Admiralty ever heard he had flogged a warranted doctor, but then the Admiralty might never hear of an incident in the distant Levant. And there was the other doubt—with McCullum once dead, so that nothing could bring him to life, Hornblower could not really believe he would torture a human being to no practical purpose. But as long as Eisenbeiss did not guess that, it did not matter.

"This is all quite clear to you now, Doctor?"

"Yes, sir."

"Then my order is that you start making your arrangements now."

It was a really great surprise to Hornblower when Eisenbeiss still hesitated. He was about to speak more sharply still, cutting into the feverish gestures of the big hands, when Eisenbeiss spoke again.

"Do you forget something, sir?"

"What do you think I have forgotten?" asked Hornblower, playing for time instead of flatly refusing to listen to any arguments—proof enough that he was a little shaken by Eisenbeiss' persistence.

"Mr. McCullum and I—we are enemies," said Eisenbeiss.

It was true that Hornblower had forgotten that. He was so engrossed with his chessboard manipulation of human pieces that he had overlooked a vital factor. But he must not admit it.

"And what of that?" he asked coldly, hoping his discomfiture was not too apparent.

"I shot him," said Eisenbeiss. There was a vivid gesture by the big right hand that had held the pistol, which enabled Hornblower to visualise the whole duel. "What will he say if I attend him?"

"Whose was the challenge?" asked Hornblower, still playing for time.

"He challenged me," said Eisenbeiss. "He said—he said I was no baron, and I said he was no gentleman. 'I will kill you for that,' he said, and so we fought."

Eisenbeiss had certainly said the thing that would best rouse McCullum's fury.

"You are convinced you are a baron?" asked Hornblower—curiosity urged him to ask the question as well as the need for time to reassemble his thoughts. The Baron drew himself up as far as the deck beams over his head allowed.

"I know I am, sir. My patent of nobility is signed by His Serene Highness himself."

"When did he do that?"

"As soon as—as soon as we were alone. Only His Serene Highness and I managed to cross the frontier when Bonaparte's men entered Seitz-Bunau. The others all took service with the tyrant. It was not fit that His Serene Highness should be attended only by a bourgeois. Only a noble could attend him to bed or serve his food. He had to have a High Chamberlain to regulate his ceremonial, and a Secretary of State to manage his foreign affairs. So His Serene Highness ennobled me—that is why I bear the title of baron—and gave me the high offices of state."

"On your advice?"

"I was the only adviser he had left."

This was very interesting and much as Hornblower had imagined it, but it was not to the point. Hornblower was more ready now to face the real issue.

"In the duel," he asked, "you exchanged shots?"

"His bullet went past my ear," answered Eisenbeiss.

"Then honour is satisfied on both sides," said Hornblower, more to himself than to the doctor.

Technically that was perfectly correct. An exchange of shots, and still more the shedding of blood, ended any affair of honour. The principals could meet again socially as if there had been no trouble between them. But to meet in the relative positions of doctor and patient might be something different. He would have to deal with that difficulty when it arose.

"You are quite right to remind me about this, Doctor," he said, with the last appearance of judicial calm that he could summon up. "I shall bear it in mind."

Eisenbeiss looked at him a little blankly, and Hornblower put on his hard face again.

"But it makes no difference at all to my promise to you. Rest assured of that," he continued. "My orders still stand. They—still—stand."

It was several seconds before the reluctant answer came.

"Aye aye, sir."

"On your way out would you please be good enough to pass the word for Mr. Turner, the new sailing master?"

"Aye aye, sir."

That showed the subtle difference between an order and a request —but both of them had to be obeyed.

"Now, Mr. Turner," said Hornblower when Turner arrived in the cabin, "our destination is Marmorice Bay, and we sail at dawn tomorrow. I want to know about the winds we can expect at this time of year. I want to lose no time at all in arriving there. Every hour—I may say every minute—is of importance."

Time was of importance, to make the most of a dying man's last hours.

ELEVEN

THESE WERE THE BLUE WATERS where history had been made, where the future of civilisation had been decided, more than once and more than twice. Here Greek had fought against Persian, Athenian against Spartan, Crusader against Saracen, Hospitaller against Turk. The pentecontors of Byzantium had furrowed the seas here, and the caracks of Pisa. Great cities had luxuriated in untold wealth. Only just over the horizon on the port beam was Rhodes, where a comparatively minor city had erected one of the Seven Wonders of the World, so that two thousand years later the adjective "colossal" was part of the vocabulary of people whose ancestors wore skins and painted themselves with woad at the time when the Rhodians were debating the nature of the Infinite. Now conditions were reversed. Here came *Atropos*, guided by sextant and compass, driven by the wind harnessed to her well-planned sails, armed with her long guns and carronades—a triumph of modern invention, in short—emerging from the wealthiest corner of the world into one where misgovernment and disease, anarchy and war, had left deserts where there had been fertile fields, villages where there had been cities, and hovels where there had been palaces. But there was no time to philosophise in this profound fashion. The sands in the hourglass beside the binnacle were running low, and the moment was approaching when course should be altered.

"Mr. Turner!"

"Sir!"

"We'll alter course when the watch is called."

"Aye aye, sir."

"Doctor!"

"Sir!"

"Stand by for a change of course."

"Aye aye, sir."

McCullum's invalid bed was disposed athwart ships between Nos. 6 and 7 carronades on the starboard side; a simple tackle attached to the bed head enabled the level of the bed to be adjusted with the change of course, so that the patient lay as horizontal as might be, whichever way the ship might be heeling. It was the doctor's responsibility to attend to that.

The watch was being called.

"Very good, Mr. Turner."

"Headsail sheets! Hands to the braces!"

Turner was an efficient seaman, despite his age. Hornblower could be sure of that by now. He stood by and watched him lay the ship close to the wind. Still came and touched his hat to Turner to take over the watch.

"We ought to raise the Seven Capes on this tack, sir," said Turner, coming over to Hornblower.

"I fancy so," said Hornblower.

The passage from Malta had been comfortingly rapid. They had lain becalmed for a single night to the south of Crete, but with the morning the wind had got up again from a westerly quarter. There had not been a single breath of a Levanter—the equinox was still too far off for that, apparently—and every day had seen at least a hundred miles made good. And McCullum was still alive.

Hornblower walked forward to where he lay. Eisenbeiss was bending over him, his fingers on his pulse, and, with the cessation of the bustle of going about, the three Ceylonese divers had returned, to squat round the foot of the bed, their eyes on their master. To have those three pairs of melancholy eyes gazing at him would, Hornblower thought, have a most depressing effect, but apparently McCullum had no objection.

"All well, Mr. McCullum?" asked Hornblower.

"Not—quite as well as I would like."

It was distressing to see how slowly and painfully the head turned on the pillow. The heavy beard that had sprouted over his face could not conceal the fact that McCullum was more hollow-cheeked, more feverish-eyed, than yesterday. The decline had been very marked; the day they sailed McCullum had appeared hardly more than slightly wounded, and the second day he had seemed better still—he had protested against being kept in bed; but that night he had taken a turn for the worse and had sunk steadily ever since, just as the garrison surgeon and Eisenbeiss had gloomily predicted.

Of course those had not been his only protests. McCullum had been as angry as his muddled condition would allow when he emerged from his narcotic to find he was under the treatment of the man who had shot him. He had struggled against his weakness and his bandages. It had called for Hornblower's personal intervention—fortunately *Atropos* was clear of the harbour mouth when McCullum regained consciousness—to calm him down. "It's a blackguard trick to pursue an affair of honour after an exchange of shots," Hornblower had said, and "It's the doctor who's attending to you, not the Baron," and then the clinching argument: "Don't be a fool, man. There's no other surgeon within fifty miles. Do you want to die?" So McCullum had yielded, and had submitted his tortured body to Eisenbeiss' ministrations, perhaps deriving some comfort from the ignoble things the doctor had to do for him.

And now all that spirit had gone. McCullum was a very sick man. He closed his eyes as Eisenbeiss laid his hand on his forehead. The pale lips muttered, and Hornblower, stooping, could only hear disjointed phrases. There was something about "fuses under water." McCullum was thinking, then, of the salvage operation ahead. Hornblower looked up and met Eisenbeiss' eyes. There was deep concern in them, and there was the least perceptible shake of the head. Eisenbeiss thought McCullum was going to die.

"It hurts—it hurts," said McCullum, moaning a little.

He moved restlessly, and Eisenbeiss' large powerful hands eased him into a more comfortable position on his left side. Hornblower noticed that Eisenbeiss laid one hand, as if inquiringly, over McCullum's right shoulder blade, and then lower down, towards the short ribs, and McCullum moaned again. There was no change in the gravity of Eisenbeiss' expression.

This was horrible. It was horrible to see this magnificently constructed creature dying. And it was equally horrible that Hornblower was aware that his deep sympathy was allayed with concern for himself. He could not imagine how he would carry through the salvage operation with McCullum dead, or even with McCullum as helpless as he was at present. He would return empty-handed, to face Collingwood's wrath and contempt. What was the use of all his endeavours? Hornblower suddenly boiled with exasperation at the duelling convention which had claimed the life of a valuable man and at the same time had imperilled his own professional reputation. Within himself he was a whirlpool of emotions conflicting with each other.

"Land! Land ho! Land on the starboard bow!"

The cry came ringing down from the fore topmast head. No one could hear it without at least a little excitement. McCullum opened his eyes and turned his head again, but Eisenbeiss, stooping over him, endeavoured to soothe him. Hornblower's place was aft, and he turned away from the bed and walked back, trying to restrain himself from appearing too eager. Turner was already there, brought up from his watch below at the cry, and by the lee bulwark the other officers were rapidly assembling in a group.

"A good landfall, sir," said Turner.

"An hour earlier than I was led to expect," answered Hornblower.

"The current sets northerly here with steady winds from the west, sir," said Turner. "We'll raise Atairo in Rhodes to port soon, and then we'll have a cross bearing."

"Yes," replied Hornblower. He was aware of his shortness of manner, but only dimly aware of its cause; he was uneasy with a sailing master on board who knew more about local conditions than he did, although that sailing master had been assigned to him to save him from uneasiness.

Atropos was shouldering her way valiantly through the short but steep seas that came hurrying forward to assail her port bow. Her motion was easy; she was carrying exactly the right amount of sail for that wind. Turner put a telescope in his pocket and walked forward to ascend the main shrouds, while Hornblower stood on the weather side with the wind blowing against his sunburned cheeks. Turner came aft again, his smile denoting self-satisfaction.

"That's the Seven Capes, sir," he said. "Two points on the starboard bow."

"There's a northerly set here, you say?" asked Hornblower.

"Yes, sir."

Hornblower walked over and looked at the compass, and up at the trim of the sails. The northerly set would help, and the wind was coming from the southward of west, but there was no sense in going unnecessarily far to leeward.

"Mr. Still! You can come closer to the wind than this. Brace her up."

He did not want to have to beat his way in at the last, and he was making allowance for the danger of the current setting in on Cape Kum.

Now here was the doctor, touching his hat to demand attention.

"What is it, Doctor?" asked Hornblower.

The hands were hauling on the maintack.

"May I speak to you, sir?"

That was exactly what he was doing, and at a moment by no means opportune. But of course what he wanted was a chance to speak to him in privacy, and not on this bustling deck.

"It's about the patient, sir," supplemented Eisenbeiss. "I think it is very important."

"Oh, very well," said Hornblower, restraining himself from using bad language. He led the way down into the cabin, and seated himself to face the doctor. "Well? What do you have to say?"

Eisenbeiss was nervous, that was plain.

"I have formed a theory, sir."

He failed, as ever, with the "th" sound, and the word was so unusual and his pronunciation of it was so odd that Hornblower had to think for a moment before he could guess what it was Eisenbeiss had said.

"And what is this theory?"

"It is about the position of the bullet, sir," answered Eisenbeiss; he, too, took a moment to digest what was the English pronunciation of the word.

"The garrison surgeon at Malta told me it was in the chest cavity. Do you know any more than that?"

That expression "chest cavity" was an odd one, but the garrison surgeon had used it. It implied an empty space, and was an obvious misnomer. Lungs and heart and the great blood vessels must fill that cavity full.

"I believe it may not be in there at all, sir," said Eisenbeiss, clearly taking a plunge.

"Indeed?" This might be exceedingly important news if it were true. "Then why is he so ill?"

Now that Eisenbeiss had committed himself he became voluble again. Explanations poured out of him, accompanied by jerky gestures. But the explanations were hard to follow. In this highly technical matter Eisenbeiss had been thinking in his native language even more than usual, and now he was having to translate into technical terms unfamiliar to him and still more unfamiliar to Hornblower, who grasped despairingly at one contorted sentence.

"You think that the bullet, after breaking those ribs, may have bounced off again?" he asked. At the last moment he substituted the word "bounce" for "ricochet" in the hope of retaining clarity.

"Yes, sir. Bullets often do that."

"And where do you say you think it went then?"

Eisenbeiss tried to stretch his left hand far under his right armpit; his body was too bulky to permit it to go far enough to make his demonstration quite complete.

"Under the scapula, sir—the—the shoulder blade."

"Land ho! Land on the port bow."

Hornblower heard the cry come down through the skylight from above. That must be Rhodes they had sighted. Here they were heading into Rhodes Channel, and he was down below talking about ribs and scapulas. And yet the one was as important as the other.

"I can't stay down here much longer, Doctor. Tell me why you think this is the case."

Eisenbeiss fell into explanation again. He talked about the patient's fever, and about his comparative well-being the morning after he had been wounded, and about the small amount of blood he had spat up. He was in the full flood of his talk when a knock at the door interrupted him.

"Come in," said Hornblower.

It was His Serene Highness the Prince of Seitz-Bunau, with a speech that he had obviously prepared carefully on his way down.

"Mr. Still's respects, sir," he said. "Land in sight on the port bow."

"Very well, Mr. Prince. Thank you."

It was a pity there was not time to compliment the boy on his rapid acquisition of English. Hornblower turned back to Eisenbeiss.

"So I think the bullet went round the back, sir. The skin is—is tough, sir, and the ribs are—are elastic."

"Yes?" Hornblower had heard of bullets going round the body before this.

"And the patient has much muscle. Much."

"And you think the bullet has lodged in the muscles of the back?"

"Yes. Deep against the ribs. Under the lower point of the scapula, sir."

"And the fever? The illness?"

They could be accounted for, according to Eisenbeiss' torrential explanation, by the presence of the foreign body deep inside the tissues, especially if, as was probable, it had carried fragments of clothing in along with it. It all seemed plausible enough.

"And you are trying to say that if the bullet is there and not inside the chest you might be able to extract it?"

"Yes, sir."

Eisenbeiss showed by his manner that he knew that those words had finally committed him.

"You think that you can do that? It means using the knife?"

As soon as Hornblower finished asking the second question he was aware that it was impolitic to ask two questions at once of a man who had enough trouble answering one. Eisenbeiss had to think a long time over the phrasing of his answers.

"It means using the knife," he said at length. "It means a difficult operation. I do not know if I can do it."

"But you hope you can?"

"I hope so."

"And do you think you will be successful?"

"I do not think. I hope."

"And if you are not successful?"

"He will die."

"But you think he will die in any case if you do not attempt the operation?"

That was the point. Eisenbeiss twice opened his mouth and shut it again before he answered.

"Yes."

Down through the skylight, as Hornblower sat studying Eisenbeiss' expression, came a new cry, faintly borne from the weather main chains.

"No bottom! No bottom with this line!"

Turner and Still had very properly decided to take a cast of the lead; they were still out of soundings, as was to be expected. Hornblower brought his mind back from the situation of the ship to the decision regarding McCullum. The latter might have some claim to be consulted on the matter, but the claim was specious. His life was his country's. A seaman was not consulted first when he was carried into the ordeal of battle.

"So that is your opinion, Doctor. If you operate and fail, you will only have shortened the patient's life by a few hours?"

"A few hours. A few days."

A few days might suffice for the salvage operation; but with McCullum as sick as he was he would be no use during those few days. On the other hand there was no knowing at present whether or not he might possibly recover after those few days, without being operated on.

"What are the difficulties of the operation?" asked Hornblower.

"There are several layers of muscle there," explained Eisenbeiss. "Infraspinatus. Subscapularis, many of them. In each case the—the threads run in a different direction. That makes it difficult to work quickly and yet without doing great damage. And there is the big artery, the subscapular. The patient is weak already and unable to withstand much shock."

"Have you everything you need for this operation if you carry it out?"

Eisenbeiss hunched his thick shoulders.

"The two attendants—lob-lolly boys, you call them, sir—are experienced. They have both served in ships in action. I have my instruments. But I should like—"

Eisenbeiss clearly wanted something he believed to be difficult to grant.

"What?"

"I should like the ship to be still. At anchor. And a good light."

That turned the scale of the decision.

"Before nightfall," said Hornblower, "this ship will be at anchor in a landlocked harbour. You can make your preparations for the operation."

"Yes, sir." Again a pause before Eisenbeiss asked an important question. "And your promise, sir?"

Hornblower did not have to think very long about the question as to whether Eisenbeiss would work more efficiently or not if he were faced with the certainty of flogging and hanging if he failed. The man would do all he could out of sheer professional pride. And the thought that his life was at stake might possibly make him nervous.

"I'll take my promise back," said Hornblower. "You'll suffer no harm, whatever happens."

"Thank you, sir."

"No bottom!" called the leadsman in the chains.

"Very well, then. You have until this evening to make what preparations you can."

"Yes, sir. Thank you, sir."

With Eisenbeiss out of the cabin Hornblower sat for hardly a moment retracing the grounds of his decision. His ship was entering Rhodes Channel and he must be on deck.

"Wind's come southerly a point, sir," said Still, touching his hat.

The first thing of course that Hornblower had noticed as he came up the companion was that *Atropos* was still braced up as close to the wind as she would lie. Still and Turner had acted correctly without troubling him about it.

"Very well, Mr. Still."

Hornblower put his glass to his eye and swept the horizon. A bold, wildly rugged coast on the one hand; on the other a low sandy shore. He bent to study the chart.

"Cape Angistro to starboard, sir," said Turner at his side. "Cape Kum abaft the port beam."

"Thank you."

Everything was as it should be. Hornblower straightened up and turned his glass upon the Turkish coast. It was steep, with bold cliffs, behind which rose a chain of steeply undulating hills.

"They're only green at this time of year, sir," explained Turner. "The rest of the year they're brown."

"Yes."

Hornblower had read all he could about the eastern Mediterranean, and he knew something of the climatic conditions.

"Not many people live there now, sir," went on Turner. "Farmers, a few. Shepherds. Little fishing villages in some of the coves. A little coasting trade in caïques from Rhodes—not so much of that now, sir. There's piracy in all these waters, on account of the feuds between the Greeks and the Turks. There's a bit of trade in honey an' timber, but precious little."

"Yes."

It was fortunate the wind had backed southerly, even by so little. It eased one of the myriad complications in his complicated life.

"Ruins aplenty along that coast, though, sir," droned on Turner. "Cities—temples—you'd be surprised."

Ancient Greek civilisation had flourished here. Over there had stood Artemisia and a score of other Greek cities, pulsating with life and beauty.

"Yes," said Hornblower.

"The villages mostly stand where the old cities were," persisted Turner. "Ruins all round 'em. Half the cottages are built of marble from the temples."

"Yes."

In other circumstances Hornblower could have been deeply interested, but as it was Turner was merely distraction. There was not merely the immediate business in hand of taking *Atropos* up into Marmorice harbour; there was the business of how to deal with the Turkish authorities; of how to set about the problems of salvage; there was the question—the urgent, anxious question—as to whether McCullum would live. There was the routine of the ship; when Hornblower looked round him he could see the hands and the officers clustered along the ship's sides gazing out eagerly at the shores. There were Greeks dwelling among the Mohammedans of the mainland—that would be important when it came to a question of keeping liquor from the men. And he would like to fill his water barrels; and there was the matter of obtaining fresh vegetables.

Here was Still with a routine question. Hornblower nodded in agreement.

"Up spirits!"

The cry went through the little ship, and when they heard it the men had no ears for any siren song from the shore. This was the great moment of the day for most of them, when they would pour their tiny issue of rum and water down their eager throats. To deprive a man of his ration was like barring a saint from Paradise. The speculations that went on among the men, their dealings with their rum rations, the exchanging, the buying, the selling, made the South Sea Bubble seem small by comparison. But Hornblower decided he need not vaunt himself above the herd, he need not look down with condescension at the men as if they were Circe's hogs swilling at a trough; it was perfectly true that this was the great moment of their day, but it was because they had no other moment at all, for months and for years, confined within the wooden walls of their little ship, often seeing not a shilling of money in all that time, not a fresh face, not a single human problem on which to exercise their wits. Perhaps it was better to be a captain and have too many problems.

The hands went to dinner. Cape Kum went by on the one hand and the Turkish coast on the other, the breeze freshening with the bright sunny day, and Turner droning on as the landmarks went by.

"Cape Marmorice, sir," reported Turner.

The coast dipped here, revealing mountains more lofty close behind. Now was the time to take in sail, ready to enter. It was the time when decisive action had to be taken, too; when *Atropos* changed from a peaceful ship, cruising placidly along outside territorial waters, to a stormy petrel, whose entrance into a foreign harbour might send despatches hastening from embassies, and might cause cabinets to assemble at opposite ends of Europe. Hornblower tried to give his orders as if he had no care for the importance of the moment.

"All hands! All hands shorten sail! All hands!"

The watch below came running to their posts. The officers, at the call of all hands, went to their stations, the one or two who had been dozing down below coming hastily on deck. Courses and topgallants were got in.

"Mr. Jones!" said Hornblower harshly.

"Sir!"

"Ease that sheet and take the strain off the tack! Where did you learn your seamanship?"

"Aye aye, sir," answered Jones rather pathetically, but he ran up both clues smartly together.

The reprimand was deserved, but Hornblower wondered if he would have administered it in just that way if he had not been anxious to show that the responsibilities he was carrying could not distract him from any detail of the management of the ship. Then he decided bitterly that it was unnecessary in any event; not one of those hurrying figures on deck gave a single thought to the responsibilities of his captain, or of what international crisis this shortening of sail might be the preliminary.

"Red Cliff Point, sir," said Turner. "Passage Island. Cape Sari over there. The east passage is better, sir—there's a rock in the middle of the west passage."

"Yes," said Hornblower. There was not much detail in the chart, but that much was clear. "We'll take the east passage. Quartermaster! Port your helm. Steady! Steady as you go!"

With the wind on her quarter *Atropos* headed for the entrance like a stag, even with her sail reduced to topsails and headsails. The entrance became better defined as she approached; two bold points running to meet each other with a lofty island in between. It was obvious why Red Cliff Point was so named; elsewhere there was a dark straggling growth of pine trees on capes and island, while on the summits could just be seen the rectangular outlines of small forts.

"They don't keep those manned, sir," said Turner. "Gone to rack and ruin like everything else."

"You say the east passage is absolutely clear?"

"Yes, sir."

"Very well."

Atropos headed in, with Hornblower giving his orders to the wheel. There was no flag flying on shore, and until one could be seen there was no question of firing a salute. From point to island the entrance extended a scant half mile, possibly less; now they could see through it, to the wide waters of Marmorice Bay, with high mountains surrounding it on nearly every side, except to the northward.

"There's the town, sir," said Turner. "Not much of a place."

A white tower—a minaret—caught the afternoon sun.

"You can see the red mound behind the town now, sir."

"Where did the *Speedwell* go down?" asked Hornblower.

"Over to port, there, sir. Right in line between the red mound and the fort on Passage Island. The fort on Ada bore sou'-sou'-east half south."

"Take the bearing now," ordered Hornblower.

They were through the entrance now. The water was smooth, not smooth enough to reflect the blue sky. Turner was calling the bearing of the fort on Cape Ada. With his own eye Hornblower could judge the other cross bearing. There was no harm in anchoring close to the projected scene of operations; that would attract less attention than to anchor in one place first and to move to another anchorage later. Jones took in fore and main topsails and headsails smartly enough. *Atropos* glided quietly on.

"Hard a-starboard," said Hornblower to the quartermaster. Round came *Atropos,* the mizzen topsail helping the turn as Jones clued it up. The ship's way died away almost imperceptibly, the tiny waves lapping against her bows.

"Let go!"

The hawser rumbled out. *Atropos* swung to her anchor, in Turkish waters. The crossing of the three-mile limit, even the entrance through the Pass, had been actions that might be argued about, disavowed. But that anchor, its flukes solidly buried in the firm sand, was something of which a diplomatic note could take definite notice.

"Pass the word for the doctor," said Hornblower.

There were many things to do; it was his duty to make contact with the Turkish authorities if they did not make contact with him. But first of all, without wasting a moment, it was necessary to make arrangements for the operation on McCullum. The man's life hung in the balance, and far more than his life.

TWELVE

Hornblower sat waiting in his cabin. "A few minutes" had been Eisenbeiss' estimate of the time necessary for the operation. It was necessary, Hornblower knew, to work as quickly as possible, so as to minimise the shock to the patient.

"In the old *Hannibal,* sir," said the sickberth attendant whom Hornblower had questioned regarding his experience, "we took off eleven legs in half an hour. That was at Algeciras, sir."

But amputations were relatively simple. A full half of all amputation cases survived—Nelson himself had lost an arm, amputated on a dark night in a moderate storm at sea, and he had lived until a musket bullet killed him at Trafalgar. This was not an amputation. It was something which would be worse than useless if Eisenbeiss' diagnosis was incorrect and which could easily fail in any case.

The ship was very still and quiet. Hornblower knew that all his crew were taking a morbid interest in the fate of the "poor gentleman." They were sentimental about McCullum, lying at death's door as a result of a bullet wound he need never have received; the fact that he was going to be cut about with a knife had an unholy attraction for them; the fact that in a few minutes he might be dead, might have gone through those mysterious doors they all feared to go through, invested his personality with some special quality in their eyes. Sentries had to be posted to keep out all the sentimental, the inquisitive, and the morbid-minded among the crew, and now Hornblower could tell by the silence that his men were waiting in shuddering silence for the climax, hoping perhaps to hear a scream or a groan, waiting as they would wait to see a condemned criminal turned off the hangman's cart. He could hear the heavy ticking of his watch as he waited.

Now there were distant sounds, but sounds in the little wooden ship were susceptible to so many possible interpretations that he would not at first allow himself to think that they might arise as a result of the ending of the operation. But then there were steps and voices outside his cabin door, the sentry speaking and then Eisenbeiss, and then came a knock.

"Come in," said Hornblower, trying to keep his voice indifferent; the first sight of Eisenbeiss as he entered was enough to tell Hornblower that all was as well as could be hoped. There was an obvious light-heartedness about the doctor's elephantine movements.

"I found the bullet," said Eisenbeiss. "It was where I thought—at the inferior angle of the scapula."

"Did you get it out?" asked Hornblower; the fact that he did not correct Eisenbeiss for omitting the "sir" was proof—if anyone had been present to notice it—that he was not as calm as he appeared.

"Yes," said Eisenbeiss.

He laid something on the table in front of Hornblower, with a gesture positively dramatic. It was the bullet, misshapen, flattened to an irregular disc, with a raw scratch on one surface.

"That is where my scalpel cut into it," said Eisenbeiss proudly. "I went straight to the right place."

Hornblower picked the thing up gingerly to examine it.

"You see," said Eisenbeiss, "it was as I said. The bullet struck the ribs, breaking them, and then glanced off, passing back between the bone and the muscle."

"Yes, I see," said Hornblower.

"And there are these as well," went on Eisenbeiss, laying something else in front of Hornblower with the same sort of conscious pride as a conjuror at a fair bringing the rabbit out of the hat.

"Is this the wad?" asked Hornblower, puzzled, and making no attempt to pick up the horrid little object.

"No," said Eisenbeiss, "that is how my forceps brought it out. But see—"

Eisenbeiss' large fingers plucked the object into successive layers.

"I have looked at these through my lens. That is a piece of a blue coat. That is a piece of silk lining. That is a piece of linen shirt. And those are threads of a knitted undershirt."

Eisenbeiss beamed with triumph.

"The bullet carried these in with it?" asked Hornblower.

"Exactly. Of course. Between the bullet and the bone these portions were cut off, as they might be between the blades of scissors, and the bullet carried them on with it. I found them all. No wonder the wound was suppurating."

"You address me as 'sir,'" said Hornblower, realising, now that the tension had eased, that Eisenbeiss had been omitting the honorific. "The operation was otherwise successful as well?"

"Yes—sir," said Eisenbeiss. "The removal of these foreign bodies and the draining of the wound brought immediate relief to the patient."

"He did not suffer too much?"

"Not too much. The men who were ready to hold him still had hardly anything to do. He submitted with good spirit, as he promised you he would. It was well that he lay still. I feared further injury to the lung from the broken ribs if he struggled."

"You address me as 'sir,'" said Hornblower. "That is the last time, Doctor, that I shall overlook the omission."

"Yes—sir."

"And the patient is going on well?"

"I left him as well as I could hope—sir. I must return to him soon, of course."

"Do you think he will live?"

Some of the triumph evaporated from Eisenbeiss' expression as he concentrated on phrasing his reply.

"He is more likely to live now, sir," he said. "But with wounds—one cannot be sure."

There was always the likelihood, the unpredictable likelihood, of a wound taking a turn for the worse, festering and killing.

"You cannot say more than that?"

"No, sir. The wound must remain open to drain. When applying the sutures I inserted a bristle—"

"Very well," said Hornblower, suddenly squeamish. "I understand. You had better return to him now. You have my thanks, Doctor, for what you have done."

Even with Eisenbeiss gone there was no chance of quietly reviewing the situation. A knock on the door heralded the appearance of Midshipman Smiley.

"Mr. Jones' compliments, sir, and there are boats heading for us from the shore."

"Thank you. I'll come up. And if Mr. Turner's not on deck tell him I want to see him there."

Some of the gaily painted boats in the distance were under oars, but the nearest one was under a lateen sail, lying very close to the wind. As Hornblower watched her she took in her sail, went about, and reset it on the other tack. The lateen rig had its disadvantages. On the new tack the boat would fetch up alongside *Atropos* easily enough.

"Now listen to me, Mr. Turner," said Hornblower, reaching the decision he had had at the back of his mind—overlain until now by a host of other considerations—for the last two days. "When you speak to them you are to tell them that we are looking for a French squadron."

"Beg pardon, sir?"

"We are looking for a French squadron. Two sail—that will do. A ship of the line and a frigate, escaped from Corfu three weeks back. The first thing you ask is whether they have touched here."

"Aye aye, sir."

Turner was not very clear on the point yet.

"Admiral—Admiral Harvey has sent us in for news. He's cruising off Crete looking for them with four sail of the line. Four will do. Enough force to make them respect us."

"I see, sir."

"You're quite sure you do?"

"Yes, sir."

It was irksome being dependent on Turner to interpret for him. With Spanish authorities, or French, Hornblower could have conducted his own negotiations, but not with Turks.

"Remember, that's the first thing you ask, the very first. Have two French ships touched here? Then you can go on to get permission to fill the water casks. We'll buy fresh vegetables, too, and a couple of bullocks, if we can."

"Yes, sir."

"Keep it in your mind all the time that we're scouting for Admiral Harvey. Don't forget it for a moment, and then everything will be all right."

"Aye aye, sir."

The lateen boat was nearing them fast, making surprising speed with the small evening wind; there was a respectable bubble of foam under her bow. She came running close alongside and hove-to, the lateen sail flapping until they brailed up the upper portion.

"Turks, sir, not Greeks," said Turner.

Hornblower could have guessed that without Turner's help; the boat's crew was dressed in dirty white gowns; they wore on their heads round red hats wreathed in dirty white turbans. The grey-bearded man who stood up in the stern wore a red sash about his waist, from which hung a curved sword. He hailed *Atropos* in a thin high voice. Turner hailed back; the jargon he spoke was the lingua franca of the Levant, and Hornblower tried to guess at what was being said. Italian, French, English, Arabic, Greek, all contributed to the language, he knew. It was a little strange to hear the words "Horatio Hornblower" come clearly through the incomprehensible remainder.

"Who is this fellow?" he asked.

"The Mudir, sir. The local Jack-in-office. Harbour master—preventive officer. He is asking about our bill of health, sir."

"Don't forget to ask about the French ships," said Hornblower.

"Aye aye, sir."

The shouted conversation went on; Hornblower caught the word *fregata* more than once. The greybeard in the boat extended his hands in a negative gesture and went on to supplement it with a further sentence.

"He says there have been no French ships in here for years, sir," said Turner.

"Ask him if he has heard about any along the coast or in the islands?"

The greybeard clearly disclaimed all knowledge.

"Tell him," said Hornblower, "I'll give him five pieces of gold for news of the French."

There was something infectious in the atmosphere, in this Oriental talk—that was the only explanation Hornblower could think of for his using the outlandish expression "pieces of gold." There was no reason why he should not have said "guineas" to Turner. The greybeard shook his head again; Hornblower, looking keenly at him, fancied that the offer impressed him nevertheless. He asked another question and Turner answered.

"I've told him about the British squadron in the offing, sir," he reported.

"Good."

There was no harm in having the Turks believe he had a powerful force to back him up. Now the greybeard was gesturing with the fingers of one hand outstretched as he answered some question of Turner's.

"He says he wants five piastres a hogshead for us to fill our water casks, sir," said Turner. "That's a shilling each."

"Tell him—tell him I'll give him half."

The conversation continued; the western sky was beginning to redden with the sunset as the sun sank lower. At last the greybeard waved in farewell, and the boat turned away and unfurled her sail to the dying wind.

"They've gone back to spread their mats for the evening prayer, sir," said Turner. "I've promised him ten guineas for everything. That gives us the right to land at the jetty over there, to fill our water casks, and to buy in the market that he'll open in the morning. He'll take his share of what we pay there, you can be sure, sir."

"Very well, Mr. Turner. Mr. Jones!"

"Sir!"

"With the first light in the morning I'm going to start sweeping for the wreck. I'll have the sweep prepared now."

"Er—aye aye, sir."

"A hundred fathoms of one-inch line, if you please, Mr. Jones. Two nine-pounder shot. Have a net made for each, and attach them ten fathoms apart at equal distances from the ends of the line. Is that clear?"

"Not—not quite, sir."

Because he was honest about it Hornblower refrained from remarking on his slowness of comprehension.

"Take a hundred fathoms of line and attach one shot forty five fathoms from one end and another forty five fathoms from the other end. Is that clear now?"

"Yes, sir."

"You can get the launch and longboat into the water now, ready for the morning. They'll carry the sweep between them, dragging the bottom for the wreck. Tell off the boats' crews for duty. I want to start work at first dawn, as I said. And we'll need grapnels and buoys to mark what we find. Nothing conspicuous—planks will do, with seventeen fathoms of line to each. You understand all that?"

"Yes, sir."

"Carry on, then, Mr. Turner, report in my cabin in fifteen minutes' time, if you please. Messenger! My compliments to the doctor, and I'd like to see him in my cabin immediately."

Hornblower felt like a juggler at a fair, keeping half a dozen balls in the air at once. He wanted to hear from the doctor how McCullum was progressing after the operation; he wanted to discuss with Turner the question of what local authorities might be likely to be present in Marmorice to interfere with his work there; he wanted to make all preparations for the next morning; he wanted to be ready with his own plans for raising the treasure if McCullum was unable to give advice; and night orders for the care of the ship in this harbour of doubtful neutrality had to be written; it was only late in the evening that he remembered something else—something of which he was reminded only by a suddenly noticed feeling of emptiness inside him. He had eaten nothing since breakfast. He ate biscuit and cold meat, crunching the flinty fragments hurriedly at his cabin table before hurrying on deck again into the darkness.

It was a chilly night, and the young moon had already set. No breath of air now ruffled the black surface of the water of the bay, smooth enough to bear faint reflections of the stars. Black and impenetrable was the water, beneath which lay a quarter of a million pounds sterling. It was as impenetrable as his future, he decided, leaning on the bulwark. An intelligent man, he decided, would go to bed and sleep, having done all that his forethought and ingenuity could devise, and an intelligent man would worry no further for the moment. But he had to be very firm with himself to drive himself to bed and allow his utter weariness of body and mind to sweep him away into unconsciousness.

It was still dark when he was called, dark and cold, but he ordered coffee for himself and sipped it as he dressed. Last night when he had given the time for his being called he had allowed for a leisurely dressing before daylight, but he felt tense and anxious as he got out of bed, much as he had felt on other occasions when he had been roused in the night to take part in a cutting-out expedition or a dawn landing, and he had to restrain himself from putting on his clothes in haphazard fashion and hurrying on deck. He forced himself to shave, although that was an operation which had mostly to be carried out by touch because the hanging lamp gave almost no illumination to the mirror. The shirt he pulled on felt clammy against his ribs; he was struggling with his trousers when a knock at the door brought in Eisenbeiss, reporting in obedience to overnight orders.

"The patient is sleeping well, sir," he announced.

"Is his condition good?"

"I thought I should not disturb him, sir. He was sleeping quietly, so I could not tell if he had fever nor could I examine the wound. I can wake him if you wish, sir—"

"No, don't do that, of course. I suppose it's a good symptom that he's sleeping in any case?"

"A very good one, sir."

"Then leave him alone, Doctor. Report to me if there is any change."

"Aye aye, sir."

Hornblower buttoned his trousers and thrust his feet into his shoes. His eagerness to be on deck overcame his self-restraint to the extent that he was still buttoning his coat as he went up the companion. On deck as well the atmosphere seemed to be charged with that feeling of impending attack at dawn. There were the dimly seen figures of the officers, silhouetted against the sky. To the east there was the faintest illumination, a little light reaching half-way up to the zenith, so faint as almost to be unnoticed, and its colour, in its turn, was so faint a shade of pink as hardly to be called that.

"Morning," said Hornblower in response to the touched hats of his subordinates.

In the waist he could hear orders being quietly given—just like manning the boats for a cutting-out expedition.

"Longboat's crew starboard side," said Smiley's voice.

"Launch's crew port side." That was the Prince's voice. He was acquiring a better accent than Eisenbeiss.

"There's some surface mist, sir," reported Jones. "But it's very patchy."

"So I see," replied Hornblower.

"Last night we were lying two cables' lengths from the wreck as near as makes no matter, sir," said Turner. "We've swung during the night, with the wind dropping, but little enough."

"Tell me when it's light enough for you to get your bearings."

"Aye aye, sir."

In that short time the eastern sky had changed. One might almost have said it had darkened, but perhaps that was because with the tiny increase in the general illumination the contrast was not so marked.

"You took a third bearing at the time when *Speedwell* went down, Mr. Turner?"

"Yes, sir. It was—"

"No matter."

Turner could be relied upon to manage a simple piece of business of that sort.

"I don't expect the wreck has moved an inch, sir," said Turner. "There's no tide here. No scour. The two rivers that run into the bay don't set up any current you can measure."

"And the bottom's firm sand?"

"Firm sand, sir."

That was something to be thankful for. In mud the wreck might have sunk beyond discovery.

"How the devil did *Speedwell* come to capsize?" asked Hornblower.

"Sheer bad luck, sir. She was an old ship, and she'd been at sea a long time. The weeds and the barnacles were thick along her waterline—she wasn't coppered high enough, sir. So they were heeling her, cleaning her port side, with the guns run out to starboard and all the weights they could shift over to starboard too. It was a still day, baking hot. Then before you could say Jack Robinson there came a gust out of the mountains. It caught her square on the port beam and laid her over before she could pay off. The gunports were open and the water came up over the sills. That laid her over still more—at least, that's what the court of inquiry found, sir—and with her hatchways open the water rose over the coamings and down she went."

"Did she right herself as she sank?"

"No, sir. I looked over at her when I heard the shout, and I saw her keel. Bottom upwards she went. Her topmasts were snapped clean off. They came up soon enough, main and fore topmasts still anchored to the wreck by a shroud or two. That was a help when it came to taking the bearings."

"I see," said Hornblower.

Dawn was coming up fast. It actually seemed—an optical illusion, of course—as if great arms of colour were climbing up the sky from the eastern horizon at a pace perceptible to the eye.

"It's light enough now, sir," said Turner.

"Thank you. Mr. Jones! You can carry on."

Hornblower watched them go, Turner leading the way in the gig with his instruments and compass, Still following behind in the launch with Smiley in the longboat attached to the launch by the sweep. Hornblower became acutely aware that despite the cup of coffee he had drunk he wanted his breakfast. It seemed almost against his will that he lingered. This dead still calm at dawn was the ideal time for an operation of this sort; it enabled the gig to take up and maintain a position with the least possible effort. The ripples caused by the boat's passage, slow though it was, spread far over the glassy surface of the bay before dying out at last. He saw the gig stop, and clearly over the water came the sound of Turner's voice as he spoke through his speaking trumpet to the other boats. They jockeyed round into position awkwardly, like two beetles tied together with a thread, and then they paid out the sweep between them, manoeuvred awkwardly again for a moment as they laid themselves exactly upon the correct bearing, and then the oars began to swing rhythmically, slowly, like the pendulum of Fate, as the boats began to sweep the area ahead of them. Hornblower's heart beat faster despite himself, and he swallowed with excitement. Around him the ship was beginning her normal life. Amid the peculiar patter of bare feet on wooden planking—a sound unlike any other on earth—the watch below were bringing their hammocks to stow in the nettings. Swabs and holystones, buckets and pump; the hands not at work in the boats began the eternal daily routine of washing down the decks. Not for the first time on the voyage Hornblower found himself experiencing a momentary envy of the seamen at their work. Their problems were of the simplest, their doubts were minute. To holystone a portion of planking to the whiteness demanded by a petty officer, to swab it off, to swab it dry, working in amicable companionship with friends of long standing, dabbling their naked feet in the gush of clear water—that was all they had to do, as they had done for an infinity of mornings in the past and would do for an infinity of mornings in the future. He would be glad to exchange with them his loneliness, his responsibility, the complexity of his problems; so he felt for a moment before he laughed at himself, knowing perfectly well he would be horrified if some freak of Fate forced such an exchange on him. He turned away, changing the subject of his thoughts; a generous slice of fat pork, fried to a pale brown—there had been a leg in soak for him for the past two days, and the outside cut would be not too salt now. It would smell delicious—he could almost smell it at this very moment. Holy Jerusalem, unless it was still spluttering on his plate when it was put before him, despite the journey from galley to cabin, he'd make someone wish he had never been born. And he would have biscuit crumbs fried with it, and he would top it off with black treacle smeared on a biscuit, thick. That was a breakfast worth thinking about.

THIRTEEN

Hornblower stood with his purse in his hand, having taken it from his sea-chest where it had lain in the inner compartment. He knew exactly how many guineas there were in it, and he was trying not to wish there were more. If he were a wealthy captain he would be generous towards his ship's company, and to the wardroom and gunroom. But as it was—he shook his head. He did not want to appear miserly or mean, but he certainly did not want to be foolish. He walked along to the wardroom door and paused there; Still caught his eye.

"Please come in, sir."

The other officers rose from their chairs; there was nowhere for them to sit unless they sat round the table in the tiny wardroom.

"I was hoping," said Hornblower to Carslake the purser, "that you would be kind enough to make some purchases for me."

"Of course, sir. Honoured, I'm sure," said Carslake. He could say nothing else, in any case.

"A few chickens—half a dozen, say, and some eggs."

"Yes, sir."

"Is it the intention of the wardroom to buy fresh meat for itself?"

"Well, sir—"

That had been the subject under discussion at his entrance.

"At this time of year there might be lambs to sell. I could have one—two young ones, if they're cheap. But an ox—what am I to do with a whole ox?"

Everyone in the wardroom had been up against this problem at some time or other.

"If the wardroom decides to buy an ox I would be glad to pay a quarter of the price," said Hornblower, and the wardroom cheered up perceptibly.

A captain who bought a share in an animal would always get the best cuts—that was in the course of nature. And they had all known captains who would pay no more than their share. But with five wardroom officers Hornblower's offer was generous.

"Thank you very much, sir," said Carslake. "I think I can sell a couple of joints to the gunroom."

"On advantageous terms, I trust?" said Hornblower, with a grin.

He could remember well enough as a midshipman occasions when wardroom and gunroom had gone shares in an animal.

"I expect so, sir," said Carslake and then, changing the subject, "Mr. Turner says that it'll be goat here, mainly. Do you care for goat, sir?"

"Young kid, stewed with turnips and carrots!" said Jones. "You can do worse than that, sir."

Jones' lantern-jawed face was alight with appetite. These grown men, continuously fed on preserved food, were like children at a gingerbread stall at a fair with the thought of fresh meat.

"Do what you can," said Hornblower. "I'll eat kid or lamb, or I'll share in an ox, as you find the market provides. You know what you're buying for the crew?"

"Yes, sir," said Carslake.

The penny-pinching clerks of a penurious government at home would scrutinise those expenditures in time. Nothing very generous could be bought for the hands.

"I don't know what vegetables we'll find, sir, at this time of year," went on Carslake. "Winter cabbage, I suppose."

"Nothing wrong with winter cabbage," interposed Jones.

"Carrots and turnips out of winter store," said Carslake. "They'll be pretty stringy, sir."

"Better than nothing," said Hornblower. "There won't be enough in the market for all we need, nor will there be until the word goes round the countryside. So much the better. Then we'll have an excuse to linger. You're going to interpret, Mr. Turner?"

"Yes, sir."

"Keep your eyes open. And your ears."

"Aye aye, sir."

"Mr. Jones, you will attend to the water casks, if you please."

"Aye aye, sir."

That was the transition between the social visit and the official issuing of orders.

"Carry on."

Hornblower went to the bedside where McCullum lay. Sailcloth pillows supported him in a position half on his side. It was a comfort to see how comparatively well he looked. The fever and its accompanying distortion of thought had left him.

"Glad to see you looking so well, Mr. McCullum," said Hornblower.

"Well enough," answered McCullum.

He croaked a little, but his speech was almost normal.

"A full night's sleep," said Eisenbeiss, hovering on the far side of the bed. He had already made his report to Hornblower—the wound showed every sign of healing, the sutures had not at least as yet caused undue inflammation, and the draining where the bristle kept the wound in the back open had been apparently satisfactory.

"And we've started a full morning's work," said Hornblower. "You have heard that we have located the wreck?"

"No. I had not heard that."

"It's located and buoyed," said Hornblower.

"Are you sure it is the wreck?" croaked McCullum. "I've known some queer mistakes made."

"It is exactly where the bearings were taken when she sank," said Hornblower. "It is the right size as far as the sweep can show. And no other obstructions were found by the sweep, either. The bottom here is firm sand, as I expect you know."

"It sounds plausible," said McCullum grudgingly. "I could have wished I'd had the direction of the sweeping, nevertheless."

"You must trust me, Mr. McCullum," said Hornblower patiently.

"'Tis little that I know about you and your capabilities," answered McCullum.

Hornblower, swallowing his irritation at that remark, wondered how McCullum had managed to live so long without previously being shot in a duel. But McCullum was the irreplaceable expert, and even if he were not a sick man it would be both foolish and undignified to quarrel with him.

"I presume the next thing to do is to send your divers down to report on the condition of the wreck," he said, trying to be both firm and polite.

"Undoubtedly that will be the first thing I do as soon as I am allowed out of this bed," said McCullum.

Hornblower thought of all that Eisenbeiss had told him about McCullum's wound, about gangrene and suppuration and general blood-poisoning, and he knew there was a fair chance that McCullum would never rise from his bed.

"Mr. McCullum," he said, "this is an urgent matter. Once the Turks get wind of what we want to do, and can assemble sufficient force to stop us, we will never be allowed to conduct salvage operations here. It is of the first importance that we get to work as quickly as we can. I was hoping that you would instruct your divers in their duties so that they could start now, immediately."

"So that is what you were thinking, is it?" said McCullum.

It took some minutes of patient argument to wear McCullum down, and the grudging agreement that McCullum gave was tempered by an immediate pointing out of the difficulties.

"That water's mortal cold," said McCullum.

"I'm afraid so," answered Hornblower, "but we have always expected that."

"The eastern Mediterranean in March is nothing like the Bay of Bengal in summer. My men won't stand it for long."

It was a great advance that McCullum should admit that they might stand it at all.

"If they work for short intervals?" suggested Hornblower.

"Aye. Seventeen fathoms beside the wreck?"

"Seventeen fathoms all round it," said Hornblower.

"They can't work for long at that depth in any case. Five dives a day will be all. Then they bleed at the nose and ears. They'll need lines and weights—nine-pounder shot will serve."

"I'll have them got ready," said Hornblower.

Hornblower stood by while McCullum addressed his divers. He could guess at the point of some of the speeches. One of the divers was raising objections; it was clear, when he clasped his arms about his chest and shuddered dramatically with a rolling of his pathetic dark eyes, what he was saying. All three of them talked at once for a space in their twittering language. A sterner note came into McCullum's voice when he replied, and he indicated Hornblower with a gesture, directing all eyes to him for a moment. All three clung to each other and shrank from him like frightened children. McCullum went on speaking, energetically—Eisenbeiss leaned over him and restrained the left hand that gesticulated; the right was strapped into immobility against McCullum's chest.

"Do not move," said Eisenbeiss. "We shall have an inflammation."

McCullum had winced more than once after an incautious movement, and his appearance of well-being changed quickly to one of fatigue.

"They'll start now," he said at length, his head back on his pillow. "You can take 'em. Looney, here—that's what I call him—will be in charge. I've told 'em there are no sharks. Generally when one of 'em's down at the bottom the other two pray against sharks—they're all three of 'em shark doctors. A good thing they've seen men flogged on board here. I promised 'em you'd give 'em a taste of the cat if there was any nonsense."

Hornblower had seen very plainly what the reactions of these twittering birdlike creatures had been to that horror.

"Take 'em away," said McCullum, lying back on his pillow.

With longboat and launch over at the far side of the bay for stores and water only the gig and the tiny jolly boat were available. The gig was uncomfortably crowded but it served, with four hands at the oars, Hornblower and Leadbitter in the stern—Hornblower felt he could not possibly endure not taking part in this first essay—and the Ceylonese crowded into the bows. Hornblower had formed a shrewd notion about the extent of McCullum's ability to speak the divers' language. He had no doubt that McCullum made no attempt to speak it accurately or with any attempt at inflection. He made his points, Hornblower guessed, with a few nouns and verbs and some energetic gestures. McCullum's command of the Ceylonese tongue could not compare with Hornblower's Spanish, nor even with his French. Hornblower felt a sense of grievance about that, as he sat with his hand on the tiller and steered the gig over the dancing water—already the flat calm of dawn had given way to a moderate breeze that ruffled the surface.

They reached the first of the buoys—a plank wallowing among the wavelets at the end of its line—and Hornblower stood to identify the others. A stroke or two of the oars carried the gig into the centre of the area, and Hornblower looked down the boat to where the divers huddled together.

"Looney," he said.

Now that he had been paying special attention to them he could distinguish each of the three divers from the others. Until that time they might as well have been triplets as far as his ability went to tell them apart.

"Looney," said Hornblower again.

Looney rose to his feet and dropped the grapnel over the side. It went down fast, taking out the coiled-down line rapidly over the gunwale. Slowly Looney took off his clothes until he stood naked. He sat himself on the gunwale and swung his legs over. As his feet felt the cold of the water he cried out, and the other two joined with him in cries of alarm or commiseration.

"Shall I give 'im a shove, sir?" asked the hand at the bow oar.

"No," said Hornblower.

Looney was sitting systematically inflating and deflating his chest, inhaling as deeply as he could, forcing air into his lungs. Hornblower could see how widely the ribs moved at each breath. One of the other two Ceylonese put a cannon ball into Looney's hands, and he clasped it to his naked chest. Then he let himself slip from the gunwale and disappeared below the surface, leaving the gig rocking violently.

Hornblower took out his watch; it had no second hand—watches with second hands were far too expensive for him to afford—but he could measure the time roughly. He watched the tip of the minute hand creep from one mark to the next, from there to the next, and into the third minute. He was concentrating so deeply on the task that he did not hear Looney break water; his attention was called by a word from Leadbitter. Looney's head was visible twenty yards astern, his long thick switch of black hair, tied with a string, beside his ear.

"Back water!" said Hornblower promptly. "Pay out that line, there!"

The second order was understood clearly enough by the Ceylonese, or at least they knew their business, for as a vigorous stroke or two sent the gig down to Looney one of them attended to the line over the bows. Looney put his hands up to the gunwale and the other two pulled him on board. They talked volubly, but Looney at first sat still on the thwart, his head down by his thighs. Then he lifted his head, the water streaming from his wet hair. Clearly he talked about the cold—that sharp breeze must have been icy upon his wet skin—for the others towelled him and assisted him to cover himself with his clothes.

Hornblower wondered how he would set them to work again, but there was no need for him to interfere. As soon as Looney had his white garments about his shoulders he stood up in the bows of the gig and looked about him, considering. Then he pointed to a spot in the water a few yards away, looking round at Hornblower.

"Give way!" said Hornblower.

One of the Ceylonese hauled in on the grapnel and let it go again when the boat reached the spot indicated. Now it was his turn to strip, to inflate and deflate his chest, and to take a cannon ball into his hands and drop over the side. Cannon balls cost money, thought Hornblower, and a time might come when he would need them to fire at the enemy. It would be better in the future to lay in a supply of small rocks gathered on the shore. The diver came up to the surface and scrambled on board, to be received by his companions just as Looney had been. There was some kind of discussion among the divers, which was ended by the third one going down in the same place, apparently to settle the point in dispute. What he discovered led on his return to Looney's requesting by signs a further shifting of the gig, and then Looney took off his clothes again to go down.

The divers were working industriously and, as far as Hornblower could see, intelligently. Later on Looney and one of his mates made a simultaneous descent, and it was on this occasion that Hornblower noticed that Looney's legs and feet, when he climbed in, were scratched and bleeding. For a moment Hornblower thought of sharks and similar underwater perils, but he revised his opinion at once. Looney must have been scrambling about on the wreck itself. There were decaying timbers down there, deep in the bright water, overgrown with barnacles and razor-edged sea shells. Hornblower felt confirmed in his opinion when Looney desired to buoy this particular spot. They anchored a plank there by a grapnel, and then dived more than once again in the neighborhood.

Now the divers were exhausted, lying doubled up and huddled together beside the bow thwart.

"Very well, Looney," said Hornblower, and he pointed back to the ship.

Looney gave him a weary nod.

"Up anchor," ordered Hornblower, and the gig pulled back towards *Atropos.*

A mile away were visible the lug sails of longboat and launch also on their return journey, coming down with the freshening wind abeam. It seemed to Hornblower as if things could never happen to him one at a time; he had hardly set foot on the deck of the *Atropos* before they were running alongside, and as the Ceylonese made their weary way forward to report to McCullum here were Carslake and Turner demanding his attention.

"The water casks are refilled, sir," said Carslake. "I used the little stream that comes in half a mile from the town. I thought that would be better than those in the town."

"Quite right, Mr. Carslake," said Hornblower. On account of what he had seen in North Africa, Hornblower agreed with Carslake that a water supply that had not passed through a Turkish town would be preferable.

"What stores did you get?"

"Very little, sir, today, I'm afraid."

"There was only the local market, sir," supplemented Turner. "The

Mudir has only sent out word today. The goods will be coming in for sale tomorrow."

"The Mudir?" asked Hornblower. That was the word Turner had used before.

"The head man, sir, the local governor. The old man with the sword who came out to us in the boat yesterday."

"And he is the Mudir?"

"Yes, sir. The Mudir is under the Kaimakam, and the Kaimakam is under the Vali, and the Vali is under the Grand Vizier, and he's under the Sultan, or at least that's how it's supposed to be—all of 'em try to be independent when they get the chance."

"I understand that," said Hornblower.

No one who had given any study at all to the military and naval history of the last few years in the eastern Mediterranean could be ignorant of the anarchy and disintegration prevailing in the Turkish Empire. What Hornblower wanted to hear about was the effect these were producing locally and today. He turned back to Carslake to listen patiently first to his account of what had been bought and what would be available later.

"I bought all the eggs there were, sir. Two and a half dozen," said Carslake in the course of his report.

"Good," said Hornblower, but without any fervour, and that was clear proof that his mind was not on what Carslake was saying. Normally the thought of eggs, boiled, scrambled, or poached, would have excited him. The untoward events at Malta had prevented his buying any there for himself. He had not even laid in a store of pickled eggs at Deptford.

Carslake droned himself to a stop.

"Thank you, Mr. Carslake," said Hornblower. "Mr. Turner, come below and I'll hear what you have to say."

Turner had apparently kept his eyes and ears open, as Hornblower had ordered him to.

"The Mudir has no force here at all worth mentioning, sir," said Turner, his wizened old face animated and lively. "I doubt if he could raise twenty five armed men all told. He came down with two guards as old as himself."

"You spoke with him?"

"Yes, sir. I gave him—Mr. Carslake and I gave him—ten guineas to open the market for us. Another ten guineas tomorrow is what we've promised him."

No harm in keeping local authority on his side as long as possible, thought Hornblower.

"And was he friendly?" he asked.

"We-ell, sir. I wouldn't say that, not exactly, sir. Maybe it was because he wanted our money. I wouldn't call him friendly, sir."

He would be reserved and cautious, Hornblower decided, not anxious to commit himself without instructions from superior authority, and yet not averse to pocketing twenty pieces of gold—pickings for an average year, Hornblower guessed—when the opportunity presented itself.

"The Vali's carried off the local army, sir," went on Turner. "That was plain enough from the way the Mudir talked. But I don't know why, sir. Maybe there's trouble with the Greeks again. There's always trouble in the Archipelago."

Rebellion was endemic among the Greek subjects of Turkey. Fire and sword, massacre and desolation, piracy and revolt, swept islands and mainland periodically. And nowadays with French influence penetrating from the Seven Islands, and Russia taking a suspiciously humanitarian interest in the welfare of Turkey's Orthodox subjects, there were fresh sources of trouble and unrest.

"One point's clear anyway," said Hornblower, "and that is that the Vali's not here at present."

"That's so, sir."

It would take time for a message to reach the Vali, or even the Vali's subordinate, the—the Kaimakam, decided Hornblower, fishing the strange title out of his memory with an effort. The political situation was involved beyond any simple disentanglement. Turkey had been Britain's enthusiastic ally recently, when Bonaparte had conquered Egypt and invaded Syria and threatened Constantinople. But Russia and Turkey were chronic enemies—they had fought half a dozen wars in the last half century—and now Russia and England were allies, and Russia and France were enemies, even though since Austerlitz there was no way in which they could attack each other. There could be no doubt in the world that the French ambassador in Constantinople was doing his best to incite Turkey to a fresh war with Russia; no doubt at all that Russia since the days of Catherine the Great was casting covetous eyes on Constantinople and the Dardanelles.

The Greek unrest was an established fact. So was the ambition of the local Turkish governors. The tottering Turkish government would seize any opportunity to play off one possible enemy against the other, and would view with the deepest suspicion—there was even the religious factor to be borne in mind—any British activity amid Turkish possessions. With England and France locked in a death struggle the Turks could hardly be blamed if they suspected England of buying Russia's continued alliance with a promise of a slice of Turkish territory; luckily France, with a far worse record, was liable to be similarly suspected. When the Sultan heard—if ever he did hear—of the presence of a British ship of war in Marmorice Bay he would wonder what intrigues were brewing with the Vali; and if Sultan or Vali heard that a quarter of a million in gold and silver lay at the bottom of Marmorice Bay it could be taken for granted that none would be salvaged unless the lion's share went into Turkish hands.

There was just no conclusion to be reached after all this debate, except for the one he had reached a week ago, and that was to effect as prompt a recovery of the treasure as possible and to leave the diplomats to argue over a *fait accompli*. He walked forward to hear from McCullum's lips how much had been learned regarding this possibility.

McCullum had just finished hearing what the divers had reported to him. They were squatting round his cot, with all the attention of their big eyes concentrated on his face, and with all their clothes draped about them until they looked something like beehives.

"She's there," said McCullum. Apparently he had been quite prepared to find that some gross blunder or other had been committed, either in plotting the original bearings or in the recent sweeping operations.

"I'm glad to hear it," replied Hornblower, as politely as he could make himself endure these temperamental liberties of an expert and an invalid.

"She's greatly overgrown, except for her copper, but she shows no sign of breaking up at all."

A wooden ship, fastened together with wooden pegs, and untouched by storm or current, might well lie forever on a sandy bed without disintegration.

"Did she right herself?" asked Hornblower.

"No. She's nearly bottom up. My men could tell bow from stern."

"That's fortunate," said Hornblower.

"Yes," McCullum referred to some pages of written notes that he held in his free hand. "The money was in the lower lazarette, aft, abaft the mizzenmast and immediately below the maindeck. A ton and a half of coined gold in iron chests and nearly four tons of coined silver in bags."

"Ye-es," said Hornblower, trying to look as if that exactly agreed with his own calculations.

"The lazarette was given an additional lining of oak to strengthen it before the treasure was put on board," went on McCullum. "I expect the money's still there."

"You mean—?" asked Hornblower, quite at a loss.

"I mean it will not have fallen through the deck onto the sea bottom," said McCullum, condescending to explain to this ignorant amateur.

"Of course," said Hornblower, hastily.

"*Speedwell's* main cargo was half the battering train of the army," went on McCullum. "Ten long eighteen-pounders. Bronze guns. And the shot for them. Iron shot."

"That's why she went down the way she did," said Hornblower brightly. As he spoke he realised as well the implications of the words "bronze" and "iron" which McCullum had accented. Bronze would endure under water longer than iron.

"Yes," said McCullum. "As soon as she heeled, guns and shot and all would shift. I'll wager on that, from what I know of first mates in these days. With the war, any jumped-up apprentice is a first mate."

"I've seen it myself," said Hornblower, sorrowfully.

"But that's neither here nor there," went on McCullum. "Looney here says she is still, most of her, above the sand. He could get in under the break of the poop, just."

From McCullum's significant glance when he made this announcement Hornblower could guess that it was of great importance, but it was hard to see just why this should be.

"Yes?" said Hornblower, tentatively.

"Do you think they can break in through the ship's side with crowbars?" asked McCullum testily. "Five minutes' work on the bottom a day each for three men! We'd be here a year."

Hornblower suddenly remembered the "leather fuse-hoses" for which McCullum had indented at Malta. He made a hasty guess, despite the fantastic nature of what he had to say.

"You're going to blow up the wreck?" he said.

"Of course. A powder charge in that angle should open the ship at exactly the right place."

"Naturally," said Hornblower. He was dimly aware that it was possible to explode charges under water, but his knowledge of the technical methods to be employed was dimmer still.

"We'll try the fuse-hoses first," announced McCullum. "But I've little hope of them at that depth. The joints can't resist the pressure."

"I suppose not," said Hornblower.

"I expect it'll mean a flying fuse in the end," said McCullum. "These fellows here are always afraid of 'em. But I'll do it."

The bulky figure of Eisenbeiss loomed up beside the cot. He put one hand on McCullum's forehead and the other on his wrist.

"Take your hands off me!" snarled McCullum. "I'm busy."

"You must not do too much," said Eisenbeiss. "Excitement increases the morbid humours."

"Morbid humours be damned!" exclaimed McCullum. "And you be damned too."

"Don't be a fool, man," said Hornblower, his patience exhausted. "He saved your life yesterday. Don't you remember how sick you were? 'It hurts. It hurts.' That's what you were saying."

Hornblower found his voice piping in imitation of McCullum's yesterday, and he turned his face feebly from side to side like McCullum's on the pillow. He was aware that it was an effective bit of mimicry, and even McCullum was a trifle abashed by it.

"Sick I may have been," he said, "but I'm well enough now."

Hornblower looked across at Eisenbeiss.

"Let Mr. McCullum have five more minutes," he said. "Now, Mr. McCullum, you were talking about leather fuse-hoses. Will you please explain how they are used?"

FOURTEEN

HORNBLOWER CAME FORWARD to where the gunner and his mates were squatting on the deck at work upon the fuse-hose in accordance with McCullum's instructions.

"You are making a thorough job of those seams, I hope, Mr. Clout," he said.

"Aye aye, sir," said Clout.

They had an old sail spread out to sit on, for the purpose of saving the spotless deck from the warm pitch in the iron pot beside them.

"Five seconds to the foot, this quick match burns, sir. You said one foot of slow match, sir?"

"I did."

Hornblower bent to look at the work. The leather hose was in irregular lengths, from three to five feet; it was typical of the cross-grained ways of Nature that animals could not provide longer pieces of leather than that. One of the gunner's mates was at work with a slender wooden bodkin dragging the end of a vast length of quick match through a section of hose. When the bodkin emerged he proceeded to slip the hose along the quick match until it joined the preceding section.

"Easy with that, now," said Clout. "We don't want a break in that match."

The other gunner's mate set to work with needle and palm to sew and double-sew the new length to its neighbour. The joint completed, Clout proceeded to apply warm pitch liberally over the joint and down the seam of the new section. Eventually there would be a hundred and twenty feet of hose joined and pitched and with quick match threaded all the way through it.

"I've picked a couple of sound kegs, sir," said Clout. "Fifty-pound kegs, they are. I have bags of dry sand to fill 'em up."

"Very well," said Hornblower.

Thirty pounds of powder was what McCullum wanted for his explosive charge, no more and no less.

"I don't want to shatter the wreck to pieces," McCullum had said. "I only want to split her open."

That was a part of McCullum's special knowledge; Hornblower could not possibly have guessed how much powder, at a depth of a hundred feet, would achieve this result. In a long nine-pounder, he knew, three pounds of powder would throw the shot a mile and a half, random shooting, but this was something entirely different, and in the incompressible medium of water, too. With a fifty-pound keg and only thirty pounds of powder it was necessary to have some indifferent substance like sand to fill the keg full.

"Send me word the moment you are ready," said Hornblower, and turned back aft again.

Here was Turner, newly come from the shore, hovering about to attract his attention.

"Well, Mr. Turner?"

Turner kept his distance, his manner indicating that he had something very private to say. He spoke in a low voice when Hornblower walked over to him.

"Please, sir, it's the Mudir. He wants to visit you. I can't make him out, but there's something he wants."

"What did you tell him?"

"I said—I'm sorry, sir, but I didn't know what else to do—I said you'd be delighted. There's something fishy, I think. He said he'd come at once."

"He did, did he?"

Things were bound to be fishy in these troubled waters, thought Hornblower, with a simultaneous disapproval of the style of that sentiment.

"Midshipman of the watch!"

"Sir!"

"What do you see over towards the town?"

Smiley trained his glass across the bay.

"Boat putting out, sir. She's the same lateen we saw before."

"Any flag?"

"Yes, sir. Red. Turkish colours, it looks like."

"Very well. Mr. Jones, we're going to have an official visitor. You may pipe the side for him."

"Aye aye, sir."

"Now, Mr. Turner, you don't know what the Mudir wants?"

"No, sir. He wanted to see you, urgently, it seems like. '*Il capitano*' was all he'd say when we landed—the market was supposed to be ready for us, but it wasn't. What he wanted was to see the captain, and so I said you'd see him."

"He gave no hint?"

"No, sir. He wouldn't say. But he was agitated, I could see."

"Well, we'll know soon enough," said Hornblower.

The Mudir mounted to the deck with a certain dignity, despite the difficulties the awkward ascent presented to his old legs. He looked keenly about him as he came on board; whether or not he understood the compliment that was being paid him by the bosun's mates and the sideboys could not be determined. There was a keen hawklike face above the grey beard, and a pair of lively dark eyes took in the scene about him without revealing whether it was a familiar one or not. Hornblower touched his hat and the Mudir replied with a graceful gesture of his hand to his face.

"Ask him if he will come below," said Hornblower. "I'll lead the way."

Down in the cabin Hornblower offered a chair, with a bow, and the Mudir seated himself. Hornblower sat opposite him with Turner at his side. The Mudir spoke and Turner translated.

"He hopes God has given you the gift of health, sir," said Turner.

"Make the correct reply," said Hornblower.

As he spoke he met the glance of the sharp brown eyes and smiled politely.

"Now he's asking you if you have had a prosperous voyage, sir," reported Turner.

"Say whatever you think fit," answered Hornblower.

The conversation proceeded from one formal politeness to another. This was the way of the Levant, Hornblower knew. It could be neither dignified nor tactful to announce one's business in one's opening sentences.

"Should we offer him a drink?" asked Hornblower.

"Well, sir, it's usual over business to offer coffee."

"Then don't you think we'd better?"

"You see, sir, it's the coffee—it'll be different from what he calls coffee."

"We can hardly help that. Give the order, if you please."

The conversation continued, still without reaching any point. It was interesting to note how an intelligent and mobile face like the Mudir's could give no hint at all of any emotion behind it. But the coffee brought about a change. The sharp eyes took in the thick mugs, the battered pewter coffee-pot, while the face remained impassive and the Mudir was going through the ceremony of polite refusal and then grateful acceptance; but the tasting of the coffee effected a transformation. Willy-nilly, the Mudir could not prevent an expression of surprise, even though he instantly brought his features under control again. He proceeded to sweeten his coffee to a syrup with sugar, and he did not touch the cup, but raised it to his lips by means of the saucer.

"There ought to be little cakes and sweetmeats, too, sir," said Turner. "But we couldn't offer him blackstrap and biscuit."

"I suppose not," said Hornblower.

The Mudir sipped cautiously at his coffee again, and resumed his speech.

"He says you have a very fine ship, sir," said Turner. "I think he is coming to the point soon."

"Thank him and tell him what a wonderful village he has, if you think that's the right thing," said Hornblower.

The Mudir sat back in his chair—it was plain that he was not accustomed to chairs—studying first Hornblower's face and then Turner's. Then he spoke again; his voice was well modulated, well controlled.

"He's asking if *Atropos* is going to stay long, sir," said Turner.

It was the question Hornblower was expecting.

"Say that I have not completed my stores yet," he said.

He was quite sure that the preliminary operations of salvage, sweeping for the wreck, buoying it, and sending down the divers, had escaped observation, or at least would be quite unintelligible from the shore. He did not take his eyes from the Mudir's face as Turner translated and the Mudir replied.

"He says he presumes you will be leaving as soon as you've done that," said Turner.

"Tell him it's likely."

"He says this would be a good place to wait for information about French ships, sir. The fishing boats often come in with news."

"Tell him I have my orders."

The suspicion began to form in Hornblower's mind that the Mudir did not want *Atropos* to leave. Perhaps he wanted to keep him here until an ambush could be laid, until the guns at the fort could be manned, until the Vali returned with the local army. This was a good way to carry on a diplomatic conversation. He could watch the Mudir all the time, while any unguarded statement of Turner's could be disavowed on the grounds of poor translation if no other way.

"We can keep an eye on the Rhodes Channel from here, sir, he says," went on Turner. "It's the most likely course for any Frenchy. It looks as if he wants to get his twenty guineas, sir."

"Maybe so," said Hornblower, trying to convey by his tone that he saw no need for Turner to contribute to the conversation. "Say that my orders give me very little discretion."

With the conversation taking this turn it was obvious that the best tactics would be to display a reluctance that might with great difficulty be overcome. Hornblower hoped that Turner's command of lingua franca was equal to this demand upon it.

The Mudir replied with more animation than he had previously shown; it was as if he were about to show his hand.

"He wants us to stay here, sir," said Turner. "If we do there'll be much better supplies coming in from the country."

That was not his real reason, obviously.

"No," said Hornblower. "If we can't get the supplies we'll go without them."

Hornblower was having to be careful about the expression on his face; he had to say these things to Turner as if he really meant them—the Mudir was not letting anything escape his notice.

"Now he's coming out in the open, sir," said Turner. "He's asking us to stay."

"Then ask him why he wants us to."

This time the Mudir spoke for a long time.

"So that's it, sir," reported Turner. "Now we know. There are pirates about."

"Tell me exactly what he said, if you please, Mr. Turner."

"There are pirates along the coast, sir," explained Turner, accepting the rebuke. "A fellow called Michael—Michael the—the Slayer of Turks, sir. I've heard of him. He raids these coasts. A Greek, of course. He was at Fettech two days back. That's just along the coast, sir."

"And the Mudir's afraid this'll be the next place he raids?"

"Yes, sir. I'll ask him so as to make sure, sir," added Turner when Hornblower glanced at him.

The Mudir was quite eloquent now that he had taken the plunge. Turner had to listen for a long time before he could resume his translation.

"Michael burns the houses, sir, and takes the women and cattle. He's the sworn enemy of the Mohammedans. That's why the Vali is with the local army, sir. He went to head off Michael but he guessed wrong. He went to Adalia, and that's a week's march away, sir."

"I see."

With *Atropos* lying in Marmorice Bay a pirate would never venture in, and the Mudir and his people were safe as long as she stayed there. The purpose of the Mudir's visit was plain; he wanted to persuade Hornblower to stay until this Michael was at a safe distance again. It was a remarkable piece of good fortune; it was, thought Hornblower, ample compensation for the freak of Fate which had left McCullum wounded in a duel. In the same way that in a long enough session the whist player found that the luck evened itself out, so it was with war. Good luck followed bad—and for Hornblower that was an astonishing admission, although he was ready enough to admit that bad luck followed good. But he must on no account show any pleasure.

"It's a stroke of luck for us, sir," said Turner.

"Please keep your conclusions to yourself, Mr. Turner," said Hornblower bitingly.

The tone of his voice and Turner's crestfallen expression puzzled the Mudir, who had not ceased to watch them closely. But he waited patiently for the unbelievers to make the next move.

"No," said Hornblower decisively. "Tell him I can't do it."

At Hornblower's shake of the head the Mudir actually showed a little dismay even before Turner translated. He stroked his grey beard and spoke again, choosing his words carefully.

"He's offering to bribe us, sir," said Turner. "Five lambs or kids for every day we stay here."

"That's better," said Hornblower. "Tell him I'd rather have money."

It was the Mudir's turn to shake his head when he heard what Turner had to say. He looked, to Hornblower's searching eye, like a man quite sincere.

"He says there isn't any money, sir. The Vali took all there was when he was here last."

"He has our twenty guineas anyway. Tell him I want them back, and six lambs a day—no kids—and I'll stay."

That was how it was decided in the end. With Turner escorting the Mudir back in the launch Hornblower went forward to inspect the gunner's work. It was nearly completed. A hundred odd feet of hose, carefully coiled, lay on the deck, and one end disappeared into a powder keg covered over with canvas which the gunner was smearing thickly with pitch. Hornblower stooped to examine what must be the weakest point, where the canvas cover of the keg was sewn round the hose.

"That's as good as I can make it, sir," said the gunner. "But it's a mighty long length of hose."

At a hundred feet below water the pressures were enormous. A minute, indetectable pinprick anywhere in the fabric and water would be forced in.

"We can try it," said Hornblower. "The sooner the better."

That was how it always was—"the sooner the better" might be found written on a naval officer's heart like Queen Mary's "Calais." Man the gig, see that all necessary equipment was packed into it, herd the divers into the bows after their last-minute instructions from McCullum, and start off without a minute wasted. Drink coffee with a Turkish Mudir at one hour, and dabble in underwater explosives the next. If variety was the spice of life, thought Hornblower, his present existence must be an Oriental curry.

"Easy!" he ordered, and the gig drifted slowly up to the moored plank which marked the accessible point of the wreck underneath.

Looney knew his business. The canvas-covered powder keg lay beside him; it was bound with line, and Looney took another short length of line, secured one end to the keg, passed the line round the mooring line of the buoy, and secured the other end to the keg again. He checked to see that the free end of the fuse-hose was properly fastened to the empty keg that was to buoy it up, and then gave a piping order to one of his colleagues, who stood up to take off his clothes. Looney laid hold of the powder keg, but it was too heavy for his spindly arms.

"Help him, you two," said Hornblower to the two seamen nearest. "See that the line's clear and see that the hose is clear, too."

Under Looney's direction the powder keg was lifted up and lowered over the side.

"Let go! Handsomely! Handsomely!" ordered Hornblower.

It was a tense moment—one more tense moment—to watch the powder keg sink below the choppy surface. By the line attached to it the seamen lowered it slowly down, the fuse-hose uncoiling after it as the keg sank. The loop of line which Looney had passed round the mooring line of the buoy made certain that the keg would sink to the right place.

"Bottom, sir," said a seaman, as the lowering line went slack in his hands. Several feet of hose remained in the boat.

The diver was sitting on the opposite gunwale; he carried a sheath knife on a string round his naked waist, and he took in his hands the cannon ball that Looney gave him. Then he lowered himself over and vanished under the surface. They waited until he came up; they waited while the next diver went down and came up again; they waited while Looney took his turn too. Dive succeeded dive; apparently it was not too easy an operation to move the powder keg to exactly the right place under the break of the *Speedwell's* poop. But presumably, down below the surface, the thing was achieved in the end. Looney came up from what seemed to be an extra-long dive; he had to be helped over the gunwale and he lay gasping in the bows for some time recovering. Then at last he sat up and made to Hornblower the unmistakable gesture of handling flint and steel.

"Strike a light," said Hornblower to Leadbitter. In all his life he had never properly acquired the knack of it.

Leadbitter opened the tinderbox, and struck, and struck again. It did not take Leadbitter more than six times before he succeeded. He bent and blew the spark on the tinder into life, took the piece of slow match and caught the fire on it, blew that into life too, and looked to Hornblower for further orders.

"I'll do it," said Hornblower.

Leadbitter handed him the glowing match, and Hornblower sat with it in his hand for a second while he checked once more to see that all was ready. He was tingling with excitement.

"Stand by with the cask!" he said. "Leadbitter, have the stopper ready."

There were four or five inches of quick match hanging out of the fuse-hose; Hornblower dabbed the glowing match upon it. A second's hesitation and it took fire. Hornblower watched the spark run along the quick match and vanish down into the hose.

"Stopper it!" said Hornblower, and Leadbitter forced the wooden stopper into the end of the hose, grinding down upon the brittle ashes of the match.

At five seconds to the foot the fire was now, he hoped, travelling down the hose, down, down, far below the level of the sea. At the far end, next to the powder keg, there was a foot of slow match. That burned at five minutes to the foot; they had plenty of time—no need for feverish haste, however great the urge to hurry.

"Over with it!" said Hornblower, and Leadbitter picked up the empty cask and lowered it gently into the water. It floated there, holding up above the surface the stoppered end of the fuse-hose.

"Oars!" said Hornblower. "Give way!"

The gig swung away from the floating keg. The spark was still travelling along the quick match, Hornblower presumed; it would be some seconds yet before it even reached the slow match down there by the wreck of the *Speedwell.* He remembered to take the time by his watch.

"Take her back to the ship," he ordered Leadbitter; he looked back to where the empty cask bobbed on the surface.

McCullum had said, "I advise you to keep clear of the explosion." Apparently the explosion of a barrel of powder, even far down under the water, created a turmoil on the surface that would endanger the gig. Beside the ship they would be a quarter of a mile away; that should be safe enough. When the bowman hooked onto the main chains of the *Atropos* Hornblower looked at his watch again. It was exactly five minutes since he had seen the spark passing into the end of the fuse-hose. The explosion could be expected at any time from now.

Naturally the side of the ship was lined with every idler who could find a place there. The preparation of the charge and the fuse had excited gossip throughout the ship.

Hornblower changed his mind about awaiting the explosion in the gig and mounted to the deck.

"Mr. Jones!" he bellowed. "Is this a raree show? Keep the hands at work, if you please."

"Aye aye, sir."

He very much wanted to see the explosion himself, but he feared to display curiosity inconsonant with his dignity. And there was the chance —a likely chance, according to McCullum—that there would be no explosion at all. A glance at his watch showed him that it was by now overdue. With an appearance of the utmost indifference he strolled forward to McCullum's bedside, where McCullum was listening to the reports of his divers.

"Nothing as yet?" said McCullum.

"Nothing."

"I never trust a fuse-hose beyond five fathoms," said McCullum, "even when I handle it myself."

Hornblower kept back an irritated answer, and gazed out towards the scene of his recent activities. In the choppy water he could just perceive at intervals the dark spot which was the keg that floated the end of the fuse-hose. He glanced at his watch again.

"Long overdue," he said.

"Water's in that hose. You'll have to use a flying-fuse after all."

"The sooner the better," said Hornblower. "How do I set about it?"

He was glad for the sake of his precious dignity that he had not waited in sight of the men.

FIFTEEN

THIS TIME SO MANY MEN were wanted for the operation that Hornblower was using the launch instead of the gig. As usual the three Ceylonese divers were huddled in the bows, but next to them on the bottom of the boat stood an iron pot of melted pitch, and beside it squatted a sail-maker's mate, and Mr. Clout the gunner sat amidships with the powder keg between his legs. The canvas covering to the keg was incompletely sewn, gaping wide at the upper end. They dropped the grapnel, and the launch rode on the little waves beside the little keg that floated with the end of the useless fuse-hose, a monument to the previous failure.

"Carry on, Mr. Clout," said Hornblower.

This was something more than exciting. This was dangerous. The divers stripped themselves for their work, and sat up to begin their exercises of inflating and deflating their lungs. There would not be any time to spare later. Clout took the tinderbox and proceeded to strike a spark upon the tinder, crouching low to shelter it from the small breeze which blew over the surface of the bay. He caught fire upon the slow match, brought it to a glow, and looked over at Hornblower.

"Carry on, I said," said Hornblower.

Clout dabbed the slow match upon the fuse that protruded through a hole in the end of the powder keg. Hornblower could hear the faint irregular hissing of the fuse as Clout waited for it to burn down into the hole. Among them now, in the middle of the boat, fire was creeping towards thirty pounds of gunpowder. If there were a few powder grains out of place, if the fuse were the least faulty, there would come a sudden crashing explosion which would blow them and the boat to fragments. There was not a sound in the boat save the hissing of the fuse. The spark crept down into the hole. The powder keg at this upper end had a double head, the result of the most careful work by the ship's cooper. In the space between the two heads was coiled the fuse, whose farther end penetrated the inner head to rest amid the powder. Along that coil stapled to the inner head the fire was now moving unseen, creeping round and round on its way to dive down along its final length through the inner head.

Clout took from his pocket the canvas-covered stopper, and dipped it into the warm pitch.

"Make sure of it, Mr. Clout," said Hornblower.

Clout rammed the stopper into the hole in the outer head. The action cut off the sound of the hissing fuse, but everyone in the boat knew that the fire was still pursuing its inexorable way inside. Clout smeared pitch thickly about the stopper and then moved out of the way.

"Now, my hearty," he said to the sail-maker's mate.

This last needed no urging. Needle and palm in hand, he took Clout's place and sewed up the canvas cover over the top of the keg.

"Keep those stitches small," said Hornblower; the sail-maker's mate, crouching over instant death, was not unnaturally nervous. So was Hornblower, but the irritation caused by the previous failure made him anxious that the work should be well done.

The sail-maker's mate finished the last stitch, oversewed it, and, whipping out his sheath knife, cut the twine. There could be hardly anything more harmless in appearance than that canvas-covered keg. It looked a stupid, a brainless object, standing there in the boat. Clout was already daubing pitch over the newly sewn end; the sides and the other end had been thickly pitched before the keg was put into the launch.

"Now the line," said Hornblower.

As on the previous occasion a loop of line attached to the keg was passed round the mooring line of the buoy and secured to the keg again.

"Hoist it, you two. Lower away. Handsomely."

The keg sank below the surface, dangling on the lowering line as the men let it down hand over hand. There was a sudden relief from tension in the boat, marked by a sudden babble of talk.

"Silence!" said Hornblower.

Even though the thing was invisible now, sinking down to the bottom of the bay, it was still deadly—the men did not understand that. One of the divers was already sitting on the gunwale, a cannon ball in his hands—that was a ridiculous moment for Hornblower to remember that he had not carried out his earlier resolution to get in a store of rocks for that purpose—and his chest expanding and contracting. Hornblower would have liked to tell him to make certain to place the powder keg to the best advantage, but that was impossible owing to the difficulties of language. He had to content himself with a glance, half encouragement and half threat.

"Bottom, sir," announced the seaman at the lowering line.

The diver slipped from the gunwale and vanished under the surface. Down there with the powder charge and the glowing fuse he was in worse peril even than before. "They've seen one of their mates blown to bits using a flying-fuse off Cuddalore," McCullum had said. Hornblower wanted nothing like that to happen now. It occurred to him that if it were to happen the launch, with him in it, would be on top of the explosion and turmoil, and he wondered what was the mysterious force that always drove him into voluntarily taking part in dangerous adventures. He thought it must be curiosity, and then he realised that it was a sense of shame as well; and it never occurred to him that a sense of duty had something to do with it too.

The second diver was sitting on the gunwale, cannon ball in hand and breathing deeply, and the moment the first diver's head broke water he let himself slip down and vanished. "I've put the fear of God into 'em," McCullum had said. "I've told 'em that if the charge explodes without being properly placed they'll all get two dozen. An' I've said we're here to stay. No matter how long we try we get the money up. So you can rely on 'em. They'll do their best."

And they certainly were doing their best. Looney was waiting on the gunwale now, and down he went as soon as the second diver appeared. They wanted to waste no time at all. Not for the first time Hornblower peered overside in the attempt to see down through the water, unsuccessfully again. It was clear, and the loveliest deep green, but there was just sufficient lop and commotion on the surface to make it impossible to see down. Hornblower had to take it for granted that deep down below, in semi-darkness at least, and amid paralysing cold, Looney was dragging the powder charge towards the wreck and shoving it under the break of the poop. That powder keg under water could weigh little enough, thanks to the upthrust that Archimedes discovered, twenty centuries before.

Looney reappeared, and the first diver instantly went down to replace him. This business was for the divers a gamble with life and death, a losing lottery. If the charge were to explode prematurely it would be chance that would dictate who would happen to be down there with it at that moment. But surely it could not take long to move the charge a few yards along the bottom and into the right place. And down there, he hoped, the fire was creeping along the coils of the fuse, sandwiched tight between the two barrelheads. The philosophers had decided that fuses were able to burn in the absence of air—unlike candles—because the nitre that permeated the cord supplied the same combustible substance that air supplied. It was a discovery that went close to solving the problem of life—a human being's life went out like a candle's in the absence of air. It might be reasonably expected soon that the discovery might be made as to how to maintain life without air.

Yet another dive. The fire was hurrying along the fuse. Clout had allowed enough for an hour's burning—it must not be too little, obviously, but also it must not be too much, for the longer the keg was exposed to the water pressure the greater the chance of a weak point giving way and water seeping in. But Clout had pointed out that in that confined space between the barrelheads the heat would not be able to escape; it would grow hotter and hotter in there and the fuse would burn faster—the fire might even jump from one part of the coil to another. The rate of burning, in other words, was unpredictable.

The diver who had just appeared gave a sharp cry, in time to prevent the next one—Looney—from going down. An eager question and answer, and Looney turned to Hornblower with a waving of hands.

"Get that man on board," ordered Hornblower. "Up anchor!"

A few strokes of the oars got the launch under way; the Ceylonese in the bows were chattering like sparrows at dawn.

"Back to the ship," ordered Hornblower.

He would go straight on board without looking back once; he would not compromise his dignity by awaiting an explosion which might never come. The tiller was put over and the launch began her steady course towards *Atropos*.

And then it happened, while Hornblower's back was turned to it. A sullen, muffled roar, not very loud, as if a gun had been fired in a distant cave. Hornblower swung round in his seat just in time to see a bulging wave overtake them, heaving up the stern of the launch. The stern sank and bow rose, the launch pitching violently, like a child's toy boat in a tub. The water that surged round them was discoloured and dark. It was only for a few seconds that the violent commotion lasted, and then it passed on, leaving the launch rocking jerkily.

"She's gone up, sir," said Clout, quite unnecessarily.

The hands were chattering as much as the Ceylonese.

"Silence in the boat!" said Hornblower.

He was angry with himself because the unexpected sound had caused him to leap in his seat. He glowered at the men, and they fell into a hushed silence.

"Starboard your helm," growled Hornblower. "Give way!"

The launch swung round and retraced its course towards the scene of the explosion, marked by a dirty patch of water. Half a dozen big bubbles rose to the surface and burst as he watched. Then something else came up, and something else, dead fish floating up to the surface, their white bellies gleaming under the sky. The launch passed one which was not quite dead; it was making feeble efforts, just perceptible, to right itself and descend again.

"Silence!" said Hornblower again—the irrepressible chatter had broken out again. "Easy!"

In silence the launch floated over the scene of the explosion. Dead fish, a stain, and nothing else. Nothing else at all. Hornblower felt a sick feeling of disappointment; there should be fragments from the wreck covering the surface, shattered bits of timber to show that the powder charge had done its work. The fact that there was none was proof that no gap had been blown in the wreck. His mind was racing into the future. Another charge with another flying fuse would have to be used, he supposed, and the most brutal threats would have to be employed towards the divers to make them put it into position. They had escaped the last explosion by not more than thirty seconds, he supposed, and they would be chary of running the risk again.

There was a bit of timber! No, it was the plank which had been used as a marker buoy.

"Haul in on that line," said Hornblower to the man pulling stroke oar. There was only ten feet of line attached to the plank—the line had been broken at that point; so the explosion had effected something, at least. It was ironical that that was all—just a marker buoy torn loose.

"Put on another grapnel and line," ordered Hornblower. They must still be close enough to the spot for the marker to be better than nothing.

Hornblower caught Looney's eye; he seemed willing enough to all appearance. It would save time if an examination of the scant results were made now.

"Looney," said Hornblower, and pointed overside. He had only to point a second time for Looney to nod his agreement and pull off his clothes again. As far as Hornblower could remember, Looney had not yet made his daily quota of five dives. Looney inflated his chest and slipped in, and the launch lay drifting. The little waves that slapped against her sides had a different quality from usual; they had not even the small amount of system arising from the wind that agitated the surface—they seemed to come from all points at once. Hornblower realised that they were the last dying remnants of the turbulence which the explosion had set up.

Up came Looney, his slender bundle of black hair bobbing beside his face. His white teeth showed in what might almost be thought to be a smile, except that of course he was gasping for breath. He struck out towards the launch, saying something to his colleagues as he did so which set them off twittering volubly. Apparently the explosion which had torn the marker buoy loose had not driven it any distance from its position. They hauled Looney on board into the bows. The chattering went on; now Looney was making his way aft over the thwarts and between the men. He was rubbing something in a portion of his clothing as he came—something which he put into Hornblower's hand with a broad grin. Something disc-shaped and small, tarnished, encrusted, and yet—and yet—

"God bless my soul!" said Hornblower.

It was an English shilling; Hornblower could only stare at it, and turn it over in his fingers. Every eye in the boat was directed at it; the men were quick enough to guess even if they could not see it clearly. Someone started a cheer, and the others took it up. Hornblower looked down the boat at the grinning faces. Even Clout was waving his hat and yelling.

"Silence!" shouted Hornblower. "Mr. Clout, you ought to be ashamed of yourself."

But the noise did not stop instantly as before; the men were too excited. But it died away at length, and the men waited. Hornblower had to think now about the next move, completely at a loss—this development had taken him by surprise and he had no idea for the moment what to do next. It would have to be anticlimax, he decided at last. For the recovery of the treasure fresh equipment would be necessary; that was certain. The divers had made nearly as many dives that day as they could. Moreover, McCullum must be informed of the results of the explosion and his decision heard regarding further steps. Hornblower even realised that there was no certainty that subsequent operations would be easy. One shilling did not make a quarter of a million sterling. There might be much further work necessary.

"Oars!" he snapped at the waiting men. The oar-looms clattered into the rowlocks and the men bent forward ready to pull. "Give way!"

The oarblades bit into the water and the launch slowly gathered way.

"Head for the ship!" he growled at the coxswain.

He sat glowering in the sternsheets. Anyone seeing his face might well have thought that the launch was returning after a complete failure, but it was merely that he was annoyed with himself at not being quick-witted enough to have had the appropriate orders ready at once when that astonishing shilling was put into his hand. The whole boat's crew had seen him at a loss. His precious dignity was hurt. When he got on board he was inclined to sulk in his cabin, but commonsense made him go forward soon to discuss the situation with McCullum.

"There's a cascade of silver," said McCullum, who had been listening to the reports of the divers. "The bags have rotted, and when the treasure room was blown open the silver poured out. I think that's clear enough."

"And the gold?" asked Hornblower.

"Looney can't tell me as yet," said McCullum. "If I had been in the launch I daresay I should have acquired more information."

Hornblower bit back an angry retort. Nothing would please McCullum better than a quarrel, and he had no wish to indulge him.

"At least the explosion served its purpose," he said pacifically.

"Like enough."

"Then why," asked Hornblower—the question had been awaiting the asking for a long time—"if the wreck was blown open why didn't wreckage come to the surface?"

"You don't know?" asked McCullum in reply, clearly gratified at possessing superior knowledge.

"No."

"That's one of the elementary facts of science. Timber submerged at great depths soon becomes waterlogged."

"Indeed?"

"Wood only floats—as I presume you know—by virtue of the air contained in the cavities in its substance. Under pressure that air is squeezed out, and, deprived of this upthrust, the residual material has no tendency to rise."

"I see," said Hornblower. "Thank you, Mr. McCullum."

"I am accustomed by now," said McCullum, "to supplementing the education of King's officers."

"Then I trust," said Hornblower still keeping his temper, "you will continue with mine. What is the next step to take?"

McCullum pursed his lips.

"If that damned Dutch doctor," he said, "would only have the sense to allow me out of this bed I could attend to it all myself."

"He'll have the stitches out of you soon," said Hornblower. "Meanwhile time is of importance."

It was infuriating that a captain in his own ship should have to endure this sort of insolence. Hornblower thought of the official complaints he could make. He could quarrel with McCullum, abandon the whole attempt, and in his report to Collingwood he would declaim that "owing to the complete lack of co-operation on the part of Mr. William McCullum, of the Honourable East India Company's Service" the expedition had ended in failure. No doubt McCullum would then be rapped on the knuckles officially. But it was better to achieve success, even without receiving any sympathy for the trials he was enduring, than to return with the best of excuses empty-handed. It was just as meritorious to pocket his pride and to coax McCullum into giving clear instructions as it was to head a boarding party onto an enemy's deck. Just as meritorious—although less likely to achieve a paragraph in the *Gazette.* He forced himself to ask the right questions and to listen to McCullum's grudging explanations of what should next be done.

And it was pleasant, later, when eating his dinner, to be able to congratulate himself on his duty done, orders given, all prepared. Those words of McCullum's—"a cascade of silver"—ran in his mind as he sat and ate. It called for little imagination to conjure up a mental picture of the wreck down there in the translucent water, with her strongroom torn open and the silver in a frozen stream pouring out of it. Gray could have written a poem about it; and somewhere in that strongroom there was the gold. Life was good, and he was a fortunate man. He slowly consumed his last mouthful of roast lamb, and addressed himself to his lettuce salad, tender young plants, sweet and delicious, the first fruits of the Turkish spring.

SIXTEEN

The Turkish spring was not going to give way to summer without a last struggle, without calling the vanished winter back to her aid. The wind blew wildly and cold from the northwestward; the skies were grey, and the rain lashed down torrentially. It drummed upon the deck, streaming out through the scuppers; it poured in unexpected streams down from points in the rigging; even though it grudgingly gave to the crew the chance to wash their clothes in fresh water it denied them the opportunity of drying them again. *Atropos* swung fitfully to her anchor as the gusts blowing down from the surrounding mountains backed and veered, whipping the surface of the bay into turbulent whitecaps. Wind and rain seemed peculiarly searching. Everyone seemed to be colder and wetter than if the ship were battling a storm in mid-Atlantic, with the deck leaking as she worked in a seaway and the waves crashing down upon it; sulkiness and bad temper made their appearance among the ship's company along with the cold and wet—lack of exercise and lack of occupation combined with the constant drumming of the rain to bring that about.

Walking upon the quarterdeck with the raindrops rattling upon his oilskin seemed to Hornblower to be a cheerless business, the more so because until this gale dropped there would be no chance of continuing the salvage operations. Boxes of gold lay over there under that wind-whipped surface; he hated having to wait through these empty hours before knowing if they could be recovered. He hated the thought of having to rouse himself from his inertia and exert himself to re-establish the good spirits of the ship's company, but he knew he must.

"Messenger!" he said, "my compliments to Mr. Smiley and Mr. Horrocks, and I'll see them at once in my cabin."

Half an hour later both watches were assembled on deck by divisions ("Half an hour I'll give you to get it all arranged," Hornblower had said), wearing only their duck trousers in the rain, the cold drops beating on their bare chests and feet. There was plenty of growling at the discomfort, but there was amusement among the topmen because every idler in the ship was there—"I'll have 'em all," Hornblower had said, "waisters and holders, gunner's crew and sail-maker's crew." And there was the excitement always attendant upon a race; and there was the compensation of seeing the three senior watch-keeping officers, Jones and Still and Turner, climbing the ratlines to take their places in the crosstrees to see that the racing was fair. Hornblower stood forward by the knight-heads with his speaking trumpet so that the wind would carry his voice plainly along the deck.

"One to get steady!" he shouted, "two to be ready! Three—and you're off!"

It was a relay race, up the rigging of each mast in turn and down again, port watch against starboard; it was the inclusion of the men who rarely if ever went aloft that gave spice to the proceedings. Soon divisions down on deck were dancing with excitement as they watched the slow ascent and descent of some lumbering gunner's mate or ship's corporal; until he completed the journey they were not free to dash to the next mast and start again.

"Come on, Fatty!"

The Pegasus-winged topmen, to whom the ascent was a trifle, leaped up and down on deck with never a thought for the streaming rain as some rival division, set free by the eventual descent of its last man, rushed joyfully along the deck to the next mast while they were forced to stand and witness the cautious movements of the slowest of their own side.

Up went the men and down, round and across. The Prince of Seitz-Bunau came shrieking round the deck, wild with excitement; Horrocks and Smiley, captains of the two sides, were croaking like crows, their voices failing them with the continual shouting as they organised and encouraged. The cook's mate, who was the last man of the port watch, was already close to the mainmast head when Horrocks, who had reserved himself to be the last of the starboard watch, began the ascent on the other side. Everyone in the ship seemed to be shouting and gesticulating. Up ran Horrocks, the shrouds vibrating with the apelike speed of his passage. The cook's mate reached the crosstrees and started down again.

"Come on, Fatty!"

The cook's mate did not even look to see where to put his feet, and he was coming down two ratlines at a time. Horrocks reached the crosstrees and leaped for the backstay. Down he came, sliding at a speed that must burn his hands. Cook's mate and midshipman reached the deck together, but Horrocks had farther to run to reach his place with his division than did the cook's mate. There was a final yell as both of them staggered gasping to their places, but the cook's mate was first by a full yard, and every eye was turned towards Hornblower.

"Port watch wins!" he announced. "Starboard watch provides the entertainment tomorrow night!"

The port watch cheered again, but the starboard watch—Hornblower was observing them closely—was not humiliated. He could guess that there were plenty of men among them who were not too displeased at the thought of tomorrow exhibiting their talents to an audience and who were already planning their turns. He put his speaking trumpet to his lips again.

"Attention! Mr. Horrocks! Mr. Smiley! Dismiss your teams."

Aft beside the wardroom door as Hornblower was returning to his cabin, there was an unusual figure, walking with slow steps under the supervision of the doctor.

"This is a pleasure, Mr. McCullum," said Hornblower. "It's good to see you out of your bed."

"The incision has entirely healed, sir," said Eisenbeiss, proudly. "Not only are the sutures removed, but I have judged it safe to remove the bristle from the wound, as the drainage was complete."

"Excellent!" said Hornblower. "Then that arm will come out of its sling soon?"

"Within a few days. The broken ribs seem to have knitted well."

"Still a bit stiff round there," said McCullum, feeling his right armpit with his left hand. He was displaying none of his usual ill temper; but a convalescent, making his first attempt to walk, and with his wound under discussion, could feel so much in the centre of the picture as to be well disposed towards humanity.

"Well it might be," said Hornblower. "A pistol bullet at twelve paces is not a welcome visitor. We thought we had lost you. At Malta they thought that bullet was in your lungs."

"It would have been easier," said Eisenbeiss, "if he had not been so muscular. The bullet could not be felt in that mass of muscle."

McCullum fished from his left trouser pocket a small object which he handed to Hornblower.

"D'you see that?" asked McCullum. It was the bullet which Eisenbeiss had extracted, flattened and irregular. Hornblower had seen it before, but this was not the moment to say so. He marvelled over it in suitable terms, much to McCullum's gratification.

"I think," said Hornblower, "that this occasion should be observed with a fitting ceremony. I shall invite the wardroom to dine with me, and I can ask you two gentlemen first of all."

"Honoured, I'm sure," said McCullum, and Eisenbeiss bowed.

"Let us say tomorrow, then. We can dine in comfort before the entertainment which the starboard watch is providing."

He retired to his cabin well pleased with himself. He had exercised his crew; he had given them something to think about; he had found a suitable occasion to entertain his officers socially; his salvage expert had returned from the jaws of death and in a better temper than usual—all this, and the *Speedwell's* treasure lay on the Tom Tiddler's Ground of the sandy bottom of the bay, with gold and silver only waiting to be picked up. His good opinion of himself even enabled him to endure the tedium of the concert given by the starboard watch next night. There were the sentimental songs which a handsome young fore topman sang; Hornblower found their glutinous sentimentality as wearisome to his soul as the music was to his tone-deaf ear. "The Flowers on Mother's Grave" and "The Empty Cradle"—the young seaman squeezed out every lugubrious drop from their funereal substance, and his audience, with the exception of Hornblower, revelled in it. And an elderly bosun's mate sang sea songs in a thunderous bass while Hornblower marvelled that a seagoing audience could tolerate the misuse of nautical terms in those songs; if his "good sail" were to "rustle" with a following wind his officer of the watch would hear from him in good round terms, and there was of course the usual landsman's confusion between the sheet and the sail, and Dibdin had never bothered to find out that a "sheer hulk" was still leading a useful existence thanks to its sheers—the term did not imply a complete hulk or anything like it. And of course the song laid stress on the statement that Tom Bowling was dead, like the fore topman's mythical mother and baby. He had "gone aloft" and everybody in the ship's company, apparently, felt the better for it.

The hornpipes were more agreeable; Hornblower could admire the lightness and grace of the dancers and could manage to ignore the squeaky sweetness of the flute that accompanied them, played by the same cook's mate whose final effort had won the race for the port watch—his services as accompanist were so necessary, apparently, that they were called for even though the port watch were officially the guests at the concert. To Hornblower the most amusing part of the evening's entertainment, in fact, was the difference in attitude between the two watches, the starboard watch as anxious hosts and the port watch as critical guests. He could congratulate himself again at the end of the evening on a successful piece of work. He had a willing and orderly crew, and a satisfied complement of officers.

And next morning came the real triumph, no less satisfactory in that Hornblower stayed on board the ship and allowed McCullum, his arm still in a sling, to go out with launch and longboat and all the new apparatus that had been constructed for the salvage operations. Hornblower stood at the side of the ship, warmed by the newly returned sunshine, as the boats returned. McCullum pointed with his left hand to a vast heap piled between the centre thwarts of the launch, and turned and pointed to another in the longboat. Silver! The divers must have worked fast down in the depths, shovelling the coins with their hands into the lowered buckets.

The boats came alongside, and a working party prepared to hoist the mass of silver on board. A sudden sharp order by McCullum halted the three Ceylonese divers as they were about to make their way forward to their own particular lair. They looked at him a little sheepishly as he gave a further order in their strange tongue, and he repeated it. Then slowly they began to take off their clothes; Hornblower had seen them stripping themselves so often before in the days—they seemed weeks ago—when the salvage operations had begun. The voluminous cotton garments came off one by one.

"I'll lay a bet," said McCullum, "they've got fifty pounds between them."

One of the garments gave out a mysterious chink as it was laid on the deck, despite the care of the owner.

"Master at arms!" said Hornblower. "Search those clothes!"

With a grinning crew looking on, the seams and folds of the clothing were emptied of coins, dozens of them.

"They never make a dive," said McCullum, "without trying this on."

Hornblower could only wonder how a naked man climbing from the sea into a boat could possibly manage to convey silver coins into his clothing unobserved, but anything was possible to human ingenuity.

"That would have made them rich for life if they could have taken it back to Jaffna," said McCullum. Reverting to the foreign speech he dismissed the divers, who picked up their clothes again and vanished, while McCullum turned back to Hornblower. "It might be quicker to weigh this than to count it. If we get it all up there'll be four tons altogether."

Silver by the ton! The sail-maker stitched sacks out of new canvas to hold it, and, just as in the lost *Speedwell,* the lower lazarette was cleared to store it. And Hornblower found there was a profound truth in the story of Midas, who received the gift of the Golden Touch not so very far from where *Atropos* swung at anchor. Just as Midas lost his happiness at a moment when the world must have deemed him the happiest man on earth, so Hornblower lost his happiness at this moment of success. For as the silver was piled in the lazarette so he came to worry about the coins. He was in no doubt about the ingenuity and persistence and skill of the seamen under his orders; nor was he in doubt about the criminal pasts of many of them, the sweepings of Newgate Gaol. Tales innumerable were told about the remarkable ways in which seamen managed to steal liquor, but the man who stole liquor inevitably revealed himself sooner or later. This was money, solid coins, and there was only a frail wooden bulkhead to keep out thieves. So, as in the *Speedwell,* the bulkheads and decks were reinforced by stout timbers nailed across them; the careful and well-planned arrangement of the stores in the hold had to be altered so that the biggest beef casks, the ones that could only be moved by block and tackle, were ranged outside the bulkheads to hinder thieves from breaking through. And even then Hornblower spent wakeful nights visualising the situation of the lower lazarette and wondering first how he would set about breaking into it and second how he would defeat such an attempt. These feelings intensified each day as the piles of sacks of silver grew larger; and they grew ten times more intense on the triumphant day when McCullum's divers reached the gold.

McCullum knew his work, no doubt about that. One day he told Hornblower of the discovery of one of the chests of gold; the next morning Hornblower watched launch and longboat start off with strongbacks erected in their sterns and blocks and tackles rigged on them, miles of line coiled in readiness, timbers, buckets, everything that human ingenuity could think of for use in this new task. Hornblower watched through his glass as the boats lay together over the wreck. He saw the divers go down and come up again, time after time. He saw the weighted lines lowered from the tackles; more than once he saw the hands begin to haul in on the falls and then desist while another diver went down, presumably to clear the line. Then at the end he saw the hands haul in again, and stay at work, hauling in, coiling down, until at last between the two boats something broke water and a yell of exultation came echoing over to the ship.

It was something quite large which was gingerly swung into the stern of the launch—Hornblower could see the stern of the launch sink and the bows rise as the weight was transferred. His calculations had already told him that a cubic foot of gold weighed half a ton—and gold was at a premium, five guineas in paper or more to the ounce. That was a king's ransom; Hornblower looked at it as the launch came pulling back alongside, a strange object lying in the bottom of the boat, half obscured by weed.

"Those must be wrought-iron bars on it," said McCullum, standing beside him while Jones fussily supervised the transfer to the ship, "and best Sussex iron at that. Steel would have rusted to nothing a year ago, but some of those bars are still whole. The weeds growing from the oak must have been a yard long—my boys had to trim 'em off before they got the tackles round."

"Easy there! Easy!" shouted Jones.

"Vast heaving at the yard-arm!" shouted the bosun. "Now, you at the stay tackle, walk away with it!"

The chest dangled over the deck, balancing on its supporting lines.

"Easy! Lower away, yard-arm! Easy! Lower away, stay tackle! Handsomely!"

The chest sank to the deck; there were little dribbles of water still flowing from inside it. The gold that lay concealed inside it would have built, armed, and equipped the whole *Atropos*, have filled her holds with stores for a year, have provided a month's advance pay for the crew, and still have left a handsome balance.

"Well, that's one of them," said McCullum. "I have a feeling that it won't be so easy to get up the other two. This is the easiest job I've ever done, so far. We've been lucky—inexperienced as you are, you will never know how lucky."

But Hornblower knew how lucky he was. Lucky that McCullum had survived a pistol shot in the ribs; lucky that the Ceylonese divers had survived the journey all round Africa from India to Asia Minor; lucky—incredibly lucky—that the Turks had been so complacent, allowing him to carry out the salvage operation in the bay without guessing what he was doing and without interfering. It was consideration of this good fortune that reconciled him at last to the worry regarding the guarding of the treasure in the lower lazarette. He was the most fortunate man on earth; fortunate (he told himself) and yet at the same time he owed some of his success to his own merits. He had been clever in his handling of the Mudir. It had been a cunning move to accept a bribe to stay here anchored in the bay, to appear reluctant to do the very thing he wanted most to do. Collingwood would approve, no doubt. He had recovered the silver; he had recovered one-third of the gold already. He would receive a pat on the back from authority even if McCullum should find it impossible to recover the rest.

SEVENTEEN

THESE MEDITERRANEAN MORNINGS were beautiful. It was a pleasure to come on deck as the dawn brightened into daylight; usually the night wind had died down, leaving the bay glassy smooth, reflecting, as the light increased, the intense blue of the sky as the sun climbed up over the mountains of Turkey. There was a refreshing chill in the air—not enough to necessitate wearing a pea-jacket—so that the increasing warmth of the sun brought a sensuous pleasure with it. During a walk on deck with his mind leisurely working out the plans for the day Hornblower soaked in the beauty and freshness; and right at the back of his mind, flavouring his pleasure as a sauce might give the finishing touch to some perfect dish, was the knowledge that when he went below he could sit down to a plate of fried eggs and a pot of coffee. Beauty all round him, a growing appetite, and the immediate prospect of satisfying it—at least they brought the realisation that he was a fortunate man.

Today he was not quite as fortunate as usual, because instead of indulging in solitary thought he had to give some attention to McCullum and his problems.

"We'll have one more try along the present lines," said McCullum. "I'll send the boys down again today, and hear what they have to say. But I'm afraid that chest is out of reach at present. I came to suspect that yesterday."

Two days ago the second of the three chests of gold had been recovered, but only after an explosive charge had blown a wide entrance into the wreck.

"Yes," said Hornblower, "that was the substance of your report."

"It's not easy to make 'em go down right in among the wreckage."

"I shouldn't think it was," said Hornblower.

In the dimly lit depths, under the intolerable weight of a hundred feet of water, to hold one's breath, suffocating, and to make one's way in among the tangled timbers, must be a frightful thing to do.

"The deck sloped away from the gap in the side, and I fancy the last explosion sent that third chest through and down. The whole wreck's on top of it now," said McCullum.

"Then what do you propose to do?"

"It'll be a couple of weeks' work, I expect. I'll use half a dozen charges —with flying-fuses, of course—and blow the whole wreck to pieces. But I must inform you officially that the result may still be unsatisfactory."

"You mean you may not recover the gold even then?"

"I may not."

Two-thirds of the gold and nearly all the silver lay already in the lower lazarette of the *Atropos*—a good second best, but as unsatisfactory as any other second best.

"I'm sure you'll do the best you can, Mr. McCullum," said Hornblower.

Already the morning breeze was blowing. The first gentle breaths had swung *Atropos* round from where she lay completely inert upon the water. Now she rode to her anchor again, with a fair breeze coursing along her deck. Hornblower felt it about his ears.

And for the last few seconds something had been troubling him. Subconsciously he had become aware of something, while he had addressed that final sentence to McCullum, like a gnat seen out of the corner of his eye. He looked over at the pine-clad slopes of Ada peninsula, at the square outline of the fort on the summit. The beauty of the morning seemed suddenly to turn harsh and grey; the feeling of intense well-being was suddenly replaced by sharp apprehension.

"Give me that glass!" he snapped at the master's mate of the watch.

There was really no need for the glass; Hornblower's powers of deduction had already reinforced his naked eye, and the telescope merely revealed what he was sure he would see. There was a flag waving over the fort on the peninsula—the red flag of Turkey, where no flag had flown yesterday, nor ever since his arrival in the Bay of Marmorice. There could be only one conclusion. There was a garrison in that fort now; troops must have come back to Marmorice—they must have manned the guns of the fort. He was a fool, a stupid insensitive idiot, blinded by his own complacency. Now that the revelation had come to him his mind worked feverishly. He had been utterly deceived; the Mudir with his grey beard and his innocent anxiety had played upon him the very trick he thought he was playing himself—had lulled him into self-confidence, gaining time for troops to be gathered while he thought he was gaining time to carry out the salvage operation. With bitter self-contempt it dawned upon him that all the work on the wreck must have been carefully noted from the shore. Even the Turks had telescopes—they must have seen all that was done. They must know of the treasure being recovered, and now they had manned the guns guarding the exit, shutting him in.

From where he stood aft he could not see Passage Island—Red Cliff Point lay in line with it. Without a word to the astonished master's mate he ran forward and threw himself into the foremast shrouds. He ran up them, gasping for breath, as fast as any of the competitors in that foolish relay race; back downward, he went up the futtock shrouds, and then up the fore topmast shrouds to the fore topmast head. There was a flag flying above the fort on Passage Island too; the glass revealed a couple of boats drawn up on the beach in the little cove there, showing how during the night, or at first dawn, the garrison had been conveyed there. The guns on Passage Island could cross their fire with those on Ada and sweep the entrance, and could sweep also the tortuous passage between the island and Kaia Rock. The cork was in the bottle. He and the *Atropos* were trapped.

Not by guns alone. The easterly sun, shining behind him, was reflected back from far off in the Rhodes Channel by three geometrical shapes close together on the horizon, two rectangles and a triangle—the sails of a big ship, a Turkish ship, obviously. Equally obvious was the fact that it could not be pure coincidence that the hoisting of the flags on the forts occurred at the same moment that those sails appeared. The flags had been hoisted as soon as the lofty fort on Ada had perceived the sails; the despised Turk was perfectly capable of executing a well-planned coup. In an hour—in less—that ship would be stemming the entrance to the bay. With the wind blowing straight in he could not hope to escape, even discounting the fact that if he tried to beat out of the entrance the guns on Ada would dismast him. Hornblower was sunk in despair as he clung to his lofty perch, glass in hand; to the despair of a man faced by overwhelming odds was added the frightful self-contempt of a man who found himself outtricked, outdeceived. The memory of his recent self-congratulation was like the echoing laughter of a crowd of scornful spectators, drowning his thoughts and paralysing his mental processes.

It was a bad moment, up there at the fore topmast head, perhaps the worst moment Hornblower had ever known. Self-control came back slowly, even though hope remained quite absent. Looking again through his glass at the approaching sails Hornblower found that the telescope was trembling with the shaking of his hands, the eyepiece blinding him by vibrating against his eyelashes. He could admit to himself that he was a fool—bitter though such an admission might be—but he could not admit to himself that he was a coward, at least that kind of coward. And yet was anything worth the effort? Did it matter if a grain of dust in a whirlwind retained its dignity? The criminal in the cart on the way to Tyburn strove to retain his self-control, strove not to give way to his pitiful human fears and weaknesses, tried to "die game" for the sake of his own self-respect under the gaze of the heartless crowd, and yet did it profit him when in five minutes he would be dead? There was a horrible moment when Hornblower thought how easy something else would be. He had only to let go his hold, to fall, down, down, to a final crash upon the deck and the end of all this, no need for further effort, the end, oblivion; that would be far easier than to face, trying to appear not to notice, the pity or contempt of his fellow men. He was being tempted to cast himself down, as Christ had been by Satan.

Then he told himself again that he was not that kind of coward. He was calm now; the sweat that had streamed down him lay cold upon his skin. He shut the telescope with a click that sounded clear amid the noise of the wind about his ears. He had no idea what he was going to do, but it was a healing mechanical exercise to set himself to descend the rigging, to lodge first one foot and then the other upon the ratlines, to make sure that despite the weakness he felt he accomplished the descent in safety. And, having set foot on deck, it was further good exercise to try to appear quite unruffled and unperturbed, the grain of dust unchanging in the whirlwind, even though he had a feeling that his cheeks were pale under their sunburn. Habit was a useful thing too; to put back his head and bellow an order could set his mechanism working again, as the stopped clock would start to tick again and would go on ticking after a single shake.

"Mr. McCullum! Belay those arrangements, if you please. Officer of the watch! Pipe all hands. Get the launch hoisted in. Leave the longboat for the present."

A surprised Jones came hurrying on deck at the call of all hands.

"Mr. Jones! Get a hawser passed out through a stern port. I want a spring on the cable."

"A spring, sir? Aye aye, sir."

It was a minute compensation for his own misery to see how a glance called forth the last three words after the astonished utterance of the first three. Men who went to sea, and ten times more so men who went to sea in a fighting ship, must be ready for the execution of the most unexpected orders, at any moment, even the shattering of the routine of a peaceful morning by an order to put a spring on the cable—a hawser passed out through a stern port and made fast to the anchor cable, so that by hauling in on the spring with the capstan the ship could be swung even though she was stationary, and her guns trained to sweep a different arc at will. It happened to be very nearly the only exercise in which Hornblower had not drilled his ship's company so far.

"You're too slow, Mr. Jones! Master-at-arms, take the names of those three men there!"

Midshipman Smiley went off with the hawser end in the longboat; Jones, running forward, bellowed himself hoarse through his speaking trumpet with instructions to Smiley, to the man beside him at the capstan, to the man aft with the hawser. Cable was taken in; cable was paid out.

"Spring's ready, sir."

"Very well, Mr. Jones. Hoist in the longboat and clear for action."

"Er—aye aye, sir. Pipe 'hands to quarters.' Clear for action. Drummer! Beat to quarters."

There was no marine detachment in a little ship like *Atropos*. The ship's boy who had been appointed drummer set his sticks rolling on his drumhead. That warlike sound—there was nothing quite as martial as the rolling of a drum—would drift over the water and would bear a message of defiance to the shore. The longboat came swaying down on the chocks; excited men, with the drum echoing in their ears, braced the lines about her and secured her; already the pump crew were directing a stream of water into her to fill her up—a necessary precaution against her catching fire while providing a convenient reservoir of water to fight other fires. The hands at the tackles broke off and went racing away to their other duties.

"Guns loaded and run out, if you please, Mr. Jones!"

"Aye aye, sir."

Mr. Jones was startled again. In a mere exercise of clearing for action it was usual merely to simulate the loading of the guns; otherwise when the exercise ended there was the difficulty and waste of drawing wads and charges. At the cry the powder boys went scurrying to bring up from below the cartridges that Mr. Clout was laying out in the magazine. Some gun captain gave a yell as he flung his weight on the tackle to run out his gun.

"Silence!"

The men were well enough behaved; despite the excitement of the moment they had worked in silence save for that one yell. Much drill and relentless discipline showed their effects.

"Cleared for action, sir!" reported Jones.

"Rig the boarding nettings, if you please."

That was a harassing, irritating exercise. The nettings had to be roused out, laid in position along the ship's sides, and their lower edges made fast in the chains all round. Then lines from the yard-arms and bowsprit end had to be rove through the upper edges. Then with steady hauling on the falls of the tackles the nettings rose into position, sloping up and out from the ship's sides from bow to stern, making it impossible for boarders to come in over the ship's side.

"Belay!" ordered Jones as the tricing lines came taut.

"Too taut, Mr. Jones! I told you that before. Slack away on those falls!"

Taut boarding nettings, triced up trimly as far as they would go, might look seamanlike, but were not as effective when their function as obstacles was considered. A loose, sagging netting was far more difficult to climb or to cut. Hornblower watched the netting sag down again into lubberly festoons.

"Belay!"

That was better. These nettings were not intended to pass an admiral's inspection, but to keep out boarders.

"Boarding nettings rigged, sir," reported Jones, after a moment's interval, to call his captain's attention to the fact that the ship's company was awaiting further orders; Hornblower had given the last one himself.

"Thank you, Mr. Jones."

Hornblower spoke a trifle absently; his gaze was not towards Jones, but was directed far away. Automatically Jones followed his glance.

"Good God!" said Jones.

A big ship was rounding Red Cliff Point, entering into the bay. Everyone else saw her at the same moment, and a babble of exclamation arose.

"Silence, there!"

A big ship, gaudily painted in red and yellow, coming in under topsails, a broad pendant at her mainmast head and the flag of the Prophet at her peak. She was a great clumsy craft, old-fashioned in the extreme, carrying two tiers of guns so that her sides were unnaturally high for her length; and her beam was unnaturally wide, and her bowsprit steeved higher than current fashions in European navies dictated. But the feature which first caught the eye was the lateen rig on the mizzen-mast; it was more than thirty years since the last lateen mizzen in the Royal Navy had been replaced by the square mizzen topsail. When

Hornblower had first seen her through his glass the triangular peak of her mizzen beside her two square topsails had revealed her nationality unmistakably to him. She looked like something in an old print; without her flag she could have taken her place in the fighting line in Blake's Navy or Van Tromp's without exciting comment. She must be almost the last survivor of the lesser clumsy ships of the line that had now been replaced by the stately 74; small, clumsy, but all the same with a weight of metal that could lay the tiny *Atropos* into a splintered wreck at one broadside.

"That's a broad pendant, Mr. Jones," said Hornblower. "Salute her."

He spoke out of the side of his mouth, for he had his glass trained on her. Her gunports were closed; on her lofty forecastle he could see men scurrying like ants making ready to anchor. She was crowded with men; as she took in sail it was strange to see men balanced across the sloping mizzen yard—Hornblower had never expected to see a sight like that in his life, especially as the men wore long loose shirts like gowns, which flapped round them as they hung over the yard.

The nine-pounder forward gave its sharp bang—some powder boy must have run fast below to bring up the one-pound saluting charges —and a puff of smoke, followed by a report, showed that the Turkish ship was replying. She had goose-winged her main topsail—another outlandish sight in these circumstances—and was slowly coming into the bay towards them.

"Mr. Turner! Come here please, to interpret. Mr. Jones, send some hands to the capstan, if you please. Take in on the spring if necessary so that the guns bear."

The Turkish ship glided on.

"Hail her," said Hornblower to Turner.

A shout came back from her.

"She's the *Mejidieh,* sir," reported Turner. "I've seen her before."

"Tell her to keep her distance."

Turner hailed through his speaking trumpet, but the *Mejidieh* still came on.

"Tell her to keep off. Mr. Jones! Take in on the spring. Stand by at the guns, there!"

Closer and closer came the *Mejidieh,* and as she did so the *Atropos* swung round, keeping her guns pointed at her. Hornblower picked up the speaking trumpet.

"Keep off, or I'll fire into you!"

She altered course almost imperceptibly and glided by, close enough for Hornblower to see the faces that lined the side, faces with moustaches and faces with beards; mahogany-coloured faces, almost chocolate-coloured faces. Hornblower watched her go by. She rounded-to, with the goose-winged main topsail close-hauled, held her new course for a few seconds, and then took in her sail, came to the wind, and anchored, a quarter of a mile away. The excitement of action ebbed away in Hornblower, and the old depression returned. A buzz of talk went up from the men clustered at the guns—it was quite irrepressible by now, with this remarkable new arrival.

"The lateener's heading this way, sir," reported Horrocks.

From the promptitude with which she appeared she must have been awaiting the *Mejidieh's* arrival. Hornblower saw her pass close under the *Mejidieh's* stern; he could almost hear the words that she exchanged with the ship, and then she came briskly up close alongside the *Atropos*. There in the stern was the grey-bearded Mudir, hailing them.

"He wants to come on board, sir," reported Turner.

"Let him come," said Hornblower. "Unlace that netting just enough for him to get through."

Down in the cabin the Mudir looked just the same as before. His lean face was as impassive as ever; at least he showed no signs of triumph. He could play a winning game like a gentleman; Hornblower, without a single trump card in his hand, was determined to show that he could play a losing game like a gentleman too.

"Explain to him," he said to Turner, "that I regret there is no coffee to offer him. No fires when the ship's cleared for action."

The Mudir was gracious about the absence of coffee, as he indicated by a gesture. There was a polite interchange of compliments, which Turner hardly troubled to translate, before he approached the business in hand.

"He says the Vali is in Marmorice with his army," reported Turner. "He says the forts at the mouth are manned and the guns loaded."

"Tell him I know that."

"He says that ship's the *Mejidieh*, sir, with fifty six guns and a thousand men."

"Tell him I know that too."

The Mudir stroked his beard before taking the next step.

"He says the Vali was very angry when he heard we'd been taking treasure from the bottom of the bay."

"Tell him it is British treasure."

"He says it was lying in the Sultan's waters, and all wrecks belong to the Sultan."

In England all wrecks belonged to the King.

"Tell him the Sultan and King George are friends."

The Mudir's reply to that was lengthy.

"No good, sir," said Turner. "He says Turkey's at peace with France now and so is neutral. He said—he said that we have no more rights here than if we were Neapolitans, sir."

There could not be any greater expression of contempt anywhere in the Levant.

"Ask him if he has ever seen a Neapolitan with guns run out and matches burning."

It was a losing game that Hornblower was playing, but he was not going to throw in his cards and yield all the tricks without a struggle, even though he could see no possibility of winning even one. The Mudir stroked his beard again; with his expressionless eyes he looked straight at Hornblower, and straight through him, as he spoke.

"He must have been watching everything through a telescope from shore, sir," commented Turner, "or it may have been those fishing boats. At any rate, he knows about the gold and the silver and it's my belief, sir, that they've known there was treasure in the wreck for years. That secret wasn't as well kept as they thought it was in London."

"I can draw my own conclusions, Mr. Turner, thank you."

Whatever the Mudir knew or guessed, Hornblower was not going to admit anything.

"Tell him we have been delighted with the pleasure of his company."

The Mudir, when that was translated to him, allowed a flicker of a change of expression to pass over his face. But when he spoke it was with the same flatness of tone.

"He says that if we hand over all we have recovered so far the Vali will allow us to remain here and keep whatever else we find," reported Turner.

Turner displayed some small concern as he translated, but yet in his old man's face the most noticeable expression was one of curiosity; he bore no responsibility, and he could allow himself the luxury—the pleasure—of wondering how his captain was going to receive this demand. Even in that horrid moment Hornblower found himself remembering La Rochefoucauld's cynical epigram about the pleasure we derive from the contemplation of our friends' troubles.

"Tell him," said Hornblower, "that my master King George will be angry when he hears that such a thing has been said to me, his servant, and that his friend the Sultan will be angry when he hears what his servant has said."

But the Mudir was unmoved by any suggestion of international complications. It would take a long, long time for a complaint to travel from Marmorice to London and then back to Constantinople. And Hornblower could guess that a very small proportion of a quarter of a million sterling, laid out in the proper quarter, would buy the support of the Vizier for the Vali. The Mudir's face was quite unrelenting—a frightened child might have a nightmare about a face as heartless as that.

"Damn it!" said Hornblower, "I won't do it."

There was nothing he wanted more in this world than to break through the iron serenity of the Mudir.

"Tell him," said Hornblower, "I'll drop the gold back into the bay sooner than hand it over. By God, I will. I'll drop it down to the bottom and they can fish for it themselves, which they can't do. Tell him I swear that, by—by the Koran or the beard of the Prophet or whatever they swear by."

Turner nodded in surprised approval; that was a move he had not thought of, and he addressed himself eagerly to the task of translation. The Mudir listened with his eternal patience.

"No, it's no good, sir," said Turner, after the Mudir had replied. "You can't frighten him that way. He says—"

Turner was interrupted by a fresh sentence from the Mudir.

"He says that after this ship has been seized the idolaters—that's the Ceylonese divers, sir—will work for him just as they work for us."

Hornblower, desperate, thought wildly of cutting the divers' throats after throwing the treasure overboard; that would be consonant with this Oriental atmosphere, but before he could put the frightful thought into words the Mudir spoke again, and at considerable length.

"He says wouldn't it be better to go back with *some* treasure, sir—whatever more we can recover—than to lose everything? He says—he says—I beg your pardon, sir, but he says that if this ship is seized for breaking the law your name would not be held in respect by King George."

That was phrasing it elegantly. Hornblower could well imagine what Their Lordships of the Admiralty would say. Even at the best, even if he fought it out to the last man, London would not look with favour on the man who had precipitated an international crisis and whose behaviour necessitated sending a squadron and an army into the Levant to restore British prestige at a moment when every ship and man was needed to fight Bonaparte. And at worst—Hornblower could picture his little ship suddenly overwhelmed by a thousand boarders, seized, emptied of the treasure, and then dismissed with contemptuous indulgence for him to take back to Malta with a tale possibly of outrage but certainly of failure.

It took every ounce of his moral strength to conceal his despair and dismay—from Turner as well as from the Mudir—and as it was he sat silent for a while, shaken, like a boxer in the ring trying to rally after a blow had slipped through his guard. Like a boxer, he needed time to recover.

"Very well," he said at length, "tell him I must think over all this. Tell him it is too important for me to make up my mind now."

"He says," translated Turner when the Mudir replied, "he says he will come tomorrow morning to receive the treasure."

EIGHTEEN

In the old days, long ago, Hornblower as a midshipman had served in the *Indefatigable* on cutting-out expeditions more numerous than he could remember. The frigate would find a coaster anchored under the protection of shore batteries, or would chase one into some small harbour; then at night—or even in broad day—the boats would be manned and sent in. The coaster would take all the precautions she could; she could load her guns, rig her boarding nettings, keep her crew on the alert, row guard round the ship, but to no avail. The boarders would fight their way on board, clear the decks, set sail, and carry off the prize under the nose of the defences. Often and often had Hornblower seen it close, had taken part. He had noted with small enough sympathy the pitiful precautions taken by the victim.

Now the boot was on the other leg; now it was even worse, because *Atropos* lay in the broad Bay of Marmorice without even the protection of shore batteries and with ten thousand enemies around her. Tomorrow, the Mudir had said, he would come for the treasure, but there was no trusting the Turks. That might be one more move to lull the *Atropos* into security. She might be rushed in the night. The *Mejidieh,* over there, could put into her boats more men than *Atropos* could boast altogether, and they could be supplemented with soldiers crammed into fishing boats from the shore. If she were attacked by twenty boats at once, from all sides, by a thousand Mohammedan fanatics, what could she do to defend herself?

She could rig her boarding nettings—they were already rigged. She could load her guns—they were already loaded, grape on top of round shot, depressed so as to sweep the surface of the bay at close range round the ship. She could keep anxious watch—Hornblower was going round the ship himself, to see that the lookouts were all awake, the guns' crews dozing no more deeply than the hard decks would allow as they lay at their posts, the remainder of the hands stationed round the bulwarks with pike and cutlass within easy reach.

It was a novel experience to be the mouse instead of the cat, to be on the defensive instead of the offensive, to wait anxiously for the moon to rise instead of hurrying to the attack while darkness endured. It might be counted as another lesson in war, to know how the waiting victim thought and felt—some day in the future Hornblower might put that lesson to use, and, paralleling the thought of the ship he was going to attack, contrive to circumvent the precautions she was taking.

That was one more proof of the levity and inconstancy of his mind, said Hornblower to himself, bitterness and despair returning in overwhelming force. Here he was thinking about the future, about some other command he might hold, when there was no future. No future. Tomorrow would see the end. He did not know for certain yet what he would do; vaguely in his mind he had the plan that at dawn he would empty the ship of her crew—non-swimmers in the boats, swimmers sent to seek refuge in the *Mejidieh*—while he went down below to the magazine, with a loaded pistol, to blow the ship and the treasure, himself with his dead ambitions, his love for his children and his wife, to blow it all to fragments. But would that be better than bargaining? Would it be better than returning not only with *Atropos* intact but with whatever further treasure McCullum could retrieve? It was his duty to save his ship if he could, and he could. Seventy thousand pounds was far less than a quarter of a million, but it would be a godsend to an England at her wits' ends for gold. A captain in the navy should have no personal feelings; he had a duty to do.

That might be so, but all the same he was convulsed with anguish. This deep, dark sorrow which was rending him was something beyond his control. He looked across at the dark shape of the *Mejidieh*, and sorrow was joined to an intense hatred, like some ugly pattern of red and black before his mind's eye. The vague shape of the *Mejidieh* was drawing back abaft the *Atropos'* quarter—the soft night wind was backing round, as might be expected at this hour, and swinging the ships at their anchors. Overhead there were stars, here and there obscured by patches of cloud whose presence could just be guessed at, moving very slowly over the zenith. And over there, beyond the *Mejidieh*, the sky was a trifle paler; the moon must be rising above the horizon beyond the mountains. The loveliest night imaginable with the gentle breeze—this gentle breeze! Hornblower glowered round in the darkness as if he feared someone might prematurely guess the thought that was forming in his mind.

"I am going below for a few minutes, Mr. Jones," he said, softly.

"Aye aye, sir."

Turner, of course, had been talking. He had told the wardroom all about the quandary in which their captain found himself. One could hear curiosity in the tone of even those three words of Jones'. Resolution came to lacquer over the pattern of red and black.

Down in the cabin the two candles he sent for lit the whole little space, save for a solid shadow here and there. But the chart that he laid out between them was brightly illuminated. He stooped over it, peering at the tiny figures that marked the soundings. He knew them already, as soon as he came to think about them; there was really no need to refresh his memory. Red Cliff Point, Passage Island, Kaia Rock, Point Sari beyond Kaia Rock–he knew them all. He could weather Kaia Rock with this breeze if it should hold. God, there was need for haste! He blew out the candles and felt his way out of the cabin.

"Mr. Jones! I want two reliable bosun's mates. Quietly, if you please."

That breeze was still blowing, ever so gently, a little more fitful than might be desired, and the moon had not cleared the mountains yet.

"Now, you two, pay attention. Go quietly round the ship and see that every man is awake. Not a sound–you hear me? Topmen are to assemble silently at the foot of the masts. Silently."

"Aye aye, sir," was the whispered reply.

"Carry on. Now, Mr. Jones–"

The gentle patter of bare feet on the deck as the men assembled acted as accompaniment to the whispered orders Hornblower was giving to Jones. Over there was the vast bulk of the *Mejidieh;* two thousand ears which might catch the slightest unusual noise–an axe being laid ready on the deck, for instance, or capstan bars being gently eased into their sockets. The bosun came aft again to rejoin the little group of officers round Hornblower and to make his report in a whisper that accorded ill with his bulk and power.

"The capstan pawl's thrown out, sir."

"Very good. Yours is the first move. Go back, count a hundred, and take up on the spring. Six turns, and hold it. Understand?"

"Aye aye, sir."

"Then off you go. You others are clear about your duties? Mr. Carslake, with the axe at the cable. I'll attend to the axe at the spring. Mr. Smiley, fore tops'l sheets. Mr. Hunt, main tops'l sheets. Go to your stations."

The little ship lay there quietly. A tiny rim of the moon came up over the mountains, and broadened momentarily, revealing her lying peacefully at anchor. She seemed inert, incapable of action. Silent men had swarmed up the rigging and were waiting for the signal. There was a gentle creaking as the spring to the cable tightened, but there was no clank from the capstan, for the pawl had been thrown out from the ratchet; the men at the capstan bars walked silently round, and when their six turns had been completed they stood, breasts against the bars, feet braced on the deck, holding the ship steady. Under the pull of the spring she lay at an angle to the breeze, so that when sail should be set not a moment would be wasted gathering stern way and paying off. She would be under command at once.

The moon had cleared the mountains; the seconds went slowly by.

Ting–ting went the ship's bell–two bells: the signal.

Feet pattered in unison. Sheaves squealed in blocks, but, even as the ear caught that sound, topsail yards and forestay had blossomed into sail. Forward and aft came brief sullen thumpings as axe blades cut through cable and spring–with the sudden end of the resistance of the spring the capstan spun round, precipitating the men at the bars to the deck. There were bruises and grazes, but nobody paid attention to the injuries; *Atropos* was under way. In five seconds without giving any warning at all she had transformed herself from something stationary and inert to a living thing, gliding through the water towards the entrance to the bay. She was clear of the peril of the *Mejidieh's* broadside, for the *Mejidieh* had no spring on her cable to swing her round. She would have to weigh her anchor, or cut or slip her cable; she would have to set sail enough to give her steerage way, and then she would have to yaw round before she could fire. With an alert crew, awake and ready for the summons, it would be at least several minutes before she could turn her broadside upon *Atropos,* and then it would be at a range of half a mile or more.

As it was *Atropos* had gathered speed, and was already more than clear before *Mejidieh* gave her first sign of life. The deep booming of a drum came sounding over the water; not the high-pitched rattle of the *Atropos'* side drum, but the far deeper and slower tone of a bass drum monotonously beaten.

"Mr. Jones!" said Hornblower. "Rig in those boarding nettings, if you please."

The moon was shining brightly, lighting the water ahead of them.

"Starboard a point," said Hornblower to the helmsman.

"Starboard a point," came the automatic reply.

"You're taking the West Pass, sir?" asked Turner.

As sailing master and navigator his station in action was on the quarterdeck beside his captain, and the question he asked was strictly within his province.

"I don't think so," said Hornblower.

The booming of the *Mejidieh's* drum was still audible; if the sound reached the batteries the guns' crews there would be on the alert. And when he reached that conclusion there was an orange flash from far astern, as if momentarily a furnace door had been opened and then closed. Seconds later came the heavy report; the *Mejidieh* had fired a gun. There was no sound of the passage of the shot—but if it had even been a blank charge it would serve to warn the batteries.

"I'm going under Sari Point," said Hornblower.

"Sari Point, sir!"

"Yes."

It was surprise and not discipline that limited Turner's protests to that single exclamation. Thirty years of service in the merchant navy had trained Turner's mind so that nothing could induce him to contemplate subjecting his ship voluntarily to navigational hazards; his years of service as sailing master in the Royal Navy had done little to change that mental attitude. It was his duty to keep the ship safe from shoal and storm and let the captain worry about cannon balls. He would never have thought for a moment of trying to take *Atropos* through the narrow channel between Sari Point and Kaia Rock, not even by daylight and ten times never by night, and the fact that he had not thought of it left him without words.

Another orange flash showed astern; another report reached their ears.

"Take a night glass and go for'rard," said Hornblower. "Look out for the surf."

"Aye aye, sir."

"Take a speaking trumpet as well. Make sure I hear you."

"Aye aye, sir."

The gunfire from *Mejidieh* would have warned the garrisons of the batteries; there would be plenty of time for the men to rouse themselves to wakefulness at their guns, to get their linstocks well alight, so as to sweep the channels with their salvos. Turkish gunners might not be efficient, but the cross fire at East Pass could hardly miss. The West Pass, between Kaia Rock and Passage Island, would not be so efficiently swept; but on the other hand the range was negligible, and with the double turn that had to be made (*Atropos* would be like a sitting duck) there would be no chance of coming through uninjured. Dismasted, or even only crippled, *Atropos* would fall an easy prey to *Mejidieh* coming down through East Pass at her leisure. And, crippled and out of control, *Atropos* might run aground; and she was only a little ship, her scantlings were frail—a salvo from the huge stone cannon balls that the Turks favoured, plunging from a height, could tear her to pieces, tear open her bottom and sink her in a minute. He would have to take her under Sari Point; that would double, treble the range from the guns on Passage Island; it would be a surprise move; and very likely the guns there would be trained upon Kaia Rock, to sweep the narrowest passage—their aim would have to be hurriedly changed and for a moment at least he would have the rock itself to shelter him. It was his best chance.

"Starboard a point," he said to the quartermaster. That was the moment, like playing his king as third player to the first trick in a hand of whist; it was the best thing to do, taking all chances into consideration, and so, the decision taken, there was no room for second thoughts.

The moderate breeze was holding; that meant not merely that he had *Atropos* under full command but also that wavelets would be breaking at the foot of Kaia Rock and Sari Point, reflecting back the moonlight visibly to Turner's night glass. He could see Ada Peninsula plainly enough. At this angle it looked as if there was no exit at all from the bay; *Atropos* seemed to be gliding down, unhurried, as though to immolate herself upon an unbroken coast.

"Mr. Jones, hands to the braces and headsail sheets, if you please."

The gunners on Ada would be able to see the ship plainly enough now, silhouetted against the moon; they would be waiting for her to turn. Passage Island and Sari Point were still blended together. He held on.

"Breakers on the port bow!"

That was Turner hailing from forward.

"Breakers ahead!" A long pause, and then Turner's high thin voice again, sharpened with anxiety: "Breakers ahead!"

"Mr. Jones, we'll be wearing ship soon."

He could see well enough. He carried the chart before his mental eyes, and could superimpose it upon the shadowy landscape before him.

"Breakers ahead!"

The closer he came the better. That shore was steep-to.

"Now, Mr. Jones. Quartermaster—hard a-starboard."

She was coming round on her heel like a dancer. Too fast!

"Meet her! Steady!"

He must hold on for a moment; and it would be as well, too, for then *Atropos* could regain the way and handiness of which the sharp turn had deprived her.

"Breakers ahead! Breakers on the starboard bow! Breakers to port!"

A chain of long bright flashes over port quarter; a thunder-roll of reports, echoing again from the hills.

"Hard a-starboard. Brace her up, Mr. Jones. Full and bye!"

Coming round now, with Sari Point close alongside; not merely alongside but right ahead with the hollow curve of it.

"Keep your luff!"

"Sir—sir—"

The quartermaster at the wheel was croaking with anxiety; she would be in irons in a moment. The headsails were flapping. From the feel of her she was losing her way, sagging off to leeward; she would be aground before long.

"Port a little."

That would keep her going for a moment. The black bulk of Kaia was plainly visible to port. Sari was ahead and to starboard, and the wind was in their teeth. They were creeping forward to destruction. But there must be—there *must* be—a back lash of wind from Sari Point. It could not be otherwise with that land formation. The headsails flapped again as the quartermaster at the wheel vacillated between going aground and being taken aback.

"Keep her going."

"Sir—!"

It would be close under the land that that air would be found if at all. Ah! Hornblower could feel the transition with the acute sensitivity of the seaman; the cessation of wind and then the tiny gentle breath on the other cheek. The headsails flapped again, but in a different mood from before; before Hornblower could speak the quartermaster was turning the wheel in agonised relief. It would only be a second or two that would be granted them, small enough time in which to gather steerage way to get the ship under command again, to gain distance from the cliffs.

"Stand by to go about!"

Steerage way so that the rudder would bite; that was what was wanted now. A flash and a roar from Passage Island—Kaia Rock nearly intercepted the flash; perhaps the shot was intercepted as well. That would be the first gun to be reloaded. The others would undoubtedly follow soon. Another flash, another roar, but no time to think about them, for Hornblower's perceptions told him of the fresh alteration in the feel of the ship. They were passing out into the wind again.

"Headsail sheets!"

One moment more. Now!

"Hard a-starboard!"

He could feel the rudder bite. She was coming round. She would not miss stays. As she emerged into the wind she was on her new tack.

"Breakers right ahead!"

That was Kaia Rock, of course. But they must gather way again.

"Stand by to go about!"

They must hold on until the bowsprit was almost touching. Wait. Now!

"Hard over!"

The wheel spun. She was sluggish. Yes—no—yes. The fore staysail was drawing. She was coming round. The yards turned as the hands came aft with the lee-braces. One moment's hesitation, and then she gathered way on the fresh tack, leaving Kaia close beside them. Sari Point ahead; no chance of weathering it on this tack.

"Stand by to go about!"

Hold on as far as possible; this would be the last tack that would be necessary. A howl close overhead. That was a cannon ball from Passage Island.

"Stand by! Hard over!"

Round she came, the rocks at the foot of Sari Point clearly visible as she wheeled away from them. A flaw, an eddy in the wind again, but only a second's hesitation as she caught the true breeze. Hold on for safety a moment more, with Kaia close abeam. Now all was safe.

"Mr. Jones! Course south by east."

"Course south by east, sir!"

They were heading into the open sea, with Rhodes to starboard and Turkey left behind, and with a king's ransom in the lazarette. They were leaving behind a prince's ransom, so to speak, but Hornblower could think of that with hardly a twinge.

NINETEEN

His Majesty's sloop of war *Atropos*, admittedly, was the smallest ship in the British navy. There were brigs of war smaller than she was, and schooners and cutters smaller still, but she was the smallest ship in the technical sense, with three masts and a captain in command, that King George owned, yet Hornblower was well content with her. There were times when he looked at the captains' list, and saw below his name those of the fifty captains junior to him, and when he noted above his name the slowly dwindling number of captains senior to him—as captains died or attained flag rank—and it occurred to him that some day with good fortune he might be posted to a frigate or even a ship of the line, yet at the moment he was content.

He had completed a mission and was entering upon another one. He had discharged at Gibraltar two hundred thousand pounds sterling in gold and silver coin, and he had left there the unpleasant Mr. McCullum and his Ceylonese divers. The money was to await shipment to London, where it would constitute some part of the "British gold" that sustained the fainting spirits of England's allies and against which Bonaparte raved so violently in his bulletins; McCullum and his men would wait for an opportunity to travel in the opposite direction, round Africa back to India. And *Atropos* was running before a heavy westerly gale in a third direction, back up the Mediterranean to rejoin Collingwood and the Mediterranean Fleet.

She seemed to be lightheartedly free of her encumbrances as she heaved and pitched on the quartering sea; after six months afloat with hardly six hours on land Hornblower's seasickness was no longer apparent and he was lighthearted on that account too, along with his ship. Collingwood had seen fit to approve of his report on his proceedings at Marmorice before sending him on to Gibraltar with the treasure, and had given him, for his return journey, orders that an adventurous young captain would approve of. He was to scour the Mediterranean coast of southern Spain, disorganise the Spanish coasting trade, gather up any information he could by personal observation of the harbours, and then look in at Corsica before rejoining the fleet off the Italian coast, where it was damming back, at the water's edge, Bonaparte's new flood of conquest. Naples had fallen, but Sicily was held intact; Bonaparte's monstrous power ended when the salt water reached the saddle-girths of his horse. His armies could march where they would, but his ships cowered in port, or only ventured forth on furtive raids, while the little *Atropos,* with her twenty two tiny guns, had twice sailed the whole length of the Mediterranean, from Gibraltar to Marmorice and back again, without once seeing the tricolour flag.

No wonder Hornblower felt pleased with himself, standing on the plunging deck without a qualm, looking over at the serrated skyline which, in the clear Mediterranean air, indicated the mountains of Spain. He had sailed boldly in within gunshot of the harbours and roadsteads of the coast; he had looked into Malaga and Motril and Almeria; fishing boats and coasters had fled before him like minnows before a pike. He had rounded Cape de Gata and had clawed his way back to the coast again so as to look into Cartagena. Malaga and Almeria had sheltered no ships of war. That was negative information, but even negative information could be of value to Collingwood as he directed the activities of his enormous fleet, covering the ramifications of British commerce over two thousand miles of sea, with his finger on the pulse of a score of international enmities and alliances. Cartagena was the principal Spanish naval base. An examination of it would reveal whether the bankrupt Spanish government had made any effort to reconstitute the fleet shattered at Trafalgar. Perhaps a French ship or two would be sheltering there, on one stage of some adventurous cruise planned by Bonaparte, to enable them to strike at British convoys.

Hornblower looked up at the straining rigging, felt the heave and plunge of the ship under his feet. There were two reefs in the topsails already—it was more than half a gale that was blowing. He considered, and then dismissed, the notion of a third reef. *Atropos* could carry that amount of canvas safely enough. Cape Cope lay on the port beam; his glass revealed that a little cluster of coasters had taken refuge in the shallows under its lee, and he looked at them longingly. But there were batteries to protect them, and this wind made any attempt on them quite impracticable—he could not send in boats in the teeth of half a gale. He gave an order to the helmsman and the *Atropos* went hurtling on towards Cartagena. It was exhilarating to stand here by the taffrail with the wind screaming round him and a creamy wake emerging from under the stern beneath his feet. He smiled to watch Mr. Turner's navigation class at work; Turner had the midshipmen and master's mates around him giving them instruction in coastwise navigation. He was trying to ballast their feather-brains with good solid mathematics about the "running fix" and "doubling the angle on the bow" and the "four point bearing," but it was a difficult task to retain their attention in these stimulating surroundings, with the wind setting the chart fluttering wildly in Turner's hand and even making it hard for the young men to hold their slates steady as it caught their inclined surfaces.

"Mr. Turner," said Hornblower. "Report any case of inattention to me at once and I will deal with it as it deserves."

That steadied the young men to a noticeable extent and made them restrain their animal spirits. Smiley checked himself in the midst of a wink at the young Prince, and the Prince's embryo guffaw was stillborn as a guilty grin. That boy was perfectly human now—it was a far cry from the stuffy German court into which he had been born to the windy deck of the *Atropos*. If ever he were restored to the throne of his fathers he would be free of the thralldom of a sextant, but perhaps he might remember these breezy days with regret. The great-nephew of King George—Hornblower looked at him, pretending to study wisely the equilateral triangle scrawled on his slate, and smiled to himself again, remembering Dr. Eisenbeiss' horror at the suggestion that perhaps corporal punishment might come the way of a reigning Prince. It had not so far, but it might.

Four bells sounded, the sandglass was turned, the wheel was relieved, and Turner dismissed his class.

"Mr. Smiley! Mr. Horrocks!"

The released midshipmen turned to their captain.

"I want you at the mastheads now with your glasses."

Sharp young eyes would be best for looking into Cartagena. Hornblower noticed the appeal in the Prince's expression.

"Very well, Mr. Prince. You can go too. Fore topmast head with Mr. Smiley."

It was a frequent punishment to send a young officer up to the discomforts of the masthead, but it was no punishment today, not with an enemy's harbour to be examined, and reports made on the shipping inside. Cartagena was fast coming into sight; the castle and the towers of the churches were visible now beyond the sheltering island of La Escombrera. With this westerly wind it was simple enough to stand right in so that from the masthead a view could be had of the inner harbour.

"Deck, there! Captain, sir—"

Smiley was hailing down from the fore topmast head. Hornblower had to walk forward to hear what he had to say, for the wind was sweeping away his words.

"There's a ship of war in the outer bay, sir! Spanish, she looks like. One of their big frigates. She's got her yards across."

That was likely to be the *Castilla*, one of the survivors of Trafalgar.

"There's seven sail of coasters anchored close in, sir."

They were safe enough from the *Atropos* in these conditions.

"What about the inner harbour?"

"Four—no, five ships moored there, sir. And two hulks."

"What d'you make of them?"

"Four of the line, sir, and a frigate. No yards across. Laid up in ordinary, I should say, sir."

In past years the Spanish government had built fine ships, but under the corruption and inefficiency of Godoy they were allowed to rot at their moorings for want of crews and stores. Four of the line and a frigate laid up at Cartagena was what had last been reported there, so there was no change; negative information for Collingwood again, but useful.

"She's setting sail!"

That was the Prince's voice, high-pitched and excited, screaming down. A moment later Horrocks and Smiley were supplementing the warning.

"The frigate, sir! She's getting sail on her!"

"I can see her cross, sir!"

Spanish ships of war had the habit of hoisting huge wooden crosses at the mizzen peak when action seemed likely. The frigate must be intending to make a sortie, to chase away this inquisitive visitor. It was high time to beat a retreat. A big Spanish frigate such as the *Castilla* carried forty four guns, just twice as many as *Atropos*, and with three times their weight of metal. If only over the horizon *Atropos* had a colleague to whom she could lure the *Castilla!* That was something to bear in mind and to suggest to Collingwood in any case; this Spanish captain was enterprising and energetic, and might be rash—he might be smouldering with shame after Trafalgar, and he might be lured out to his destruction.

"She's under way, sir!"

"Fore tops'l set! Main tops'l set, sir!"

No sense in courting danger, even though with this wind *Atropos* had a clear run to safety.

"Keep her away a point," said Hornblower to the helmsman, and *Atropos* turned a little to show a clean pair of heels to the Spaniard.

"She's coming out, sir!" reported Horrocks from the main topmast head. "Reefed tops'ls. Two reefs, I think, sir."

Hornblower trained his glass over the quarter. There it was, the white oblong just showing above the horizon as *Atropos* lifted—the reefed fore topsail of the *Castilla.*

"She's pointing straight at us now, sir," reported Smiley.

In a stern chase like this *Atropos* had nothing to fear, newly coppered as she was and with a pretty turn of speed. The high wind and the rough sea would favour the bigger ship, of course. The *Castilla* might contrive to keep the *Atropos* in sight even though she had no chance of overtaking her. It would be a useful object lesson to officers and men to see *Atropos* making the best use of her potentiality for speed. Hornblower looked up again at sails and rigging. Certainly now there could be no question of taking in a third reef. He must carry all possible sail, just as the *Castilla* was doing.

Mr. Still, as officer of the watch, was touching his hat to Hornblower with a routine question.

"Carry on, Mr. Still."

"Up spirits!"

With a powerful enemy plunging along behind her the life of the *Atropos* went on quite normally; the men had their grog and went to their dinners, the watch changed, the wheel was relieved. Palos Point disappeared over the port quarter as *Atropos* went flying on into the open Mediterranean, and still that white oblong kept its position on the horizon astern. The *Castilla* was doing well for a Spanish frigate.

"Call me the moment there is any change, Mr. Jones," said Hornblower, shutting his glass.

Jones was nervous—he might be imagining himself in a Spanish prison already. It would do him no harm to be left on deck with the responsibility, even though, down in his cabin, Hornblower found himself getting up from his dinner table to peer aft through the scuttle to make sure the *Castilla* was not gaining on them. In fact Hornblower was not sorry when, with his dinner not yet finished, a knock at the door brought a messenger from the quarterdeck.

"Mr. Jones' respects, sir, and the wind is moderating a little, he thinks, sir."

"I'm coming," said Hornblower, laying down his knife and fork.

In a moderate breeze *Atropos* ought to be able to run *Castilla* topsails-under in an hour or two, and any reduction in the wind was to the advantage of *Atropos* as long as she spread all the canvas she could carry. But it would call for judgment to shake out the reefs at the right time, without imperilling spars on the one hand or losing distance on the other. When Hornblower arrived on deck a glance told him that it was time.

"You are quite right, Mr. Jones," he said—no harm in giving him a pat on the back—"we'll shake out a reef."

The order sped along the deck.

"Hands make sail!"

Hornblower looked aft through his glass; as *Atropos* lifted her stern he could get the *Castilla's* fore topsail right in the centre of the field. The most painstaking thought could not bring a decision as to whether or not it was any nearer. She must be exactly maintaining her distance. Then as the topsail hung dizzily in the lens he saw—he was nearly sure he saw—the oblong broaden into a square. He rested his eye and looked again. No doubt about it. *Castilla* had decided that was the moment to shake out a reef too.

Hornblower looked up at the *Atropos'* main topsail yard. The topmen, bent over the yard at that dizzy height, had completed the untying of the reef points. Now they came running in from the yard. Smiley had the starboard yard-arm, and His Serene Highness the Prince of Seitz-Bunau the port. They were having their usual race, flinging themselves onto the backstays and sliding down without a thought for their necks. Hornblower was glad that boy had found his feet—of course he was wild with the excitement of the flight and pursuit; Hornblower was glad that Smiley had adopted that amused paternal attitude towards him.

With the letting out of the reef *Atropos* increased her speed again; Hornblower could feel the renewed thrust of the sail upon the fabric of the ship under his feet; he could feel the more frantic leap of the vessel on the wave crests. He directed a wary glance aloft. This would not be the moment to have anything carry away, not with *Castilla* tearing along in pursuit. Jones was standing by the wheel. The wind was just over the starboard quarter, and the little ship was answering well to her rudder, but it was as important to keep an eye on the helmsman as it was to see that they did not split a topsail. It called for some little resolution to leave Jones in charge again and go below to try to finish his dinner.

When the message came down again that the wind was moderating it was like that uncanny feeling which Hornblower had once or twice experienced of something happening even though it had not happened before—the circumstances were so exactly similar.

"Mr. Jones' respects, sir, and the wind is moderating a little, he thinks, sir."

Hornblower had to compel himself to vary his reply.

"My compliments to Mr. Jones, and I am coming on deck."

Just as before, he could feel that the ship was not giving her utmost. Just as before, he gave the order for a reef to be shaken out. Just as before, he swung round to train his glass on the *Castilla's* topsail. And just as before he turned back as the men prepared to come in from the yard. But that was the moment when everything took a different course, when the desperate emergency arose that always at sea lies just over the horizon of the future.

Excitement had stimulated the Prince into folly. Hornblower looked up to see the boy standing on the port yard-arm, not merely standing but dancing, taking a clumsy step or two to dare Smiley at the starboard yard-arm to imitate him, one hand on his hip, the other over his head. Hornblower was going to shout a reprimand; he opened his mouth and inflated his chest but before he could utter a sound the Prince's foot slipped. Hornblower saw him totter, strive to regain his balance, and then fall, heavily through the air, and turning a complete circle as he fell.

Later on Hornblower out of curiosity made a calculation. The Prince fell from a height of a little over seventy feet, and without the resistance of the air he would have reached the surface of the sea in something over two seconds. But the resistance of the air could have been by no means negligible—it must have got under his jacket and slowed his fall considerably, for the boy was not killed and was in fact only momentarily knocked unconscious by the impact when he bounced off the main shrouds. Probably it took as much as four seconds for the Prince to fall into the sea. Hornblower was led to make the calculation when brooding over the incident later, for he could remember clearly all the thoughts that passed through his mind during those four seconds. Momentary exasperation came first and then anxiety, and then followed a hasty summing up of the situation. If he hove-to to pick up the boy the *Castilla* would have all the time needed to overhaul them. If he went on the boy would drown. And if he went on he would have to report to Collingwood that he had left the King's great-nephew without lifting a finger to help him. He had to choose quickly—quickly. He had no right to risk his ship to save one single life. But—but—if the boy had been killed in battle by a broadside sweeping the deck it would be different. To abandon him was another matter again. On the heels of that conclusion came another thought, the beginnings of another thought sprouting from a seed that had been sown outside Cartagena. It did not have time to develop in those four seconds; it was as if Hornblower acted the moment the green shoot from the seed showed above ground, to reach its full growth later.

By the time the boy had reached the sea Hornblower had torn the emergency life buoy from the taffrail; he flung it over the port quarter as the speed of the ship brought the boy nearly opposite him, and it smacked into the sea close beside him. At the same moment the air which Hornblower had drawn into his lungs to reprimand the Prince was expelled in a salvo of bellowed orders.

"Mizzen braces! Back the mizzen topsail! Quarter boat away!"

Maybe—Hornblower could not be sure later—everyone was shouting at once, but everyone at least responded to orders with the rapidity that was the result of months of drill. *Atropos* flew up into the wind, her way checked instantly. It was Smiley—Heaven only knew how he had made the descent from the starboard main topsail yard-arm in that brief space—who got the jolly boat over the side, with four men at the oars, and dashed off to effect the rescue, the tiny boat soaring up and swooping down as the waves passed under her. And even before *Atropos* was hove-to Hornblower was putting the next part of the plan into action.

"Mr. Horrocks! Signal 'Enemy in sight to windward.'"

Horrocks stood and gaped, and Hornblower was about to blare out with "Blast you! Do what I tell you," but he restrained himself. Horrocks was not a man of the quickest thought in the world, and he had failed entirely to see any purpose in signalling to a vacant horizon. To swear at him now would simply paralyse him with nervousness and lead to a further delay.

"Mr. Horrocks, kindly send up the signal as quickly as you can. 'Enemy in sight to windward.' Quickly, please."

The signal rating beside Horrocks was luckily quicker-witted—he was one of the dozen men of the crew who could read and write, naturally—and was already at the halliards with the flag-locker open, and his example shook Horrocks out of his amazement. The flags went soaring up to the main topsail yard-arm, flying out wildly in the wind. Hornblower made a mental note that that rating, even though he was no seaman as yet—lately a City apprentice who had come hurriedly aboard at Deptford to avoid something worse in civilian life—was deserving of promotion.

"Now another signal, Mr. Horrocks. 'Enemy is a frigate distant seven miles bearing west course east.' "

It was the sensible thing to do to send up the very signals he would have hoisted if there really were help in sight—the *Castilla* might be able to read them or might make at least a fair guess at their meaning. If there had been a friendly ship in sight down to leeward (Hornblower remembered the suggestion he had been going to make to Collingwood) he would never have hove-to, of course, but would have gone on tearing down to lure the *Castilla* as near as possible, but the captain of the *Castilla* was not to know that.

"Keep that signal flying. Now send up an affirmative, Mr. Horrocks. Very good. Haul it down again. Mr. Jones! Lay the ship on the starboard tack, a good full."

A powerful English ship down there to leeward would certainly order *Atropos* to close on *Castilla* as quickly as possible. He must act as if that were the case. It was only when Jones—almost as helpless with astonishment as Horrocks had been—had plunged into the business of getting *Atropos* under way again that Hornblower had time to use his telescope. He trained it on the distant topsail again; not so distant now. Coming up fast, and Hornblower felt a sick feeling of disappointment and apprehension. And then as he watched he saw the square of the topsail narrow into a vertical oblong, and two other oblongs appear beside it. At the same moment the masthead lookout gave a hail.

"Deck there! The enemy's hauled his wind, sir!"

Of course he would do so—the disappointment and apprehension vanished instantly. A Spanish frigate captain once he had put his bowsprit outside the safety of a defended port would ever be a prey to fear. Always there would be the probability in his mind that just over the horizon lay a British squadron ready to pounce on him. He would chase a little sloop of war eagerly enough, but as soon as he saw that sloop sending up signals and swinging boldly round on a course that challenged action he would bethink him of the fact that he was already far to leeward of safety; he would imagine hostile ships only just out of sight cracking on all sail to cut him off from his base, and once his mind was made up he would not lose a single additional mile or minute before turning to beat back to safety. For two minutes the Spaniard had been a prey to indecision after *Atropos* hove-to, but the final bold move had made up his mind for him. If he had held on for a short time longer he might have caught sight of the jolly boat pulling over the waves and then would have guessed what *Atropos* was doing, but, as it was, time was gained and the Spaniard, close-hauled, was clawing back to safety in flight from a non-existent enemy.

"Masthead! What do you see of the boat?"

"She's still pulling, sir, right in the wind's eye."

"Do you see anything of Mr. Prince?"

"No, sir, can't say as I do."

Not much chance in that tossing sea of seeing a floating man two miles away, not even from the masthead.

"Mr. Jones, tack the ship."

It would be best to keep *Atropos* as nearly straight down wind from the boat as possible, allowing it an easy run to leeward when its mission was accomplished. *Castilla* would not be able to make anything of the manoeuvre.

"Deck there! The boat's stopped pulling, sir. I think they're picking up Mr. Prince, sir."

Thank God for that! It was only now that Hornblower could realise what a bad ten minutes it had been.

"Deck there! Yes, sir, they're waving a shirt. They're pulling back to us now."

"Heave-to, Mr. Jones, if you please. Doctor Eisenbeiss, have everything ready in case Mr. Prince needs treatment."

The Mediterranean at midsummer was warm enough; most likely the boy had taken no harm. The jolly boat came dancing back over the waves and turned under *Atropos'* stern into the little lee afforded by her quarter as she rode with her starboard bow to the waves. Here came His Serene Highness wet and bedraggled but not in the least hurt, meeting the concentrated gaze of all on deck with a smile half sheepish and half defiant. Eisenbeiss came forward fussily, talking voluble German, and then turned to Hornblower to explain.

"I have a hot blanket ready for him, sir."

It was at that moment that the dam of Hornblower's even temper burst.

"A hot blanket! I know what'll warm him quicker than that. Bosun's mate! My compliments to the bosun, and ask him to be kind enough to lend you his cane for a few minutes. Shut your mouth, Doctor, if you know what's good for you. Now, young man—"

Humanitarians had much to say against corporal punishment, but in their arguments, while pointing out the harm it might do to the one punished, they omitted to allow for the satisfaction other people derived from it. And it was some further training for the blood royal to display his acquired British imperturbability, to bite off the howl that a well-applied cane tended to draw forth, and to stand straight afterwards with hardly a skip to betray his discomfort, with hardly a rub at the smarting royal posterior, and with the tears blinked manfully back. Satisfaction or not, Hornblower was a little sorry afterwards.

TWENTY

There was everything to be said in favour of keeping *Castilla* under observation for a while at least, and almost nothing to be said against it. The recent flight and pursuit had proved that *Atropos* had the heels of her even under reefed topsails, so that it could be taken for granted that she was safe from her in any lesser wind—and the wind was moderating. The *Castilla* was now a full thirty miles dead to leeward of Cartagena; it would be useful to know—Collingwood would certainly want to know—whether she intended to beat back there again or would fetch some easier Spanish port. Close-hauled she could make Alicante to the north or perhaps Almeria to the south; she was close-hauled on the starboard tack, heading south, at this moment. And there was the possibility to be borne in mind that she did not intend to return to Spain as yet, that her captain might decide to range through the Mediterranean for a while to see what prizes he could snap up. On her present course she could easily stretch over to the Barbary Coast and pick up a victualler or two with grain and cattle intended for the British Mediterrancan Fleet.

Hornblower's orders were that he should rejoin Collingwood in Sicilian waters after looking into Malaga and Cartagena; he was not the bearer of urgent despatches, nor, Heaven knew, was *Atropos* likely to be an important addition to the strength of the fleet; while on the other hand it was the duty of every English captain, having once made contact with a ship of the enemy in open water, to maintain that contact as long as was possible. *Atropos* could not hope to face *Castilla* in battle, but she could keep her under observation, she might warn merchant shipping of danger, and she might with good fortune meet some big British ship of war—in actual fact, not make-believe—to whom she could indicate the enemy.

"Mr. Jones," said Hornblower. "Lay her on the starboard tack again, if you please. Full and bye."

"Aye aye, sir."

Jones, of course, showed some surprise at the reversal of the roles, at the pursued becoming the pursuer, and that was one more proof that he was incapable of strategic thought. But he had to engage himself on carrying out his orders, and *Atropos* steadied on a southerly course, running parallel to *Castilla's,* far to windward; Hornblower trained his glass on the topsails just visible over the horizon. He fixed the shape of them firmly in his memory; a slight alteration in the proportion of length to breadth would indicate any change of course on the part of the *Castilla.*

"Masthead!" he hailed. "Keep your eye on the enemy. Report anything you see."

"Aye aye, sir."

Atropos was like a terrier now, yapping at the heels of a bull in a field—not a very dignified role—and the bull might turn and charge at any moment. Eventually the captain of the *Castilla* would make up his mind that a trick had been played on him, that *Atropos* had been signalling to non-existent friends, and there was no guessing what he might decide to do then, when he grew certain that there was no help following *Atropos* up just beyond the horizon. Meanwhile the wind was still moderating, and *Atropos* could set more canvas. When beating to windward she behaved best under all the sail she could carry, and he might as well keep as close to the enemy as the wind allowed.

"Try setting the mainsail, Mr. Jones, if you please."

"Aye aye, sir."

The main course was a big sail, and the little *Atropos* seemed to take wings under the tremendous pressure of it when it was sheeted home, with the tack hauled forward to the chesstrees by the united strength of half a watch. Now she was thrusting along bravely in the summer evening, lying over to the wind, and shouldering off the hungry waves with her starboard bow in great fountains of spray, through which the setting sun gleamed in fleeting rainbows of fiery beauty, and leaving behind her a seething wake dazzling white against the blue. It was a moment when it was good to be alive, driving hard to windward like this, and with all the potentiality of adventure at hand in the near unknown. War at sea was a dreary business usually, with boredom and discomfort to be endured day and night, watch and watch, but it had moments of high exaltation like this, just as it had its moments of black despair, of fear, of shame.

"You may dismiss the watch below, Mr. Jones."

"Aye aye, sir."

Hornblower glanced round the deck. Still would have the watch.

"Call me if there's any change, Mr. Still. I want to set more sail if the wind moderates further."

"Aye aye, sir."

A moment of exaltation, come and gone. He had been on his feet nearly all day, since dawn, and his legs were weary, and if he stayed on deck they would grow wearier still. Down below there were the two books he had bought at Gibraltar for a badly needed guinea—Lord Hodge's *Statement of the Present Political Condition of Italy* and Barber's *New Methods of Determining Longitude, with Some Remarks on Discrepancies in Recent Charts.* He wanted to inform himself on both subjects, and it was better to do so now than to stay up on deck growing more and more weary while the hours passed.

At sunset he emerged again; *Castilla* was still holding the same course, with *Atropos* head-reaching upon her very slightly. He looked at those distant topsails; he read the slate that recorded the day's run, and he waited while the log was hove again. Surely if *Castilla* intended to put back into Cartagena she would have gone about by now. She had made a very long reach to the southward, and any backing of the wind round to the north—a very likely occurrence at this season—would nullify much of her progress so far. If she did not come about by the time darkness set in it would be a strong indication that she had something else in mind. He waited as the sunset faded from the western sky, and until the first stars began to appear overhead; that was when his aching eye, straining through the glass, could see no more of *Castilla.* But at the last sight of her she was still standing to the southward. All the more reason to keep her under observation.

It was the end of the second dogwatch and the hands were being called.

"I'll have the main course taken in, Mr. Turner," he said.

He wrote his night orders by the faint light of the binnacle: the ship to be kept close-hauled on the starboard tack; he was to be called if the wind shifted more than two points, and in any event he was to be called immediately before moonrise in the middle watch. The gloomy little cabin when he retired into it was like a wild beast's lair with its dark corners where the light of the lamp did not penetrate. He lay down fully clothed, endeavouring to keep his tired mind from continuing to try to solve the problem of what the *Castilla* intended to do. He had shortened sail, as she would probably do. If she did not, he had the heels of her and might overtake her in daylight. If she did anything else, if she tacked or wore, he was doing what was probably best to find her again next day. His eyes closed with fatigue, and did not open again until someone came to tell him the middle watch had been called.

The west wind, dying away though it was, had brought a slight overcast with it, enough to obscure the stars and deprive the small moon, almost in its last quarter, of most of its light. *Atropos,* still close-hauled, was now, in the lessening wind, only flirting with the waves that came onto her starboard bow, meeting them elegantly like a stage beauty extending her hand to a stage lover. The dark water all around seemed to fall in with the mood and to murmur pretty conventionalities. There appeared no imminence of blazing death. The minutes passed in warm idleness.

"Deck there!" That was the masthead lookout hailing. "I think I can see something, sir. Right away on the starboard bow."

"Get aloft with the night glass, youngster," said Turner, who had the watch, to the master's mate beside him.

A minute passed, two minutes.

"Yes, sir," came the new voice from the masthead. "It's the loom of a ship. Three miles—four miles—fine on the starboard bow."

The night glasses trained round more forward.

"Maybe," said Turner.

There was a tiny patch of something darker than the surrounding night; Hornblower's night glass could tell him no more than that. He watched it painstakingly. The bearing of it seemed to be altering.

"Steer small!" he growled at the helmsman.

For a moment he wondered if the patch was really there; it might be something his mind suggested to his eye—a whole ship's company could sometimes imagine the same thing if the idea was once put in their heads. No, it was undoubtedly there, and drawing across *Atropos'* bows, more than could be accounted for by any wavering of her course with bad steering. It must be *Castilla;* she must have swung round at midnight and come hurrying down wind in the hope of pouncing on her prey by surprise. If he had not shortened sail she would be right on him. The Spanish lookouts were not up to their work, for she was holding on her course.

"Heave-to, Mr. Turner," he said, and walked across to the port side to keep the *Castilla* under observation as *Atropos* came up into the wind. *Castilla* had already lost most of the advantage of the weather gage, and in a few minutes would lose it all. The slowly moving clouds overhead were parting; there was a faint gleam of light through a thin patch, further darkness, and then the moon shone through a gap. Yes, that was a ship; that was the *Castilla*, already far down to leeward.

"Deck, there! I can see her plainly now, sir. On the port quarter. Captain, sir! She's wearing round!"

So she was. Her sails gleamed momentarily bright in the moonlight as they swung round. She had failed in her attempt to surprise her enemy, and was making a fresh one.

"Lay her on the port tack, Mr. Turner."

The little *Atropos* could play catch-as-catch-can with any big frigate in this sort of weather. She swung round and headed into the wind, her stern to her pursuer again.

"Masthead! What sail has the enemy set?"

"She's setting her royals, sir. All plain sail to the royals."

"Call all hands, Mr. Turner. Set all plain sail."

There was still enough wind for the addition of courses and royals to lay *Atropos* over and send her flying once more. Hornblower looked back at *Castilla's* topsails and royals, silhouetted now against clear sky below the moon. It did not take very long to determine that now *Atropos* was gaining fast. He was pondering a decision regarding shortening sail when he was saved the trouble. The silhouettes narrowed again abruptly.

"Deck there!" hailed the masthead. "Enemy's hauled her wind, sir."

"Very well! Mr. Turner, wear ship, if you please. Point our bows right at her, and take in the fore course."

The terrier had evaded the bull's charge and was now yapping at its heels again. It was easy to follow the *Castilla* for the rest of the night, keeping a sharp lookout during the periods of darkness lest she should play on them the same trick as *Atropos* had played once. Dawn, rising ahead, revealed the *Castilla's* royals and topsails an inky black before they changed to ivory white against the blue sky. Hornblower could imagine the rage of the Spanish captain at the sight of his pertinacious pursuer, dogging him in this fashion with insolent impunity. Seven miles separated the ships, but as far as the *Castilla's* big eighteen-pounders mattered it might as well be seventy, and moreover the invisible wind, blowing direct from *Atropos* to *Castilla*, was an additional protection, guarding her from her enemy like the mysterious glass shield that turned the hero's sword in one of the Italian epics. *Atropos*, seven miles to windward, was as safe and yet as visible as the Saracen magician.

Hornblower was conscious of weariness again. He had been on his feet since midnight, after less than four hours' rest. He wanted, passionately, to rest his legs; he wanted, hardly less, to close his aching eyes. The hammocks had been brought up, the decks swabbed, and it only remained now to cling to *Castilla's* heels, but when any moment might bring the need for a quick decision he dared not leave the deck—odd that now he was safely to windward the situation was more dynamic than yesterday when he had been to leeward, but it was true. *Castilla* might come to the wind at any unforeseen moment, and moreover the two ships were driving into the blue Mediterranean where any surprise might be over the horizon.

"I'll have a mattress up here," said Hornblower.

They brought one up and laid it aft beside the weather scuppers. He eased his aching joints down onto it, settled his head on his pillow, and closed his eyes. The lift and send of the ship were soporific, and so was the sound of the sea under the *Atropos'* counter. The light played backward and forward over his face as the shadows of sails and rigging followed the movement of the ship. He could sleep—he could sleep, heavily and dreamlessly, while the ships flew on up the Mediterranean, while they called the watch, while they hove the log, even while they trimmed the yards as the wind came a little northerly, moving round ahead of the sun.

It was afternoon when he woke. He shaved with the aid of a mirror stuck in the hammock nettings; he took his bath under the wash-deck pump and put on the clean shirt that he sent for; he sat on the deck and ate cold beef and the last of the goodly soft bread taken on board at Gibraltar, somewhat stale now but infinitely better than ship's biscuit; and the fresh butter from the same source, kept cool so far in an earthenware crock, was quite delicious. It struck seven bells as he finished his last mouthful.

"Deck there! Enemy's altering course."

He was on his feet in a flash, his plate sliding into the scuppers, the telescope in his hand without conscious volition on his part. No doubt about it. *Castilla* had altered to a more northerly course, with the wind abeam. It was not very surprising for they had run a full two hundred miles from Cartagena; unless the *Castilla* was prepared to go right up the Mediterranean far to leeward of all Spanish bases, it was time for her to head north to fetch Minorca. He would follow her there, the terrier harassing the bull, and he would give a final yap at the bull's heels outside Port Mahon. Besides, the *Castilla's* alteration of course might not portend a mere flight to Minorca. They were right on the track of convoys beating up the Mediterranean from Sicily and Malta.

"Port your helm, Mr. Still, if you please. Maintain a parallel course."

It was only sensible to stay up to windward of *Castilla* as much as possible. The intense feeling of well-being of five minutes ago was replaced now by excitement, a slight tingling under the skin. Ten to one the *Castilla's* alteration of course meant nothing at all, but there was the tenth chance. Eight bells; hands mustered for the first dogwatch.

"Deck there! There's a sail ahead of the enemy, sir!"

That was it, then.

"Get aloft with you, Mr. Smiley. You can go too, Mr. Prince."

That would show His Serene Highness that a punishment cleared the record in the navy, and that he was being trusted not to risk any more monkey tricks. It was a detail that had to be borne in mind despite the flood of excitement following the masthead report. There was no knowing what that sail over there, invisible from the deck, might imply. But there was a chance that it was a British ship of war, fair in *Castilla's* path.

"Two sail! Three sail! Captain, sir, it looks like a convoy, dead to leeward."

A convoy could only be a British convoy, and a convoy meant the presence of a British ship of war ahead there in *Castilla's* path.

"Up helm and bear down on the enemy. Call all hands, Mr. Still, if you please. Clear for action."

During all the long flight and pursuit he had not cleared for action. He had not wanted action with the vastly superior *Castilla*, and had been determined on avoiding it. Now he hoped for it—hoped for it with that tremor of doubt that made him hate himself, all the more so as the repeating of the order brought a cheer from the men, the watch below pouring on deck for duty with expectant grins and schoolboy excitement. Mr. Jones came bustling up on deck buttoning his coat; apparently he had been dozing comfortably through the afternoon watch. To Jones would fall the command of the *Atropos* if any accident should befall him, if a shot should take off his leg or dash him into bloody fragments. Odd that the thought of Jones becoming responsible for handling *Atropos* was as disturbing as the rest of it. But all the same Jones must be brought up to date on the situation and told what should be done. He did it in three sharp sentences.

"I see, sir," said Jones, pulling at his long chin. Hornblower was not so sure that he did see, but there was no more time to spare for Jones.

"Masthead! What of the convoy?"

"One sail has tacked, sir. She's standing towards us."

"What d'you make of her?"

"She looks like a ship of war, sir. I can only see her royals, sir."

"Mr. Horrocks, make the private signal and our number."

A ship standing towards *Castilla* could only be a ship of war, the escorting vessel. Hornblower could only hope she would be one of the larger frigates, able to meet the big *Castilla* on something like equal terms. But he knew most of the frigates Collingwood had—*Sirius, Naiad, Hermione*—thirty-two-gun twelve-pounder frigates most of them, hardly a match for *Castilla's* forty four eighteen-pounders unless well handled, and unless *Castilla* fought badly, and unless he himself had a chance to intervene. He strained his eyesight staring forward through his glass, but the British ship was not yet in sight from the deck, and *Castilla* was still running boldly down before the wind. Clearing for action was nearly completed; they were casting loose the guns.

"Signal, sir!"

Horrocks was ready with the book as the masthead reported the flags.

"Private signal correctly answered, sir. And her number. She's *Nightingale,* sir, twenty eight, Captain Ford, sir."

Almost the smallest of the frigates, with only nine-pounders on her maindeck. Please God Ford would have the sense not to close with *Castilla.* He must outmanoeuvre her, keep her in play, and then when *Atropos* came up there could be some pretty tactics until they could shoot away some of *Castilla's* spars and take her at a disadvantage. Then they could rake her and weaken her before closing in for the kill. The captain of the *Castilla* was showing proof of having grasped the essentials of the situation; caught between two hostile ships so that he could not avoid action if it were forced on him he was plunging down at his best speed to the attack on the one most accessible to him; he was still carrying all sail to bring him most quickly into action before *Atropos* could intervene. He could well hope to batter *Nightingale* into a wreck and then turn on *Atropos.* If he succeeded—oh, if he succeeded! —it would be a terrible problem for *Atropos,* to decide whether or not to accept action.

"Ship cleared for action, sir," reported Jones.

"Very well."

Now his glass picked her up; the distant sail, far beyond *Castilla.* As he looked, as the topgallants appeared below the royals, the royals disappeared. *Nightingale* was shortening down to "fighting sails" ready for action. Hornblower knew a little about Ford. He had the reputation of a good fighting captain. Please God he had discretion as well. Ford was far his senior in the navy list; there was no possibility of giving him orders to keep clear.

Castilla was still hurtling down upon *Nightingale.*

"Signal, sir. Number Seventy two. 'Engage the enemy more closely!'"

"Acknowledge."

Hornblower was conscious of Jones' and Turner's eyes upon him. There might be an implied rebuke in that signal, a hint that he was not doing his best to get into action. On the other hand it might be a mere signal that action was imminent. *Nightingale's* topsails were over the horizon now; close-hauled, she was doing her best to come to meet *Castilla.* If only Ford would hold off for half an hour—*Atropos* was steadily gaining on *Castilla.* No, he was still hurrying to the encounter before *Atropos* could arrive; he was playing *Castilla's* game for her. Now *Castilla* was cluing up her courses; she was taking in her royals, ready for the clash. The two ships were hastening together; white sails on a blue sea under a blue sky. They were right in line from where Hornblower stood staring at them through his glass; right in line so that it was hard to judge the distance between them. Now they were turning, *Nightingale* paying off before the wind as *Castilla* approached. All the masts seemed blended together. Ford *must* keep clear and try to shoot away a spar.

A sudden billowing of smoke round the ships; the first broadsides were being fired. It looked as if the ships were already close-locked in action—surely it could not be. Not time yet to take in courses and royals; the sooner they got down into action the better. Now, heavily over the blue water, came the sound of those first broadsides, like the rumbling of thunder. The smoke was blowing clear of the fight, drifting away from the ships in a long bank. More smoke billowing up; the guns had been reloaded and were firing away, and still the masts were close together—had Ford been fool enough to lock yard-arms? Again the long rumble of the guns. The ships were swinging round in the smoke cloud; he could see the masts above it changing their bearing, but he could not distinguish ship from ship. There was a mast falling, yards, sails, and all; it must be *Nightingale's* main topmast, hideous though the thought was. This seemed like a lifetime, waiting to get into action. Cannon smoke and cannon thunder. He did not want to believe the glass was really revealing the truth to him as he looked, the details becoming clearer as he approached. The two ships were locked together, no doubt about it. And that was *Nightingale,* main topmast gone. She was lying at an angle to *Castilla's* side, bows towards her.

The wind was still turning the two ships, and it was turning them as if they were one. *Nightingale* must be locked against *Castilla,* bowsprit or possibly anchor hooked into *Castilla's* fore chains. All *Castilla's* guns could bear, practically raking *Nightingale* with every broadside, and *Nightingale's* fire must be almost ineffectual. Could she tear herself loose? There went her foremast, everything, over the side; almost impossible to tear herself loose now.

The men at the guns were yelling at the sight.

"Silence! Mr. Jones, get the courses in."

What was he to do? He ought to cross *Castilla's* bows or stern and rake her, come about and rake her again. Not so easy to fire into *Castilla's* bows without hitting *Nightingale;* not so easy to cross her stern; that would put him to leeward and there would be delay in getting back into action again. And the two ships were still swinging considerably, not only with the wind but with the recoil of their guns. Supposing that as he took *Atropos* to lie a little clear they swung so that *Nightingale* intercepted his fire and he had to work back again to windward to get back into action? That would be shameful, and other captains hearing the story would think he had deliberately stayed out of fire. He could lay his ship alongside *Castilla* on her unoccupied side, but her slender scantlings would bear little of *Castilla's* ponderous broadside; his ship would be a wreck in a few minutes. And yet *Nightingale* was already a wreck. He must bring her instant, immediate relief.

Now they were only a mile from the locked ships and running down fast. Years of experience at sea told him how rapidly those last few minutes passed when ships needed each other.

"Muster the port-side guns' crews," he said. "Every man, gun captains and all. Arm them for boarding. Arm every idler in the ship. But leave the hands at the mizzen braces."

"Aye aye, sir."

"Pikes, pistols, and cutlasses, lads," said Hornblower to the eager men thronging round the arms chests. "Mr. Smiley, muster your topmen for'rard by Number One carronade starboard side. Stand by for a rush."

Young Smiley was the best fighting man of them all, better than the nervous Jones or the stupid Still or the aged Turner. It was best to give him the command at the other end of the ship. Aft here Hornblower would have things under his own eye. And he realised he was still unarmed himself. His sword—the sword he had worn at the court of his King—was a cheap one. He could guess its temper was unreliable; he had never been able to afford a good sword. He stepped to the arms chest and took a cutlass for himself, drawing it and dropping the scabbard discarded on the deck; looping the knot over his wrist he stood with the naked blade in his hand and the sunlight beating down in his face.

Now they were closing on *Castilla;* only a cable's length apart and it looked closer. It called for accurate judgment to come close alongside.

"Starboard a point," he said to the helmsman.

"Starboard a point," came the repetition of the order.

Discipline kept the helmsman entirely attentive to his particular duty, even though *Castilla's* port-side gunports were opening, even though at that close range the gun muzzles were glaring straight at them, and the faces of the gunners could be seen through the ports looking along the guns. Oh God, it was just coming!

"Now, starboard slowly. Bring her gently round."

Like the end of the world that broadside came, ripping and smashing into the ship; there were screams, there were frightful crashes, the sunlight was full of dust particles flung up by the hurtling cannon balls as the splinters whizzed through the air, and then the ship sidled into the powder smoke jutting forth from the gun muzzles. But he must think about only one thing at this moment.

"Now! Hard a-port. Braces there! Back the mizzen tops'l!"

There was a tiny gap between the sides of the two ships, closing by inches. If she struck violently she might rebound and open the gap again; if her forward way was not checked she might scrape forward and swing. In the loftier sides of the *Castilla* the gunports were above the level of those of the *Atropos*. The dish-shaped *Atropos* had no "tumble-home" to her sides. Her bulwarks would make contact—he had been counting on that.

"Starboard side; fire!"

The infernal crash of the broadside; the smoke whirling round, the orange-painted side of *Castilla* torn by the carronade balls; but not a moment to think about it.

"Come on!"

Up over *Castilla's* side in the eddying smoke pierced by sunbeams; up over the side, cutlass in hand, wild with fighting madness. A distorted face looking up at him. Strike, swinging the heavy blade like an axe. Wrench the blade free, and strike again at this new face. Plunge forward. Gold lace here, a lean brown face gashed by a black moustache, a slender blade lunging at him; beat it aside and strike and strike and strike with every ounce of strength, with all the speed possible to him; beat down the feeble guard and strike again without pity. Trip over something and recover again. The terrified eyes of the men at the wheel looking round at him before they ran from his fury. A uniformed soldier with white crossbelts extending his arms in surrender; a pike appearing from nowhere beside him and plunging into the soldier's unprotected breast. The quarterdeck cleared but no time to breathe; shout "Come on!" and plunge down onto the maindeck.

Something hit his cutlass blade and sent a numbing shock up his arm—a pistol bullet, most likely. There was a crowd of men massed round the mainmast, but before he could reach it a surge of pikes from the side broke it up into fleeing fragments. Now a sudden rally on the part of the enemy, pistols banging, and then suddenly opposition ceased and Hornblower found himself glaring into a pair of wild eyes and realised that it was an English uniform, an English face although unknown to him—a midshipman from *Nightingale*, leading the boarding party which had stormed into the *Castilla* along *Nightingale's* bowsprit.

He could stand there now amid the wreckage and the dead with the madness ebbing out of him, sweat running into his eyes and blinding him; and yet once more he had to clear his mind and brace himself. He had to stop the killing that was still going on, he had to organise the disarming of the prisoners and the herding of them against the ship's side. He had to remember to say a word of thanks to Smiley, covered with blood and smoke, when he met him on the gangway forward. Here was the huge bulk of Eisenbeiss, chest heaving, the bloody cutlass like a toy in his vast hand. The sight roused his wrath.

"What the hell are you doing here, Doctor? Get back on board and attend to the wounded. You've no business to neglect them."

A smile for the Prince, and then his attention was demanded by a thin-nosed long-faced rat of a man.

"Captain Hornblower? My name's Ford."

He was going to shake the proffered hand, but discovered that first he must slip the cutlass lanyard from his wrist and transfer the weapon to his other hand.

"All's well that ends well," said Ford. "You arrived in time, but only just in time, Captain."

It was no use trying to point out to a senior the senior's errors. They shook hands there, standing on the gangway of the captured *Castilla*, looking round at the three ships clinging together, battered and shattered. Far down to leeward, drifting over the blue sea, the long trail of powder smoke was slowly dissipating under the blue heaven.

TWENTY-ONE

THE CHURCH BELLS of Palermo were ringing, as always, in the drowsy heat of the morning. The sound of them drifted over the water of the bay, the Conca d'Oro, the golden shell which holds the pearl of Palermo in its embrace. Hornblower could hear them as he brought *Atropos* in, echoing round from Monte Pellegrino to Zaffarano, and of all musical noises that was the one that annoyed him most. He looked over at the senior ship, impatient for her to start firing her salute to shatter this maddening sound. If it were not for the church bells this would be almost a happy moment, dramatic enough in all conscience. *Nightingale* under her jury rig, the clear water gushing out of her as the pumps barely kept her afloat, *Atropos* with the raw plugs in the shot holes in her sides, and then *Castilla,* battered and shot-torn, too, and with the White Ensign proudly flying over the red and gold of Spain. Surely even the Sicilians must be struck by the drama of this entrance, and for additional pleasure there were a trio of English ships of war at anchor over there; their crews at least would gape at the proud procession; they at least would be sensitive to all that the appearance of the newcomers implied; they would know of the din and the fury, the agony of the wounded and the distressing ceremony of the burial of the dead.

Palermo looked out idly as the ships came to anchor, and as the boats (even the boats were patched-up fabrics, hurriedly repaired after being shattered by shot) were swung out and began new activities. The wounded had to be carried ashore to hospital, boatload after boatload of them, moaning or silent with pain; then the prisoners under guard —there was pathos in those boatloads of men, too, of a proud nation, going into captivity within four gloomy walls, under all the stigma of defeat. Then there was other ferrying to be done; the forty men that *Atropos* had lent to *Nightingale* had to be replaced by another forty. The ones who came back were gaunt and hollow-cheeked, bearded and dirty. They fell asleep sitting on the thwarts, and they fell asleep again the moment they climbed on board, falling like dead men between the guns, for they had laboured for eleven days and nights bringing the shattered *Nightingale* in after the victory.

There was so much to do that it was not until evening that Hornblower had leisure to open the two private letters that were awaiting him. The second one was only six weeks old, having made a quick passage out from England and not having waited long for *Atropos* to come in to Palermo, the new base of the Mediterranean Fleet. Maria was well, and so were the children. Little Horatio was running everywhere now, she said, as lively as a cricket, and little Maria was as good as gold, hardly crying at all even though it seemed likely that she was about to cut a tooth, a most remarkable feat at five months old. And Maria herself was happy enough in the Southsea house with her mother, although she was lonely for her husband, and although her mother tended to spoil the children in a way that Maria feared would not be approved by her very dearest.

Letters from home; letters about little children and domestic squabbles; they were the momentary lifting of a curtain to reveal another world, utterly unlike this world of peril and hardship and intolerable strain. Little Horatio was running everywhere on busy little legs, and little Maria was cutting her first tooth, while here a tyrant's armies had swept through the whole length of Italy and were massed at the Straits of Messina for an opportunity to make another spring and effect another conquest in Sicily, where only a mile of water—and the navy—opposed their progress. England was fighting for her life against all Europe combined under a single tyrant of frightful energy and cunning.

No, not quite all Europe, for England still had allies—Portugal under an insane queen, Sweden under a mad king, and Sicily, here, under a worthless king. Ferdinand, King of Naples and Sicily—King of the Two Sicilies—bad, cruel, selfish; brother of the King of Spain, who was Bonaparte's closest ally; Ferdinand, a tyrant more bloodthirsty and more tyrannical than Bonaparte himself, faithless and untrustworthy, who had lost one of his two thrones and was only held on the other by British naval might and who yet would betray his allies for a moment's gratification of his senses, and whose gaols were choked with political prisoners and whose gallows creaked under the weight of dead suspects. Good men, and brave men, were suffering and dying in every part of the world while Ferdinand hunted in his Sicilian preserves and his wicked queen lied and intrigued and betrayed, and while Maria wrote simple little letters about the babies.

It was better to think about his duties than to brood over these insoluble anomalies. Here was a note from Lord William Bentinck, the British Minister in Palermo.

The latest advices from the Vice Admiral Commanding in the Mediterranean are to the effect that he may be expected very shortly in Palermo with his flagship. His Excellency therefore begs to inform Captain Horatio Hornblower that in His Excellency's opinion it would be best if Captain Horatio Hornblower were to begin the necessary repairs to *Atropos* immediately. His Excellency will request His Sicilian Majesty's naval establishment to afford Captain Horatio Hornblower all the facilities he may require.

Lord William might be—undoubtedly was—a man of estimable character and liberal opinions unusual in a son of a duke, but he knew little enough about the workings of a Sicilian dockyard. In the three days that followed, Hornblower succeeded in achieving nothing at all with the help of Sicilian authorities. Turner was voluble to them in lingua franca, and Hornblower laid aside his dignity to plead with them in French with *o's* and *a's* added to the words in the hope that in that manner he might convey his meaning in Italian, but even when the requests were intelligible they were not granted. Canvas? Cordage? Sheet lead for shot holes? They might never have heard of them. After those three days Hornblower warped *Atropos* out into the harbour again and set about his repairs with his own resources and with his own men, keeping them labouring under the sun, and deriving some little satisfaction from the fact that Captain Ford's troubles—he had *Nightingale* over at the careenage—were even worse than his own. Ford, with his ship heeled over while he patched her bottom, had to put sentries over the stores he had taken out of her, to prevent the Sicilians from stealing them, even while his men vanished into the alleys of Palermo to pawn their clothing in exchange for the heady Sicilian wine.

It was with relief that Hornblower saw *Ocean* come proudly into Palermo, vice admiral's flag at the fore; he felt confident that when he made his report that his ship would be ready for sea in all respects in one day's time he would be ordered out to join the fleet. It could not happen too quickly.

And sure enough the orders came that evening, after he had gone on board to give a verbal account of his doings and to hand in his written reports. Collingwood listened to all he had to say, gave in return a very pleasant word of congratulation, saw him off the ship with his invariable courtesy, and of course kept his promise regarding the orders. Hornblower read them in the privacy of his cabin when the *Ocean's* gig delivered them; they were commendably short. He was "requested and required, the day after tomorrow, the 17th instant," to make the best of his way to the island of Ischia, there to report to Commodore Harris and join the squadron blockading Naples.

So all next day the ship's company of *Atropos* toiled to complete their ship for sea. Hornblower was hardly conscious of the activity going on around *Ocean*—it was what might be expected in the flagship of the Commander-in-chief in his ally's capital. He regretted the interruption to his men's work when the admiral's barge came pulling by, and still more when the royal barge, with the Sicilian colours and the Bourbon lilies displayed, came pulling by to visit *Ocean*. But that was only to be expected. When the flaming afternoon began to die away into the lovely evening he found time to exercise his men in accordance with the new station and quarter bills—so many had been the casualties that all the organisation had to be revised. He stood there in the glowing sunset watching the men come running down from aloft after setting topsails.

"Signal from the flag, sir," said Smiley, breaking in on his concentrated thought. " 'Flag to *Atropos*. Come on board!' "

"Call my gig," said Hornblower. "Mr. Jones, you will take command."

A desperate rush to change into his better uniform, and then he hurled himself down the ship's side to where his gig awaited him. Collingwood received him in the well-remembered cabin; the silver lamps were alight now, and in the boxes under the great stern windows were strange flowers whose names he did not know. And on Collingwood's face was a strange expression; there was a hint of distress in it, and of sympathy, as well as something of irritation. Hornblower stopped short at the sight of him, with a sudden pounding of the heart. He could hardly remember to make his bow properly. It flashed through his mind that perhaps Ford had reported adversely on his behaviour in the recent action. He might be facing court-martial and ruin.

At Collingwood's shoulder stood a large elegant gentleman in full dress, with the ribbon and star of an order.

"My lord," said Collingwood, "this is Captain Horatio Hornblower. I believe you have already had correspondence with His Excellency, Captain. Lord William Bentinck."

Hornblower made his bow again, his feverish mind telling him that at least this could not be anything to do with the action with the *Castilla*—that would not be the Minister's business; on the other hand, in fact, Collingwood would keep strangers out of any scandal in the service.

"How d'ye do, sir?" asked Lord William.

"Very well, thank you, my lord."

The two lords went on looking at Hornblower, and Hornblower looked back at them, trying to appear calm during those endless seconds.

"There's bad news for you, Hornblower, I fear," said Collingwood at last, sadly.

Hornblower restrained himself from asking "What is it?" He pulled himself up stiffer than ever, and tried to meet Collingwood's eyes without wavering.

"His Sicilian Majesty," went on Collingwood, "needs a ship."

"Yes, my lord?"

Hornblower was none the wiser.

"When Bonaparte conquered the mainland he laid hands on the Sicilian navy. Negligence—desertion—you can understand. There is no ship now at the disposal of His Majesty."

"No, my lord." Hornblower could guess now what was coming.

"While coming out to visit *Ocean* this morning His Majesty happened to notice *Atropos,* with her paint all fresh. You made an excellent business of your refitting, Captain, as I noticed."

"Thank you, my lord."

"His Majesty does not think it right that, as an island King, he should be without a ship."

"I see, my lord."

Here Bentinck broke in, speaking harshly.

"The fact of the matter, Hornblower, is that the King has asked for your ship to be transferred to his flag."

"Yes, my lord."

Nothing mattered now. Nothing was of any value.

"And I have advised his lordship," went on Bentinck, indicating Collingwood, "that for the highest reasons of state it would be advisable to agree to the transfer."

The imbecile monarch coveting the newly painted toy. Hornblower could not keep back his protest.

"I find it hard to believe it necessary, my lord," he said.

For a moment His Excellency looked down in astonishment at the abysmal junior captain who questioned his judgment, but His Excellency kept his temper admirably all the same, and condescended to explain.

"I have six thousand British troops in the island," he said in his harsh voice. "At least, they call them British, but half of 'em are Corsican

Rangers and Chasseurs Britanniques—French deserters in British uniforms. I can hold the Straits against Bonaparte with them, all the same, as long as I have the good-will of the King. Without it—if the Sicilian army turns against us—we're lost."

"You must have heard about the King, Captain," interposed Collingwood, gently.

"A little, my lord."

"He'd ruin everything for a whim," said Bentinck. "Now Bonaparte finds he can't cross the Straits he'd be willing to reach an agreement with Ferdinand. He'd promise him his throne here in exchange for an alliance. Ferdinand is capable of agreeing, too. He'd as lief have French troops in occupation as British and be a satellite—or so he thinks at present—if it would mean paying off a score against us."

"I see, my lord," said Hornblower.

"When I have more troops I'll talk to him in a different fashion," said Bentinck. "But at present—"

"*Atropos* is the smallest ship I have in the Mediterranean," said Collingwood.

"And I am the most junior captain," said Hornblower. He could not restrain himself from the bitter comment. He even forgot to say "my lord."

"That is true as well," said Collingwood.

In a disciplined service an officer was only a fool if he complained about treatment received on account of being junior. And it was clear that Collingwood disliked the present situation intensely.

"I understand, my lord," said Hornblower.

"Lord William has some suggestions to make which may soften the blow," said Collingwood, and Hornblower shifted his glance.

"You can be retained in command of *Atropos*," said Bentinck—what a moment of joy, just one fleeting moment!—"if you transfer to the Sicilian service. His Majesty will appoint you commodore, and you can hoist a broad pendant. I am sure he will also confer upon you an order of high distinction as well."

"No," said Hornblower. That was the only thing he could possibly say.

"I thought that would be your answer," said Collingwood. "And if a letter from me to the Admiralty carries any weight you can hope, on your return to England, to be appointed to the frigate to which your present seniority entitles you."

"Thank you, my lord. So I am to return to England?"

He would have a glimpse of Maria and the children then.

"I see no alternative, Captain, I am afraid, as of course you understand. But if Their Lordships see fit to send you back here with your new command no one would be more delighted than I."

"What sort of man is your first lieutenant?" demanded Bentinck.

"Well, my lord—" Hornblower looked from Bentinck to Collingwood. It was hard to make a public condemnation even of the abject Jones. "He is a worthy enough man. The fact that he is John Jones the Ninth in the lieutenants' list may have held him back from promotion."

A wintry twinkle appeared in Bentinck's eye.

"I fancy he would be John Jones the First in the Sicilian navy list."

"I expect so indeed, my lord."

"Do you think he would take service as captain under the King of the Two Sicilies?"

"I would be surprised if he did not."

That would be Jones' only chance of ever becoming a captain, and most likely Jones was aware of it, however he might excuse himself for it in his own thoughts.

Collingwood entered the conversation again at this point.

"Joseph Bonaparte over in Naples has just proclaimed himself King of the Two Sicilies as well," he remarked. "That makes four Sicilies."

Now they were all smiling together, and it was a moment before Hornblower's unhappiness returned to him, when he remembered that he had to give up the ship he had brought to perfection and the crew he had trained so carefully, and his Mediterranean station of honour. He turned to Collingwood.

"What are your orders, my lord?"

"You will receive them in writing, of course. But verbally you are under orders not to move until you are officially informed of the transfer of your ship to the Sicilian flag. I'll distribute your ship's company through the fleet—I can use them."

No doubt about that; probably every ship under Collingwood's command was undermanned and would welcome a contingent of prime seamen.

"Aye aye, my lord."

"I'll take the Prince into my flagship here—there's a vacancy."

The Prince had had seven months in a sloop of war; probably he had learned as much in that time as he would learn in seven years in an admiral's flagship.

"Aye aye, my lord." Hornblower waited for a moment; it was hard to go on. "And your orders for me personally?"

"The *Aquila*—she's an empty troop transport—sails for Portsmouth immediately without convoy, because she's a fast ship. The monthly convoy is assembling, but it's far from complete as yet. As you know, I am only responsible for their escort as far as Gibraltar, so that if you choose to go in a King's ship you will have to transfer there. *Penelope* will be the escorting vessel, as far as I can tell at present. And when I can spare her—God knows when that will be—I shall send the old *Temeraire* to England direct."

"Yes, my lord."

"I would be glad if you would choose for yourself, Captain. I'll frame my orders in accordance with your wishes. You can sail in *Aquila*, or *Penelope*, or wait for *Temeraire*, whichever you prefer."

Aquila was sailing for Portsmouth immediately, and she was a fast ship, sailing alone. In a month, even in less with fair winds, he could be setting foot on shore half an hour's walk from where Maria was living, with the children. In a month he might be making his request to the Admiralty for further employment. He might be posted to that frigate that Collingwood had mentioned—he did not want to miss any opportunity. The sooner the better, as always. And he would see Maria and the children.

"I would like orders for *Aquila*, if you would be so kind, my lord."

"I expected you would say that."

So that was the news that Hornblower brought back to his ship. The dreary little cabin which he had never had time to fit out properly seemed sadly homelike when he sat in it again; the sailcloth pillow supported once more a sleepless head, as so often before, when at last he could force himself to go to bed. It was strangely painful to say good-bye to the officers and crew, good characters and bad, even though he felt a little spurt of amusement at sight of Jones, gorgeous in the uniform of a captain in the Sicilian navy, and another at sight of the twenty volunteers from the ship's company whom Jones had been permitted to recruit into the Sicilian service. They were the bad characters, of course, laughed at by the others for exchanging the grog and hardtack of old England for the *pasta* and the daily quart of wine of Sicily. But even to the bad characters it was hard to say good-bye—a sentimental fool, Hornblower called himself.

It was a dreary two days that Hornblower waited for *Aquila* to make ready to sail. Bentinck had advised him to see the Palace chapel, to take a carriage out to Monreale and see the mosaics there, but like a sulky child he would not. The dreamlike city of Palermo turns its back upon the sea, and Hornblower turned his back upon Palermo, until *Aquila* was working her way out round Monte Pellegrino, and then he stood aft, by the taffrail, looking back at *Atropos* lying there, and *Nightingale* at the careenage, and the palaces of Palermo beyond. He was forlorn and lonely, a negligible passenger amid all the bustle of getting under way.

"By your leave, sir," said a seaman, hastening to the peak halliards —a little more, and he would have been elbowed out of the way.

"Good morning, sir," said the captain of the ship, and instantly turned to shout orders to the men at the main topsail halliards; the captain of a hired transport did not want to offer any encouragement to a King's captain to comment on the handling of the ship. King's officers would only grudgingly admit that even admirals came between them and God.

Aquila dipped her colours to the flagship, and *Ocean* returned the compliment, the White Ensign slowly descending and rising again. That was the last memory Hornblower was to have of Palermo and of his voyage in the *Atropos*. *Aquila* braced round her sails and caught the first of the land breeze, heading boldly northward out to sea, and Sicily began to fade into the distance, while Hornblower tried to displace his unaccountable sadness by telling himself that he was on his way to Maria and the children. He tried to stimulate himself into excitement over the thought that a new command awaited him, and new adventures. Collingwood's flag lieutenant had passed on to him the gossip that the Admiralty was still commissioning ships as fast as they could be made ready for sea; there was a frigate, the *Lydia*, making ready, which would be an appropriate command for a captain of his seniority. But it was only slowly that he was able to overcome his sense of loss and frustration, as slowly as the captain of the *Aquila* made him welcome when he was taking his noon sights, as slowly as the days passed while *Aquila* beat her way to the Straits and out into the Atlantic.

Autumn was waiting for them beyond the Straits, with the roaring westerly gales of the equinox, gale after gale, when fortunately they had made westing enough to keep them safe from the coast of Portugal while they lay hove-to for long hours in the latitude of Lisbon, in the latitude of Oporto, and then in the Bay of Biscay. It was on the tail of the last of the gales that they drove wildly up the Channel, storm-battered and leaky, with pumps going and topsails treble-reefed. And there was England, dimly seen but well remembered, the vague outline to be gazed at with a catch in the breath. The Start, and at last St. Catharine's, and the hour of uncertainty as to whether they could get into the lee of the Wight or would have to submit to being blown all the way up-Channel. A fortunate slant of wind gave them their opportunity, and they attained the more sheltered waters of the Solent, with the unbelievable green of the Isle of Wight on their left hand, and so they attained to Portsmouth, to drop anchor where the quiet and calm made it seem as if all the turmoil outside had been merely imagined.

A shore boat took Hornblower to the Sally Port, and he set foot on English soil again, with a surge of genuine emotion, mounting the steps and looking round him at the familiar buildings of Portsmouth. A shore loafer—an old, bent man—hurried away on twisted legs to fetch his barrow while Hornblower looked round him; when he returned, Hornblower had to help him lift his chests onto the barrow.

"Thank'ee, Cap'n, thank'ee," said the old man. He used the title automatically, without knowing Hornblower's rank.

No one in England knew as yet—Maria did not know—that Hornblower was in England. For that matter no one in England knew as yet about the last exploit of the *Atropos* and the capture of *Castilla.* Copies of Ford's and Hornblower's reports to Collingwood were on board *Aquila,* in the sealed mailbag in the captain's charge, to be sent on to the Secretary of the Admiralty "for the information of Their Lordships." In a day or two they might be in the *Gazette*, and they might even be copied to appear in the *Naval Chronicle* and the daily newspapers. Most of the honour and glory, of course, would go to Ford, but a few crumbs might come Hornblower's way; there was enough chance of that to put Hornblower in a good temper as he walked along with the wooden wheels of the barrow thumping and squeaking over the cobbles behind him.

The sadness and distress he had suffered when he parted from *Atropos* had largely died away by now. He was back in England, walking as fast as the old man's legs would allow towards Maria and the children, free for the moment from all demands upon his patience or his endurance, free to be happy for a while, free to indulge in ambitious dreams of the frigate Their Lordships might give him, free to relax in Maria's happy and indifferent chatter, with little Horatio running round the room, and with little Maria making valiant efforts to crawl at his feet. The thumping of the barrow wheels beat out a pleasant rhythm to accompany his dreams.

Here was the house and the well-remembered door. He could hear the echo within as he let the knocker fall, and he turned to help the old man lift off the chests. He put a shilling into the shaky hand and turned back quickly as he heard the door open. Maria was there with a child in her arms. She stood beside the door looking at him without recognition for a long second, and when at last she spoke it was as if she were dazed.

"Horry!" she said. "Horry!"

There was no smile on her bewildered face.

"I've come home, dearest," said Hornblower.

"I–I thought you were the apothecary," said Maria, speaking slowly. "The–the babies aren't so well."

She offered the child in her arms for his inspection. It must be little Maria, although he did not know the flushed, feverish face. The closed eyes opened, and then shut again with the pain of the light, and the little head turned away fretfully but wearily, and the mouth opened to emit a low cry.

"Sh–sh!" said Maria, folding the child to her breast again, bowing her head over the wailing bundle. Then she looked up at Hornblower again.

"You must come in," she said. "The–the cold. It will strike the fever inward."

The remembered hall; the room at the side where he had asked Maria to marry him; the staircase to the bedroom. Mrs. Mason was there, her grey hair untidy even in the curtained twilight of the room.

"The apothecary?" she asked from where she bent over the bed.

"No, Mother. It's Horry come back again."

"Horry? Horatio?"

Mrs. Mason looked up to confirm what her daughter said, and Hornblower came towards the bedside. A tiny little figure lay there, half on its side, one hand outside the bedclothes holding Mrs. Mason's finger.

"He's sick," said Mrs. Mason. "Poor little man. He's so sick."

Hornblower knelt beside the bed and bent over his son. He put out his hand and touched the feverish cheek. He tried to soothe his son's forehead as the head turned on the pillow. That forehead–it felt strange; like small shot felt through velvet. And Hornblower knew what that meant. He knew it well, and he had to admit the certainty to himself before telling the women what it meant. Smallpox.

Before he rose to his feet he had reached another conclusion, too. There was still duty to be done, his duty to his King and country, and to the Service, and to Maria. Maria must be comforted. He must always comfort her, as long as life lasted.